Beloved Betrayer

THE BOOK OF THE EIGHTH SEAL

ROBERT MYRON OSTMAN

EDITED BY BRENDA B. BERGGOETZ

To my mother,
Hazel Sarah (Pumphrey) Ostman,
who always wanted me to become a minister,
and
to my wife, LaRue
and
my children,
ever supporting, never complaining:
Neal, Wayne, and Jayne.

With special gratitude to
Brenda B. Berggoetz,
for her sterling work of editing.

Contents

One   *A Good Year* 1

Two   *Getting On Board* 13

Three   *From The Past* 21

Four   *A Story Told* 36

Five   *Early Life* 48

Six   *Messages* 67

Seven   *Adventures Away From Home* 76

Eight   *In Rome* 89

Nine   *Home At Last* 106

Ten   *Back In Rome* 115

Eleven   *Letters From Home* 140

Twelve   *To Judea* 192

Thirteen   *Searching For Yeshua* 206

Fourteen   *The Story Of John* 229

Fifteen   *Yeshua's Healing* 244

Sixteen   *Meeting Yeshua* 259

Seventeen   *A Commission And A Trap* 292

Eighteen   *A Birthday, A Funeral, And A Wedding*............................ 312

Nineteen   *Among The Disciples*......................................320

Twenty   *Stories From Bethany*...................................... 338

Twenty-One   *Greetings For A King*...................................... 345

Twenty-Two   *Jewel Of The Future*.......................................355

Twenty-Three   *In The Hall*.. 377

Twenty-Four   *The Trial And Death*...................................... 397

Twenty-Five   *Moments Of The Past*...................................... 408

It was hot outside the bus window. The sweltering breeze made small whirlwinds of dust rise from the roadway like small tornados. John's mind drifted, as it often did in times like these, to his early days in Des Moines, Iowa. The stillness and heat in Jerusalem could match any summer day in his hometown. Much was the same, except for the flies - they were more abundant here than back home - must have been the use of insecticides that kept them down in Des Moines.

John could hear the friendly chatter of his students in the background as his mind drifted toward home. This was his last trip to Israel. After this, he would be desk-bound for a good while as Professor John Clyford of the University of Bradenton. He pondered just how his name looked on his office door and how many people mispronounced it when asking for him. It seemed rather simple to pronounce, but there were always those who asked for Professor "Slyford" or even "Clyfford". Bradenton - not a large school as universities go - was one with a good staff and fine reputation. He was proud of his many years with the school and hoped for many more. His mind drifted on.

"John, where are you?" He could hear the question asked again. It was Jean…Jean Tanagra, his co-worker on the team. She, too, was headed back to school. Now, as he recalled, she was one of the few people who got his name right the first time. She had flown in from a small school in Arizona to help on the project. One of the reasons for her joining the team was to gather data for her Master's Program on Early Jewish History.

"John, are you asleep at a time like this?" She shook him gently.

"No, just thinking about Iowa, and yes, I'm just as pleased with our discovery as the rest of the team," he answered as he anticipated her thoughts. "You know we have a lot to do yet: making sure all the equipment is itemized and transferred back to the University, unpacking the finds, keyboarding the finds into the computer, not to mention submitting our own financial reports…"

"Oh, I don't want to hear about all that. What I want to know is the chances of these finds being authenticated yet this season." By Jean's tone, he could tell she was in earnest.

"After all, some of my reports and papers are dependent on this as a possibility. Well, as near as I can tell, they look very good. No doubt there will be some who hold other views." John well remembered his first discovery in Egypt which took almost five years to bring into the textbooks because of minor bickering among the authorities.

"Some things I've learned from previous trips: stay with the find, make contact with the International Science Museum as soon as the data line is open, and never let anyone take total possession of your find." He was going to add something when the bus lunged forward and they were finally under way. Next stop, the airport in Jerusalem. From there it would be a long flight to New York.

The noise of the bus made normal conversation an impossibility, so most of the team settled down to await some sign of the airport. The distance wasn't long and soon the airport was in sight. The usual traffic problems kept the bus from clearing the area after arrival at the airport, but after that, all proceeded well.

Events passed smoothly and the usual troublesome losses and misplaced items never occurred. Even at customs there was only a short delay. In fact, the loading of equipment and protection of the find went well, and the plane lifted off precisely on time.

The flight was uneventful - what might be called a "good ride" by those who fly frequently. During the flight, John took advantage of the time to review the happenings of the past year; it had been a good year. In fact, the last six weeks had been the best of the year. Just six weeks to work a site was a short time, but the short program had been designed as a course to familiarize the new students with onsite conditions. It had been that and more. The program had produced enthusiasm for the work and knowledge needed for those interested in advanced archaeology. It also gave John a chance to get away from his desk, led to the meeting of his co-worker, Jean, and to the finding of a crypt.

He went over his log of the past events: days and times onsite, personnel involved, photographs taken, negative numbers, plans and site layouts, plot and strata measurements, infrared and x-ray techniques, as well as the using of a hand-held computer to aid his cataloging of these items and events. This computer allowed him to communicate with the science community anywhere in the world through the use of the International Science Foundation Satellite, or ISFS. The use of this sort of high-speed information management had eliminated the old method of tedious recordkeeping on the site. He could remember when he had many record books filled with shorthand notes that had to be transcribed before the project closed. But now, in the plane, he was placing this information into the host computer at the University with ease. He, like Jean, was fascinated by their lucky find. As the plane moved ever closer to New York, his mind kept going back to the events of the last few days.

The digs had the look of any other site and was near an old Biblical reference to land once thought to be a potter's field. However, it wasn't the one presently known to Christians as the burial plot of Judas Iscariot, as that was somewhat north of this site. Yet some of the old writings contained sketches of this area as a potter's field. Even so, after the wars fought in and around Jerusalem, no amount of recordkeeping by any of the early historians seemed without suspect.

The maps used at this location were from private collectors which came into John's possession through his uncle, also a collector of artifacts. In fact, this very uncle started John on the road to archaeology through an early introduction to this collection. Through the courtesy of his uncle, these maps had been put to good use during the past six weeks.

Because of the political climate at this time, the Israeli Government had granted only a short stay. Yet six weeks had been enough and all else was just "icing on the cake". In addition, the contract held with the Israeli Government by Bradenton University granted removal, transportation, and study time of any "finds" for a period of one year after discovery. This contractual obligation was one of the many benefits of the International Science Community Bylaws agreed to by member nations in early 2000 AD.

The old international rivalry and clandestine approach toward archaeology had been overcome by the desire for knowledge. Today, each host country permitted study of the finds outside of it's jurisdiction for a specified time period. In this case, at the end of one year, the finds must be returned to the Israeli Government for inclusion in the ISM with those of the same era. The ISM is the repository of all science information, and is similar to an international library from which any country can withdraw artifacts and other scientific data. Each country supplied funding for this form of science banking around 2000. No longer is it possible for an underdeveloped country to withhold from the science community information and data that would benefit the world.

The site was opened with care, and each student had followed his instructions well. Jean helped with the overall task. Every meter of the area and strata had been carefully photographed and labeled. Every data bit about the site and discovery had been transmitted through the satellite to the university. Everything was done to prevent oversight or lapse of data that might cause rejection of an unusual find.

THE FIND

Days went by without finding any more than the usual objects in similar areas. But the students were enjoying the thrill of the activity onsite and gaining on-the-job training necessary for future use either as teachers or field representatives.

The team had just settled down for an afternoon break when a sudden shower occurred. After the shower, some mending of the site had to be done, and during this cleanup, a small drain hole in one of the plots was discovered. It was a small trickle of water into a hole that led to finding the most important item of the dig. After carefully surveying the area near the hole, John decided to vacuum away the debris and photograph an inner ledge leading to the hole. The telecommunication video camera was set up and satellite communication code numbers for the university were keyed into the terminal; all was ready. The removal of debris led to an opening into a crypt. The crypt contained human remains. An educated guess placed the date of burial at or near 60 AD. In the crypt were the usual things considered necessary for those who believed in a hereafter, an idea not held by all Jews of that day.

The crypt was clean. There was no indication of attempted robbery or stripping as was the case of so many of the early graves. A cursory investigation of the contents indicated the remains was a male, wealthy, and wearing robes indicating a high office. From rings on the fingers, there was an indication that prior to burial, care was taken not to desecrate the remains. That is to say, the people seeing to the burial were friends and had some love for the deceased.

The remains also indicated the individual had died from old age. In addition to the remains, the contents of the crypt were straightforward and acceptable evidence of the time, except for one item. That item was a rather large gold-encased scroll. To those identifying the contents of the crypt, it seemed totally out of place in both time and location. It was only seconds for the new item to be named the "Golden Scroll".

As each item was carefully lifted from the crypt and cataloged, the Golden Scroll held the chief interest. Except for the scroll, a hurried inspection of the other items led to the finding of an inscription on one of the rings. Although dimmed by wear, the inscription was legible and found to be in Greek. The translation read, "The Lord Our God Is One Lord - Judas Marcus Annaeus Lucius, a servant of the living God - 737 - 812."

Well, the announcement of this translation sent a shock and thrill throughout the team. The camp was alive with rumor. John remembered the many questions that were and suppositions made. Who was Judas Marcus Annaeus Lucius and what was his part in history? Why the strange mixture of names? Only time and the contents of the Golden Scroll would tell. Yes, the Golden Scroll was the find of the day, if not the find of the century. It was, John thought, the highlight of the entire trip, and could become the focus of many a debate when its' secrets were deciphered. John went to the field office terminal, entered the code word, WGAGIP, and transmitted the news of the discovered Golden Scroll and rings to his colleagues at Bradenton. To Professor Charles Eddington he sent, "Research the Lucius family of Rome - time, 737 to 812 AUC and after. See you soon. Closing site. John."

Under his direction, the remains were sent to the forensic medical department at Bradenton for study. If there was a clue, even a small one, as to the identity of the remains, they would find it. The scroll was carefully packed in a stainless steel tube and vacuum-drawn to prevent deterioration due to atmospheric changes. After assigning the international science code number for the item, some detailed cataloging was done by those assigned to the site by the Israeli Government. The worth of the find was established, liability insurance secured, the project was closed, and the little band was ready for home.

THE GOLDEN SCROLL OF POTTERS FIELD

As the plane moved across the sky, John thought of the sealed tube in his carry-on luggage under the seat. In his opinion, the Golden Scroll was of great wealth, not only for the gold casing but for the message that it might contain. As time passed, he thought of the unlikeliness of this expensive scroll sequestered in an unmarked grave.

What was the reason? Was it the owner's or was it concealed by another in the grave to avoid its destruction by enemies? Did the person stowing it there hope to recover it at some later date? Had the sacking of Jerusalem prevented that? A sudden change in flight brought John back to the present.

Jean sat beside him next to a window. She was going over notes taken at the site. He could see her proficiency on the lap terminal and the confirmation of the data being transmitted to her school. He hoped she would finish work on her thesis and join him at Bradenton, but up to now, he had made it a point not to mention this possibility.

"You know, Jean, this could be one of the few good finds of the year, if not of the century." She nodded without looking up from the log of the six weeks' work. "I want you to help me see this through to the end. Do you think you can find time to join me at Bradenton?"

She looked up from her work. It was a very good offer and she knew it - a chance to become acquainted with new staff at Bradenton as well as new experiences in presenting a distinct find. Nonetheless, she was hesitant about accepting.

"You know I would love to but must complete this paper before I can consider it."

He looked at her for a short moment. "Look, let's put it this way - I need your help and would be glad to assist you in the completion of your work. Besides, there's all the necessary research programs for completion of your thesis at the library. What do you say?" For more than just the reasonableness of his request, he hoped she would agree. He waited.

Jean liked him; she enjoyed his company when the day's work had been completed and he had been cooperative and helpful during the expedition. As much as she wanted to - just for the excitement of the find - she knew her Master's Program was first.

"Gee, I'd like to, really I would, but I must report to Mirage U first. If I can get time, I'll be there with bells on."

He nodded assent, deciding not to press the matter. He had reached a decision to wire the head of the Department of Archaeology at Mirage U when he reached Bradenton and ask for Jean as an assistant. In this way, maybe he could gain her help and yet not disturb her program. As he thought about this, he could feel the plane lose altitude and was aware of the change of airspeed. They were approaching New York.

Soon after the plane touched down, everyone passed through customs and the sad goodbye's took place. Each person, somewhat sad the trip and exploration was over, was nonetheless happy to be home. John and Jean lingered a little longer than the others. John kept the carry-on bag containing the Golden Scroll with him. There was enough time for them to celebrate the success of the adventure at one of the small refreshment stands along the concourse. The boarding call came, and they boarded their flights home.

The flight to Des Moines was short. It seemed John just sat down when the "buckle seat belts" came on alerting the passengers that landing was imminent. After landing, John claimed his baggage, picked up his car, and was on the final lap home. As he drove, he glanced at the bag beside him. The excitement was still there. What secrets did the scroll hold? Then he thought of the remains shipped before he left - what had the people in forensic medicine deduced? As the car hummed along, he knew he would soon be back at the old room where he would enjoy a good shower and something to eat at his favorite restaurant, then early to bed, for tomorrow would be a busy day.

After a few miles of open highway and some turns through the campus of Bradenton, he arrived at the ivy-covered apartment. John parked and started unloading. The first item removed was the sealed cylinder containing the Golden Scroll. When it was safely placed in an easy chair, John brought in the rest of his gear. He noted that it was early and phoned maintenance to pick up the rest of the equipment at the airport. Tomorrow would be check-in day. Thank heaven for the new system - it was just a matter of code numbers and personal identification and none of the old equipment accountability.

John settled down on the couch - just for a minute. When he awoke, it was near dinner time, yet groggy as he was, he decided to shower and shave. Feeling better after the shower, he followed his first thought, dressed, and headed for his favorite eatery which was only a short drive from his apartment. He liked the people who ran the little restaurant. His meals were usually taken from the menu that rarely changed. One of the things he really liked was that once he was fond of something, he knew it would always taste the same, no need to fear the cook would decide to experiment. John liked things with a certain constancy; he was, after all, a man of simple taste and habit. He had often used constancy as a reason for not marrying.

The restaurant wasn't busy for that time of evening. John was seated and served immediately. Although of slight build, John always tried to keep an eye on his weight and, except for special occasions, avoided desserts. But this was a special occasion, therefore his favorite dessert of apple pie a la mode finished the dinner. After all, one doesn't return from an adventure in Israel every day. John was just finishing when he heard his name called. Looking up, he recognized a colleague approaching his table. It was Dick Jeremy, head of the Forensic Medicine at Bradenton.

"Hey, John, so you're back?" Dick held out his hand, "How did it go?" They shook hands. Dick motioned the waitress to bring him coffee. "You finished?"

"Yep."

"Glad to be back?" Dick continued.

"Right again." John set his cup down, anticipating more questions. The waitress brought another cup, and Dick sat down at the wave of John's hand.

"Just dropped in for a cup of coffee before I head home. Say, about that find…"

"Glad you dropped by and saved me a call. I was wanting to remind you not to let any of this out to the press." Dick nodded. "You know how they jump to conclusions. I hope everything arrived in good condition. You know how things are in the field. I thought I sent it early enough for some preliminary study before I got home. So what did you find?"

"Yeah, everything was shipshape, and I filed a prelim report just yesterday. It's probably waiting for you at the lab - you been there yet?" Dick took a drink and waited.

"Nope, and from here I'm going to hit the hay; I'm beat. I've got a little time now, so brief me on the contents of the report." As tired as he was, John wanted some news about the remains. Dick sipped his coffee. "Everything is sketchy this early in the game, John. Briefly, we found that the skeleton is of a male Caucasian, about 80 years old who died of old age. There's no indication of broken bones or missing members. We haven't made any serious study of the clothing or rings as yet. That will have to come later."

"Any special or strange things found?"

"Well, we agree with your first reading of the inscription on the ring, but nothing else at present. The lab will study the materials, dyes, and weave...hey, I know you're tired so we'll pick it up some other time."

John was tired and showing it, shower and short rest notwithstanding. "Yeah, I'll be in touch, and thanks, Dick." They separated and John left, once again, a satisfied customer.

Upon entering the apartment, he suddenly remembered his baggage and clothes. One chore he didn't relish was unpacking. Time taken on this task brought the clock around to near bedtime, and even with the nap, John was ready for a good rest. Before going to bed, he took one last look at the steel container housing the scroll. The container was equipped with a sensitive vacuum and humidity indicator to monitor its internal condition. John checked this indicator; all looked normal - no change of pressure or humidity since the closure - he set it in the easy chair. After updating his log, he placed it beside the container along with the rest of the papers needed for the next day's clearance. Pleased with the general look of things, he headed for bed.

And the evening and the morning were the first day!

THE OPENING

The sunlight falling across John's eyes woke him early; he was one of those early risers and never liked to sleep in when things were ahead. Once awake, he was unable to remain in bed - neither body nor mind would let that happen. After the usual shower, he was ready for breakfast. To avoid coming back to the apartment after breakfast, John decided to take everything with him. With this in mind, he stowed the steel tube, his logs, and accounts of the trip in the trunk.

The vehicle had made the trip so often during his tenure at Bradenton it seemed to guide itself. Breakfast was one of the better meals in John's book. He liked to take his time during breakfast, and often headed out early just to have extra time. There was something about the smell of bacon in the early morning air that pleased him. By the time he arrived, John was ready for almost anything - bacon, eggs, ham and toast, or even biscuits and gravy. There was much of the farm boy left in him after all his years of learning. As he recalled, sitting there alone, this was break time for all students and many of the faculty had left for vacation or projects such as his.

Breakfast over and back in the car, the sense of adventure surged through him once again. Just to analyze the scroll would be exhilarating in itself and the thought that it might hold some secret of history not yet told was mind boggling. But that was just what his keen instinct told him - *somewhere in that container was a message to be deciphered.*

The laboratory was the most modern building on the campus and an impressive sight. Its architecture was rather formal with the building rising from the ground like the pyramids of old. The base of the structure was supported by massive columns creating parking space. John turned down the lead-in ramp and stopped to place his ID card in the data cross-check sampler. With clearance given, the automatic gate rose to permit his entry. Once in the area, he made a few turns and moved up ramps to his regular parking space. It was a short walk to the elevator and then down the hallway to the laboratory.

Two of his colleagues in the laboratory gave him a big hello. They had been on the receiving end of the data transmitted from Israel and were anxious to see what he brought back from the land of the Hebrews. The first to hold out his hand was Professor Charles Eddington, head of the Ancient and Modern Foreign Languages Department. He brought to Bradenton one of the best minds in his field. The second to give John a manly hug was Ancient Religious History Professor Edward Stuart, also an able man in his field. John was accepted as an equal in and among these men of science. Greetings over, the stainless steel tube was placed on a spotless bench for vacuum release and opening.

"Say John, give us some details about the mysteries of the project." Although Ed spoke, both of the men were filled with curiosity. It wasn't everyday a colleague returned with such success. John took his time, and while he prepared for the days' work with the find, brought Ed and Chuck up to date. As often happens, more questions came out of the telling of the discovery than were answered.

"The big story that was really born out of rumor is the connecting of the name Judas on the ring of the remains with Judas Iscariot. And even when I explained that such a connection wasn't remotely possible, the rumors persisted." John continued to move about the laboratory while speaking, but said no more on the subject.

"You know, John, we did some research on the Lucius family…" Ed was first to speak after the commentary by John.

"Yes, what did you find?"

"Not much, other than there was an early philosopher named Apuleius Lucius, AD 125; he was from Madauros in Munidia. In general, the Lucius family was a long line running into early times. In addition, it had its share of notorious personages, a grandson of Augustus carried the name Lucius, and believe it or not, three Popes accepted the name Lucius," Ed laughed, finding humor in the latter observation.

"But nothing on a Judas Marcus Annaeus Lucius around 737 to 812 AUC?" John moved the steel tube around on the bench.

"Nothing, but I suspect he was the great, great, great grandfather of this philosopher, Lucius Apuleius - or Apuleius Lucius - whichever. The computer is still looking for a match in history. So much for that, let's see what you got!"

Before releasing the seals, the room was brought to the proper humidity and temperature by the system. When all was ready, the terminal showed an all-green board.

"Well, John, you have the honor of starting the process," Chuck stated. "Everything is ready." John waved his hand and they all turned to the problem before them.

The new process was different from that of days gone by. The container lay in a totally controlled environment. The hours or days of waiting for aged materials to soften and become pliable enough to inspect had gone with the turn of the century. Now, in a matter of seconds, or at the most, minutes, the material was softened to the right degree for manipulation, not to the extent that awkward human motion could be used, but within the scope of computer-controlled robots. Unique robot fingers moved minutely to prevent damage to even the most delicate materials.

While they watched, the robot fingers opened the stainless steel container and extracted the Golden Scroll. There it lay exposed for the first time. Each man was fascinated by its beauty. Simply made, the gold casement was embossed with Aramaic symbols and characters, and was closed by eight seals of some sort of wax-like material across a hidden seam. It was at this moment that Ed spoke softly so as not to break the apparent spell cast by the first views of the Golden Scroll.

"It could well be called 'The Book of the Eighth Seal.'"

"How is that?" whispered John.

"Well, the name would be born from Rev. 4:1 if you will. As I recall, the statement reads thus, 'And I saw in the right hand of him that sat on the throne a book written within and on the backside, sealed with seven seals...' This was the only book ever mentioned. So this could be called 'The Book of the Eighth Seal' as there are eight seals on this scroll."

John looked at him for a moment. "Boy, you're the romanticist aren't you? Yet, you just might have a good title at that."

The gold encasement was of high quality gold leaf which suffered from each touch of even this delicate instrument. As the machine positioned the scroll for selection of an entry point, sensors gave notice of the material's fragility. The computer integrated this information into delicate movements at the weakest point of the gold foil. A ruby laser beam knifed through the gold foil near the seals where the scroll had the least inscriptions.

Each man held his breath as the casement slowly came open, exposing the scroll to human eyes for the first time since the originator had sealed it. The machine stopped to allow the material to reach a stable environmental condition.

Each portion of the scroll was carefully placed before a high-speed character analyzer and recording heads. The recording heads moved into position to copy any data on the scroll as it was exposed layer by layer. The heads had the capability to accept any impressed data, registering color spectrum isolation, infrared, ultraviolet, electromagnetic waves, and high frequency sound reflections. The papyrus was pulled through matched pairs of pinch rollers while the heads scanned both sides of the material. The scanning was done in a traverse and longitudinal mode, as well as a 45-degree bias to the material. Every millimeter of the material was checked for character intelligence, as well as texture, fiber content, and age. All of this was supplied to the host computer in the old capital of the United States in Washington.

The host computer in the Archives Building was part of the present International Science Museum, or ISM. It was there all data was transmitted; each bit of data was compared with myriads of other bits of all languages of past and present. Just to authenticate a find and decipher it, the age of documents, the kinds of material and ink used, and each character were examined. When finished, the data would be in the memory of the host computer, complete with audio/visual restructuring of the impressions the originator had put on the scroll. In some cases, the system synthesized and displayed information the originator had not wished to be known, such as errors and erasures. Nothing was left to chance. This work was so thorough that rarely was any human adjustment made to the final results. Then, the machine selected a proper preservative for the papyrus and applied it automatically. The document was now protected for centuries of viewing and study.

The men turned to a big screen display to see just what the ISM machines had been able to decode from the information presented to it from the Bradenton system. Each man sat in a high-backed captain's chair; a console permitting changes to data on the display was before him. Selected passages could be recalled for study and printouts made at will by any one of the three. They settled back to be the first to view the handwritten linguistics of previous centuries.

As they watched, the computer reconstructed the material and form of the original papyrus and exhibited the date of fabrication as 60 AD. The gold encasement had been formed some time after that - approximately 63 AD, with the actual encasement of the scroll at 65 AD. The data showed the ink used to be of the same era and of the same locale, with a high probability of it being a Palestinian manufacture of the Egyptian pigments. The character structure was the block style of the Aramaic languages used throughout southwest Asia by the Jews of the early first century AD.

The study indicated the document was prepared in haste as some of the characters showed less care than others. There was a marked difference in the characters in the latter portion of the script. In addition to the mark of haste, the data lifted from the surface of the papyrus indicated that the weather was warm, even hot, where the writing had taken place, as some stains of sweat were present. At the very end of the document, the material showed signs of human tears being spilled on it as the writer moved his stylus across the surface. The response from the Archives computer placed the document in the era and time suggested by its language. That is to say, the scroll was indeed authentic and not a later fabrication. It was no counterfeit; the material was genuine.

As to the writer, no authenticity could be granted for there was no memory data to compare this document with; no other writing either in style, linguistics, or content was presently in the system memory. This was a new and entirely distinct author, yet he carried the same topical matter as that of the Christian New Testament. The data indicated that the content was nearly synoptic with the information presented in the early writings of the four Gospels. The author did indeed live in the same era as the early Christian writers. It was the questions about the person himself that the data left as unsolved.

The building was silent except for the soft noises of the computer and display unit. They sat spellbound in front of the consoles and occupied by thoughts of the information displayed on the eight-by-ten foot screen at the end of the room. An "Information Processing" notification was displayed, indicating a break time for the viewers. Processing some types of information could take an hour or more, and where the information wasn't straightforward, the processing time often extended to days. But this wasn't one of those cases and everyone knew it - it would take less than an hour. They gathered at the bench where the Golden Scroll lay protected by a plexiglass dome. While standing there, they discussed the different possibilities that might be disclosed through translation.

Chuck brought their random thoughts home. "The name on the ring, that's the hooker. Could Judas Marcus Annaeus Lucius be Judas Iscariot? If he is, John, it looks like you have a winner here, and my guess is that the text will be controversial no matter what."

"If this is what I think it is, some Christian beliefs may be disturbed," Ed interjected before John had time to comment.

"How's that?" John asked.

"Well, first, if this person is Judas Iscariot, then it's obvious he didn't commit suicide in Jerusalem. After all, the ring dates are after the accepted dates for his death of 33 to 36 AD. And second, the age of the remains, as Dick told you, was about 80 years. Of course, I've no way of knowing, but to some of us, there always has been a feeling of a missing link between the story of Judas and his time and place in history."

John was silent while studying the Golden Scroll. Even as it lay on the bench, its beauty was awe inspiring, but why was it saved from the many ages of destruction and pillage - that was the enigma? Did it really hold some detail of the early Christian era not yet known, as Ed hinted, or was it just a listing of items bought, sold, or traded during those times? And why didn't the writings on the gold foil make sense, as they surely didn't at first study?

John turned from the bench and looked out the window. "I hope you're both right, that it is a good find and that it does focus some light on the past. How it was located was pure chance. Just as I transmitted from the site, if it hadn't been for a sudden rain, we probably wouldn't have discovered it." The others followed his glances outside the room and turned to get a better view of the trees on the campus.

"You know there is one person I wanted at this premiere unveiling and that is Jean Tanagra. She deserves much of the credit for the location and care of the find."

He turned from the window. "If we had more time between decoding and presentation, I'd have her fly up from Arizona and join us."

"You want us to put this thing on hold, John?" Ed asked. "You know we still have control here at the console."

"That's right, John. One or two more days really doesn't mean much to the world out there." Chuck was always one to understand the feelings of others. "After all, the world has waited for nearly three thousand years for this moment, what's a day or two more?" There was a little tone of irony in his voice; he was never in favor of waiting for anything at any time, even in a grocery checkout line. Yet he wasn't one to overextend himself as to personal preference over another's wishes. And once a decision was made, he would stick to it without a whimper.

"Alright, let's get a reading from the computer as to storage; if this unit will hold all the information so that the lines from ISM are clear, we'll go on standby for twenty-four hours." John looked at each man for assent; both nodded in agreement. And with that, John, who had the greater knowledge of the system, keyboarded in instructions to check memory space. The display flashed for a millisecond and then confirmed all data bits were in the host computer. After confirmation, Bradenton's computer compared character space and indicated that it could hold all the data. John was satisfied and he knew he could move without losing any of the data.

"It's looking good. This will let me do some things I've put off by coming here this morning. I really hadn't expected to get into the ISM system so soon; usually, they are very busy this time of the year with all the extracurricular studies going on." He made a simple adjustment and forced the storage.

"This is great, and I know Jean will be pleased to be here for the exposé. He shut down the system and looked at the clock - it was almost lunch time.

"Look, let me make this call. I think I can have her fly here yet this afternoon, and if so, we can put the system online tomorrow morning." John was confident she would come once he told her of the possibilities of this find. First, he must notify the head of the Archeology Department at Mirage and ask for her release from the obligation of the Master's work for the rest of this project.

With that in mind, he stepped over to the intercollegiate high-speed data line and keyed in the request for Jean's release. It was only a few minutes and he had the answer he wanted. The machine gave him hard copy stating that. He placed a long distance call to Jean. It was a short wait when he heard the familiar voice on the line.

"Jean Tanagra, what can I do for you?"

"Hello Jean, it's John Clyford. How did you sleep last night?" John asked. Not waiting for her answer, he hurried on. "How would you like to come to Bradenton and be here at the translation of the Golden Scroll text?"

"You're kidding! You know I'd *really* like to be there!" She was excited. "Say, do you know something I don't?"

"Well, you might say that I have a confirmation from the head of your Archaeology Department releasing you from the Master's Program for the duration of this project. That is, if you want to come."

"I'll be there as soon as I can catch an afternoon flight. The only thing that will hold me up is the afternoon traffic." She was grateful for the chance to work on the project. While she listened to his remarks, she thought of the clothes she would have to take along.

"…I'll be waiting at the Des Moines airport…" John continued, "…and don't worry about accommodations as we have plenty of room here on the campus." He thought of the empty apartments open for the use of visitors during summer vacations.

"Well, we had better cut this short if I'm to catch the early afternoon flight." She listened for his final goodbye's and hung up the phone. She'd have to hurry to make arrangements to leave Mesa yet that afternoon. First, she had to check her clothes. For the second time in her life, she really wished she had more dresses. Jean had always been a more pragmatic type of woman, maintaining a wardrobe of less-feminine clothes while leaning toward suits and slacks, a kind of ready-for-action collection of ready-to-wear items.

Jean had always been part tomboy anyway, never afraid of the outdoors, and if facts were known, she really preferred it that way. Yet, she was practical enough to know femininity still counted and always was neat in both body and living quarters. While thinking of these facets of life, she quickly selected the lighter side of her wardrobe to take on the trip. Jean wasn't one to spend time on decision making, and once the selection was made, into the bags things went.

She started to shower, and although she never liked to, she decided for the sake of time to wash her hair in the shower. Afterward, she considered herself in the mirror: face - not too bad, figure - very good. She thought she had seen worse for women her age.

As she put the final touches to her makeup, she studied her face a little more. Just what was this sudden concern for her looks anyway? It was just a meeting with a co-worker on a project she had left less than two days ago. Was there more to this meeting than she really wanted to admit? Although John had been very nice during their stay in Israel, he'd never shown any particular interest in her other than as a personal friend and assistant on the project. He was nice though…

The phone rang, waking her from the mental drifting. It was the airline confirming her tickets for the afternoon flight. This notice caused another flurry of action as she finished preparations for the trip. After all, to catch the plane was the first step in the saga!

John hung up the phone and turned to his colleagues who had been standing by.

"I suppose this means we'll start this project again tomorrow, right?" asked Ed.

John thought a moment, "I think in all fairness we should wait until she's had a chance to settle in before we start. And besides, I was hoping I could talk you two into dining out with us tonight." He turned to get their agreement.

"Well, it's okay with me as I don't have anything special on this evening," Chuck said, and smiled with a twinkle in his eye, "and besides, I'd like to meet this girl who has stolen your heart." He was a good judge of human emotions and thought John wasn't aware of just what was going on, like many a bachelor before him.

"It's not like that; I'd do the same for any male assistant. You know that, right Ed?"

Ed smiled and threw an arm around John's shoulders. "I'm sure that's the case. I believe you, but like Chuck, I'm anxious to meet this girl. So count me in."

"So let's go to lunch before time runs out and you don't get to the church…oops, I mean to the airport on time." Ed and Chuck turned away to go to their cars.

It was the responsibility of the project leader to make sure the equipment was stowed and electronic interface modems were secured for the night. While the others moved to go, John transmitted the shutdown data bit word to ISM and closed the lab. He joined the others at the outer door, slipped the keycard into the lock, and notified security they wouldn't be back that evening.

They walked down the hall to the elevator and from there to the cars. Each man was glad to be part of the adventure and full of confidence. Just before splitting up, they discussed lunch plans. John was for his favorite eatery, while Ed liked a more formal place. It seemed Chuck really didn't care one way or the other.

As often when great minds must make a critical decision with minimal statistics, so was the decision for the place to eat. While John and Ed failed to agree, Chuck secured a coin from his pocket and said, "Heads we go to John's favorite place, tails we go to Ed's."

With that, the coin flashed in the light of the garage to land in Chuck's hand; he turned it over on the back of his other hand and removed the hand covering it. All gazed at the coin. It was heads. The place to eat was settled in less time than it took to talk about. They split up and headed for the little restaurant that all knew was John's favorite.

It didn't take long for them to arrive. They were in the restaurant, seated, given menus, and ordered in less than ten minutes. The food was brought in less than that. While eating, thoughts of the find came up as a natural subject of men interested in their work.

"John, there are several things that puzzle me about this find," Ed said while laying down his knife. "Don't you think the Golden Scroll seems grossly out of place in that type of crypt?"

"You know that's one of the things that bothered me when we made the discovery, but there're others. It didn't seem consistent with the times - but then again, if the scroll had been placed in the grave before the sacking of Jerusalem, there's a good chance it would have remained undiscovered until now." John took time to motion to the waitress for more coffee. "I suppose the text will give us the answer to that question."

"Well, I fail to see how. After all, there's a high probability the originator and person stowing the scroll had little control over what happened to it after that." Ed continued his thought. "It's almost as if there was some force protecting it from harm, and I guess that's just a little bit of religious thought creeping into the idea."

Neither of the other two said anything, so Ed continued, "It seems to me that it might be a case of the right place and the right time. You know, like something that was prophesied to happen - a kind of 'so let it be written, so let it be done.'"

"Personally, Ed, I think you're an incurable romanticist and an idealist to boot," Chuck finally was far enough along with his meal to join in the after-coffee discussion, "and just think, all of this garnered from bits and pieces. You want to know what I think?"

"Yes, just what does a guardian of ancient foreign languages think?" asked John.

"Well, I think you'd better hurry or you'll be late to meet the flight from Mesa."

The other two glanced at their watches and for the first time realized that the luncheon engagement had almost taken more time than John had to spare. John left before the waitress came with the check, after giving his portion of the bill to Ed and asking that he do the honors for him. Now not in any hurry, they settled back for one more cup of coffee and smiled at one another as John moved with a speed not exactly characteristic of him.

"You know Ed, the romanticist in me says that our friend and colleague has entered into 'the tender trap' as the old song used to say."

"I think you're right, Chuck, and you know the interesting part is that he doesn't seem to know it." Ed continued to stir his coffee even after the need had passed. "As his friends, I think we should monitor this situation with care. We should look this young thing over carefully because we wouldn't want good old John to take one giant step for himself at the expense of the rest of mankind." His face showed an impish grin.

"Your assessment is without flaw, Ed, and as of this moment, we should retire to a neutral corner and prepare for the main go." With that, they left for Bradenton.

CHAPTER TWO

Getting On Board

The time spent getting to the airport seemed a little longer than usual, but the digital readout on the dash indicated this wasn't the case. It took no longer than usual and John was soon walking up the concourse toward the gate for the flight from Mesa. This time compression was one of the mental tricks that often occur when there is a desire to get something done in a short time.

John noticed there were others waiting, a good indication the plane hadn't arrived and the line indication on the display confirmed this. He chose a seat near the windows that faced the runway and plane parking area. The usual amount of travel brochures were in the racks near at hand, but he wasn't interested in going. He was interested in who was coming.

According to the display, the flight was only ten minutes from touchdown which gave John a few minutes to think of a greeting that was apropos. This wasn't the usual situation for John; he often greeted students and parents alike on arrival for college or special occasions, but this was different. The biggest difference was that in those greetings, they tried to impress him, while in this case, he wanted to impress Jean. And how to do this gracefully was another matter. While he was considering the alternatives the plane arrived. No more time to plan a greeting, it was now in the hands of the gods.

He watched while the plane snuggled up to the ramp. Then turning, he walked to a position where he could see the passengers disembark, and yet remain unseen himself - he just wanted to see her first. It was a silly idea, but he gave in to the impulse and stood just out of view as the passengers came through the concourse entrance. As he waited, several people passed near enough to cause him to change position. He kept scanning the crowd entering the concourse. Suddenly, there she was. Jean was taller than some of the other women who greeted loved ones and friends at the entrance. She stopped for a second or two looking for a familiar face, and upon seeing none, looked a little disappointed. It gave John a feeling of warmth to see her disappointed because she didn't see him.

She was a nice-looking girl, he thought as he moved through the crowd to greet her. She stood near the ticket stand waiting for him. John liked what he saw. Jean had the briefcase that doubled as an overnight case in Israel with her. She was wearing a dress; funny, it was the first time he had seen her in a dress. In the six weeks at the site, she wore military-type jump suits and boots. From where he was, he could see she had nice legs to go with the rest of a well-formed body.

As he approached, the crowd parted and Jean saw him. She smiled pleasantly. She was pleased; it was the first time she had seen him in anything other than a pair of khaki shorts and field boots. He looked more handsome in his business suit and low-cut oxfords than he had in the field dress.

Yep, John thought, she was better looking than he remembered. They both stood looking at each other with a new respect.

"Gee, I'm glad to see you, John. I thought maybe you couldn't make it, or had forgotten me." She was first to speak.

He could hardly believe his ears. Forget her! That wasn't ever going to be in the cards, John thought, but merely stated, "No, I've been here for some time. I've always been one to be on time, it's one of my good habits. You're looking great! Did you have a good flight?"

She nodded a vigorous yes and hoped she didn't sound too anxious when she spoke before. "Do you have additional luggage?"

"Yes, I guess we had better find it and be on our way."

She thought she sounded more like herself - the initial tension was gone.

He led the way down the concourse and down an escalator to the baggage turnstile. She recognized her luggage and he lifted it from the turnstile; they turned quickly and headed for the parking lot. He carried her luggage and she carried her briefcase.

Once in the car, they were on their way to Bradenton. The traffic was congested as most industry and local stores had ended their workday. Traffic delays gave John a chance to tell Jean about the Golden Scroll, its removal from the container, the careful unrolling of the material, and the application of preservatives after the data had been secured by multi-head scanning. She listened intently, and for the first time noticed how gray his eyes were; they were nearly the color of the stainless steel tube he was talking about. He continued while nodding to get a better view of the traffic around them. His glances toward her were quick as he gave most of his attention to driving conditions.

He talked about the scroll's authenticity, making sure she understood it was for the material alone and not the content. He continued with the information the Forensic Medicine Department had supplied about the remains found in the crypt. He knew she would be pleased to hear of these developments as some of her thesis was dependent on this aspect of the trip to Israel.

While he talked, they moved out of the city traffic and onto the highway. "Well, what do you think of our project so far?" He looked at her a little longer now that they were on the open road. She was a handsome woman. He noticed she wore a little more makeup than before which he liked.

"I think it's great, and the confirmation of the material can only mean that whatever its text contains will be accepted, if not as true, at least as timely." There was little doubt in her mind now that she would secure an MA in Ancient History. The acceptance of the scroll would be a definite plus for her. "And, of course, I'm pleased you asked me to the translation. By the way, you did mention something about on-campus accommodations…" she hesitated, "I hope so, as I haven't made any other arrangements."

"You know I wouldn't leave you out in the cold, or is it the heat," he said with a smile. "There're plenty of apartments open for use by anyone visiting the university during this time of the school year. I'll guarantee that I've found one you'll like. If not, you can use mine."

"I'm not hard to please. After all, my apartment at Mesa isn't a castle, and as you know, I can live as rough as anyone on a dig." As she spoke, she noticed he turned into a beautifully landscaped area…at last, the campus of Bradenton.

"Well, this is my 'digs', so to speak. I don't know how it compares with Mirage but I like it, and I hope you will, too, as long as you're here."

She had a comfortable feeling about the campus as he drove through the winding streets. It had the look of earlier generations - something of the early 20th century - each street was a concrete replica of a prior horse-drawn carriage pathway. It definitely wasn't one of the clean and sterile layouts of the later colleges. It had something more to offer than just a place to attend for an education.

"This is very nice, I can see why you have thought so much of it." She remembered when he spoke of Bradenton while on the site, his voice always had a strong expression of pride. "I think it compares favorably not only with Mirage, but with any other campus in the land."

Even while she spoke, he pulled up in front of a small apartment which was like many of the others in the block. They were neat and well built and reflected an architecture of the early 20th century, even as the streets had.

"Well, here we are, your oasis in this desert of learning at Bradenton. This is your pad for the duration of this project…" he hesitated, "unless you don't like it. If that's the case, I'll be glad to make other arrangements."

He came around and opened her door and waited. Luggage in hand, he led the way to the apartment. He took a pass key from his pocket and opened the door. She noticed and wondered how many others had similar keys. They went in - it was nice although exhibiting a completely masculine decor.

"This is Professor Smith's residence, but he is on Sabbatical and won't be back the rest of the year. Mine is nearby, so I thought if you find it adequate, you might stay here." John looked at her for confirmation. He was much like a little boy asking for a wish and afraid it wouldn't be granted. She had been looking around while he spoke.

It was very nice compared to her apartment in Mirage, but why bring up unpleasant things? "It's great, John, and if I can use most of the things here, it'll work out fine."

"Oh, everything is at your disposal. By the way," he added quickly, "the school has a cleaning staff on duty throughout the summer. Each apartment is taken care of when the resident is out, but you must select the day. A call to maintenance will suffice; there's no reason for you to do those kinds of chores." John turned to leave.

"Hey, I almost forgot. Here's the key. The phone number is on the phone, and mine is next to it. Should you need anything, just give me a ring. If I can't supply it, then I know someone here who can."

"Thanks for the key," she laughed, "I was wondering how I would get in and out."

He smiled at the thought and as they moved toward the door, he told her about his colleagues. "I hope you get rested enough to have dinner with us tonight, say about eight?"

"I not only accept, but consider it an honor. I'll be ready for dinner. That snack on the plane just wasn't enough for a working girl like me."

"Well, I'll leave you to get settled and see you at eight." With that, John stepped through the doorway, gave a salute, and was on his way. She closed the door and leaned against it. She still didn't know where his apartment was, but was sure she'd find out before this project was over.

Six o'clock came around slowly for John - another expanded time function - he had been ready for the evening when he left Jean. He tried to busy himself with the project needs, but found different mental pictures of the scheduled evening interrupting his concentration. He finally gave up trying and gave in to dreaming of the dinner and evening to follow.

He was jolted to reality by the phone ringing. His first thought was that Jean might be calling with some need. He moved at a speed above his normal pace and nearly knocked over a lamp on the phone bench.

"Hello, is that you, Jean?" He felt a little chagrined after asking the question, which proved to be more so when he heard the voice on the other end.

"Hell no, it's not Jean," came the resonant voice of Ed. "Where have you been, and why haven't you let us know the evening plans? How do you expect us to look like gentlemen without knowing the dress code?" Ed could be humorous even without intending to if the situation was right. He and Chuck had presumed John would be at his apartment and thinking of things other than the next day's program.

"Hey, that's right. I forgot to tell you the time and place. It looks like around eight at The Shadow's." He thought of Chuck. "Say, is Chuck there with you?"

"Yep, I'll let him know, but you know The Shadow's isn't cheap. Are you sure you're not overdoing it on the first evening - kinda like setting a precedent that's hard to follow?" His voice had a ring of disbelief as John was one of simple tastes and The Shadow's wasn't normally his bag. And besides, this would mean a change of dress for both Chuck and himself, but then again, anything for a colleague and the cause.

"Well, I don't think so," John answered. "Maybe I'll write it off as part of the project expenses. Hey, if you and Chuck can't afford the spot, it's okay with me. I wouldn't want you to do anything you might regret. Besides, I can take care of myself."

"You're kidding. We wouldn't miss this evening for all the tea in China," Ed quickly added. "We'll be there at eight or shortly thereafter, and if we aren't, you can start without us." Ed waited until he heard John say goodbye and hung up.

"Hey, Chuck, it's The Shadow's of all places, at eight or thereabouts. I wonder what's gotten into our boy, Johnny?"

"Sounds good to me. I've always wanted to go there but never had a reason good enough to override the expense. This does the trick." He started toward the door. "I guess I'd better begin the process of changing this worm into a butterfly. See you later. Hey, we'll ride together."

"Boy, what we don't do for a colleague," Ed returned as Chuck closed the door.

A quarter of eight found John at the apartment door. Jean let him in and turned to get a light jacket that matched her dress. To John's surprise and delight she was ready and, if the truth were known, waiting. She fairly well disguised the possibility, though, with a pretense of a last minute makeup inspection. He thought she looked great and said so. She thanked him and returned the compliment. They were in the car and on their way in less than five minutes. The trip across the campus was pleasant, and they didn't see any other car leave at that time. John drove by his apartment just to let Jean see his lodgings, and also went by the apartments of Ed and Chuck. The lights were out in both apartments so John assumed they had left for the lounge at The Shadow's.

John made a quick turn or two and then onto the highway heading for the restaurant. The parking lot was nearly full when they arrived, an indication that The Shadow's was living up to its billing; it was one of the better night spots.

They entered through a huge brass door that opened on a large foyer. The decor was done in early Spanish tradition, complete with heavy oak furniture and knights in armor. Some historic maps and paraphernalia were attached to the walls, while gaslights gave an atmosphere of an early Spanish castle.

The maitre'd had the reservation in John's name. The second waiter led them to a table already occupied by his colleagues. They rose when Jean and John approached the table. John performed the introductions.

"This is Edward Stuart, Doctor of Religious History, and Charles Eddington, Doctor of Foreign Languages, both Modern and Ancient. And gentlemen, this is Jean Tanagra of Mesa, Arizona." John felt pretty good about the introduction for he hadn't muffed it, a real accomplishment for him as in the past he had often forgotten the names of his closest friends during an introduction.

The Shadow's was a restaurant for the gourmet as well as the casual diner. This allowed John to show his expertise in ordering - a reflection of world travels. He did this with style and good taste. His Spanish, although not as good as Chuck's, was more than adequate. They all agreed his selection was to their liking - the wine included - no debate about that.

As they waited for the main course, Ed and Chuck put John on about accomplishments in his field, and, of course, his world conquests in love. Jean enjoyed their harmless dialogue and understood for whom this was intended. She felt that John was somewhat nonplused and wanted her to know that none or very little of their prattle was true. She at first played the innocent party, but slowly changed her attitude and came to John's defense. Jean let the playful duo know that she held John in high regard, in spite of their fun. After that, John seemed to enjoy the little tête-à-tête Ed and Chuck were having.

During this exchange, Jean was careful to address them by title or surname as a matter of respect. "By the way, Jean, please call me Ed."

"That goes for me, too," Chuck remarked hurriedly. "No, don't call me Ed, use Charlie or even Chuck if you like. But not Ed. If there was only one Ed in the world, that would be enough."

Now he was putting Ed on, Jean thought, but she was pleased. She knew both men had been studying her intently during the early evening, and the use of their Christian names meant a form of acceptance into a rather select circle of bachelors. She understood that these men were, from their long acquaintance with John, reacting as older brothers might. Whether John really wanted this solicitude was not readily apparent, but by his unspoken body English, she presumed not. The meal was nearly over before talk of personal histories came to light and serious talk of the next day's work came about. Jean listened intently as the three, almost oblivious of her, argued back and forth about the still-hidden mysteries of the scroll. Most of the arguments rested on pure conjecture covered with romantic ideas of the past.

The talk slowed down for a minute and Ed finally remarked, "It's okay for you young people to stay up until the wee hours of the morning, but as for me, I'm headed for the sack. How about you, Chuck?"

As if a signal that all the questions about the "femme fatale" were answered, Chuck joined Ed.

"My thoughts exactly, Ed. First, let me say that I've had a very enjoyable evening, and Jean, it's been my pleasure meeting you." He took her hand and held it a moment. "I'm looking forward to working with you on this project, so don't let John keep you out too late."

"Don't listen to him, John, keep her out as long as you like," Ed said, with a twinkle in his eye as he winked at Jean. "I know I would, and Jean, like Chuck, it's been my pleasure. I think I can say for the both of us in the old Navy tradition, welcome aboard!" With that said, he gave a slight bow and clicked his heels together and turned to follow Ed.

"Thanks, the both of you have been the epitome of decorum for gentlemen in a mixed crowd," Jean laughed. She could give as good as she got.

"Hear! Hear!" exclaimed Ed. "Chuck, the lady speaks with a silver tongue - let's partite. Good evening and we'll see you bright and early in the morning." They turned and left without further ado.

"They're something else," John said with some admiration in his voice. "We've worked together for quite awhile. You know I did my undergraduate, graduate, and doctorate work here at Bradenton, and I've known them all that time. I've never yet found them to steer me wrong on anything."

"Well, from this evening I can say they aren't dull professors." Jean waited. John turned and looked at her intently.

"The truth now, did you have a good time this evening? And was the apartment alright, or should we look for something else?" His voice held a serious tone.

"Yes, to the first, I've had a great evening, and yes to the second, the apartment is fine, and no, we won't look for anything else."

John placed the check on the head waiter's tray, and said something to the effect that everything had been fine. He reached to help her place her light jacket over her shoulders before leaving the restaurant.

"Maybe you ought to put on your jacket; it gets cool here in Iowa in the evenings, somewhat cooler then Mesa, I'll bet." John left the decision to her.

"No, it's just a short distance to the car and in there I'll be fine." She let the reference to Mesa go by.

As John closed the door on her side of the car, he noticed the clock on the dash. "It's later than I thought and we have to make sure the system is online by eight tomorrow morning."

It was a short drive to the campus. John walked her to the door of the apartment, took the key from her and opened the door. It was helpful that he knew where the light switches were as he went in and looked around, then walked back to the door.

"Well, everything looks okay; hope you rest well. As for me, I'm still wide awake."

Jean walked across the room, removed her wrap, and sat down. "So am I. Sit down a minute."

John did. They were soon in deep discussion about the Golden Scroll and the remains found at the site. Time slipped by.

"Holy cow, it's later than I thought…hey, I said that before!" He laughed at the repetition, and stood up and moved toward the door. Jean followed.

"How about picking me up for breakfast?" She saw he liked her suggestion immediately and was glad she had asked.

"Hey, that's right, you don't have any wheels. Okay, but I'm an early riser so breakfast with me might come a bit early," he warned.

"That's no problem; give me a time and I'll be ready."

"How about seven?"

"That's early?" Jean laughed softly but continued hoping she didn't sound too disrespectful. "Fine, I'll be ready, and John, thanks again. It was nice." He nodded and left; she closed the door and locked it.

As Jean sat on the edge of the bed, she thought of the start of the day in Mesa, the phone call from John, the flight to Des Moines, their meeting at the airport, and the evening out. It all seemed somewhat like a dream - things moved so fast - all in less than fifteen hours. She reached for the little quartz clock and set it for six thirty. She didn't want to be late the first day on the project, but in reality, she didn't want to miss breakfast with John. As she lay back and stretched, she wondered where it would all end.

John entered his apartment pondering the day as he went. Much had gone as he liked. The boys had behaved themselves as professors ought, the meal was great, and Jean had won hands down. He didn't set his clock as he always had the ability to awaken within five minutes of the time he decided was needed before he went to bed. With the light out, he was asleep sooner than he expected.

John woke up on time. He checked the time and calculated how much he could spend at getting ready. His mind had wakened him with time to spare. He disliked being rushed at any time but especially in the morning. He dressed in sport shirt and slacks, and was ready to meet Jean for breakfast. It was seven when he headed for Jean's apartment, and rang the bell five after seven.

Jean was ready. She was wearing slacks and blouse nearly matching John's and they remarked about it. As they left, she picked up her briefcase - it would serve as her purse today. It was a short ride to the restaurant. He told her that though it may not be elegant, the food was good, and the people who ran it were nice.

They were enjoying breakfast in a short time. John explained that he had breakfast here off and on for nearly fifteen years and that he never regretted one meal here, which was more than he could say about some of the highly-advertised places along the road.

Jean admitted that what she had was very good and the coffee was above average. In many cases, she thought the coffee made the meal, and rested her case for or against a number of eating places on that alone.

"I always take more time at breakfast than the other meals; it's one of my idiosyncrasies. I like to plan the day and lay out what I believe I can accomplish before problems occur."

He settled back, knowing they had some time before the system had to be online. "As soon as we leave, I'll take you to security and have them issue you a temporary ID card. The card actuates the special locks on the lab doors and the parking gate as well."

John had nearly forgotten the need for special recognition to enter the laboratory. He said that was one of the advantages of taking time at breakfast; had they been in a hurry, they might have forgotten the security office call before going to the lab. Not that it was any great sin, but it would have been time lost, and he didn't like any unnecessary motion.

"Did you bring your identification and code number from Mirage?" John asked.

"Yes, they're in the briefcase."

"Good, it will take less time to check for clearance when you present them." He took one final sip of coffee and stood up, "Let's go, just in case there may be some delay." John paid the bill and they left to arrive in front of the security building after a few quick turns along the campus streets.

The secretary took Jean's badge, code number, and other control cards from Mirage University. She stepped over to an interface system and typed in the necessary information for the International Security forces personal check. She came back in a matter of minutes with a temporary badge and key card for the laboratory. Jean signed the release for additional information and they left.

They drove directly to the laboratory. He stopped just outside the building where Jean could get the best view of the structure.

"What do you think of our little lab here at Bradenton?" He asked with pride.

"I'm impressed, to say the least. It looks to be the newest of your buildings and of the most modern design." She studied the layout with some respect. Some money and thought had gone into this building.

"There's a secret about this building, or at least few outside the school know about it. Every inch outside and inside the Laboratory for Anomaly Research was designed by people here at the school. No outside architecture or engineering help was used or consulted during its design and construction. Even some of the laborers were students, many who have now graduated and occupy responsible positions in industry." With each sentence, she could sense the pride he had being part of the institution that accomplished so much with its own personnel. She said nothing but she had a strange sense of being part of the scene as well.

He drove down the ramp, stopped and inserted his keycard in the scanner. The gate rose and he drove into his parking place. He noticed Ed and Chuck's machines were not there and told Jean so, while pointing out their places, names and all. They proceeded upstairs to the main lobby. He was about to use his ID card to open the door, but decided to check Jean's newly-issued card instead.

"Try your card. Security should have made a personal print of your history on the scanner by now. If not, I'll use my card."

Jean placed the ID card in the scanner - just a few milliseconds and the steel door opened. The lab had an airlock system that functioned automatically to hold dust and humidity to a minimum within the main test and review area. The clean rooms were maintained where needed, although a change of clothing wasn't necessary in this section.

While they were standing in the interlock area, John turned to Jean and remarked, "In addition to the building design and some of the actual construction, this laboratory and its security system with its computer complex was developed by the university personnel. This building and its contents, as it is today, cost the university one hundredth of what it would have had outside contractors designed and built it." He continued with pride, "The money saved was used in part to build one of the best-equipped labs of its type in the world. I might say that we are proud of this accomplishment."

"I've never heard of a school and its students doing more for its own betterment. And I'd be proud to be part of this, too, had I been here at the time."

The interlock had stabilized while they were talking, and the clearance light came on. The door opened, letting them enter in the clean rooms and high tech area.

The Golden Scroll lay on the bench under a plastic dome. John could hear Jean gasp as she saw the scroll for the first time in its clean condition. The gold seemed to have a fire of its own in the lab lighting which gave a glow of mystery to the scroll.

"Oh John, it's beautiful!" was all she could think of saying.

As they stood admiring the scroll, the interlock door opened and Ed and Chuck came in. Both had briefcases with them and, placing them on the consoles nearby, turned to greet the two admirers of the scroll.

"Well, aren't you the early birds," Chuck mumbled as he walked by. He was never at his best in the morning before coffee. "I'll bet neither of you slept all night; if not, how could you be here so early?" It wasn't really early, but Chuck played the scene to the hilt.

Ed got a cup of coffee from an automatic vending machine that was part of the lab equipment. He saluted the couple in silence by raising his cup in a skoal position; he wasn't much until he had at least two cups of coffee down. At least that's what he claimed.

Each man, including John, started to set up and clear the consoles for the action of the day. A short beep notified John that the International Science Museum system was free. He immediately keyed in the code of the day. The code word for Bradenton was really a lockout word to secure against any pirating of information by external hackers; he waited for the confirmation from the host system at ISM.

"Jean, I want you to take the console next to mine. We will work together for the first few hours and after you get the hang of it, you'll be able to operate the console to isolate any special items of interest." He then turned to his console and the one next to it.

"Well, guys and doll, it's near the time to look into the text of the Golden Scroll. When you're ready, give me a word check, and we will be on our way into the past." He then studied his master control for Ed and Chuck's word check, and slowly dimmed the lights in the laboratory so the big screen at the end of the room became the predominant feature. All four now sat staring at the display as the words and images slowly became visible. The automatic decipherer, translator, and interpreter sections of the system turned on the speech synthesizer. For the first time since the originator had prepared the scroll, man began to see and hear its content and meaning.

The display was a vertical split screen presentation; the original Aramaic characters appearing on the left side, while the transliteration appeared on the right. The display automatically adjusted and English comment lines were printed with the most appropriate word to complete sense of the transliteration inserted in italics. This, in turn, let the speech synthesizer give vocal expressions and articulations of the translated text of the scroll.

The high speed decoder continued to scan the laser mega-bit disk to provide the display date. The first words displayed on the screen and spoken by the speech processor were: *"Hear, O Israel: the Lord is our God, the Lord is one."*

CHAPTER THREE

From The Past

"Hear, O Israel: the Lord is our God, the Lord is one."

These were the first words uttered by the speech synthesizer. The program moved the display arrow to the precise location of each Aramaic character. During the translation, the program selected the most appropriate syntax to give meaning to the inscriptions. Possible words and phrases that were also acceptable alternatives to complete variations of meaning were automatically keyed to the display for reference. Color coding was used to help the viewer follow the process on the display - red for Aramaic characters, and green for English. The background for the scroll was a parchment tan and white for the translation.

The room was filled with an electricity of anticipation. In the darkened room, the light from the display made grotesque patterns of color on the polished walls. These changing patterns added to the sense of mystery. Those watching were fascinated by the information displayed on the screen, and even though trained to react only to scientific stimuli, none moved to touch any controls before them. They were totally engrossed in this audio/visual presentation from the past.

The characters scrolled down the display, Aramaic from right to left in reverse order, while the translation was from left to right. As the translation continued, the speech synthesizer supplied the following aural output:

I, Judas of Kerioth, the last Apostle in man's sight, yet the first and most beloved in the sight of God, do herein set my hand to describe the happenings in my life. Last of the twelve in man's sight because of the lies by the Master Deceiver that will be included in books yet to be written. First before the countenance of God, yea, even before Simon Peter, for I, the one chosen before time began, followed the instructions of the Angel of the Lord and betrayed the Messiah.

Yet, it is because of this act of loving obedience to God that I fear possible destruction of this book by the Apostles. Therefore, I have commissioned Apuleius Lucius, my stepbrother, to inter this scroll with my body. I pray God it will survive, some day be discovered, and thereby remove the stain placed against me by the Master Deceiver, even Satan.

These are things revealed to me, Judas of Kerioth, a humble servant of Almighty God.

In the beginning all was null and void. From this, the Spirit of the Most Holy moved to create all things seen and unseen. Those things acting and those things acted upon; those increasing and those decreasing; those that are mass and those that are force; all these things the Spirit of Almighty God, the a priori substance that is neither contained nor containable, except by his own will; created and set into motion without diminishing or increasing His essence.

Even all life created He them, both spiritual and secular, and He forever divided them. And to the spiritual He gave the capability of moving about freely among His creations without encumbrances of any kind; neither mass, force, or time tethered them.

One of these spiritual beings became so enamored with himself that he fought against God and was forever cast from Almighty God's presence. He, even him, became the Master Deceiver of all mankind.

In the secular worlds, Almighty God formed all manner of animals and growing things, and He gave them capability to move about freely though each was subject to mass, force, and time as well as each to his own kind. Man and woman; unto the likeness of His Own essence created He them. He granted them that part of His essence that He gave to no other animal - intelligence. And with his intelligence man could do great and wonderful things, both good and evil. It was man's special gift of intelligence that made him aware of the difference between good and evil not known to other animals.

After a time, man was told by the Master Deceiver that his intelligence made him equal to God, and man believed the Deceiver. Man then chose to exercise this intelligence in a way of evil, even unto disobedience. This disobedience made Almighty God extremely wroth and He hid His face from man. This caused man great hardships; toil, sweat, and death were his through disobedience.

And man's intelligence caused him to search for Almighty God. Man looked unto the sun, stars, mountains, seas, growing things, animals, and even unto things and images made by his own hands. Then the Master Deceiver influenced man's intelligence, and man claimed all these things were God, but it was not so!

Even long after time began, Almighty God saw man looking everywhere for Him, even unto many generations, and had compassion on him. Almighty God wished that man should return to Him, but the Master Deceiver wanted not this to happen and confused man when he looked for God, saying: "Lo, this is God and that is God, and God is in this place or in that place; or God exists not; yea, even God is man himself."

And man believed the Master Deceiver and used his intelligence to look here and there, but he did not find God.

And Almighty God knew that man could never come to know Him without help as the gift of intelligence He gave man created a great void that man could not bridge. It was in this wise that God caused part of His essence to become man, and the first God-man stood among men. Through His essence, God made man, and gave intelligent man a bridge to come to Him.

But the sting of man's disobedience was yet upon God for He was a just God, and because of this desire for justice, He required that which man could not give - the return of the gift of godliness. The very gift that man lost when he first listened to Satan, yea, even from his first disobedience. Hence, God required the return of His essence from the God-man in reparation for the disobedience of all intelligent mankind.

It was necessary for Almighty God to create and sustain the lineage of the God-man through the generations of man, even unto the day the essence would be imparted to the man-child. This child was Yeshua.

So it was willed and so it was done! From the first man, even Adam, through all the generations of man until the fulfilling of the time for the essence to be moved unto man, even unto Yeshua. Almighty God knew that reparation would require return of the essence from Yeshua without stain. Indeed, it would require the surrendering of his mortal life, for only in this wise could the essence be returned.

Since the Master Deceiver wanted not this to happen, he caused man not to believe in the message of the Kingdom of God from Yeshua, but to believe that Yeshua was really

God on earth rather than the essence of God in man. And man again listened to Satan and began to worship Yeshua as God, hence man forgot Almighty God and worshiped the essence of God in man. God knew that man, listening to the Master Deceiver and using his free will, would never find cause to deliver Yeshua up for death, and it was so.

Therefore, Almighty God masked His essence in man so that only few knew who He was, and prepared a betrayer of Yeshua. A man who would not listen to Satan, and of his own free will, offer his life and yea, his very soul, to betray Yeshua and send him to his death.

To one and only one, in all generations of man, could this act be entrusted! This would be him who was to be the Beloved Betrayer, even such a one as I, Judas of Kerioth!

And so it was that my life was joined with that of Yeshua, even before the beginning of time, through Cain and all generations, even to this same hour. So it was revealed and so it was done!

The display showed some electronic noise as the system searched for the next portion of the scroll that matched the same text. It soon picked up a new source and the display continued…

It was during the reign of Gaius Julius Caesar that my grandfather, Simon of the house of Levi, met with one Johnathan of Judah, to sign a contract of marriage. My grandfather for his son, Simon, to wed the niece, Ruth, of the house of Johnathan's late brother, Joshua. Johnathan acted as contractor for Ruth, his ward, as her father had died before his time, leaving his family unto his brother's care as it was written.

So it was written and so it was done. When Simon of Kerioth, my father, was of age and had sufficiency, he took a wife, Ruth, the niece of Johnathan. It was into this household I and my twin brother, Ishmael, were born in 736, followed two years later by my sister, Anath. I was considered the oldest by mother, but only the midwife knew such a thing as a certainty.

I was the more aggressive and stronger, while Ishmael was more artistic. I sometimes envied his ability to copy things he saw on either papyrus or in clay. I often reminded him, as did father, of the writings of the law:

"Ye shall make you no idols nor graven image, neither rear you up a standing image, neither shall you set up any image of stone in your land, to bow down unto it: for I am the Lord your God."

Often mother would come to his defense saying, "Isn't this a gift from the Lord? Is it right to place a bushel over a candle and stumble in the dark? Who are you to judge, oh, husband and son? Take care that you don't read into the law that which isn't intended."

Father, who was wise in these matters, would leave it be, commenting only, "That which is of God is beyond the discouragement of man, if it is such as you say, then His will be done. Let the boy alone, Judas." This kindly reprimand increased the envy of my brother for God had given me no such talent. But even with these inner feelings at times, I loved Ishmael as myself, and through the early years, we were inseparable.

As early as I can remember, father, a Levite, was the Kohen of the house of assembly in Kerioth. His was the good fortune to be an only son and of a good talent Father made a good living as a merchant in early times. He was first in Kerioth as a representative officiating during the high holy days of penance. Later, father was chosen to be one of the select officers of the temple, and we moved to Jerusalem, where it was his good fortune to attend several high priests during his lifetime - but I go before my story.

My memory of things about me began in Kerioth. It was the village of my youth. In summer, Kerioth suffered from a pall of dust raised either by the passing caravans or by a hot wind that often blew in from the Desert of Paran in the south. If not from these, then in seasonal changes the winds came from the Desert of Shur, and the many herds of sheep and goats passing through to the cool hills above the town stirred the dust from the sun-baked streets. Rarely was the air clear in Kerioth.

Most caravans passed through Kerioth going to and from Judea and Egypt. All stopped to enjoy the water of the Kerioth well. The air was filled with the cries of the camel drivers as they watered their animals before entering the Desert of Paran. Often the cries of slaves chained to the animals were heard, each in his own tongue, each with the same request - water. Our well was renown for its sweet water; even the Roman troops, when given time from their protectorate tasks, liked to come to Kerioth to rest and drink from the spring water of the well.

As lads, Ishmael and I often spent many hours sitting on the wall near the well listening to the commands exchanged between Centurions and their troops. Sometimes, we would drop behind the wall and play soldier and even copied the verbal utterances of the soldiers. It wasn't long before we could understand much of the Roman tongue, and often listened to their stories of battles in and near Judea. Like most soldiers on foreign soil, they disliked being there - the people, the command, the heat, and nearly all else that went with life away from their own land. Yet, we could tell from the bits of talk we heard on the wall that some like the girls and wine of this land as much as those of other Roman provinces.

Like the dust in the air, rumors were constant and abundant. They were supplied in every tongue - Greek, Aramaic, and even Egyptian. Their content carried the imagination from politics of the time, through religions, to current events. As youngsters, we received a liberal education while simply sitting on the wall near the well.

When not sitting in front of our Rabbi studying the Law and Prophets, we would spend as much time on the wall as other children did in games. It was our favorite game, memorizing as many of the foreign words as we could. Many times we would write down inscriptions found on passing caravans and later translate them. It was this game that let us move into foreign circles when we grew older. By the time we were in our teens, we had a basic familiarity with several languages of the day.

It was a great surprise to us when father came home from the Bet ha-knesset and announced he must go to Jerusalem. He had been chosen for the high position of first attendant to a priest of the course of Abia - Zechariah by name. This, of course, was a position that tradition would never let him turn down. He was to attend Zechariah in the burning of incense in the temple; a service to God selected by lot. The burning of incense was the embodiment of prayer, and during this time, the people prayed for forgiveness of their sins. It was a high honor for the priest chosen might only perform this ritual once in his lifetime, and father was to attend Zechariah on this special occasion. We were justly proud - father was the first from Kerioth to do this thing.

Father prepared to go and stay the week of Zechariah's course. Father's servant, Atonis, would of course attend him, and the two would stay until his obligation was over. After that, he would return to Kerioth to take up his duties as before.

Mother longed to see the Holy City and asked to go with him but was denied. She accepted the denial readily as the household required her care, and under the law, that was her first duty.

"But husband of mine, the nights are long without you by my side; can even God ask that a man and wife be put asunder?"

Her arguments often rested on facts of life rather than the law. To her, many times love must triumph over the law, and justice must always prevail. Here her argument was simply based on wanting to go to Jerusalem.

"Your argument is well taken, oh wife of mine, but that portion of the law you lean upon indicates that asunder is not a short term separation such as the trip to Jerusalem, but instead, the lifelong separation one from the other as in divorce. May I ask, would you leave your own household to a handmaiden and your children to a slave, just to see Jerusalem and then ask God to bless such a frivolous adventure?" Father knew of her desire to see the hidden mysteries of the great marketplace.

"There is a time and place for all things, let it be so, and do not wish to tempt the Lord God." With that, the conversation ended and father continued to prepare for his trip to the temple.

As children, we sat in quiet wonderment for it was not often a Kohen from a town as small as Kerioth was called to perform such a fine task. We knew as his children we would gain in stature in the community, that is, in the sight of the other children. Our playmates would want to know everything father told us of the great temple and in detail what happens in its many courtyards. We knew waiting for him to come back would seem long.

Our waiting would not seem as long as the trip to Jerusalem would to father, and as we owned neither horse nor ass at that time, walking was his only mode of travel.

Jerusalem lay some thirty miles to the north of Kerioth, a good three days' walk over miles of caravan trails. It was true there were some good roads built by the Romans but these connected some major cities and forts, and Kerioth was neither. The trails were not easy ones, but they did pass through Hebron and Bethlehem. Both of these towns offered a good place to rest and obtain fresh water.

Father was welcomed into the Zechariah household as one of the family once lost - now found. He was treated like a brother and had set before him all that he needed for the time of attendance.

During the days before the ritual, Zechariah and his wife, Elizabeth, spoke of their great sadness for they were well up in years, and yet had no children. They recounted how they had ever lived in accordance with the Law and Prohibitions but Elizabeth remained barren. Their sadness was indeed great, and father joined them in many prayers for relief from this mark of shame. Time became short, for soon Zechariah must perform the ritual of the burning of the incense as it was his course to do.

"Come, let us set aside the troubles of this household and prepare for my task," said Zechariah. "The Lord has indeed blessed me for even in old age I have been granted the honor to serve."

"I find it no small honor, oh Zechariah, would that I could be so honored," father said in deep respect for the man about to attend to the incense. "It's I who am fortunate, as the Lord placed your hand in mine when I was chosen to assist in your preparation and am therefore twice blessed for it."

"How so, Simon, that it is a twofold blessing for you?"

"First, that a person from the small village of Kerioth is chosen of all the cities of Judea, and second, that I was chosen to serve you. Isn't that true? Am I wrong in my thoughts on the matter?" Father was one not wanting to force his thoughts on others.

"To praise and thank God is never in error, Simon, but may it never be for things undeserving." With that said, Zechariah ended the subject. "Let's be on our way to the temple."

The distance wasn't a long one, but Zechariah wasn't in a hurry, and walked as one deep in thought. Father noted Zechariah was oblivious of the many tradesmen and soldiers that brushed against him in the early hours of the day, but said nothing.

The temple could be seen from nearly all parts of the city; it rose to a towering height of 150 feet. It was said by some… "to be one of the most beautiful buildings in all the world", and well it should be as Herod used forced labor to build it. Some labored without pay and others, it was rumored, received only bread to eat. All this done while taxing the people for money to adorn it with gold, silver, and precious stones. It was whispered Herod built the temple more for his glory than that of the God he was supposed to serve.

Herod was now up in years and in poor health; he feared his family, local politicians, and loss of his kingdom. A kingdom that only existed by the will of Rome - every Jew knew that. His fear of being deposed was well known to those studying the prophets; it was said that a leader would rise from the house of David to lead the children of Israel to freedom.

In his illness Herod wondered - freedom from whom? His only answer wasn't freedom from Rome, but freedom from his rule - a new king to replace him! His belief in this prophesy led him to cruel and evil crimes against his family, friends, and the people. The people murmured against him and excluded his name from their prayers.

This was the scene and time in Jerusalem when Zechariah and father entered the gate and passed through the court of the gentiles. Father walked a step behind Zechariah even as it was written, "Let the lesser follow the greater into the temple, and no man stand above his station."

The wicks of the lamps were ready to be trimmed and the incense was ready for the ritual. Father assisted Zechariah with his travel clothes. This was the first day of the burning of the incense. The multitudes had already gathered in the courtyard to pray to Almighty God for forgiveness of their sins and the fulfillment of the prophesy that a Messiah would soon come and lift the heel of the gentile from their necks.

When Zechariah came before the people, the call was given. All, even as one man, fell on their knees and placed their foreheads on the ground.

"Hear our prayer, oh God of our Fathers."

And Zechariah answered, *"Hear, O Israel: the Lord is our God, the Lord is one."*

Zechariah entered the Holy of Holies. His time in the Holy of Holies was to be short; all the people feared that he might be struck dead if he was not of a contrite heart. The time went by slowly and yet Zechariah didn't appear. Soon all knew he tarried longer than any had done before. The people outside began to murmur - they feared God had rejected the incense and struck Zechariah dead. Woe unto them, had the sins of the people rested on Zechariah and found too great? They trembled with such a thought; they knew not what to do.

Who was to call them from the prayer position? Father, who was the chief attendant, stood outside the great curtain, for no man save the high priest can approach the Holy of Holies, and he, only on the day and time appointed.

Each man remained bowed down and searched his past for sins not confessed. To each with face to the ground, it seemed that God was punishing them for sins already confessed. Their bodies sweat as the sun caused the heat of the day to set upon them. Still they remained awaiting the benediction. Where was Zechariah?

Just when all seemed lost, the curtain parted and Zechariah appeared.

He motioned for father to approach for he could not speak. His face was white and he trembled with great fear and shock. From his motions, father understood that he should give the benediction, and did so. The people rose to look upon Zechariah. They saw a man of great need. He was as one that had suffered a stroke; his tongue clove to the bottom of his mouth, and he only made animal-like sounds. He couldn't form words he had used since childhood. All his efforts were in vain; no one understood him. Tears ran down his face as he knew what he wanted to say but couldn't cause his tongue to free itself. He was greatly undone.

Many were struck with great fear for it was surely an act of God. Others said that Zechariah's age had finally come upon him; he was too old for such an undertaking. Soon all left the temple courts. Each carried a different story of the event to his home. Many traveled throughout the city telling the story as they went, and some even throughout the countryside to foreign lands.

The officers of the temple carried the news of this event to Annas and Caiaphas who found little comfort in it. They came and viewed Zechariah. Later, the seventy was called to rule on the qualification of Zechariah as there were at that time twenty-two such temporary disabilities which could cause loss of duty. The ruling came that should Zechariah recover before his course was through, he could return to his priestly duties, but then only after testing.

Father attended to the needs of Zechariah. After removing the raiment of his office, Zechariah dressed in his street clothes. At last Zechariah became stable enough to ask for writing instruments and a surface to use. They were brought and placed before him; he then wrote down the following description of the happenings within the sanctuary. All this father told to us when he returned from Jerusalem.

Zechariah wrote he was visited by an angel of the Lord. The angel stood at the right of the altar of incense. Zechariah's heart nearly failed him at the sight, and he was greatly troubled; fear and trembling fell upon him. But the angel said that he should fear not as his prayers were heard and Elizabeth would have a son. Yet more, the angel said - that Zechariah should call his son's name John, and he would be a happy child and, because of him, many others as well. His son had a destiny to fulfill, and therefore must never drink either wine or strong drink all the days of his life; even the Passover wine he shall not have. He shall be filled with the Spirit of the Lord, and upon hearing him, many people shall turn from their evil ways and return to the God of their fathers. Yea, even many of the children of Israel.

And John bar Zechariah would have the power of Elijah to turn the hearts of the fathers unto the children, and the disobedient to the wisdom of the just; and even make the people ready for the coming of the Messiah.

Upon hearing these things, Zechariah wrote he felt some misgivings that the angel had selected him, and yes, even Elizabeth, as they were both late in years. Knowing the difficulties given to late childbirth and the raising of a child so late in life, he was concerned. Now, he said, he believed what was said, but for Elizabeth, as she would surely laugh at this - his news of this day.

Whereupon the angel became greatly agitated and said that he was indeed the angel Gabriel, one who stands in the presence of Almighty God and had been sent to tell these glad tidings. The angel continued saying, therefore, not only because of your unbelief, but also the attempt to lie and place the blame on Elizabeth, you shall be struck dumb as of this moment and shall remain so until the day these things come to pass.

All this Zechariah wrote on the tablet. He was then relieved of his duties by Annas.

Father helped Zechariah through the city to his home, pausing many times to explain Zechariah's ailment to those who stopped them to talk to Zechariah.

When home, father called the family of Zechariah to his side. The tablets were shown to the family. Zechariah motioned for father to be his voice and relate the story, even as it happened that day. The family was distressed and gave many sacrifices for relief from this sign but to no avail. The loss of speech caused Zechariah great hardship because his blessings were shut up within him and only signs of the blessings could he perform.

There was much joy and sadness in the house of Zechariah that day and those that followed. The joy over the announcement, and great sadness that Zechariah couldn't tell of the great happening himself.

After some time, father went to Zechariah and told him he must return to his family for we were in need of him. He asked for his release to return. Zechariah released him from his obligation, blessed him, and sent him on his way with gifts for his services.

When father returned, the household gathered, as was the custom, to welcome the master of the house. Mother had a meal prepared for the occasion and the family received him and Zechariah's blessings. After the meal, the household gathered again, even the servants, into the courtyard and father told us all as he had seen and heard. And all wondered what it meant, but not as much as Ishmael and I. The household was in great wonderment for these were indeed strange signs that were occurring among the people.

Father went about his duties in the local house of assembly, but all was not the same. His acceptance in Jerusalem set him apart from the others, and he was sought out when strange stories were told by the hill people and herdsmen. He was now called upon to explain numerous tales of animal multi-births to changes in the sky, and falling stars. Many stories were brought to our house, and we as children, were privy to them by remaining silent in the background while each was told. We wondered just what these stories meant.

But none of these stories were of greater wonderment than those we heard from the passersby who stopped at the well. Here was the great fountain of all sorts of attractive tales of human activities, all told in believable fashion by foreigners from every land. It was here we heard our first story of the child later to be known to me as Yeshua of Nazareth.

One morning in 747, Ishmael and I rose early as the night had been oppressively hot. And even before the sun rose, we went to the well. We had often done this before to catch sight of the early morning caravans and troops traveling through Kerioth. It was from these early morning travelers the freshest rumors and news of the trail could be learned. We took our usual place on the wall near the well, and listened to the gossip of the day. Each had his own story or version of a story to tell. Although it was of the same origin, it seldom was told in the same context, and Ishmael and I often laughed at the differences between these stories. At the same time, we never really knew which was true for all were told by their carriers as the truth of the prophets of old.

Each storyteller wanted to tell his story to anyone who would listen, and two young boys of eleven were no exception. The fact that we listened, and this with a show of wonderment, often gave a power of eloquence to the teller, and the stories, although often told along the trail, became as new for him as they were for us. With this kind of audience, the teller would add to his tale the necessary body movements he thought would make up the difference between his command of the listeners' language and his own. The stories often became plays with the teller playing all the parts as he would weave his tale of human experiences to mythology. Many of these stories were adventures, some love stories and some tragedies, but irrespective of time and setting, they were all true - so each claimed.

It was this morning, as the dust in the heart of Kerioth had settled some, that Ishmael and I sat on the wall listening to the calls of the drivers, that a young man resting against the wall spoke to us.

"I salute you in the name of the Lord our God. Would you lads know of the household of Simon the Kohen of Kerioth?" He spoke slowly as if in fear we wouldn't understand him, and he was surprised by Ishmael's quick answer.

"May the Lord be with you. We know of him and his household, but it isn't wise to reveal the whereabouts of another's home to strangers in these days of oppression. What is your need of him? What's your name, good sir?" Ishmael was always quicker with his tongue than I, but always spoke with respect.

"Aye, that's a good teaching for all when Herod lives in fear of his own people. My name is Abidan of the house of Benjamin but it is a story of good and curious tiding I carry from the house of Zechariah to one Simon of Kerioth. Simon has found favor in the heart of Zechariah, and he longs to see him again." The young stranger was showing his tiredness as he came from Jerusalem late the night before.

"It is well, we know of Zechariah. Come follow us to the house of my father, Simon." With that said, we jumped from the wall and led the young stranger toward home. While Ishmael walked along with Abidan, I ran ahead to announce his coming. I saluted father as was the custom and blurted out the news.

"A stranger now comes with Ishmael, father, and has told us he brings news from Zechariah." I was quite breathless from running ahead.

"Go, find your mother and tell her we have the honor of a visitor with news from Jerusalem. Prepare water for his feet and wine for his stomach." Father accepted the news with some surprise. I went to do his bidding but was back in time to see Abidan and Ishmael enter the house.

Abidan saluted father and said, "I, Abidan, from the house of Benjamin, and humble servant of Zechariah, greet you and bring you tidings from him. His concern is of you and your family, and his blessings on your house." The young man stopped for a moment and father held up his hand.

"Welcome, Abidan, but pray rest and sup with us before you reveal your tidings. I know the trip from Jerusalem is a tiring one having made it myself."

The servants brought cool water and a change of clothes for Abidan as was the custom of the house. He was led to a closet where his ablution was completed in privacy. After washing, he dressed in the fresh clothes and sandals supplied him. His trail clothing would be washed and ready for him when he left the house. When he reappeared, he looked pleased for no man wanted to bring the soil of the road into another's house.

"Come, let us move to the cool courtyard." Father turned and with his hand directed Abidan toward our small but well-kept courtyard. The courtyard was an oasis from the heat of the house during midday. Both mother and father spent many summer hours there.

Abidan looked more comfortable after his washing and accepted a position near father. Mother sat some distance away as was the custom, but listened with great interest of any news from Jerusalem. The servants brought food and wine that Abidan might be refreshed and feel welcome.

"When you are rested tell us the news." Although not pressing Abidan, father, like mother, was anxious for news from Jerusalem. Father wanted news in the religious vein, while mother was more interested in political attitudes of the people of Jerusalem.

Abidan, now somewhat recovered from the trip and little sleep, was ready to tell his story. He leaned forward from his position on the couch: "The message concerns an event unknown until now. I now tell the part not yet told," he said with strength in his voice. This was his account: Elizabeth conceived. She hid in the hill country of Judea for five months; the place was known only to Zechariah and her maidservant. In the sixth month of her sojourn in secret, her kinswoman, Mary, from the house of David, a cousin, found her by a revelation of the Lord.

It was with great surprise Elizabeth received Mary into her hiding place. As Mary greeted her, Elizabeth became aware of the babe she was carrying moving in her womb. She testified that the babe recognized the salutation from Mary.

Mary told of the visit from an angel of the Lord and her selection of all women to be the instrument for the birth of a son to be called Yeshua. Elizabeth was greatly disturbed as she knew Mary had no man but was betrothed to one in Nazareth. Mary told Elizabeth that the child was Spirit given; Elizabeth, knowing of her own good fortune, believed the words of Mary. Mother listened to this news with some show of skepticism and turned her head away from Abidan so he might not see her doubt. But Ishmael and I recognized this little quirk and held it in mind.

Mary told the mighty things Yeshua would do for his people when the Spirit came upon him. She told her cousin of the wonders that were revealed to her by the angel.

When she finished, the Spirit came upon Elizabeth and she foretold things revealed to her. The women rejoiced in the message of hope the Lord had shown unto them - even that Yeshua was the Messiah. Mary stayed with her cousin nearly three months and then left for her own city, Nazareth, where her betrothed, Joseph, of the house of David, lived.

Abidan told how he came by this knowledge and how the thing came to pass; even how Elizabeth presented Zechariah with a son. Zechariah's household and kin were joyful over the removal of the curse of barrenness from Elizabeth as she had walked in the Law and Prohibitions all her days.

He told when it came time to present the babe to the Lord, and circumcision was to be done, his name had not yet been told the relatives and friends. All those present called him Zechariah, after his father, as was the custom since the ages. But Elizabeth said not so - for his name should be John, even as the angel commanded. The relatives and people murmured at her words and turned to Zechariah and asked him what the name should be. Zechariah asked for his tablet and wrote the name John; when this was done, Zechariah's tongue was loosened and he was able to speak, yea, even as before. And all present marveled as he had perfect speech without any time needed to educate his tongue.

Fear came upon them and dwelt round about them, and all these things were noised about throughout the hills of Judea. And all that heard them stored them in their memory and hearts saying, "What manner of child shall this be?"

Abidan also told how the Spirit of the Lord came upon Zechariah, who prophesied, saying that John would accomplish great and wondrous things, and many people should follow his voice and become changed. Zechariah prophesied all these things that day.

Abidan then said, "All these things I was told by Zechariah to reveal to you and your household, as I am his humble servant." With that, Abidan relaxed from his speaking position on the couch.

Father asked him many questions about these wonders and listened to many comments about the babe and how Zechariah believed in his vision. How both he and Elizabeth praised the Lord with songs of old. All these things we heard while we sat at the feet of Abidan; Ishmael and I were filled with the adventure of the tale. Mother listened in her quiet way, but was more interested in the goings and comings of the court of Herod and Roman politics. When Abidan finished with the tale, she begged him to tell her the news of the social world in Jerusalem. Abidan asked forgiveness for he had no first-hand knowledge of such things; his was the message of the new government of Israel, a government yet to be established as its' leader was not yet born.

Father heard Abidan out and then asked him to stay for the passing of the holidays, as it wasn't possible for one to travel on the day of rest. Abidan agreed, but would be gone the following day, for he had others to tell this story to, as commanded by Zechariah. His time was short, or so he said, and he had a great distance to travel, although to where he didn't say. Father gave him the evening blessing and we retired to our rooms.

Abidan had been gone some months when a messenger arrived requesting father's presence by Zechariah. Zechariah had passed all priestly tests and was found clean under the law, and was reinstated in the course of his fathers.

While the messenger waited outside the gates, father called the family to him and announced that he was wanted in Jerusalem. He was willing to go if and only if the family could go as well. Here we could see mother's influence. Mother, who was never one to let a chance for success go by, began the mental preparation for the move. Father gave the messenger his blessing and sent him on his way with the news that he would come to serve as he had before.

Mother was happy for the change. Life for her in Kerioth was too close; she secretly admired the Roman lifestyle. She always wanted to move to a larger and more metropolitan community, and Jerusalem was the answer to her longing.

She earlier had pressed father to go to the temple in Jerusalem and seek a position there, but father merely stated, "Shall the servant of God choose his place of servitude like a common peddler chooses his house of business? Is it not written that he who doeth My will among the least is greater than those who doeth it not in mighty places? Woman, don't cry lest God take away what he has surely given us."

Mother accepted father's words but deep within her hoped for just such recognition as now had come about even without father's petitioning. She moved to set her house aright.

Much was to be done, and preparing the household for the trek to Jerusalem was no easy task as mother wasn't one to shirk her responsibilities. The next day we were sent by cart, bag and baggage, to our Uncle Joshua on mother's side. There we were to stay until all was ready for the move.

Mother went with father to study our new quarters in Jerusalem. It was to be the family abode for many years, if not for life. Before entering the gate, father placed the mezuzah, carefully removed from the house in Kerioth, on the gate of the new structure. Once in the house, mother quickly assigned quarters to master, children, and servants. All this preparation to move to the holy city was predicated, so father said, on the hope that a census decreed by Augustus Caesar wouldn't reach Judea for another year.

The census, and coincident taxation, was one implemented in Rome in 741 and had been moving throughout the empire. The census started in Rome, moved north and west to Gaul, Hispania, and by sea to Egypt. From Rome it also moved east through Illyricum, Macedonia, Asia, and Syria. Nearly six years had passed since Augustus ordered the count - this wasn't an overnight operation.

The census was taking longer than expected outside Rome as many of the provinces were slow complying. Father said Herod had received the edict earlier in 744 from Quirinius to start the census in Judea, but stood on 'rex socius' and didn't start until the beginning of this year, 747. I could remember the order being read at the well in Kerioth by Herod's messenger.

In the order, Herod imposed additional obligations on his subjects. It was rumored he wanted to gain information that he would hide from Rome - the count of military-aged men. All males twenty to fifty years old were to register as of old, that is, they were to return to the city of their fathers in accordance with the law. So it was that men fit for military service and some of their families moved about the land to obey the edict of Herod.

During this time, much commerce and family life was in turmoil in Herod's kingdom. The confusion caused by men trying to meet an outdated religious law that King David had brought into being in this day was horrendous. Father said it was a wonder the Romans permitted such disruption within their empire, but Herod would be Herod.

With the census and taxes for Rome, the old fox added the gathering of the temple tax - a redemption gift - so he said. This additional tax collection required both Roman and Jewish collectors and scribes. The time to accomplish this task was long - longer than within other provinces. Father said such a census in accordance with Jewish law could take nearly two years in cities like Jerusalem, but in Kerioth, not so long.

The preparation for the move wasn't completed yet when word was received that this census was to be taken throughout the kingdom. Since the decree for taxation came from the Roman political system, no man could avoid it, and because it was in accordance with Jewish law, it required every man to register in his own city. In father's case, it meant we couldn't move to Jerusalem until the census and taxation of Kerioth was completed as it was father's own city. How long this would be wasn't clear, for the Roman system was riddled with sluggards and ne'er-do-wells that maintained their positions through bribery and trickery - not service.

When dealing with the Jewish nation, no great pressure was brought to bear on behalf of the Jewish populous. There was always pressure from Rome to get the job done, and always at the expense of the Jewish people - never the Roman citizen.

So it was that father recognized the need for a change of plans concerning the coming move to Jerusalem. All would have to be thought out again. Mother was consulted for the needs of the household. The question was, how long could we live in our present condition of disarray? She knew the answer even before asked; it was her life to know the needs and wants of her family. All of this she knew and without hesitation spoke of the acceptance of our condition as one of short duration. Maybe a week or two, then the house must be resettled; it would be necessary to accept family and guests who would come to Kerioth to be counted and taxed in accordance with the decree.

It was her final decision that all should be put back in order; the children would return from the house of Uncle Joshua, father would go to Jerusalem alone again, and from thence return to take his household there after the census.

She recognized the family obligation to those who must make the long trip to Kerioth and needed a place to stay. It was, she said, a God-given duty for one to assist any of the family during this period of trial. What must be, must be, and all else should be put aside. Who could tell when we might be in the same position, needing help and a place to stay during some dire event after the move to Jerusalem?

Father listened to her wise words and made the changes necessary to delay his return to Jerusalem. Our family was from Kerioth many generations and it was here we would be counted. Father was one of the first to meet all the requirements of the census, both Roman and Jewish. He soon was counted as a military man, paid his tax, and received his mark and papers. It was the mark and papers that told other taxation checkpoints throughout the area that he had been counted and taxed. Any man without the mark and papers was subject to loss of freedom and loss of property. The mark made on the back of father's hand was of a dye that lasted for nearly two years - this I can remember even to this day.

Mother prepared for any and all relatives who might appeal to us for shelter and food during their stay while taking part in the census. During this time, our house was a beehive of activity, and many brothers, brothers-in-law, as well as aunts and uncles together with cousins that we had never seen before or since, came and stayed with us. None stayed long and all offered father gold for that which his house had done for them. All this father turned aside, for what is it that a man does for those he loves, an act of family grace to be likened unto a product sold by a common merchant? Each family came and went as they complied with the census and taxation. They arrived in weary condition but left with clean raiment, food, and refreshed for the trek back from whence they came, all giving salutations upon arriving and family blessings when leaving.

It was during this family excitement that a messenger came once again from Zechariah requesting father's help. Father prepared to go to Jerusalem alone. Mother would manage all the household and family obligations during his absence. He was to return as soon as he had a clear view of Zechariah's needs. Giving his blessing to all, he and one servant, Atonis, left for Jerusalem.

The road was filled with people on their way to and from other cities, even as the decree stated for men of military age - each unto his own city. People jostled one another for position on the road, and the dust, heat, and crowded conditions caused the temper of even the most upright traveler to flare now and again. Father and Atonis had traveled this same road not long before, and they noted the great differences in the travelers met this time with those met before. Each seemed to have lost his patience with the other, and the salute and friendly greeting was not often heard. Instead, the cries of the young, bellows of the beasts of burden, and the shouts of the drivers were predominant.

It wasn't long for the heat to take its toll, and many of the very young and old were sitting along the road. Although this was mainly a movement of the young, family responsibilities forced them to bring along members that were young and old. Many of the men of military age couldn't leave their families behind on a trip that might take weeks to complete. So it was that a great share of Herod's subjects found themselves on some road far from home, nearly in want, and bewildered because of his secret call to arms.

The sun shone on those still able to travel, and those not, with little mercy. Sweat came freely from whatever activity and caused the dust to cling to every part of the body. Both father and Atonis were more than willing to rest before they reached Jerusalem. Even with an early start, they hadn't traveled as far as before. The distance from Kerioth to Jerusalem was nearly thirty miles over rough roads, but the conditions made it seem longer.

As the sun went below the hills, they approached the small town of Bethlehem. The possibility of improving their lot very much by traveling in the dark seemed doubtful. From previous trips, father knew that to continue on and try to reach Jerusalem yet that day was hardship not required by the lack of urgency. To do so meant traveling the last eight miles in total darkness and thereby be subjected to road hazards and robbers who were preying on unhappy pilgrims traveling to be counted.

Father decided they should tarry overnight in Bethlehem even as many others were doing. Since it was still in the first watch of the Roman order, father and Atonis searched for lodgings wherein they might wash off the dust of the road, secure food, and rest in safety.

Finding an inn that still had rooms for let was not an easy task; therefore, to increase the chances of locating a place to rest, father instructed Atonis to search another part of the town while he stayed near the well. It was Atonis who located a small inn at the north edge of Bethlehem on the route to Jerusalem. Father was greatly pleased with this report, for it meant they could be through the town and on their way to Jerusalem early in the morning. Atonis led the way and father made arrangements for the nights' lodging and supper.

Once in the room, Atonis helped father with his bath and change of clothes and soon followed with his own change. When both were rested, they entered the dining chamber where guests were served the meal of the house. With prayers of thanksgiving said, they ate in silence. They no sooner finished dining than the weariness of the day's travel fell heavy upon them and they retired for the night.

Sleep did not come easy that night as father's mind was not at rest; much troubled him about leaving his family once again. But this was not true of Atonis, as once he had fulfilled his obligation to father, he fell fast asleep across the threshold of the chamber door.

When sleep finally came, it was fretful; father seemed to hover between a half-awake and half-asleep condition, with dreams so real that he felt he was fully awake at times, but never sure. Then all would fade away and simple quietness would reign supreme for what seemed a short period. Then the cycle would begin again.

It was during one of the quiet periods that he was aroused to the state of being half awake by what seemed to him a loud knocking on the gate of the inn. Father felt he was dreaming but arose and went to the window of the chamber. Looking out at the dimly-lit street below, he saw a man leading an ass with a woman sitting thereon. In the weak light, he couldn't see their faces or tell their ages. From the man's speech, father determined he was from an area known as Galilee far to the north of Jerusalem.

"Innkeeper, Innkeeper, have you a room for a weary pair? My wife and I have traveled from Nazareth these days past; she is near her time and we need a room for her." The man's voice showed genuine concern for his wife and the possibility of her delivery yet with the watch.

"I'm sorry, my friend, but my inn is full. In fact, many have shared rooms with others to ease their discomforts. There is none I can ask to give up any more as guests of the inn. Some of them are equally as bad off as you and your wife. Some have come further distances without the aid of animals. Blind are some, and have to be led or stumble along the road using only a stick for safe guidance." It was during this speech by the innkeeper that the woman on the ass cried out. Her husband went to her aid, and then rushed back to the innkeeper and asked if there was at least room in the stable for his animal. The innkeeper said yes, and that he was welcome to it at no cost, and was sorry he could do no more. Father was about to waken Atonis to offer his quarters to the couple, when the man said no more and straightway led the animal with the woman on its back to the stable.

All became quiet again, and the moon went behind a cloud to darken the street below. When father looked again, there was no movement near the inn; he returned to his bed and wondered if it had all been a dream. It wasn't long before he finally fell asleep again, or had he been sleeping and now dreaming he was sleeping?

As he slept, it seemed he dreamed another dream. When he turned to rest his side, through the open window he saw a glow in the sky over the distant hills to the east of Bethlehem. A rather strange glow, like that of a large fire, yet not so much like a fire as a cloud-covered sunset. It lacked the proper look of a land fire glow; the light seemed to originate in the heavens and move toward the earth - a brush fire wouldn't cause this.

All was quiet except for the soft chanting by some of those yet traveling through the night. Father could make out only little of the chant which seemed to be one of praise. It came floating through the night air from those on the road nearest the glow in the sky. The song of praise, as near as his sleepy condition would permit his mind to accept, was not one of the ancient chants but of a new and different origin.

"Glory be to God in the highest, and on earth, peace and good will toward men."

He thought the words were carried on a sweet melody but the distance was too great for his understanding it all and recalled how many of those traveling at night often sang to help one another follow the road during the darkest hours. This simple act let those near know all was well and that robbers had not attacked the little band of night travelers. As he watched and listened, his eyes closed and he slept again.

Suddenly, noises of a gathering crowd in the street below came through the window. He went to look out the window, and there in the street below was a gathering of shepherds milling about and talking excitedly among themselves, repeating a story of some strange happening in the hills not far from Bethlehem. It was odd, father thought, that these men were in town yet their flocks were nowhere in sight. As he watched, the shepherds moved to the back of the inn by the stable in the same direction the couple took in his first dream.

The shepherds talked agitatedly among themselves, unable to refrain from gesturing and waving their arms about. Father, not being familiar with all the hill dialects, could make little of their stories as they repeated them to one another.

"Oh, Thomas, why do you continue to doubt? I tell you I saw them with my own eyes and heard them as well…'in Bethlehem you shall find him,' one said to the other."

"And I, too, Josiah, heard the singing in the heavens by a multitude of angels. It was a sign for us to hasten to see this thing that has come to pass in Judea this night," he paused to take a breath, "here we are come, even to the place described to us, and here is the babe…"

"Let us hasten and see this thing that was told to us, for he is to be in the stable of this very inn." With that said, they turned toward the stable. After the shepherds were gone for awhile, father became extremely tired and turned back to his bed. It was as though he hadn't reached his bed and he was fast asleep again.

Yet a fourth time, after the call of the fourth watch, he was wakened to hear the shepherds leaving the stable. They were very excited about the happening of the night, and talked loudly among themselves as to how lucky they were to be chosen first to know and see this thing that was wrought by the Almighty God. As they separated, he heard them call encouragement to one another and promise to tell everyone they met of this night.

Father was greatly curious about their excitement and planned to ask the innkeeper about the strange happening of this night before he left Bethlehem in the morning. As he again turned from the window, he noticed Atonis had slept through all he had seen and heard. His head had no more reached his pillow and he was again fast asleep.

C H A P T E R   F O U R

A Story Told

Atonis woke father with a gentle touch. The sun was yet to appear as the time was in the fourth watch. Father, having paid for their lodging and supper the night before, was free to start the trek to Jerusalem. Most people in the inn were still sleeping when father and Atonis left. As they walked along, the air was somewhat cooler and the road less crowded. Even after a fretful night, father had regained strength for the next few miles. Talk between he and Atonis helped the miles pass.

It was during an early part of their conversation that father recalled his desire to speak with the innkeeper about the happenings of the night before. Yet, they were too far away to turn back and learn if the events were real or just parts of dreams. It wasn't worth the loss of time, so they continued along the road trying to gain as much distance as they could before the heat of the day. Since Jerusalem was only eight miles from Bethlehem, father reasoned they would be there by noon.

The people along the road were just as disrespectful of one another as before and father wanted to be away from the coarseness of the crowd as soon as possible. Jerusalem would soon be seen from a rise in the roadway. As they neared it, the press of the crowds increased until it seemed the entire Jewish nation was on the road from Jerusalem to other cities in the kingdom, more traveling *from* the great city than *to* it. Everywhere were young and old striving to reach the cities of their fathers elsewhere in the country.

It was high noon when they finally approached the house of Zechariah. They were tired and covered with the dust of the road. As they approached, a young servant of Zechariah recognized them and ran into the house to announce their coming. Zechariah came out and met them at the gate. "I salute you. May the peace of God rest with you and your days be long on the earth. Come, refresh yourselves. I'm glad you honored my request during this time of trial. Come!"

"God be with you and your household, Zechariah," father answered, bowing to him.

Zechariah, paying little attention to their disheveled appearance, ushered them through the gates into the house. It was obvious he was happy at their arrival and wished to talk to father as soon as he was refreshed.

Father, always concerned for the needs of others, especially his servants, waited until Atonis was cared for within the servants' quarters before continuing with his own comforts. When this was done, father proceeded to clear away the dust of the road, and accepted the clean raiment and sandals brought for him, as many others had done before.

Refreshed, he went into the inner chambers, and finding no one there, went to the small courtyard he visited many times before during the burning of incense. He saluted Zechariah and his family. They were assembled for the noonday meal. As a guest, he was expected to join them. When the blessing was said, the family took of the food, each in his order and station, with father first, being the only guest in the house. Father ate small portions as was the custom, only to be asked to increase his amount or he would disgrace the house of Zechariah by his hunger. After the meal, praise was given for the food and kindness of God for the safe journey of father and blessings were said for father's family.

Zechariah had Elizabeth present their son, John, to father. The boy was now about ten months old. He was a sturdy baby with a good pair of lungs, or so father thought. Zechariah and Elizabeth expressed their joy for the gift of a son in songs of praise to the God of their fathers.

After their song, Zechariah gave father a detailed accounting of the events that led up to the presentation of John. He spoke of the announcement of the birth of a son to Elizabeth's cousin Mary, of the house of David. Much of this Abidan had told sometime before but discretion kept father from mentioning this to Zechariah.

Zechariah told how Joseph and Mary just passed through the city the day before on their way to Bethlehem. He spoke of their taking the noonday meal with him and how they refused to stay overnight even though Mary was great with child. He expressed sadness because of the refusal, but accepted their feeling of urgency to be in Bethlehem yet that night as an angel of the Lord had told them it was there a son would be born unto them. Their not staying to rest weighed heavily on his heart.

No word had come from them through the night, even to this hour. It was Zechariah's servant, on his way to Bethlehem, who saw father approach the gate. After learning father had slept in an inn at Bethlehem, Zechariah stayed his servant until he could ask father if he had perchance heard of a birth taking place in Bethlehem. Of course, Zechariah understood only too well that at times such as these, with the press of the multitude caused by the decree, it was unlikely such news would be worded about. After all, a birth of a babe at a time like this just meant additional taxes. Yet, Zechariah was a man of faith and he had seen a miracle in his own life - God could show the way. It was indeed the will of God and Zechariah's good fortune that father came from Bethlehem that very day. Zechariah asked father to tell all he knew of that night in Bethlehem.

As Zechariah spoke, the Spirit moved father and he remembered the couple who stopped at the inn that evening.

"Your words cause me some woe, for much of a strange and fretful night comes upon me. Would I could return to that time and cause the events to happen again knowing what has been revealed to me this hour." Father was greatly disturbed at the news.

Zechariah bid father to tell his story. Father told them of the experiences along the road, of the many people on the road and their impious and disrespectful nature. He told of the strange tiredness he and Atonis had experienced as they approached Bethlehem, and how it was his decision to stay the night there. He described the great numbers of people in the small town of Bethlehem, and the difficulty of finding a room for a night's rest. He told of their search and finding the inns within the city full and overflowing. He included the finding of the inn by faithful Atonis and their rest therein. His story continued with their partaking of the evening meal as guests of the inn, of the strange tiredness that once again overtook them after the meal, and how they fell asleep early in the first watch.

"Zechariah, it's from this point that I'm troubled, for surely God showed me things I just now understand. Woe is my heart. I feel as one who was lost without knowing it. Even as it's written by the prophets, 'The sheep shall not know they are lost, for only this is known to the shepherd.'" Father was indeed greatly distressed; only the encouragement of Zechariah caused him to continue.

Father then told of the half-asleep, half-awake condition during the night, and how he was troubled by dreams, some so real he couldn't tell reality from dreams. He told of this first partial awakening by the voice of the man leading an animal with a woman setting thereon. Of the man's request for a room for his wife who was great with child. And how the innkeeper had rejected them because his rooms were filled to overflowing. He remembered his urge to rouse Atonis and give his room to the couple, but the man asked the way to the stable and moved away before he could turn and notify the innkeeper that they could have his room. He continued by recalling how they moved toward the stable and after that, all was again quiet and he fell into a deep sleep.

"Oh Zechariah," Elizabeth cried upon hearing this part of the story, "it must have been them, and they did reach Bethlehem safely as it was the will of God." She was greatly distraught at the possible discomforts of her younger cousin at the time of her deliverance. "Would we had forced them to stay the night, or I had gone with her to act as midwife in her time of trial. That she should be alone without family near is indeed a great trial for one in travail. Oh, woe is me, for I'm one that knew of her great coming before any other."

Elizabeth's distress was so deep that father and Zechariah feared for her life because of her age. Zechariah told her maidservants to tend to her needs, and bade father not continue until she had recovered from her discomfort. He then called his trusted servant to him and ordered him to secure an animal from the stable, and be ready to fly to Bethlehem, even unto the inn whereof father spoke.

When Elizabeth had recovered, Zechariah asked her to prepare her maidservant and all that was necessary to ease Mary's discomforts while in the early days of her time with the babe. And Elizabeth was buoyed up and did as he requested. She gathered those things, most oft needed by a young mother in those times, and after praising God for his graciousness in permitting her this small deed, gave them to her maidservant for Mary. After learning the whereabouts of the inn, she gave her servant a blessing and sent her along with Zechariah's servant to Bethlehem.

When she returned from her task, Zechariah asked father to continue with his accounting of the stay in Bethlehem. Father continued the story beginning with the second time he was awakened by the strange glow in the sky to the east of Bethlehem, in the area where the local herdsmen were watching the sheep through the night. How, in his sleepy condition, he first thought it was a brush fire in the hills, but as he continued to watch, he saw the light seemed to come from the heavens and not from the ground as in a land fire. As he watched, the light suddenly grew in brightness, and even in his sleepy condition, he became afraid. While he was engrossed with the scene, he became aware of a soft chanting of a song of praise to the most High God. The chanting seemed to come from the hills wherein the light was most bright. He then recalled the words and tune of the chant and sang it for Zechariah.

"Glory to God in the highest, and on earth, peace and good will toward men!"

The chant was repeated over and over, but from whence it came he couldn't be certain. At the time, he considered it to be from some of those who traveled through the night on the dark roadway. As he watched and listened, the sky darkened and all became quiet, and he returned to his bed to fall asleep again. And so ended his reconstruction of the second awakening.

"It is indeed as it was written, and even the angels shall sing praises to Almighty God for the deliverer of Israel from their evil ways. You, Simon, have been the blessed one among us, for you unknowingly have been the one chosen as the first teller of the good news. Our blessings are upon you, for you have brought the news of the boy king of Israel," Zechariah said and bade father to continue with his story.

Father told of his fretfulness the rest of the night. He was wakened a third time from his sleep by the voices of men below his chamber window. Going to the window, he saw below in the bright moonlight a group of shepherds standing near. As they spoke, he was able to understand little, for some spoke a dialect unknown to him. But what he heard and understood gave him cause for wonderment.

The shepherds were greatly excited as they truly believed they had seen a miracle. They spoke of seeing a host of angels in the heavens singing praises to God on high. And how an angel appeared to tell them of the birth of a Messiah and true messenger of God. Each shepherd, although in different areas of the fields, had the same message revealed to him. A message which told him to leave his flock and go into the city of Bethlehem to a stable and see this thing that had come to pass. While they spoke thus, they moved in the direction of the stable, and the night was once again quiet. Father recalled how he then fell across his bed in exhausted sleep.

When father awoke the fourth time it was still very dark as the moon had started its fall from the sky. It was the shepherds leaving the inn that had caused him to waken. They left the stable in great spirits and the talk among them was how they had been part of this wondrous thing that was revealed to them. When they left, all was quiet and father fell fast asleep again, not waking until Atonis placed his hand upon him. Father told how God masked his intent to seek out the innkeeper and see if these were facts or dreams, and hence his travel to Jerusalem forthwith.

Upon hearing all this, Zechariah and Elizabeth fell on their knees in humble praise to the most High God for the news brought to them from Bethlehem.

NOT IN A MANGER

It was on the third day of father's stay that Elizabeth's maidservant returned from Bethlehem with news of Mary and the babe. Elizabeth was joyful at the news and hastened to Zechariah to tell the story. However, it was from the mouth of the maidservant that all was spoken. Father was invited to hear and study her words as was the custom of that day. She told about the trip and how they made haste even as they were instructed. They didn't spare the animals. Their trip was with the flow of the travelers which greatly helped their progress. They were in Bethlehem within the day and they arrived before the first watch.

They proceeded to search for the inn described by father and found it straightaway. The press of the multitude was very great and the innkeeper was in demand for many sought rooms for the night as before. Although the decree from Herod for a census of all men who could bear arms was considered a tragedy for some, it was like the rain from God, not so for all. Many of those offering services to weary travelers were seldom so lucky; the flow of gold followed the masses on the road. Even in some of the smallest towns, new money came in with the request for men to return to the cities of their fathers.

Among those so favored were shopkeepers, money changers, innkeepers and the like. Not all were cursing the taxation, even though they too had to pay new taxes and register for the military themselves.

The innkeeper, not knowing their mission, gave them permission to visit the stable, and by his attitude, gave the impression that others had come to see the stable and inquire about the birth the night before.

The maidservant followed the innkeeper to the stable. Her heart nearly failed her when she found no one there; only the beasts of burden were within the structure - she made sure of that - there was no sign of an ass among the animals in the stalls. Upon finding this, she caused the manservant to inquire of the innkeeper what had happened to the couple and babe who were there just the night before.

The innkeeper remembered the event and couple quite readily. "It was indeed singularly strange," he remarked, touching his hand to his forehead.

The innkeeper told them of the great feeling of compassion that came over him when he beheld the couple's plight. It increased from compassion to wonderment when the shepherds visited them late that night and told their strange story of angels appearing unto them in the hills. He admitted he couldn't sleep through the night. He heard the cries of the newborn during the early hours and he was moved by the sound. His heart wasn't of stone and wouldn't let him rest. He prayed for forgiveness for his failure to make room for them.

During his prayer, God revealed that he should have them move from the stable unto a small house he owned near the north side of the city. And so it was that he offered them temporary shelter in a humble home he owned, and there they could stay until her time for purification would come. In fact, his heart was so penitent he decided to let them stay as long as they wished, and so it was that Joseph, concerned for Mary and the newborn, accepted his offer for a period agreed to between them. The innkeeper caused his servants to assist the new family in moving from the stable to the house at the edge of Bethlehem. It was there he bade the servants to go to see Joseph and his family. With these instructions and the blessings of the innkeeper, the servants went to find the cousin of Elizabeth. They found them even as the innkeeper told them, and after saluting them in the name of Zechariah, they presented the gifts and performed the services as they were instructed.

Mary's heart was full of happiness. She told them all that had happened the night of the birth of her son; even the things she considered miracles. She showed them the babe peacefully sleeping in his crib. Mary accepted the gifts from Elizabeth with a grateful heart, praising God and thanking him for so good a cousin as she.

Although Mary and Joseph didn't speak of their needs, the handmaiden told of their lack of many things. Joseph hadn't made the trip prepared to stay for long in Bethlehem. Yet, the lack of service and questionable birth records was making the stay longer than he had planned. They had expressed a fear they might have to stay in Bethlehem as long as a year or longer. Because of this possibility, Mary wanted their relatives in Nazareth to know of their misfortune. She appealed to Elizabeth to notify her family of the possible additional time in Bethlehem. All this the maidservant told Zechariah, Elizabeth, and father.

Mary and Joseph sent their blessings to Zechariah and his house. They commanded the maidservant to convey their humble request that Zechariah honor their house by performing the ceremony of circumcision and naming of the child.

The servants tarried until the handmaiden was no longer needed and then, after accepting the blessing of Mary, left straightaway for Jerusalem and their master's house.

The maidservant said that Mary was well and the babe was taking nourishment. After telling the story, she was dismissed and given new raiment to replace those soiled on the trip from Bethlehem.

Both Zechariah and Elizabeth were happy and sang praises to God for the request that Zechariah had received from Mary. They began preparation for the trip to Bethlehem in that same hour.

During the time of preparation, father and Zechariah talked of the possibility of a move to Jerusalem. Zechariah told father of his need for someone to help him in the temple as he was approaching an age in life that required the steadiness of a younger hand. He told father of speaking to Caiaphas about his need for assistance, and that Caiaphas found no law against such action. Father expressed his gratitude for considering him as his special attendant, and asked when such a need would be required. Zechariah said as soon as father could move to Jerusalem. Father was eager to join him in the office of the temple and asked for a blessing that he might prepare for his trip back to Kerioth. And so it was done.

As the time for leaving Jerusalem approached, Zechariah bade father to delay his departure until the time of the circumcision and they would travel together as far as Bethlehem. It was Zechariah's will and pleasure that father help him in the ceremony of circumcision and see firsthand that which had come to pass.

So it was that after seven days passed, father traveled with Zechariah, Elizabeth, and their servants to Bethlehem. Both Zechariah and Elizabeth, being up in years, rode animals while father, Atonis, and the household servants walked, as was the custom.

When the entourage arrived at Bethlehem, the press of those traveling under the edict of taxation was still great. Zechariah, who had relatives in Bethlehem, sent his servants on ahead of this party to his kinsman to salute them in his name and tell them of their great need for lodging that night and more. His servant returned within the hour, saying Zechariah and his family would be welcome to stay under his kinsman's roof as long as need be. And so it was that lodging was provided for Zechariah and his household, and they were guests of his kinsman during the time of the naming and circumcision of the babe called Yeshua. Father and his servant, being known to the innkeeper, found suitable quarters in the inn as before.

It was on the morning of the eighth day that Zechariah and Elizabeth went to the house wherein Joseph, Mary, and the babe were staying. Father arose early to join them in accordance with Zechariah's request. And so it was done according to the law; on the eighth day of the babe's life, the circumcision and naming occurred. Zechariah gave praise and sang songs of benediction after the naming of the child. Father looked upon the child and thought him beautiful as babes are apt to be. Father heard all these sayings and held them in his heart; these and much more he told to us when he came home to Kerioth.

When the ceremony was over, the household of Joseph and Mary thanked their cousins for their coming from Jerusalem in answer to their request. Father and Zechariah exchanged blessings and parted; father and Atonis left that same hour for home. Because of their age, Zechariah and Elizabeth tarried at their kinsman's a fortnight before returning to Jerusalem.

Father arrived home just nine days from the time he left to go to Jerusalem. Mother met him at the gate for she had great desire to see him. Father and Atonis were given time to refresh themselves; mother attended to father's needs while Atonis was cared for in the servants' quarters.

It was near the supper hour and all was ready. After an ablution to remove the stains and care of the road, father gave blessings that all was well with us. During the meal, he told us of all he had seen and heard, much about his night in Bethlehem, the couple that stayed in the stable at the inn who later turned out to be Elizabeth's cousin, and the rest of his adventure. All this we heard in great wonderment, for Israel had been waiting for a Messiah for many centuries. Yet Ishmael and I kept these things in our hearts wondering - could one so close to us and so poor be the Messiah all Israel waited for?

Father then spoke of Zechariah petitioning him to move to Jerusalem and there assist him in the temple for the rest of his life as a priest. Mother was pleased, as she had her mind set on the move before father went to see Zechariah. Later, when Ishmael and I were alone, we talked about the events father revealed to us that night, and marveled at what it all might mean.

In the intervening weeks, between father's announcement and the actual move, life for me and Ishmael almost returned to normal. We again visited our favorite haunt on the wall near the town well. Everyday that was free of lessons or work, we were positioned where we could hear the talk between the many different well users. Much of the talk between the Roman soldiers was either about their homeland and their hope to return there, or the border skirmishes with the Zealots.

Although we as a people were against the occupation of our land by the gentile hordes, yet, we as boys of twelve were too young to be totally against all the young soldiers we saw so closely. Both Ishmael and I covertly admired their lean bodies and clean-shaven look. Yes, and even their uniform had some appeal to us. When no one was looking, we often played soldier and the loser of the game had to play the Roman the next time.

Time moved slowly that summer because of the readying of the household for the move to Jerusalem. We thought it would never come about.

The display suddenly changed and became garbled. This was followed by a flashing red indicator denoting temporary loss of text continuity and data input. After a short delay, the system automatically switched into the character search mode, and each character of Aramaic on the scroll was again compared with that in the ISM memory.

John and his colleagues knew this operation would take some time and decided to take a break. Much of the day had sped by while they were watching this part of early Christian history unfold. Their thoughts were full of questions about what they had been privileged to see and hear as the first persons since the scroll's writing. John raised the lights in the viewing room, and admitted his amazement and delight with what he had seen on the display. He noted it was time to report to security if they were going to stay over into the evening hours. It was hard for them to realize that they had sat through nearly five hours of data displayed through the system. The four considered they had seen enough for the day and decided to return in the morning after a good nights' rest. With that decided, they agreed to an evening of good food and discussion of the things seen and heard from the scroll and left the laboratory after securing it in accordance with the proper rules and codes.

After securing the facility, John and his colleagues left; all admitted being tired from the days' activities. All were extremely captivated by the strange turn of events as none had the remotest idea this scroll would contain what they saw and heard. Even as they stood by their cars ready to head home, they couldn't refrain from throwing questions back and forth.

John finally said, "Look, there's no use standing here as tired as we are and talking about the Golden Scroll. Let's meet at my favorite haunt, have dinner, and talk there. If we're still interested in reviewing the data, then we can adjourn to my place, have some drinks, and stay as late as we feel the urge."

"My thoughts exactly, and I know the subject lends itself to hours of discussion, and this isn't the time or place," seconded Ed.

"Ok, say when!" interjected Chuck. They turned to Jean as if she should supply the missing time. She was silent during the repartee, and was now sought out for comment.

"Since I'm riding with John, I've no preference to either time or place. My only request is that I have enough time for a good shower and rest before we take up the sport of dialectics." Her comments caused some eyebrows to raise.

"Hear, hear, I think we have heard the best suggestion of the day," Ed said, with a soft whistle. "I'm sure something can be worked out." He smiled and made a move to go. "Did I hear a time?"

"I vote for seven - all in favor say aye!" The ayes carried. They agreed to meet at John's favorite eatery at seven. With that agreed upon, Ed and Chuck moved away and Jean joined John for the trip across the campus to her apartment.

"This has been one day to remember, Jean, and I can hardly keep from going back this evening and trying to call up the rest of the scroll." John's voice showed the excitement of adventure as he carefully guided the car into the apartment complex and pulled up in front of her door, jumped from the car and went around to open the door on her side. Nice, she thought again.

"By the way, Jean, seven isn't too soon, is it?"

"No, if I thought so I would've objected. After all, I'm not that easy to please, and will speak for myself when the need arises." She moved to the doorway, opened the door, and went into the small foyer. She looked back with a smile. "John, it's been one of the most memorable days of my life, and I too wonder just what some of the text really means. I know both Ed and Chuck can answer many of my questions about the material, but I really doubt if we will have time to get into a long catechism of the scroll."

He thought she looked tired, and wondered if he looked the same even though he was quite stimulated by the data displayed that day.

"Look, I think you're right but every little bit helps. Get some rest and I'll pick you up near seven, ok?"

"I'll be ready and waiting, and John, thanks for including me in this project." With that, he left and she closed the door.

John drove to his apartment. Once inside, he flopped down on the couch for a few winks. Before completely relaxing, he set his watch for six-thirty and passed out. The next thing he heard was the low beeping of his watch waking him. He fought going back to sleep and headed for the shower. In twenty minutes, he arrived at Jean's apartment, pressed the doorbell, and Jean appeared ready to go.

"Well, how about that?" John asked, not intended as a question, but more as an old saying borrowed from a baseball broadcaster of many years ago. They were across the campus in good time, and soon in the parking lot of the restaurant, which was rather vacant. This meant quick service, which John liked - he wasn't one for waiting. Glancing around the parking lot, John could only see Ed's car. This meant one of two things: either Chuck wasn't there yet, or he decided to ride with Ed. It turned out to be the latter.

Once inside, they were seated in a round booth that provided plenty of room for all. With a small crowd, the ambient noise level was low, and all heard well over the background music.

Tonight things were different - all was done to expedite the meal, and get to the coffee and conversation. Each had pent-up questions about the translation; each in his own way thought his most important. Even before the meal was over, some questions were asked and answers sought.

"I think what we've seen and heard to date has been above average in both context and content." Ed was first to speak. "The machine is doing a great job in selection of syntax and comparing the Aramaic to other languages. I've seen some things I would have constructed differently, especially in tense and color, but all in all, the translation has been very good."

"The main theme is approached well, from the ancient religions' standpoint that is. And until I've had a chance to study the text more closely, I think it all sounds plausible as well as extremely interesting." Chuck always had a bit of the romanticist in him, and the thoughts of mystery increased the romantic appeal for him.

"Even if not true, and I'm not proposing this is the case, it seems as if we actually moved in time to those days in early Christianity, and it's a religious experience I've never had before. I, for one, have been truly fascinated by the approach of the storyteller, whomever he might be." He kept stirring his coffee during his entire statement.

"You're going to wear out both the spoon and cup if you don't stop the stirring," John said. "Well, as the archaeologist, I find the dates expressed by the author a bit more interesting. But I believe so far the text agrees with the age of the papyrus and inks used in the preparation of the document." He had hoped for a little more reference in the text to things seen by the author, that is, buildings described in a little more detail, or descriptions of land and conditions of the environment.

"Personally, I agree with you, John, but it seems the author is more interested in what is happening and to whom, rather than structures and land conditions," Jean added onto John's thought.

"Yet, there was that bit about the height of the temple in Jerusalem; granted, a small item and nothing to build a reputation on, but at least something. And Chuck, do you really think it's possible for Judas to write this long discourse in the latter time of his life, and under the stress of the moment?"

"Well, everything so far indicates the author believes he is Judas, and the unique thing is that one must remember whomever it was, he wrote without fear of his life at that moment, but did fear the loss of this instrument he is writing in the short prologue."

Jean interjected, "But Chuck, remember the remains found in the crypt was that of an old man. The bones have a great deal of porosity indicating advanced age."

After a brief pause, Jean continued, "Remember, John received the prelim report from Dick Jeremy to that effect. Yet, as I recall, the accepted and traditional view is that Judas died by hanging when he wasn't more than forty to fifty years old. How can we justify attributing this scroll to Judas if the body and scroll were interred together?"

"Your point is well taken. I really don't know…from what we've seen, we can't really tell what this difference between the author's words and the traditional views means." Chuck was deliberate in his choice of words, almost like a lawyer choosing statements that couldn't be said to mislead the listener. "We'll have to wait and see if the author presents a solution to this problem. From the start, the author is at odds with traditional views anyway. His early concern was that he would be branded in history as a turncoat, not as a coward. Again, it's too early in this document to judge the origin of the author. I've the feeling that none of the others would've dared to attempt to write such a piece. In addition, the overall familiarity with the author's family history also belies someone else telling the story."

"I might add, that so far, the translation indicates one and only one author," said Ed, "if that helps any."

"Of course, it does relieve some of the strain that was experienced in the early writings when canonicity of certain versions was acclaimed. And if this consistency of style remains, the probability that it's indeed the writings of Judas Iscariot - that is, a man from Kerioth - is very good." Chuck was cautious about declaring loyalty for the moment. No one interrupted, so he continued, "but, for the moment, let's get back to Jean's question about Judas having time to write this lengthy instrument in the latter hours of his life. Well, it's early to tell, but my considered opinion is, that to accomplish that much effort by hand would take longer than the early Christian story of his immediate death from hanging permits. Of course, this again brings us back to traditional beliefs based on text from the other apostles. That is to say, they leave the impression that Judas died within the hour of betrayal; this may not be the case. The respected version simply says, "And he cast down the pieces of silver in the temple and departed, and went and hanged himself." Now, I ask Ed, does this early text necessarily establish immediacy as fact?"

"No, almost every translation accepted as valid leaves the exact time that Judas took his life for the reader to decide. The accepted view by exegetists is that a broad sense can be taken, but I'm sure you know more about the traditional religionists' views than I do, Chuck."

"The established Christian view is that he hung himself within a few minutes after throwing the money to the temple floor; however, this may or may not be the case. It may very well be that he lived after the crucifixion and resurrection." Chuck looked at John, and continued. "The greatest thing about this is that if it's truly what the author claims it to be, we have in our possession the oldest existing writing from that period. And I shouldn't wonder that it is absolutely priceless, correct John?"

"Yes, I would think so, and the very thought of it lying there in the laboratory is beginning to give me the willies. Tomorrow we'll have to place it in the vault." John was concerned now, as were the rest, as it was beginning to look like they had treasure beyond compare - at least among those in the world of Christianity. They each sat thinking about this aspect that suddenly dawned on them during the discussion.

The earliest versions of religious writings extant were some 400 years after this was originated. The scroll predated the Codex form and its successor on Vellum, and the oldest accepted portions of any manuscript now rested in the old British Museum with a minimum price tag of over $5 million. What they had at the university was undoubtedly priceless.

While they sat wondering about this possibility, the waiter cleared the table next to them and this signaled time to leave. They arose silently and moved to pay their bills. Once outside, they gathered about John's car. "Well, what's it going to be, over to John's place for continued discussion, or home to bed and early to rise and see what tomorrow brings?" Ed asked.

"I say we all meet at my place and talk awhile," John said with a questioning look. The answer was a silent nod by each. With that, they entered the waiting cars and headed for John's apartment, Ed and Chuck together, and Jean and John in his car.

The trip from the restaurant wasn't long, and both cars pulled up in front of John's apartment at nearly the same time. The conversation between the occupants in each car had continued, and as they got out of the cars, it continued up to the door and into the apartment.

After entering, Jean thought for a moment that she was in her own apartment; the configuration of the interior was the same. This apartment was also fitted with masculine furniture and objects of use, but a little more on the modern side. Jean took her time looking around as she wanted to know more about John Clyford, and this was one way to learn about him. She had to admit he was neat, but she knew the local university maintenance people were assigned the cleaning job. The small living room contained an adequate couch and some overstuffed chairs with a coffee table resting between them where they all sat.

John called out the list of liquid refreshments available, everyone ordered something different, and he joined the group by sitting in one of the overstuffed chairs.

"For openers, the author seems to believe he is a select personage in the scheme of spiritual things and I'd say from what we've seen and heard up to now, he is sincere," Ed paused to take a sip of his drink. "But I'm sure the traditionalists would never buy it."

"Why not?" asked Jean.

"Well, for one thing, it takes Satan, the great Deceiver, out of the picture, so to speak. The evil act he is supposed to cause is lost and the basic of good and evil concept in religion is also lost." Ed stopped for a moment as if trying to construct an acceptable idea that all would understand, and possibly, find palatable.

"Some traditionalists support a fundamental idea that Satan entered into Judas and caused him to betray his master. Now, this does a couple of things for the rest of the twelve. That is to say that through the heart, as the ancients believed, the mind was controlled. This, of course, meant that none of the others were affected and were free from any stigma that might have developed in later years from this act."

"In addition, they must hold that Judas followed the Master Deceiver's suggestion about the betrayal of his own free will. As far as we've seen in the author's prologue, he also believes in his own action being free, but he is offering the proposition that he was acting under the direction of Almighty God; a completely different matter - theologically.

This would be hard to swallow by most believers who would probably, either wittingly or unwittingly, opt for the scroll's destruction today, even as he feared in his time."

Ed hesitated. None of the others offered side comments, so he continued. "Of course, there are those of a later school of rationalization who hold Judas believed whole-heartedly in the Messianic tradition. That is to say, he expected, as did most Jews, the Messiah to lead Israel from under the Roman boot into political and religious rebirth greater than that experienced in the reign of David - a complete Kingdom of God here on earth where all nations would honor Israel and come to worship Yahweh. All this happened during his lifetime, in fact, there is little doubt that the others believed this as well. When he finally realized this was slow in coming, he thought to force the hand of his mighty teacher. To do this, it's held by some he decided to place Yeshua in such an untenable human position that he must bring down the heavenly hosts for support. With this support, Judas believed the Kingdom of God would be established on earth in his lifetime. Although an interesting rationale, there is nothing in the New Testament to support such a position."

"Which brings us to a change of subject - that of protection of the Golden Scroll. I think it's worth a small fortune, as possibly the earliest copy of those times, and true or not, it should be copied," Chuck had finally interrupted Ed.

"Well, it's really the property of ISM, but since we have some idea of what it might be, I agree that tomorrow we should put it in the vault. But are you suggesting some additional measures, Ed?" John was always open to suggestions from his colleagues.

"Yep, I say we have the capability in the lab for generating a legal facsimile, and I think we should use it. As you know, methods of recreating the necessary material in needed quantities - papyrus, inks, gold foil, and even the aging process - to provide a nearly perfect product is in-house. In fact, I've seen some of the items produced by the lab in some of the finest museums in the world, and few viewing them can tell the difference from the original." There was a sense of urgency in his voice as well as some pride. What he claimed was true, the school had produced copies of some early writings and artifacts now in many of the great museums throughout the world. It was no mean accomplishment. "I think you, as director, should expedite the necessary communiqués to ISM for serial numbers to this effect."

"I believe Ed has a serious thought, John. It would be foolhardy for us to continue this operation without some insurance; by that I don't mean money, but a backup item that we could keep here at the university," Chuck added before John could reply to Ed's comments.

John got up to make some notes for the communiqué with ISM in the morning. "I agree, I'll start the necessary encoding first thing tomorrow. This will delay the review for a few minutes."

While making the notes, John noticed it was near twenty-four hundred hours. "Holy smoke! I think we should call it a night, and get some sleep as it's been some day. We'll meet at the lab at eight o'clock and continue the project." They all started milling around.

"It's alright by me," said Ed, as he placed his empty glass on the coffee table. He turned to Jean, "Well, how did you like your first day?"

"I'm having a ball, and maybe sometime I'll be able to contribute some. It's a fascinating adventure to say the least. And I agree with you, some better care should be taken of the scroll. Have a good night, Ed." Jean was standing and ready to go. "Say, I wonder if I could beg a ride. That way John wouldn't have to go back out?"

Ed was quick to offer his services, "My pleasure, ma'am, but I'm hoping you won't mind riding with the likes of Chuck." Chuck made a face, but Ed ignored it and continued, "I hope John doesn't mind; I thought he might have made plans to take you home. I wouldn't want to cut in on his gal!"

"It's alright Ed, I was going to do just that, but if Jean doesn't mind, I don't," John tried to be nonchalant about it, but he was wondering why she had suggested the ride with the others. "Remember, I'll pick you up tomorrow morning, Jean," John called as they left his apartment and entered Ed's car.

She nodded assent, waved, and got in the front seat next to Ed. Chuck jumped in the back and they were off, while John watched. He stood a moment and looked over the campus; it was a good night, and the day had gone well, and now for a good nights' rest.

And the evening and the morning were the second day!

John and Jean had breakfast together and arrived at the laboratory at nearly the same time as the others. They all went up to the lab and gained entrance at the same time. Ed went for his usual cup of coffee from the machine, while Chuck put his briefcase on the console by his chair.

"Good morning one and all. I hope you slept better than I did," Chuck commented. Although he looked well, his actions gave the impression that he had a restless night.

"Good morning, Chuck, John, and Jean," said Ed, his cup raised high in salute, a thing Jean seemed to remember from yesterday. She wondered if that was his usual form of greeting, even to his students.

"Good morning all," said Jean.

John nodded his greetings to everyone, but was already at the console to call up the line from ISM. It was from them he would get serial and code numbers as well as the sixteen-bit security word of the day. Once online, he transmitted the request to make two facsimiles of the scroll, declaring the need for instruction and study by the school.

There was some time taken to cross check Bradenton's rights to and need for two copies. The message from ISM was displayed on the video screen before John. In accordance with regulations, it would take some time to authorize reproduction of the scroll. John turned from the console and held up his hands to let everyone know that all was done in that regard. "Well, it's up to the council as to whether we are free to make copies or not," John said as he rose from the console. "Ed, I think you might as well see just what is needed for the reproduction of the scroll and just what funding is required."

"Ok, I'll do just that."

"Chuck, didn't we get hard copy of the material reviewed yesterday?" John turned to Chuck who was at his position.

"Yes, we have three copies, and they are all collated and ready for use." He held up some of the paper from the computer. Since all was text, there was no green bar.

"Good, I think we should lock them up in the security file when we aren't working with them." John watched the display for an answer from ISM while he spoke about the hard copies. Jean moved to the console she used the day before and put it online.

John remained at his console. Each was occupied with directions John had issued. The object of all this activity, the Golden Scroll, lay in the environmental chamber. John set in the code of the day, took control of the robot, and gave the commands to manipulate the robot arms, allowing him to place the scroll back into the stainless steel container.

The robot answered every touch of the control console with inerrant precision. By minute moves, the scroll was lifted from the table and stowed in the container. The top was replaced and pressure and humidity were drawn again to ensure long-lasting protection. All this was done as insurance against possible damage even though the scroll had been treated with preservatives to protect it against most laboratory handling procedures. But John thought - *better safe than sorry*. After the unit had been checked for atmospheric safeguards, it was placed on a cart and John took it into the vault next to the laboratory.

This vault held most of the irreplaceable artifacts of the university. Here they were sealed and held under controlled atmospheric conditions as required for their specific age and condition. The vault was secured by an electronic latching system that was key-card controlled. The security department and the keycard holder had to have matching identifi-cation data. This was done by a high-speed thumbprint reading system. One and only one person could open the vault, and that person had to be the one with a matching thumbprint.

John placed his card in the transmitter, notified security that he wanted in the vault, and placed the item there for safekeeping. After confirmation of his thumbprint, the bolts on the vast door opened and he pushed the cart into the vault. He then placed the stainless steel container with the Golden Scroll on the storage shelf. The monitor in the vault sent a video of this procedure to security. In addition, the change of displacement and mass were registered within the security computer. Once this was established, nothing could be added or removed from the vault without energizing the alarm in security. All these precautions were electronically controlled from within the vault so that no external power was needed to maintain the constant monitoring of the vault's contents, regardless of the external power conditions, either present or not present, so that loss of power, even to the entire university, wouldn't jeopardize the security system of the vault. John knew it was a good system.

John moved the cart outside and closed the vault door, inserted his keycard and placed his thumb in the scanner; the security clearance came through promptly. He returned to the lab where Jean met him in the doorway with the news that ISM had transmitted the authorization for fabrication of two scrolls.

"There wasn't any difficulty in securing the go-ahead. The serial numbers and security code of the day was also transmitted at the same time so I think Ed can call the prototype specialists and have them study the scroll and draw up the design figures and costs. There was one thing, though. They needed a name for the item, and the Golden Scroll wouldn't work, they said, although not why. So I transmitted the name as 'The Book of the Eighth Seal.' Is that agreeable? Ed thought you would agree."

John thought she had handled the receipt of the transmission very well, and had a good handle on what was happening in the project to date.

"Yes, that sounds like a good working title for the document; I was wondering what we might call it anyway." He was pleased, it sounded like a good title to disguise its contents. After all, there would be plenty of time to delineate later.

"Ed, did you get the information about the authorization from ISM?"

"Yes, and I'm already drawing up the in-house order for the engineering and design phase of the reproduction of the scroll alias, 'The Book of the Eighth Seal.' The design and material control people will be here tomorrow to study it." He continued filling out forms.

"Fine, I guess everything is shaping up much as I had hoped. Let's put the system online and see if it has found text continuity." He started keyboarding, received a ready display and indication that the program had functioned properly again, and called to Chuck, "Are you ready, or should we go ahead without you?"

"Yes, I'm ready and don't *ever* start without me!" Chuck slid into his captain's chair and gave a thumbs up sign. John lowered the house lights, inserted the final command word, and the screen came alive with characters as the first words formed in English were simultaneously produced aurally, *"Hear, O Israel: the Lord is our God, the Lord is one."*

THE STRANGER

The move had been completed early in the summer of AUC 748, and Ishmael and I celebrated our twelfth birthday in our new home in the famous city of Jerusalem. Not being of the wealthy class, our home wasn't far from the marketplace of the gentiles, and mother, fearing for our safety, forbade us to go there alone. We were permitted to cross through the marketplaces on our way to our teacher's home with our faithful servant, Apius.

Apius, like Atonis, was a Greek that had attached himself to my father's house after being freed from a passing caravan. He, like Atonis, had been sick beyond use to the slave traders and was left at the Kerioth well to die.

Ishmael and I brought his pitiful plight to the attention of father. We knew he couldn't bear the suffering of any human being far or near. This being near his doorstep, he took action to relieve the poor man's discomfort. With father's care, Apius became whole again but wouldn't leave the house of one so generous. Both Apius and Atonis became trusted servants of our household. Their love for father was often shown in their deeds of trial and danger for him and for our family.

Being inventive children, we would play tricks on Apius; we often managed to break a sandal thong while in the marketplace, thus allowing us more time to study the strange world of the foreigner and gentile. It was there I caught the first glimpses of a handsome stranger who would later become a dominant figure in my life. As a young boy is apt to do, I couldn't turn my eyes away. I stood staring at this lithesome figure of a man; he moved among the gentiles and tradesman with the ease of a king. I thought he was a king of some foreign land. He strode through the crowd with head held high as though he was master of all about him. Just as he turned to glance in our direction, Apius recognized our little game and bade us to be on our way or he would surely tell the mistress, my mother, of our behavior. Fearing this would end our adventures, we quickly moved through the crowded marketplace and continued on our way to teacher Shedeur's home.

I was excited by the sight of such a man, and asked Ishmael, "Did you see him?"

"See whom? I saw many a curious and interesting person, but how am I to know…" he retorted.

"Ishmael, come, don't play with me. The one who stood taller than the rest and strode with such grace and authority; surely, you noticed him in your crowd of the curious?" I was sure he, like me, had seen the same person.

"Judas, I saw no such person. All were interesting, but none more than any other. The next time you see him, if ever, tell me so I, too, can gaze on him." His voice contained the ring of truth I had come to know as part of Ishmael's honesty. But why hadn't he seen the stranger? Wasn't he immediately in front of him even as I? I couldn't leave it be, this sight unconfirmed, so I turned to Apius.

"Apius, Apius, did you see the kingly person who stood taller than the rest of the crowd, and moved with the look of strength and…" I was about to continue when he shook his head and turned his eyes away such that I couldn't see if his answer was truthful or not. It was strange I was the only one that had seen the handsome stranger, but by that time we were approaching the courtyard of our teacher's house and my mind returned to the studies of the day. But even before my mind returned to the lessons of the day, I had the feeling that I would see the stranger again.

A SECRET CIRCLE

Life in Jerusalem moved at a much faster pace than in Kerioth, and sometimes not to my liking. But on the whole, the family was better off and mother was much happier with her lot. She soon became one of the leaders of a circle of Jewish women courting the Roman women of the officers and officials stationed in Jerusalem. The Roman women secretly admired the natural beauty of their Jewish counterparts and were willing to spend large amounts of gold for beauty aids and potions. The Roman ladies vied for acquisition of one which they thought was the true secret of the beauty shown by the Jewish women. They would often make additional concessions once finding a Jewess who brought some improvement to health and good looks. Hence, some Jewish women found themselves included in many Roman social gatherings with fine Roman clothes and jewelry to wear and eventually keep. Income derived from this trafficking in health and beauty aids raised the living standards of some Jewish families.

But often a price was paid by those families involved in this traffic with Romans by the isolation from many Zealot circles. Because of this, some families wouldn't associate with Romans or those close to them in any way. But mother wasn't one to be easily intimidated and held to her socializing with the Romans as her right. In addition, she liked their life-style in a guarded way.

Father, on the other hand, was bound by the law and traditions of the people and disliked her fraternizing with the gentiles, as he was apt to address them. To him, Romans, Greeks, Assyrians, and the like were all outside the law and lumped into one word - gentiles. His point was that the wife and family of an officer of the temple shouldn't cater to the whims of those outside God's blessing; however, mother persisted in these visits until father gave her an ultimatum to either disengage from her practices or go before the council.

I can remember how shocked Ishmael and I were when mother agreed to go before the council and defend her right to continue her avocation as a beauty consultant to the officer's wives. Father was more agitated by her decision than she was frightened of facing the council in all its majesty. When the day came, mother prepared herself in accordance with the Prohibitions. Ishmael and I hid from the world outside for fear of God striking us dead once beyond the mezuzah. The day came and went without incident, and when mother and father came home, she was jubilant for she had won her case. Father was obviously not pleased but had to follow the ruling of the council. No more words were spoken in the house about the incident, but mother went on her way preparing potions and visiting the Roman households as did each of the women in her beauty circle. She now became the leader of the largest and most integrated group of women servicing the Romans.

It was some months later when, while playing with comrades, we heard of our mother's confrontation with the Jewish council. It became the talk of the children of the other women in the circle. We were last to know of this adventure. Mother was a heroine, and to our playmates, was at least a minor star in the Jewish heavens, even as Esther was a major one. It was she who proved to the council that each woman in her circle had available to them secrets of Roman politics that were known to no others. Political thoughts and acts not yet published even among the most influential Romans were theirs for the listening. All this information could be gained only through personal contact, a spy system above suspicion and reproach, able to function everyday.

Mother proved that it was this sort of early warning system that had saved many a patriot from the Roman sword and crucifixion. She held that to cut off this communication link wasn't the will of the Lord, but that of stiff-necked men who would put the law before the love of God for his people. When she finished, none of the council could face her, and it was the great Rabbi Hillel who dismissed the case against her. We were proud of mother and her circle of beauty consultants from that day forth. And after confronting her with this story, she said we must be silent about this and must tell our friends to be the same. The incident left a mark on my memory and a separation from the strictness of the law. It was for my young heart the key of understanding many of the mysteries of the ancient writings.

We had been at our new home long enough for family life to recover from the shock of living in Kerioth to that in Jerusalem. Father accompanied Zechariah to the temple every day of Zechariah's course. It was after one of these days that father told us of another strange happening in the temple. After the evening meal, father called us all together and told us of the happenings of the day.

For some time, father had noticed an old man, well up in years, always in the temple. He would greet every young couple who presented a male child to the Lord. When given permission, and there were some who didn't, he would raise the child up in his arms and repeat a benediction, and sing praises to the Lord for letting him live so long as to see the child he then held. Father was never near enough to hear the entire song of praise, but had often wondered about the old man's daily visits to the temple. When Zechariah was not about the cares of his office, father asked him about the old man and of his strange procedure of greeting each new couple. "Zechariah, what is this thing I see everyday in the temple; the old man who greets each young couple presenting their firstborn to the Lord? I've observed he is here every day, never fail, and repeats a song of praise over each one."

"It's Simeon, and it's his custom. By his own word, the angel of the Lord revealed that he wouldn't die until he has seen the consolation of Israel. And he has since made a trip to the temple each day of his life, and greeted each young couple presenting their first son to the Lord. He is very old, some say he's nearly one hundred and fifty years old. Yet, his strength is maintained through the belief that someday he will see the true Messiah. I have heard him say that same song of praise for the sons of many in my time here, and many before my time has he said. If one can believe his story, he hasn't seen the Savior of Israel yet, for he still lives." Zechariah wasn't greatly impressed by old Simeon's presence.

It was while they were talking that a young couple came forward to present their young son to the Lord. And Zechariah recognized them as his niece, Mary, and her husband, Joseph, from Bethlehem. Father also recognized them. Mary had finished her days of purification and now brought Yeshua to the house of the Lord, even as it was written in the law, "Every male that openeth the womb shall be called holy to the Lord."

Mary and Joseph saluted Zechariah and father. They recognized father as the one who assisted Zechariah in the circumcision. Zechariah saw that they were in need of money for they were poor this day after the trip from Bethlehem, and presented them a pair of doves to satisfy the law. Mary and Joseph accepted the gift with grateful hearts, and so the law was met with respect to a sacrifice.

After the presentation, as they turned to go, Simeon asked to see the babe. Mary agreed, and Simeon took him up in his arms and blessed God.

While holding the child, Simeon repeated the song of praise that father heard in part before: "Lord, now let your servant depart in peace, according to your words; my eyes have seen your salvation, which you have prepared before the face of all people. A light to lighten the gentiles, and the glory of thy people Israel."

Joseph and Mary marveled at those things which were spoken of Yeshua by Simeon. Zechariah showed some puzzlement at hearing these words, as they weren't the same as before. Simeon changed the blessing to identify the child as he had no other. Then father said Zechariah also praised the Lord for his timely view of this happening. Then Simeon blessed them, saying, "Behold, this child is set for the fall and rising again of many in Israel, and for a sign which shall be spoken against; yes, a sword shall pierce through your soul also, that the thoughts of many hearts may be revealed."

Simeon then turned to greet another couple that came into the temple for the same reason. Zechariah asked Joseph and his family to tarry at his house for a time to rest the babe from the trip. He said Elizabeth would be grieved if they didn't stay, so she could see and visit with Mary, her cousin.

It was from this appeal that Joseph and Mary decided to stay at the house of Zechariah. As they turned to go, there was one Anna, a prophetess, the daughter of Phanuel of the tribe of Asher. She was very old, had lived with a husband nearly seven years from her virginity, was a widow of about eighty-four years, and served God with fasting and prayers night and day. Now father had seen her often in the temple, and knew well the story worded about her. Yet she wasn't alone in these strange acts as others, both younger and older, did equally mortifying things. Father, like some others, had grave doubts about their usefulness, and wondered if the Lord considered them true sacrifices.

Anna likewise praised the Lord and gave thanks that she saw the babe. She spoke of Yeshua to all of them who looked for redemption in Jerusalem; after praising God again, she also turned to follow her calling even as Simeon had. Father marked her as one to search out someday, as he wanted to know more of her story.

After the blessings of Anna, the family went with Zechariah who guided them to his house by a different route; they stayed there for a fortnight and then returned to Bethlehem. All these things father told us about the unusual happenings concerning the babe named Yeshua and his parents in the temple that day. Our household wondered just what it all meant, and Ishmael and I held private discussions about these things, vowing never to forget them as young people are apt to do. Later, father told us how it was rumored that Joseph and his family went directly to Nazareth; this wasn't true, but it was this wise:

While in Zechariah's house, Joseph said he must return to Bethlehem as he had accepted a position in a carpenter's shop there. The innkeeper agreed to their staying in his house for longer at a minimum rent. Zechariah told Joseph of better things that could be found in Jerusalem, and told him to stay there until he could arrange for a new position for him. Joseph agreed to wait awhile longer before going back to Bethlehem. But that night, the angel of the Lord appeared to Joseph saying they must return to Bethlehem even as it was written in Isaiah: "The Lord still has need of the child in Bethlehem, for because of his presence there, priests shall bring presents unto you, and these priests shall be from the land of Sheba, even unto the far East. And they shall come by the brightness of thy star rising in the heavens; they shall bring gold and incense, and show forth the praises of their god."

So it was that Joseph and his young family returned to Bethlehem after a sojourn with Mary's kinswoman a fortnight, and did not return to their first home in Nazareth as was supposed. Joseph and Mary kept these things in their hearts and obeyed the angel of the Lord.

All these things father saw and heard as they happened. Father told us of all these things as they came to pass, and we wondered what manner of child this was to be?

Later, when some time had passed, Ishmael and I came to question him about Simeon. When I was permitted to speak, I asked father what happened to Simeon.

"What is your question, Judas? What is there to know?"

"But father, you said that Simeon asked the Lord to let him die in peace. Did he do so, or is he still alive?" I couldn't help but wonder if he collapsed at that moment as the Lord honored his prayer. I was not alone as Ishmael also wondered about the strange pleading of the old man.

Father considered my question for some time. "Son, he didn't die at that moment, in fact, I saw him approach another family that very day. When I left the temple, he was still moving about the courtyard in good spirits. Your question is well put, and I'll look for him again when I go to the temple. Ask me again." Ishmael and I decided to surely do this.

Time dragged for Ishmael and me in Jerusalem. We missed going to the well, our perch on the wall, the passing parade from all walks of life, and in it, the interesting faces and fanciful stories. We had none of these in Jerusalem, and we were still not permitted access to the marketplaces where at least some of the romance and pain of life moved by.

Some said this city was the crossroad of the east and west - the center of commerce. Our teacher told us that during restive times, Jerusalem had a population of nearly fifty thousand, and when the high holy days were upon the city, nearly six hundred thousand were in and about the great city's walls. This number was incomprehensible to us, but the crowds during the holy days were not. People from every nation in the world came to Jerusalem on these days in accordance with the mitzvoth.

Our first year in Jerusalem was slow even though the city was a large and thriving community. It was true for later years, also. It was during one of the slow days late in the year 749 that mother came home early from serving some of the more influential women in Roman society. She was called there by several of the women in her clientele. They told her of an important social event to be held at Herod's palace. The word being that several men from the East, who were worthy of being counselors to kings, were now approaching the city. They had sent consuls ahead to announce their arrival. It was rumored that these were Magi or wise men skilled in the reading of the heavens, and given to divination.

From their consuls it was learned they represented some great kings in the East and had with them a large entourage of both men and animals. Herod, not knowing their intentions and wishing to avoid challenges to his place in the scheme of things political, proclaimed a holiday in their honor. It was this proclamation that had the Roman ladies scurrying for new and better beauty aids. Mother and her ladies of the circle rose to the demands and prepared different and more exotic formulas for their patrons.

As each day went by, more and more rumors were mingled with fact, each more exciting than the other, and all built on hearsay. Mother told us all every evening these men of vision were said to be high priests of an ancient religion from the former Persian empire.

The consuls told of their masters' mission to follow ancient and hidden mysteries about the coming birth of a prophet - a child among the people of Israel. One who, they said, would be the head of a spiritual kingdom that should some day conquer evil, raise the dead, protect his followers from evil, act as a mediator between his followers and his father, and at the end of time, judge the good and evil of the world.

Our teacher, and the priest as well, were greatly disturbed by this news, fact or fiction. Caiaphas and Annas went before Herod and told him to withdraw his proclamation for it was written in the law: *Hear, O Israel: other nations hearken to diviners, but as for thee, the Lord thy God hath not suffered thee so to do.* They warned Herod that these strangers were known followers of the ancient Persian sun god and his son, Mithras - an abomination - they should not enter the holy city, let alone be entertained by the king.

Mother heard Herod was about to withdraw his proclamation and not permit these foreign ministers entrance to the city when his chief steward brought news of another sort.

The steward claimed that he had it on good authority that this was not the true mission of these men. It was so rumored that these men of wisdom desired an audience with the now-aging Herod the Great on an entirely different matter, one which would bear upon his political position in the empire. The Roman ladies whispered that the enemies of Herod, called the Sicarii, whom he feared more than the Romans, told a different story about the visitors. According to them, it was to find where a boy king of the Jews now lived and present him gifts. Upon hearing this, Herod trembled from fear and rage, so some said, and he hardened his heart against the call of Caiaphas. Hence, he issued his proclamation and the entourage was encouraged to come into the city and to the court; Herod must know if the rumors had any substance.

Herod was beside himself, for he was old, ill, and in great fear of losing his rule in the latter years of his life. The court was in a great deal of unrest; many of his enemies supported the rumors about the boy king. Many of those closest to Herod feared for their lives because of his maniacal outbreaks against anyone whom he presumed was part of a conspiracy to overthrow him. These outbursts became so frequent that even his own family feared death at his hand should they wander from his side. Although the Roman ladies were not frightened by his outbursts, they were reminded that he was still the appointed ruler as far as Rome was concerned, and therefore it necessitated some courtly appearance on these occasions. It was for this event that some of mother's clientele were preparing; many were wives and mistresses of the local Roman officials and men-at-arms.

THE VISITORS FROM THE EAST

The following were days of preparation and expectation; Jerusalem hadn't seen such a visit for years. Herod's soldiers moved through the marketplace clearing undesirables from the streets. A small army of prisoners and slaves cleaned the city. An edict was read along the main thoroughfares to all subjects of his domain stating who could and who couldn't line the streets when the visitors from the East came into the city gates.

We, as young lads of thirteen late in 749, were to remain inside unless we had special permission by being part of the receiving committee or moving to and from our teacher's home; the latter being an action that even the great Herod didn't want to disturb for fear of the people. Instructing the young was still one of the laws Herod knew wasn't taken lightly by his subjects. To interfere with the age-old responsibility of every family to instruct the young in the ways of their fathers would cause greater unrest than even he wanted at this time. So it was that the young students in Jerusalem could move about during the entry of the visitors. From later visits, mother told us which gate and the route the visitors would use. And so it was that we were once again perched on a wall high above the streets of Jerusalem to see the great caravan as it came into the city.

In they came, foot soldiers dressed like some of those we saw when on the wall near the Kerioth well, many carrying long, curved swords held next to their bodies by sashes of many colors which had special meaning to the different tribes of nomads from which each may have come. They wore no special armor and carried only light shields.

Following them were horsemen on animals the like we had never seen. These animals were light in color with long, flowing manes and moved with such grace that they made the Roman war and chariot horses look like field animals. After these came the entourage of camels with the Magi mounted in high-backed saddles covered with rich silver and gold brocade. Their clothes and headwear were of fine silk with gold and silver threads woven in the cloth, and the sun nearly set them afire to the eye as they came into the city. The crowd murmured as they went by for few had seen such a display of wealth.

On and on they came! Following the camels came a herd of elephants. Some carried saddles with single riders armed with different articles of war. And one, the largest elephant we had ever seen, carried a howdah covered with fine tapestry of gold and silver brocade. It was covered with mysterious characters and inscriptions in a language that neither of us had ever seen; no, not on any of the animals that passed through Kerioth.

Fastened to the howdah were leather cases with compartments in them, and protruding from the leather compartments were several three-legged objects. From our vantage point, we couldn't see their total construction or surmise their use. One thing was sure - the items on the animal were of great importance to the Magi as it was surrounded by protecting troops. Even though displaying less opulence than some of the other animals, this elephant and its appointments were watched and guarded more than the others. It seemed to us that they guarded it as we were taught our forefathers guarded the Ark of the

Covenant when it was moved from place to place. This animal and its fittings induced in the viewer the feeling that its secrets were of great religious significance.

As the procession passed, I noticed one rider stood out from the rest. He rode near the elephant carrying the strange instruments. He stayed near the animal as though he had a personal interest in its welfare. He made circles around the animal while he watched its every move; he even reached up from time to time and checked the fittings. His horse was a beautiful cream color with a golden mane. His saddle was less ornate than some of the others, but had a distinct marking different from the others in the entourage. He sat on his horse as none of the others. His body moved and rippled with the motion of the animal. As he drew near, I recognized him as the same stranger I had seen in the marketplace some months before. When close enough to see us plainly, he wheeled his horse and made an expert rider's maneuver in the street below and upon coming about to face me, he smiled and raised his hand in a salute. I knew he had seen me, there was no doubt about it, but I was so engrossed in watching him that I forgot to nudge Ishmael. I remembered Ishmael told me to call his attention to the stranger if I ever saw him again - well, *this* was the time.

"Ishmael, come and look! I see the stranger that was in the marketplace before!" I pulled his arm to get him to look across my finger now pointing at the stranger slowly disappearing in the group. "Look, Ishmael, look, don't you see him?" But even while I pointed at the stranger, another rider came between us and the stranger.

"I'm sorry, Judas, but I still didn't see the person you were pointing at. After all, there are many fine-looking riders in the parade." What he said was true; there were many formidable-looking riders in the group. And it was my lateness in calling Ishmael's attention that was to blame, not his lack of trying. I knew that I would see the stranger again without doubt; so far, I was the only one to notice him and he me.

While I pondered this, an ancient saying of the prophets came to mind, "…and I will find thee and thee alone shall know me, and because of this many shall fall away from thy side." Could this be some sort of sign? Even at this young age, I began to feel the pull within that I would be given some worthy task to perform by the Lord.

From their numbers and trappings one could only surmise they were people of great wealth and power. Who else would dare cross the desert with so much glitter displayed knowing great bands of thieves and robbers abounded there? Even the Romans moved aside to let those from the East pass. The Roman troops didn't register the awe the subjects of Jerusalem did, and with good reason. After all, once the Roman soldier had experienced the celebrations in Rome, all else was trivial; the Romans respected but were never awed of any other force in this part of the world.

The court of Herod the Great was the scene of much entertainment, and the Roman ladies were asked to attend many of the functions nearly a week long. Mother was asked by her patrons to sit among them during the formal introduction of the visitors from the East. The Magi were presented to Herod with all pomp and ceremony at his command. They presented Herod with many gifts and he them. Afterward, it was told that Herod feigned illness so he might have a private interview with the visionaries, but they would have none of it. Because of this, mother and the ladies of the court saw and heard all.

There were among the Magi three held in high esteem - Cyrusnabu, Dariusnergal, and Xerxesninib - master Magi or priests of Mithra. Standing with them, mother said, was a man like she hadn't seen before. He stood at least a head taller than the others and, as near as she could tell from her vantage point, was much younger. He was powerfully built and extremely handsome, as the whispers of the ladies testified. His clothing was different in texture and markings, and woven into the cloth were strange signs and symbols the like of which mother said she had never seen. It was he who did the interpretation for the others and the court, as the Magi spoke only a Persian dialect of Aramaic unknown to the court of Herod. When asked, he said his name was Shalazar. Even as mother told these things, my heart beat faster. Could this be the same person as the stranger I saw before? Soon I became lost in the story and forgot about him. Herod questioned diligently about their reason for coming to the land of Judea, a part of his kingdom. The one called Cyrusnabu spoke for the rest through Shalazar.

"In accordance with our ancient writings, we have come in search of a prophet. Even as given in the scripture of Zarathustra, a child shall be born in the land far to the West, even Judea. He shall be raised up by Ahura-Mazda to defeat Ahriman." Here he stopped and Shalazar interpreted for the court. All were puzzled but remained silent.

"We have seen his star for many days, even the time of two years we have traveled across mountains and deserts, and have followed it to Judea. We have yet a distance to go as his star still moves before us. Yet, we tire and would rest here in Jerusalem." Cyrusnabu would have continued but Herod raised his hand with the courtesy of the court.

"This child then, is not, nor is likely to become the king of the Jews?"

"This is so. His kingdom is not of this world but for it. He can only be king of the Jews if they will let him…"

Upon hearing this, Caiaphas, who was standing near, turned his back on the visitors. His face became pallid either from rage or fear of Yahweh at this verbal abomination. He and Annas gathered the Sanhedrin and left the palace forthwith. Herod was displeased at this but gave no sign lest his visitors misinterpret his actions. So it was that the enmity between the house of Hanan the high priest and Herod grew. When murmurs of the court had diminished, Cyrusnabu continued his discourse.

"He will be a mediator between his father and his followers, and aid them in their struggle against evil, lies, and other works of darkness. He and he alone will judge all mankind at the end of the age; his followers will be given everlasting life with Ahura-Mazda in paradise, while the wicked will fall into outer darkness forever." Cyrusnabu was very animated during his speech.

Herod was greatly relieved to hear this and he smiled and spoke in his most beguiling way. "It's easy to see that this child is one who deserves honor from the house of Herod. I would honor the young prophet, also. I would have a word about his whereabouts - is this revealed unto you?"

"Aye, but this is not yet known as fact. It is for us to follow his star, and through it and only it, can we discover the place of his birth. The time of his birth is now for every man has a star and his is now in its zenith over Judea." The three Magi gave the sign of Mithra, bowing to the East.

"Your words have quieted my heart, though I am grieved that I cannot hear his place of birth from you. Nonetheless, I beg you to stay, rest, and refresh yourselves in the pleasures of my court." Herod gave them freedom of his court. The wise men withdrew to separate rooms in the palace. Herod wasn't completely satisfied with their words, and called his chief steward to him.

"These men have given me no cause to doubt them, yet your story still causes me grief. Call to me Caiaphas and Annas; I would have word with them about these things."

Herod then demanded of them the place and date of birth of this new prophet. He had reasoned that should his guests be lying, he would know without doubt when the child was found. He was still troubled, and secretly all Jerusalem with him, about the rumor that this child would one day rule Judea. The Sicarii had struck a dagger of doubt in Herod's heart.

Caiaphas and Annas, as well as many lesser priests, searched the ancient writings for details but found only the place of birth; none could but guess about the date. The place, Bethlehem of Judea, for thus it was written by the prophet, "…and thou Bethlehem, in the land of Judea, for out of thee shall come a Governor that shall rule my people Israel." To this all agreed, yet though they searched diligently, they found no reference to the time of birth. Herod was greatly distressed at this but knew from the words of the Magi the child was nearly two years old even as they had said.

Now the festivities continued without loss of excitement. Some wondered why the stay of the Magi was so short as many of the formal court events lasted longer. Rumor was that the visitors found Herod and his courtly play not to their liking, and decided after a polite stay to move on following their route to the west. It was then the visitors from the East left the court of Herod, not because they found the court wanting, but that they had seen the star change position and moved to follow it.

When Herod heard the star had appeared to move once again and lead the Magi elsewhere, he sent his priest and consuls to look for the star. The nights were clear and the sky filled with the glory of God. After great searching, all returned and told Herod there was not a star in the heavens that was brighter than any other to the eye, and that it would take the Lord God or his chosen servant to tell one from the other. They held that no man could do this, and that the Magi were indeed hoodwinking the Great Herod.

Herod became very angry at this news from his seers and vowed to find the child, but he didn't show his anger, remembering he had asked the Magi to return and tell him of the child's whereabouts. All these things mother told us that the women talked about while receiving their beauty treatments. It was said that Herod didn't want to honor the young child rumored to be the next king of the Jews, but that Herod secretly instructed his soldiers to slay the young child as soon as they found him. Upon hearing this, mother was greatly grieved and told father of this rumor among the Roman ladies.

Both father and mother believed the young child might be the kin of Zechariah born in Bethlehem under the strange circumstances we all knew some two years before. Why they had decided thus I never quite knew, for the thought that the babe born to Mary to be the king of the Jews wasn't likely.

Father, acting on belief and the encouragement of mother, went that same hour to the house of Zechariah and told him this story and of the rumor. He feared for the child, and the acts of Herod as well. Zechariah was greatly troubled, as he, like father, was privy to the revelation and strange signs concerning the son of Mary and Joseph.

Zechariah thanked father for the news and gave his blessing to give to mother for her listening to the court news. Father returned and told us that Zechariah was preparing one of his servants to go and warn Joseph and Mary of possible danger to the young child.

We later learned that the servant had left that same hour but was prevented from leaving the city, as were all other Jewish subjects under the dominion of Herod. Herod wanted no one to find the young child and warn his parents before he had found him. And so it was that no warning was delivered from Zechariah's household to Joseph and Mary.

ANOTHER STORY

Mother wasn't so easily put off. When she heard of Herod's edict preventing his subjects from leaving Jerusalem and traveling to Bethlehem, she devised a plan she hoped would save Yeshua. She called Apius to her, and in father's presence, asked Apius if he would ignore the edict and try to reach Bethlehem. This meant his passing through the guarded gates to the South. At first, father would have none of it, fearing for the life of his good and faithful servant, but mother reminded him the restriction was against Herod's subjects only, and Apius wasn't one of them. He was, at that time, a voluntary servant of father and his house and a Greek by birth. He was in actuality a Roman citizen, a free man.

Apius was anything but reluctant; he disliked Herod and was very compassionate to the young, even as Ishmael and I knew. Apius was given raiment befitting a Greek trades-man and instructions to join with the entourage of the Magi. He was to remain as discrete as possible, yet to find the whereabouts of the child before Herod's spies could do so. After warning Joseph and Mary, he was to return home and tell us of all that transpired during his trip. So it was written and so it was done; Apius prepared for the adventure and left to join the Magi from the East.

Before the entourage of the Magi left Jerusalem, Herod had a change of heart. Fear-ing that the Magi had heard the rumors about his not wanting the young child to live and might not return to his court, nor send a messenger unto him of the discovery of the child's whereabouts, he offered his guards as protection for the young prophet when they found him. But the learned and experienced visionaries were wise men and saw through this ruse and refused the accompaniment of his guards. Herod became angry, but not knowing their power and sway in Rome, was cautious not to offend them, and withheld his guards and bid the wise men leave his court in peace with the blessing of his people.

They hadn't left the city gates when Herod called his special spies to him and assigned them to watch the foreigners; he trusted them not. He couldn't forget the rumor and say-ing of the prophets about a new leader of Israel to come out of Bethlehem. The entourage left the city and among them were Herod's spies and our Apius; the spies were charged with returning with the child's whereabouts. Some thought the child was a prophet of the Persian god, while others, including Herod, thought he was the anointed one of Israel.

It was sometime later that Apius told us the strange story of the sighting of the star and honoring of the child by the mystics. During his travels with the Magi, Apius learned they all left at the same hour and traveled the same road our family used some years before. He told of his passing through the guards without question. His forged papers and clothing gave him good cover, and with the help of the travelers from the East, he was not troubled.

The Magi followed the birth star that only they could see. This Ishmael and I knew as we tried to see the great star they spoke about in Herod's court, but like many others, saw no difference in the starlit sky.

Apius told how the master diviners stopped many times on their way to Bethlehem to aid those who were ill. How they had potions that worked many times on those too ill to move. Later, we remembered how their good deeds were talked about many days after they had left Judea.

He continued about the magical instrument these strange men from the East used to view the sky. They took it from a huge elephant and placed it on the ground; a three-legged instrument it was, with many strange wheels that they turned by hand to position it. And how they moved the animals back and quieted them so the earth about and near the instrument was very still. Several men looked into the instrument while making mark-ings on papyrus, and each compared his writings with the others, and then how they con-sulted large charts of the heavens. These charts were like maps of the sky and were drawn on strange material - like cloth - but like none Apius had ever seen before.

When all were satisfied with that shown on the charts and their writings, they care-fully repacked the instrument and charts and placed them on the back of the same animal. Then and only then did they move along the road toward Bethlehem.

Apius said when some peasant saw these things they did and asked what they saw in the instrument and was it a thing of the gods, the mystics said they saw many stars in the heavens, more than could be seen by any other men. Plainly visible among these stars was the birth star that had guided them across the desert and mountains even unto Jerusalem and now unto Bethlehem. It was in this wise they checked the motion of the birth star against the permanent position of all the other stars on the chart. Thus, it was even the smallest movement of the guiding star that led the way to their destination.

Apius, who had become acquainted with one of the mystics, asked the name of this wondrous instrument and said one called it Xerxesninib. He didn't know the name of the instrument for it was of ancient times, but that among them it was called "Ontosas-troblabos", or the thing to view the heavens. They told how it had been handed down through the generations even from an age before their fathers knew how to express time. And the ancient scribes wrote the instrument was given to the learned of their people as a gift from the servants of Ahura-Mazda, yea, even from a passing silver ship that sailed the heavens as ships now sail the seas.

Many who heard these things were in great awe of these strangers from the East, but some thought they were full of spirits and told nothing but tales to confuse the people. Apius told us boys, after much pleading on our part, that these men were as wise as his Greek forefathers and more. Ishmael and I marked these words and often spoke of them.

THE END OF A JOURNEY

It was late in the year of 749 that Ishmael and I heard the rest of the story from Apius. He came to know of these things through his travels with the Magi and stated that the visionaries followed the star only they could see, as even the priests and soothsayers of Herod's court couldn't see this sign in the sky locating the child. It was said the Lord God masked the vision of those without the wondrous instrument so they might not see the star and avoid harming the child. So Herod's spies followed the wise men to find the child.

Apius was a great storyteller and held the family's attention throughout this tale. He said each day at the same hour the Magi took their instrument from a golden case, set it up, and checked the charts for motion. When the star ceased to move, it stood directly over the house wherein Joseph and his family abode. This location they communicated to no man; neither Apius nor Herod's spies knew where the household of Joseph was.

The visionaries were jubilant when the star stopped and they set up an encampment outside Bethlehem. While Apius waited nearby, they chose three from among them - the chief priests Cyrusnabu, Dariusnergal, and Xerxesninib - to go and see this thing that had come to pass, even as their scribes of ancient Persia had written. Apius brought this to our attention knowing of our young boyish curiosity - with them was the tall and impressive figure of the man mother knew as Shalazar, and again, it was he who gave meaning to the words between the Magi and Joseph and Mary.

The Magi held a special ritual of thanksgiving to Ahura-Mazda for his graciousness; this Apius witnessed. In this, Shalazar took no part. They then left for Bethlehem and their servants with them. Apius, and those he now knew as Herod's spies, followed them at some distance. Soon they arrived at a small house with a carpenter's shop attached thereto. Here Apius saw and recognized Mary and Joseph, but they not him.

Before Apius could speak with Joseph, the servants of the Magi saw the young child with Mary. The servants and men-at-arms made way for the three chief priests forcing all others aside including Apius and Herod's spies. While Apius was not offended by this act, Herod's spies were and became unruly. With no Roman soldiers nearby, the servants and soldiers of the Magi restrained Herod's spies. Since the spies were disguised as wayfarers and held no special articles of identification, the men-at-arms decided to hold them until the Roman authorities could be contacted and arrest them. Their cries about being under special orders of Herod made no great impression on the men from the East. They were summarily marched to the encampment outside Bethlehem, and Apius saw them no more until he returned there with the others. Apius said it was because of this that Herod's spies failed in their mission, and Herod didn't receive early news of the child's whereabouts; his use of spies was thwarted by the power of the Magi and God. Because of this peculiar circumstance, a large crowd of people drew near to the small house of the carpenter's family. They were in awe of the might and glitter of these visitors and murmured about these happenings as they strained against the Magi's servants to see what was happening.

Apius, having befriended some of the members of the mystics, was permitted an intimate view of what transpired. Mary brought Yeshua, now nearly two years old, unto the men. The Magi bowed to Yeshua as one greater than they and marked him as a great priest among priests - Prince of Princes, Light of Light, Prophet of Ahura-Mazda, the long-awaited one, and the anointed one of the sun. They presented him, through Mary and Joseph, many gifts brought from the far East. Among these were gold coins, silver chains, frankincense and myrrh. Apius remarked that such wealth he hadn't seen by any. All these things they did without the one called Shalazar as he neither knelt nor gave homage.

Mary and Joseph were greatly puzzled by this show of adulation by the Magi and wondered if these things were not an abomination unto the Lord. Yet they were simple people and were afraid to deny these priests from the East that which they had traveled so far to do. As the evening wore on, Mary and the child tired, and because of this, the Magi moved back to their campsite outside of Bethlehem. Apius said many of the townspeople came to see what it was that caused such a distinguished group to call on a simple carpenters' family. Much talk was heard in and about the household of Joseph about the strange high priests of Mithra and their giving of gifts unto the young Yeshua. Not all were pleased at this show of pomp and ceremony and the words about the child. Some were jealous and considerable talk moved about the crowd that the priests should know of this worship by the followers of Ahur-Mazda. To many, this was not in accordance with the law. Some fell away from the household of the carpenter, and held ill will in their hearts against him. Some held that no good thing could come of this adulation of the Magi, and it was these Apius feared the most for they could be bought.

When young Yeshua was to bed, Apius approached Joseph and Mary. When they saw him, they were greatly pleased; they recognized him even with his change of clothing. He spoke to them of the urgent matter of the child's life and the rumors of Herod's threats against him. Both Joseph and Mary were reluctant to believe such things, and were not so eager to leave Bethlehem. They had lived there now over two years and Joseph had gained much good will in carpentry throughout Bethlehem. His was a good business and the Lord had indeed blessed them as befitted good and faithful servants.

Because of these comforts and the sudden gain of wealth from the gifts of the visionaries, they would not give Apius their word on going into hiding. Apius left them late that night with only a word of thanks from them to mother and the house of Zechariah for their concern. Apius was grieved for these were not the words he wanted to bring mother.

Apius told how he traveled from the little house to the encampment of the Magi. He feared that their act against Herod's spies would bring censure on them and, feeling this way, he approached the camp determined to warn them not to return to Jerusalem. He was met by the perimeter guards, and because of language difference, his warning was nearly lost. His words to the guards were overheard by one who later called himself Shalazar.

As Apius recounted his story, I could hardly refrain from interrupting, but strict upbringing caused me to remain silent. Yet, I knew I would someday ask Apius about this person he talked with and mother had identified in Herod's court. Was he the stranger I had seen before? My boyish curiosity was a force to be reckoned with on this matter!

Apius told of Shalazar bringing him before the high priests and of the spies still being held by the guards. He told them of his commission to warn the child's parents of the danger to Yeshua by Herod, and of what might be a hidden danger to them as well. They were not greatly disturbed by his news but, as he could see by their attitude, they were greatly suspicious of Herod and his request for news of the young child.

Apius was permitted to join their table; they recognized in him the friend he claimed to be. Apius told of their true mission as they saw it. They told of ancient rites and how through them they received inspiration of the scriptures. How from these spiritual insights they deduced the story of the coming of a new prophet of Mithra. How for many days they studied the coming of a new star in the heavens, its date and place among the others. All this, they said, through the instrument and charts he had seen before.

They set their mathematical tables to track the star's motion, and much to their wonderment, it moved and changed its position even as it was written. The instrument and charts from days gone by were without error. Some time passed before they could convince those in power to set aside funds for a large caravan needed to follow the star in accordance with the scriptures. At last, those in high order of priesthood believed their interpretation that a new prophet was born and to be found in a foreign country within the empire. It was indeed strange that the prophet of Mithra was to appear in a distant land, but the writings were convincing and only those of true faith could see this thing come about. So nearly a year after the first sighting of the star, the caravan left Babylon to follow it thither.

It was then Apius said they revealed to him that Shalazar was not one of them. As they passed through many foreign lands and terrains in their quest, they came into great difficulty with a fever and it was then Shalazar joined them. It was he who saved many of them and was accepted as one in the search for the young prophet. It was only because of their exhaustion and low provisions that they asked for Herod's hospitality. It was because of this and only because of this, and they were amazed that anyone could believe they came so far in search of a Jewish boy-king. And to hold they came to honor such a person was political madness. Indeed, all such thoughts were political suicide if heard by the wrong Roman authorities, and besides, everyone knew there was only one ruler and that was Augustus Caesar! To express interest in someone else anywhere in the empire was to invite charges of treason and possible death.

To their minds, the young child had more to fear from Caesar than from Herod. If this talk of a Jewish king traveled to Rome and was taken seriously, no stone would be left unturned to find the boy and destroy him.

These men turned to Apius and questioned him as to these things. How did the Jews come to believe they were seeking a boy-king of Israel? Apius told them of the rumor by the Sicarii and how the aged and addled Herod believed this rumor. It was in Herod's makeup to protect his image before Caesar, and therefore, he was more concerned in finding the lad and destroying him to show Caesar that he was a friend indeed.

They shook their heads in disbelief, and asked if Herod knew only Rome could appoint regents over Judea and elsewhere, why then could he believe such rumors? How could it be possible that this small family from a town called Nazareth cause the mighty Augustus to honor their son with a tetrarchy? And since Herod had already presented his will to Caesar, wasn't it fair to conclude that his sons would be given preference in this selection? Apius said they continued to discuss these things until the lamps were refilled, and came to no other conclusions than someone was hoodwinking Herod! All this concerned them not for they were only interested in the finding of a new prophet of Mithra.

THE FLIGHT TO EGYPT

Because of his timely warning, Apius was given a robe of great wealth and given an honored place at their table. The table represented the feast of the eternal fire, the god they called Atar. Consecrated bread and wine was passed from the honored sage to all at the table, this they claimed was the body and blood of Atar, and after reading of prayers of adulation, the sounding of a bell signaled the end of worship. These men were full of great joy and only with some difficulty controlled their desire to return immediately to their own country with the news of this event. The one called Shalazar sat near him and provided the needed interpretation, although he took no part in the ritual. After the love feast, Apius was asked to stay yet that night. It was while resting that Apius was wakened by calls of the guards. The encampment was aroused, lamps lit, and the high priests talked excitedly among themselves. From Shalazar, who was nearby, Apius understood these mystics had experienced dreams and visions like those he had heard us tell of Daniel some years before.

From their excited conversation, Shalazar deduced that each had experienced the very same scenario - the Jewish God, Yahweh, had spoken to them. This was indeed strange, but each recalled the same words of identification, "I, Yahweh, God of the Jews, warn you of Herod. Hear me, o men of Media, return not to Jerusalem, nor send to Herod any message concerning the child. Go thither to your own lands, and go quickly."

They didn't know what to think as Yahweh had no strength to them. Yet, being men of wisdom and courage, considered it the spirit of Ahura-Mazda in the character of Yahweh to warn them of these things. So it was that yet in the third watch they consulted their writings about these things.

The interpretation of these visions and dreams confirmed what Apius had told them - they shouldn't return to the court of Herod but should depart from Bethlehem by a southern route. After some discussion, they agreed to leave before the next watch was called out. They asked what should be done with Herod's spies? On his answer, they decided to release them that night for they didn't want to break the laws of the land.

Yet, because they feared retaliation from Herod, they prepared a powerful potion which was forced upon the spies. This potion caused the spies to forget many things common to them for a fortnight, so the spies returned to Jerusalem only after the wise men, Joseph, and his family left Judea. As it was told, no one, not even the watch, knew when the entourage left or in which direction they went. This wasn't true for all as Apius was privy to their time of leaving and the direction but remained silent on the matter until this story was told. All these things he told us as he had experienced them.

Mother was grieved to hear Joseph gave no word to Apius about their plans, and after showing her gratitude for his services, sent other servants to deliver the word to Zechariah. It was with great sadness that the people of the road told of hearing from distant lands that a great caravan from the East, one of great wealth and strange instruments, had been set upon by evil and cruel robbers in the mountains and all save one were lost. Even all animals were destroyed and the riches taken. Yet, one rider escaped and took with him the strange instrument and charts. Of him no more was heard, and the instruments and charts were lost to the people forever. When I heard of the possibility of one escaping, my heart leaped as I could see only one who was able to perform such a feat - the man called Shalazar. I didn't tell Ishmael of this thought as I knew he would laugh, but kept it in my heart as one does a story about a hero. All this Ishmael and I heard from the road travelers.

After a time, Mary sent a messenger to Zechariah telling him of the events that happened after the visit of the Magi. The messenger told this story, and it was this wise. Mary and Joseph wondered about all these things - the visit of the Magi, the gifts from them, and the words of Apius about the evil intentions of Herod - and pondered these things in their hearts. That same day the Magi came, yet even that night the angel of the Lord appeared unto Joseph in a dream saying, "Arise, take the young child and mother, and flee into Egypt and be thou there until I bring thee word, for Herod will seek the young child to destroy him." The messenger told that Joseph awoke, and remembering the words of

Apius as well, woke Mary, also. That same hour they packed all they could take with them for the stay in Egypt. They believed it would not be long for Herod was old and in poor health.

Mary called her trusted servant of Zechariah, and gave to him much of the gold, silver chains, and other gifts they couldn't take to Egypt, to deliver unto Zechariah. It was in this wise that Zechariah held the gifts given by the Magi for Joseph and his family. Joseph and Mary gave thanks unto the Lord for the warning and departed that same night for Egypt. The servant told Zechariah how the angel of the Lord said they must sojourn in Egypt until the death of Herod. Mary told the servant to tell Zechariah that he shouldn't try to find them lest one of Herod's spies might waylay his servant and find them. But she assured him she would transmit timely messages about their welfare unto him and others. She asked Zechariah to convert many of the gifts from the Magi into the coinage of the land and supply it when requested by her in Egypt. She didn't know what they would do to maintain a home in the years in Egypt. All this the trusted servant was commissioned to tell Zechariah and his household. These things we heard through Zechariah and Elizabeth. So Zechariah became the administrator of those things given to Yeshua by the Magi, and Zechariah converted the gifts into gold and silver as he was commissioned. This is how Zechariah and Elizabeth knew of the well being of the child all the years he sojourned in Egypt. Mary and Joseph sent blessings for their kindness and care during this trial.

When Zechariah heard these words, he called father, told all these things about the family of Joseph, and even some of Joseph's kin were dependent on Zechariah for news.

Mother told us how the ladies of the court told that Herod waited a fortnight and when he didn't hear from his spies, he was extremely wroth. He called his elite guard together and sent them to search for his spies and the child and to bring them to him. His first command to slay the child was tempered by the fear of the people as it would be much more discrete to bring the boy and his family to the palace. It was at the palace indiscretions could be kept from the eye of the public. So it was the elite guard was ordered to do.

On their return, they reported no success in either and Herod became angry again and many were fearful, even his elite guard. In the madness of his anger, he ordered them to slay every male child in and about Bethlehem under the age of three but older than six months. Herod recalled the age of the child from the words of the Magi.

The guard left and searched and destroyed every male child in that age group in all of Bethlehem and surrounding coastal towns. Herod thought the young couple might have hidden the young boy in a nearby town. When his troops returned, he was relieved and truly believed he had accomplished his goal. He had little fear of the noise of the people to Rome, as he would tell Augustus he had caused little destruction to preserve the will of Rome. He was right, for as it was written by the prophet Jeremiah, there would be great mourning and weeping because of the loss of the children in Bethlehem.

Later, Herod became uneasy when the captain of his guards found no family in and about Bethlehem known as Nazarenes, but had the good fortune to find out, through an offering of gold, that such a family recently resided there. Some were eager to tell what they saw and heard; after all, it wasn't often Bethlehem had such noble visitors. From them, the captain learned that a carpenter and his family recently left there, and they had been there nearly two years. The townspeople remembered their son was born during the census.

"And where are they now?" Herod asked his guard.

"According to the informant, they are even now on their way to Egypt."

"Then the child still lives!" Herod remarked in rage. He reasoned the family must still be on the road and within Judean borders. He summoned his fastest horsemen and ordered them to pursue the family now known to him through the words of his guards.

"Ride with extreme haste, spare not your horses, find this Nazarene family and bring them to me. Gold and honor to the man!" He stopped short of ordering the boy destroyed as he knew of the propensity of the people and the Sicarii after the debacle at Bethlehem - the people he feared not, but the Sicarii was another story. It was the Sicarii with their secret orders and dagger men Herod feared most. He would have this family from Nazareth brought to the palace and there, where no other eyes could see, end the child's life.

Herod was a crafty man and realized it was possible with such an early start the family might escape his hand. He feared an overt action against the family in a foreign country, but not a covert one. Therefore, he concluded that his guard might be unable to find the family before they reached the border, and gave orders to his master spy to follow the family wherever they might go. So it was that a master spy, Mizzah, went with the elite guard. Some weeks later, we heard from mother through her clientele, word had leaked out that the special guard returned without success, and the family had arrived safely in Egypt. Yet, the rumor was, the master spy hadn't returned.

Some months went by and the year turned over without word from Mary. Then Zechariah called father to him and told him a servant arrived from Egypt and carried with him messages from Joseph and his household which revealed the difficulties encountered by Joseph and Mary in their flight from Bethlehem. How, as they prepared for their journey, one of the members of the entourage, one Shalazar by name, called upon them. It was through him they joined the Magi and traveled with them, and under their protection, to Egypt. The messages continued with the news of the changing of their raiment, blending in with the group to avoid suspicion, and accepting the use of strong animals to carry their goods. All this good will coming from the Magi who still looked upon Yeshua as the new prophet the writings had revealed to them.

Mary added the entourage was overtaken near Hebron by an elite guard from Herod who halted its way to Egypt. She, Joseph, and Yeshua perched high above the ground in a covered howdah, heard them speak to Shalazar of their desire to find a Nazarene family of three, how Herod was waiting to bestow great honors upon the boy and his family, and since the Magi had been reported seeing the family, they wondered if they had knowledge of their whereabouts. In addition, they spoke of Herod's great hurt because of the Magi's failure to return and give him word of the child's whereabouts as they were thought to do.

She heard Shalazar offer his deep-felt apologies to Herod for their apparent rudeness. Knowing Herod to be the wise man he was, he would understand their great haste as the result of visions and dreams which instructed them to leave Judea and travel to Egypt, where they would find rest and the place for worship of their god. The captain of the guards gave his word to return this message to Herod, but persisted in his quest for information about the Nazarene family. Mary was afraid that all was lost as Shalazar did indeed know of their whereabouts as it was he who had suggested they join the entourage. But she called upon the Lord to save them and Yeshua from the hand of Herod.

Shalazar produced a writ from the Magi and reminded the captain that the visitors from the East were given diplomatic immunity from this kind of scrutiny by Caesar himself. The captain was duly impressed, and after studying the document, permitted the entourage to proceed. So the household of Joseph moved through Judea into Egypt, and with them, unknown to the Magi, was Herod's master spy, Mizzah. We heard these things as we were privy to the household of Zechariah, mother's beauty circle, and Herod's palace gossip.

The people of Jerusalem heard of the cruelty of Herod to those in Bethlehem and surrounding towns. They murmured against such evil deeds and ceased remembering him in their prayers. In the temple, Zechariah heard talk against Herod and asked God not to hold them accountable for his crimes as Herod grew sickly and near infirmity during the last days of his life and the people were afraid of him and none said prayers for his body or soul.

The days went by and our lessons took much of our time and we saw less of our sister Anath as she was about women's work. In the beginning of 750, father enrolled us in a small class under the famous teacher Hillel. It was our good fortune to come under the tutelage of such a great teacher because of the wise counsel of Zechariah. We were studying under Hillel but a little while when all Jerusalem heard of Herod's illness growing worse and many people were afraid for none knew who would replace him on the throne. So the people waited for Herod to die, as the family of Joseph and Mary did in Egypt.

C H A P T E R   S I X

Messages

Many worried about the young family of Joseph. Zechariah and his kin and the kin of Mary and Joseph gave many offerings on their behalf. Each family awaited news from those so far from home exiled in Egypt even as those before the exodus. We also awaited word from them. Some time passed before word reached Zechariah and his house about Joseph and his family. When nearly everyone had lost hope of hearing, a traveler came to the house of Zechariah. He gave careful study of the house before he presented himself, and used great care in announcing his mission. It was he who brought messages from Joseph and his household. Zechariah was quick to understand his concern as Herod's spies were still about. Nevertheless, Zechariah welcomed the messenger into his house and, as was the custom, provided him with new clothes and refreshment before asking him to impart the news. This we heard through father who was present at the time.

The messenger was grateful for the kindness shown by Zechariah. He was a rough man of the sea though not a sailor. He was a maritime trader and had seen nearly every port in the world, and his trading was the reason for his trip to Jerusalem. His name was Ohad, and he was from an ancient sea town of Pulesium on the coast of Egypt. He became a messenger for Joseph and his family only by chance. He and Joseph became friends because of similar sea occupations. As he told it, Joseph didn't find carpentry so plentiful in that section of Egypt and had turned his hand to ship building. Those along the coast found him good at his trade and soon he was in charge of men reconditioning ships near Pulesium. It was in this way Ohad met and became a close friend of Joseph and his family. So it was that Ohad and his family frequently visited the household of Joseph.

During their many conversations, Joseph often remarked of his hope to return to Galilee soon, as Mary was beginning to show the care of it all. She longed to be once again in Nazareth, the village of her people. Joseph told Ohad the story of their eldest son's birth and of the strange things that surrounded it. He told of how his life with Mary started on a series of strange events and of the choice he made; he spoke of the rumor about his son becoming the next king of Israel and how, because of it, he had to leave Judea for fear of Herod. All these things Joseph told Ohad in such honesty that he was taken by it.

Then came a time when Joseph was greatly worried about Mary, and desired to get word to her kin that all was well and that they were safe. Yet, even more, he wished to get Mary word from her family, for she was very homesick. When his business in Jerusalem needed attention, Ohad gave his word to act as the messenger unto the family of Zechariah, and through them, Mary's other kin. He was at their service as a return messenger even as he had promised Joseph. The messages were both verbal and written. A small packet of letters sealed with Joseph's family seal Ohad gave to Zechariah. These were opened and read to the family and father.

The message gave thanks to the Lord for the messenger and the household of his family. She first expressed her complete trust in Ohad, and begged Zechariah to have the same respect for him. She told how her family traveled with the Magi throughout the trip, and how these good men protected them from many evils along the way.

She wrote of the frightening experience caused by one called Mizzah, a mean and spiteful man who had joined the entourage surreptitiously. From whence he came she wasn't sure but afterwards, the men in the camp rumored that he was a spy from Herod. His mannerisms were of one who had a mission of evil; he was given to taking much spirits and always sought to be near Yeshua. It was some time after the entourage was in Egypt that Mizzah managed to cause a guard assigned to watch over Yeshua to become drunk.

While this guard was thus indisposed, Mizzah came into Joseph's tent and tried to stab Yeshua. The cries of Mary wakened Joseph and he wrestled with Mizzah, but alas, he was too strong for Joseph. Only through Shalazar's intervention was Mizzah disarmed and subdued. By this time, the entire camp was aroused, and the evildoer and the drunken guard were brought before the high priests of Mithra. On Mary's identification, Mizzah was tried for his attempted assassination of Yeshua and found guilty by the assembly. So it was within the hour he and the guard who became drunk with him was hung outside the camp.

When morning came, Mary said she and Joseph searched for Shalazar but to no avail. It was said he had left the group but would indeed join them again soon and they, that is the Magi, would confer Mary's blessings upon him then. Joseph and Mary were heartily sorry they could not do this themselves but it was not to be so.

She continued how these men of vision had taken to Yeshua and would have him go with them unto their country. And had they not been so honorable a group, they might have easily taken him from them. Yet it was their constant study of the scriptures that led them to do otherwise as another brilliant moving star appeared in the heavens. A star that caused them to doubt their original interpretation of the ancient writings concerning the birthplace of a new prophet. There occurred among them an excited and animated debate of what this new star meant, that is, by its position and brilliance. Because of it, they halted the great caravan for many days while they all studied it.

After some study of the heavens and the maps thereof, they announced that Yeshua wasn't the great prophet of Mithra they had first believed. Because of these new findings, they were anxious to follow this new and more promising star, one that even now moved toward their own land, and which they now thought would take them back to their land and locate the prophet they searched for. They had traveled a long way from their land, and were near the city of Pulesium. They left Joseph and his family with great sadness. Joseph offered to return all the gifts they still had of those presented to Yeshua, but the Magi would have none of it, and after securing a place for Joseph's family, left for their own land.

Mary continued telling of her deep and abiding love for her kin in Galilee and Zechariah's household as well. She also made special note of those things Apius had done for them so long ago, how she was very lonely in this country of Egypt, and how she believed that they must stay until Herod was dead even as the Lord directed. Yet, she was with her husband and would not have it otherwise.

She wrote of Yeshua and how he grew in stature and knowledge. He showed great interest in all things as many of his age are apt to do. While watching him play, she wept many times for those children of Bethlehem, as she had heard from travelers of the atrocity by the men of Herod. Her heart was heavy and many doubts were upon her, and she longed to talk with her cousin, Elizabeth, about these things.

Mary wondered why the Lord had laid upon her heart such things. Why had Herod been so disturbed by the news of Yeshua's birth? Had all those other children died to save Yeshua's life? Couldn't he have saved theirs by staying in Bethlehem? Hadn't the prophets called him the Messiah, and the Prince of Peace? Was this then the price? Where would it all end? Where was the God of our fathers, for she saw him not in this place.

Zechariah could see the tear stains on the letter; his household was in great sorrow for Mary. Zechariah's voice trembled as he continued until the end of the letter. She wrote of many things in and near Pulesium and tried to lessen the impact of her needs, but to all of us, and Zechariah's household, it was all too evident that she was in distress. She closed by asking for news of them all, and for remembrance unto the Lord in his house in Jerusalem.

Zechariah sent servants that same day unto all Mary and Joseph's kin with this news about the family and their whereabouts. With this, he sent the strict admonition to take care not to reveal anything to those not close, as Herod still looked for Yeshua and his family.

Some time later, Zechariah asked and received family news which he prepared for Mary in hopes it would relieve her loneliness. He reminded her of the monies he held for her, and when the need arose, to send a messenger for same. All these things were written to Mary and Joseph and placed in a packet carrying Zechariah's seal. So it was that within a fortnight Ohad was on his way from Jerusalem. All these things we knew as father told them to us yet that same day.

Days of our bar mitzvah grew close and Ishmael and I were busy with our studies. Our efforts to please father and our teacher caused us to forget the stories about Mary and her family, but not those about Herod.

All Jerusalem was aware of his condition. It was in the year 750 that word came that the Great Herod was sick even unto death. Yet he continued his evil and cruel ways. It was rumored that he was evil to look upon and none of his family wanted to go unto him. It was said he had a great fear that he would die alone and after death, none would grieve his passing. Because of this fear, he demanded that his sons remain at his beside, and called unto him many of the great men of the Jewish nation. Once in his presence, he had them shut up in the great hippodrome in the city, surrounded by men-at-arms. He then gave a command to his lieutenants to kill these men when he died. This, he said, would give a justifiable mourning at his funeral. Some in the temple asked the Lord not to hold the nation responsible for his acts, and others requested his quick demise.

It was during the evil hour that he died and those that heard said it was indeed justice. It was to the credit of his elite guard that the hateful deed of killing those held in the hippodrome was not fulfilled. So it was that the nation rejoiced at his passing and gave thanks for the lives of the men freed by the guard.

Because Herod had changed his will several times before he died, all the people wondered who would be declared the new ruler as Herod had three sons. The people waited on Rome to chose the leaders of Israel in those days. Augustus Caesar then divided Herod's domain among his three sons: Archelaus became the Ethnarch of Judea, Herod Antipas the Tetrarch of Galilee and Perea, and Phillip the Tetrarch of the fifth Province. In this year, Ishmael and I became fourteen years old. Father was selected again as a chief among the attendants to the high priests, mother's circle watched the goings and comings of Herod Archelaus, and Ishmael and I continued to grow in understanding of the law.

The year passed by quickly. Archelaus tried to follow in his father's footsteps and be claimed king by Augustus, but the people rebelled. A large group of influential Jews went to Rome to protest his claim to kingship. Augustus agreed after reading the will and listening to the people, and appointed him Ethnarch over one half of his father's domain; Judea, Idumaea, and Samaria. Because of his arrogant manners and cruelty, he had troubles immediately and everywhere in Judea during the years of 750 and 751. Some said that fear and hatred preceded and followed his name in nearly every country in the empire.

During these years, little was heard from Joseph and his family in Egypt. It was reasonable to believe they had heard of Archelaus and his cruelty. It was known that Joseph and his family now lived in Pulesium, and had grown accustomed to life there. Through Zechariah, we heard Mary had two more sons, James, and the other, Judas, even as I was.

In the spring of 753, father visited Zechariah on matters of priestly course. While they talked of the possible return of Joseph and his family, a messenger appeared at the gate. He saluted and told them he brought messages from Mary. Zechariah called his family together and, after the messenger was refreshed, he handed a packet bearing Joseph's seal.

Zechariah dismissed the servant and opened the packet. It contained a letter from Mary. She began by sending blessings to them all then commented on many things about their life in Egypt: how they had become familiar with language and customs in Pulesium, how there was a synagogue, and how their little family had grown to like the people. Since her last message, much had happened. Joseph and Ohad had joined forces and developed a good shipping business. Joseph was the shipbuilder and Ohad, the maritime trader.

The message told a strange happening that disturbed both she and Joseph. Things had come about such that time nearly made them forget their original reason for being in Egypt. It was on the eve of a celebration of their financial success that Joseph had a dream. After he awoke, he told Mary an angel of the Lord appeared unto him saying, "Arise, and take your family and go into the land of Israel; for they are dead who sought the young boys' life."

When Mary heard these things, she was much disturbed. Both she and Joseph realized how well they were established in Pulesium and didn't care for the thought of beginning life again in Nazareth. The idea of maintaining a ship building occupation and business was out of the question, as Nazareth was nearly fifteen miles from the Sea of Galilee. It would mean starting over as a carpenter in a small town. This meant a definite loss of income, and it meant a loss of a lifestyle they had become accustomed to in the past six years. This was a serious blow to their plans but the command was not to be ignored.

Mary's message included a commission for the messenger to secure a sum of gold and silver from Zechariah. It was from the sale of the gifts the Magi had given them. Zechariah later gave this sum to the messenger. Mary was concerned they wouldn't have enough money to care for the young children on their return home.

She wrote they knew of Archelaus and his cruel ways, but they didn't fear him as much as they did the people of Bethlehem and the surrounding territory. Even in Egypt, they heard of the killings and how the people were told the executions were caused by their refusal to reveal the whereabouts of the Nazarene family who had lived among them. Some of their closest friends in Bethlehem had sons put to the sword and they, being unable to take revenge on Herod, still looked for the family of the carpenter.

It was this family who had left in the middle of the night that brought the sword upon them and their sons. Their leaving without word left many people without defense against the guard's questions as to when they left and where they went, and because of this, cost them their sons. After all, the king had declared them to be possible insurrectionists and outlaws, and anyone who refused to help with their capture or withheld information was subject to loss of his son and/or his life. Because of this, the survivor's cries to the Lord were identical to those recorded in Jeremiah, the prophet, saying let their sons' blood be upon the son of Mary and Joseph, and many planned to exercise family justice according to the law against the family of Joseph should they pass through Bethlehem again.

Now, Mary understood their desire for justice and had some misgivings about traveling through the town of Yeshua's birth. She not only feared for Yeshua but the other children as well. Joseph and Mary prayed about this but received no answer to their prayers, and because of this, decided that Joseph didn't understand the dream correctly and they shouldn't travel through Idumaea and Judea to Galilee.

Mary wrote of Ohad's great sorrow at the news of their return to Nazareth and the loss of Joseph as a business partner. It was Ohad that suggested they should return to Galilee by ship. He had sailed from Pulesium to Caesarea many times and found it pleasant that time of year. So it was that Joseph prepared his family for departure within a fortnight of receiving Zechariah's message and gold.

Zechariah followed Mary's wishes and gave his blessing to Ohad, asking God's blessing on his trip to Egypt. And so it was the things and gold Mary requested returned to Egypt. Father then came home and told all these things, and we kept them in our hearts for many days. Like Zechariah, we were disappointed that Joseph's family wouldn't pass through Jerusalem as we hadn't seen them for nearly six years as it was nearly 753.

So it was we heard Joseph and his family sailed from Pulesium to Caesarea and from thence by sea to Ptolemais. From Ptolemais, they traveled in high spirits along the road to Asochis. There they rested and enjoyed the scenes of home once again. It was a short walk from Asochis to Nazareth and their new home, and other than seeing them on the high holy days, little was made known to us about their life in Nazareth.

Ishmael and I continued our studies under Hillel that summer and for the following eight years it was our good fortune to sit at his feet. Hillel was advanced in years, and his nephew, Gamaliel, a learned and righteous man, had already taken over many of his classes. It was in 759, when we were nearly twenty-three years old, that the great teacher dismissed us and after showing our respect to him, we were ready for other things. Ishmael wanted to increase his knowledge and proficiency in art forms, while I was ready to study the field of commerce. So we petitioned father to send us to Rome to learn these arts and sciences from our kin in Rome. It was shortly thereafter, about the year 761, that Gamaliel was commissioned to relieve Hillel. It was a sad time for those who had set at the feet of Hillel.

After some pleading by mother, father wrote his brother in Rome about these things. His brother, Benjamin, was involved in commercial shipping trade and was of good standing in the Roman community. It was to him we appealed for assistance and housing in this venture. The days seemed to drag as we waited for a message to arrive from Uncle Benjamin in Rome.

To pass the time, Ishmael and I would walk to the great marketplace in the heart of the city. On our walks we often talked of the strange things that happened to our family. If not of those directly related, then to those who were family friends such as Zechariah and his family who had become very close to our household since we moved to Jerusalem. Their son, John, was often seen by us at play when we visited Zechariah's household during breaks between the holidays. It was also during this time we noticed that Zechariah and Elizabeth were aging more than earlier and slowing down more as the young lad grew. It seemed they had decided with the birth of John their lives had fulfilled their purpose.

When we were twenty-four, John was approaching thirteen and just six months older than his kin, Yeshua. Father had assisted Zechariah even more than before and Zechariah didn't show the strength he had when he received the announcement of John's birth. Caiaphas decided that Zechariah's course must end soon. Father was asked to remain as the attendant to the next priest, and Zechariah knew his time for release was near.

PREPARATION

The feast days were upon us again; the temple was the scene of near madness. Pilgrims from every country flocked into the city and brought with them many different customs and mores which they wanted to apply in the temple. The guards and priests were called to give guidance and keep order within its holy walls. Many carried their sacrificial animals across their shoulders and waited impatiently for their turn before the priests.

Father was called with the other priests to serve; the mass of people pressed greatly against the gates. All the priests of the house of Hanan were called to serve; Zechariah was called to serve even though he wasn't well. Father showed signs of wear as the hour for the family celebration approached. Mother had the household set aright for our celebration. Others of our kin and friends were ready as well.

As in the past, the household of Joseph from Nazareth made the trek from Galilee and were housed by Zechariah. They did this each year since they returned from Egypt. Ishmael and I often visited with Joseph's children during these times, and when the holiday permitted, argued politics and religion with others our age. Since we were grown, we cared less for the children and their games, but still went to Zechariah's and gave them greetings of the day.

When there, as youngsters, we often stayed and helped entertain some of the children. Among them was Yeshua, the eldest of Joseph's family, which now included James, Judas, Joses and Sarah.

Now Yeshua was rather precocious, that was understood - Mary wouldn't let anyone forget it. She would sing his praises to anyone who would listen, and some of those who wouldn't. As children growing up, Ishmael and I grew tired of hearing of his deeds, and we were not alone.

Mary seemed not to notice the turning away of the others because of her incessant motherly coaching and reminding him of his special calling. Many times the other children frowned and turned away from their brother, and to speak in truth, it often reminded me of writings about Joseph and his brothers. Even Elizabeth, Mary's closest ally in this story of Yeshua's birth and John's as well, tired of Mary's continual comment to and about her eldest. Many noted how little attention she gave to her other sons while doting on Yeshua.

Even Joseph, a quiet and patient man, would finally comment, "Mary, if you don't stop this devotion, Yeshua could be hated by his family. You will cause his early death with these inculcations. Beware, God will not accept your placing this child above Him!" But for reasons of her own, she paid little attention to his admonitions.

Ishmael and I often heard her call Yeshua *Emmanuel* or *Messiah*, even though we knew his name was Yeshua, a common one if there ever was one. As children at play often do, we would tease him about this title, but as time went on, we ceased this form of childlike fun. Time gave us a chance to see the sadness in his eyes, a result of his mother's love and belief in his calling, we thought, and often thanked the Lord our mother didn't have this obsession.

Mary would delight in telling anyone about his quick learning of the law, always claiming, even at an early age, his great insight of all the scriptures. But Mary wasn't a learned Pharisee, and her knowledge of the law was no better than any other woman of the day. Her views of his knowledge weren't conclusive and suffered from the eye of a doting mother - so many of the family said.

So it was that Ishmael and I were familiar with many of the things said about Yeshua at an early age. We could see his character being formed early on by his mothers' insistence that he was the Messiah! Whether he believed it or not at his young age, or wanted to believe it or not, wasn't apparent to us. Our social contacts weren't close enough, nor long enough, to give us a clear idea of his true character and secret wants. But Mary's acts caused us to wonder and we asked our teacher about these things. He remarked that all women hoped and prayed their son would be the Messiah, and further reminded us that no man knoweth where, when, or who would be the deliverer of Israel.

Pesach passed by quickly that year and Joseph's family left Jerusalem for their trek to Nazareth without delay. At last, with the days calmer, father had time to tell us of many strange things he saw and heard in the temple during the feast days. These stories were always of great interest to us. The stories of many foreign delegates who came to the temple to follow the law and their strange approaches to it were told and retold by father.

IN THE TEMPLE

It was on one of these occasions he told us of Yeshua and the Chachamin in the temple. Father said the story was told to him thusly: It was the custom of Joseph, as we knew, to permit his older children to travel with other kin on the way home from the festival. Each child was to get permission to do this from Joseph and the accepting kin before a day's journey had passed. After the family had made its pilgrimage to the temple and was returning, they discovered that their eldest, Yeshua, wasn't among them. Joseph and Mary were very concerned for the young lad. They sought him among all those who made the trip with them from Nazareth, but to no avail. They were greatly distressed not finding him among even those who had left the temple later.

Yeshua was but twelve, and because of the press of the crowds leaving the city, wasn't easily seen. After diligent searching among those traveling back to Nazareth, Joseph and Mary returned from a goodly distance to Jerusalem. They searched for Yeshua among those in Zechariah's household, but none had seen him. Even Zechariah became concerned that Yeshua wasn't among the guests and relatives still in his house.

Under some distress, Joseph, Mary, and Zechariah went to the temple to seek him there. They asked many of those still there, but none in the outer courts had seen him. It was in the inner court within an inner circle of Chachamin they found him. These were asking him questions as to the whereabouts of his parents, and why he hadn't sought them out. Some said they asked him deep and thoughtful questions on the law as well as the prophets, but this Zechariah didn't confirm or deny, and Mary was full of these words.

Joseph remembered the fourth commandment and rebuked Yeshua for his lack of thought for them. He, as the eldest, should have set the best example for the others, yet what had he done?

Mary then asked, "Son why have you dealt with us thus? Behold, your father and I have sought you sorrowing!"

Father said young Yeshua rose from where he and the sages and officers of the temple were engaged in the discussion, and said unto them, "How is it that you sought me? Don't you know I must be about my Father's business?"

Father continued that neither Joseph nor Mary, nor the officers of the temple understood his words. The officers told of their attempt to find the lad's parents as they were parents also and knew only too well of their concern. All agreed that three days was indeed too long for a son to be away from his father's house without their knowledge. Their worries increased with each day but he gave them no word of who he was or how he came there; none among them knew about the Galilean lad. Zechariah was much undone, for had he still been in office, he would have known of the venture, but alas, such was not the case.

One Malcus, a chief steward of Caiaphas, told of taking Yeshua to his own home to care for him and returned him each day, hoping thereby to bring about just such a reconciliation as had happened. Joseph was very grateful for this care of his errant son, and offered Malcus a token of his feelings but it was refused. After some discussion, Yeshua submitted himself unto his parents and left the temple with the reluctance of the young bound for adventure. The family left Zechariah and joined those on the road to Nazareth.

Father continued to wonder as to these sayings by the young lad. What did he mean, his father's business, when all knew his father was a carpenter and shipwright? It was said that many of his relatives questioned why Yeshua would do such a disobedient thing and thereby cause his parents discomfort. I kept these things in my memory unto this very day.

ON THE WAY TO THE MARKETPLACE

The day was stifling and the dust of the street near the marketplace choked one with every step. Ishmael and I walked on the shady side of the street on our way to the marketplace. We talked as we strode along to the place of the gentiles of many things that day, the hope for a letter from Rome, the prospects of a new life in the world city, and eventually about the incident father told us about Yeshua in the temple.

"Ishmael, don't you think it strange what is said about Yeshua, and do you believe some of these things?" I asked Ishmael as we walked along. I was deeply troubled by some of the news about Yeshua. While waiting for his answer, I drifted back mentally to the stories about the announcement of Yeshua's birth - from angels and all that, also of the Magi and the story of the killings of the boys in and around Bethlehem by Herod's men. It all seemed so distant some eleven years ago.

It was strange that his parents and their close friends never commanded much respect prior to his birth. No one, neither kin nor friend, ever gave special notice that Joseph and Mary were special people. Oh, they were just and upright and of good character and followed the law without fail. Except, as all knew, Joseph had made an exception for Mary before their marriage. Yet even now, after all the great noise and claim by Mary that Yeshua was the savior of Israel, little had changed. Only Mary was enamored by these things and dreamed of their eventual recognition by all others.

"I don't know what to believe, and that's the honest truth. Wasn't it just a short time ago Yeshua was in the temple with the Chachamin, and wasn't it told that he confounded them with his understanding of the law? Yet, it's mighty strange no one from the temple has sought out Yeshua, at least I haven't heard of such."

"Nor I. Even father hasn't made any great effort to contact Joseph about this mysterious event in the temple. I know if I had accomplished as much at that age, father would've let the family and friends know from here to Rome." I turned to look at Ishmael and watched as he studied the forms before him. He had a natural way of looking at things that instructed his hand and eye when working on papyrus. His copy of things before him, either large or small, was a delight to see. His drawings were lifelike when compared with others trying the same transposition. He was in truth a gifted person.

"Remember as father told us that while in the temple, Yeshua became so interested in the law with the sages he forgot to return to his parents. But I think it exceedingly strange, for most of the sages would have instructed the lad to return to his parents before the first watch. And again, father said Joseph and Mary didn't miss him at first, and it then took three days to find him. Now, both of us have traveled with our parents many times to distant cities, and one of the important instructions was to report to them at prayer time. Isn't that so?"

What Ishmael said was true. Many times when traveling with our parents, we had to report at a predetermined time. To do otherwise was being disobedient and not in accordance with the law, as stated, "Honor your parents, that your days may be many on the land which the Lord gave you." Even in Leviticus, it's stated, "You shall fear every man his mother and his father, and keep my Sabbaths. I am the Lord your God."

"How then is it that one claimed by some to be the Son of God chose not to report to his parents and cause them so much anguish? Isn't this dishonor?" I asked Ishmael as we continued our journey. But alas, I could see he was already occupied by some other thought; his eyes were fixed on the scene before him. The questions about Yeshua would remain unanswered this day.

The marketplace was busy as always during this time of day, and the colors and sights were a changing kaleidoscope to his artistic senses. I knew to ask him to continue the dialogue was of little use; he was already pondering colors and shapes.

I turned to survey the scene. As we walked by the booths and shops, we could hear bits and pieces of conversations from customers and merchants. Our interests separated us, as often happened when Ishmael became more interested in some things than I and would wonder off to his own pursuits. The concern of these happenings lessened through the years, and wasn't as traumatic as in earlier days. Besides, it often provided different subjects to talk about when we met again.

I could see a small crowd ahead moving to follow some itinerant speaker, and as I moved closer, I could hear him advocating freedom from Rome and its tyranny. He was a Zealot from the hills and urging the males, young and old, to join he and his comrades in the cause of freedom. It was a very dangerous thing to do in Jerusalem during these times as some had been arrested, convicted, and even crucified for just such rousing speeches.

Even as he spoke a troop of Roman guards approached. The crowd, taking notice, dispersed quickly and the speaker left the scene, also. The guard swept the street clean of people, forcing them to move on ahead or back against the shops. As the guards moved by, the crowd closed in behind them, both Jew and gentile, shouting and shaking their fists at the disappearing soldiers.

But the speaker was gone and didn't return. The soldiers had accomplished what the command wanted without bodily harm to Roman, foreigner, or Jew. Not that this was a particular goal of the men of the garrison, but it made reporting of the day much easier with no lives lost versus one that had to justify even one soldier lost.

CHAPTER SEVEN

Adventures Away From Home

After the troops had passed, the crowd became even more unruly. They were like a group of students who had the master leave for the day, and knowing he wasn't to return, became pranksters, each showing his most violent side. And so it was with the crowd; struggles broke out in nearly every direction, cries of those inflicting bodily harm on some and cries of those set upon filled the air around me. I became disoriented and knew not which way to turn. My thoughts were not only of my welfare, but that of Ishmael as well.

During this melee, I was forced into an alcove between two small shops, and was there set upon by two men with knives. They had spied my money pouch and were determined to have it, even if it cost my life. They were foreigners and evil looking as well. They brandished their knives and forced me further and further into the alcove. As I stepped back, I passed a doorway. Suddenly, the curtain that was across the doorway was drawn aside, and a man stepped between me and the would-be robber assassins. He intercepted their deadly strokes with his own body, and with a command, frightened them such that they lost interest in me, my money pouch, and their intent on robbery. They both dropped their knives and turned and ran out of the alcove as if Satan himself was after them.

I stood there transfixed for a moment fully expecting the stranger to fall mortally wounded at my feet, but it was not so. Instead, he turned and smiled at me. It was the same stranger I had seen twice before - the very same. His size and manly grace that first caused me to notice him wasn't diminished by our closeness. He was very handsome indeed, and well above the average height and build of most men. Although not a giant, he was tall and looked to be very subtle with the capability of moving with great agility. He was dressed differently from those of Jerusalem and from foreigners who managed booths along the streets of the marketplace. His clothes didn't follow the style of the Roman or Asian, neither were they of any tribe of Israel. Even the cloth was different, not home spun nor of fine silks of the Orient, but something in between. It had a quality of light about it that made it shimmer even in the shadows of the alcove between the shops. He wasn't armed, but carried a long whip similar to one used to drive teams of horses as on a large chariot, yet not the same. He made no motion to use it on the would-be assassins as his figure and voice had completely unnerved them.

I was relieved when I saw he wasn't harmed and felt his grace and agility accounted for this, but later was to puzzle over this a great deal. "Verily, you have saved my life this day, and it is only right that I should know your name so I can ask blessings of Almighty God on you and yours." I was still shaken and deeply disturbed by the turn of events within these few moments. I remembered mother's telling us years ago of the man called Shalazar who traveled with the Magi and interpreted for them in Herod's court. Could this be him?

"I would know to whom I'm indebted!"

"Ah Judas, son of Simon of Kerioth, it's of no value for you to know my name. It's only that I should know you and your destiny. Oh, Judas, you are a man among men, but it's not well for you to know of events before their appointed time and place. And my name is one of them."

His handsome face had a look of true concern, one who realized that I was indeed important to him, and that he knew more of me than I of myself.

"Judas, I ask you to search your soul and remember this meeting, for some day we will meet again and I'll then ask for a favor in kind. Will you remember this moment, Judas, or will you, like many others, leave me to face my dilemma alone?"

"As the Lord is my judge, I'll never forget your act of this moment. But how come you know me when we've never met before? Are you from distant kin I don't recognize?" I cried with all the emotion of one still under the influence of the traumatic moment. How could he ask such a question? What man could forget one who saved his life? And what man wouldn't want to repay in kind? I was indignant at his comparing me in a group that had failed him, and wondered of his knowledge of my name and place of birth.

"Hold, Judas, ask not for your God to judge you or your actions before their time. Don't ask for that which will come hard upon you before you are forty-five years old. It's well enough for you to say you'll remember this day, and I mean no disparagement of your character with this statement." He stopped and gazed deeply into my eyes. I was as a child in returning his gaze; I couldn't turn away, absorbing every line and angle of his face.

Strangely, while I looked into his face, my mind suddenly thought of Ishmael and I realized he, too, might have been attacked by some of the mob. My heart rose in my throat as I thought of something happening to Ishmael. Yet the stranger's voice brought me back to the moment with him.

"Ah Judas, I have known of you before time began, and have seen your progenitors come and go even unto this hour. Hear me, your part in the book of life was written before Adam fell and the curse of the mark of Cain; even before the curse upon Canaan, it was known to those in heaven. But alas, my time is nearly gone! I must tend to other things, and Judas, don't wonder about Ishmael, for he is well, and has already returned home and is awaiting you. Judas, this day are you bound to me twice, once for yourself and once again for your brother, but don't tell him as it's not time for him to know this. Farewell, Judas, and remember, we will meet again, and this more than once." With that, he moved quickly through the curtain from whence he came and was gone from my view.

As soon as I recovered my senses, I went through the doorway wherein he disappeared, hoping to get another glimpse of him. When I stepped into the room, it was empty; he was nowhere in sight. I hurried out on the street, where a strange sight struck me; it was no longer morning, but afternoon. The shadows were already creeping across the street indicating the sun was in the lower quarter. Where had the day gone?

I hurried homeward, while my mind burned with the scene just played by the stranger and me. How could I ever be the same? His last words burned themselves into my memory. "I've know of you before time began." What did they mean? Also, the strange statement that, "…you're a man among men," was all so confusing. And who was this stranger whom even robbers' weapons didn't harm? The world was suddenly not the same. I wanted to see Ishmael and hear his story of the morning and early afternoon.

As I walked through the gate, I could see Ishmael running toward me. His face showed honest relief when he saw me. He fell upon my shoulders as he was more emotional than

I, yet this was the first time we experienced a testing of our bond as twins and I, too, felt the blessing of God that kept us safe and together.

"Ho Judas, where have you been? I've grieved about your delay, and was about to send Apius and Atonis looking for you," his voice shook with emotion. I pushed him off and looked upon his face; he had been truly distressed by my lateness. I was anxious to hear his story because of the words of the stranger, "fear not, for your brother has been spared for your sake." Spared from what?

"Aye, it's I who was concerned about you, not knowing if you escaped the irate mob. Tell me, what befell you this day?"

"Ah Judas, this has been one exceedingly strange day. Things that should be weren't, and those that shouldn't be were. Where shall I begin?"

"At the beginning," I said, trying to make some light of the adventure.

"Ah, where we were separated! I became compelled to search into the depths of the foreign market corner, but I can't say why. As I wandered deeper and deeper into the strange part of the market, I was drawn to a display of some fine tapestry in a small shop. The proprietor was a small ugly man who moved about on a crutch. When he saw me admiring the tapestry, he told me in halting Aramaic that the most beautiful of his stock was inside. He said he kept them there out of the weather and bright sun as they were so delicate that their beauty would be undone by such elements.

"I was so enamored by the beauty of those displayed outside, I couldn't resist the opportunity to see any that might be more beautiful than those. I didn't notice people about me, or the increase of street noise in front of the shop. And as he drew the heavy curtain aside for me, I stepped into the darkness of his small shop. After a moment, my eyes adjusted to the dimly-lit room, and there before me was one of the most beautiful curtains I've ever seen; his statements about it were indeed true. I wanted to question him about the price of such a fine piece and turned to do so, but as I did, I found he was gone and instead, two men faced me with knives drawn. I shouted for help but couldn't be heard over the noise of the mob outside. They laughed at my helplessness. I was in the power of some evil men. They made it known to me they wanted my money and would kill to get it. I moved toward the rear of the shop hoping to find an escape. I discovered another door and moved as quickly as I could toward it while they tried to cut off my escape.

"Just as I neared the doorway, they lunged toward me with knives flashing. It was at that moment, a large fellow stepped into the shop from that very doorway. It was he who intercepted their blades. He spoke but one word, they dropped their knives, and ran full of fright through the outer door into the street and were gone.

"What should've happened didn't. I feared for the stranger's life and expected him to be mortally wounded, but as he turned, I saw he was unharmed. An unusual thing as even though he stood with his back to me during the attack, I could see the knives plunge into his body. I was frightened even as the attackers. Here was a strange person and I wondered if he was devil or angel."

Ishmael continued, "While my thoughts were still unsettled, he smiled and spoke in a soft but deep voice, "Fear not, Ishmael of Kerioth, as no harm will come to you this day." His voice had a reassuring quality that I was willing to believe, and found my heart returned to normal as soon as he spoke. What manner of man was he? As I stood like a child surveying him, he moved toward the doorway. He was exceedingly handsome in facial features, one that any artist would want to sculpture. He stood at least a foot above me, and his body was strong and muscular, even as those early Greek statues. I couldn't recognize his native land from his bearing or dress. He was not of our people but whether Greek, Roman or Oriental I couldn't tell. Even his dress was strange to me; the material wasn't of anything I've seen before as it glowed unnaturally in the darkened room. He was a most unusual man to look upon."

Ishmael stopped for a moment as if to reflect on the description he gave. "Surely, Judas, he was an angel of the Lord, for who else could stand the blows of the robber's knives and not be harmed, and who else, save one of divine background, could know that I was your brother, having never seen me before?"

He looked quizzically at me, "Aye Judas, what is the meaning of all these things taking place around us? Can it be true that our God is preparing a way for Israel to rise again and give us a king, even as the prophets of old wrote?"

I felt the same mood of expectation as did Ishmael. He was right in wondering what it all meant. But I couldn't tell him of my true thoughts and of what the stranger told me. Listening to Ishmael, I agreed with the stranger. This wasn't the time for such revelations. Instead, I turned away and answered only the questions of the day.

"Ishmael, whether he was an angel or not, I cannot tell. Do you remember the first time in the marketplace when we were young and with Apius, and my asking you if you saw the tall stranger in the crowd? Well, it's the same person that I saw then, Ishmael - the very same!" I could see he was reflecting on the past.

"And again, when we were on the wall watching the procession of the Magi arriving through the city gates. Don't you remember my calling to you about a handsome stranger among them? Oh, surely you remember those events. He is one and the same I tell you!"

"Aye, I remember those times, Judas, but remember, I didn't see him then. Besides, how do you know the man I saw is the same one? How can you know this when you weren't there to see him?" His question forced me to make a decision to tell him of my adventure with the same stranger. I wouldn't hold to the word of the stranger. And so it was that I told Ishmael all about my harrowing escape from would-be robber assassins just as he had in similar fashion.

"Let's go into the courtyard and rest awhile and I'll tell you what happened to me." And with that, I led the way into the cool courtyard. The house was empty and only the servants remained. Mother was with her beauty clients, father in the temple, and Anath, who was soon to be wed, was being tutored elsewhere in the womanly arts.

I called Apius and asked him to see to refreshments for us. He was a good man and well schooled in the arts of running the household. He could get things done and quickly. Yet he, like many of the other Greeks who had become slaves or servants because of unfortunate circumstances, had a very good education in all the sciences and social graces of the day. As we grew up, he often was in our confidence and was one that never betrayed us to our parents or any other authority once his word was given. The big problem was that he wasn't quick to commit himself to such obligations. He didn't take the giving of his word lightly, which made both Ishmael and me admire him all the more.

It wasn't long before he had set before us some cool wine and fruit, and we refreshed ourselves before resuming our discussion of the activities of the day.

"I should like Apius to hear our adventures. Would you agree to that Ishmael?"

"I not only agree, but would also like to hear his comments. You know he often has a different view of the cause and effect of such things." Ishmael's remarks were well taken.

"Apius, come, sit here in the shade and listen to my story." He turned and sat beneath a nearby tree. I sat opposite both of them and rested on a bench near a small pool wherein goldfish played among some lily pads. The pool was there when we moved into the home some years before and although it looked cool, it contributed little to the real cooling of the courtyard. "I'll tell you my adventure first, and then Ishmael his, and we will see what we can make of them." I looked at Apius as I spoke as Ishmael had already told me his adventure.

"Yes, master Judas, I'll listen and explain what I can from ancient Greek legend."

And so it was we told Apius about our adventures that morning and early afternoon. Everybody listened intently as I told my adventure in detail. They were silent after I finished, each occupied by his own thoughts. I then asked Ishmael to relate his experience for the sake of Apius. As each story was told, Apius's expression changed from one of mild interest to one of great expectation. He followed each change of action in our stories with increased interest. After awhile, he leaned forward and spoke.

"It would seem that this stranger is one and the same person that you saw some years ago in the marketplace. Ah, I remember it well now! It was a strange sight and I didn't want you to know that I, too, saw him that day." He shook his head slowly from side to side, as if he still wanted to deny the possibility of the event some ten years before. "As I recall, he was a striking figure of a man, both handsome and well proportioned in body."

"Aha! I always thought you saw him that day, Apius, even if you didn't admit it. But what of this new event; isn't it also *too strange* to be a coincidence?" I was encouraged by his admitting he also saw the stranger so many years before. I knew now that this person wasn't just a figment of my imagination. He did exist and others could see him!

Apius leaned back against the tree and closed his eyes. "In ancient writings, the gods are both good and evil, even as man is. The gods often use the forms of humans and animals to communicate with man. The forms taken, either man or animal, may be such that man considers them ugly or beautiful. Yet again, it may be the gods make themselves appear unto man as they wish, and men don't recognize them as they are, but as he wishes them to be, that is, the god desiring to cause man mischief may take upon himself the figure of the most beautiful, while the god desiring good for man may take on the form of the most ugly. The first, it is said, is to confuse man, because it is one of man's great failings that he believes only good things come in beautiful forms, and therefore is easily led astray. So those that practice evil often hold beauty before man to ensnare him."

Being assured of our attention, he went on. "While in the second, it's written the gods choose the ugly form to test the power of the good man to see goodness in that form. It is held by some to be a game played by the gods. Do you follow me, masters?" Apius opened his eyes to see if we were indeed listening, as he had experienced us playing tricks on him before. We both shook our heads although I wasn't sure our background of our God permitted us to fully understand his Greek point of view.

"It seems each of you has the feeling the act or the stranger was a good deed, and I must agree. Your ancient writings say this good deed is generated by a good source; therefore, you draw the conclusion the angel of the Lord intervened and saved your lives."

After a brief pause, Apius continued, "In Greek lore, it's possible for the evil source to cause a good thing, if indeed the end is intended to produce an evil result. Therefore, I say unto you, beware of the things that have happened to you this day, as they may be just an omen of things yet to come which aren't good. The real question is why have you been thus protected from evil? Aye, it's this that troubles me! Hear me, Master Judas, I have deep feelings at the moment for you. These things you have experienced are not for the weak in spirit. Pray to your God that you may have strength to endure the travail that may come upon you!" And with that said, Apius rose and left us before we could speak.

The change in Apius even while he spoke was a shock to us, as we had expected him to tell us of the writings of the Greeks. Instead, he acted nearly as a prophet of old! We were at a loss for words and sat looking at one another without moving. What changed Apius, and what gave him the feeling that all wasn't well with the events of the day? Hadn't we both been saved from an evil deed? Where then is the foreboding which caused Apius to fear the future?

His comments and reaction to our stories remained with us for many days. Ishmael and I often discussed the strange comments of Apius. Nothing was said during the evening meal about the unusual happenings of the day; it was then I decided to keep a log of all the things I thought were important and might have bearing on the future. It was from this log that much of this epistle is written. So it was at the age of twenty-three I started this record of my life and the events that followed even to this hour.

ANOTHER VIEW

It was then the display became garbled again and the system automatically switched into search mode. The search lamp indicated the system was looking for the next coincident characters which would again make sense.

John punched up the delay control bit and proceeded to shut down the entire process and turned to those at the consoles. He was tired and felt they were, also.

"We all deserve a rest," he said with some feeling. "The last few hours of this travel into the past has been very eventful, and I for one am ready for lunch. So I'm going to take the system offline until we have some lunch and rest a bit."

"I'm with you; I'm not used to working without a coffee break."

Chuck and Jean shut down their control consoles. Jean went to the printer and checked to see that all copies were present. John pressed the control panel switch to raise the lights in the lab; the long vertablinds in the windows slowly repositioned to let in the sunlight. As sunlight filled the room, the interior lighting was adjusted to balance the light spectrum for daylight values. The net result was a room lit to the correct intensity and color balance without the harsh shadows and bright spots or open-air lighting. In one easy move, the lab went from the darkness of a theater to that of a beautifully-sunlit room.

"We all agree then?"

The others indicated assent; they prepared to leave for lunch. John had warned them that all precautions must be taken to preserve the integrity of the program. All printed matter must be filed as classified material. Each was responsible for hard copy. John notified ISM of the shutdown.

They moved through the air interlock and into the hallway. John closed the door, inserted his keycard, and notified security that the laboratory was cleared. The security department replied and secured the lab against a change in mass or temperature. It was one of many failsafe systems used against forced or accidental entry. John joined the others waiting in the hallway. They walked along in silence into the elevator and out to the cars, each occupied by thoughts of his own as translated from the Golden Scroll.

They automatically returned to John's favorite restaurant. Both cars pulled up at nearly the same time and the four entered the eating place together. They completed the meal in cautious silence. The conversation began with the dessert and coffee.

"Boy, I'm glad to get this coffee. I thought we'd never take a break," Ed said, setting his cup down. I'm a Java-junky, to turn a phrase, and like to take breaks."

"I'm sorry, Ed, I'm not one who is hung up on the food and drink items of the day, so I'm apt to forget that some are. And I think most of us were deeply interested in the deciphering of the scroll." John was one who believed some things should not interfere with the motion of progress on an assignment. Jean noted this while they were on the site in Jerusalem. He had an intensity for the completion of any project which overrode many of the common and accepted pastimes of the day. He frowned on the relaxed way some of the schools went about their archaeological projects, and often stated so in no uncertain terms.

"Well, personally, I'm glad the computer went into search mode. I was getting hungry. Even though the scroll and its contents are of great interest and, of course, importance, I really think we should set aside a regular break period for both rest and lunch from now on. I'm sure it would benefit everyone," Jean said in a rather positive manner. She expected some controversy about this suggestion but was surprised John and the others agreed. It was then set up as part of the routine for the translation of the scroll; coffee and lunch breaks would be part of the daily routine. The computers would be programmed in real time to notify them and prevent them from becoming so engrossed as to forget the time.

"After all the many years of being taught that the religious world is flat, it's hard to believe it could be anything else. Yet, this writer intimates it is round and more secular than religious, and there is a hemisphere other than the commonly-accepted view of Christianity." Chuck was the first to open the conversation on the subject of the scroll's contents. He often spoke in metaphors. "Being a believer from the old school, I find it a little far out, but I'm willing to see what the author is about. I have some reservations about the transliteration program, and I think I will rework some of the language in the future. The syntax, where the old text verbiage and the new are intermixed, doesn't aid understanding, but fundamentally, the program is working well. How do you feel about the religious events as described by the author so far, Ed?"

Ed had been listening to Chuck with the same interest as the others. Each was respectful of the other's area of expertise. In this case, the question was directed to the expert on ancient religious history, and all were interested in what he might say about the revelations that had opened new thoughts about the reports in or left out of the Gospels.

"It's too early to make anything but an educated guess as to the ideas presented therein, yet I must admit the story line *is* different from the traditional view. It's the first time more than twelve hundred words have been found written about Judas, all in the first person, and not all derogatory."

"How about that?" John came through with his usual comment.

"Yes, an autobiography by Judas would be a find beyond even the most heretical imagination. In traditional writings, he is treated as a despicable character, and even his introduction in the book of Matthew is followed by the phrase, 'who also betrayed Him.' Of course, this is held by some to be an added phrase - as a kind of afterthought. None of the other disciples are treated in this manner. And even though Simon Peter was one who denied his master, 'And the master said unto Peter, verily I say unto thee, that this night, before the cock crows, thou shalt deny me thrice.' Again, he is given special attention, as Yeshua recognizes Satan in Peter."

Ed stopped for a moment.

"What's the point, Ed?"

"Yet, with these two great revelations in the presence of the others, he is never addressed as 'Peter, the one who denied the master three times,' or as 'Peter, the one who contained Satan.' This approach of the writers seems to be used to reinforce the apparent evilness in one and not the other." Ed stopped and took up his coffee cup; he motioned for the waitress to bring a refill.

"But what has this to do with the text of the present scroll?" asked Jean.

"Not much, other than it shows little understanding or sympathy for the second most important character in the story of Christianity, which is what the writer of the scroll is implying. The gospels have always been rather silent on some of the events and places between well described major events." None of the others interrupted, so Ed continued.

"That is to say, what happened in the life of Yeshua between his twelfth year and his approximate year of baptism is left to conjecture. His twelfth year is a fixed number, that is, the writer testifies as to when Yeshua appears in the temple before the doctors, but evidently didn't know, even though he lived with the man for at least three years, or thought it irrelevant to state Yeshua's age when he was introduced to the world as the Son of God at his baptism by John." Ed stopped for a moment as the waitress poured coffee for all.

John nodded as he listened, "You know, I never really gave that any thought. What is your opinion about these things?"

There was no doubt that Ed enjoyed the attention of the moment. He sipped his fresh coffee before continuing, "Personally, I have always considered the time of baptism more important than his appearance in the temple at the age of twelve. After all, a great share of Christian belief hangs on the baptism, not his appearance in the temple. I'm hoping that this writer will shed some light on these cracks in the planking, so to speak. There's just too much information to assimilate in such a short time. Even if some of it isn't true, the fact it exists is mind boggling. The portion about the Magi observing the 'star of stars' is intriguing to say the least, and John, how do you see this as possibility? Could there be a third encounter event and in that timeframe?"

John wasn't in any hurry to commit himself to comment on this question, but feeling he was caught up in the dialogue, picked up his spoon and had at it.

"It's pretty well known that archaeology has discovered many areas throughout the world which provide enigmas as to the possibility of higher forms of intelligence having some kind of intercourse with human beings. To what degree and what time is still just conjecture."

John continued, "Some of these are recorded in stone, land masses, art forms and other unique forms conveying possible intelligence. As you well know, Ed, there are some Mayan art forms that point to the possibility of that race knowing space vehicles, and the Old Testament writings of Ezekiel have often been held by some to be sightings of space beings. I've no real evidence to support this position, and other than using pure imagination, can only conclude it might be some form of optical instrument. There isn't any solid evidence that any early societies had the capability or know-how to design and build such instruments. As indicated by the writer, it was used with charts of the skies to locate and mark the movement of the heavens. In this case, it was used, so he wrote, to track one certain star which the users believed indicated some event of great importance to them. The birth of a prophet was known to their ancients when they started on their trek across the miles of desert and mountains. The real kicker is, did the story of the boy king of the Jews to be born under a star come from this ancient Persian story or did the birth of a prophet come from the Jewish lore?" John rested his case; it had been a long speech for him. He normally spoke little during these combined gatherings.

He waited for someone to comment on his final question but none did, so he continued, "If the language is correct, and I see no way to prove it at this time, I would accept the author's thoughts on the instrument. He doesn't seem to be explicit as to what the instrument was, which is to his credit, for if he had been, it might have led to a suspicion of a later contrived forgery." The restaurant was nearly empty, but they took little notice.

"As it is, we must assume he and his brother were totally unfamiliar with the telescope and celestial navigation, and that along with the rest of the people of that time, believed that the diviners of the East were guided by a bright moving star. And even though they couldn't see it themselves, believed that by an act of spiritual insight, the Magi were permitted privy to its motion." John took a sip of his already-cold coffee, but for the moment paid little attention to that fact. "This is told in the Gospels, but in history, there isn't any corroborating evidence to support such during the dates supplied us."

"It's always been an enigma that no one else in the world noticed or made any entry in their records of a bright moving body in the heavens. Now, it wasn't that there weren't people watching the sky, for almost all navigation on the sea at that time was done by landfall and celestial observation. Yet none of the seafaring men of that day scribed in their logs anything near this sort of phenomenon ever occurring. This, I believe, adds to the consensus that the event was one of spiritual and not secular import. Of course, that is a religious precept and not one of archaeology." He ended his statement with a nod to Ed.

Ed accepted the nod as one turning over the floor to another speaker, and gave this observation, "I agree it enters the realm of religion when reaching for an explanation of the star and its necessity in the scheme of things. It is one of those items that was often added in the story of travel, even before the Gospels were written. In early religions of many nations, gods of all kinds left their places of abode to guide mankind, or some select nation, through some distant and uncharted land or sea. Even in Exodus, the Hebrews believed and wrote that a pillar or cloud led them by day, and pillar of fire by night, yet neither of these were seen by any other nations of that day. Or we may say that they were never recorded as a phenomenon. These special occurrences were common in tales on religions of the day," he said with some emphasis on the part of the historical quality of the different religions.

"But what do you think of the loss of the instrument and charts? And who do you think the stranger is, at least as Judas sees him at the moment?" asked Jean. The stranger seemed a little more romantic to her than the story of the star.

Ed turned to look at Jean, "I really believe, at this moment in the translation, we can only say the author is a little confused by the events of the day. His thoughts at first were that the stranger was a messenger of God, an angel if you will, but with the inclusion of the short comment by Apius, there's some indication that doubt is creeping into his mind about the identity of the stranger."

He continued to address the subject while the others looked at the time. "I'll say he believes the stranger isn't a trick of his mind, as he was beginning to doubt his own belief in this stranger's existence until both Apius and Ishmael admitted they too had seen him. And not only that, but they also saw him in nearly the same form, that is a handsome and well-built male. There are at least three persons that now have had a glimpse of the stranger and all have been marked by the close encounter." Ed stopped here and looked at his watch. "Although I've no real insight in this writing, I believe from the opening statement, we can safely conclude that the stranger is either Satan, the Master Deceiver, or one of his obedient servants. As to the truth of this deduction, only time and more of the translation can tell. And speaking of time, I see we better get back and put the equipment online. What do you think, John?"

"Yep, boy, time has really slipped by. I've notified the security department that we will be entering the building soon after lunch, and we had better save any more of the dialogue for later in the evening." They paid their separate checks, left the restaurant, and drove to the laboratory where they entered after being identified. John turned on all the equipment and they returned to the consoles. In went the code of the day, the vertablinds closed, and the interior was ready for viewing. They watched the display as the next portion of the translation appeared and listened to the output of the speech synthesizer. The output started with the same key words as before and then moved into the story line.

THE ROAD TO ROME

It was later that evening when father called the family together for a special announcement. Neither Ishmael nor I knew what the subject might be, but our sister, being a born tease, tempted us with the idea of a letter from our uncle in Rome as father had indeed received a letter from his brother welcoming us into his family for as long as we might like to stay. With that announcement, all remembrances of the events of the day and warnings of Apius were forgotten; our thoughts turned to the preparation for the trip.

Mother had many things to warn us about, from Roman women to the sinful places of the street. She was full of enthusiasm. The thoughts of her boys in Rome, the greatest city of the day, was enough to bring her to the highest activity. So much to be done and clothes to prepare; after all, she didn't want her brother-in-law to think she had no mind of style. Since the trip was to be partly by land and the rest by sea, there were needs for both.

We planned to travel from Jerusalem to the seaport town of Caesarea and there catch a ship bound for Rome. Joppa and Azotus were port towns closer to Jerusalem than Caesarea, but they were somewhat seasonal ports and the chance of consistently securing passage to Rome from them was less than at Caesarea, so Caesarea it was.

Ishmael and I were joyous over our good fortune, but at the same time, grieved we were leaving those we loved for such a long trip. We wished we could take Apius with us, but father said his status with us in Jerusalem was not the same as it would be in Rome, and therefore we should not take the chance of his being bound over in Rome. So it was that our dear friend and confidant was to stay home while we sailed away.

Mother claimed the days for preparation flew by, but we thought the day for departure would never come. Yet the day did come, and we stood with our family in the courtyard to receive father's blessing on a bright warm day in the spring of the year. Mother and Anath wept greatly when the hour arrived, and father fell upon our shoulders asking the Lord to bless and keep us from harm, and return us in safety to them. It was the first time I really noticed father was aging. It was as though I saw him as he really was, a truly good man who worked hard to provide for the family, and deep in him was the love that, only on these occasions, came to the surface enough for each of us to know.

Our horses were ready for the trip. We said our final blessings on each of those left behind and stepped aboard our animals. Apius, the faithful one, was to travel with us to Caesarea, see that all went well, and then bring the animals back home. As we left, we experienced the pull of adventure of Rome and all it stood for in the world, and the longing to remain among family and friends. Soon, Jerusalem faded from view and we were elated to be on our way to the capital of the world.

The distance to Joppa was about fifty miles and this following the roads from Jerusalem to Emmaus, there rest the animals, and then through Lydda, up the road to the coast and Joppa. It was for us to be a three-day journey. Ours was not one of great urgency, that is to say, we had no previous date for sailing, and it was only upon arrival at Joppa we could negotiate for passage to Rome. It was Apius who convinced us that forcing the animals at a harder pace wasn't wise, and of no avail. A ship would either be there or it wouldn't, and all our impatience wouldn't make it otherwise. We accepted his advice as we often had, and held ourselves in check. To pass the time during the trip, we relived the strange happenings of the last few days.

The review of the past and the new country route to Emmaus made the time on the open road seem shorter. We arrived in Emmaus near noon. Emmaus was an ancient town having much history and yet a fair amount of trade being on the route to Joppa and Caesarea. We went to the well and watered our animals. Here we left Apius to tend to things and went to the marketplace. We found fresh fruits and dates as well as some goat's milk. We listened to the rumors at the well before we moved on. We returned with the food and enjoyed our first meal on the road. After resting the animals during this noon meal, we set out for Lydda which was but nine miles away from Joppa. Joppa lay on the sea coast of the Mediterranean; it was also an ancient port town which had been used as the port for the movement of food stuffs for the interior of Judea, but since that time had fallen from the list of main port because of the shallowness. It was Joppa that had the port for smaller ships of the Mediterranean. We hoped to reach Joppa by the following day. If this happened, it was then onto Caesarea and to find a ship.

Apius warned us that it would be in the late hours of the second watch before we reached Joppa, and because of not knowing the city, we had best seek shelter along the road and enter the city in the light.

And so it was when evening came, we moved our animals off the roadway onto the near hillside. Here, close to our animals and possessions, we ate our evening meal, then after asking blessings of the Lord on our loved ones at home and for us on our trip, we laid down and went to sleep. Apius and some servants he had brought to help drive the animals back to Jerusalem stood guard during the night. It was rumored along the road that small bands of robbers were active in the area, but none bothered us that night. Ishmael and I slept a dreamless sleep until Apius woke us in the early hours of the morning.

We gave thanks for our rest and asked blessings for that day, ate some of the fruit and goat cheese with some flat bread we had purchased the day before, and were ready to proceed to Joppa.

As we approached Joppa, we had our first glimpse of the Mediterranean Sea. Neither of us had ever seen so large a body of water before this. It was beautiful, yet somewhat awesome for such land-bound people as we were. The sea stretched as far as the eye could see, and as we looked down on the city, we could see the ships approaching from distant ports.

Oh, it was a romantic place for those not acquainted with life near the sea. Apius warned us again about the rowdiness of the seafaring men and their families. He had seen them in action during his lifetime when he was first taken as a slave, and he was transported by ship from his homeland. Many ports of call had he seen in his younger days when taken from Greece and sold in Egypt.

We moved through Joppa as quickly as the animals would permit, and turned northward toward Caesarea - our final destination on these shores. We followed the coastline northward for some miles. During this time, we could see the sea from the coastal rises along the route. Caesarea lay only one days' travel from Joppa and was within our reach at a leisurely pace.

And so it was, we reached the largest port city in that part of the country early in the day. It was Apius, following father's orders, who found us a place to stay until we could secure passage on a ship to Rome.

We were comfortable in a small inn near the seafront; from here, we could walk to the market and the docks. Only a short time passed before we discovered that finding a ship going directly to Rome wasn't an easy task. Most ships were sailing shorter routes this time of the year. It was possible to secure passage on ships sailing for other destinations and then change ships at those ports for further extensions even to Rome. Because of this, Apius advised us to lay out a new route.

A week had nearly passed before we found a captain who had news of a ship which would sail from Cyprus to Lycia and then to Crete. It was there, the captain said, we would have the best chance of catching a ship to Sicily and then to Rome. He warned often ships that went to Crete stopped at Athens and there another ship could be found to sail to Rome.

But this time of year, the seas weren't favorable for a trip so extensive as one from Caesarea to Rome. Oh, it was done, but not without considerable risk. We returned to the inn somewhat discouraged by our discovery, but what must be must be. We brought this news and some sea charts along with us to show Apius, for he would surely know which would be the best for us.

Apius studied the charts for the better part of the evening, and finally decided that, if the connections were possible, a route from Caesarea to Paphos, a port city on the island of Cypress, would be the first leg of our journey. This port, although not holding the possibility of direct passage to Rome, would have many ships sailing to the port city of Myra in the province of Lycia and would be our second leg of the voyage. With the prevailing winds, we could then catch a ship for the island of Rhodes and its port city.

Apius heard during his travels that many ships plied the waters between Rhodes and the island of Crete, and one of the busiest ports on the island of Crete was Phenice. Many ships docked there from all parts of the world and it offered the best possible passage to Rome. But should this not be possible, then we would have to accept passage to Syracuse on the east coast of Sicily, and from Syracuse, we would be able to find passage through the Straits of Messina to Rome.

So it was marked on the charts by Apius, and we rolled the charts and placed them with our other things. We decided to make every effort to locate a ship going from Caesarea to some city in Cyprus, and hoped it would be Paphos. Should this not be the case, Apius showed us how to read the charts well enough to find our way if we were forced, by some act of nature, to land at some port not defined as one of the major ones.

And so it was, after the evening meal and prayers of the day, Ishmael and I lay quietly in our room at the inn, each pondering just what this adventure would bring in the next few years. The strange surroundings and noises outside our window made sleep hard to come by, but at last it overtook two weary travelers.

Apius woke us early the next day in the fourth watch. We were dockside before the sun rose over the water. As each ship docked, we approached the captain and asked when he would put out to sea again and his destination. Each gave an answer that wasn't one we wanted, so we continued our search all day, breaking only for a noon meal and prayers.

Late the next day we finally found a ship which was bound for Cyprus and, in fact, to Paphos. The ship wasn't one of the most sturdy construction but it seemed seaworthy to us. Apius somewhat reluctantly gave his consent to our choice and, after paying for passage, we returned to the inn for our charts and belongings. The ship was to sail with the next tide, which left us no time for lingering with our old friend and faithful servant, Apius. We were very grieved to take leave from him, and wept some on his shoulders as we gave him our blessings. He returned the blessings with a prayer of his own to the gods of Greece. We gave him a message for father that we were well and on our way to Rome. Apius gave us money he had secured from the sale of some animals that father didn't want returned. It was this amount that kept body and soul together until we arrived in Rome and our uncle's house.

Apius remained dockside until the ship was under way and sailed into the distance. Even as his figure grew smaller we could still see him waving to us.

It was late in 759 when we last saw the shores of Judea. When we couldn't see the shoreline, we settled down midships for the trip to Paphos.

The ship was ladened with market goods and carried few passengers; Ishmael and I huddled next to the mast to keep away from the spray. I wasn't one who felt ill at ease on the water but poor Ishmael was soon very ill and didn't want to move at any cost. The ship was old and didn't move quickly, and I knew even a short trip would seem like a long one.

The captain sailed by landfall navigation by day, and stars by night. In either case, weather and clearness of the sky was an aid to navigation and as soon as a change in the weather limited these, the captain was one to sail ever closer to shore. Yet the weather didn't change and the clear sky gave him the best sailing conditions he had for many a year, or so he said. The captain, therefore, put up as much sail as he could and moved the old ship toward Cyprus hoping to reach Paphos in two days.

We reached Paphos in the time the captain predicted. Here again, we were blessed on our adventure - the finding of another ship for us by the captain. Our captain knew the master of a ship sailing for Myra in Lycia and suggested we might save time in the long run by taking it rather than waiting for a ship sailing directly to Rhodes. We agreed and gave the new captain our passage money. We sailed on the tide for Myra.

The ship was newer and a somewhat better sailing vessel; the time was lessened by favorable winds and sailing methods of the crew. We arrived in Myra in less than three days, and after making the necessary changes to the cargo and passengers, we were again headed toward Rhodes. On the trip from Cyprus to Myra, Ishmael had time to become ill again, but found it less difficult. He was beginning to get his sea legs, or so I hoped.

We remained on board the ship at Myra to protect our belongings from possible looting by many evil-looking waterfront people. We said our prayers and ate little to keep from expending our stores. I found it better for Ishmael to eat very little while on the water and most of that being dry foods. It seemed the more liquids he consumed, the greater his chances of being ill.

The trip from Myra to Rhodes was shorter than that from Caesarea to Cyprus. Although we passed more ships along the way, there were less landmarks, and navigation depended on the sun by day and stars by night. The captain had confidence in his ability to follow the stars and sailed a true course for Rhodes. In less than one day, we approached Rhodes, and we landed shortly thereafter a tired but happy duo for we were making time.

In Rhodes, the ship was emptied of cargo and fresh water and food was placed aboard. The cargo was then replaced and we were ready to sail for Crete. We managed to get more supplies from peddlers along the dock and were prepared for the trip as well as we could anticipate; we sailed the next day with the tide. The trip from Rhodes to Phenice in Crete was nearly three days in length. All aboard fared well except Ishmael who was ill most of the way. Early on the fourth day we docked at the port city of Phenice. Here we learned we must again find another ship, for this one was to return to Rhodes with new oil from Crete. We asked the captain's advice on finding another ship headed for Sicily and he directed us to another part of the island where he said would be our best chance to get passage to Sicily.

We traversed the island and found a large ship sailing for Syracuse. The captain told us the trip was one that took nearly five days in good weather, so he advised us to bring extra food and water. Upon hearing this, Ishmael nearly fainted. We paid the master and joined many others from all parts of the world. The ship sailed within the day. Ishmael was not alone in his illness this time, as many of the new passengers were troubled by the ship's motion. Ishmael ate little and I feared for his health before the voyage was over. The master took pity on me and said, with a great deal of humor, that he hadn't lost a passenger to sea sickness yet, and doubted he would in Ishmael's case.

We had no sight of land for nearly four days. The more we sailed without sight of land, the more I admired those of the sea. The captain held his course by the heavens, the weather favored us, and we made good time. The land mass that came into view on the fifth day was later identified as Sicily. It wasn't long before we landed at Syracuse. I helped Ishmael off the ship and he managed to rest on land and eat a full meal. We were at last nearing our goal, the famous city of Rome. It was now just a matter of finding a ship leaving for Rome and the voyage would be finished - a thing that Ishmael had prayed for since we left Caesarea. Poor Ishmael, I felt he had held up well for all his trials. Each time we landed, he thanked God for the safe passage and prayed for the strength to continue.

A ship headed for Rome wasn't hard to find for many were interested in the trade that Rome offered; it was one of the greatest cities in the Empire and its activity in maritime trade was already legendary. Rome was the seat of world government, social life, and trade. Uncle Benjamin had long ago established his business there as a sea trader. He was a son of a slave who had risen from nothing to high acceptance in this world - a man who, even though a Jew, wheeled some power in his circles of commerce and some in government. It was to his home we were going to live and study while assisting him with his business.

The ship we boarded was ready to sail the hour we arrived, and so it was that we were on the high seas headed for Rome more quickly than any of the other transfers. We were on the water four days before the sailors announced that Rome would soon be in sight. Passengers crowded the fore part of the ship for their first glimpse of this wonderful city.

CHAPTER EIGHT

In Rome

Rome was not only a beautiful sight, but it was also a welcome one. We had been nearly seventeen days on the voyage from Caesarea to Rome and for most of those, Ishmael had been ill. We were two weary young adventurers from the hinterland of Judea. The year had changed date during our voyage as it was early 760 when we sighted Rome, and now Ambivius was ruler of Judea. We had followed our progress on the charts that Apius marked for us, and were happy that all had gone well with us. We prepared our song of thanks to God when we landed. We had our letter of introduction from father to Uncle Benjamin and with it, the instruction from Uncle Benjamin on how to locate his home.

After the ship docked, we proceeded to follow his directions, but soon found we had little sense of direction as marked on his maps. We knew if the marketplace was near the waterfront, we could find some of our people and they would help us find our way. We strode through the port side of the market and listened to the traders and market people.

We had not walked far when we heard the distinct Hebrew song of praise for good fortune, and following the sound, discovered a young lad moving through the crowd selling freshly-made cakes. He was a handsome lad and full of life by the sound of his voice. Ishmael and I hadn't heard such a song since leaving the doorstep of our home.

"We salute you, oh singer of such joyful music," Ishmael said. "We would ask for blessing on your efforts and would ask in return some directions as we are new in the city."

"I salute you as well, and if I can be of some service to you, say on." The lad spoke in good Aramaic, a thing we hadn't expected.

"We are nephews of one Benjamin, the sea merchant of this fair city, and would ask directions unto his house. My name is Ishmael, and this is my brother, Judas, and we are just come from Jerusalem." Ishmael paused and smiled as pleasantly as he could after his trying time at sea. "We would care to know your name and the house of your fathers?"

"My name is Ocran of the ancient house of Asher, and I know of your uncle." He accepted our statements as true as he noticed our dress and travel-worn appearance. "I don't know where his house is located, but my father, Pagiel, will know, and his servants can lead you unto the house of your uncle. So come, let us go to my father's house and he can instruct us." He turned and motioned us to follow, and strode off at a pace that was the mark of the young and strong. It was not long before I called to him, asking him to shorten his stride as both Ishmael and I hadn't recovered from the sea voyage. He recognized our discomfort, and helped carry Ishmael's belongings, for he indeed was the least steady of the two of us after our voyage. We were now on the last leg of our trip to Rome; soon we hoped to be in the friendly arms of our relatives.

Young Ocran passed through the crowd and around corners effortlessly. It wasn't long before the waterfront and dock area disappeared from our view and we were completely lost in the immensity of Rome. Everything was different; each sight and sound was a new experience. Never had we seen such a diversified populous. People from every corner of the world jostled us from every side. Even the smells were different; the odors of foods being prepared for the afternoon meals wafted through the heavy air of the city.

Just when it seemed that we had nearly reached the end of our strength, Ocran topped a long hill, and there standing before us was his father's house. While we struggled to gain access to the gate, Ocran ran on ahead and reappeared with two strong servants who assisted with our things. He led us to Pagiel, his father. We exchanged greetings and blessings, and he bid us to rest and refresh ourselves in the custom of the house of Asher. We expressed our gratitude and accepted his offer. After washing and changing clothing, we were ushered into his presence again.

We expressed our desire to see our uncle as soon as possible. Pagiel ordered his servants to provide us food and wine, bidding us to stay with him a fortnight and tell him of the news in Jerusalem. His request was made with such kindness and longing to hear about the place of his birth, as he too was from Judea, that we set aside our wishes and agreed to stay yet awhile longer. It was Ishmael who pointed out that we couldn't stay a full fortnight as we were expected within the month of Annas which was but a week away.

To do otherwise would cause great worry to our uncle. Pagiel offered to send one of his servants to tell Uncle Benjamin that we were in Rome and would soon be there. Yet we thought it not wise to do so, and offered to stay some time less than a fortnight. He agreed and had his servants prepare a room for us where we rested until the evening meal.

After the meal, we all gathered with Pagiel's family in a most beautiful alcove near the main room of the house. We explained our trip to Rome with our hopes of furthering our knowledge and experience. Pagiel remarked that this was indeed a laudable endeavor and prayed that we would succeed. He remarked that should we find our labors going for naught, to apply to him and he would be pleased to assist us in his own field.

As we could see, his true interests were not in our future, but in our past. It was news of Jerusalem that he was intent on hearing. We talked late that night. Ishmael and I spent the better part of the next few days and nights telling him of the changes in and about Jerusalem since he had been there as a young man. He was very grateful for the news of the old city and often thanked us for our honoring his request.

By the end of the week, we had told him nearly everything we could remember about Jerusalem and the nearby towns, and after thanking him for his hospitality, asked once again to be led to the house of our uncle. He was grieved to see us go, and asked us not to forget his hospitality by returning often to talk more of Jerusalem and its people. He then called his servants and had them help us prepare for the trip across Rome.

OUR NEW HOME

The following morning we took leave of Pagiel and his house and followed his servants to the house of our uncle. We were awed by the size and splendor of our uncle's house. It was indeed one that would stand out among many of the most wealthy if found in Jerusalem. It was impressive with its spaciousness and well-kept gardens. He was also a man of exceeding kindness we were to find as we stayed with him for the next five years.

As we approached, his servants came to meet us, bringing fresh rose water for our use. We greeted our uncle from the gate. He saluted us with his blessing and blessings on our father's house. We, in turn, offered our prayers of thanks to the Lord for the safe journey and the goodness of our uncle. Nor did we fail to acknowledge his letter to father and convey father's blessing on he and his house.

He greeted us with the custom of his house, and a formal introduction to his family. Refreshed, we were ushered into the main part of the house.

Now, Uncle Benjamin wasn't as old as father, being the younger brother. His attitude and lifestyle had always been different than father's; he was adventuresome and father wasn't, hence, the difference we immediately recognized.

He stood before us in Roman attire of the day, as did the rest of the family. I suppose this was registered on our faces and he laughed at our surprise, after all, in Judea seldom would a Jew accept friendship with a Roman let alone his dress. Here it was different; they had left some of the traditions of the Jews. We met each member of the family with our Aunt Rachel being first to supply greetings from her household. The cousins were then next, each in accordance with her age as Uncle Benjamin had no sons.

After these formalities were completed, and before we could press our case on the possibility of some sort of work to pay our way, he asked about life in Jerusalem. He, like our new friend, Pagiel, wanted to know all about the happenings in and about Jerusalem. What news from the Holy City was the word! The first few days were occupied by the exposé of all we could remember of our lives in Jerusalem.

We told him of the strange happenings of the last few years: about a story of a coming Messiah that was worded about in the city, of the birth of John to one of the priests of the temple, of the boy known as Yeshua, of the strange Magi from the East who came to the court of Herod, and of Herod's cruelty to the people of Bethlehem and nearby towns as a result of this visit. All these things we told him and found that our stories were well received, especially our adventure with the stranger. Uncle Benjamin was greatly caught up in these stories and often asked us to repeat them, even to the smallest details.

It was some days after our arrival that word was finally spoken of our possible occupation while with him. Uncle Benjamin was in no great hurry to place us in any type of labor, yet he was wise enough to have planned for our time with him. Even before we arrived, and after he wrote father, he already formulated a routine for us both. Ishmael was to attend the school for the arts as he wished and help in the shops in the evening, and I was to work in the main accounting house of the large overseas trading company. Both of us were greatly pleased with his generous offer.

Time passed rapidly for us in Rome - Ishmael with his visits to the school of the arts, and I working in a warehouse in the port side of the city. There was always something new in the time spent at our new home. We were very happy with our lot, and were apt to forget about those at home. Uncle Benjamin often reminded us of our obligation to those at home, and wasn't above asking us about letters sent to them on special occasions. He persuaded us to include messages about our lives in Rome to those waiting to hear. In turn, we were far from last to seek out the return letters when ships docked from Judea.

Sometime afterward in the year 763, father wrote of the aging of Zechariah and Elizabeth. This letter also contained details of the death of our teacher, Hillel. It caused both Ishmael and me unhappiness, as he was truly a great and righteous man. Father wrote of his grandson, Gamaliel, taking over and maintaining the formal classes that Hillel started so many years ago. We were happy that Gamaliel was chosen as successor, for he was also a true and learned man. It was later in life that I was to meet Gamaliel again, although it wasn't known to me at the time of father's letter.

Father was deeply concerned that neither Zechariah nor Elizabeth was well and were now under the care of their servants. Their young son, John, who wasn't yet seventeen, wasn't the stable person father saw in his early age. He was headstrong and seldom at home with his parents, who seemed not to take any offense at his strange behavior. It was as though they knew of his inner desire to be away, and often said when he was small that he had a mission to fulfill, yet admitted to not knowing what it was. Of late, father wrote John would disappear into the desert for days, sometimes traveling with a group called Essenes and often living on only locusts and dates. Although the Essenes were known to me, I never considered them politically important, and remained skeptical of their religious intent.

Later that same year, another letter grieved us even more when father announced his dear friend and confidant, Zechariah, had died, and Elizabeth was stricken as well. Father's heart was sorely stricken by the situation and in a later missive from mother, she said she was greatly concerned about father's health as well. This she had written without his knowledge. She accounted how father had taken Zechariah's death as a devastating loss, and when Elizabeth died some months later, father was greatly troubled again. She was troubled and asked for Ishmael and me to return as soon as possible. She expressed the hope our return would reawaken in father the desire to live. The letter then continued to describe the happenings of John. He was consumed by the desire to become a prophet, as one of old. He had forsaken friends and family, and had taken up residency with the Essenes who lived in the desert near the great hills of Jerusalem. There he remained after the death of his parents, and none of the family had seen him since. Woe is the family of Zechariah for his household is no more. It was a great weight for us and we talked with Uncle Benjamin about our return.

A NEW FRIEND

It was in the same year, on one of the trips to the docks, when I was run down by a chariot. It all seemed like a dream at the time. It happened in this wise: I was on my way to the counting house in the early morning. As was my habit, I was deep in thought about the days' accounts and the many ships that were scheduled to sail that day. To this was added the trying news of father's condition at home. It was necessary to make sure the manifests of each ship was properly documented and the cost of every item aboard was on the ledger. Each of these had to be copied and submitted to the Roman tax agent for his approval and from these, the copies for the captain of each craft were made.

It was while contemplating these and other problems that I stepped into the path of an oncoming chariot. It was driven rather recklessly by a young Roman legionnaire. To look up and see the chariot bearing down on me was a rude shock indeed. I made every attempt to escape but wasn't quick enough to avoid the unpleasant impact from one of the horses. The horse struck me on the shoulder. I was thrown to the roadway like a shaft of wheat thrown by the wind. All around me became dark and still for a few moments. When I came around, I found the face of the Roman just above me. He was a handsome young man and his face swam in and out of my vision. I realized some pain in my shoulder and other parts. Although not apologetic, he was concerned enough to stop his hurried ride through the street to come to my aid. He had drawn his chariot to the side of the street and left a passerby holding the horses while he was at my side.

"What say you? Can you understand me?" were the first I managed to recognize from the fog which enveloped me. He was interested in my capability of understanding Aramaic as he could tell by my appearance that I was Jewish. It seemed strange that he would be so concerned in the running down of a foreigner as Romans were not above letting these things go by as happenings of the day.

"Aye, I can understand you, sir," I managed to answer. "But I'm afraid all isn't well with my shoulder. It pains me a good deal," I continued, not waiting for him to answer. "Pray, tell me, have I been here long?" My thoughts were of my appointments with the ship's captains and the manifests I must prepare. With his help, I struggled to my feet.

"Come, I'll help you to my chariot and will see you are taken care of before you continue on your way." With that, he helped me up where I was able to sit on the edge of the chariot's platform. "My name is Apuleius. I'm a physician stationed here with the 100th Cohort, and I'll be glad to look at your injury. I'm sorry I've contributed to it."

This was something new. He was different than most Romans. I was in some discomfort from the collision and welcomed any relief he might be able to provide. Although there were some Romans who had compassion for all foreigners, it wasn't commonplace, and with the troubles in the East, the tendency was just the opposite with respect to us Judeans.

Without waiting for a direct answer, either yea or nay, he removed my outer garment and carefully felt my shoulder and the surrounding area. His fingers were soft and skilled. He moved my arm in the directions indicated to satisfy himself that nothing was broken or out of place. He saw no need for any great worry about my writing capability, but admonished me to take care not to aggravate the injury. While he spoke, I noticed how young he was to be an officer in the Roman army. His appearance made me wonder about the words of the stranger who had saved my life before, "Farewell, Judas, and remember, we will meet again, and this more than once." Could it be that this young Roman was in some way an ally of the stranger?

"How is that you speak Aramaic so well, and what is your name?" He asked the question as one who was used to asking questions and expecting answers. He could recognize by my tongue that I wasn't one of the longtime residents of Rome. "How came you to be here and what is your duty?" He waited for answers while studying me from a position near the chariot. He placed his one hand on the sword hilt, while he stroked his face with the other.

"Judas ben Simon is my name. I was educated in Jerusalem by one of the best teachers of the language, and often present in the court of Herod the Great. I'm pleased that you consider my use of the language worthy of your remarks. I'm here in Rome to study the methods of accounting of the maritime trade for my Uncle Benjamin, owner of the shipping trade and a sea merchant of some renown. Perhaps you've heard of him?" It was my turn to ask questions.

His face and eyes showed that he recognized my uncle's name, although I couldn't tell by his expression whether he considered it a blessing or a curse. He continued to study me for some time and I remained seated on the edge of his chariot the whole time of this inspection. It was as though he was looking at a new and strange illness in someone brought to him through an accident, and an accident it was that brought us together.

"I believe I should take you to your uncle's house and let him decide if you are fit for service. You seem a bit shaken, and rightly so, and I'm not one to leave any man to his own devices if not well." With that said, he propped me against the front of the chariot and standing behind me to prevent me from falling, took the reins from the passerby and drove the chariot. Apuleius knew where the house of Benjamin, the sea merchant, was without a doubt. As we moved through the city, I became aware of how the world looked to a Roman in a chariot. Most people stepped aside to permit the chariot to pass; none cared to stand in the way of the oncoming horses and vehicle. The drive was a short one and nothing was said by either of us during the trip.

We stopped at the gate of the house of Uncle Benjamin and Apuleius helped me through the gate. A servant of the house greeted us and then immediately ran to tell of my apparent misfortune. Uncle Benjamin came in haste. He paused long enough to recognize the Roman and give him proper greetings. He addressed me in Hebrew, as we were apt to do when there were those present who were not party to what was discussed.

"Oh Judas, what has happened, and why is the gentile present?" My uncle was grieved at my appearance and let it show in his voice. His eye's moved from me to the Roman and back trying to solve the puzzle of my return from the counting house so soon and on the arm of a legionnaire.

"Greetings uncle, and don't worry. I've just received a minor injury to my shoulder. I'll be fine when rested." I answered in Aramaic as I felt to follow my uncle's use of Hebrew would be disrespectful to Apuleius, who had just shown concern for me. "I was struck in the shoulder by a horse and knocked to the ground. This is Apuleius, a physician from the 100th Cohort stationed here. It was he that came to my aid." I carefully avoided mentioning it was his chariot which had caused the accident.

"Come, be the guest of my humble house, Apuleius, for I must thank you for your care." He motioned that we should follow him into the garden. Apuleius hobbled the horses, a military habit I later learned. He then turned and followed us into the garden.

In these times, it was rare such an offer was made from a Jew to a Roman, and even rarer still when such an offer was accepted; however, I had the impression Apuleius was a different kind of Roman. Although his walk and manner was that of the Roman military, his attitude and demeanor was gentle in nature. The garden was pleasant, and we sat under some of the olive trees near a pool. I couldn't sit as straight as I would have liked, but tried not to give the impression of an invalid to my uncle. After he was assured I wasn't greatly injured, he then instructed his servant to bring refreshments for us, and sent a runner to notify the counting house that I wouldn't be there for a few days. He was confident the others could take care of the business at hand while I was on the mend.

Uncle Benjamin continued the conversation about the accident. "Judas, just what caused you to be so careless on your way to the counting house?"

"Alas, I was admittedly not paying attention to things about me. In my mind, I was already at the counting house going over the tasks of the day, uncle." I was uncomfortable under this continued questioning, but knew it was his custom that came from the care he took of the business. "It shall not happen again."

"Our bodies are a gift of the Most High and not to be carelessly placed in danger, Judas," he persisted.

"Let me say something on behalf of your nephew, Benjamin," Apuleius spoke. "It was my chariot that ran him down, and I must admit to some recklessness in the accident. This has been a lesson to me as I'm sure the results could have been more serious."

Upon hearing this, Uncle Benjamin seemed somewhat relieved. "Ah Judas, this is something you didn't mention but seeing as how Apuleius came forward with this part of the story, it is good." He turned to Apuleius and graciously said, "We are thankful for your kindness on behalf of Judas; many wouldn't have reacted so, and accidents can and do happen to one and all. He is the son of my brother in Jerusalem. He came to stay with us to learn the finer arts of accounting. It's incumbent on me to ask your father's name."

It was then I realized I didn't know the family name of my new acquaintance.

"Indeed, I'm the son of Lucius, the Senator of the third district," said Apuleius. "I must be on my way, as I still have an appointment with the commander at the station. After two years, I've received orders that I am going to Jerusalem for a tour of duty." He stopped for a moment, then continued, "I hope this accident may be of mutual benefit." He rose and saluted in a manner of grace in Roman custom. Turning to me, he smiled and held out his hand in a gesture indicating he hoped all was well. "I don't believe you're seriously injured, and with some rest, will be good as new. I would appreciate your company as I've much to learn of the customs of your people in Judea. If your uncle can spare you from your duties, I would like you to sit with me in study of the things I would like to know. Do you think it could be arranged?" He looked from me to Uncle Benjamin.

"Ah yes, Lucius, a name above names in governmental circles. Your father is a man of good heart and kindness toward our people. It is well we met, although not so for Judas." Uncle Benjamin laughed lightly. "I'm sure Judas has earned some free time. How can my house be of service to you, Apuleius?"

"The service of your nephew is all that is desired, for in him and his command of languages, I see the information I need. I would have him visit with me from time to time so that I may learn the customs and language of Judea." Apuleius seemed anxious to settle the thing and be on his way.

"Aye, it is written, let no man interfere with the gathering of knowledge. And so it is that my house and Judas are indeed at your disposal. Please give my regards to your father."

"It is well. I'll have my servant bring notice of the time and places," said Apuleius. "Till then, Judas, have a care where you walk." Apuleius turned and strode out of the garden gate to where his chariot waited. He raised his arm in a mock salute and was off.

It was through the accidental meeting of this day that Apuleius and I became great friends, even nearly unto brothers. Yea, even greater than some brothers we became. From that day on, Apuleius and I met frequently and exchanged many thoughts about our different cultures, he learning the ways of our people and I the ways of Romans. We met at first at the courtyard of Uncle Benjamin's and later, near the small pond in the foyer of the great house of Apuleius Lucius, the father of Apuleius the younger. The time was considered well spent by both parties. I learned to accept the liberal lifestyle of the Roman with all his confusion about gods in his history, while I attempted to explain the unwavering belief of our people in only one God with the rigorous adherence to the Laws and Prohibitions handed down by Him through the ancient writings.

Time passed swiftly, with both Ishmael and I very intent on vocations and avocations as well. Nearly three years had passed since we arrived in Rome. Ishmael had accomplished much in his field, and I often went to see him in the street of the artisans. Ishmael never brought his work to the house as uncle wasn't one to accept the making of images; this wasn't in accordance with the Torah, and even though on the liberal side, uncle still held some things inviolable. It was as Ishmael said, "It's not the image that is the fault, or the making thereof, but the sin comes from falling down before them!" His thought was that many people hadn't made images but had purchased them and fell down before them; here was the transgression.

I'd become very proficient at keeping books and was able to pay for our stay at the house of my uncle. It was through Apuleius that I became the keeper of accounts for Romans outside my uncle's business. This provided additional income and it was from this money that I was able to send gold to my family in Jerusalem. They needed it more than I because of the new taxes imposed by Ambivius, and because of father's illness.

In early 764, after nearly five years in Rome, the letters from home reminded us of father's failing health. It was then we asked our uncle for his blessing and requested release from his house. This he did with great sorrow, for he was fond of us. The tone of the letters told us of the urgency in returning home soon. It was then we discovered we were leaving Rome far richer than when we arrived. We had accumulated some personal property and wealth. Uncle Benjamin agreed to hold these until we would know of the conditions that faced us in Jerusalem. Much depended on the taxation of our people.

We spent much time preparing for the trip back to Jerusalem. Ishmael was greatly disturbed for he knew he couldn't take his artwork with him to Jerusalem. Uncle Benjamin pleaded for him to stay, his artwork was still in the hands of those at school, and illness on the sea all caused him to cry out at his dilemma. His desire to stay with me and that of seeing father again overcame his want to stay in Rome; it was that year we set sail for home.

It was during this preparation for the trip home that a strange turn of events occurred. The time was short, barely a week before we were to sail. It was then I noticed Ishmael was not his usual happy self. He wasn't present at mealtime, a sign of his not being well from boyhood. Within a short span of two days Ishmael was indeed very ill. He was taken with a fever and all our prayers and supplications failed to relieve his suffering. The suggestions of many were tried, but to no avail. As his condition worsened, he became more persistent in his wish to be home. Yet it seemed ill advised to travel, not knowing how serious his illness was, as we knew from our first trip he wasn't a good sailor. It was this concern for Ishmael I expressed to Apuleius.

"I'm afraid for Ishmael, but he desires to see father and home, even though he is ill; he won't hear differently. I'm greatly grieved."

"Come Judas, I've some news that will lighten your cares. First, I'd like to look at Ishmael, and second, I've been saving a surprise…I've been granted early leave to join the men at Fort Antonia in Jerusalem. I've already secured passage on the same ship you're sailing on. It's possible, if Ishmael isn't fully recovered by the time we sail, I can attend him on the trip." He spoke with happiness, "Let's go and see what can be done."

It was as though Almighty God had answered our prayers once again. My heart leaped for happiness as I felt Apuleius was indeed a good physician, and I couldn't be more pleased to find him as a companion. We hurried to Ishmael's bedside where Apuleius studied his condition. After some time, Apuleius came to me and said he would need some potions from his service bag. He left only to return later with the needed supplies. He had Ishmael take the potions and then sat by his bedside to watch over him. Apuleius, the young Roman physician, sat through the night watching Ishmael, the Jew. It was then I realized that he was a physician first and Roman second. His was a heart that God surely looked on with favor.

It was late the following morning when the fever broke and Ishmael rested quietly. Apuleius rose from his chair, walked to the entrance way, and motioned for me to follow.

"Your brother has found favor with the gods; the potion has reduced the fever. I believe he will recover enough to accompany us to Jerusalem." His voice was firm but lowered, "He must rest as much as possible before we start on the trip. Keep him in bed and I'll come as often as I can. I must go and prepare for the trip."

"I'm grateful for your kindness and help, dear friend. Pray, will you have time to get ready?" I wanted to be reassured he would indeed be on the same ship when we sailed.

"Yes, I've but a few things to attend to and those are affairs at arms. All else is in readiness." He turned and left quietly, saluting Uncle Benjamin who had been watching us as he was also concerned about Ishmael. I followed Apuleius to his horse and bade him good day. Returning to the house I told uncle what Apuleius had said about Ishmael's recovery and his need for rest. Uncle Benjamin sang a short praise to God for Ishmael's recovery, and then prepared a blessing for Apuleius. He called his servants together and reminded them that Ishmael wasn't to leave his bed until Apuleius returned.

Ishmael was one of the favorites with the servants and all wanted the honor of caring for him. I knew he would be in good hands; I thanked Uncle Benjamin for his thoughtfulness and asked to be excused for I too was up most of the night. And so it was that Ishmael had been made whole again by Apuleius and was ready for the trip to Jerusalem. I didn't know it then, but this same affliction was to affect my life again.

The night before sailing, Uncle Benjamin set a feast for us, gathered his family about him to sing praises for our good times with him, and asked God's blessing on us and our father. Uncle Benjamin also prepared gifts for his brother and the rest of the family in Jerusalem; these we took with us. His generosity was indeed great, and Ishmael and I were nearly overcome by it. We sang praises for his kindness and the use of his house while in Rome. It was late when we went to our quarters that evening.

THE SEA AGAIN

We were wakened early the next day by the servant of the house; the early meal was ready. By the time we ate, Uncle Benjamin and many family members formed an entourage that went with us to the dock. As the tide came in, the master of our ship notified us we must be away. Ishmael and I fell upon Uncle Benjamin's shoulders and wept. It was thought to be the last time I would see him and he sensed this with a heavy heart. I asked him to forgive any and all sins, known and unknown to me; this he did with a true heart.

We loaded our things on board, and were shown the area of the ship we were to occupy on the trip from Rome through the Straits of Messina even unto Syracuse in Sicily. Poor Ishmael was already showing his weakness for sailing. I was again grieved by his discomfort, and wondered if we hadn't left Rome too soon after his attack of the fever. It was during my thoughts about Ishmael I heard the shout of commands given on the dock. Looking to see, I discovered it to be a contingent of Roman soldiers coming up the gangplank, and with them was Apuleius.

While watching them board, I noticed two other ships maneuver alongside the dock. One full cohort of Roman soldiers was standing ready for embarking. I was told later by Apuleius that these were replacements for some of the men stationed in Jerusalem and thereabouts. The system of rotating troops was the order of the day; this relieved some of the grumbling in the outposts of the Roman army.

Our ship was soon filled and moved away from the dock to take up anchor in the harbor awaiting the other two. We were to travel as a fleet of three ships from Rome to the coast of Judea. The knowledge of this left us somewhat relieved as there had been word of sailing vessels being attacked by bands of sea robbers. These plundered the captive ships and made slaves of all able-bodied men on board. It was a fate worse than death - so the rumors were along the coasts.

The boarding of the troops took the rest of the day, so we sat riding anchor, waiting to clear for travel. Early the following morning we sailed with the tide. Our captain, who was the most experienced in these seas, commanded the lead vessel in the small convoy. It was a sight to see, as the ships maneuvered to stay in line and in sight of each other.

The trip soon settled down to the routine of sea travel: sleeping, eating, watching the sea and sky, and returning to sleeping again. The only real relief from the monotony of it all came from conversation with other passengers, and watching games of chance played by them which Ishmael and I were forbidden to play. Conversation meant the chance to talk with Apuleius again which was some time later since he was responsible for the well being of the soldiers on board this ship, and some, like Ishmael, were not good sailors.

Our first conversation came when I finally got to speak to Apuleius about Ishmael; he was in poor straights early in the trip. Apuleius came to our quarters and looked at Ishmael, announced that he would live even if he didn't think he would, gave Ishmael a potion for sleep, and ordered him to eat only dry meals or breads for the rest of the voyage.

"It would be wise for Ishmael to take to walking about the ship as soon as possible; it is through exercise he can retain his needed strength. If he doesn't do so, we will surely have to carry him off the ship when we reach Judea. You must see that he tries each day,

Judas." Apuleius knew of my love for Ishmael, and he knew I would try to do this thing. "And how are you on this trip?"

"Ah, I've always been a good sailor, and enjoy the ship's motion, so far as it's not too violent." This was a true statement for I enjoyed the trip we made some years before.

"Well, let's hope that events favor us on this trip, as not only this ship but the others as well are loaded to the gunnels and heavy seas would cause great concern. I'm glad we have the good fortune to travel together, Judas. We've yet to finish our discussions about the religions of man." Apuleius was an educated man, and willing to debate a good subject without losing sight of good will and companionship.

"I, for one, will sing songs of praise for every good and quiet day on this trip, and will plead for the will of God to favor us with a strong breeze to carry us with good speed to Sicily." I was enthusiastic and showed it.

"Ah Judas, why only to Sicily? Do you fear your God has only the strength to see us safe to the first port of call?" I could see he was baiting me in his usual way. "Could it be you have some doubts?"

"You can make jests, but it's not for me to question the will and strength of our God. Nor is it for you to assume that I'll not plead for his guidance and keeping for the whole of the voyage, for I surely will. It's not that God cannot do these things, but that I cannot think of each step of the care and goodness needed by both you and me. Pray, tell me, Apuleius, how do the Romans appeal to their gods in these matters? And, for that matter, which god do you select?"

"You know well, Judas, I'm not one to follow the early gods. I don't pray to any, be it Mars, Jupiter, or an unknown. I have and will continue to follow the sayings of Epicurus as sung in the poems of Lucretius. Secondly, I hold that Stoicism fills the needs of the active man. There is place for both in my life, Judas, but not one for the prayer and supplication to some god that pays no heed to the needs of man. In Stoicism, I find the independence from supernatural surveillance and command that you seem to need."

I was about to answer when a call for the physician was sounded from the troop quarters. He rose immediately from our position and strode away to answer the call. He took no time for an answer and just waved his farewell. Apuleius was part of the medical group assigned to the troops on board, and when they arrived in Judea he would accompany them to the post in Jerusalem. I watched him go and reflected on his answer. Oh Apuleius, I pray you will never need the help from those greater than men, for it is then you will find fault with the philosophy of Stoicism and its companion, Epicurus.

The first day ended with Ishmael feeling somewhat better after the potion. The only sound which disturbed the night was the call of the watch from ship to ship - a system used by the master of each ship to maintain contact and distance through the night watch. Once we became used to this lonely call from the watch, we both slept soundly.

The next morning and the following five were similar; I encouraged Ishmael to walk about the ship as much as possible and it seemed he was the better for it. The winds were contrary and the time for the voyage from Rome to Sicily was lengthened by one full day. We were on the sea five days before passing through the Straits of Messina. Our landfall was the port of Syracuse; here, all three ships were docked and troops and passengers were sent ashore while fresh water and provisions were brought aboard. At the same time, the ships were cleared of goods brought from Rome and the animal dung as well. The troops were marched to a holding area, while the passengers were left to their own devices. This re-supply of the ships for the longer leg of the voyage from Sicily to Crete gave us time to walk about the city. From the stories we heard in Rome about the history of Syracuse, we could understand why this once-great city was so important to the world. Its people were as mixed as those in Rome, and the crowds as animated.

We were notified when all three ships were refitted and ready to sail. We moved our things on board and watched while the troops embarked, once again divided between the three. We left on the tide the next morning.

Although I watched the troops closely, I didn't see Apuleius among them. The thoughts of him not being aboard was unsettling for I hoped for continued conversations with him to pass the time away. Finally, late that evening, Apuleius made his appearance and, relieved, I greeted him as I would a brother.

"Ah, dear friend, I was afraid you were detained or transferred to another ship. As for me, the trip would have been a boring one without you aboard."

"Well, you know the life of a soldier. Ours is not one to question, but one to do as commanded. In this case, I came aboard with some of the men not feeling well, as the command isn't one to leave men ill or incapacitated. Each man has his position in this exchange of force with those now in Judea, and it's the duty of the command to see they arrive to fulfill the order of the day." His words came from one who knew his duty, and was willing to do what was necessary to see it was carried out. He continued softly without gestures. "There are some that suffer from ship motion even as Ishmael, but none so bad as to be left in Syracuse. But had it been so, those too ill to travel would've been left there, and their places taken by some from garrison. The complement would be the same in number and position when we arrived in Judea. All the same, I, too, am glad I've been able to stay aboard this craft. For a moment, I thought the commander might move me to another, but to my good fortune, this didn't happen."

While Apuleius and I talked, Ishmael moved over to the side of the ship, and Apuleius, seeing him up and about, shouted to him.

"Ishmael, how is it by you so far on the voyage…do you have your sea legs yet?"

Ishmael turned from the side and facing Apuleius, made an ugly face, then turned back to the side of the ship. Although not a good sailor, Ishmael tried to be one, and for this I thought all the more of him. I often wondered if I could do as well under like conditions.

"He's much better so far on this trip that I know," I remarked. "Don't be deceived by his mannerisms. I'm sure he is grateful for the potion you gave him."

"Good, I had hoped his unsettledness would ease. Judas, I must leave now and attend to Army matters. Take care until we meet again." With that, he turned and walked to the far end of the ship where the troops were settled.

I shouted, "God go with you," really not knowing why. This was our first meeting from beginning to end after leaving Syracuse.

Through the following days on the way to Crete, we had many hours of good dialogue about nature and man, he expressing his beliefs and learning from philosophers and poets of Greece and Rome, and I expounding on the holy writings of our people the Law of Moses, and its strength throughout the history of our people.

The days were pleasant early into the voyage. Good winds moved the three ships along in fine fashion. Early on the fifth day we sighted Crete, and within the first watch, were in the port city of Fair Havens. The winds favored us mightily and God answered our prayers for a safe journey. Ishmael and I sang songs of thanks to our God, and asked for continued good favor from Him. Many from other religions made way for us and often showed interest in our prayers. Some weren't so kind and remarked it was a waste of time, after all, wasn't the God of the Jews under the Roman eagle?

The convoy remained dockside long enough for all passengers, troops, and animals to disembark. The troops were marched through the countryside to allow them to regain their strength, and the horses were exercised to prevent leg soreness. We enjoyed the layover, but were glad to be called back to the ship at the end of the third day. We stood by and watched the troops and horses embark, then stepped on board for the next leg of our voyage to Cyprus. With each destination, we grew more and more impatient to be home.

The distance from Crete to Cyprus was long but the winds remained with us and the time was short. The sailors remarked how well the voyage went, and many told of trials and tribulations before it was over. Some weren't so happy about the ease of the trip, and declared we could still pay for this apparent good fortune. I paid little attention to their old sea tales and accepted the pleasant trip in good humor. We landed at Paphos after five days. The ships were again emptied, cleaned, and made ready in just one day.

It was while in Paphos that the captain called us to him. He told us that because of the military on board, he was forced to change his route which would add time to our voyage. The master said his orders were to set sail for the city of Tarsus in Cilicia. We were not pleased, but not sufficiently unhappy to look for another ship. Some passengers, who were traders and merchants, left the ship that same hour to find other accommodations. It was learned the other two ships were to sail directly to Caesarea, and only this ship, which was the commandants' vessel, was to sail to Tarsus. Upon learning this, we discussed the possibility of changing ships, but in the final analysis, decided to stay with this ship.

The following day we sailed for Tarsus. We weren't underway a full day when the weather changed with unbelievable quickness. The sky closed in on the ship. The clouds, once high and fluffy, were now lower, dark, and foreboding. The wind began to move about, not blowing in one direction. The waves, which were easy swells just minutes before, became covered with whitecaps. Even the sea changed color. What was emerald green all about us became dark, almost black. The winds continued to raise, blowing first fore and then aft, then athwart ship. The ship wallowed because of its burden. The weather closed down until we could barely see the fore and aft part while standing amidships.

The sailors took in all sails but those needed to keep the ship from turning broadside to the great swells. Ishmael and I called upon the Lord for his protection. We lost comprehension of things about us, as even in the first watch it became as dark as night. Rain blew across the ship, pelting man and beast; it stung the skin where not protected. We pulled our cloaks over our heads and huddled down as close to one another as we could since we couldn't see each other and could barely hear our shouts when mouth to ear.

The hearts of many of us trembled from the fierceness of the storm. Many cried out to their gods even as we did, each wondering what great sin he had committed to cause his gods to bring this upon him. Some who weren't so inclined cursed the storm. It was then I recalled the words of the sailors earlier when talking about the fine sailing conditions, and how we might yet pay for them before the voyage was over - so it was now.

The sailors moved to tend the ship. They were dimly-lit figures sometimes seen against the curtain of rain, but never heard over the howling wind. Lightning and thunder were continuous. The decks became slippery and we clung desperately to each other and to the fittings in our quarters. I had never seen such a storm on land, no, not in all my life.

Because of the darkness of the storm, time was lost; we became tired of the effort to avoid being washed overboard. Even though being bathed with cold sea water, sweat ran down our faces and bodies. Ishmael began to show signs of weakness because of his recent illness. Once his grip on the rigging relaxed, and only through desperate measures was I able to keep him from sliding from his perch of safety. After that, I found a sturdy piece of rope and looped it around him and tied him to the rigging. This I hoped would protect him should my grip fail. I prayed most diligently to the Lord that we would be spared.

After awhile, the wind lessened and we could see figures moving about the ship. As we lay in our partly-protected area, the strong figure of Apuleius appeared, moving along the deck from one fitting to another until he reached us. With the wind calmer, we could hear one another when talking mouth to ear.

"I had to see if you were alright as it hasn't fared well for some of the troops and animals. Two horses fell and injured their legs and we may have to put them to the sword to end their misery. The captain said the blow is not over, only resting for the next trial of the sea. I must return to my men. Don't wander from your place of safety and pray to your God for deliverance, as many ships have been lost in a lesser storm than this."

I placed my mouth to his ear and thanked him. "May God go with you."

He had taken but two steps when a mighty gust of wind carried him across the open deck to the gunnel. The ship lunged violently, and Apuleius disappeared over the side. Pushing against the wind with all my strength I was able to reach Apuleius's side. While hanging onto the ship rigging, I grasped the front of his tunic, which was held in place by a military harness. As we struggled, the wind seemed to increase in ferocity and force. All seemed lost; we were tiring from the force of both sea and wind. I was determined not to let go of my hold even if it cost my life. I could hear him shouting for me to let go and save myself, but this I would not do. I asked the Lord God to save us if it be his will, and if not, to accept us both in the bosom of Abraham. *"Hear, O Israel: the Lord is our God, the Lord is one."*

SAVED AGAIN

It was getting darker and none of the rest of the crew could hear our cries. Just when all seemed lost and in the darkest hour, a helping hand was stretched forth and managed to grasp the tunic of Apuleius and pulled both he and I back upon the deck. It was a superhuman effort for such a thing to be done. Such an effort to pull us on board like small children from a quiet pool would require the power of ten men. I turned to see who was so powerful and aware of our danger so as to answer our cries.

Once again, I recognized the stranger met before in an alleyway in Jerusalem so many years ago. Even in the dark of the storm I recognized him.

"Oh Judas, must I forever save you from your generosity and carelessness? Yours is not a life to waste, even for friends. Your destiny is one more important than the lives of one or two. Yours is for the lives of millions. Judas, hear me, your time has not yet come. Till we meet again, and this we will, farewell." The stranger then moved quickly across the deck and disappeared in the sheet of rain increasing each moment.

Apuleius, who heard part of the strangers' words, looked at me for answers to what happened. I motioned that I didn't know what the words meant. He rose carefully and proceeded back to his quarters and I returned to where Ishmael lay, still tied and exhausted.

After this, the storm continued to abate and soon the sea was quiet for a second time. The sailors moved about the ship checking for damage and removing the water she had taken. It was from them we understood the worst was over and they expected no more severe weather for the remainder of the voyage. It was then we sang praises to the Lord and blessed his Holy name.

The sailors were right; the sea became calm again, and the wind and rain ceased. The sunlight once again bathed the ship and sea with its warmth and brightness. The passengers and troops appeared on deck to dry out and warm themselves in this gift of the Lord. Some were penitent and smote their breasts, singing praises to their several gods, while others still cursed the storm for all their discomforts. We sang praises to the Lord, and asked for the forgiveness of those who were still not resolved. They didn't know the Lord had spared them for the sake of others. Woe, be unto those who don't hear and fear the Lord as they are the hopeless ones.

The sea continued to remain quiet and the ship moved through the water at a fine rate. In less than three days, we were docking at Tarsus, a mighty coastal trading city. It was here the ship must dock for repairs it had sustained in the storm. Even as Apuleius said, some of the animals were injured beyond healing and had to be destroyed. These must be replaced before the ship could sail again. Time was also needed to take the troops off and exercise them again. So it was we were to remain in Tarsus for some time.

While searching for things of interest in Tarsus, we happened across a middle-aged Jew in the marketplace. He said his name was Bela Ard, of the house of Benjamin, a Pharisee, and was anxious to hear of the happenings in Rome and in the holy city of Jerusalem as well. Because of this, he offered us quarters in his home. We knew the ship would be in dock a few days while being refitted, and accepted his gracious offer. We joined him in the walk to his home after we had secured our belongings.

His house was in the Jewish quarter of Tarsus. His wife, Tirzah, of the house of Dan, had presented him with a son just six years before. He was the only child, a very bright one with a strong will. The child had been presented to the Lord as Saul, although his father often spoke to him as Paul, a Roman name for Saul. It was easy to see that family life revolved about the young lad. Even at this early age, he was receiving instruction in Greek and Hebrew languages, and could recite the history of the Exodus in detail. In him, I could see a true soul of the Jewish people being maintained in the foreign environment. His was a true family with parental love to keep all traditions alive.

We were guests in the household of Bela Ard for the remaining three days. We spent many hours describing the city of Rome and our visit with our uncle, as well as the history of our family in Jerusalem. Ishmael told them of the miracles which happened in Jerusalem some five years before, and the rumors about the birth of a Messiah sent to free Israel from the yoke of the Romans. They listened with great wonderment, but reserved opinions on our stories. During our stay, we were treated as family, and when we left, Bela Ard presented us with gifts for our father. He called for the blessing of the Lord on us and our father's house, asking God to relieve father of his illness. For some reason, we were drawn to this man for he was just and upright among a heathen land. I promised to write him when we reached home. We gave thanks for his kindness and left his household with many songs of praise. The Lord had treated us well while in the city of Tarsus.

AN UNANSWERED QUESTION

At the appointed date, we arrived to embark on the final leg of our trip. The ship was loaded with troops and animals when we arrived. We boarded just as the master issued the call to cast off. The ship headed nearly due south when leaving Tarsus. The weather was with us once again. The ship was relieved of some of the cargo and rode higher in the water. Apparently, this made her handle better in the brisk wind.

Caesarea lay some four hundred miles to the south of Tarsus. With good winds, we would land in three days. We were jubilant! By the grace of the Lord, we would soon be in Judea again. Now, we wondered if our earlier letters ever reached home, and if Apius would be waiting for us at the dock; our feelings were of great anticipation.

The next four days went slowly. Each day we became more impatient with the slowness of the ship. As we were approaching Rome, we had the same feelings as five years ago, when we were waiting for sight of a port in like manner. Our hearts were afire with excitement of the moment. On the morning of the fourth day, we said our prayers and listened for the call that meant land was sighted.

Apuleius, our constant companion, stood by when "land ho" was given. He was happy for us but not so for our pending separation. We had become closer than most brothers after his near-death during the storm, and mutual admiration because of it sealed the friendship. We were a strange combination: he, a Roman legionnaire, and I, a Pharisee, both near political opposites. He represented the government holding Jewish life in the balance, and I was one of those so held. We knew his life would put us apart; he would be assigned to Fort Antonia with days of adventure in the hills of Judea, and these were often dangerous for the men were away from the protection of the fort.

"Apuleius, dear friend, I fear for you in these hills of Judea. I'll pray for your safety on all your missions." I felt a great loneliness as the ship approached the coast of Judea. "We must ever keep close and when possible, you must take leave and visit us in my father's house. Promise me you'll remember to do this?"

"Ah, I couldn't do otherwise. How can I forget the person who offered his life to save me from the sea? Never fear, Judas, if there is any way we can be together, I'll be there." He hesitated. "Judas, I'd like to remind you that even though we have been on this trip four days after the storm, we haven't talked about the rescue, nor have I forgotten the strange person who rescued us. I looked at every passenger and asked many questions of each, but found none that looked like him, or was as strong as he." He searched my face for some clue to the stranger. "And what of the strange words he spoke, and how did his voice carry over the storm even when we couldn't hear one another at the same moment? I tell you, Judas, this shakes my faith in Stoicism, but there must be some logical answer." He looked closely at me for an answer that would make sense to him as a Roman.

"Judas," he continued, "can't you tell me about this strange happening? Isn't there still time before we dock?" Even though we spent many hours discussing the life and purposes of man, I couldn't tell him of the feelings I had experienced when faced with these strange personal happenings. They made little sense to me and I was of a people who had a great history of mysticism. A history of the Lord our God moving men and elements to gain some discrete end. There wasn't time to bring his knowledge up to my view and this was a gap only time would close.

"I can't give any answer that would please you. It is one of the mysteries and requires belief in things you've already said aren't possible. It would be, at present, a step you aren't willing or able to take. Maybe in time, Apuleius, things will be different, and then I'll provide the answer. At least, you will come to the point of truth necessary to understand these things. For now, dear friend, let it be. Please don't press me and let's part with this as a new subject to be explored when we meet again."

He was silent for a long time, his eyes exploring my face for a glimpse of some hidden key to the mystery of that event.

"So be it, Judas, but I'll not let you dissuade me for long. When we land at Caesarea, I'll report to my troops and we will make a forced march to Fort Antonia. It will be some time before we meet again. I wish you and Ishmael well, and hope you find your father in better health than that revealed to you. And if wishes can secure wants and desires, may my wish for your good health and our continued meetings be fulfilled." He held out his hand in the style of the Roman soldier, and I took it in the same manner. I met his firm grip with one of my own.

"May God go with you, Apuleius," said Ishmael. He had often been by my side during our discussions, but seldom said anything, being more interested in his reflection on art than of politics and history. Apuleius was evidently pleased with the statement of Ishmael, and also offered him his hand.

He turned on his heel, his boots making a scraping noise on the deck, and left us. I was sure we would meet and become traveling companions again in greater adventures than these on the sea. Why I felt this I wasn't sure.

The ship was fast approaching the port as we started to gather our belongings for disembarking. As we worked to place things in order, Ishmael remarked without looking up, "You've never told me of the strange event between you and Apuleius during the storm,

Judas. I remember when you left me and went to the side of the ship, but the wind and rain was so severe at that time, I couldn't see what happened. Then you were able to make your way back to our place of safety but never said anything of an adventure near the rail. What are you keeping from me?" He looked up with his final question. I was looking at myself in a copper mirror. To not tell him was like denying my own conscience.

"I'm not keeping anything from you. What happened is still an enigma to me and I must bear it alone awhile longer. I'll tell you on our way home from Caesarea." I continued to gather our supplies, gifts for home, and other belongings in readiness for departure.

"It's alright, but you'll have to tell me, we've always shared our fortunes and misfortunes, Judas." He was appeased by my answer, and didn't press me about the near-tragedy at the rail of the ship during the storm.

As we gathered our possessions, the ship docked. The military complements were first to disembark. I couldn't see Apuleius. I was heartily sorry for that; I'd wanted to give him one last salute before we separated. Following them went the horses and cavalry units, and last, we left with the remaining passengers. The dockside hadn't changed much over the past five years as the people, ships, and smells all seemed much the same.

In our last letter home, we arranged to meet Apius at the same inn we occupied when waiting to leave some five years before. Although we never received an answer before we embarked and set sail for Judea, we truly believed Apius would be waiting for us.

So it was that we strode down the long dock toward the street of the waterfront inns with this expectation. We were somewhat burdened down with our gear and gifts for those at home, yet the completion of a successful voyage left us lighthearted and full of songs of thanks to the Lord. To us, the day was much brighter and the breeze sweeter here in Caesarea. Oh, it was good to be back in Judea. Ishmael and I couldn't help from smiling and greeting everyone along the street; ours was the good life! We moved as quickly as our loads would permit, singing softly as we went.

It wasn't long before we stood in front of the inn we occupied before our adventure. It looked the same, the owner hadn't changed the exterior; however, as to the interior, we couldn't tell. I glanced up at the window which permitted us to see the ships in the harbor when there before. I could see the figure of Apius standing there and waving to us. I called Ishmael's attention to this and in a moment, Apius was gone, and in another moment, he was beside us.

It was a time of great love, this greeting. We fell upon each other's shoulders and wept without shame. It was a joyous occasion.

We all attempted to speak at once, asking questions, and not listening for answers. It was Apius, as usual, who suggested we take this conversation up in the inn, and with that suggestion, he called some servants standing nearby watching the reunion, and they took our things into the inn. We followed, Ishmael on one side of Apius, and I on the other.

We hadn't been in the room long when the mood of Apius changed to one of somber realism. The lightheartedness of the moment gave way to concern for the family, especially father. Apius slowly related that father's condition was serious indeed, and we must not tarry long in Caesarea. He brought extra servants and animals to afford us maximum swiftness in returning to Jerusalem. When he left, father was asking for us and pleading with the Lord to let him live until we should return. He wanted to give his blessing to us, even as his father had before him.

"Oh Judas, I've brought our fastest horses for you. They are the best in the stable and will carry you without complaint. Early in the first watch tomorrow you must be away to your father's house. I'll remain here and see all is brought to you. You must travel quickly and lightly to reach your father's side before it's too late." His voice shook with emotion. His love for father was very deep, and I knew he wanted to be at father's side during these last hours as well; he was indeed giving much of himself to do as father asked. "We must not tarry for the many tales you have to tell can wait. Rest and refresh yourselves and then be on your way."

"Is father as ill as that?"

"Yea, he is suffering from a fever and at his age cannot survive long, but all is the will of the Lord your God."

We arose early the next day. The servants, under the direction of Apius, prepared the animals for the trip. Taking only those things needed, we left after a few words with Apius. We rode directly to Joppa and from there to Emmaus. Apius was right; these animals were strong and willing. From Emmaus, we followed the main road to the gates of Jerusalem. The distance was nearly eighty miles from Caesarea to Jerusalem, and this we had traveled in good time.

CHAPTER NINE

Mother met us as we rode through the gates. We dismounted and ran to meet her.

"Mother, God turn his countenance unto you, and give us your blessing!" I approached her as an obedient son. Ishmael, the more emotional son, wept openly.

"Oh Judas, God has remembered me this day. He has returned my sons to me," she said with the emotion of a mother receiving her returning sons.

We cried for the joy of the reunion. "Come, let's hasten to see your father; he is now waiting word of your return. Take care, he isn't the man he once was. He's had a long illness, but he wouldn't let me tell you of this until these last days. Oh Judas, I fear for his life." She was greatly distraught, and my heart nearly failed me at her words. All seemed unreal; when we left five years ago, father was well and strong, though tired. And now she was saying he wasn't the same man and near death. I was anxious to see for myself!

"Let's go to him, I must see myself all that brought you to this unhappy condition."

We turned to enter the house. It was good to pass through the doors again, even if the situation wasn't a happy one. Walking through the courtyard and passages brought back memories; five years didn't seem long, but the heart often finds it so. We walked along without further conversation. The house seemed strangely quiet. The servants moved about with great care in respect to the master who now lay near death.

Before reaching father's bedroom, I decided it would be best to remove the dirt of the roadway before we greeted him. It's not polite for a man to carry the filth of the road into another's house; we learned this from the very man now very ill.

Mother agreed and we proceeded to the guest room where we refreshed ourselves and put on the clean raiment brought to us. It was like old times. It was good to be home, and the feel of clothes reflecting Jerusalem was good. The servants brought us wine and dates, as well as other foods; mother had seen to that realizing we had not eaten much nor often since we landed in Caesarea. We ate little and hurriedly.

"It's good to be back, isn't it, Ishmael?"

"Aye, that's the truth, but my heart goes out to mother, and my fears for father increase by the minute," he returned. We were ready in a short time. Mother came to greet us in the courtyard. She, too, had changed her clothes. Together we proceeded to father's room; all was quiet in the house.

We entered his room quietly. It was as I remembered it. Little had changed while we were away. Although I was in father's room very little, the sparseness of its contents always intrigued me. Even Ishmael and I had more things about. His room contained only his bed, which he now occupied, a table which held a copy of the law, two chairs for the table, and a commode. The room had the finest tapestry, the most beautiful of the house.

We could see him by the light coming through the window. How small he looked. It seemed he had shrunken both in size and weight. His beard, which was salt-and-pepper colored when we left, was now snow white. His face no longer had the high color of the priest we once knew, but bore the pallor of one near death. I was greatly distressed to see my father in such a state. Woe unto me, for I hadn't been the son I should have been.

Mother called softly to him; he slowly opened his eyes. He was a very tired man. His gaze fell on us. Tears welled up in his eyes and ran down his cheeks. He weakly raised his hands to give us his blessing. Ishmael and I knelt at his bedside, heads bowed to cover our tears. Father rested his hands on us and weakly said, "Thanks be to the Lord, for he has let my sons appear before me once again. Now I know what Jacob felt so many years ago."

Ishmael wept and said, "Father forgive us for our misdeeds and accept our blessings, and those of Uncle Benjamin."

"Yes, father may we have your forgiveness and blessing. We have come from Rome to be at your side. We bring the blessings of Uncle Benjamin and his household." I quickly added, hoping uncle's news would give him interest to rise above his illness.

"My sons, my sons, how can I forgive naught? Is it for me to find fault with my own? No, blessings you most certainly have, but forgiveness only can come for transgressions, and these I don't find." The speech tired him even more, and he released his hold on us and rested heavily on the pillows. His breath came in short gasps. He was indeed a very weak man. The illness had taken its toll.

"It's we who are grateful father, for we have been blessed more for your guidance when young and now forgiveness when older." My eyes filled with tears again, and I couldn't form more words. I was, like Ishmael, completely undone. Even after being forewarned by Apius and mother, this homecoming was more than I could bear.

Mother came forward and with the servants, rearranged father's bed and told us to retire as he was too tired to continue. We left and went to our old room, and there sang songs of thanksgiving for our timely return. We asked the Lord to look with favor on father, and if it was the Lord's will, to restore father to health. But even as we sang, we weren't to know his will wasn't in agreement with our wants and pleasures, for father grew steadily worse. And before the third watch, mother summoned us to his beside and even then, that same hour, his spirit left him.

Great sadness came over the household for many days. And as required by the law, the family mourned my father's death. His death was noted by those he served in the temple, and many priests came to honor father. Mother's inner circle of women supplied her with great comfort in the days that followed. Ishmael and I acted in accordance with the ritual of days. Mother, being a strong woman, took over the household and moved to set the house aright after father's death.

"Sons of mine, you are now given to do whatever must take you. Only a wise person releases those near and dear to them so they can make their own way. Both of you must go your way in life, while I must do what is wanted of me by my lord, your father. It's here I'll stay. You may go or stay as it pleases you." She knew we had planned to return to Rome when father improved, not really knowing how serious his illness was at the time. And now that he died, she wanted us to know we were free to pursue our original course.

"Oh, mother of mine," said Ishmael, "I've received all that Rome can teach me, so it's here I'll remain and serve you as best as I can."

His words struck a chill in my heart as I had wanted to return to Rome with him. As twins, we were nearly inseparable since birth, experiencing many of life's trials, goals, and honors together; each one for the other. Now, my heart was heavy as I wanted desperately to return to Rome, but didn't want to leave Ishmael.

"Oh Ishmael, your words strike me a serious blow, I thought you would return to Rome. But if this be your will, I'll not force mine on you. Stay with mother and represent me to those I love. As for me, I'll return to Rome."

My words seemed to be a sword unto us all for mother and Ishmael hoped I would stay and set up a business in Jerusalem.

AN OLD FRIEND

The voice and mystery of Rome and the magic of the business world alien to that here in Jerusalem called me even more now that father was gone. I was more determined than ever to see the inner workings of the finance of the empire, and this could only be done in Rome. So it was to Rome for me!

While at home studying the accounts of the family after father's death, I sat in the family study just off the courtyard. I completed the financial affairs that would provide mother with a comfortable income for the rest of her life. Father had been a good provider and had inherited a goodly sum of land from his kinfolk. When placed in the best light, the investments would give mother a life's estate. To this end, I had used the knowledge gained in Rome, and was very proud of the accomplishment.

I completed letters to Uncle Benjamin and Bela Ard, the father of Saul, even as I promised. I told them of father's death and the family wellbeing. As I was finishing, a servant came to me with the news that a young stranger stood without the gate, and would have a word with me. The servant asked if he should admit him into the house; it wasn't the usual practice to permit strangers into the gate unless the master of the house had given word to do so. As I was acting as mother's representative in meeting those who came to see the family, I told the servant to have the young man wait, and I would see him directly. I finished my work on the estate and returned the books to the library.

I went directly to the gate to greet the stranger. As I approached, I could see he was very thin and burned brown by the sun. He was young, not more than eighteen. He wore the strange clothing of the desert hill clans; it was a tunic of camel's hair and secured with a belt of skin - like that worn by those called Essenes. Over his shoulder was slung a leather thong with a small pouch and wine bottle, which I later found contained only water. Wine had never touched the lips of this young lad, no, not even that served during Pesach. His hair was long and fell in ringlets over his shoulders, and his face was covered with a soft beard that had never been shorn. As I came nearer, he saluted me in the fashion of the day.

"May God find favor with you, Judas." His speech was of one born and raised locally. His eyes were dark brown, and burned with an inner light that one might take to be caused by the fever. He had the look of one with great intensity about things yet to be done.

"God be with you, stranger. How do you know my name and I not yours?" I asked, for I couldn't recognize him as one of the family or friends. He could have been a passing friend of father's and not known to me, having been away nearly six years.

"Don't you know me? I'm John, the son of Zechariah." It was then I suddenly realized who he was - John, the young boy I had seen grow from a babe to about ten years old. He had changed a great deal from the full-faced little lad I knew to the near-gaunt young man with fire in his eyes that stood before me now. The more I looked into his eyes, the more I knew he had the Spirit of the Lord resting on him.

"Forgive me, John; it has been some time since we were together, and you've grown into a man of some stature. Accept my humble house as your own, and I'll tell mother and Ishmael you're here. Come in and refresh yourself; the servants will attend to your needs." He looked tired and in need of a change of clothing. His sandals were of the worst sort. "Come, you know the way to the vestibule; the servants will have the things you need."

I placed my arm across his shoulders and we strode through the garden and into the house. I directed the servants to attend to him, and then went to mother's room.

"Mother, we have a visitor who wishes to express his feelings to you. He has been away from the city and just now heard of father's death. Come, you will be surprised to see who it is." I had decided not to tell mother who it was before I went to her room.

"And who might it be at this hour?" she asked as she joined me in the walk to the courtyard. When she was seated and comfortable, I brought John to greet her. Ishmael came from the lower part of the house and I stopped him.

"Come with me to greet an old friend and playmate, Ishmael." And together we went to John. He was now refreshed and in different clothing. Ishmael, with the eye of an artist, recognized John immediately.

"John, dear friend, accept my condolences for the deaths of your parents. May God be with you." Ishmael threw his arms about John in a brotherly way, truly glad to see him. Ishmael had given John the greeting of remembrance I had forgotten to do in my surprise in seeing him. John was very happy to see Ishmael again and expressed this in his greeting.

"John, forgive my loss of memory when we first met, for I, too, regret the loss of your parents; they were always kind to us and we loved them as much as our own. Now we must go to mother."

When mother saw John, tears of joy ran down her cheeks, for she thought him lost forever. He was like one of her own. It was mother who helped take care of John when he was very young; she and Elizabeth often spent many hours together.

"My son, where have you been? My heart has been sorely pressed on your account, as I promised your mother to look after you if she couldn't do so. Why have you done this unto us?" He came to her and fell at her knees, a penitent and humble person.

"I bring you my condolences. I always considered Simon an uncle, he was a dear man and a true one unto my father. Forgive my ungenerous act, Ruth, but I was consumed by the Spirit of the Lord and must be away unto the desert. It was there I was told by the angel of the Lord to prepare for a greater work. It wasn't a simple thing to explain, so I left without revealing this calling to anyone. If I've caused you any suffering, it's a stripe I must bear and only the forgiveness you can give will remove it." As he looked up at mother, his eyes burned with a fire of a Zealot and more. He was concerned for mother and her unhappiness, but still held the firmness of one committed to a task yet to be completed.

"Ah, my forgiveness you have and more; you have my blessing on your quest. I believe you have been chosen for a task greater than we know. I pray God will give you the strength to fulfill it. Oh John, the Spirit of the Lord has revealed to me this hour that your name will be spoken for many generations to come; yea, even forever." Mother's face shone with the Spirit of the Lord and things yet to come were revealed to her. John accepted these sayings with no apparent change of expression, but Ishmael and I were greatly affected as we had never heard mother speak this way.

We were the ones who showed our wonder and later sang praises to the Lord. Mother was as one in a trance, and the Spirit was upon her as she continued. "Woe unto your enemies and blessed be your friends; yours will be a short life, but given for the Glory of God. He alone will sustain you, for friends and loved ones will not be able to offer you strength or comfort. Yours is the lonely road of the proscriber and it will be on your head. Oh, John, yours is a troubled road. God go with you, let none deter you, as a world in great need awaits your message." At that, mother fell forward, and would have fallen had not John been at her knees. He caught and lifted her with ease. For all his gaunt look, he was as strong as rawhide. He carried her to her bedroom which he remembered for the days when he stayed here as a lad.

He placed her on the bed and I called for the servants. Ishmael and I were greatly disturbed, both at her prophesy and her sudden swooning after saying these things. It was then I thought of my friend, Apuleius. I had great confidence in his treating of illness. While the servants made mother comfortable, I sent Apius to the fort to look for Apuleius, although I realized the unlikelihood of his being there or being available. We stayed with mother while John retired to a secluded place to pray and sing praises to the Lord for the prophesy just heard. We could hear him singing softly well into the evening as we waited for mother to recover and for word from Apius.

Time seemed to drag; mother stirred only little in fretful sleep, and since father's illness, we were concerned about her more than before. On each move, the servants came to her side in anticipation of her needs should she waken. Ishmael and I were afraid to leave her side; we had never seen her thus. Pillar, her most trusted servant for many years, finally sent us away in fear that we would do more harm than good staying there.

In our room, while waiting, Ishmael again mentioned the incident which happened aboard the ship during the storm. He avoided asking about the incident during the memorial to father, but since he knew of my intentions of returning to Rome, wanted to know all about it.

"Come Judas, won't you tell me what happened during the storm before you leave? Why do you refrain; haven't I always been honest with you about my life? Is there anyone you can trust more than me?"

"Aye, you're right. We've always been open in our dealings, and this should be no exception. It's only that I didn't want to worry you that I held back." I stopped for a moment. We were sitting near an open window so that I might see Apius should he return, and if Apuleius was with him, to run to the gate and welcome him to my father's house.

While still watching for Apius, I continued, "As you recall, the sea had turned vicious that morning and battered our ship. When the first break in the storm came, Apuleius came to see how we fared. He was concerned about you."

"Yes, that much I know."

I really didn't know how much he knew as I had tied him to the rigging before the worst of the storm and he lay there, eyes closed, with his cloak pulled over his face.

"Yes, I thought as much. As he turned to leave us, a mighty gust of wind carried him overboard. I then left you, as I feared for his life. When I took my first steps toward where he had disappeared, the wind caught me and lifted me over the side as well. I ended up within an arms' reach of him."

Ishmael nodded. He was struck by the danger of the situation once again; he was an excitable person and this story brought vivid memories of the storm to him.

"I only saved myself by clutching the rigging of the ship as I went overboard. It was then I saw Apuleius also in the rigging. With some effort, I was able to reach him and grasp the front harness of his breast plate. Both he and I were locked in a life-and-death struggle against the storm. I was determined not to see him lost. In a few moments, both of us could tell that I wouldn't be able to save us."

Ishmael looked away and swallowed hard.

"He then cried out as best he could in the howling wind that I should let go of him and save myself. This I was determined not to do, and shook my head to his request in order to save my breath to extend my effort against the storm. I cried unto the Lord to spare us from the sea. So it was Apuleius, the Roman Centurion, and I, the follower of the God of Abraham, fought, not against one another but *for* one another. I prayed for God to spare Apuleius, if not me, because he was a man of great talent in medicine - his life could do more good than mine."

I could see Ishmael took offense to what I said and was about to inject some word, but I continued.

"It was during this silent prayer that he cried out again, that I should leave go and save myself, but I would not hear of such. Yet I realized I was becoming extremely tired and if the storm didn't lay soon, I would be joining him in the sea forever.

"It was at this precise moment the stranger appeared beside us, grasped both of us, lifted us as if we were babes, and placed us on the deck in one motion. I recognized him as the same person we had met before. Oh, Ishmael, he must have had the strength of ten men.

"Even though the wind was howling fiercely, and the sea roaring like a lion, I was able to hear this rescuer. He spoke to me in a low and resonant voice - I was able to hear him distinctly. He spoke thus: 'Oh Judas, must I ever save you from yourself. Yours isn't a life to waste, even for friends. Your destiny is more important than the lives of one or two; yours is for the lives of a multitude. Judas, hear me, your time has not yet come. Till we meet again, and this we will, farewell.' With that, the wind lay for a moment and he moved quickly across the deck and disappeared into a sheet of rain that followed. Apuleius and I were exhausted from the ordeal. My breath came in such short gasps that I didn't have strength to call after the stranger, not that he could have heard me in the noise of the storm. When rested, Apuleius left for his quarters and I returned to your side."

Ishmael sat spellbound.

"This is the story: after the storm, while you were too ill to move about, I searched the ship for this person. I asked all who understood me if they had seen such a person but none had. I'm sure that my life is not my own to do with as I choose. Ishmael, laugh if you will, but I feel, like John, I have a mission. It is in Rome I hope to find it."

Ishmael sat engrossed in the tale. I didn't tell him of the questions Apuleius raised and his insistence on answers that I couldn't give. We were both silent for awhile; he was first to speak. "Judas, what does it all mean? First, the prophesy by mother about John, and now, you tell me this story about your adventure on board the ship. Is this truly the time for the Messiah, and is the Lord going to reveal him to His people as was foretold so many centuries ago? Can you, I, John and mother be part of His plan even today?"

He was about to continue the questions, but I held up my hand.

"Hear me, dear brother, my heart is full of wonder at these things. Wonder even from the days of father telling us about the birth of both John and Yeshua. Remember the strange circumstances of those births and announcements of each?" Ishmael shook his head as he remembered the fascination we had with the story of the star we couldn't see, the shepherds and their story of angels singing in the heavens, the slaying of the children in Bethlehem in the year following, and many more stories that were still told. Ishmael, however, hadn't given up on his search for reasons for my words about Apuleius.

"Judas, wasn't it so that you asked the Lord to take Apuleius to Abraham's bosom should his life be lost? Isn't it a sin to think this way? He isn't one of the chosen of the seed of Israel." He was greatly perplexed at the thought of such a request being made.

"Aye, but consider this, it's written, 'Moses did cry to the Lord to remove which he had brought against Pharaoh. And the Lord did according to the word of Moses, and the frogs died out of the Land.' Notice, the Lord heard the cry of Moses and blessed his request even though Pharaoh was an enemy of the Lord and not a circumcised one. Let me pose this to you, if the Lord heard and honored Moses' request against an enemy, then how is it a sin for me to ask for the life of a friend, be he Egyptian or Roman?

"Now hear me, this man would've risked his life for me, and were he of that mind, would've prayed to his god for help for me in a like situation. Am I a lesser creature of the

Lord that I should deny the same request of my God? Aren't we Pharisees, and shouldn't we know the law and interpret it? What man wouldn't ask God's blessing on his flock of sheep? Are sheep any more circumcised than a gentile? Woe is he who sets the law above the needs of man."

It was a long speech for me, but I found I was caught up in the feelings of the moment; his questions were the very same ones I was asking myself.

Ishmael looked somewhat placated for the moment but not for long. "Ah, I see you've pondered this for some time. Your answer raises more questions. I know of no answers, but I'm sure the Lord will direct you as you search for them. But what of the stranger? Is he an angel of the Lord?"

I was about to answer when I saw Apius approaching the gate. He was alone! My heart sank for I hoped he would bring Apuleius with him. I rose and left Ishmael in thought; I moved quickly through the halls and met Apius at the gate.

"What ho, Apius, where is Apuleius? Didn't you find him?" He simply nodded as he dismounted.

"Alas, I located him, or at least his maniple. The officer in charge told me Apuleius was out in the hills with his unit. They will be in contact with some renegades for the remainder of this month. When he returns, the commander said Apuleius will be reassigned to a unit stationed elsewhere. He couldn't give me directions because it was a military matter. It's with great distress I tell you, and ask forgiveness for returning without him by my side." He was unhappy knowing how strongly I desired to have Apuleius look at mother.

"Come, Apius, don't worry about it, what must be must be, and you cannot cause things to happen beyond your control. Go and rest with my blessing."

I was distressed at the news. I was hoping to see Apuleius before leaving for Rome, and wanted him to help mother, but now neither seemed likely. My thoughts turned to mother. I left the gate and slowly strode into the house. As I walked head down, I became aware of someone beside me. It was Pillar. She came from mother's room looking for me. She saluted me as was the custom for a maidservant.

"Judas, I've words for you. Your mother has recovered from her ordeal and wishes to see you." She turned to lead the way, and I hurried my pace to reach the bedroom.

Mother was resting on a bed of pillows. She was a small and pretty woman. Some of her color had returned, and looked no worse for the experience. She was strong and always had been. Mother's inner courage was a thing of beauty, and because of it, was the keystone of her political circle - the circle of beauty consultants which operated covertly in Herod's palace. Even now they operated in the court of Herod Antipas II. She managed to avoid discovery and prosecution of any of the group through changes of administration.

Mother held her arms open to me. "Come Judas, come here and sit by my side. Judas, I fear for you, even as I do for John," she said after a time.

"You needn't be so apprehensive, mother. Rome isn't the evil place some would have you to believe, and besides, Uncle Benjamin is still there as friend and counselor," I casually remarked to ease her fears.

"It's not Rome I fear Judas. It's something hence I fear. Your trials will begin soon. I know of strange things in your life. Some you haven't told me as Ishmael has confided in me of his deep concern for you. Why haven't you told me? Haven't I been your confidant throughout your life? Have I ever betrayed you?"

My surprise kept me from speaking. What had Ishmael told her? I stood silently studying her face.

"It's because of these stories that I've come to the Lord many times on your behalf. As the Lord has given his servant, I've seen dimly, even as with John, things yet to come.

It's of these things I must warn you. Yours will be a role such as none has ever played in all Israel. Many will come to your side as friends, but most will fall away when your trial begins. Your trials will be such it will seem Almighty God has given up your soul. Satan will be known to you, and this, personally. I pray God you will prevail against the Great Deceiver. Oh Judas, as a mother, my very soul trembles at the things I see so dimly. Have a care." She clutched my hand with great force. I was undone! I couldn't understand all this, first her speaking about John and his mission, and now unto me.

"Oh mother, I am truly undone. I wouldn't have you troubled by these things. I didn't know Ishmael was troubled by these events, and hardly enough to carry them to you." I took both her hands in mine and squeezed them gently. "Your words to John and I have troubled me as I have no comment on these strange happenings. Don't hold it against me because I held these things from you as I felt they would bring you naught but grief. Isn't it right for me to do so? Can your distress relieve the rush of life as it will be? How then can I, as your son, carry everything to you, and to what end? Mother, for your prayers and supplications I'm grateful, but I wouldn't want you to worry about things to come; they aren't in our hands. Now, let's not carry on like this; it's not good for you. Consider it closed; I'll do as it's given me and trust in the hand of God."

After a bit she became more calm and resolute.

"So, mother, as your finances are now in order, I'm off to Rome." I bowed low and kissed her; she answered with a soft stroking of my head. After a moment in embrace, she relaxed and we parted.

Mother, realizing she couldn't deter me from the trip to Rome and what I thought was my destiny there, gazed at me for some time. She then spoke softly the words that, although I didn't know it at the time, were to strike me like the edge of a sword later in life.

"Thou hast said; that thou doest, do quickly!"

I stood silently considering her words. They were strange and not her normal sayings - like one repeating a line from an ancient writing. Where had she heard such a short saying? I would mark it in my heart.

She then gave me her blessing and turned her head away so I might not see the tears that forced their way through tightly closed eyelids. Oh, mother, I knew even though you tried not for me to do so.

I left her bedroom with a sad and wondering heart, and prepared to leave for Rome that same hour.

Once in my room, I told Ishmael of the things which passed between mother and I. I commissioned him to be the head of the household and surety for mother as I was leaving for Rome within the week. He was greatly distraught. He had wanted to have the family come and see me off. This I told him I wanted to avoid and told him of mother's words reflecting her desires on the matter, "Thou hast said; that thou doest, do quickly." Neither he nor I could understand her strange words, but I told him she would have me leave quickly and not tarry, which I planned to do. It was to my mind that separations should be as short as possible, while returns should be as long and warm as possible.

I called Apius to me and told him of my plans and needs for the trip. He was sad to hear of my decision to leave so soon, but he set about with the servants to get things ready. It was then I remembered John! John was still in the guest room. I went to see him.

After telling him of mother's words, I spoke of my trip to Rome. "John, I'm leaving within the week. I wish you well, and should we not meet again, I give you my blessings now. It may be that our destinies parallel each other. Both of us may be called upon to give much for the needs of others. May God go with you, and may the angel of the Lord be your right hand." I gave him my hand.

"Judas, I'm sure we will meet again, and when we do, it is you who will experience the first encounter. May the Lord go with you, and may His countenance be ever toward you. As for me, I go again into the desert to communicate with the Spirit of the Lord." He turned and saluted Ishmael who had just come into the room.

Ishmael saw that he too was prepared to leave and added his blessing. "May God be your guide and armor against all evil. And John, should you pass this way again, consider this humble house as your own."

John, the son of Zechariah, left that same hour.

Ishmael stood by the window and watched him leave. He, like me, wondered what was in store for the young lad. "Dear Judas, my heart is torn as if from my own body at the news you are so persistent. Isn't there any way to change your mind?" He turned toward me and I could see the unhappiness on his face. Oh, how much he looked like me! How many times people had mistaken us for one another. But how different in thought.

"It's written that man must listen to his heart to live a happy life, and wise is the man who's heart reflects the will of God. My heart says I must go to Rome. It's there I'll find some of the answers to the enigmas found in my life. Parting from you, dear brother, weighs heavy on my heart. I would be sure of your blessing before I go, even as you have mine. May God protect you and guide you in all things. May your art grow and bring you good fortune and the love of God. Till we meet again, dear playmate, know that I love you greater than any other." My eyes were very wet indeed after my comments.

"What must be must be. May the Lord bless and keep you from all harm. Till we meet again, let our letters keep us together." We fell upon each other's shoulders and wept; for us, parting was like the separation of one soul.

It was with some sadness I finished preparation. Ishmael and I remained close through the remaining days. Anath came home and was told all that had happened and wondered about everything. She was a good woman and stood by in deep unhappiness as I prepared to go. I was sad when I looked upon her as I realized how little I really knew about my only sister. Some day, I thought, I'll make it up to you, dear Anath.

By the middle of the week, mother was strong again and was at the gate when I was ready to depart. The great question for me was the need for someone to accompany me on the trip. It was now I realized how much I took Ishmael for granted. Mother was insistent that I take Apius with me, and although he was willing, I felt he would be of greater value helping mother here. He was a good man and knew the operation of the entire household better than Ishmael or I for that matter. In the end, I decided to take no one.

The last days were busy ones and they passed quickly. Soon, I said goodbye to all and with Apius by my side, left the great city in early 766. The trip to Caesarea was uneventful and we made good time.

As luck would have it, we stayed at the same inn as before. Apius and I waited for a ship which would make the voyage. When it arrived, I secured passage, and after loading my belongings on board, gave Apius my farewell with a commission to take care of the family. His heart was deeply troubled and he fought tears as he thanked me for my blessings and promised all should be well with them or he would die trying.

The call of the master separated us - he on the dock and I aboard the ship. The ship sailed out quickly and I was en route to Rome. What would be there for me?

CHAPTER TEN

Back In Rome

The voyage was uneventful and I arrived in Rome within the month. Uncle Benjamin's servants met me at the port. The ride to his house was like old times. All seemed the same; I was home in Rome. The only difference from the year before was the loneliness because of Ishmael's absence and, of course, Apuleius.

Uncle Benjamin greeted me as he would his own son, had he one. He conveyed his sympathy and that of his household on the death of father; his was double grief as father was his only brother. We talked many hours about father and the early years they spent together in Judea. His reminiscing about father caused me to miss Ishmael even more.

With this loneliness always present, I found that work at the counting house was a great help, and spent more and more time there. Yet, even the counting house had its moments of discomfort. To relieve these moments of unhappiness, I grew interested in the history of Rome and its religions. I walked the city over while studying the statues and houses of worship erected to the many gods, some still honored and some not. The young Roman had grown away from ancient ways, most were free thinking and only paid lip service to these gods, both living and dead, during festival days. Yet, some put great store in the power and sympathy of the gods and provided great noise during the festivals. Some made great noise with cymbals, trumpets, drums, and loud, incessant wailing of incantations that were obscene in themselves. With these, some performed obscene gestures that caused me to turn and flee, asking God to forgive me for the witness of such abominations.

The year was 768 and I had started to feel at home in the atmosphere of Rome. I became close to Uncle Benjamin during the passing months and he toward me. He conferred the ring of his house on me and I wore it with pride. He was a well-respected businessman known throughout the city for his integrity and fair dealings in all things. He had the respect if not the love of many Romans. It was from him I learned to deal with the Romans and understand their attitude toward us Jews. That's not to say I liked their view, but I understood it and dealt with it skillfully.

The letters from home told of many adventures in the holy city. Both mother and Ishmael wrote faithfully and I tried to be the same but wasn't always consistent. Time passed well for me, and the letters grew in number. Because of the distance and method of travel, the letters were more often than not late and sometimes out of sequence. Some would be as much as weeks out of sequence, therefore, I didn't always make sense of the immediate delivery. Because of this, I carefully saved all, placed them in order, and would read them again. It was like visiting with those at home, and I often found new meaning in each letter or increased understanding of the old. As the number grew and I reread them, I began to realize a change in the mood and character of Ishmael.

His letters began to reflect more and more the feelings of the Zealots. It was a new role for him. Normally, as I remembered him, he wasn't one to become involved as things of beauty moved him more than political reality. Yet, I could see the difference in his letters and the little pieces of artwork that annotated them. These often said more to me than his text.

Ishmael wrote he saw and talked to Apuleius a time or two; the last meeting was in the marketplace. Apuleius was now an officer of some rank, and commanded a unit of nearly twelve medical offices and aid men. Ishmael was glad to hear that I had returned to Rome and said he was due back in Rome on rotation that very year. This news made my heart jump at the thought of seeing Apuleius again.

It was 772, and I suddenly realized I had been in Rome nearly six years this second time. I was becoming very Roman. A cosmopolitan Jew in the great city of the Empire at the old age of thirty-five.

It was while considering this that suddenly a great loneliness overcame me for the things of home and those I missed most. I was ready to leave Rome, but I'd made a contract with my uncle to continue as his head accountant for four more years, and unless some severe hardship occurred at home, I was to remain with him and complete my contract. This was the law. Uncle Benjamin was wealthy, or so it seemed, and had moved to a place of prominence in the political scene, or at least as prominent as a Jew and foreigner could be in the days of Tiberius. Yet, because of the political climate, there was always a feeling of insecurity. Jews were always envied if and when they moved into high circles of politics, and this was Uncle Benjamin's condition. We both knew that it took only one incident to cause the feelings of the great city to turn against the Jews. When this happened, wealth and integrity meant nothing. All could be lost in the snapping of the fingers. It was because of this insecurity I looked toward Jerusalem, but a contract made is a contract fulfilled, so I was taught, and a contract made and blessed by God was a binding one.

After learning Apuleius might be coming back for a rest from the wars, or the policing of Judea, I began to watch the ships coming from Judea. I learned most of the east trading schedules and began watching and hoping to know of his probable landing and tried to be on the dock when his group arrived. It was from Uncle Benjamin I heard of the troops coming home. It would be a joy to greet and talk with Apuleius once more.

I began to wonder if the policing of Judea had made any noticeable change in Apuleius. What if the life as a soldier in contact with the enemy, and they being Zealots, had turned him against Jews? My heart sank at the thoughts he might not enjoy my company because of his combat experiences. The thought of losing a friend because of these stupid skirmishes with some over-zealous Jewish patriots created some anger in me. I didn't know why as I wanted a free Judea as much as anyone. It was the way it was being brought about that caused me hurt. The constant harassment of the Roman soldiers in Judea and thereabouts, and the consequential loss of innocent life because of the retaliation of such harassment was the real crux of the matter. I secretly felt these acts against the Romans would bring nothing but great disaster to all the Jewish nations. I then prayed to God that it wouldn't be so.

The days passed slowly after Ishmael's letter. I searched the list of ships from the east for those from Judea. I listened to the gossip of the mariners along the docks, always waiting to hear of a ship arriving from the port of Caesarea or even Joppa, not knowing which port of call the ship might egress from. The waiting and watching gave me a bit of relief from the otherwise mundane operations of the counting house. I was confronted one day with the news that two ships lay just outside the harbor in the breakwater waiting for entry into port. Both had just arrived from the east, and both may have been from Judea.

The first ship docked before noon. I had completed the entries on my accounts early enough to be there waiting. As the boat docked, I could see the crew move to tie up. The first off was the military; of these, first came the sick and injured, then, those with the fever and like illnesses. After that, those that were ambulatory, and with them came the aid men, giving them a steady hand. After these, came the physicians who gave the commands for the care of the incapacitated. It was in this latter group I recognized the figure of Apuleius.

The flow of the rest of the military, their horses, and equipment onto the dock prevented me from reaching Apuleius. It wasn't wise for a Jew to interfere with the movement of military personnel even for the most personal reasons. I stood afar trying to keep Apuleius in sight. I managed to follow his progress from the ship down the dock to a staging area. It was here they were assembled for a short march through the streets of the city before receiving their dismissal for leave. It was the custom of the day to recognize the returning soldiers with some sort of expression of gratitude, and regardless of how small the contingent, the people were ready to throw flowers and shout praises to those passing by.

I watched as the troops moved out of view. I turned and left the dock. Walking to the counting house I knew I wouldn't see Apuleius the rest of that day, so I might as well work on the manifests and bills of lading. I knew very well he had family obligations that must be kept before friends and acquaintances and this was as it should be. Yet, even while working, my mind kept wandering to Jerusalem and things of home, and from there to Apuleius and his arrival. When would I see him and what would be his comments about the skirmishes and troubles of Jerusalem? What would he tell me of my family?

The lack of concentration caused me to go over figures and names of ships on the bills of lading more than once. It was a relief to see the last of the manifests completed and the books closed for the day. The next several days were similar scenarios. After nearly two weeks, I decided I would try to see Apuleius and left the counting room early. I would return home, then cross town to the home of Lucius the elder to see if Apuleius was there.

I started for Uncle Benjamin's house and walked down the familiar streets on my way there. Always a bit preoccupied with my thoughts, I stepped into the path of an oncoming chariot. The chariot was drawn to a sudden halt to avoid running me down.

"Ho there!" a familiar voice cried. "Don't you care for your life, man?"

I looked up and there, standing braced against the front of the chariot and holding the reins of the now-rearing horses, was my dear friend, Apuleius.

"Apuleius! Ho, ho, Apuleius!" I couldn't have been more surprised.

"Judas!" He struggled to get his team under control. He was still a handsome man, and the years spent in Jerusalem had hardened him and added color to his body. He was the picture of a Roman legionnaire. With the horses calmed, he jumped down and ran to greet me as of old.

"Judas, what luck, I was just on my way to your uncle's to see you!" His breath came in short gasps reflecting the effort spent in bringing the team under control. "So, we meet again, and nearly in the same manner. Some day, if you don't change your dreaming while walking, you're going to visit the bosom of Abraham sooner than you want."

He was as happy as I. He embraced me in the manner of the Romans; an act rarely done to Jews, and ever more rarely done in public. But he always considered me as a brother more than a friend, and because of this refused to abide by the customs of the day.

"Ah, Apuleius, I went to the dock the day you arrived and saw you disembark but couldn't get nearer than the length of four spears. The crowd pressed hard to see your cohort leave the ships. I was proud to be among them, and thanked God that you were safe. I heard from the other ship captains that ships were due in Rome, and letters from Ishmael told of your possible return."

"Come Judas, ride with me, and we will go to your uncle's house. I've much to tell you. Perhaps when you are free we can spend a day or two near the sea discussing some of the things that happened while we were apart." With that, he pulled me up and started his team down the street toward my uncle's.

The ride was just as hectic as I remembered the first one to be some years before. The chariot rattled down the streets and through alleyways at nearly breakneck speed. People scattered like sheep before a runaway wagon, with the usual fists held in the air after we passed by those forced to turn aside. Not all people cared for the military and even less considered their use of chariots in a reckless manner in good taste. But most were more than willing to forgive the returning soldier of his misdemeanors.

It must have been a comical scene to those we passed, a legionnaire driving like demons were about to overtake him, and a Jew hanging onto the chariot for dear life - he in his public dress and I in my robes, and the wind whipping both costumes. I held my peace throughout the drive, but had my doubts of arriving home in one piece.

At last, Apuleius slowed the chariot and let the horses blow themselves. He was proud of his skill in handling the chariot, and turned to look at me still clinging to the handhold in the front of the chariot.

"Stand free, Judas, lean against the curveboard and let go of the handhold. I promise not to give the horses their head again." He flashed a smile. "It's truly good to see you. This separation wasn't to my liking but the military being what it is takes precedence over personal wants. I was extremely sorry to hear of your father's death, and wished many times I might have met him and the rest of your family. The times I was free I spent in study and only met Ishmael twice. Hence, I've little to tell you about your family."

TROUBLES IN THE WIND

It was good to see Apuleius again; next to Ishmael, there wasn't another person that meant so much to me. I did as he suggested and released my white-knuckle hold on the front edge of the curveboard. He held the team in check as he said he would. As we approached the main thoroughfare, he suddenly turned away from the street that led to Uncle Benjamin's house. He took a roadway which led up the hills and overlooked Rome.

"What's this, Apuleius? What do you have in mind?" I asked, but he just smiled and continued uphill.

"Have you ever seen the city from the hills?" And without waiting for an answer, continued, "It's one impressive sight, Rome. We have the time, so I thought we could reminisce while looking down on Rome." He reined the horses, and brought the chariot to a stop on an overlook that jutted out from the mountain. I'd never been so far up the mountain and the view was astounding. The people looked like ants and the houses and temples like toy boxes. The port lay before us with miniature ships floating like toys in a boys' pond.

"It's beautiful; I've never been this high before."

He took a small basket from the floor of the chariot, and strode to a flat rock large enough for several people to sit and enjoy the view, even though we were alone. He set the basket down; in it was the making of a feast, or so I thought.

"Mother was glad to have some of this ready for me; the family treats me well since my return. It's their way of showing their love for a son home from the wars." He laughed lightly and placed some of the food and wine bottle on a small scarf. "The servants could've taken care of all this, but then, who needs them? After being out in the fort and away from servants, the need for privacy outweighs the desire for pampering."

He took some of the foodstuffs for himself and passed the rest to me for selection. In days gone by, I wouldn't have eaten without washing, but now it seemed different. So it was that when in Rome do as Romans do included bending the old laws. By his attitude, I could see that he had planned this and wanted me to join him in this little repast. We ate away and talked between bites.

"This is my favorite spot to view the seat of world politics. It must be the way the gods see man - so small and unknowing of what each other is doing, hurrying here and there trying to accomplish things that make little difference to the overall picture, most completely oblivious of the gods, and the gods able to reach down and change the course of every one of their little plans. From here, we can see one man fighting another on one corner of the street, and on another corner of a different block, a couple making love. Those involved are in separate worlds, neither able to see the other, while we, like the gods, can see both. Even the mighty Caesar cannot see as we do this moment. There is one great difference between us and the gods, Judas. We can see only that which sight will permit, but the gods see all. Their sight isn't limited to the need for daylight and open spaces. They can see what is hidden from us by rooftop and cover. Someday man may also see thus." He paused for a moment, and when he began again, started with a new subject.

"In my younger days, I came up here when things depressed me, and often found the view removed those feelings. This is my temple, my piece of hallowed ground."

I couldn't help admiring his choice of location, as it provided a panoramic view of the great city. The feeling of being isolated from the happenings below, yet able to enjoy the several personal adventures of the people below made one feel a sense of power.

"Aye, Apuleius, it's a grand feeling and one of the more spectacular views. I can see that with other teachings you could ascribe many religious happenings to this place. I envy you. I have no such place of hallowed ground here in Rome. Mine lies far to the east in Jerusalem. Here I must make do with my prayer shawl and commitment to that which is essential to every Jew, the remembrance that God is one and everywhere. I pray I need no spot of hallowed ground, no more than those of ages past. My heart still cries out for the temple on high holy days. Oh, where art thou, O God, that I cannot find thee? What mountain is high enough or sea deep enough to hide thee? I pray these things but the longing is still there."

I suddenly remembered that I wanted to know why he brought us here on the hill. "Enough of this, Apuleius, what really brings us to this spot? Surely a small lunch out of doors wasn't the object of this trip. After all, we could've eaten in the gardens of my uncle's house as well as here."

He sat quietly looking out across the city below; it was as though he was elsewhere. I waited for his return to the present and an answer to my question. He wasn't the same. Six years ago he would have answered the question without much thought, but today he sat in considerable thought. His breathing was of one completely relaxed, the deep rhythm of one near sleep. He didn't move from this position nor turn to look at me.

"You're observant as always, Judas. I brought you here to look at my retreat. It's a place I've held dear from my youth. Always, rain or shine, I've come to this spot when troubled by things about me. You're the first person I've brought with me; yours is an honor granted to no other. But Judas, I am deeply troubled by events of the last few months." He turned to look out to the southwest part of the city and I could see his face as the sunshine fell directly on it. His face showed his concern. "All isn't what it used to be in Jerusalem. In only the six years you've been gone, the conditions between our government in place there and your people has deteriorated greatly." He stopped and shook his head to express the negative side.

"The former Procurator, Annis Rufus, has been replaced by Valerius Gratus, a most unreasonable man. His presence has done nothing to alleviate the discomforts and unhappiness of the peoples of Judea. His highhandedness and offensive manner has strained the relationship between the zealous patriot and the lawful government of Rome."

He shifted his position to face me while continuing his statement. "In Jerusalem, the situation has been increasingly intolerable for your people, especially on the high holy days. In the last year, small riots have broken out because of this intolerance and I see no diminishing of these troubles, and I don't blame the people for their actions. That's not to say it's proper and lawful, and that some aren't fostering and promoting this condition to their advantage, Romans and Jews alike." He pounded his fist on the rock nearby.

"Mind, Judas, this isn't to be repeated outside our confidence. As a legionnaire, I would be suspect of treason for less than these statements. In the past few months, itinerant preachers and teachers of your people have called for them to repent and return to the God of their fathers. All in all, this is harmless enough when taken as a religious calling, but the trouble is that some feel this is a call of nationalism as well. Whether this is in accordance with your beliefs is not of great concern to me or of my command in Judea. What is of concern is the forming of bands that strike some of the outposts and then fall back into the hills and let the people bear the brunt of the commands' response."

He stood up and paced back and forth across the rock. He rubbed his cheek. "When I left, we were forced to increase patrols and the number of men stationed at each post. This has been reported to Rome and the high command. Judas, this sort of flaunting of power with force, regardless of how small or of what intent, isn't taken lightly by those in power. Take heed, one of these days Rome will lose patience, rightly or wrongly, and will place the boot-heel of the legions on the neck of the Jewish people. Remember, it wasn't but less than a century ago that Pompey took Judea, and if these fanatical elements continue to grow, the hand of Rome will move once again to destroy all Judea."

"Ah, so it is, and I'm aware of the signs of the times, Apuleius. But to separate religion from nationalism is not to be. By the Laws and Prophets, we are to serve one God, and under him, the chosen ones of the nation. The young are taught to understand this as a commandment and a right granted to them by a power greater than that of Rome."

What he said was true, and had been apparent to me as the news of many tongues here in Rome could be heard repeating. I continued, "When those young itinerant teachers, as you call them, speak, the young listen with their hearts and not with their heads. It has ever been that way. Listen Apuleius, our history has been a struggle to adhere to this precept. Think of the many times our people have been enslaved for one reason or another. Yet through all this, we have remained faithful in our way to the God of our fathers."

He raised his hand, "Judas, it has been a long eight years, our separation. I was a young and inexperienced physician who left you on the dock of Caesarea in 764. The time has caused me to wonder, for I have seen much in that time. I've saved the wounded on both sides. I've seen the most trivial reason used to incite riot and armed conflict. In every case, both sides have been losers with your young Zealots losing the greater share, some dying, some in prison, and some sent to Rome as slaves. For what? Consider if you placed all your young men-at-arms they would still be no match for the legions. Why then is it that some are so easily persuaded to move in that direction? Tell me, Judas!"

As he finished his commentary, he turned to face me again so he could hear better as the wind now coming up the hill made a rushing sound. It reminded me of the statement of who causes the wind to blow and from whence its direction - it comes from the Lord and only He can give it direction and purpose.

His words struck great fear in me, as I knew the young Zealots, yea, even some by name. Would that I could change one man's thoughts about my people and their great yearning for freedom!

"You are a reasonable man, Apuleius. But you must understand it's not the Roman government, or even for that matter, Caesar, that's the goad. Remember, my people have suffered under the heavy hand of others since our father's time. First Egypt and Assyria, then Persia, then the Hellenized Lagids and Seleucids, and finally Rome. Even before Rome was, our people resisted political and religious intolerance of others, ever seeking to understand our own faults which caused our God to turn away from us. Even now, there is strong hope our God will one day rise up and provide us with a Messiah to throw off the yoke of the oppressor, whoever it might be. The young Zealot holds no idea that he or his brothers-at-arms can win a struggle against Roman legions. Oh no, Apuleius, it's the thought that someday, God will rise up and cause a great calamity which will make the difference. Oh Apuleius, when the heart believes this possible, then odds mean little! Yes, even life itself becomes a small price to pay for the future when all will serve God and enjoy the fruits of this kind of servitude. Can you follow this, Apuleius? Is it so hard to see?"

"Ah yes, but why is it not just acceptable to believe that, since someone has to rule, why not the will of your God that it is Rome?"

It had been some time since I had such a fine argument. I enjoyed the thoughts of Apuleius. He knew some of the things held by some of my people, and this was one of them. I could see I had his attention. "Ah, there's the rub. Some search the law for an answer to this question. But the Zealots are not such a group; they hold that a good and gracious God wouldn't permit a people outside His blessing hold his people for long. They acknowledge no leader or master but God, with rulers set in tune with the law. Some prefer death for themselves and their families to serving those outside God's blessing. Their numbers mean little when they feel their cause is just and the will of God."

I continued my refute. "Remember, our people fear them at times nearly as much as do your troops, as they've used terrorist methods against the adherents of Rome and all those suspected of laxity in the law. It's not easy for good people to fight a terrorist group of their own kind. The game played is a deadly one. Some don't know who is friend and who is foe! With this, you aren't troubled; at least all not Romans can be assumed to be the enemy. Others must live within the circle; they cannot go home after a skirmish. Don't be harsh on the people, for even in Rome you have suffered from the changing of the guard wherein the citizenry don't know who holds control over life and death. How say you?"

Our conversation on this and others like it went on into the afternoon, and the sun moved behind the hills. As the shadows grew longer, the air grew cooler. Apuleius finally moved to go, gathering up the things spread out before us. He moved deliberately. "We must talk again about this. Sometime soon, in our lifetime I believe, there will be a great deal of bloodletting over this cause, and valid or not, the Jewish nation will suffer greatly. Mark me, many who aren't combatants will be asked to choose in order to save life and family. Pray that your God will give them the right choice." He continued to talk while placing the basket in the chariot. We stepped aboard and were off.

Suddenly, the speech synthesizer output became garbled and the screen lost all intelligence. The system switched to search mode. The system was offline while it tried to recapture the lost characters and sync words.

A sigh of exasperation came from John as he pressed the delay button and proceeded to shut down the entire process. He turned to those at the consoles, and with a gesture, indicated that he was tired and welcomed the break.

A glance at the elapse time meter indicated they had been online for nearly four hours, which had been previously decided was enough to stay with the program. John proceeded to notify the university that he was taking the computer offline for the rest of the day. They had been on the job eight hours. It was time for rest until tomorrow.

They moved through the air interlock and into the hallway. John closed the door, inserted his keycard and notified security the lab was cleared for the rest of the evening.

And the evening and the morning were the third day!

CONTRACTUAL OBLIGATIONS

The next day everyone arrived together, and had minimum delay in identification by security. Once in the laboratory, documents were retrieved from the safes, and consoles were set up for the next phase of the decoding of the Golden Scroll. There was some quandary about the system finding the lost sync words, but the system was functioning well up to the moment it left the line. All hoped the system would retrieve the story line.

John inserted the answer to the original query of the day before and after the system started, the lights lowered, the screen became alive with intelligent prose, and the voice synthesizer became audible again. The ancient world became a thing of the present.

The trip to Uncle Benjamin's house was a short one. "I'll not greet your uncle and his family this time, Judas. Give them my regards and promise I'll see them soon. May all be well with you and think on what I've said this day."

I stood leaning against the curveboard and watched Uncle Benjamin's house come into view. After we stopped, I hurriedly stepped down and turned from the chariot.

"Hold, Judas!" Apuleius called, and grasped my arm in a tight grip; it was then I realized just how strong he was. "Hear me before you go. I would have you come and stay at my father's house while you complete your contract with your uncle. A chariot and servant can be yours while you're there, if you want. It would mean a great deal to me to have someone near that has seen the things I have these last few years. There's none in my house that has. You know there's no one I would rather have near than you, dear friend. I asked you to consider this offer made in friendship and out of loneliness. Approach your uncle about this matter and I will await your answer." He released his hold and moved off.

"Never fear, I'll not sleep well this night. Some of your words about Israel are as a chill in the night. I'll consider your offer; it's an honor I would enjoy. I will lay this before Uncle Benjamin. May God be with you till we meet again."

He nodded again and drove off into the dusk. I stood at the gate musing what had just occurred between us. The bond that started some years ago was as strong as ever - the years at Fort Antonia hadn't changed anything - my heart sang.

"Judas, come, your uncle awaits you," I heard from behind me. I turned to see one of the servants motioning for me to follow. He led me to Uncle Benjamin on the terrace. He looked older somehow, or was it that I saw in him myself growing older?

"Greetings, uncle, and how is it by you?"

"Ah, I've been waiting for you. You didn't come directly home from the counting house." Uncle was troubled at times by my freedom of movement. Not that he would curtail it, but that he thought it somewhat dangerous as there was an element of citizenry who would just as soon take your life for your purse as not. I was always grateful for his concern and often thanked him for it.

"Don't fear, uncle, all was well with me today. In fact, the reason for my lateness was the chance meeting with Apuleius. You remember the young physician who cared for Ishmael before we left for home? He's home from Jerusalem for a rest. It did my heart good to see him again. He sends his greetings and promises to visit soon."

He nodded assent; he remembered Apuleius and his cure of Ishmael. I didn't mention the offer made by him about a change of living quarters. I was aware that something was bothering Uncle Benjamin and in deference to his age, I withheld my wants.

"I would have a word with you." He started with a simple statement, but I still knew he was troubled. "What are you going to do with your life? Haven't I treated you well?" I could see that he was in earnest. What was on his mind?

"That is without question, uncle." I answered without hesitation, as it was true in every way. Uncle Benjamin had been and still was a great help in all things. I had made my way in the business world and had a going enterprise of my own. He had been like a father to both Ishmael and me during our stay, and was my contact with the Jewish tradition and family during my stay. "I've tried to be worthy of your kindness and protection, haven't I?"

His eyes were brimming with tears as we talked. "Judas, since your father's death, I've held great feeling for you, and had I a son, I would have been pleased if he were a copy of you. Yet I have none to carry on this name and business. I've brought prayers and supplication to the Lord that you might find it in your heart to take the place of the son I don't have. Haven't I given you the family ring to show you are as my son? I have no wish to deny you freedom of choice, but only wish to present my wants for your consideration."

He stopped and turned to instruct the servants to light the lamps for the evening shadows were beginning to fall about the house. On the great table were copies of many of his most active accounts. These I recognized because of my work with them. I didn't answer his questions about his giving me the family ring, but waited patiently for him to continue. I had accepted it out of great respect for him and his family. He knew without my answering that I had understood the possible significance of this acceptance, yet he knew of my desire to return home. He knew this meant I wouldn't stay in Rome always.

"Judas, is it your will to finish out the remaining four years of your contract?" he asked while still giving instructions to his servants.

"Aye, uncle this you know. A contract fairly made is one to be kept. Have I indicated any less?" Although I was beginning to fear his motives, I still remained silent about the offer to move to the Lucius household.

"Ah, it is good. In the past few weeks I could sense a new longing to be gone to Jerusalem, am I not right?"

"Yes, but this I've turned aside to meet my obligation unto you. And I must admit that I would be gone at the end of the four years. My heart longs to see Mother, Ishmael, Anath, and to serve God in the temple once again. This I am sure you can understand." He sat resting against the large table without moving, his eyes watching my face for signs known only to him. His fingers traced out little patterns on one of the books.

"Judas, Judas, you are my right hand, as you have been for nearly ten years. You've never failed me in any account, nor has any customer or client said ought but good about you. Your books are error free, and your overseeing of detail has lessened loss of funds through any dealing made with anyone be he Senator, free man, or slave."

He stopped and glanced around the room as one seeing that no one else was within hearing distance of our conversation. "And, Judas, you of all people know the strengths and weaknesses of my ventures. It is these I must discuss with you this night."

Aha! *Now* I knew what was on his mind. Since I had been back, and after studying his books, I knew some of those ventures weren't doing well. In fact, the shipping trade had fallen off considerably in the last five years. Some said it was because of piracy while others said the taxes were too high. The truth was that Uncle Benjamin was in trouble with some of his ventures. It was this he had to bring to light if he wanted to survive; I waited.

He leaned across the table to pick up a packet of letters which were held together with a ribbon of golden cloth. "First, I have heard from Ishmael and your mother in the last few days, and their letters leave under the impression that you haven't written them as faithfully as you should. And I hope you will correct this oversight. Your mother is my age, nearly sixty-one this year. You must take time to write, Judas. She fears for you and wants to know of your welfare enough to ask me about you. This ought not be, Judas. I wouldn't want her to think I have captured your time to the extent you can't write."

He laid the packet down and picked up a new letter and handed it to me. "Here is one that just arrived this morning. It's from your mother. It carries her mark of urgency, Judas. I will retire while you read it. If it is something that must be attended to soon, this talk can wait," he turned to go.

"No need to leave, uncle. She may ask about you and comment on your household."

I broke the seal and unrolled the packet. It was preserved as all letters were that traveled by ship with a waterproof outer covering. The letter was tearstained and the hand writing not as sure as mother's usually was. It read in part, "Dear Judas, it is with great grief that I tell you of Ishmael's misfortune…" My eyes moved faster over the page. What was this? What had happened to Ishmael? "He was solicited to do artwork for one Jonas bar Nebat, a close friend of one called Barabbas. It was during the delivery of the artwork he was found during a raid by Roman guards. It was said that Jonas bar Nebat and his chief, Barabbas, were leaders of local Zealots responsible for great damage to Fort Antonia."

Who was Jonas bar Nebat? And Barabbas? Neither of these were known to me! And what was the damage done to the fort? Strange that Apuleius didn't mention it.

"Ishmael was placed under arrest with the others, but Barabbas was warned and escaped. Ishmael now languishes in the prison at the fort. I was able to secure permission to see him through some of my clients. Ishmael tells me he knew nothing of this matter and was only there to complete his art for Jonas. The Roman officer in charge will not release him and has turned a deaf ear to my pleadings. His time for tribunal review is but two months hence. I've seen all my political friends but to no avail. My heart is sore grieved and a great fear rests upon me for Ishmael's life." Her letter continued to describe the prison and conditions of his discomfort. My heart trembled for I knew Ishmael wasn't one of great physical strength and couldn't stand such hardships. The letter became more pleading…"Judas, I'm at a loss as to what to do. I pray each day for both my sons. Where have I gone wrong? Why has the Lord stricken me thus? Judas, our hopes rest with you and the Lord. Can't you come home and do something to secure his release?" The letter was no longer concerned with anything else. I was undone! I turned to Uncle Benjamin and cried out that all was lost.

"Judas, how say you?" He hastened to my side.

"Alas, it's Ishmael. He has been arrested and accused of collaborating with some Zealots who are guilty of damaging the fort and causing bodily harm to personnel there. He claims his innocence, and I know of no time he has lied about such things. He is an artist, not a soldier or insurrectionist." I was truly grieved at the news. The idea of my twin being in some prison came hard upon me; it was as though my own body was even with him. I slumped into a chair and handed the letter to Uncle Benjamin, and he scanned it for a time.

"All isn't lost Judas, I will go on the morrow to see some friends who have some power in the civil government of Rome. Perhaps they can intercede for Ishmael. I'll talk with all I know who may have some sway over such things. Don't despair, God will find a way. We must ask for his love and justice." With that, he returned the letter and gave me an embrace. "I must go to my family, and we will pray as one to God. *Hear, O Israel: the Lord is our God, the Lord is one.*"

Speaking thus, he left the room to prepare for the evening meal. I was to join the family as was my habit, but this night my appetite left me with the first words of the letter.

My soul was in great torment. I was so far away from the scene. It would be days, if not weeks, before I could get to Judea by sea. But a messenger, with good horsemanship, could get across land to Judea in much shorter time. My restless mind, searching for an answer, thought of Apuleius. Here might be the answer. God does provide help through gentiles, even as He did for those of ages past. I must go and plead my case with Apuleius.

A FRIEND IN NEED

I called Johnathan to me. Johnathan was the first servant of Uncle Benjamin's household. He had taken messages to Apuleius for me several times before. This time I would go, but I needed his help in finding my way through the city. I told Johnathan to prepare two horses; this was done, and we were soon on our way.

It was early evening and the streets crowded. This was a festival week, and a great number of merrymakers were roaming the streets. Mixed in with them were the usual amount of ruffians who preyed on the unsuspecting pilgrims who came for the celebration. Many of the ruffians were men with prices on their heads and would stop at nothing to steal and rob anyone of horse, money, or life, if they saw an opportunity. Some order was maintained during these times by patrols of guards that moved through the streets on an hourly tour. Yet with the city being large, the patrols seldom made more than two passes during a watch. The ruffians soon learned this weakness in citizen protection, either by observation or by spies among the guards, and took every advantage of the time between tours of the guards.

Johnathan armed himself with a Roman short sword before we left the house. Because of his rank and placement in the household, he was permitted to carry such a weapon, and was authorized to use it should anyone attack him while fulfilling his appointed task. I was grateful for his armed condition and held my horse close to his; I trusted him with my life.

The press of the crowd was great; many merrymakers, well into the wine, staggered when they walked. The oil lamps and fire brands in the niches of building walls cast eerie shadows on the walls of the houses in the narrow streets. The shadowy figures painted by firelight became giants that moved in grotesque patterns as the night breeze pulled the flames.

The force of the crowd was so great that Johnathan thought it better if he took the lead from my horse and looped it through a waist belt; this way the horses were less apt to be separated. I was in agreement and thankful he had the presence of mind to do this. The trip across the city was much slower than I had experienced while riding in the chariot the day before. As the trip wore on, my admiration of Johnathan increased. Every situation that seemed to be troublesome he was able to avoid; this meant sometimes going around it and at other times meeting it head on. When things became ugly a time or two, he was quick to show he was armed and willing to use the short sword if necessary. It was clear to me why Uncle Benjamin chose him as one of the master servants.

We continued to move through the city; Johnathan changed course several times to avoid riotous mobs roaming the streets. I became totally confused and thought if anything happened to him I would be at the mercy of the crowd, and doubted if I could find my way home even in daylight, let alone in this darkness. We finally broke out of the city proper and climbed upward, moving away from the close movement of the pilgrims and those with evil intent. The way became darker, as little light was supplied along the roads at the edge of the city. Johnathan spoke no word, but moved along the dimly-lit road with confidence. At last, we stopped in front of a massive gate set in a stone wall. Johnathan struck a large cymbal with his sword and two servants stepped from the small niche in the wall.

"Who goes there; who strikes the cymbal at this hour?" called one of the servants. I could see in the light from an oil lamp he carried that he was also armed. "Who would rouse the household of master Lucius?"

"It's Johnathan, the servant of the shipping merchant, Benjamin, and with me is one Judas of Kerioth of Judea. It's his wish to speak with Apuleius." Johnathan spoke with firm tones of one who knows his degree of importance with respect to the other. This was recognized between the servants of masters. "The matter is of some urgency."

"Stand firm, and we will take this message to the house." It was now a matter of waiting for his master to permit entrance. I had never been to the home of Lucius before and had some misgivings about this meeting, but what must be done must be done. I must see Apuleius before morning as this was a matter of great urgency. Every passing hour could lessen Ishmael's chances for life.

As we sat on our horses, we could see the servant carrying the lamp walking to the main house. I was surprised that soon afterward there was a scurrying of people; several came toward us with lamps. One of the figures came faster than the others as his lamp moved about in the breeze caused by his motion.

"Judas, Judas! Friend, is that you?" he shouted and called to his servants, "Open the gates and let these men into the courtyard!" As I entered, he shouted to me, "Judas, what brings you here at this hour?"

The huge gates swung open. Johnathan and I rode into the estate of Lucius, a nobleman and statesman of Rome. Apuleius was happy to see me, this much I knew.

"Apuleius, dear friend, it grieves me to come to you at this hour, but troubles are upon me. I am truly undone." I said no more until the servants were some distance away.

"Judas, what is the trouble that weighs so heavily on you? You've come to the right person, for haven't we shared as brothers nearly all things?" He and I turned to walk up the pathway to the house. "Come, but first meet my family, as they have heard that it was you at the gate. After all I've said, they're anxious to meet the person who saved my life."

"Apuleius, have a caution, I'm not dressed for such a meeting. I'm somewhat distressed and this may be perceived by your family. Can't we postpone this meeting?"

"Nay, I'll not be put aside. Wouldn't you like me to meet your family in any dress and especially in time of trial? Don't be so humble, Judas, you're as a brother to me, and so I'll introduce you. Come, the family is in the great room." With that, he turned to go and gave me no time for further resistance. We left the front hallway and entered into the connecting rooms which led to the great room as he called it. The house was large and magnificent. Well-trimmed lamps placed around the room and hung on the walls gave ample light to each hallway and room. The major part of each room was made of marble. The floors were filled with mosaics of both animals and flowers. I had never seen such a fine home. As we came to the great room, I could see members of his family on comfortable couches. The center of the room was heated by a charcoal burner of large expanse and beautifully wrought from iron and brass. A low table supported dishes of fruit and sweets. Wine goblets were visible, also.

I felt greatly out of place in my common attire, but Apuleius wouldn't be put off. I could feel their careful observation of this man from Judea; I was the one who had so much influence on the son and brother of this family.

Apuleius strode confidently into the room while I followed behind a pace or two. He first stood before his parents, and after saluting them in the style of the Roman household, proceeded to introduce me unto them.

"Father, mother, here is the man who saved my life while nearly ending his own on our voyage to Judea. Without his holding my breastplate, I would have surely perished in the sea. Judas, the man from Kerioth." He moved to one side and I stepped forward. "Judas, my father, Apuleius Lucius and mother, Marcia."

His father nor mother rose from their places on the couches; this was as it should be.

"Judas, the man from Kerioth, we have heard much of you. Our home is yours and our gratefulness can never repay you for saving our son's life. You must ask of us anything you will and we will try to fulfill your request. Join us now as one of the family." The senior Lucius spoke for both parents as Marcia held out her hand in the custom of the day.

"You must tell us of your family and your stay in Rome. We would hear more of the news of the east. Much of what we hear is so controlled by the government we don't know what to believe these days."

"The pleasure of this meeting is hard upon me for I was not intending this to happen. I've not dressed for such an introduction, and can only ask for your indulgence for my appearance at this hour and in this attire. I am humbly your servant and hope for your continued kindly thoughts toward me." With that said, I bowed to the master and found Apuleius moving me along to meet the rest of his family.

First were three sisters, some older than Apuleius, and by the men nearby, I understood they were married. Each was fair to look upon and after seeing Apuleius, I could see this as a family type. The older sister, Julia, was married to Cordus who sat next to her. He was a big man and wore military clothes. The second sister in age was Paulina, a very attractive girl, and unmarried for reasons I couldn't tell as she was also pretty. The youngest sister, Lollia, was the most beautiful of all the girls and had I been younger...

I carefully saluted each one and greeted them with respect. Apuleius had no brothers; he was the only son of Lucius the elder. It was the reason for the great concern of the family when Apuleius left for the Army. On him rested the name of the family. There were others in the room, aunts and uncles of both sides of the house, but I found in my state of concern over Ishmael, I couldn't remember their name even long enough to return greetings when we met later in the evening. I was torn by the need for common courtesy and respect to Apuleius and his family, and my need to speak to him of Ishmael's plight.

After answering questions and exchanging pleasantries, Apuleius excused himself and guided me to a room which held a great many scrolls; it was a fine library. He stated I could tell him of my troubles without fear of interference from family or servants.

"It's Ishmael; his life is in danger if I can't secure help for him," I blurted out, as I struggled to pull our mother's letter from my cloak. I walked to one of the lamps. I proceeded to read the letter, leaving out parts that were not pertaining to the issue of incarceration. "Oh, Apuleius, you are the only one here in all of Rome who can help me. You alone know the circumstances there in Jerusalem, and about the justice by the military general there. Is there anything we can do to secure his release? He's not now nor has he ever been a member of the Zealots, and by no means has he ever contrived to harm the Roman forces in Jerusalem. Ah, Apuleius, I am truly without hope."

"It sounds serious, Judas, this I'll admit, but there is hope. I've known those stationed at the fort to release prisoners on technicalities, but this has only been accomplished by certain amounts of gold given to those in charge, and these supplied under cover of night and through servants who have often been slain to keep the secret of the transfer of the gold. It's possible, but we must be quick; no time can be lost." He turned and walked to and fro while deep in thought. "I'll appeal to father for help through his connections with the Senators, but in the meantime, we must find a way to secure the gold necessary. Have you asked your uncle?"

"Not as yet, but I will ask him forthwith. Can we reach Jerusalem in time to make the transaction before Ishmael comes to trial?"

"If we can secure the gold within a fortnight, I'm sure someone can get it to Jerusalem in time." Apuleius continued to walk up and down. "Your mother says his trial will not be until two months from the date of her letter; this doesn't give us much time, but it can be done. Judas, this makes it imperative that you come to stay here until this is resolved. Please come and stay with us." He was very much concerned about Ishmael as he liked him and understood his sensitivity to things in the world.

"It's with a heavy heart I return home; I'll not sleep well this night. We must be up early and applying our time to this cause. As I return now, may the God of Heaven be with us and may the release of Ishmael be His will." I moved from the lamp light and followed Apuleius into the great room where I proceeded to salute the members of the family and take my leave. Apuleius led me through the hallways to the outside where Johnathan and the horses were waiting.

"Until the morrow, Apuleius, farewell."

"Aye, and Judas, have faith in your God; all is not lost." I thought his statement was different than I had heard from him before, but didn't dwell on it. We turned our horses and headed down the lane and through the gate to the road below. Now, I must confront Uncle Benjamin.

Johnathan slipped a lead from my animal through his waist band and we started through the city. Because our return wasn't so urgent, he chose a different and quieter route. We rode along in silence. He wasn't one to inquire about things outside his confidence. The way he chose was further from the main part of the city, and the crowds were less inclined to be rowdy.

It was well after the second watch when we arrived home. We were greeted at the gate by the servants on watch even as at the house of Lucius. After being recognized at the gate, we entered the courtyard. Johnathan waited for me to dismount and took the reins from me.

"Hold, Johnathan, you have my blessings and thanks for this night. I can see why uncle has placed you over the household. How long have you yet to serve?" I was curious about his life and service to my uncle.

"My time is yet two years, and then, according to the Law of Moses, I shall be free. But I have no unhappiness here, the master has always treated me well. I accept your blessing with a glad heart, but have done nothing above that which I am asked. Should there be anything I can do to serve you again, master Judas, I remain your obedient servant." It was the first time I had heard Johnathan make comments unsolicited.

"May God go with you, Johnathan, and I'll remember your offer of service." I turned and strode into the house and to my room.

I wasn't long in preparing for bed, and after prayers, wherein I asked Almighty God to give me strength to meet the coming trials, I prayed that Ishmael might find favor with God. At last I lay down to rest. The cool breeze came in through the open window, and I wondered what Ishmael was going through this moment. As I thought of these things, my eyelids became heavy and sleep came upon me.

Sleep was not sound and I turned and tossed half awake and half asleep. Dreams came to me about Ishmael as a young boy romping with me on the wall in Kerioth. Even later times when we would talk together of the things we had planned when we became great men of wisdom. Then the dreams changed and I was transported back to Jerusalem. There I saw Ishmael lying in an unkempt cell. He was with many others. His clothes were badly torn and he was untidy. His beard had grown until it was hard to know him as he was never like this. I was greatly distressed at his discomforts.

I moved about the cell, but no one seemed to notice me. Large rats traveled across the floor of the cell; they moved freely into and out of holes in the stone walls. There was little sign of food, and water was in basins by the door. Here the rats would pause to drink.

Ishmael was deep in his prayers; some others were as well, yet others cursed the day they were born. Some turned on those praying and railed out on those whose faith yet called them to ask the Lord for help and blessings. I could hear him ask for blessings on his family - mother, sister, and me. My heart could hardly refrain from crying at his thoughtfulness. Here he was in great discomfort and still thinking of his loved ones. Only after pleading for the blessing of God on all others did he then ask to be relieved of his burden - should it be God's will. It was then I realized how good a man Ishmael really was. I wasn't so sure I would've done the same were I in his sandals.

As I stood in the cell, a light moved through the passageway; it was a lamp carried by the guards. The guards stopped at each cell and took from each some prisoners. On they came, and finally paused at the cell in which Ishmael was confined. The captain of the guards called out names of those who were to be taken from the cell. Each man cowered in his cell, even Ishmael was unwilling to be among those taken out this night. The captain sent men into the cell to bring them out, slammed the door closed, and moved on down the cell block. Ishmael was not one of those taken.

A noise outside my window awoke me. I was perspiring heavily and my breathing was rapid. I turned over and fell asleep again only to find I was yet in the same cell with Ishmael. The time had changed though. Many of those in the cell were now gone; only Ishmael and three others remained. By their conversation, I reasoned they were part of the Zealot group which had caused Ishmael's downfall. It was also evident he held no ill will toward them for his misfortune. He took responsibility for his actions and only asked that God might forgive him for his carelessness of the property given him - his life. For all knew it was a sin to act in such a manner as to lose one's life without just cause. It's a fool who places his life in danger without knowing the outcome of his actions.

As I watched Ishmael move about the cell, pacing first to one end and then to the other, I noticed the coming of the guards again. They moved through the passageways without stopping at any other cells, but came directly to the one that held Ishmael. The captain called for Ishmael to come forward. My heart moved in my chest and I tried to have them see me, but to no avail. I wasn't visible to them; in my dream I wasn't in the party, just watching the event. Ishmael came forward, head high and prepared to meet whatever might come as a man who knows he is innocent of any wrong and at peace with the God of Abraham, Isaac, and Jacob. What was happening? I could follow them only so far and then I couldn't see what was about to happen to Ishmael. I cried out to the Lord, and then I awoke again. It was near morning and I was frightened; the fear for Ishmael was great upon me. What did all this mean? Why was I permitted to see only part of what might happen?

I fell upon my knees once again and asked the Lord to save Ishmael. I then bathed, said my morning prayers, and immediately went to have an audience with my uncle. Upon entering the main room I discovered he had already departed for his conference room. It was there he and the government officials made arrangements for shipping to be processed for the months ahead. There he would attempt to gain the ear of someone who might help secure Ishmael's release. He left without hearing my words about the dream.

I went to the accounting and shipping office. The day did not go well as my thoughts kept wandering to the dream and Ishmael's plight. Would the day never end? At last, I couldn't contain my feelings any longer and went back to my room where I waited for word from Uncle Benjamin.

A NEW CONTRACT

Uncle Benjamin wasn't in conference long after I came home. I heard his voice giving commands to the servants soon afterward. He came directly into the garden to see me. I could tell by his face that all wasn't well.

"Judas, I was unable to secure any direct word of help, and all are of the opinion that it will take a large amount of gold to accomplish this release. As you know, the charge against those arrested is a serious one."

"Aye, uncle, but what is to be done? I cannot see my brother lost for the want of a price." I told him of the dream I had the night before. Neither he nor I could give meaning to it. But I was sure that it revealed the urgency of the matter. "Can't you secure the gold from your business?" It was only the desperation of the moment that caused me to cry out.

"Aye, but to do so will cost me much and may jeopardize the livelihood of this family. Would you ask me to do this, Judas?" He placed the question in such a manner that I would be responsible for the choice between my brother's life and the well being of his family. It was clear he didn't want to make such a decision.

"This isn't a fair question, uncle. How can I deny an opportunity to save Ishmael? I must appeal to you to act even as you would for your brother, my father, were he in the same plight. What must be done to secure the money?" My intentions were clear - I would ask uncle to do this thing. Ishmael's life was of great importance to me, even as Uncle Benjamin's family was to him.

"Judas, I would be willing to secure the money by placing my funds in the hands of those who will give us the gold if, and only if, you will agree to remain here with me and operate the business until the money is once again in balance. Will you do this?" His voice had a curious ring to it. It almost sounded like he was to gain greatly by this tragedy. I was wary of his quick offer to secure the funds if I would stay and operate his shipping business.

"Dear uncle, what is this? How long would this be to recover the amount of gold you might sign for and set the books aright?"

"I can say that if all goes well, your obligation will only be for six more years. And consider this, Judas, all may come to you as I would make you my son." He took down some parchment from the table in the other room and brought it into the garden. He started to write a formal contract for me to sign, binding me for the gold needed for Ishmael.

"Hold uncle, I have yet to talk to Apuleius. I went to see him last evening and his father agreed to see if there was a way to apply pressure from the Senate to gain Ishmael's release." I would hold off signing any contract until I knew if Lucius the elder had brought news, good or ill, from the Senate. "I must go to Apuleius and see what answer is gained by his father; if nothing can be done, I will sign and work for you until the money has been recovered."

Deep in my heart I felt some misgivings at my uncle's offer, but at the same time could realize his concern for this family so far from Jerusalem. Losing a great share of his fortune could mean hardships for his family and putting his business up as security in these times in Rome was indeed risky.

"I beg your leave, uncle, as I must see Apuleius and hear what news his father has for me. It may be that he has had some good fortune in this regard." Saying thus, I left my uncle and once again sought out Johnathan.

It was but a short time until Johnathan and I were on our way to the house of Lucius. The crowds were every bit as unruly, but in the daylight, it was much less trying. With light to our favor, we moved across the city in much less time.

The home of Lucius appeared even more palatial than at night. The high walls and huge gates set the scene for the home that was some distance from the road. All this I couldn't remember for in the dark, the forms took on other dimensions. We stopped at the gate once again and announced our presence as before. It wasn't long before we were riding up the lane to the same spot as just a few hours before. Apuleius was there to greet me. His face showed his concern and gave me the first impression that all was not well.

"How goes it, Judas? Can your uncle gain access to the necessary gold?" His question led me to understand that his father wasn't able to apply any pressure through the Senate. My heart fell and it was reflected in my face.

I dismounted and walked with Apuleius across the porch into the house. Nothing more was said until we reached a spacious garden. Apuleius led the way to a group of stone benches. Here we sat and discussed the happenings since we had parted. I first told him of my dream and how I felt whatever is to be done must be done with haste. Then I told him of Uncle Benjamin's offer to secure the gold and how I would be held to a contract that would keep me from joining him in the return trip to Jerusalem. His face showed the great disappointment and sadness that my uncle would ask such a thing. I then asked him what news his father had brought from the Senate. He told how his father set in conference with several Senators on the subject of the release of a Jew from prison. But all turned a deaf ear; if he were a Roman subject, then the matter was a simple one, but as it was, none wanted to risk disfavor with the commandant of the fort. None would take any action to bring attention unto them. His father was greatly disturbed to find this fear among the Senators, but gained no other person to listen to his cause.

I held my head in my hands. The world seemed to rest on my shoulders even as it was said to rest on the shoulders of Atlas.

"Alas, it's written, I am my brother's keeper. I'll sign to stay with my uncle for the added time if it will afford gold for my cause. I must appeal to you, dear friend, as I have need of a fast horse and trustworthy servant to carry the gold to mother. You alone know to whom and how the gold is placed in the hands of those at Fort Antonia. Do we have such a man, and can we get the gold to Antonia in time?" Apuleius came near and placed his arm across my shoulders in an attempt to comfort me.

"Yes, I know of such a man. He is an expert horseman and can be trusted with all the gold we have, and he will get there in time. All this I guarantee!" His statement was made in such a positive tone that my interest was whet; I lifted my head to look at him.

"And who is this man of quality?"

"Me!" He said this with no gesture at all.

"Are you mad? This can't be, you can't risk your life in this scheme! If something would happen, I would lose two of the most important people in my life - first Ishmael, my only brother and twin, and then you, second only to him. No! There must be someone else we can trust who is nearly as brave and experienced in these matters. You cannot go, dear Apuleius, you have your parents and loved ones to think of as well. On your head rests the family name. You are the only son! No, your offer is a generous and brave one, but not realistic or practical." My mind reeled with the thought of both Ishmael and Apuleius in some difficulty - that would be too much for my heart.

"Stand to, Judas, who am I, some boy who hasn't yet seen outside of his own back gate? Am I not one who has spent more time in combat than both you and Ishmael together? Wouldn't I go any place in this empire if so commanded?" He looked much taller when he spoke thus, and the questions he asked were far from being unreasonable.

"Who has the better right to go; who has more skill and knowledge of Roman law? Ah, Judas, I didn't live among your people completely blind to your teachings. I found many things that are more reasonable in your religion than in all the gods in Rome. But hold, that doesn't mean I follow all the precepts, especially that you are the chosen race of the world. Yet that some are their brothers' keepers and with them rest the duty to aid them when in need is without fault. This I feel toward Ishmael and will follow it to the end. Judas, I don't know who is my brother, for I have none, but some day we may find one who will tell us who is and who isn't, and from that, we'll be able to tell who is. But Judas, all this is for naught if we have no gold!" Apuleius stood before me, legs spread apart and hands on hips. He was the picture of a man asserting his rights.

"You have spoken well. Would that I was such a speaker. Some day I shouldn't wonder you will be a Senator. I can't take away your right to be your brothers' keeper, and it's not for me to say who is or who isn't. I've always considered you one, and would have died that day in the water with you. Should anyone have denied me the opportunity to save you, I would have resisted greatly. I stand as one who is torn between the grinding wheels of pain, as you have feeling for both Ishmael and me. If I suggest that I'm the one with the greater right to go to Ishmael as I am his brother, wouldn't you object?" Apuleius started to comment, but I held up my hand.

"Interrupt me not, Apuleius! Hear me out; see how this is to me. If I should go and fail, and it cost me my life, what have I gained? If I go and succeed, and it cost me not my life, what have I lost? Don't you see, I would sign away six years of freedom to get the gold. Six years here in Rome without you and Ishmael would be an exile my soul couldn't stand. I would be better to give my life for Ishmael than suffer here alone." My voice shook near the end of this comment. I was near overcome by the thoughts of it all.

"Alas, my friend, I can't but feel your great distress, and I, too, would have you by my side in Jerusalem. Yea, all isn't lost. Sign for the money for there's a chance I may be able to get an equal amount from my father at a later date, and with that we can buy your contract and free you and this even before I leave for Jerusalem." His words were like honey to a bear. My heart sang praises to the Lord for such a solution was indeed a favor from Him. It was true every contract must be fulfilled, but it was also true such contracts of servitude could be bought and sold. Once the obligation was met, I was a free man.

"Ah Apuleius, this is good news, for it would please me for such to come about. I'll go first to give my prayers of thanks, and then go to my uncle." I rose in much better spirits and went straightaway to Johnathan and the horses. We mounted, waved to Apuleius, and were on our way.

We traveled across the city and through the crowds. The people were in great spirits again; this was the high day of the festival. As we rode through the city, we came upon a large and boisterous group carrying large drums and cymbals. Just as they came alongside, they struck such a din that my horse bolted, and before I could regain control of the reins, he had his head. He was a powerful animal and I found staying on him was just as important as gaining control. Johnathan saw my plight, but the crowd had closed in around him and he was unable to reach me in time to prevent the runaway. The crowd held him so close that in a short time I had lost sight and sound of him. My horse was in full gallop, and I had no control of his direction. My life was a ride left to the animal and God alone. The horse, having made this trip before, was headed for the stable without fear of life or limb.

A CONTRACT OF DIFFERENT SORTS

I had just about given up ever controlling the animal when from my left side a rider approached, reached down, and caught the loose reins. He pulled the horse to a walk and held him in check until the animal became calm, kept the reins, and didn't offer them to me.

I turned to see who this savior and expert horseman was and discovered it to be the stranger I had met several times before. He was as handsome and tall as I remembered some six years ago during the rescue at sea. What did it all mean?

"Ah Judas, must I save you again from your own folly? When will you learn? Here, follow me!" With that, he gave me the reins and turned up a side street which eventually led to the road that Apuleius took to his point of overview of the city the day or so before. We wound up on the road and then the trail to the very spot Apuleius said he used so often when he was in despair - his temple of rest, so to speak.

The stranger reined his horse and I followed. He made no attempt to dismount. I sat completely overcome at seeing him again after nearly six years. I kept looking at him in an attempt to align his appearance with some land, country, or peoples, but to no avail. His features defied all placement. He looked as one that could fit in many places and times.

While I studied him, he studied the city below. He finally spoke, "It's a beautiful city, but an evil one, Judas. The evil outweighs the good here. The temples are filled with all sorts of ungodly practices. When the gods look down on it from high, even as we do now, do you think they constantly check the balances for good and evil? How far can the scales be tipped toward evil before the god's destroy their own creation?"

He turned slowly and looked at me with some curiosity. "If the gods destroy their own handiwork because man is evil by choice, or does evil things, who then is the loser and who is the winner?"

My mind began searching through the law for an answer to his question, even as I had been taught by Hillel, but even before I had formulated an answer, he held up his hand indicating he expected no answer.

"This isn't for you to answer now, Judas. The time will come when it will be crucial to do so, but not now. I brought you here for other reasons. Isn't it true that you have a problem which is pressing you?"

"Aye, it's my brother, Ishmael. It's his plight that causes me great grief." I let my gaze drop and wondered where this man fit into the scene.

"What manner is his plight, and why the great concern; have you no faith?" A slight trace of a smile crossed his lips. I couldn't tell if it was formed by amusement or scorn.

I told him of the imprisonment and probable death sentence over Ishmael. "We had hoped to bribe the prison officials and thereby gain Ishmael's freedom. Every minute counts, and your holding me here delays the possibility of securing the necessary gold to obtain his release. So sir, if you cannot contribute to the solution of this problem, then let this conversation end and I'll be on my way. My uncle now awaits me to sign a contract to gain the gold necessary to bribe the officials. Time is short and so is my patience!" My trial of the past days gave me strength to speak plainly, even to this imposing figure.

"Hold Judas, give me but a moment of your time, at least the same amount that would have been lost if I hadn't stopped your horse."

The statement made me realize I was indebted to him for his forthright action just a few moments before. My face must have shown my sadness at not recognizing my debt before this; he smiled, indicating he knew my desire to express my lapse of politeness. And with that came the thoughts of Johnathan wandering about the city looking for me.

"Don't wonder about Johnathan, he understands the horse better than you. He will continue on his way to your uncle's and there hope to find you and the horse. And so it will be! But consider it not, for the crowd has him tightly held for awhile yet."

His statements gave me the feeling that he either knew these things were about to happen or he had control of them and would make them happen. Was Johnathan really held fast in the crowd? How would he be so long as to find me at the gate when I am here on the hill? Who is this man, if a man he is?

He maneuvered his horse such that we could face each other; this aided our conversation.

"Judas, isn't it your brother that I saved from the assassins' blades some years ago? It's on his behalf I'm here by your side. I can help you, Judas. That which I did before I can do again! Can't you give an old friend some time? It may be to your advantage and that of your brother, also!"

As he spoke, visions of these events passed through my mind. He had saved Ishmael this I knew. Could he again? "I'm at your service; if you have ought to tell me, speak on. I'm in your debt at least fourfold unto this day." I held the reins tightly now; he sat like a statue.

This man and I were no more than a foot apart; his voice carried well without any strain. "Hear me, your problems are simple to solve, but it won't be without some cost to you. Are you interested?"

"Yes, speak on!"

"I've heard of your difficulty from several sources and have the power to help your brother even as I did many years ago. It will be for your sake I do this, not his. Judas, I've deep respect for you and your faithfulness to your promises before your God. Because of this, I'll accept your hand on any agreement with me. No other contract is necessary. Hear me, this I'll do, Judas. I'll see that Ishmael is released from prison and free of all charges against him this day, even this same hour, if you will give me your word to my conditions." He stopped and waited for me to respond. I couldn't believe he could deliver Ishmael free as he said, but remembered the strange happening in Jerusalem many years ago. Yet, even this hour? He was here and Ishmael was there!

I was like a child. "Tell me, what are these conditions?" Many things went through my mind as I sat waiting for this man to state the conditions. What was his real motive? Was it good or evil in the long run? But would it really matter?

His voice suddenly brought me back to the moment. "All these things I will accomplish for you, Judas, but you must give me your word before your God that you will accept this condition," he hesitated, looking hard at me. His eyes were without mercy in them; whatever the condition, he meant for it to be kept. "You must supply me with thirty pieces of silver - on demand!"

I rocked back on the horse as if someone drunk; I couldn't believe what I heard. Thirty pieces of silver? What did he take me for, someone daft?

"Ha! This is the demand? Are you toying with me? Isn't my brother's life worth more than thirty pieces of silver? I have more than that in gold in my money pouch. I'll give it all to you, yes, even the pouch as well, if that is your demand! There's no need to set my word by the Lord. Here, take my pouch, and all that is therein!"

I quickly untied the pouch and was attempting to hand it to him, when he moved his horse away so the pouch wouldn't touch him. His face grew dark; I suddenly feared I had offended him although that wasn't my intent. I became afraid if he withdrew his offer, then what would happen? I let my arm drop to my side and waited for him to speak again.

"Do you take what I offer so lightly? It's your brother's life which hangs in the balance. I have offered to save him this day. Do you believe I can do this or not? You must decide before we can strike a bargain." He moved closer again; I could see his powerful build. I knew deep from within he wasn't one to trifle with in this matter.

Suddenly, my heart trembled; I didn't know what manner of man he was, good or evil, but decided I must trust him to do that which he said, the small sum not withstanding.

"Accept my request for pardon, sir, as I'm yet overcome by the news of my twin's plight. I accept that you can do as you say. Please say on, I'm your servant."

"Hear me, Judas! This demand isn't for *any* thirty pieces of silver! It's for one and one *only*, and this is the contract - the thirty pieces must come from the treasury of the Sanhedrin in Jerusalem and from no other place, and this on the day I choose." His face showed a strange look of one gaining in strength as my decision was about to be given.

The Sanhedrin - how would I ever get thirty pieces of silver from them? I might as well try to get them from the temple treasury itself.

"How can I refuse such an offer? Isn't there some other thing I can do to assure you of my good intent?" Something just didn't seem right.

"Yes, you must never reveal and forever conceal where or how you came to secure Ishmael's freedom to anyone; the bargain is between you and me. Hear me once again!" He rose as high as he could and looked down on me from his height. "Believe this, that which I do, I can undo! Thus it's given to me! How say you?" He held out his right hand, and I struck his hand with mine in solemn agreement. The instant my hand struck his, I felt a momentary numbness in my hand. It was strange indeed, but soon left and I thought no more of it. Later in life I would remember this sealing of the contract with my right hand.

As our hands struck, the wind began to blow up the mountain side and dark clouds formed quickly, followed by great flashes of lightning. The sky became dark as night. The storm made me lower my head and cover my face with my cloak to avoid its force. My horse became nervous and I reined him hard about to place his hind quarters to the storm. After this, the storm left suddenly, the clouds lightened, and all became quiet. I looked up to assure myself that the stranger had understood my belief in him but neither he nor his horse was in view, nor was the mountain. Instead, my horse moved forward and I found I was approaching my uncle's house some distance from the mountain lookout I had just occupied with the stranger.

What had happened in that brief storm I couldn't say, but there was Johnathan running toward me, shouting his thanks to God for my safe return. It was as the stranger had said!

"Ah, master Judas, may God be praised for your safe return, and will you forgive my negligence, as I knew this might happen. Forgive me, I pray!"

Johnathan was indeed a penitent person, but he wasn't at fault any more than the horse. If there was any fault, it was mine.

When I went to dismount, I found I was extremely tired and somewhat weakened by the ordeal and the concern for Ishmael. "Johnathan, help me to my room and advise my uncle that I cannot see him until I've rested. I'm all undone, Johnathan."

Johnathan helped me to my room; I lay down on the bed fully clothed. Then he left straightaway to tell uncle I had arrived safely but tired and begged time to rest before meeting with him. I said thanks to the Lord and fell into a deep but troubled sleep.

While I slept, I dreamed I was transported again to Jerusalem. I found I was standing once again in the cell with Ishmael. There were still some with him in the cell. Things had grown no better or worse with him. The cell was as filthy as before. While I surveyed this scene, the guards came through the passageways. They again stopped in front of the cell and called Ishmael's name. He strode forward once again. The guards formed about him and they went down the passageway. This time I was able to follow them. He was brought before the commandant of the cell block. Here was read the charges against Ishmael. The captain asked Ishmael how he pleaded, and he answered "Not guilty."

The captain turned toward a tall figure in the shadows and repeated Ishmael's answer. From the tall figure came the command, "Release him!"

The captain grudgingly acted on the command of the half-hidden figure, and the chains were struck from Ishmael. The captain of the guards told Ishmael that as of this day he was free to return to his home. Ishmael turned to thank the person in the darkness and found him gone. Even though I couldn't see him, I knew the stranger had accomplished that which he told me he would. I saw Ishmael leave the prison in the arms of mother. My heart cried out with thanks unto them, but they couldn't hear me.

Before the scene faded completely, the face of the stranger came before me; he was smiling and said with softness, "Remember, Judas, what I do, I can undo. Be not deceived, every word of your bargain is sealed in the heavens. Think not to avoid it." The scene faded and I slept soundly.

It was yet another day when I awoke. I had slept through the rest of that day through the night and even unto the next day. After ablution and morning prayers, I went to the lower rooms where the early morning meal was taken. Here Uncle Benjamin was with his family. After salutations, I joined in the early meal. With the meal over, Uncle Benjamin was anxious to proceed with the plans of the day. He led the way to his study.

"You have slept nearly two full days; I hope you're sufficiently recovered to discuss our arrangements. I've been anxious to get and deliver the gold to you for Ishmael's release. I must have you sign the contract before I can go into the city and secure the loan and gold. Time is short, Judas." While he talked, he walked over to a large table and rummaged through some of the scrolls and papers on it. It almost seemed as though he knew what and where to look, but didn't want to seem too anxious. So for some time, he shuffled papers and other items about. It was during this time that I spoke to him.

"Dear uncle, I've decided not to provide any bribe for Ishmael. The risk is too great!" I spoke with great assurance that he would be interested in this news.

"Judas, how came you to this? There is no risk too great for the life of your brother! It is written, 'You are your brothers' keeper.'" His face changed from the kindly look I was accustomed to unto one of great concern. I couldn't tell whether it was for his own interests or that of Ishmael. He moved to a chair and sat down as one not completely comprehending my statement.

"Hear me. This isn't a time for careless talk. We must make haste if we are to get the gold to Jerusalem."

"It's not idle talk, uncle. Last night I had a dream and in it I was transported to Jerusalem even as in the first one. Yet this time, it was different. This time I was able to see where Ishmael was taken. He stood before the magistrate, and there accused of the crime of treason. But instead of being led to the place of execution, there stood a person I was unable to see clearly, who demanded Ishmael be released. And so it was done. I was permitted to see Ishmael join mother as a free man. I believe this dream is one of good omen. I won't act on this need until I again receive another letter from mother. If the urgency is still upon us, then will I sign the contract." Even as I spoke, his countenance fell. His eyes took on the look of one not only disappointed but as one betrayed. He was at that moment a very unhappy man.

"It's not easy for me to accept this change of heart. I've spent the better part of two days appealing to those who might help us, and yes, even applying pressure on some who didn't want to. I've set up meetings with the wealthy to gain this gold for Ishmael's freedom, and for what? Is this the thanks I receive for this effort? Remember Judas, the second appeal may fall on deaf ears among my friends."

I had never seen my uncle in such a state, but I had enough business experience to understand his words very well. What he said was true, the next time, if there was one… that was the key. If I believed this to be remotely possible, then I would take the offer and store the gold until needed; that would only be common sense. But the trouble was, I believed implicitly in this stranger's word and my dream. In essence, to believe and do otherwise would violate the contract made to the stranger, and this I couldn't consider as his warning still held me captive, "…that which I do, I can undo."

His hands shook until the contract he held was nearly destroyed. He didn't wait for my answers to his questions but left the room immediately. I stood for some time contemplating the strange turn of events, yet knowing I had made the right decision.

It was while standing there I thought of Apuleius. I suddenly remembered he was still without notice of these things; here I had slept away nearly two days. I had to let him know as soon as possible. I also had to fulfill my contract and that meant to the counting house for the day. I called Johnathan to me and told him to take a message to Apuleius.

Johnathan was mounted and away before I left for work. I was sure of my decision with respect to Ishmael's plight, and moved along the streets of Rome to the shipping lanes and counting houses. The day wore on slowly. All the operations which were once interesting were now just labor. My thoughts kept wandering to the meeting this evening with Apuleius. What would be the best way to break the news to him about not attempting to get money to Jerusalem? I must have written the same ship's manifests several times before I was satisfied that all was in order. Everything seemed to move as in a dream.

At last, the final ship was loaded and sailed on its way to some distant port; all the documents needed for our records were sealed and safely sent to the port authorities. My day was closing.

I started my usual walk through the city toward home. I hoped Apuleius would find me before I reached the house. I would like to talk to him before another discussion with my uncle. I reasoned that Apuleius knew my route well enough to find me at this hour. If this didn't happen because Apuleius hadn't received my message, then I would go home and have Johnathan get a horse ready for me. All this was being turned over in my mind when I heard someone calling my name.

"Judas, can't you hear me?" It was Apuleius. He was astride a horse and leading another. "Here, climb aboard and we will ride to the lookout point."

I mounted the animal and we were off in the direction of the lookout. We rode at an easy pace, and neither of us made any remark. The weather was pleasant and the ride restful. We arrived at our destination, dismounted, and moved to the outer edge of the rock to get the best view of the city and port.

"So Judas, you're a day late. I waited a full day, not knowing whether you would come with the gold. Have you succeeded in securing the gold, and if so, when shall I start for Jerusalem?" He hadn't turned to look at me during this part of our conversation.

"Ah, Apuleius, things were revealed to me that force a change in plans. Some of these I cannot reveal, but would have you believe as I do that all is well with Ishmael!"

He became interested and changed position so he could look at me without giving up the view of the city below. He said nothing but his eyes were alert to any change that might show in my face.

"You remember me telling you of the dream about Ishmael where I could sense the urgency of the matter? How I witnessed Ishmael being taken from his cell to another place? And that I wasn't able to see where or for what end this was? Do you remember this?"

He followed my story and shook his head in the affirmative but remained silent on the matter.

"Well, when I left you two days ago I headed for home. While crossing the city, a large crowd of minstrels passed beside us, and my horse bolted. I wasn't prepared for this and lost control of the animal. He galloped through the city with me hanging on for dear life. When he at last became quiet, I found I was home." I was careful not to tell of the meeting with the stranger in accordance with his admonition. Yet I remained determined I would tell all to Apuleius someday. I continued, "Johnathan was unable to help me because of the press of the crowd, but knowing the horse would return to the stable, took a shorter route and met me at the gate. It was there I found the excitement of the runaway had completely exhausted me. I then went to rest and didn't wake up until this very morning."

"It was during this exhausted sleep that I had another dream about Ishmael. I dreamed I was once again in his cell. The guards came and took him away again, but this time I was able to follow. They took him to the commandant of the cell block who asked how he pleaded to a set of charges just read. Ishmael pleaded not guilty. It was then a stranger, standing in the background and with his back to the group and me, demanded that Ishmael be released. The commandant showed his dislike for the decision but the chains were struck and Ishmael set free. All this I saw in my dream, and even this also: I saw Ishmael leave the prison and fall into the arms of mother a free man! Apuleius, I truly believe that Ishmael is even now a free man and that the next letter will tell me this. My heart is full of thanks to God for all things done on his behalf. Can't you believe as I do, that we don't need to pay any bribe?"

He lowered his eyes that I might not read his thoughts. "Judas, I'm not one given to dreams and visions. I've little understanding of them or their place in our waking hours. From your ancient writings, it's been one way your God gave your people glimpses of the future - or so it's claimed. Who am I to cast dispersions on what your dream may tell you? But I've reservations on these matters. Mine are one of a soldier, not a priest. In matters of war, the future often lies in the hands of the enemy and not the gods. I hold your brother is as precious to you as anyone on this earth, and therefore abide by your decision to wait until you hear again from Jerusalem. I follow you in the matter, Judas, and will ever believe as you would wish. But have you approached your uncle about changing your abode?"

"Thank you for your trust in what I must do. There is no indication of faith born out of misgivings. I cannot say at one time that I believe in my dream and in the next, set out to secure gold for the rescue. Either I believe and live by it or I don't. There can be no in-between. As to the possibility of joining you at your father's house, I've spoken about it but Uncle Benjamin wasn't very receptive.

"Yet, I must tell you he has acted very oddly upon hearing the news that I wouldn't sign the contract to secure the gold. I couldn't tell if it was because of the feelings he had for Ishmael, or the possibility of having me under contract for another six years. But this I know, I'm willing to move whenever you supply servants to bring my belongings thither." I went on to describe my uncle's reactions to the news of that morning, and how he became so agitated and left the room without giving me the honored salute of all good families.

We mounted and discussed the coming move and what could be done with our time after the move. We rode to Uncle Benjamin's house where I dismounted and Apuleius gave a salute and wheeled the horses about and left. I watched him pass through the gate and then I turned to go into the house.

Uncle Benjamin met me at the garden entrance. The garden was a place I found most restful, and often went there to say my prayers of thanksgiving to the Lord of Hosts. Uncle Benjamin knew this was my habit, and was seated under one of the trees there. He greeted me and I saluted him as I always had; we passed pleasantries. I wanted to leave and have a moment to myself and therein thank God for saving Ishmael, but uncle, by his action, wanted to speak of other things.

"Judas, have you considered the need for continuing the search for gold to aid Ishmael, or have you placed all your hopes on a dream?"

"Dear uncle, even as Jacob had faith in his dream, and Joseph in his, so I also have in mine. Ishmael is released at this very moment. Can it be that you would doubt the word of Joseph and Jacob? It's odd we can accept the words of scriptures about the dreams of others not even known to us, and yet reject those so near and dear." Once started, I couldn't contain the feelings that raised from his opening statements. "What would you have me do, destroy the faith in my dream by building wealth to save a man no longer in need of such help? Isn't this a sin to reject the revealed word?"

He sat for some time; he was a shrewd man with a great sense for business. He knew he had found favor with the Lord since I joined him. His wealth had increased some measure and there was a great possibility it would continue as long as I remained his servant.

The thoughts of my leaving weren't pleasing to him, and I began to see his real motives in this case was not necessarily that I sign the contract to save Ishmael, but to stay on for six more years. This I had decided not to do - Jerusalem called too strongly.

"Judas, you have but four more years and then you will be free of all encumbrances placed on you by your stay in my house. Yet, I would that you might find it in your heart to stay awhile longer. It would please me a great deal to have you as one of the family. If this isn't to be, then accept my blessings and return as you will. Your words about your dream are well chosen and I have no right to suggest your actions are improper. Consider the words never spoken, and sup with us once more."

"I'm pleased you have accepted my decision, and will join you this evening. But I am moving to the house of Lucius yet this week. It's there I will remain until I go to Jerusalem." He realized I wouldn't be moved from my intent and silently made motions of his understanding.

"God go with you, Judas, and may your decision be one that you never regret." He turned and went into the house to prepare for the evening. We spoke no more of the letters, dreams, or of my decision. I left the house that week and took up residence with Apuleius.

CHAPTER ELEVEN

Letters From Home

I continued my service to Uncle Benjamin for the rest of that year and the following three years while residing at the house of Lucius the elder. I went to visit my uncle on all the sacred holidays and feast days.

During the first few weeks of my stay with Apuleius, a letter came from mother; it was carried from my uncle by Johnathan. It was the first communiqué I received since my decision not to secure money for the bribe. When I received it, I called to Apuleius, and we went into the garden where I read the letter in his presence.

It opened with the usual greetings, "Dear son," and followed with asking the blessing of God on me and Apuleius. After the opening lines, she told of the miracle which had taken place and the date to the day of my meeting with the stranger. It was in this wise:

> "Ishmael is free, dear Judas! Free of all charges! Those with him haven't fared so well as they have been taken away even to Rome or some other province to be sold as slaves. Would that you could find them and secure them as your servants? Remember, it's written, 'let not thy brother be a bondsman unto the stranger, and turn not aside, as thou art thy brothers' keeper.' Ishmael was brought from his cell on the day before the Sabbath and presented with the charges against him. The commandant of the prison asked him how he pleaded. Ishmael replied not guilty. The commandant was about to send him with the others for sale into slavery, when a stranger spoke unto him. His words were simply, 'Release him.' And so Ishmael's chains were struck from him and he was released that same hour. I was informed that he would be released through a dream I had the night before and, believing this to be a token, went unto the prison to greet him whereby he was released unto me. We've been singing praises unto the Lord and will remember this day forever."

"So it is and so it always has been, Apuleius. The things of this world aren't as they seem. What say you now about my dreams?"

"It's exceedingly strange, that I must admit, but as far as it being more than this, I must reserve unto myself. In any case, you should thank your God that all has turned out well with Ishmael. And I'm one that will send a tribute to Mars for the good fortune you have been granted. How is it, Judas, that you can tell it was the grace of your God Jehovah, and not the grace of another?" He was happy for me and Ishmael. He smiled at his own comment about the gods. I, on the other hand, was horrified.

"Apuleius, don't say such things! I fear for you! Your question makes no sense; there is no God other than Yahweh! This is written in every man's heart whether he knows it or not. Even yours, Apuleius, and someday there will come to you this revelation. This I'm certain and pray continually for you. My concern for you lies heavy on my heart." I spoke to him as never before, always afraid of placing a barrier between us that could not be overcome. Even this faded away and I spoke to him about this belief in the gods of the day.

"Hear me, I will never press you about this thing for I know yours is a different culture, but I will and in fact must answer all questions about our traditions, so Apuleius, find no fault in me for this."

After studying me for sometime, Apuleius said, "I find no fault in your views, and I have always wanted to know more of your people and their God. I have a great amount of Roman and Greek history to compare with your teachings. Things that are known to me will someday be stumbling blocks even to you. It may be that I will come to your Yahweh better than you think, and fear him as much or more than you. Till then, listen with an attentive ear." I was happy he hadn't seen my chiding him as offensive.

"I must leave now, as I must read this to uncle so that he will restore me unto his bosom. He has felt somewhat distrustful of my decision not to attempt to rescue Ishmael. I will return soon and we can plan for the day." With that, I saluted him and left. Outside I found Johnathan waiting although he had given no previous sign he would do so.

At a sign from me, a servant brought a horse. I mounted and joined Johnathan in the ride to my uncle's house. We rode side by side in silence. Johnathan wasn't one given to many words, and carried his opinions to himself well. Neither was he a gossip, and what he overheard in the household was held in strict confidence. He finally broke the silence as we moved away from the crowded part of the city.

"Master Judas, is it true that you are going to Jerusalem soon?" I knew he overheard my discussion of such a possibility with Apuleius.

"Yes, Johnathan, it's my intention to return home as soon as my contract is fulfilled. My heart still lies in the land of Judea, and the call to see my family is still hard upon me. But why do you ask?"

"Forgive my impertinence, master, but I stay at your uncle's house because I have no other place to go, and for me, there was no place other than Rome until you and Ishmael came. As I heard of the things of the east, I came to want to see such places." He held his horse in a slow walk as he talked. "Will you take me with you when you leave?"

"Aye, Johnathan, but I'm not one who has anything to offer a man of your skill. I would be glad to have you accompany me to Jerusalem, but can only offer you guidance there, and you would have to make your own way."

"Ah, it's good, I wouldn't burden you, but would serve you willingly to gain the chance to see the holy city."

"It's settled then. I'll speak with Apuleius, and if he has no objections, you will join us." He expressed happiness at my comment with increased speed of his mount. It wasn't long before we reached the gates and I turned the animals over to Johnathan for care. Shortly afterward, I stood before Uncle Benjamin in his study.

"Greetings uncle, may the Lord be with you this day." He sat in his great chair. He returned the salute without looking up from his books.

"Uncle, this day Johnathan brought me word from mother. It's part of her message that I would share with you." I took out the letter and proceeded to carefully unroll the weather-beaten covering. "She sent word Ishmael is safe and has been released from prison even as I dreamed so many nights ago. These are her words, '…Ishmael is free of all charges, dear Judas. Those with him have not fared so well, for they have been taken away unto Rome as slaves, or to be sold as slaves elsewhere. Would you find them and secure them as your servants…' And so it was as the dream had its meaning. Ishmael is now free even as my dream foretold. God has been with us and even as Joseph had his dream, so I have had mine."

Uncle Benjamin's face showed his relief as he was really fond of Ishmael.

"It's a blessing for which we all must give thanks, Judas." He struck his breast as a sign of one truly repentant of any thoughts to the contrary. "But Judas, how goes it with your new friends and family? Will you remain with Apuleius even as you have said?"

"Aye, so it is my intention. But uncle, don't think harshly of me. I'm still indebted to you and wouldn't do other than fulfill my obligations. The high holy days I will always spend here with you but be gone when the contract is completed. It is off to Judea and there to see mother and Ishmael."

"God go with you then and come to me when you can. This house is yours as ever." We then moved to the garden and talked of many things of the shipping trade and home. The time moved without either of us noticing it and soon it was time for the evening meal. I left after the sun began to set and had Johnathan bring my horse from the stable. I mounted and turned toward the home of Apuleius.

I spent many pleasant hours after that with Apuleius and his family. The remaining years on the contract to my uncle passed swiftly and without incident. In fact, the four years were so filled with new adventures in and about Rome that I didn't spend all the high holy days with my uncle at all, but those I did were kind in nature and remembered unto this day.

Under the tutelage of Apuleius, I became a good horseman, and although it wasn't my nature, I learned the art of the sword and shield. Many of the tools and actions of war became known to me. I began to see, from early on, why and how the Roman legions were able to control so much of the world. The officers and young men in the legion were dedicated, and even though some elements were corrupt, the heart of the army was well trained, confident, hardened, and willing to conquer. The more I saw of the awesome power of the legions, the more I felt the Jewish nation was never to leave its rule. Each prayer hour, I began to pray for guidance and a way to instill acceptance of the rule of the Romans, for the will of God was yet to be done.

As time moved on, Apuleius and I became closer and closer, until we were nearly as inseparable as Ishmael and I had been some years ago. I went with Apuleius to receptions, weddings, royal court proceedings, military reviews, and yes, some religious rituals. Through all this, I had the opportunity to become more familiar with several languages.

I found during these times that Apuleius couldn't resist calls of the sick and injured. Sometimes the wealthy and sometimes the poor; it made no difference to Apuleius. All who were ill or injured were patients. He was a caring person who was willing to extend himself to see all was done for each patient. Sometimes this meant sleepless nights and tiring days of service for no compensation other than knowing he had done his best.

On many of these calls to relieve suffering I accompanied Apuleius. From these, I began to learn the Greek names of the human anatomy and the tools used by him for remedy of human ailments.

I learned he had a quick mind and spent no small amount of time going over what medical texts he could find in the libraries of Rome. He had a keen sense of curiosity and I often found we traveled miles, yes, even days, to places where new cures were heard to have happened. It wasn't uncommon for him to wake me in the wee hours of the night and ask if I wanted to accompany him to some part of the back country in hopes of finding a new cure for some illness that puzzled him.

It was a compelling force for him. Even the cures claimed by the priests of the day were often part of his curiosity. His key words of life in the medical profession were what, where, when, how, and why. He carried a small tablet on which he kept notes of medical events he saw. The book contained not only the successes but also the failures of medical treatments. It was in his book that he kept those histories of recoveries he considered valid medical cures, and those he considered rare happenings wherein the patient wasn't really ill but claimed the gods had cured him. His faith in the healings by the priests was weak, and their applications of incantations, prayers, and potions nearly always suspect. When he heard of a healing through the touching of the springs from the mountains, or of the burning of incense to the gods, he became highly suspicious. Often he found the illness was brought on by a sudden need for gold by the cured patient. Gold which the priests paid to the patient to fain illness. Each of these patients played their part to deceive the untrained eye. Every time he discovered this shill game, he lost more and more faith with the religions of the day.

"I would go a long way just to learn a new method or potion to cure some illness; just to bring relief to those who suffer is a reward in itself. But Judas, what sort of man are these who use their religion to deceive the sick and take their money as well? Are they not the greater enemy to man than those who carry the sword?" He was sincere in his remarks.

"Aye, but isn't it a thin line between the good life offered by the religions of Rome and the wholesome body pledged by the men of medicine? And what are those ill to do when medicine fails? It's normal for man to move from the natural to the supernatural when belief in the natural gains naught. Is this not so?"

He failed to answer, but remained attentive.

"It isn't that man does this in error, just that he addresses the wrong god for help. There will be a day, dear friend, when you will accept what I say as the truth, even for you."

"Ah, you and your eastern religion. If your god is so powerful, why are the Jews under the heel of the Romans? Could it be you have been appealing to the wrong god as well?" He smiled for he knew my concern for his way of life and his distance from all forms of religious thought.

"It's not for me to question the power of God. Who am I to be able to know such things? Wouldn't any god be small indeed if man could know his power and turn of mind? As to the position of our people under the Romans, it's for us to bear, as we know the sins of the fathers are often visited on the sons. This I'll say and no more - mark me, Apuleius, Yahweh will permit Rome to hold his people as subjects only so long as it fits his will. When this time passes, nothing will hold them captive, no, not even the invincible legions."

"Ha, I see I have touched a tender spot - forgive me, I have nearly overstepped the bounds of our friendship. I didn't intend you any hurt. It's the frustrations of the day which have me unhappy. I've no right to hold your people's hardships over you. Come, let's discuss our coming trip to Judea." And with that, the talk between us turned to pleasant thoughts of Judea.

I completed my obligation to Uncle Benjamin in the year 776, but remained in the household of Lucius as a guest until 780. Those four years passed so rapidly that neither Apuleius nor I remembered our solemn resolve to return to Judea. Even Apuleius had to be reminded that his commission in the legion still was in effect. It seemed sometimes that the powers that be set aside his calling date time and time again.

It wasn't until 780 that a call for doctors for the army of the east included his name, rank, and unit. Even then he was given the option of serving in Judea as before or taking some new assignment elsewhere in the Empire. His decision to return to Fort Antonia wasn't news to me, although it was pleasing to know his intentions hadn't changed.

During the four years I was a guest at the household of Lucius the elder, I became more and more like the Romans. After I left the services of Uncle Benjamin, I paid less and less attention to the formal attire of the east, and took on the dress of the Romans. The clothing was very comfortable and allowed one to show rank. The family of Apuleius provided me with all I needed and more. From the funds I earned and invested in other ventures, and some care in managing them, I was able to increase my wealth and still live without being a burden on the Lucius household. In fact, to speak in earnest, I provided some valuable household commodities to the family.

Even as early as the first year at the household, the family soon found I had expertise in managing funds. It was in that year the senior Lucius gave me control of nearly all the family assets. By the time we decided to leave Rome, I had successfully increased the wealth of the Lucius family two-fold. Of course, I was amply compensated for this work and held in high esteem by all.

THE NEXT PROCURATOR

Apuleius and I talked of the changes I had seen over the years from 766 to 772; the death of Augustus and installation of Tiberius at the age of 56, and of his changes and the dislike of the people for some of them. In five years, the mood had changed from a conquering nation to one of peace. The people were better off than before but were still complaining. For us, it was a good time after 772, and we went everywhere - to the games and banquets of all those in power. I saw the mighty power of the Roman legions when fully assembled for festival days and on the birthday of the emperor. I visited the ancient Roman ruins and heard all the historic songs of the people. It was a time of learning.

During these times of 772 to 780, a strange event happened that affected my life. It happened in this wise. Because of a returning conquering hero and the change of the prefect over Judea, all Jews were affected. The returning hero was the young nephew of Tiberius, one Germanicus. Now the word was that Tiberius really liked the young leader of his armies in the north, but at the same time, like those before him, feared well-liked generals.

Because of the power and wealth of Lucius the elder and because he was a Senator of good standing, he and the members of his family were expected to attend many of the celebrations of the court. Yet there were so many the old man often begged to be excused from one or the other and sent Apuleius to represent his family. I, being a close friend, was often invited, if not directly, then indirectly as a confidant of Apuleius. It was on one of these occasions while with Apuleius, I was fortunate to see the leaders of the troops from the wars of the Black Forest - the German wars they called them. The honor was for young Germanicus and several of the generals and lesser leaders of the armies. The celebration, although tiring for old Tiberius, was attended by him to avoid the ill will of the people.

So it was that Apuleius and I were present at the great court celebration for the return of young Germanicus, a favorite of his troops. If one thing disturbed the ruling Caesar's in the history of Rome, it was the great influence a heroic general had over seasoned troops.

As so often happened, the power of the armies vested in the general rights to the throne. Each Caesar felt the need to honor a victorious general, but at the same time, feared his power over the army. Hence, it was to their advantage to see these men of valor were honored, paid their gold, and then sent to areas outside of Rome as soon as possible.

Now Germanicus, so it was said, wanted to continue his battles with the Germans and present to Tiberius and the people of Rome victory, spoils, and slaves. But Tiberius felt it better not to spread the lines too thin, and therefore recalled Germanicus. And so honor it was for young Germanicus. This was his week of honor before Caesar found another post for him in the empire.

For several weeks, great parties were held for him and the people were delighted. Tiberius, although nearly sixty-one and tired of the pressures of governing, gave the impression that he was well pleased with it all.

It was at this party I saw the great Tiberius, and with him the trusted Prefect of the Praetorian Guard, Sejanus. Even at a distance I took an immediate dislike for the man. He reminded me of Herod in looks and actions. He was ever near Tiberius, and often spoke for him. I believed he took on himself more than was necessary for his title.

I also saw the young hero, Germanicus, and some of his trusted lieutenants. Two of these were head and shoulders above the rest. One was an olive-skinned Centurion who walked with authority among the others. He remained aloof to the entertainment and studied Tiberius with great interest. I noticed there was more than just a passing interest between Sejanus and him.

He was slightly taller than most, was powerfully built, and walked with the grace of one born in a foreign court. And so it was, as his name was Pontius Pilate Telesinus, a Spaniard by birth, whose parents were of near nobility and of the clan Telesinus. His parents were of good background, but hardly of the high court, though it was said he was a direct descendant of Pontius Telesinus, the great Sammite general. He was handsome with a clean-shaven face, and his eyes were a flashing dark brown, almost black. He was an exceedingly good soldier, or so it was said throughout the court. Many stories of his valor, true or not, bought or not, preceded him to the court and they wanted to see this winner of hearts and battles. It was rumored that he was the one to watch as he was ambitious.

It wasn't hard to recognize him in the crowd and I marked him well as one not to cross. He had the look of one who knew the full extent of his authority and was willing to use it for his own benefit without regard to Rome.

With him was another Centurion whom I didn't recognize. The two were very close and often whispered to one another during the celebration. I asked Apuleius who this second Centurion was; he replied that he knew him only as an equal to Pontius Pilate in rank, had seen many battles with Germanicus, and was thought to be of good family here in Rome. Apuleius said his name was Publius Cornelius Minor. He was physically much different from Pilate. He was nearly blonde with the striking blue eyes like those clans of the north. It was whispered he was the better tactician of the two, but was less ambitious and more studious, with a better feel for justice. As I watched both, I had the feeling that of the two, P. Cornelius was the better in dealing with people. The more I watched Cornelius, the more I had the feeling I would meet him again, or hear of his exploits among our people in Judea. Why this feeling was so recognizable I wouldn't know until much later in life.

Both men moved about the court with ease, and were assigned couches near Germanicus. The byplay between old Tiberius, Germanicus, and the evil-looking Sejanus was friendly, but behind the words of each lay some hidden meaning not clearly recognizable as either threats or honors. Each was vying for position with respect to the many leaders and Senators in the court. The party went well with entertainers, musicians, and dancers from all over the empire displaying their talents.

Wine and good food was abundant and slaves from the far corners of the empire served the guests. Here and there I saw the good souls of Jews in bondage carrying food, preparing special dishes for their masters, and being treated with kindness for the most part. It caused my heart to bleed, seeing my brothers in bondage. Yet my thoughts went back to all those not faring as well outside the Dung Gate in Jerusalem. Yes, in our own country and under Herod, some had less than these slaves.

I followed Apuleius in paying respects to General Germanicus, as was the custom for the elite families of Rome to do. I wore none of my Jewish jewelry and, save for my beard and hair style, none knew I was from the house of Israel.

It was rumored some weeks later, after the celebration, that polite pressure was brought by Sejanus on Tiberius to have Germanicus sent elsewhere. Sejanus, it was whispered, had his eye on the throne and feared Germanicus even more than Tiberius. Now Tiberius was an old man, and beginning to lean on Sejanus more and more. Tiberius was disenchanted with the pains of governing and spoke of retiring to Caperea. It was this Sejanus saw as a great opportunity to gradually move from Prefect of the Praetorian Guards to the throne. One thing was sure, this young and well-liked General of the Armies, Germanicus, must be gone from the scene. So it was written and so it was done. A writ was presented to Tiberius to send Germanicus to the east and he signed it. The people were unhappy with the decision and petitioned the Senate to do something about this unfair act, but many were already under the influence of Sejanus and refused to stand and be counted.

Germanicus, the young, bold, victorious nephew of Tiberius, was given a new assignment in the east, some said Alexandria, that same year - 772. It was with great sadness that the people heard Germanicus fell ill while there and died. Rumors flew like wildfire that he had been poisoned at the hand of followers of Sejanus. Because of his strange death, Tiberius feared the Senate and the people, and held a high ceremony honoring Germanicus. The funeral was imposing with Tiberius being the loudest in lamenting his loss. Strangely enough, Sejanus wasn't present and some said it was his hand which caused the deed.

It was Sejanus who spoke of the poisoner as one Cnaeus Piso, an appointee of Tiberius in Asia Minor, but held the line that Germanicus was already plotting against Tiberius. No one came to know the truth of the matter as Piso committed suicide to save himself and his family a cruel death. It was through Sejanus that the Senate was held at bay and the people without recourse.

Sometime after these happenings, it was learned of Pilate's wooing Claudia, the Emperor's stepdaughter, and later still, that Pilate became the husband of Claudia. Tiberius, at the suggestion of Sejanus, gave Pilate the position of Procurator of Judea as a wedding present. So Valerius Gratus was recalled and Pilate was scheduled to take his place.

The year of Pilate's move to Jerusalem was to be 778 or 779 at his choice.

A CALL HOME

The life at the house of Lucius the elder was a new experience for me. I was for a time the center of attention. But this soon passed as I adjusted to Roman customs and spent time studying the history and customs of these people. Whenever possible, I would wear Roman dress to make the others feel more at ease.

I even studied some of their religions. Ever remembering the words of the prophets, "Take heed to thyself that thou be not snared by following them." I studied the gods of the Greeks and Romans and how the people worshiped them - the creations of man. My prayers of thanks went to the Lord for saving me from such sins.

After a morning of such study, I heard Lucius say, "What's this I hear, Judas? Have I been deceived by your manner; I thought you were one of us, and now I hear you and Apuleius are planning to leave? What has been said to cause such a change in plans?"

Although his mood seemed lighthearted, I knew he was against the move. It was no secret that he had used his influence to keep Apuleius home these last few years, even though he knew there would be a time when Apuleius would have to report.

"Ah, don't think me ungrateful, Lucius, for this isn't so, but we both recognize the call of the army. It's this that has finally brought the action you now address. As you know, I have ever wanted to return to Judea to be once again be with my loved ones. This cannot be seen as a whim, as all have the longing to see family and friends of the past. Your acceptance of me has been a boon to my heart, and if it were not for family and friends in Jerusalem, I would remain in Rome. Rome has been good to me and time has moved by rapidly. It's now 779, and I have been in Rome longer than I planned by four years."

"Just how long has it been?"

"The first time here was 760 through 765, that was five years, and the second time was from 766 to the present - 779, nearly eighteen years of my adult life has been lived in Rome. Just to think, I'm 43 years old."

"It's a long time to be away from loved ones, Judas, and I'm sure they await your homecoming with great desire. Your presence in our household has been pleasant for us as well. I'll watch you leave with great sadness, yet with the hope you will find all well in Jerusalem. I want you to consider my house as a place of refuge should such ever be needed. And if you should ever tire of the old city, remember us here in Rome. May the gods provide you with good winds for your trip home. And Judas, keep a watchful eye on Apuleius for an old man who loves his only son."

His eyes filled with tears as he spoke in a trembling voice. I felt his deep emotion as Apuleius was his only son, and this could be the last time they would be together.

"Your request will be foremost in my mind, Lucius. Apuleius is as dear to me as Ishmael." I found my own voice unsteady as I continued. Lucius had always been kind to me; he was a man of sensitivity and graciousness. "I find this coming departure from your household trying also, good Lucius, but the call of home lays hard against me."

With that I took my leave from him. It was a short walk to my room in this magnificent house. As I entered the hall leading to my room, a servant stepped forward, saluted and handed me letters from Judea. He indicated they had just arrived by ship. I took the letters and entered my room. I stepped near the window to get better light. Eager fingers tore off the weatherproof cover.

These were letters from mother. Ah, what would a lonely man far from home do without an understanding and faithful mother? She had never failed me. And here again was the latest as she saw and heard it in Jerusalem.

"Dear Judas, It has been nearly a year since I received any news from you in Rome…" My thoughts drifted off and I began to reflect on the previous letters from home. Could it have been that long since I wrote a letter?

It's not that I didn't have good intentions. I reviewed the past happenings as written by mother in Jerusalem. Ishmael had been released from prison some years before, in 771 or was it 772, and he settled down to his arts. He took up making unique pottery for the market with some of the Roman clientele of mother's beauty circle. She had written how well his work was done, and how much more he was paid for his creations than others in the city. How he longed to see me. In the following years, she often spoke of Anath and her children, nieces and nephews still not seen by me. How happy Anath was and how well off her family was; she had married well.

Throughout the several years from 771 until 779, she often wrote of these things. Only rarely did she write of her health. And only through Ishmael's occasional letters, I knew she wasn't as well as in days gone by.

My mind returned from the wandering and I remembered the letter still in my hand.

"Why haven't you written? We long for news from you and the politics of Rome." Aha, that was mother. She was always interested in the political picture, especially as it might affect our people. She never lost her interest in local politics as well. All were the same to her, the things that happened in Rome were important to the people in Judea. "When you write, you must include the latest about the changes in power there. It's to our advantage to know who is to be sent here as we know from our sources Valerius Gratus is to be replaced. The big question is by whom? We need someone who is just and sensitive to our causes."

It suddenly came to me that I knew little of Valerius as I had been in Rome most of his rule. And now mother wrote he was to be replaced soon.

I knew who would replace him! It was all over Rome. A younger man, Pontius Pilate, was being prepared for the task of overseeing Judea, and more especially, Jerusalem. A man some said was strong-willed and confident, a man fresh from the wars who could bring some order to the old city if anyone could, while others openly expressed the feelings that he wasn't the man for the position as he was any man's dog. He was one who was willing to change attitudes and loyalties on political issues if the price was right.

I knew that Valerius Gratus was to be recalled, or so it was rumored among the Senators. And from the night of honor at the return of Germanicus, I knew Pontius Pilate Telesinus. I knew him by reputation and person as well, but with mother's letter came the realization that I might come to know him better as time went by. It was easy to recognize I would be under his authority in Jerusalem when I returned.

Things aren't different now, Judas, times haven't improved the political climate between the Romans and the Zealots. The number of small skirmishes have increased. If it's God's will, may peace reign until a deliverer is sent to us. There are those who teach the time is nigh for the deliverer to come. Many are wondering just what it all means.

Many itinerant teachers now travel about the country calling to the people to repent and cry to God for this strong arm to lift the yoke from their shoulders. One such self-styled teacher is Zechariah's son, John. He has left the fold of his father's house and even now travels about crying for people to repent of their sins. I haven't seen him for nearly two years, but have heard from friends he has a moderate following. He moves about from the Jordan to the desert.

He claims he has received a commission from God that he is to prepare the way for one who will indeed be the Messiah. It's said that he really believes the deliverer will be the Son of the living God. Yet he never says who this person will be, but it's thought among his followers he knows the selected one. It's told that many of his faithful have called him aside and asked him to reveal who the deliverer is, but he merely says God will make it known in due time.

Some think he's mad or possessed, while others hold he is one truly touched by the hand of God. None dares to call for his censor for if he is mad or possessed, then it's a matter for the Sanhedrin, and if he's blessed and filled with the Spirit of God, who can stand against him? He stands well within the law and speaks even as the prophets of old. He demands ablution from all his followers; all that believe his message are washed in the water. All must wash where water is sufficient to cover them from head to foot in flowing water. If there isn't sufficient water to do such, then they must go where there is. It's to the Jordan for most as he doesn't wash in still water. Judas, this strange washing of each of his followers marks them from the others. They are sometimes referred to as the washers.

He calls for harsh training by his following and presents the view that God wishes all to follow strict mortification of the flesh. His followers are a motley crowd, consisting of rich men as well as beggars. Their dress is a mark of distinction as well, as they wear the simplest of clothing, often sackcloth and rough skins. These they hold about them with simple leather belts or flaxen ropes. When not barefoot, they wear sandals. Most are very thin and many are sickly. Because of his promises of a coming Messiah, the poor and sick crowd about him. They, more than any others, find in his words strength and hope to endure their hardships.

His words have had great sting in them for those living lavishly without thought of body or soul, and a thorn in the side of the high priest and the family of Herod. I fear he is a marked man, and I pray he will be spared, yet his cries against Herodias and Herod won't go unnoticed. Oh, Judas, I wish you were here to speak with him. Alas, ours is a troubled time.

Her letter closed with the news of the rest of the family. But my mind was filled with the strange things she wrote of John. I carefully folded the letter and stored it with the others. Each letter was adding to the desire to see those in Jerusalem. I opened the next letter to read mother's comments of the things happening at home:

Dear Judas, It's now 777, and things are becoming more antagonistic here. Each day, the oppression becomes greater, and many do speak openly against Rome. Strange things are heard among the people. The name of John, the son of Zechariah, is on the lips of an increasing number. God has granted John a following. He preaches the time is near at hand and tells his followers to prepare for the great coming of the Messiah. Ishmael has heard him several times - preaching and washing those who repent and follow his doctrine. It was at one of those meetings and bathings along the Jordan near the town of Bethabara, which Ishmael had followed for a day or more, that a strange event took place. Ishmael came to me with this tale and trembled when he told me of this event. He went to hear John tell of the coming of the Messiah as before. Ishmael is part dreamer you know and recently found some comfort in the sayings of John, the little boy I once knew, now a "voice crying in the wilderness." In these days, my heart is filled with foreboding; these are times of great good and evil, and John preaches, saying, "Repent ye; for the kingdom of heaven is at hand." What is the meaning of this, Judas? What is the kingdom of heaven?

While Ishmael watched, some cried out at John to be received into his following and prayed for forgiveness even as he prescribed. Some say he washed many that day, others not so many; Ishmael held less than one hundred. Not all were interested in belonging to his sect. There were some officers of the temple there as well as Sadducees and Pharisees. They were watching the washings of the penitents.

Some cried out against John; they wanted to know on whose authority he proclaimed this message. So it was that some Levites from the temple raised their voices over the crowd, and asked, "Who are you, John bar Zechariah, that you should say these things?" Some had heard of his sayings in the desert and were curious of his qualifications. Few knew of his lineage or his formal training. Some heard the poor and unlearned near the temple claim he was Elias reincarnated or some other great prophet. Others claimed him to be the Messiah! All these rumors flowed among the people like water from a hidden spring.

John, not taken aback by their shouts and questions, answered boldly, "I'm not a Messiah." They were glad to hear this for others had been stoned for saying such. "Neither am I Elias nor a prophet of old; I'm just a small voice of God crying in the desert and here near the Jordan."

Ishmael said John became angry with the hecklers in the crowd and shouted back, "O you generation of vipers, who has told you to challenge these sayings? Who asked Elias his qualifications? Why come to me, what have I done? If I'm wrong, prove me so, if not, go back to your masters, for here I am and here I stay."

Of these things and more John accused them and as anyone so berated, some fell away a goodly distance to see what it was all about. It was said that those who stayed saw no sacrilege, as the washings were done in flowing water and covered the entire body. Ishmael said of those standing on the bank some argued among themselves the value of what John was doing. Some expressed feelings in shouts at those being washed by John.

From the near bank came a shout, "John, John bar Zechariah!" It came from a small man with a great voice - a voice that rolled like thunder from his small frame. Some of the crowd stepped aside and craned their necks to see the owner. How could such a voice come from so small a man?

To their surprise, a second man no bigger than the other, shouted in like manner "Ho! John, John bar Zechariah!" His voice was like the first, thunder from a cave. "What's this washing all about? Would you have us all do this thing?"

John was as amazed as the others at what he heard, but continued washing and merely returned with a shout of his own, "Aye, it is so!" But even at best, his voice was thin compared to the other two. The first called again, "Ha! And how about King Herod and Herodias? They, too, I suppose?" Some that heard laughed while others looked over their shoulders; the King had spies everywhere these days. Who were these two with the voices like thunder? They should have a care - they might not have them long - heads had rolled for less than this kind of remark.

"Aye, even them, and the more so! For the sake of Israel. Isn't it written the people shall bear the sins of the King? Would that they repent and lift God's hand from us!" John wasn't afraid of the King's spies - so Ishmael said. John was the voice of truth - the ancient pact Israel and God made when they wanted a king was still viable. Every King, regardless of how selected or placed on the throne of Israel, was blessed by God and the people were held accountable for his actions. Many had brought petitions against Herod to the seventy and felt Israel's troubles came through the house of Herod. Some of the crowd encouraged John and others smote their breasts as a sign of contrite hearts.

"Ha! And I suppose you would have Caiaphas and Annas here in the Jordan with these other sinners?" The other man who was a near copy of the first spoke. Gasps and sharp cries came from the crowd - some ground their teeth and others shook fists - such things weren't to be considered. Wasn't it written the priest was without sin after the atonement sacrifice? How could he enter the high holy place if sin was his companion? The crowd now wanted to hear John's answer.

They murmured against the question, it had no answer. It was self incriminating - all knew if the answer was aye, then it meant the high priest was sinful and unclean before the alter of God, and if nay, then it meant John's teachings weren't valid for all and some didn't need to repent. The crowd, now into the dialogue, waited for John's answer. So did some of the officers of the temple who stood nearby. One who stepped forward was Malcus, a trusted servant of Caiaphas. He came close to the bank to improve his chances of hearing John's reply.

"Aye, so it must be done!" John called in a clear voice.

Upon hearing this, Malcus clapped his hands together and scowled fiercely, then turned and stomped away. He had his words to tell Caiaphas. Some moved away and toward the road back to Jerusalem. They had no intentions of being seen there any longer. Still others stood by John. The two hecklers turned and strode away - they had their fun for the day. So it was that John was marked by Malcus and the friends of Herod as a troublemaker.

John demanded many things of his followers as he washed them, saying, "Your sins are forgiven you even unto the God of Abraham, Isaac, and Jacob." And those washed for forgiveness praised the Lord.

Ishmael said later some of the Pharisees murmured against John, saying, "How can there be forgiveness of sin without sacrifice?"

John ceased to teach his doctrine of preparation and rested among the people on the bank. As Ishmael moved through some of the new converts, he heard much confusion. It was a curious thing for many didn't know what to do with their new life and none had gone this way before. It was they, the newly-washed ones, who could band together to follow John bar Zechariah, but many couldn't do so because of their obligations and returned that same day to Jerusalem. Even so, the following of John soon grew but most were those poor who had little and expected less. After resting, John started his teaching and washings again. Ishmael decided to stay awhile longer, watch more closely and perchance, let John know he was there. Later, a man stepped from the edge of the crowd and approached John.

A MAN CALLED YESHUA

Mother's letter had a break in the pages, and I had to fit the pieces together before I could continue reading:

Ishmael said he didn't recognize the intruder at first. He was dressed commonly enough. He was well kept with clean body and hair without knots, as some of John's followers often had. Ishmael said the stranger moved with grace and possessed an air of majesty although his clothes showed no rank. The crowd murmured for it was the custom for all to accept their place in line, yet this man stepped forward without recognizing this custom. Some in the crowd whistled and hissed at this. Some recognized him, and whispered he was from Galilee and that was the reason for his apparent shortness. After all, many knew what kind of men the Galileans were.

He was first to speak, "John, John bar Zechariah, don't you know me?"

Ishmael said John studied the man with some care, and answered he didn't know him. Afterward, Ishmael said he truly couldn't understand this as the old story was told, John knew Yeshua before he was born. Nonetheless, John claimed ignorance.

As the man approached, he spoke again, "John, John, have I changed so much since our last meeting? I'm Yeshua of Nazareth, the son of Joseph, your kinsman. Your mother and mine were cousins. We often played together. Have I really changed so much in these few years?"

Suddenly John became very agitated. "Yeshua, Yeshua," and raising his arms and moving forward to meet Yeshua, John embraced him. It was then Ishmael also recognized Yeshua.

"Ah, now I know why my heart leaped at the sound of your voice. It moved even as it did in mother's womb so many years ago. Ah, many times I've cried out for you in the desert. The coming of one greater than me."

John stepped back and looked at Yeshua again. "How is your mother and your father? Is all well with them? I've not seen them for many years, but my heart has always held them in good stead."

Yeshua stepped deeper into the water. "John, I've come from Galilee. I heard along the way of your sayings. Mother is well but father is at rest with his fathers. I know of your parents and mother, also. It is well. But hear me, my work is to begin here in Bethabara. It's here I would be washed even as those before me."

Ishmael said upon hearing this, John became confused. Some of those standing near lost some faith in his teachings at that moment. John spoke quizzically, "But this cannot be, all my work is predicated on forgiveness of sins, it would be for you to wash me and not otherwise. My washing is simply with water unto the preparation of your coming. It's *I* who would be baptized of *thee,* and this with the spirit." John turned to be in a position for washing. "Can't you wash me with the spirit? Where is it written that the greater shall be subject to the lesser? Can a man repent and be washed for that which he doesn't have?" Seeing that he had gained nothing in the exchange, John moved up out of the Jordan as a symbol of his reluctance to wash Yeshua. Ishmael saw and heard but said he didn't understand it.

Yet Yeshua wouldn't be put off. "Hear me, John, some of these things even I don't understand, but it must be so for now. This is to fulfill the writings."

Now Ishmael searched his memory for any such scripture but could remember none that required a man to be washed in the Jordan; repenting of sins - yes, but washing in the Jordan - no. And while Ishmael and the others watched, Yeshua removed his outer garments and stepped into the Jordan and John did likewise. There the washing of Yeshua took place.

After this, John was filled with the Spirit of God and cried out to those present, "Behold, the Lamb of God, who takes away the sins of the world. This is He who comes after me who is greater than me. Hear, O Israel, *here* is your Messiah!" When those present who could hear, and Ishmael included, heard these things, they were shocked and greatly puzzled. None of his followers had heard John speak thus; always before this, he refused to identify the one who was to follow and be the Messiah. Some were taken by fits; some said it was the Spirit of God upon them. As Ishmael watched, Yeshua came up from the water, and at that moment, there was a loud rushing of the wind; clouds formed overhead. Ishmael and many others became afraid and hid their heads under their cloaks. It was during the rushing of the wind that Ishmael heard strange sounds like voices, but not completely so. In an instant, the wind quieted and all present murmured about the strange turn of events. Some heard a voice say, "You are my beloved Son, in whom I am well pleased."

Ishmael couldn't recall such was what he heard. Some claimed that this wind and voice was accompanied by the appearance of a dove-like creature which flew from the heavens and rested on Yeshua; to this Ishmael couldn't agree for he had his cloak over his head and saw nothing of this strange event.

Ishmael pressed close to the two as he wanted to speak with Yeshua; he now recognized him as the son of Mary even as he had said. Yes, the very one you had played with at Zechariah's so many years ago.

While Ishmael was still present, John was taken again by the Spirit and brought forth two of his followers. He said unto them, "Behold, the Son of God." This he said in such a manner that Ishmael couldn't tell if it was the truth or a wish.

Ishmael couldn't believe this, John claiming Yeshua to be the Son of the living God - this was near blasphemy! Not a son of God, but *the* Son of God! This was talk of the gentiles. *"Hear, O Israel: the Lord is our God, the Lord is one."*

The two who were followers of John, namely men from Galilee, unknown to Ishmael, stood before Yeshua.

Upon seeing them, Yeshua said, "What do you want?"

And one answered, "Where do you live?"

Yeshua then said, "Come and see." And Ishmael said they turned without a word to John and followed Yeshua.

I couldn't believe my eyes. What was she writing about? I remembered the words of Mary many years ago, but I had put them aside as wishful thinking; all Jewish mothers had this failing, mine as well. The problem in mother's case was that she had two sons at the same time - who would be the Messiah? We often laughed at this as we grew older. I returned to the letter.

> Ishmael was overcome with the happening and couldn't speak to Yeshua, but was certain it was indeed the son of Joseph and Mary. Ishmael hurried back from the Jordan to tell me straightaway. He was in a state of some agitation. His curiosity is greatly aroused. He wants to follow the others and see what might come to pass. Oh, Judas, I wish you were here as I fear Ishmael will also leave me and follow Yeshua. I leave you with this Judas: can it be that in our own midst is a Messiah? Have a care, son, and don't tarry long in Rome. It's here things of the world will be formed; this God has revealed to me."

It was here the letter ended. News about the family and Anath's children, my nieces and nephews, seemed of little importance after this event. I stared at the script before me and hastily read of the happenings again before placing it with the others.

Now all else seemed of little importance and what I wanted was to read more of the happenings in Jerusalem. I eagerly reached for the rest of the packet. There were more letters therein. I quickly opened the next and studied it for dates. It was the dates that made all things relevant. I couldn't see any; how long had it been between this one and the other?

It opened as the others:

> Dear Son, these are times of change, Judas. My heart trembles with fear of the unknown. My prayers are that my sons may not be caught up in an ill-founded movement. I can still remember the stories about Judas of Galilee and his brothers. You should remember him, too, for you were nearly twelve at the time. It's with a heavy heart I write that Ishmael has left your father's house to join with the curious following Yeshua bar Joseph.

> He has taken only those things necessary for bodily comforts. He asked my blessings on his venture which I reluctantly gave. And now I have no sons. You are in Rome and he is following after Yeshua. Who will look after me in my old age? Oh, Judas, when will you return?

> I must tell you what happened before Ishmael left. It was thus, Ishmael came to me full of excitement, even as he did years ago when he found a new subject to sketch. He was on fire with desire to sketch Yeshua. Some now call Yeshua a teacher, yet he is untrained and never sat before a great one. Nonetheless, Ishmael was caught up in the excitement of the time and became his only thought; he would wander throughout the city looking for Yeshua.

> It wasn't more than a week after he saw the strange ablution of Yeshua that Ishmael found Yeshua traveled from Bethabara to a small house in the lower part of Jerusalem. There he prepared for a mission into the wilderness; he returned to Bethabara, left his followers, and went into the wilderness alone. This was for renewal of Spirit, and he wouldn't allow any followers to be with him in these days.

> This strange proceeding wouldn't leave Ishmael be. He took provisions and followed Yeshua into the wilderness and he was gone nearly a fortnight. After he returned, he rested for a fortnight and then left again to seek Yeshua. It was then he heard from Yeshua's followers that he was still in the wilderness. They were greatly grieved about this, but none would break their word and follow their master for he had admonished them otherwise. Judas, imagine, our Ishmael traveling into the desert to seek someone? He was gone nearly forty days!

> Oh Judas, when he returned he wasn't the same. He was like one born again. His words were like hot irons as he told me of the strange things he saw and heard while standing afar off from Yeshua in the desert.

Here mother stopped and the papyrus showed signs of tears on the page. In the next portion of the packet was text written in Ishmael's own hand.

> I asked those I knew as followers of Yeshua where he had gone. At first, they refused to tell me of his whereabouts, yet as I persisted, they told me he was in need of solitude and went into the wilderness to commune with God. This wasn't uncommon among holy men of the day as even John bar Zechariah spent many days in the wilderness looking for Spiritual food from the Lord.
>
> The followers of Yeshua were very forceful about his need for peace. He had refused the accompaniment of even his closest followers. Those I later identified were two principals called James, and his brother, John, said to be sons of Zebedee - all from the town of Bethsaida near the lake of Gennesaret. They were quick to tell me that it was called the Sea of Galilee by those who sailed and fished on it.
>
> With forceful remarks about their leader wanting peace, and since I wasn't one of them, they had no legal right to prevent me from following his footsteps into the wilderness. Indeed, some were afraid he might be set upon by robbers and thieves and thereby come to some evil, and when they found I was determined to follow him, most gave their blessings. I hoped I might find him before harm came his way, yet strangely enough I had no fear for my own wellbeing. My only thought was that I must once again see Yeshua, the one I knew as a babe so many years ago, the lad who later visited the house of our father each Passover. This is the one John claims to be not only the Messiah and the deliverer of Israel, but the one true Son of God!"

I looked up from the page. My mind reeled with the immensity of such a claim, not that we hadn't had those who claimed to be the Messiah before. But to claim to be the Son of God is to diminish His power. Only the gentiles claim living beings to be gods or sons of gods. Where can John's mind be? Was he addled by his stay in the desert?

Yet at the same time, I remembered the tales told by Mary about Yeshua, and how she tenaciously held to her claims about his Messiahship and godly gifts. She only - through all the years, and regardless of the family's derisions - held him to be other than human. The rest of their kin and other family members gave no sign of recognizing powers above those of man. Only Mary persisted.

> I returned to the page in my hand where Ishmael continued:
>
> If this is blasphemy, and some say it is so, then surely the Sanhedrin and the seventy will call for the stoning of both John and Yeshua when they hear of these things. If it's true, then you cannot tarry in Rome as you are needed here. Ah Judas, would that you were here that I might ask you to explain these things. When this is done, I'll go to Gamaliel and he will set it right in my mind.
>
> But for now I must find Yeshua. I moved along the path Yeshua had taken; the trail he left was as one being led by the Spirit, not one of direct intentions. He walked slowly and I found many signs of meditation and prayer. Here and there were signs of his prayer rug place on the ground. It was nearly a week before I came upon him in a grove some distance away. Here I determined I wouldn't intrude on his solitude and need to communicate with God. From this point on, I remained some distance from the lonely figure. I determined that where he would go, I would go, and as long as he stayed in the wilderness, so I would stay. It was food and water that would be the final limit for me, and I thought for him, also.
>
> The days passed with monotonous regularity. I tried to make as many mental sketches of this solitary figure as I could. Judas, Yeshua is a quiet and godly man. I wished then I had brought my sketching materials with me but this wasn't to be

as I had only taken time for the necessities. So it was that I must make as many mental notes of the different postures of him as I could. It would be from these I would create drawings for you. Oh Judas, this land is harsh.

It was just a fortnight when my dwindling supplies gave me cause to wonder how long Yeshua would wander in the desert in search of spiritual comfort. I couldn't see that I could stay longer. Because of this, I returned to Bethabara and from thence home. I returned home and told mother of my finding Yeshua and of his apparent need for solitude. I spent another fortnight resting and gaining strength from the ordeal in the desert. Another week passed before I was strong enough to again go in search of Yeshua, as I had it on good authority he was still there.

My soul wouldn't let me rest. I must see him again. There was something lacking in these first drawings which made me want to see this lonely figure again. I set out again with minimum supplies to find him. His followers at Bethabara told me he hadn't returned yet; armed with this information, I set out once again.

Nearly thirty-one days had passed since I first began this odyssey. The Spirit of the Lord came upon me and I was led to high ground that looked down on the floor of the wilderness. It was there I saw him. He was indeed as I had pictured. For all his fasting, he seemed well and strong. His ability to remain well and alert on a minimum of food was evident to me even from a distance. I was puzzled. Was it as written about Elijah, "…So he went and did according unto the Lord… and the ravens brought him bread and flesh in the morning…" Could it be also for Yeshua? Even as I fell away from the lack of food, he didn't seem to.

I began to wonder if I would be able to return to Bethabara, and at night I would dream of things not in this land. I would be transported back home, to my room, and to good things to eat and drink. Sometimes this would happen in the long oppressive days as I watched the lonely figure before me. As I became weaker, I became more and more subject to these daydreams and visions. A mirage?

It was during one of these mental lapses that a strange thing happened before me on the land. I could see Yeshua resting on a large flat rock not too far in the distance. The heat caused the lonely figure to shimmer in my vision. As I watched, I could see two figures, one on the rock and one standing nearby. The change in scene caused me to rub my eyes in hopes I could bring the two figures into one, as I had seen no one other than Yeshua since leaving Bethabara. But try as I might, the two remained so, both shimmering in the heat of the day. The time knots counted to be thirty five days that he had been in this desert. How much longer, Oh Lord?

I moved forward to enhance my chance to either eliminate the second figure or to identify him, if indeed there was a second person. I moved forward with care of one approaching an enemy. I was soon within good sighting and could hear the speech of both, the desert being a quiet place in the heat of the day. I studied the second person with great interest. Who else would be as foolish as myself in coming into this wilderness to see a lonely teacher from Nazareth?

As I studied the figure, dear Judas, I became aware of an overpowering feeling of remembrance. The figure was tall and well built, and a great deal larger and more muscular than Yeshua. He was dressed in a strange uniform of some foreign country. That was when I realized who it was; it was the stranger whom we had seen before! The same one who had saved us some years before from the assassins. I couldn't have been more overcome! Could I trust my senses? I couldn't tell if this was a trick of the desert or my mind. Did they know I was within earshot? They made no motion that I was near them.

Suddenly, I heard the stranger whom I'll now call Shalazar speak. He said, "You say you are the Son of God. If this is so and you are hungry, command these stones to become bread." I was able to see a smile on his lips even from where I was hiding. Yeshua was white from the lack of nourishment; it was plain to see he was hungry and in need of food.

He slowly raised his head from a position of prayer and looked directly into the eyes of Shalazar and said in a steady voice, "Man shall not live by bread alone, but by every word that comes from the mouth of God."

Shalazar wasn't satisfied and continued his questioning. "But pray, isn't it so that gods don't hunger or thirst? See, it's even known to you that I don't hunger or thirst, and yet, I see by your actions that you're both hungry and thirsty. Tell me, Yeshua, are you as some say, the Son of God?"

Yeshua accepted his questioning without showing rancor and replied, "You know." Judas, this wasn't the answer I expected. The meaning was neither yea nor nay as far as I could reason. Shalazar asked no more and turned away. Suddenly, the desert wind blew such that the sand caused me to hide under my cloak.

When the wind lay, I looked from under my cloak to see a strange sight. It was as if I had been transported unto the holy city. I stood high above the ground and my feet rested on a cloud. I could see Yeshua standing with Shalazar on the highest portion of the temple, and they, too, were comfortable. Neither they nor I feared the height, and we could see the rest of the land below. Many people and animals looked like ants on the earth below.

Then Shalazar said to Yeshua, "Come, you have answered well, but you have left me some doubt. If you're the Son of God, cast yourself down and don't worry, for it's written, "He shall give his angels charge concerning you: and in their hands they shall bear you up, lest at any time you dash your foot against a stone."

It was the first time I could remember Shalazar quoting the writings of the ancients, and that not too well. His question and quotation caused my heart to quake. Who might this Shalazar be?

Yeshua was patient. He again showed no anger against him when he softly said, "You know more than you pretend not to. What is your need for proof of any kind? Haven't we been locked in combat before? You know it's also written, "You shall not tempt the Lord your God." It's not yet time for you to show your strength over the world. Ask what you will, for the strength of God is ever in my hand."

When he finished speaking thus, a great wind came again, and I turned away from the scene to hide my face. When the wind died, I looked again for Yeshua and Shalazar. And what I saw I now write. Three of us were as on a high mountain; there were none higher that could be seen. I stood some distance from them, and neither looked my way. Below us were many things of the earth. It was as though all the kingdoms were laid out below us. The nations were so many that I couldn't tell their kinds. Even many were of such opulence and glory that I could hardly look upon them for their color and hue. Some were very old, even like unto the past, and some were of the present, while others were like unto things yet to be seen by man. Below us lay all the power and beauty of this world. My eyes burned from all I saw.

As I stood transfixed by these things, I heard Shalazar say to Yeshua, "All these things I will give you, if you will just fall down and worship me." My heart fluttered at these words, and even more he said, "All this power will I give you and the glory of them; for it's delivered unto me, and to whomsoever I will, I can give it. Hear me, all shall be yours if you will worship me this day."

Who was this Shalazar who offered the world and all that was in it to another? Were my teachings wrong? Who has possession of the earth but the creator God? Didn't the writers say, "The earth is the Lord's and the fullness thereof, the world, and they that dwell therein?" What manner of being was this man?

Dear Judas, it was just said by him, "All these things will I give you." Aren't these the property of God? Oh Judas, my mind reeled again from the statement of Shalazar. What does, "for that which is delivered unto me" mean? Who delivered the world and all that is in it, the things of God, unto the hands of this Shalazar? Who had such power?

What amazed me even more was that Yeshua wasn't taken aback by these statements but accepted them as true! He didn't question Shalazar's claim of supremacy over all. I stood as one turned to a pillar of salt. I couldn't move as I watched these titans exchange remarks.

Then Yeshua spoke, "Leave me, you deceiver. It's written, 'You shall worship the Lord your God, and him only shall you serve.'" Then, Shalazar stumbled backwards and would have fallen if Yeshua hadn't prevented it. Shalazar writhed as if in great pain. He looked as one stung with a lash of lead tips. He fell to his knees.

Suddenly there was a loud peal of thunder and the sky was filled with light. The desert floated up to greet me once again. Shalazar was gone! Yeshua knelt in prayer. We were alone in the desert as before.

As I watched, a stairway appeared extending from the clouds to earth and I beheld angels of the Lord moving upon it. As they moved, they sang songs of praise for Yeshua and ministered unto him. They provided for his every want and he grew in strength of body as I watched. And I could see him grow in the Spirit of the Lord.

Then I fainted and when I awoke, Yeshua was gone. Had I dreamed all these things? Was it too late for me to find my way out of this wilderness? I struggled to my feet and I left the desert straightaway trusting the Lord would guide me. I hurried in the direction I thought would lead to Bethabara. I arrived there in great need of sustenance and fell into the arms of the waiting followers of Yeshua, where one lifted me up and carried me unto a house used by the followers. It was a secret place for all now feared the arms of the high priest and friends of Herod. The followers gave me care until I gained strength. I told them of the things I saw and heard in the wilderness. Few believed my story.

Some of those present praised God for the news that Yeshua was well and had found new and greater strength in the Spirit of God even as I have testified unto you in this letter. I remained with them a full week, and then left for home. It is from my room I write this letter to you. Oh Judas, my heart is full of wonderment! Were these things real or imagined? This I know, Judas - there was no other human at the temptation but me! Hurry home! These are the times that make a man's heart burn with the desire for fulfillment of the ages. Israel is about to be relieved from the yoke of the Romans; God is in his seat of Justice.

As the letter closed with a blessing upon me and the household of Uncle Benjamin, my legs grew weak from the news in Ishmael's letter. I sat on the edge of the windowsill to gain greater light on the pages before me. I read and reread portions of the letter and studied the sketches that annotated the edges. Had Ishmael gone mad while in the desert? Parts of his story were nearly incomprehensible and parts were approaching blasphemy! The attributes of God were being assigned to a living man, that was blasphemy, there was no other way to put it. And there was the part about the stranger, and here I agreed with

Ishmael, his name should be Shalazar. For the stories of mother, Apius, and yes, even Mary indicated this was one and the same man. How true it was I could but surmise. The conversation between Shalazar and Yeshua, as told, bore the marks of one under the influence of the harsh wilderness and lack of sustenance. Who could believe these things?

Oh Ishmael, what have you really seen? Even now I wondered if Shalazar was the one who rescued Ishmael. Had he been the one who said to me, "Believe this, that which I do, I can undo! Thus it's given to me."

My mind swam with the force of this thought. Who was this Shalazar I contracted to save Ishmael from prison? My hand still stung from the handshake that sealed the bargain, and now shook as I set the letter aside and searched through the packet for another missive from Ishmael. Before opening another, I checked the date of Ishmael's letter.

This letter was dated the spring of 777, still the year of the washing of Yeshua, and the beginning of John's public sayings. Yes, it was true, some of them who visited the holy city during the great feast brought back tales of the young itinerant preacher, now called John the washer, who called the people to repentance. And now Ishmael's letters testified to that, but these were nearly two years old! Where had they been? Why have they come so late? Was it another case of pirates in the shipping lanes, or had some minor Roman officer caused the delay of Jewish communication?

Searching through the packet, I found another written by Ishmael, and in it were sketches of the scenes of the very happenings described in the previous missive. These were of greater detail. The sketches gave added meaning to his words. They depicted the washing of Yeshua by John, the dove poised above Yeshua, and the scenes of his trials in the Judean desert south and east along the Dead Sea.

The likeness of John was without flaw, but that of Yeshua brought no remembrance of the lad I knew so many years ago. The figure of Shalazar was like that of the stranger I saw in Jerusalem, on the sea, and in Rome. Was it really Shalazar or had Ishmael conjured up this figure while under distress in the desert? I couldn't help but study the sketch with great interest; I wondered if Apuleius would recognize this figure and face as a likeness of the man who rescued us from the sea? I would show him these when he returned.

The face of Yeshua Ishmael drew showed considerable patience and kindness, or so I thought. It was the face of a godly man. I could recognize the face of mother and some of the others in each sketch. Ishmael was very proficient at his craft. I wondered what father would have said of these sketches if he was alive.

After studying them for some time, I turned to the script which had been rolled and placed in the packet. His letter began:

Dear Brother, when will you return? Mother and I are hard pressed to know what keeps you in the city of the gentiles." I quickly looked the page over for a date; it was at the top of the first sheet, 778, nearly two years to arrive here in Rome.

It's here that God has made known some of his mighty works. I have been permitted to see the washing of Yeshua, and was the only one present in the wilderness when Shalazar placed before Yeshua some strange questions and propositions. Some are being blessed by the things done by both John and Yeshua.

I cannot rest, Judas. My room is like a prison. My soul cries out for knowledge. I must be with those that are in search of that which was lost.

His letter moved on after two or more sketches on the same page. First, a sketch of an older man with great strength which was annotated as, "Simon bar Jona, a fisherman." The second was of two men standing side by side, "James and John, sons of Zebedee, also fishermen." The third was a sketch of another man, "Andrew, the brother of Simon."

The letter continued without reference to the sketches as I read on:

I traveled once again to the town of Bethabara and sought Yeshua. I was told that he left Bethabara a few days before. I had heard from some that he cured illnesses of some, but evidently not all. When leaving, he had selected four men to follow him. The first two I had mentioned in a letter before, James and John, and Andrew and his brother Simon were selected while he was still in Bethabara.

With these at his side, Yeshua went to the city of Bethsaida and from thence to Cana for there was a wedding in the house of a friend of his family he desired to attend. Now Bethsaida was known round about as the "house of fish" as in truth it was a fishing village. It lay west of and close to the Sea of Tiberius in the land of Galilee and was some four days' journey on foot from Bethabara.

As I rested on my travels toward Bethsaida, I spoke with an old man near a well by the roadside. He claimed he knew of the five, but they had grown to seven in number. When I asked how this was, he told a story of what he heard at the well while they were resting.

While yet on their way, Yeshua found Philip who was also from the city of Bethsaida, even as were Andrew and Simon. They went only a little way when Philip found Nathanael and said to him, "We have found the one Moses and the prophets wrote about, one Yeshua bar Nazareth, and the son of a carpenter named Joseph." It was said that Nathanael questioned the truth of this statement, but he followed Philip and met Yeshua.

When Yeshua saw Nathanael, he remarked, "Look, an Israelite indeed in whom there is no guile."

Nathanael was taken aback by this greeting, and remarked, "From where do you know me?"

The teacher answered, "Before Philip called you, while you were still under the fig tree, I saw you."

Nathanael was surprised at this as he hadn't seen anyone while he was resting under the tree. What manner of man is this who can see things before they appear on the horizon? After all, the hill and tree hid all from the road.

The old man said they all claimed the Spirit of God rested on Nathanael, and he answered as God gave him knowledge, "Teacher, you are the Son of God, and the King of Israel!"

Now the old man said that some along the road heard Nathanael say these things and murmured against them as Yeshua didn't rebuke him. There were those who took a different meaning from the words. Some who heard this knew all were sons of God, even as the writings proclaim, but also knew this Nazarene wasn't the king of Israel. They laughed at Nathanael's remarks; after all, even the least in Judea knew Israel wasn't a sovereign nation anymore, and hadn't been so for nearly two centuries. Israel had no king now and wouldn't have until the Romans were thrown out of Judea. Besides, he stood before them without the least mark of royalty - he had no entourage or men-at-arms to support him - unless you could call these fishermen from Galilee such.

There was no king of Israel, even Herod Antipas wasn't a king of the nation, as he was on the throne of only part of his father's land. And wasn't this the will of the Romans, the old man asked? How then could this young Nazarene be called the King of Israel? Why hadn't he denied this, for all knew that Herod would surely hear of these claims and seek to arrest him? The old man continued to babble on about these things, sometimes serious and sometimes laughing. Ah, dear brother, neither I nor the old man at the well could explain these words about Yeshua.

TO A WEDDING

He was a rascal this old man. He said the one called Yeshua said to Nathanael, "Because I said unto you, I saw you under the fig tree, you believe? You shall see greater things than these. Listen, I say this. Later you will see heaven open, and the angels of God ascending and descending upon the Son of Man."

And so it was, the old man said, that none of his followers knew the meaning of these words. All these things I heard from the old man as I sat by the well.

I reached Bethsaida, but not finding Yeshua, I moved on to enter Cana. It was here I found him with his followers and a group of curiosity seekers. The curious were from all walks of life and included hecklers as well as supporters. I joined the curious but didn't have the chance to speak with Yeshua and ask him of his family.

Ah Judas, I wish you were here. I have many questions about these happenings. It's still in my mind to set at the feet of Gamaliel and have him tell me the straight of these things, but for now I must follow my heart.

I was on the road four days and the journey tired me greatly. I found a goodly spot, pulled my cloak over me and fell asleep early the fourth evening. I was awakened by the noise of a passing group of entertainers. As my vision cleared, I saw they were part of a wedding party. Weddings in this small town of Cana were not common affairs. All joined in. Many of the shops closed for such an occasion. The wedding party contained not only family members of the bride and groom, but neighbors, friends, and the curious like me. All were there to support the couple in this, God's first sacrament. There were dancers and wine bearers, and musicians with tambourines, cymbals, and lutes. Then came the priests and teachers of each family. There was much merrymaking and chanting of traditional songs and blessings. It was this lifting up of the spirits which had awakened me.

I moved away from the passing parade and went to the river to wash and give thanks. I recognized that this might be the wedding in Cana that I was told Yeshua would attend. I prepared as best I could to attend it. When I finished at the river, I could still hear the merrymaking, then came upon the wedding party. I stood at the outer edge of the crowd to see without being seen as I had nothing for the family, nor had I proper attire. As I watched, the wedding ceremony took place and the young couple became man and wife. The wedding feast then began in earnest. The food and wine was provided by the family and all were invited to join in the well-wishing party. The feast ran on throughout the day and for nearly five days thereafter; I remained there throughout.

It was a typical feast with the crowd wasting as much food and wine as it consumed; as the days wore on, many became more drunk than sober. Both food and wine began to dwindle as no one was turned away. As some portions became less, the guests began to murmur against the household for want of more wine and food. I wasn't one to indulge as I only wanted to speak with Yeshua.

During the first five days and nights of the feast, I hadn't seen him but was told he was expected. I began to search for Mary for if I couldn't talk to him, perhaps I could present myself to his mother. I believed that she would remember me; after all, our families met on the high holy days many times as you recall.

It was during the thoughts of our families intermingling I suddenly realized both you and I, Judas, were better acquainted with Yeshua than any of his followers. We had known about him before his birth, and we played with him when he was a small child. We had seen him on many visits to the temple on Pesach. How could it be that he has chosen for his followers those who knew him the least? Not that I really care! Is it that those who know won't believe he is the Son of God?

Each night I didn't find him at the feast I lay awake pondering these things and wished you were here to settle these things in my mind as you used to. You were my confidant and I yours. My soul cries out for you, dear brother.

Here the letter was smudged and on some of the pages were small sketches of the feast and guests in less-than-attractive poses. From his sketches, it appeared many of the guests were in strong drink; the bride and groom showed fine clothes and jewelry worn by them which led me to believe the wedding was of a well-to-do family. The letter continued:

It was on the eve of the sixth day, one day before the Sabbath, the wine was nearly exhausted. As was the custom, the feast was enlivened by the songs, dances, riddles, and histories of the families. The large water pots were kept filled with fresh water to wash the faces, hands and sometimes feet of the guests. As each guest called for water, it was placed into separate bowls for their use. Because of the heat and revelry, the demand for water was high, and it kept many servants busy.

While I watched from some distance, I saw some guests were agitated. I moved closer to see and hear what concerned them. I determined it was caused by a lack of wine. It seemed the brides' household hadn't expected as many guests as had appeared and therefore was running out of wine. It was common practice to keep an additional supply of wine on hand, but warm weather and heavy drinking had nearly depleted this supply. The honored family was about to be without enough wine for their guests and there were several more days yet in the wedding festival.

The disgrace of such a happening was upon the household. The father of the bride appealed to one of the women standing near the family crest. I noticed she was directing the servants in the preparation and execution of the wedding party operations. As the father of the bride talked to her, I suddenly knew it was Mary. She was the same as I had remembered.

Here the letter ended and Ishmael had added a sketch of Mary. I recognized her with ease; it was like looking into the past. She hadn't changed as much as some women are apt to in later life. Her hair was long and fell over her shoulders. She wore the festive dress of those invited to a wedding.

Ishmael's letter continued to bring to light the events back home, but I drifted back to the last time I was home. I couldn't remember the last time I saw Mary. I knew it wasn't at father's funeral as none of Joseph's household came. It was a thing remembered by mother and I, but not one to cause ill will over. Joseph and his family came to show respect to Zechariah, but after that, Mary hadn't visited us even though she and her family still made trips to Jerusalem each Passover. Mother made one trip to Nazareth when Joseph died, and other than that, little contact was maintained with the carpenter's family. We heard of their comings and goings through friends who lived in Nazareth. I could see from Ishmael's sketches she was as unchanged as was mother for her age.

I unrolled the letter further and it continued with the story of the wedding at Cana:

After seeing Mary, I was determined to seek her out and ask about her family. So it was that I came close to her when the steward of the wedding expressed his concern for the lack of wine. The wedding guests were sufficiently inebriated that he had the servants cutting the wine with water. None of the guests seemed aware of the dilution and all were enjoying themselves, but even that was now nearing an end. There just wasn't enough wine base for more cutting with water. Soon it would be more water than wine and even a person under the influence of the wine would tell the difference between wine and the diluted drink.

It was obvious that the more diluted wine the people drank, the more sober they became, and as they became more sober they began to pay more attention to the taste of the wine. Some were already complaining that the wine was too new and not as good as the first that was served. Something must be done and quickly.

After this, Mary, in hopes of easing the strain of the situation, looked for her eldest son. Surely he would know what to do! As she moved through the guests and the crowd outside the wedding circle in search of Yeshua, I was able to greet her. I saluted her, and she, although in a hurry, returned the greeting with good will. She hesitated for a moment and her eyes indicated a slight recognition when they met mine, but that quickly faded as her mind was on the problem at hand.

"Mary, don't you remember me? I'm Ishmael bar Simon. My mother is Ruth."

She turned back from her quest and came to me.

"Ishmael, ah Ishmael, it's been some time. Now I know why you looked familiar to me. It does my heart good to see you, but I must find Yeshua; have you seen him?" She stood by me while searching the crowd for him. She stopped one of the servants and remarked to him, "Go to the house of Nathanael the elder and look for Yeshua. When you find him, tell him his mother has need of him." The servant left the wedding party immediately. He didn't ask the way as he was of the town and knew the location of the Nathanael household.

This done she turned again to me. "It's been a long time, and why are you here in Cana? How is your dear mother? Is she here? Where is your brother, Judas? And wasn't your sister, Anath, married some time ago?" All these questions came tumbling from her lips.

"I came from Bethabara seeking your son. Mother is well and does often ask of you and your family." I told her about not seeing you for nearly six years; how you were in Rome with Uncle Benjamin following an accounting career, and even now applies this to the sea trade. I added how we hoped you would return soon. "Anath is a mother of two already." The servant hadn't returned but the steward moved about seeking Mary as he believed she was securing more wine.

He approached saying, "Dear Mary, have you been able to get more wine?" His question was spoken sharply and I was irritated at this; she took no offense.

"It's in the hands of the servants. All will be done within the hour." She showed great confidence in the capability of her eldest to do what she asked. The steward was satisfied and left to soothe the guests.

Here, because of some soil and loss of words, I had to study the manuscript from Ishmael with care. He rambled on in great detail I thought and presented a lengthy dialogue between he and Mary. Why he did this I wasn't sure, but I read on:

"I hear this is the wedding of one Nathanael, a follower of Yeshua, isn't that true?" I asked. The old man at the well said this Nathanael was following Yeshua.

"Yes," she answered, "yet it's odd that he is being wedded."

"Why is that?"

"Well, I heard him say he is willing to follow Yeshua as one following a master. This means his leaving his bride for the sake of his teacher. One wonders what the world is coming to, for in my day, a groom was permitted and expected to remain home with his bride even from the calls of war! And to leave her bed for a new teacher was never thought to be in accordance with the law." She turned to look after the servant; there was no sign of him.

Her observation was an interesting one - a marriage starting out with the groom leaving his bride to follow a teacher didn't indicate a full house.

We moved to a shady spot. "Tell me of your family, Mary. Mother won't rest until I've told her all."

"Ah, your mother is a good woman, but where to begin?" She told me of her family of seven children. Yeshua, the eldest, never took to carpentering and was somewhat of a dreamer. His wasn't the hands and mind of a builder. She went through her thoughts about Yeshua and all the wonderful things he was to accomplish. His understanding of the Law and the Prophets was, even at a young age, too great a thing to waste in a carpenter shop. She couldn't keep from extolling his accomplishments over the other children. It seemed that James, the second son, was taught the trade, while Joses, Simon, and Judas, carrying the same name as you, were still too young to do such work. It was shortly thereafter that Joseph was killed trying to free a trapped servant from a collapsing building. Soon afterwards, Yeshua left the household and began to roam the countryside in search of the Spirit of God. It was as though his father's death had released him from the family obligations.

She told me how Joseph had no brothers to look after his family, so her sons-in-law continued the business with the help of James. They had hard times as the money from the gold and gifts of the Magi was long gone. The family missed the hands of Yeshua, but when asked, he simply said he must follow the Spirit of God. Her daughters married well, and the sons-in-law have often given all manner of things to the family. It wasn't more than two months ago that Yeshua left the house finally in search of John bar Zechariah. She paused here and looked again for the servant she had sent for Yeshua. Her eyebrows knit together, showing her concern at the lateness of the hour.

"Did he tell you of finding John?" She didn't give up the search for the servant but held her head in the direction of the gate.

"Aye, he told me some strange things; much of this I don't understand. He arrived just three days ago; he was aware I had to attend this wedding. Oh, why hasn't the servant returned and Yeshua with him?"

Finally, the servant and Yeshua were approaching. Several men were with him; three I knew from Bethabara - Simon, James, and John. It was later I learned who they were - brothers of Yeshua - James, Joses, Simon, and Judas. I remarked at the time that you bore the name of Judas as well. But, dear brother, the similarity between you and he ends with the name. This you'll see from the sketches.

Here, Ishmael added sketches of the other men. I agreed that Judas, the brother of Yeshua, and I weren't close in resemblance. I looked at each of the sketches closely. It seemed the longer I looked, the more real they became. I knew in my heart that someday I would meet these men, and not only meet them but have intimate dealings with them. It wasn't known to me presently, but the feeling of camaraderie was keen.

Later, I found two others to be Nathanael, the bridegroom, and one named Philip. These were the men the old man at the well spoke about. Some were followers and some weren't. It seemed that Yeshua was less popular with his own brothers than with those less familiar with him. When I approached some of them later, his brothers were quick to identify themselves as relatives and not followers.

On the whole, most of his followers were those of different towns, all Galileans, and less likely to have known him in his early life. Several were nearly ten years his senior. Many were of the fishing trade, while some weren't.

Yeshua strode quickly up the street and through the gate to the house of the wedding. He came directly to his mother who moved but a few feet from me. He was much shorter than you or I, and much lighter in frame. He saluted his mother as a dutiful son; she acknowledged his greeting but was interested in his lateness.

"Where have you been? Wasn't it agreed that you were to attend this wedding feast as the eldest of my house? Have I asked so much so often that you couldn't leave your studies and followers long enough for this?" She didn't wait for his answer. "It's unhappiness that's upon us as the wine is in short supply. The good name of Nathanael suffers. New guests have arrived, and I've not allowed for such. The steward has asked me to secure more wine; can you secure the needed wine?"

He stood with his left hand on his chin while his right rested on a walking staff; he stood nearly eye to eye with his mother - he wasn't taller than she. His clothing was similar to that which I had seen at Bethabara when he was baptized; he wore no festive dress - nor any of his followers. I could see his brothers were dressed for the occasion. Why Yeshua and his followers refused to don festive garb wasn't known to me; perhaps because of the lateness of the hour of their coming.

He spoke with some care. His voice carried the twang of the Galileans even as did his parent's. His voice was manly but not deep. He had changed some since I saw him at the baptism and in the desert. I couldn't express what the difference was; it was more a feeling than an observation.

"Peace mother, what have you told these people? Have you not understood?" He waited. Judas, it seemed to me from his speech that he was accustomed to Mary making remarks as to his capabilities to others. You remember, the things about his superhuman capabilities - how he was the Son of God and all! From his questions and attitude, he acted as though she had placed him in one of those situations. It didn't sound like he was angry; he just wanted to avoid demonstrations.

"Son, haven't I asked for help? Is it so disturbing I should do so?" Ah Judas, from this I knew she understood his meaning as well. She continued as I recall now, "It is written, 'Honor thy father and mother that all will be well with thee.'" She lowered her head as one expecting refusal. "My request is only that wine be found for this wedding. If there is some in this village, maybe it can be brought forth. I'm but a woman in need of help." It seemed to me she knew her son well. She looked much like mother when she played the game of helplessness - ah Judas, mothers are given to these things!

Yeshua looked about the festival while not moving from where he stood near me. He gave no indication that he recognized me, and Mary, who was still occupied with her problem, didn't introduce me. Now some of the others whom I had met at Bethabara quietly nodded unto me, but this was done without Yeshua's knowledge. None of those near, neither followers nor brothers, joined in the festivities.

Yeshua finally spoke, "Aye, so it's written and so I've done. Whatever there is between you and me isn't to be told everyone, remember, my time hasn't come yet. Hold your tongue. All is given for good and not for entertainment. But go and feel relieved as it shall be done as you ask." Upon hearing this, Mary gave him a kiss and moved away in good spirits.

She stood erect among the other women as she turned to the servants nearby. "Whatever he says for you to do, do it!" she said, and waved her hand in Yeshua's direction. Having said thus, she welcomed each of her sons with a kiss and walked again among the ladies of the party. She strode off as one who knows all is well with the world and she had completed a task set before her. Judas, regardless of what we may think, Mary had great confidence in Yeshua.

After she directed thus, the servants crowded around Yeshua as they wanted to please the host and the steward; it was his pleasure that influenced their lives.

Before this, the servants filled the water pots used for washing and refreshment. At the time, there were six of these standing in the vestibule. Some of these weren't filled when Mary called the servants to her side. It was as though they would never be filled as the heat of the day was upon the guests and they constantly called for more water to relieve the heat. The water carriers were bringing water from the village well as fast as they could, but couldn't keep them filled for the celebration.

Yeshua told his brothers and followers to stay awhile where they were. Not being one of the group, I followed him to the place where the water pots stood. Here he noted how much water was in them. He left the vestibule and returned to his followers. The servants and I followed.

He spoke to them quietly, "Hear me, perceive, and believe for this is done through the will of God. All this and more you shall see from this day on."

He turned to the chief servant, "Stop taking water from the pots, and fill them to the brim. When they are full, cover them, use no more from them for washing, but come and tell me of your success." Upon hearing this strange request, the servants ran to the well and proceeded to fill the pots as quickly as they could. None wanted to hear the chief steward call for water for the guests. Yeshua and his followers moved to the shade of a tree and there rested while this took place.

Ah Judas, it was a sight to see, servants running to the well and back as fast as they could. The festival in full swing. Time was running out - the Sabbath would soon be upon us. All would rest on the Sabbath.

Soon thereafter, the leading servant came to the group, saluted Yeshua, and told of their success in filling the pots. The steward had placed a hold on the water drawn from the pots. They awaited other instructions. Yeshua and his group went to the vestibule and there moved away from his followers a short distance. He stood for sometime in deep reflection and prayer, or so it seemed to me. The veins on his forehead stood out from the concentration of his will. Time passed slowly for those who watched. He then returned to his followers and called the head servant to him.

"Uncover the first filled and bring me a dipper of the liquid." This he did with haste. He took the dipper and gave thanks to the Lord for all things and tasted of the liquid. This I assumed to be water, but he didn't ask for water but instead used the word "liquid." After a drink, he gave the dipper to his followers and they likewise drank from the dipper. All were elated at the taste of the contents of the dipper. He then handed the dipper to the servant saying, "Return

to the first pot and fill the dipper again and take it to the steward of the feast."
This he did.

A cry of surprise was heard as the master of the festival tasted the liquid in
the dipper. All this had transpired without his knowledge, that is, the filling of
the pots and the drawing from one of them. He was delighted with the taste and
strength of the contents. It was he who identified it as wine of the best character.

As I stood near, I could hear the acclamation of this new wine. The master of
the wedding celebration called loudly for the groom. It was then the young man
called Nathanael stepped forward in his wedding attire. The master spoke to him
in a hearty voice, "Ah Nathanael, you rogue, what have you done? Here we have
been singing the praises of your feast and the wine for nearly six days and nights,
and now you've supplied a wine better than before. Why, dear friend, have you
kept the best wine until last?" He raised his cup unto the ceiling in a happy salute
to the groom. "Here is to the goodly surprise and may they always be thus."

Nathanael didn't answer him as he was not aware of these things either. He
left the hall and found Mary and Yeshua and gave thanks for the gift of additional
wine.

The guests drank heartily, and even the little ones drank from the water pots.
There had never been such a wedding party in Cana before and many said, "Nor
will there ever be again!" Many of the townspeople promised not to forget this
day of the wedding of Nathanael. Even before I left Cana, there were different
stories told about the source, goodness, and plentifulness of the wine - the latter
being best. Some accused others of exaggerating the stories of the feast but all
agreed it was one wedding not to be forgotten.

The wedding festival lasted through the Sabbath and unto the seventh day.
Like most weddings, it started on the sixth day so that many of the townspeople
could take advantage of the Sabbath to come to the wedding. The wine lasted
until then and more. All the guests praised the fine food and wine set before them
by the host. Many stayed the full days of the festival, and many came and went
as the wedding party continued, yet none knew of the drawing of the wine from
the water pots.

Ah Judas, it was the water carriers and servants who told of the strange happening that day at the wedding. It's their testimony that is still heard about the
village of Cana. It was known that even the servants and slaves had wine to drink
from the water pots and it was said the wine didn't give out until the last guest left.

And thereafter, when water was then added to the pots, all was water again.
Yet it was months before the water from the pots lost the tang and flavor of wine.
The servants said the pots were magic and often said people who drank from them
on the anniversary of the wedding would still feel the affects of the wine.

I, Ishmael, drank of the wine drawn from the water pots, and Judas, it was
truly wine of good report. There can be no doubt that the Lord of hosts delivered
unto the hands of Yeshua power to change things from what they are to what they
aren't.

"Wonder not, for greater than this you shall see, for as the Father is in me so
I can do that which is new." This he stated unto them. They accepted this as an
indication of his kinship with the Lord even as he had said. But some murmured
that he was Elisha returned, while others remembered the deeds of Moses. And
I recalled the words some heard at the washing at Bethabara, "This is my son in
whom I am well pleased." All this I saw and heard as I have written unto you.

Judas, Judas, it's as if one sees the beginning of a new era for Israel. Come home dear brother, come home.

And so the letter ended with pleas for me to come back to Judea. There were still other letters in the packet. I wandered over to a couch near the west window and there lay down to look at the rest. My head was in a whirl. All this wasn't present-day news, all had been held somewhere for nearly two years. Why? Was it an act of God or man? The letter was dated for some reason. And it was by this date on each letter I knew the history of things in Judea. Here it was 780, and I'm reading for the first time letters two years old. If his letters were this slow in getting to Rome, how long had it taken for mine to reach Jerusalem? And how long for them to find their way to Ishmael? His last letter was dated 778 and I looked again through the packet for another from him; this time I hoped for a later date.

In the packet was a letter from him dated 779. The letter began as the others:
We have missed your letters, and have longed to see you. May the Lord's countenance shine on you. Much has happened since I last wrote about the wedding of Nathanael in Cana, where the will of the Lord was manifest in the changing of water into wine. The people present at the wedding still retell the story.
But as time moves on, the story is told differently. It was as I described to you even to the last detail. After the wedding, Yeshua moved among the people of Cana, and they who heard of the changing of water into wine wouldn't leave him alone. All wanted to see him do other feats of magic, even as the traveling magicians of the Chaldaeans and Egyptians did as entertainment.
Some came a goodly distance when they heard of the changing of water into wine, and from this, concluded Yeshua could and would cure their different ills. They heard the Spirit of the Lord rested on him. Most who came to Cana were extremely poor and were the unclean ones. Some crowded the marketplace of Cana, and the merchants murmured against them. Most were unable to purchase anything and continued to beg by the wayside.
While Yeshua taught these the Law and Prophets, they remained in the streets. The merchants of Cana finally picked one of their number to speak against the crowds of poor, and held Yeshua to blame for their coming and polluting the marketplace. Many of the unclean had contaminated the vessels of oil and wine used for the sacraments, causing the merchants to destroy both contents and vessels or sell them at a much-reduced price. The people of Cana were angry at Yeshua and the poor and unclean, and the Pharisees brought cause against them because of the law. It was then Yeshua and his family made their way to Capernaum.

TO CAPERNAUM

In all this time, I hadn't found it convenient to introduce myself to Yeshua, for when he wasn't surrounded by the sick and poor, he was with his followers. It was strange to see the separation held by his brothers from the followers. Noticing this division, I decided not to make myself known unto him. I remained on the outer edge of his followers but didn't become one of them.
As the press of the crowd became great, Yeshua, his family, and followers left Cana as quickly and quietly as they had come. I followed them to Capernaum where Yeshua, Mary, his brothers, and his followers went to the house of the mother-in-law of the one called Simon.
Capernaum was a goodly-sized town which lay on the northwest shores of the Sea of Tiberias, which the local people called the Sea of Galilee. Because of its

size, being thirteen miles long and five across, some of the Romans called it the Lake of Galilee. It was a marketplace for the produce of nearby country farms and was blessed with a fine, small harbor, and the ever-present customs house. The country's produce were floated across the opposite shore for sale in the territory of Tetrarch Philipus. The greater share of the income came from well-watered farms.

Soon after entering Capernaum, Simon made a turn into the courtyard of a small house that was lined only with a hedge of twigs and palm leaves and reflected the poor of the city. In the near part of the yard, by a small garden, hung fish nets drying for the next days' catch. Simon held up his hand as a signal for all to stay outside the courtyard as he went in alone. I stood at the outer edge of the followers and as evening was near, I wasn't noticed by many. Simon wasn't long in his mission; he returned with the news that all was ready for the guests. He stationed himself at the gate and passed only those he considered followers or family.

I could hear him call out, "Ho there!" now and again as someone approached whom he deemed not part of the honored clan. There were many of the poor and disabled pressing to see Yeshua and have a word with him. Yeshua passed into the courtyard; after that, James and John also stationed themselves at the gate. They were small men with fierce voices and this alone was enough to hold back many of the curious and sick. It was while watching these two in action that I suddenly remembered who they were. Judas, they were the two hecklers at the washing of Yeshua! The small men with the voices like thunder itself; the very same. All this time at Cana I failed to recognize them, but here they had raised their voices at the crowd - like thunder again. So why had they become party of this man?

The crowd wasn't to be so easily turned aside as many came a goodly distance to see this man they had heard about from others. To them, Yeshua might be the only help the Lord provided. Some raised loud and mournful cries for help but these men weren't to change in their self-appointed task. Their master would have rest; they would see to that. Some of the poor, seeing that their cries wouldn't be heeded, turned aside toward the marketplace to beg, while others too tired and sick lay down outside the courtyard wall where they would stay until Yeshua returned. As the crowd dispersed, I finally presented myself to the followers at the gate.

"Ho, what have we here? Here's one of the wealth from the land of Judea, and from the look of things, he has traveled from Jerusalem. Who are you and what do you want with us?" The words came from the one called Simon as he stood by the gate. Dear Judas, I was amazed that he didn't seem to recognize me. We had just met some weeks ago in Bethabara. But I gave no notice and met him as a stranger, not knowing whether he had some special reason for this apparent forgetfulness. I had no real reason for seeing Yeshua other than curiosity but I couldn't really give that as the driving force which brought me to seek him. What could I say to the staunch defender of Yeshua's right to rest and well being? While I stood without words, and he peering at me from half-closed eyelids, Mary came forward.

"What happens here, Simon? It's time for you to enter the house; your wife Saria, and your family would have a word with you." Simon's face changed from the look of one studying a potential enemy to one hearing good news. He saluted his master's mother as one with great adoration.

"Come now to your family. I'll tend to this." She pointed to the house, making it plain that he should enter as soon as he could.

Mary turned, looked through the shadows and asked, "Who stands at the gate?"

I moved to where the light fell across my face to give her a better look at me and said, "It's me, Ishmael, and I would come in to see the family in a quiet moment."

"Ah Ishmael, come in and don't be afraid of these people - they're well-meaning fellows. Some would give their lives for Yeshua and would see his wellbeing isn't left to the press of the crowds. Come and enter the house for there is yet room for one more." She turned and led me into the little house now filled with the families of Yeshua, Simon, his mother-in-law, and the followers.

As I followed her into the house, there was some murmuring when they saw me as I wasn't one of them and my dress set me apart from them. This difference of garments caused them to be suspicious for, even as I had heard, there were spies of the high priest in nearly every corner of the country. These spies were used to keep the leaders informed of any self-acclaimed teachers, as there was much talk of a Messiah rising up to lead Israel from under the heel of the Romans.

"Ah Judas, things have changed. Not all of the house of Hanan considered the rule of the Romans outside the will of God. Some teachers point to the ancient trials of the people under the gentiles as the necessary penance for the people leaving the laws of God while others believed the time had come for the Lord to accept his people's suffering as enough and bring forth a leader even as Joshua and Moses before him to unite them and bring the freedom and greatness they once knew.

It's because of these differences in beliefs of penance fulfilled and penance due that some are happy with their lot and some not. Even now, dear brother, the Sadducees and the well-to-do class bend their rules to accept the rule of the ungodly. On the other hand, the Zealots will not bend and suffer greatly. From them comes the call to resist to the end for a leader will come and soon. Because of these words rumored about, the followers of new and unfettered teachers must keep a vigil against strangers who bring with them a sense of spies among their little band of believers. And because of this, their attitude changed toward freedom of speech and action. They were reticent to speak of their true beliefs and hopes for the future. It was this I had hoped to overcome without becoming a follower of Yeshua. I hoped to document their simple ways and complete sketches of them and their meetings and hear them recite their adventures.

Mary made no formal introduction of me to the group. Instead, she motioned for me to move to a place in the corner of the largest room of the house now to be used as the dining area. Even as I took a place standing among the least, I yet could see the young people and women actively preparing the evening meal. The lamps were lit and hung from small nails driven in the ceiling beams. Other lamps were placed about the room where the most light fell on a large table pulled to the center of the room. The smoke from the lamps hung near the ceiling and worked its way through the cracks in the roof to the sky above. I counted, as best I could, the people present. Excluding the children and Simon's immediate family who were not at the wedding feast in Cana, there were some twenty or so that stood in the room waiting the evening prayers before the meal; hardly what you would call a multitude. Most of them I didn't know at this writing.

I looked up from the letter to see the light had faded some. Time was slipping by. Between reading and reminiscing, the better part of the afternoon had gone. Outside the window all seemed quiet. I returned to the letter. Ishmael wrote on:

Call to evening prayers was answered without special arrangement; each person used the space available as best he could. *"Hear, O Israel: the Lord is our God, the Lord is one."* The cry of the poor outside echoed the call to worship.

After prayers, preparation of the meal continued. For this occasion, a large table had been assembled from simple carpenter sawhorses with rough-hewn boards placed on them. Benches had been constructed similarly. A quick count revealed not all could be seated at the table; several recognized this while the meal was being prepared. Where I stood, I could hear the murmur of those interested in the seating arrangements speak to one to another. Many were interested in who would sit next to whom. It became a matter of protocol, and I, who was the least of those present, had no interest in this but was in the attitude of those present. It became evident that the family members and followers had differing opinions as to who would be seated where, and especially who would be next to Yeshua and his mother.

The meal was prepared without the help of Mary. Instead, she was treated as the honored guest in the household of Sarai, the mother-in-law of Simon. Sarai was busy directing the younger women and children as the preparation continued.

Fresh flowers were brought from the garden to grace the table, while many of the young in-season vegetables were washed and set on the table. Fish, the meat of the poor, was served with a flat cake of barley. Everything was brought to the table in baskets covered with leaves of the plants used for this purpose.

During this time, Yeshua was on the roof in prayer. It was his wish to be alone for a period of prayer and meditation. His wish was a command to his followers, and because of this, the group below held their conversations in low tones. Except for the occasional command given by the women, the level of household noise was low. Even those that were curious about the seating whispered among themselves.

The preparations finally completed, one of the youths was sent to tell Yeshua that all was in readiness for his meal. The lad scampered up and down the ladder signifying he had accomplished his task. Soon, Yeshua came to the ladder and descended. Eager hands reached to help him. A clean outer garment, just washed the hour before, was placed over his shoulders.

For a man who lived and worked in this sun-filled land, he was very pale in color. He was smaller than I had first thought, small in bone and small in height and weight. His hands weren't rough and worn as those of a carpenter, nor was he heavily muscled as one who spent his young life using an ax, foot adz, and saw.

He moved from the bottom of the ladder to his mother's side and said, "Mother of mine, come sit with me at the table," while he led her to a place of honor. He then sat, or semi reclined, at her side. This selection of his mother at the head of the table seemed to indicate to the others that the family was to be seated at the table while the followers were to take positions on mats around the table. Ah Judas, you should've seen it. There was a wholesale movement of people. The murmur grew into a clamor as the followers claimed the right to serve their teacher as a right above the family. Theirs was a rightful claim in the tradition of master to student.

By tradition, it was their closeness with their master that caused many of them to leave households and follow even as we did Hillel so many years ago. Do you remember, Judas? It wasn't uncommon to see many pupils providing the teacher or chosen one complete care. Each pupil was given this honor on selected days; I can remember this often included the seeing to his needs and wants from sunrise to sunset. Bathing and anointing with oil on the holy days was also part of this ritual. I can remember it was a prized expression of love between teacher and student. No pupil, neither you nor I, would have relinquished his turn to do these services for his teacher, and to be passed over was taken as a reprimand in our day, eh, Judas?

It was from this tradition that Simon, who was of the old school, spoke out against his loss of position to serve Yeshua, his master. Being placed at a distance from him on the floor, where he couldn't pass the food to his master, or provide for him the water to wash his hands before the meal, was an affront to him and denial of his right. He couldn't show his love for Yeshua; this was his day of service, and he wouldn't relinquish it even unto Mary.

"Look upon me, master! I'm your servant of the day. Why am I forced away from your table?" He stood with his head down and spoke in a manner that showed his complete rejection. "Oh, woe is me, that I should see this day!"

The room became quiet and everyone waited for Yeshua to speak. Before he spoke, the one next to him, his brother, James, rose and spoke to Yeshua.

"Am I not your brother, and isn't it written that the stranger shall not take over rights which are reserved for the family? Who has the greater right to sit at the table, and isn't it so of the others? Where is it written the stranger shall inherit the place of the son?" He had no more spoken these words than the rest of the family began to join in the clamor of family rights over those of the strangers.

Yeshua took note of the noise, raised his hand for quiet, and spoke, "Who is the family and who the brother? Hear me, I say unto you, he who hears my words and follows me, he is my brother. And they who believe my words, believe the Father that sent me. It is they who are my family. For it is time for my earthly family to know that my work is not of this world. Hence, to the brothers of my body, through my own mother, you, too, can be part of the family through belief and following me, but those who care for this life more than the Kingdom of God, they aren't my brothers. It's for them to make the decision this day. Those who will follow me - they shall be seated at this table, and those who don't shall not.'

"I saw Mary lean on her eldest son's breast and strike her right hand against her own breast. She spoke with a quiet attitude, "Is this mission now come to term, even as you've said? Haven't I seen and heard you grow and play as the others? My son, there's yet time to withdraw those words. Remember, at some time, everyone on earth needs family. The Lord created man and woman to be fruitful and multiply; isn't this the saying?"

She continued and he made no motion to interrupt her, "Your brothers mean no harm, yet because of their closeness to you, some find these things difficult to accept. Some have heard me tell stories of old about your strange announcement and birth. Yes, even some have envied the special recognition by the Magi, and later, the special treatment you were given while yet in your youth." Some now shook their heads in agreement with the words of Mary.

"It's not their fault that these feelings come upon them, but mine. I was the one who repeated these strange and wondrous happenings as any other proud mother. Remember, even as your special gifts from the Lord have raised in you the need for goals not understood by us, these same gifts have raised in us the feelings of being rejected by the Lord. Isn't it written of the brothers of Joseph in like manner? 'And Joseph dreamed a dream, and he told it to his brothers, and they hated him more…' Are these, your brothers, so different from those of Joseph? Yeshua, I pray you, don't persist in this request but consider for my sake, for isn't it written that Joseph said unto his brethren, 'Now therefore, be not grieved, not angry with yourselves, that ye sold me hither, for God did send me before you to preserve life.'

I could see this request by Mary came hard upon Yeshua. His eye's became dark and sad. He looked upon her as a son driven by the love for his mother and respect for her wishes. At that moment, he was distressed for he was torn between the commission of the Spirit of the Lord given to him at his washing at Bethabara, and the love for his family. Ah Judas, his lips trembled as he studied the group at the table. All remained as they were and waited his comment.

"Mother your love for your family is as it should be but it blinds you to things of the Spirit. My heart is greatly grieved that this should be so, and of these things I've been aware, yet things of the flesh I can forgive but those of the Spirit I can not. The things my brothers feel against me are of no importance and have no substance, and I forgive them of this, even as Joseph forgave his brothers. But those that don't believe I am sent by the God of our Fathers to do that not yet done is to deny him that sent me. It's not yet given to me to forgive them for this denial. Hear me, those who would be my brothers and of my family must deny themselves and follow me."

This story by Ishmael was more than a simple family squabble - here was the new thought of Yeshua believing himself to be the Son of God! I read on:

Yeshua had no more spoken these words than one of his brothers called James rose and spoke to a very quiet crowd in the little house.

"Can it be that I have heard these things? Are my brothers ashamed of their place in the plans of the future? I've no quarrel with the Spirit of God, whether my place is among the high or low. Dear Yeshua, I will follow you even unto the ends of the earth. Here, brothers and followers, I make my stand." He left his seat at the table and came to his elder brother and kissed him. Yeshua was pleased with him. James then took a place behind Yeshua, showing his servant position unto him.

The others leaned to and fro whispering among themselves. One was selected to speak for the others. He was called Joses by some and Joseph by others. He rose and faced his mother and elder brother, for he was sitting along the long side of the table, while Yeshua and Mary were at the head of the table. Although this would have normally been the seat of the head of the household, or Simon, the son-in-law of Saria, yet he had, in honor to his master, arranged the seat for Yeshua.

Joses was a dark-skinned man, somewhat younger than Yeshua. His hair and beard was worked in ringlets. He had much dark hair on both head and face. His hands showed he was a man of labor, and was not afraid to accept responsibility. It seemed his brothers understood this and accepted him as their spokesman.

He waited for some of the murmurs to subside and then spoke, "Yeshua, all of us are younger than you, and therefore yet to experience that which calls you. When you left the house of our father to take your call, and this wherever it might lead, some of us had to pick up the load for the income of the household must be earned. It was by our hands that mother was kept in needs and away from torments of want. The family you left was on its own devices. The spirit that called you to your work, whatever that may be, called some of us to answer to the needs of the family. Have we misunderstood this? Have our actions been improper? Is it not written, 'Better is a dry morsel, and quietness therewith, than a house full of sacrifices with strife.' And haven't we done this to prevent strife among us while you were away? Hasn't mother been cared for while you were gone? Who has seen to this? Are we to be held accountable for this as evil? Why now must we make a choice in these things? Isn't it written, 'He that tills his land shall have plenty of bread, but he that follows after a vain person shall have poverty.'"

Joses paused for a moment, there was no other sound as those present hung on his every word. Judas, I could have been swayed by either. Where was the fault?

Joses continued, "It's written, 'Whosoever robs his father and mother, and saith, it's no transgression; the same is the companion of a destroyer.' But I say to you that leaving the household of the father and mother without necessary support is the same as stealing from them. Hear me, Yeshua, it's our choice to remain with the family and support our mother. If this be other than God's will, we fail to see it!" He ended his homily by bringing his fist down on the table.

During this speech by Joses, many of the group were swayed one way and then the other. I couldn't help but see the need of Mary remained after her eldest son left. And, even as an outsider, I could see the need for some of them to work and maintain the household. Even as we had left our mother in good standing before we left for Rome, so ought the eldest son provide for his mother. But somehow this wasn't the case, but that he left the household in less than a strong condition, if not without support altogether.

Judas, I listened with great interest as the family talked of this and that. They argued about such things as the money for the high holy days and the money needed to meet the taxes on the property. These were irrefutable taxes held payable each year by the house of Hanan and the chief priests, Herod Antipas, and the Roman government. Any of these could cause the householder to lose both living quarters and, in some cases, freedom. These were serious needs of the day, and to this was added the need for food and high holy sacrifices. The brothers were adamant about these needs and the lack of responsibility they believed Yeshua had shown toward them and Mary. Whether these accusations were true wasn't known to me, dear brother, but their concern for them was true as I was present when these things were made known.

For yet a little while these things were argued among the brothers, and then one moved away from the others and came to stand near Yeshua.

"While it's true Yeshua left our household in a questionable fashion to us and some admit not to have the spiritual quickening he has, how then can any of us denounce his actions? Would it be different if the same call came to us? No, it's not for us to say which is right or wrong in this act of following the Spirit of the Lord. We must be tolerant of these things, for haven't many prophets of old left their families to bring God's message to his people? If this is the call of the Lord, who can stand against it? I, for one, cannot call for rejection because of the law, and as I see it, the call is higher than the law."

With that said, he moved closer to his brothers Yeshua and James. It was during the course of his speech I heard the others call out to him; he was one called Judas. Aye, Judas, just as you are so called in our family. Some of the others called him traitor to his mother's cause. So far, Yeshua and James said nothing. Later, when they left the house for Nazareth, I still heard them murmuring harsh words against him for changing sides during the heated arguments.

Mary wept quietly but openly to see her family torn by this position taken by brothers, some willing to follow Yeshua, others forming resistance to his request. Mary raised her hand and tried once again to find a peaceful solution to this family difference.

"Is there no room for the natural family in this calling of yours, Yeshua? Must it be a choice so severe?" She turned to look upon him with pleading eyes showing the pain of a mother watching dissolution of the family.

Yeshua accepted her question and finally signed to all for quiet. "The time has come, dear mother, for me to leave my family and start the work of my Father which is in heaven. Whether this leads isn't clear, but what is clear is that things of this world aren't to interfere with this calling. Yea, I must travel where the Spirit takes me, and verily, even the foxes have holes, and the birds of the air have nests, but I have nowhere to lay my head from this day forward. The home and family once held so dear to me, must not now be as a weight to carry. Mother, I commend you to those who choose to stay with the land. To those who choose to follow me, step to the table and partake of this supper."

There was a moment of silence as those brothers who had chosen not to follow Yeshua sat unable to justly understand the full meaning of his words. One by one, they who had reasons to refuse the request to follow him rose and left the table, and those who were followers came forward to take their places. Many I didn't know, but of them who accepted his offer, I could see James and Judas, his brothers, James and John, the sons of Zebedee, Simon and Andrew, sons of Jona, Philip, and Nathanael, the former bridegroom; these I knew from the wedding in Cana.

Here the letter was annotated with small sketches of those seated around a large, roughly-made table. The sketch plainly showed the group with Mary seated at the head of the table beside Yeshua. I could see the lamps and room described by Ishmael; even on some parts of the scroll were sketches of the wedding and the people present.

It was the sketch of the stranger and Yeshua in the desert that held my attention the longest. Ishmael was right, the sketch of the stranger was easily recognizable as the person I had made the contract with to gain Ishmael's release. My heart trembled with fear as it was now plain this man was one of great power in this world. I fumbled through the rest of the roll to find the next words from Ishmael. I finally found the continuation.

Except for the prayers and washing of hands, the meal was started and finished under harsh silence. The tone and mood of this meal was greatly different from that at the wedding in Cana. Much bitterness was shown on the faces of the family members, yet Yeshua made no sign that this wasn't to be tolerated.

When the meal was finished, the prayers said, and the table cleaned, Yeshua lifted his mother from the table. He kissed her, bid all others to remain within the house, and led her to the little garden outside. She still was greatly upset by the things that just came about before her and leaned heavily upon him. As they left the room, the silence was broken by those unhappy with the news that they were not part of the meal in the traditional sense.

Charges and countercharges were hurled back and forth like stones meant to hurt. Feelings were running high; of the followers, Simon, James, and John were standing with feet spread apart and fists clenched, ready to defend their newly-gained position against any and all. The sense of brotherly love wasn't present. It wasn't a scene to my liking so I quietly moved to the back of the room. Here I could see and hear without taking sides.

Those of the family who weren't joining the followers soon tired of the threats and counter threats and gathered outside the gate of the little house without waiting for the return of Yeshua and Mary.

A CALL FROM HOME

Ishmael's letter continued and I changed position to increase the light on the page.

I moved through the door into the area between the gate and the house to consider my next move. While there, I heard those outside challenging a new person at the gate. Simon was called to the gate to represent his mother-in-law and her household. Simon moved to the gate to see who the intruder might be. I could hear the conversation between Simon and the stranger. My heart leaped, dear Judas, for I heard the familiar voice of Apius.

Who stands without the gate, and what is your business with the household of Tirzah?" It was the rough voice of Simon. He spoke for Tirzah, as next of kin. Her husband, Caleb, of the house of Judah, had been lost at sea some years before. Simon spoke again, "Can't you see we are about a family affair?"

"Aye, I care not to disturb you. I'm Apius, a servant of the household of Simon of Kerioth, and even now seek his son, Ishmael. Word has been given me along the way from Bethabara and Cana that he might be found among you who are followers of Yeshua of Nazareth. I'm sent by his mother to seek him out. Can't you give me your ear on this matter?"

"Say on, but I know of no such a one. If he is among us, we have no knowledge of it." He turned away from the gate and called to the followers, "Is there one Ishmael of Kerioth here? If so, let him speak and be recognized by this man."

There was a murmur among the group for none knew me and were curious that a servant would be sent to find one who might be among them. When I moved forward, the murmur grew louder for they had been suspicious of me from the beginning, not knowing if I was one of the temple spies. It was then Simon remembered our meeting at the gate some time before.

"Ho, it's you then, the one from Jerusalem. Wasn't it Mary who spoke for you at the gate? Behold, this man waits without for word of you. Go and speak with him." He had the others step aside and I passed through to greet Apius who was astride one of our horses and led another.

"Ah, Apius, it's good to see you, and what brings you in search of me?"

"Ah, Ishmael, it's your mother who prevailed upon me to seek you out. She hadn't heard from Judas these many months and is concerned that you have forgotten her, also. Won't you return with me now as she longs to see you again?"

"Is she well then?"

"Aye, but her heart is nearly broken for she longs to see you and Judas. Can't you give up this venture for awhile and come home?"

"I can't give up the quest, as I thirst for more knowledge. You remember Yeshua, Apius? He played around your knees when he visited with us. He is a strange one - this teacher. I can't come with you, but this I'll do. I will write mother and tell her of the adventure. And I'll give you this packet to send to Judas."

So I mounted the horse brought by Apius and left the house of Simon's mother-in-law. I accompanied Apius to a small inn and lodged there until I finished this letter and others. I trust him to carry these to mother and then send to you after mother has read them. I then wrote mother and explained the want to follow Yeshua until I had enough sketches to complete a series on his travels. Oh, Judas, his is an interesting life, and he is one truly touched by the hand of God, this I believe. As to how much of this is for the betterment of the people of Israel I don't know, but I must follow this course and find out the difference he can bring, if any.

I stayed with Apius in the inn without returning to the little cottage for nearly a fortnight. I'll return to the cottage and seek Yeshua as soon as I've completed this task and sent Apius on his way. I asked Apius to stay with me as a messenger and companion. His would be the task of transporting my letters to mother and you. He is an able horseman, as you well know, and I trust him with my life. I'll close this packet now and send it back with him. May the God of our Fathers cause his countenance to shine upon you always, and may you return soon to Jerusalem.

The packet contained more sketches, ones of the followers at the gate, and of Apius on the horse. Ah, Ishmael was indeed one who was blessed with the hand of the artist. His sketches were pleasing to the eye and told the truth of form and facial structure. I could see Apius on the horse as if I were there with him. The sketches were dated 778. So the year had turned while Ishmael was with Yeshua and his followers in and about Bethabara, Cana, and Capernaum. This seemed to account for the time between letters, but it didn't explain the reason for the lateness of these to me in Rome. Why had they all come at one time? Tears came to my eyes as I now understood mothers' concern about him and, of course, me.

I placed the packet with the others on the table near the window. Some time had passed as I read these letters from home. The sun had moved around and was now in the near south, and it was time for the noon meal. Yet, I thought of the other letters still in the packet, and what other news they contained of Yeshua, his followers, and Shalazar.

The next text I found was different in structure from the others; Ishmael had changed the subject. He opened the letter with a date as if he wanted me to know he was aware of the passage of time. It was dated 779; therefore, nearly a year had passed since he wrote it. These sheets were as stained as were the others, showing marks of being written under poor conditions.

Dear Judas, how I long to see you again. This has been a time of great change in me and I would that I could speak directly with you. Have you received my other letters or have they been lost somewhere en route? I hope all is well in Rome. Mother says in her notes that I receive through Apius that she hasn't heard from you either. Have the gods of the gentiles enslaved you? We await with longing your coming home. I'll assume you have read the other letters and won't repeat their contents. I've seen Yeshua, and was present at some strange happenings.

I sent Apius on his way with the blessing of God. He was to deliver the letters to mother and from her hand to the ship for Rome. It's my prayer that you received these in good condition, but I've heard strange stories about the sea lanes and the loss of many ships headed west; even those carrying the Roman eagle aren't safe. With pirates and storms, only the will of God guides our letters to their destination.

Apius has been gone some days now, and I've been following Yeshua and witnessing the things which happen about him. These I'll relate to you, but because of the dangers of travel, I'll break these letters into small missives and thereby I may prevent loss of much of the information at one time - should that be the case.

There are rumors that a new procurator is to replace Valerius Gratus. The countryside is alive with these rumors, and all are wondering who it will be. There are those who say he will be a taskmaster to our people yet there is hope among us that this won't be true. I suppose you know of these rumors as well, and may even know who the next procurator will be. If it's possible, Judas, send us such news.

A low noise of a street band caused me to look out the window. I saw nothing of importance in the street below. A small band of merrymakers soon passed the gate in celebration of some lesser dignitary's birthday.

While watching the scene below, I saw Apuleius arrive. He was in uniform and carried his courier papers, and I knew then all was in readiness for our trip to Judea. My heart sang with praises of thanks to the Lord as I had found favor in his eyes and was at last on my way home. Ah, to see mother, Ishmael, Anath, Apius, and Atonis again. To once again be among the sights, sounds, and smells of Jerusalem!

My thoughts returned to the letters - what of these? I had no time now to write for to do so wouldn't gain anything, after all, I would arrive in Jerusalem the same time as any letter - the same ships were used to carry documents and passengers. It was settled then. I wouldn't try to answer these letters but concentrate on getting things in order for the trip.

While I thought of the necessary preparation and the time needed for it, I looked again at the letter still in my hand, and decided to finish reading it before Apuleius came upon me. It continued with Ishmael's recounting of the happenings after Apius left him in Capernaum. He told of his sending Apius in search of additional inks and papyrus - he still had other notes to transcribe. He explained how his mind was full of the events and times of Yeshua and his followers. And so it went:

Even before Apius left, I was aware the Passover was near at hand. It was the beginning of Nisan and I would return to Jerusalem to keep the law. I decided to keep the horse with me and be able to stay in Capernaum longer if necessary.

After Apius left, I rode to the house of Simon's mother-in-law, where I hoped I would see Yeshua and his followers. I supposed they would be going to Jerusalem for the feast, and I would follow them at a distance on horseback. When I arrived at the gate of the house, I was greeted by the eldest son of Simon, Joseph, who told me that Yeshua, his father, and the rest left for Jerusalem nearly a week before.

I was told by the boy that Yeshua wanted to celebrate Pesach and seeing as it was a four-day journey from Capernaum, as he would travel only as fast as the sick would allow, they had left early on.

It seemed Yeshua's brothers, except for those called James and Judas, ridiculed the thoughts that one so near to them, even one of their family, could be the Messiah. They accused him of being a dreamer and placing his personal wants and desires before the needs of the family. They wouldn't change their thoughts on this. It was with this attitude in their hearts they took Mary and proceeded unto Nazareth the town of their birth. There, they, too, would prepare for the trip to Jerusalem.

Joseph said there was much sorrow shown during the separation of Yeshua and his brothers, and Mary was greatly grieved by this rift in the family. Yeshua and his followers left Capernaum with many sick and poor in their group, while his mother and the brothers went to Nazareth. I reasoned those with Yeshua would travel slowly because of the needs of those with them. I, on the other hand, had a sturdy horse that would carry me to Jerusalem in good comfort and less time.

I returned to the inn and there compiled some of this letter, secured my belongings, and left within the hour. As I started from Capernaum, the roads were beginning to clog with the pilgrims hurrying to the Holy City. It was always so during the time of the first Feast. Even on horseback, normal travel time was extended for the press of the crowds on the roadways. The wretched, poor, blind, and infirm sat along the wayside calling out for relief. It was enough to cause any sturdy heart to pause and thank the Lord for his love and care. Many called to be carried along to the Holy City, and here and again some strong lad would praise God for his strength and choose one to carry as far as he could. It was then for the others to offer their strength to the poor and ill. All this I saw on my way to Jerusalem.

It was well within the normal riding time to get to Jerusalem from Capernaum in two days. But with the press of the crowd, I was held to a slower time of three days. I didn't see the others during the trip. Yet here and there along the way I heard bits and pieces of stories of his kindness unto those ill and disabled. Some even made claims of immediate healing of those disabled for many years. Others scoffed at these stories, saying those who believed them were suffering from wine or mad from the want to believe in the coming of one that could do these things. I heard these things but kept them to myself, and reserved my opinion on their truth.

I was on the road for two days traveling with the multitudes when I came to the Gate of the Sheep, the one on the roadway from Capernaum to Jerusalem. The thought of being home again kept me from stopping and listening to other tales of those who saw Yeshua. I must be home in time to prepare for the feast.

I let the horse have his head as he was from our stables and was more than willing to move toward his stall once within familiar surrounding of the city. He carefully stepped through the throngs of people, other animals, and ox-drawn carts. He moved with an easy canter where the streets permitted this, and I, free from the necessity of guiding him, studied the colorful throngs. Ah Judas, people from all over the world could be seen in the crowds moving to and fro within the city's gates. Passover was the time of excitement - new sayings, new rumors, new products, and also new and bigger woes for the city.

Even with increased watchmen and Roman guards throughout the city, there were still reports of lost children, robberies, and yes, even killings during this time. Many of the local people were unhappy with the trends of unlawfulness during this the most special of holy days. Some merchants complained to the high priest about these things, but were the first to recognize the increase in their income caused by the influx of the people. They always wanted something done to the others but not their business places. Restrict the others but not those who were patrons of their booths, was the cry of the oppressed.

A MAELSTROM IN THE TEMPLE

As you know, Judas, with many kinds of people come different kinds of money, languages, customs, and understandings of the law. Remember the many arguments that occurred - they haven't lessened any these days. The temple guards are hard pressed to keep the pilgrims in line. Usually, when the language barrier arose, those not understanding one another raised their voices as if an increase in volume would solve the problem. It was therefore, dear brother, just as we have seen so many times when we were young, a continual din from morning to night.

I rode on greatly interested and somewhat amused at the scene about me, while leaving my horse to his own choices as to when and how fast he should travel. I was home in my beloved city and that was all that really mattered. The urgency of the moment had left as familiar sights, sounds and odors came to me.

And now, I'll relate a strange incident to you. The closer to the temple I came, the louder and more agitated the people were. This increase in animation roused me from a daydreaming condition I had fallen into while enjoying the spectacle before me. Here and there I could catch bits and pieces of excited conversations.

One merchant nearby posed a question to another, "What right did he have to do such a thing to us?" I recognized him as one who brought artifacts into the street near the temple. He had been on the street many years.

"Yes, on who's authority; I saw none of the high priest's men present." The man seconding the question was one of the money changers that sat in the Court of the Gentiles. I recognized him from the many years before. It was Zichri, ah, he had made a good living at his money changing stall. Now, he was angry and his beard bobbed up and down as he spat in all directions while he spoke. He waved his arms in the fashion of one near flying, and I thought it somewhat humorous to see old Zichri in such a state.

I reined my horse closer to the group in such a fit of crosstalk. Everyone was talking and no one was listening; it was worse than a flock of chickens with a fox nearby. What had happened to cause such a thorough sense of indignation among the merchants on this holy week? I raised my arm as a signal and rode closer to Zichri, hoping he would see and hear me.

"Zichri, why are you in such a state? Has someone robbed you or given you brass for gold?" My making light of his predicament wasn't to his liking. He raised his fist in answer to my prodding; he was in ill humor. His face was contorted and red with the flush of anger.

"Laugh if you will, Ishmael of Simon," he knew me soon enough, "it wouldn't be so a few years ago. These itinerant teachers of the coming of a Messiah have raised every listener unto a self-righteous Joshua!" He was right, Judas. Since you have been gone, many are moving the people. He continued to bellow, "Each of these believes he has the finger of God resting upon him; each believes it's his appointed task to take action against law-abiding citizens that don't agree with his interpretation of the law. Mind, each one believes this even if he breaks the law to do it. Aye, it's a bleak day for honest merchants when any passing teacher can take the law in his own hands and destroy property."

He went on muttering about things that happened this very morning. All of this wasn't clear to me so I decided to pursue the story. Even as he spoke, others joined in agreement with him, each gesturing with flailing arms and grinding teeth. They were an unhappy lot. The more I studied them, the more I realized that all were part of those who had booths in the Court of the Gentiles.

Many were milling about and dragging parts of their booths with them. Some of the booths were damaged beyond repair. The scene was one of havoc; men and animals seemed in a contest with others for attention. The animals were bawling and bleating, while many of the booth operators were loudly claiming some of their own had stolen from them during the melee. They stood outside the temple gate demanding their rights, yet were afraid to enter again without support of the guards.

"Haven't we given portions due to the house of Hanan? Hasn't Caiaphas received his tax from us, and hasn't Valerius Gratus set him in place? If the house of Hanan is displeased, then let them come to us."

It was Zichri that spoke again. "Is it possible to have all these from distant lands here even in the temple and not have just cause to exchange moneys; has the house of Hanan suddenly changed the law? Isn't the shekel and half shekel still the yearly payment to the temple treasury? Isn't foreign money still unclean for temple use?"

His questions tumbled through his trembling lips, and the more he spoke of what he thought was an injustice, the more violent he became. His words didn't ease the tension of the moment. Others joined his expressions of unhappiness with some of their own complaints.

"He shall be ours when he comes out of the temple!" someone cried, and the crowd roared its approval, and a small group of men went to find stones.

"Zichri, Zichri," I called at the top of my voice, "I hear your complaint and those here with you, but who and what is the cause of this unhappiness?" I didn't know if he could hear me over the crowd, so I rode as close to him as I could. Bending down, I cried to him, "Zichri, hear me! What is the cause of this anger among all these merchants? Has someone cheated old Caiaphas of some yearly tax?"

"No, you don't understand! Haven't I said it wasn't an officer of the temple that descended upon us like a madman? Mind you, it was even one of lesser learning than a Levite. It was one named Yeshua, of all places, from the land of little - Galilee. Let me ask you, Ishmael, what good thing has ever come out of Galilee?"

"All this caused by one person? All this destruction and excitement? How was it done, Zichri?" I couldn't believe that one so mild mannered as Yeshua had caused this uproar. Surely there must be some mistake! This I said, dear brother, because I couldn't believe Yeshua, the soft-spoken teacher I had seen in Cana and Capernaum, could cause this havoc. A man who, so said by John, believed in forgiveness of faults in others, and this even in his enemies.

"Yea, he is a madman! He comes into the temple court and surveys the money changers, honest merchants all, at work, as is our custom and right. He then becomes excited and irate - from what cause, I don't know - for he neither asked for nor needed to change his coins into temple ones. He and his followers left the court for a short time and then they arrived again."

Zichri continued, "This time, he carried with him a cat-o-nine-tails made of rope; all this he did without just cause, this I swear. He and his followers alike, although they carried nothing, went to the highest steps of Solomon's Porch and there he shouted, in a sort of battle cry, 'Hear me, take these things hence,' pointing to the sheep, oxen, and doves offered for sale to those who were unable to bring such with them from far countries, 'make not my Father's house a house of trading!' His father's house, ha, what claim has he more than the rest of us? Aren't we all son's of God? It is written by Isaiah, 'But now, O Lord, thou art our father; we are the clay, and thou are the potter as we all are the work of thy hand.'"

"What happened then?"

"Before any of us knew what he was about, he came like a madman, shouting and swinging his whip from side to side striking both man and beast alike. Every man looked unto himself. Many were hurt from the whip and the press of those trying to escape his blows. Innocent and guilty alike, of what I don't know, were driven to cover themselves. Yes, even those seeking only change were trapped in the melee. Some animals were lost and even now must be slaughtered as unclean as they received hurt from the rush of others during the excitement. Many others were hurt, even as I, when he overturned their booths and tables. All these things he did while shouting a writing of old that made little sense to those not having time to do his bidding, 'The zeal of thine house hath eaten me up!'

Zichri stopped to take a breath. Then another man stepped before him and spoke to me almost as excitedly as did Zichri. He was an Alexandrian Jew by his dress and mannerisms. "All this I can attest to. What's more, I and others like me, visitors to this great city, were also put upon by this self-styled judge. What was my sin? I had just come into the court when he descended on the booths. He didn't ask me if I were one making his father's house a trading house! No, he struck me with a whip just as he did the others; where is the justice in this?" He turned to look at the crowd as he asked the last question, and they answered him with verbal agreement.

Ah, Judas, I felt ill at ease I tell you.

By this time, Zichri had recovered his wind enough to continue his story - which he did as though the other man hadn't spoken at all. "He continued to do this terrible thing with no authority other than his own thoughts of self-righteous indignation. After things were well under way, his followers gained confidence from his action and joined in this unlawful maelstrom. Oh, we shall appeal to Caiaphas about this, and to the Roman authorities as well - although the Romans could care less about our internal disturbances. This man has overstepped his robes of the teacher. If he is a teacher, what does he teach his followers - how to destroy property and harm merchants in their earning of bread? Who's to pay for all this loss? I understand that neither he nor his followers have even as much as a shekel among them. Oh, woe is me! Does he think this act of madness will survive long in the memories of us who have a right to deal in the court? Besides, what is this affair to you? Are you one of his followers?"

Ah, Judas, he had me for a moment. "No, I'm not, but I've heard of him, and seen him do mysterious things."

Zichri shook his fist and yelled back, "Aye, why didn't he do one this time?" The others took up the cry, "Aye, if he is such a miracle maker, let him do one for us - put our booths back and make our animals worthy of sacrifice again!"

I continued as best I could over the noise of the crowd, "He may have the Spirit of God in him at that. Have a care, Zichri, and you others as well, that you don't overstep your rights. Call back those who would find stones. Stoning is for serious crimes of blasphemy, not for overturning booths and the like." I was now determined that all reasonable doubt should be supported against such serious actions by the disgruntled merchants. After all, much respect had always been given to teachers, and their actions were not always understood at the time of occurrence. It was plain to see Zirchi wasn't pleased with my words and continued on his way.

Zichri continued his harangue, "We'll see what the high priest says of this and we'll be back at our stands yet this week! We will file charges against this lawless band of ruffians from Galilee; this kind of act may be acceptable there, but not here in Jerusalem." Many joined him in search of the captain of the temple guards; it was they who had brought this bedlam to an end. They had moved against Yeshua and his followers sufficiently to seal them from the others. They now held Yeshua and his few followers in protective custody on the steps of Solomon. Except for them, I think the crowd would have moved against Yeshua in this outer court.

I knew he was right. The merchants would be back in the court within the week, and I remembered how often the Galileans were thought of as rowdy and untrained people. It was also true that neither Yeshua nor his followers had kept ought for themselves, but had given every shekel unto the poor and infirm along the way. Even the money James and John received from their mother was placed in the common fund and dispersed among the needy. As I see it, dear Judas, they have no one held accountable for their group funds and none seems to know what funds come in and what funds go out.

Their system is totally chaotic. When things occur that require money, such as paying the tithes for sacrifices, all must search through their purses for coinage to meet the obligation. Sometimes enough is found and sometimes not. Someday one must be selected to monitor funds for the group, as they have little financial skills.

While I was yet mulling over this turn of events, Zichri and the others appeared with the captain of the guards. With him were some Sadducees and Pharisees, and some other teachers. As they turned into the gate of the court, I dismounted and followed them as I was now curious what might befall Yeshua.

While I followed at some distance, the group led by Zichri crossed the court to the steps of Solomon. Here Yeshua and his followers were now seated and he was instructing them in the law. When the crowd drew near, three of his followers, Simon, James and John, rose to stand between the crowd and their master. There was little to fear as the guards stood between the crowd and the three with Yeshua.

The group with Zichri stopped just before reaching Yeshua and his men. Zichri prodded the captain to take Yeshua by force as he had claimed he had a right to justice, as it was written, "It's forbidden to convict on circumstantial evidence alone, witnesses must be brought forth."

Zicri pointed out that Yeshua had taken no hard evidence against those he whipped and therefore moved without just cause. The Sadducees were in agreement and knew they had many witnesses against the acts of Yeshua. They had the right, under the law, to arrest Yeshua for acting outside the law, but they were reluctant to do so because of the approaching holiday. Instead, they hoped to discourage those who followed Yeshua through exposing his lack of understanding the law.

"Teacher, under whose authority did you bring the lash against these people? And how do you know they are equally guilty of perversion of the house of the Lord?" These were the first questions asked by the leader of the Sadducees. Some of the crowd echoed his questions saying that some had done no wrong. Aye Judas, you might have been led to believe there wasn't a guilty one among the entire lot. But you and I know differently, as we have seen many of them smile at the gains made at the expense of the pilgrims from foreign lands. Those whose understanding of the exchange rate of some coins wasn't strong. Ah, how many times I remember some of these old timers whispering down the line one to another about the easy pickings they had among the pilgrims. Both you and I know there's many a rotten grape in an old cluster. Yet it was true that some of those injured were pilgrims and totally innocent of wrong-doing. Their major crime was just being there.

Yeshua stood calmly behind his three defenders and looked very tired but resolute. "Am I a criminal that you bring the temple guards against me? You ask by whose authority I've moved against these merchants, and I would ask you, by whose authority did they set up booths in the court of the temple? It is written, 'Even them will I bring to my holy mountain, and make them joyful in my house of prayer.' Who then among you has dared to change this; who has changed the house of prayer into a bazaar? Woe be unto those who would make the immediate want king over the infinite!"

Hearing these words, I saw the Sadducees and officials of the temple were somewhat troubled as none could recall who had started the buying and selling in the courtyard of the temple - the practice was before their time. To them it had always been so, and none questioned it before the law.

The group fell back from Yeshua and talked among themselves when one stepped forward again to speak with him, "Your words cause us some concern and we admit we cannot of ourselves answer your question, but pray, answer us this, do you know who changed this house of prayer into a bazaar, and if so, why didn't you take your case against them? Are you above the law? It is written, '...and if you don't warn him to avoid his wicked ways, his blood will be on your hands.' Where is the warning for these?" With those words, the leader stepped back and waited. For once, dear brother, the crowd was quiet.

Later, I learned the speaker was one called Nicodemus - a Pharisee of good standing and a member of the Sanhedrin.

Suddenly, there was a good deal of jostling and noise from some of the animals still loose. My attention was drawn away from the debate as I had to sidestep a bull calf that was bearing down upon me. When I again joined the crowd, I found I hadn't heard Yeshua's reply and Nicodemus was speaking again.

"Your answers are insufficient, we will go to Caiaphas! Yet we don't want to be confused on this, so give us a sign of your authority to do these things. Has your teacher been the venerable Hillel or his grandson, Gamaliel?" It seemed to me that Nicodemus wasn't concerned with a sign as much as Pharisaic authority; a name Caiaphas would accept.

"Oh, you who would continue to do that which isn't pleasing to the Lord, of what use is a sign to you? I don't speak from the teachings of Hillel or of Gamaliel, but from Him who sent me. Hear me, destroy this temple and in three days I'll raise it up again!" On hearing this, some became very angry. Nicodemus felt this, turned on his heel and returned to where the others stood near me. I could see his anger. He spoke unto Zichri and the others in low tones.

"This fellow mocks us as he says if we destroy this temple, which is yet in building these forty and six years, he will raise it up in three days!" His anger was carried over in his speech and manners; the crowd soon became as angry as he. They milled about asking what manner of answer this was to a civil question about his authority to act.

None understood his words, even I couldn't reason his remark - what had this to do with his authority? As I studied the faces of his followers, I could see they were also without understanding and were taken aback by this saying. The temple officers were now convinced he was of some danger to the house of the Lord and said among themselves, "Surely one who thinks he can raise up this temple in three days can also believe he can destroy it in like time. We must report this unto Caiaphas as there is real and great danger in such a mind."

They turned to look upon him again, not knowing what to think - was he a madman as Zichri and the others claimed, or one addled? I stood nearby and did likewise wonder. Some whispered that he did speak in great disrespect for all agreed that only God could do such a thing; therefore, they planned to charge him this day for his utterances as they could all bear witness, but there was some fear in them because Pesach wasn't a time to accuse another of crimes.

The officers promised to bring this charge before the Sanhedrin and Caiaphas and took their leave with no other action, Yeshua continued his teaching on the steps of the temple, and Zichri and the others grumbled but slowly dispersed and set upon the path of repairing and installing new and better booths outside the wall. I knew it wouldn't be long before they would be in the Court of the Gentiles again.

It happened even as I have written, Judas. Whether I heard the truth from the mouth of Zichri I don't know, and the meaning of Yeshua's words about the temple was and still is a mystery to me, so I keep these things in my heart, making no decision about them. During all the excitement, I nearly forgot I was on my way home, but after some of the noise had gone, I returned to my horse and made my way home.

I was at the gate of home within the hour. Apius met me and took care of the horse. Atonis was also there and provided me with water to wash away the dust of the road. Mother was told I had arrived and came to meet me in the garden.

"Dear son, it does my heart good to see you again, would that Judas was with you, but then I must not be selfish as God cares not for those so inclined." She fell on my shoulders and I kissed her.

"Mother, I've had strange things befall me and have little time to tell you of these. Many of these I've written to Judas and even now have great news for you and him." I began to realize how tired I was and the garden gave me the feeling of protection and restfulness I had missed. I told mother of many of the things I had written to you and added some of the things not in the letters to you because of space and weight. These I'll tell you when we are together again. As time passed, weariness came upon me and at last I excused myself and took to my room.

QUESTIONS ANSWERED

I was awakened by the call to morning prayers. *"Hear, O Israel: the Lord our God is one."* It was a familiar and blessed sound after a good night's sleep. It's good, dear brother, to be home and feel the love and warmth of family and to again be among surroundings of old. I do wish you would come home soon. It's as if I were a divided soul; I'm not whole with you so far away. Do you know that I still meet old acquaintances who yet mistake me for you? Oh, yes, our identities still remain nearly interchangeable.

Ishmael's letter continued, but my vision was too blurred with tears of longing to see him to read any further. Oh Ishmael, how I long to see you and home, but don't lose heart, it won't be long now, for even as I finish this letter, I can hear Apuleius telling his family of his recall to duty. The household is in an uproar. All the servants are in a festive mood scurrying here and there as a great farewell feast is in the making. Lucius the elder won't let this occasion pass without having friends and relatives bid Apuleius Godspeed and safe return. I couldn't weep for things that were to change and I returned to the letter.

The day and many like it followed, dear brother, as the Passover days came and went. The Roman's had moved extra men into the area and added checkpoints as before. I went to the temple as was the custom and saw Yeshua with his followers. Later, I saw him again teaching in the temple. There always was a small group of pilgrims and others listening to his exposition of the law. The followers I knew were always present listening as well, but I had the feeling they were on the lookout for any that might threaten their master. I observed all this from afar, still not being of a mind to become a follower of Yeshua.

I was unable to follow all the travels of Yeshua as mother and the household needed me. It isn't that I didn't want to, but mother was to be cared for and I wasn't a follower committed to him as is one who is a disciple.

Apius had become enamored with some of the stories of Yeshua and begged me to give him leave to hear him. I was kept informed of the exploits of Yeshua through Apius. Now remember these things I write are but hearsay and through the eyes of a Greek.

Apius told me that some pilgrims who heard were converted to his teachings, and offered him much gold to go to their countries and teach their fellow countrymen. This Yeshua steadfastly refused to do, often saying, "It's not right to take the children's bread and cast it to the dogs." Apius was taken aback by these words, but later rationalized them and what was meant by them through his Hellenistic teachings. I was unable to find an easy answer to such a strong remark unto the pilgrims, as I saw some were indeed sincere about their needs. Who had the greater need for his teachings, those who had never heard, or those who had heard and refused to heed them? Mary often quoted an angel of the Lord, "Behold, I bring you good tidings of great joy, which shall be to all people." Why then is it said that he is so secretive, and why not give his message to all people? There's more misunderstanding to this than the writings of old, I think.

Apius said some claimed Yeshua did great miracles before them, but he, Apius, wasn't able to witness any of these. Some pilgrims claimed he was the Messiah and would have others believe as they did. It was this desire in some that caused them to ask him to teach in their lands. But Apius said all wasn't as it seemed, for some were filled with wonder at the great mysteries done by Yeshua, yet they hadn't seen them firsthand. Even those who claimed to have seen these mysteries had never seen the mysteries done by the Chaldaean and Egyptian magi of old. They were, as Apius said, a gullible lot.

There are many teachers in Jerusalem these days. The most venerated of these is Gamaliel, the grandson of our old teacher, Hillel. Yet, Judas, I've heard talk of one called Nicodemus, a Pharisee, the same who challenged Yeshua in the temple, who has the Spirit of the Lord in him. His followers insist he is well grounded in the Law and Prophets yet hasn't the narrow interpretation of some of his contemporaries.

One day, some followers of Yeshua came to me as they had heard and seen some of the sketches I made of others. They wanted me to sketch their teacher, but at the same time feared he wouldn't permit such. They didn't know of the sketches I had sent you. How I remember your chastisement of my efforts and the repeating of the law about the making of images. It's from this calling I cannot turn; it's a millstone about my neck and I asked the Lord to forgive me for this weakness. It was this willingness to do that which I am forbidden that caused me to search out Nicodemus. I'm older now, and perhaps I can understand what he teaches of this mitzvoth, prohibiting the making of images.

So I asked one of his followers, Joseph ben Arimathaea, where I might find his master. He wasn't willing to tell me without my word to hold this in strict confidence. After an agreement, Joseph led me through the streets of Jerusalem by night to the upper city where those of wealth resided. Here in a fine, gardened home was the teacher Nicodemus and to him I put my question and cause of my heartache.

"Greetings, Nicodemus, and may God be with you! May your house be blessed for accepting me." I was grateful for his audience.

"How can I be of service to you? Joseph tells me you are Ishmael of the house of Simon, a good man and officer in the temple for some years. I remember him well, a good man and true."

I noted Nicodemus was a small man, neither old nor young; he was one that age had been kind to and therefore I wasn't able to place his age. "I would hear your question and maybe we can both learn something from it."

"Hear me then, Nicodemus. I'm greatly troubled. From my youngest days, I've been granted a gift of art. I can and do create likeness of all things, and this on scrolls, stone, and wood. Yes, even clay I have worked. Yet, I know well the commandments. Now, is this gift given to me to be a trial for my life, or is it one that I may use for the good of all? Isn't there a difference between making an image and that of making an image for use as an idol?"

"Son, there are many gifts of God. These may be varied; one of these is music. It's not music that is found as an abomination to the Lord, but the use of music for the releasing of evil in man. It's also true of art. The making of images on any medium is in itself not of consequence, but the making of images for those who would bow down unto them. Remember, it's obedience that's the first law of all things. Wasn't it the command of the Lord that caused Moses to make a fiery serpent and set it upon a pole? Wasn't it an act outside the commandment not to make graven images? It wasn't held against Moses, the making or causing of the image of the serpent, as it was his greater duty to obey the command to make the image. Hear me, Ishmael, don't create any image that may be used for the replacement of the Lord God of Israel. Don't make them to sell or for free; remember, their use will be held against the maker as well as the user. Go and fear not the honest work of your hands." He was an understanding teacher. My heart leaped at his words and it was as if I was a slave given freedom. I gave him my blessing and went my way rejoicing.

It was sometime later that I heard of Nicodemus once again. The story was told to me by Joseph of Arimathaea. The story was in this wise. Nicodemus was a teacher of goodly stature in Jerusalem and was a member of the Sanhedrin. He was, as I had learned from my meeting before, a man who desired to know the truth of all things of God. The deeds and sayings of Yeshua had been brought to him by others. He was greatly curious about the teachings of one who had caused such bedlam in the Court of the Gentiles just before the Passover. He would have come directly unto Yeshua but for the press of the Sanhedrin in these matters. Most of the council was of a mind not favorable to accept any news about Yeshua. It was because of this and the want to know more about this renegade teacher from the boorish country of Galilee that caused Nicodemus to seek out Yeshua in the night.

With their cloaks closely about them, Joseph of Arimathaea and his teacher, Nicodemus, walked through the streets of Jerusalem to find Yeshua. The dark of the night wasn't the kindest time to walk the streets and alleyways of Jerusalem. The lower city had elements of human degradation that weren't above foul play. It was known but to a few the whereabouts of Yeshua, as he had no home of his own in Jerusalem. He wasn't without a place to rest as some of the poor and well-to-do alike would have him stay under their roofs. God's blessing was upon any house having a teacher therein, so the old writings said.

Through careful questioning, Joseph of Arimathaea had found the abode of Yeshua. He was the guest of one Mary Magdalene. Mary was from Magdala, a city on the shores of the Sea of Genesaret. She had moved to Jerusalem some years before and was known among the more well-to-do for fine perfumes and ointments.

Mary had a small garden in which she grew some of the most exotic plants in the eastern world. Through blends of these and other plants, she produced beauty products of great demand. As you remember, Judas, her clientele was nearly as elite as mother's. She had gained prominence in the world of Jerusalem's aristocracy.

Mary of Magdala was admired by many of the young and wealthy of this and other cities. Her perfumes and ointments brought high sums. Her home was built by a wealthy foreigner, and constructed at her insistence in the lower side of Jerusalem. It was often debated among the wealthy why she held such an idiosyncrasy, for all knew she could maintain a home in the upper city, but it seemed she was more comfortable among the poor of the land, and that's where the house was built. It was here Yeshua and his followers found a friend when she opened her home to them. Care was always taken when leaving and entering the house to avoid possible disclosure to the spies of the high priest and others. Different ways through the city were used to throw off any energetic followers.

Through the streets of the poor and sick, Joseph of Arimathaea led his master unto the house of Mary Magdalene. Yeshua sat among his followers when Joseph of Arimathaea and Nicodemus came upon them. They were challenged by the three followers - Simon, James, and John. Although not well known to Yeshua, he told his followers to permit them to enter and join the lessons of the evening. Joseph and Nicodemus came into the lamp-lit room. One of the followers, James, recognized Nicodemus as a teacher that had held in reserve his decision of the teachings of Yeshua while others of the Sanhedrin where calling for his censure.

Nicodemus spoke thereafter, "God be with Yeshua, and blessing on this house. We are come to ask of you of these things we hear have come to pass." Nicodemus spoke for both he and Joseph of Arimathaea, his disciple. It was Joseph that had brought the first news of the mysteries of the man from Galilee to Nicodemus. What Joseph heard troubled him. Nicodemus had listened to his troubled disciple with great interest, and had attempted to answer the questions of life after death and the salvation of Israel but found his own knowledge in question; therefore, Nicodemus planned to seek out Yeshua and ask these questions for himself.

"Ask and it shall be answered unto you, Nicodemus."

"We know you are a teacher of some controversy, but we hear you are one from God and has His Spirit upon you, for no mere man can do the things that are spoken of you. Our question is of the kingdom of God. How can it be that man born of woman can see the kingdom of God, as it's written, 'There is no man that hath power over the Spirit to retain the Spirit; neither has he power in that day of death.'"

"It's even as written, 'No man born of woman as man can see the kingdom of God, and no man has power over the hand of death, for it's the will of God, and the length of life is in man's control as well as God's.' Hear me, I say unto you, except a man be born again, he cannot see the kingdom of God."

Nicodemus mused over this for a moment, then asked, "I accept your words but don't understand them. A man comes from woman as a babe, how then can a grown man enter his mother's womb and be born again?" Nicodemus smiled, for he at first thought Yeshua was trying him. "Hasn't it ever been so?"

"Aye, so it's been and so it shall be. A grown man cannot enter the body of his mother and be born again a child." Then Yeshua smiled as one teaching a child.

"It's written in Daniel, 'And the kingdom and dominion, and the greatness of the kingdom under the whole heaven, shall be given to the people of the saints of the most High.' Are all to know the kingdom of God? Who might these saints be?"

"The kingdom of God isn't for all men, and the saints are those that believe what I bring. But here I pose you a question, for I'm told you are a wise man and a Pharisee of good standing. What have you been taught and what do you teach?"

"From the time of Moses, it has been thus. Moses received the oral law on Sinai, and delivered it to Joshua, and Joshua to the elders, and these to the prophets, and these to the men of the great temple. He that keeps the law is a child of God, and he shall be considered to life after death, and he that does not shall be chastised by eternal punishment when he dies." Nicodemus held his head high while saying these things as he was of one mind. The law was the fence that separated the Pharisee from those who didn't know the law. It was the law and the adherence to it that had saved Israel from all the ungodly religions of the world throughout the centuries. Yea, even through the many years the children of Israel were in bondage, it was the law and belief in one God that had sustained them and kept their children from straying. Could anything less than or more than this be expected of man? "Thus I teach among men," finished Nicodemus.

Now Nicodemus was a proud man; this was apparent. Not proud to the extent of being unmindful of God's dislike of pride, but the pride that comes from doing what God has called him to do.

Yeshua studied Nicodemus then remarked, "It is good, but Nicodemus, who can keep the law, and if they don't keep it, then who can be called the saints of God?"

"None can keep the law, for it's written that no man is above the law. The saints are hidden from us."

"But the kingdom of God is for the saints. These are the children of God, even as Ezekiel said, 'I will sprinkle clean water upon you, and you will be clean. A new heart also I give you, and a new Spirit will I put within you and I will take away your stony heart.'"

Yeshua stopped for a moment and drew a line figure of a fish on the ground. He looked up and continued, 'Notice it isn't the world but the love of it that condemns, and it's not the law that condemns you, but the love of it. Some find in the law a refuge to avoid relief of those in need - they indeed have stony hearts. Mark me well, oh Pharisee, some who love the law say the unclean shall receive no help from them, secretly keeping the law as a shield against doing good. Woe unto those who use the love of the law as an excuse for not bending down to aid a fallen brother! It seems to me, Nicodemus, it would be far better that they did so without knowledge of the law. Don't you agree, Nicodemus?"

Nicodemus returned part way and spoke softly, "Aye."

"Hear me, Nicodemus. Except a man be born again of water and of Spirit, even as it was said of old, he cannot enter the kingdom of God."

Yeshua showed signs of the Spirit while he spoke to the teacher from Jerusalem. His followers smiled and shook their heads in agreement with his every word. They were caught up in his teaching and were also of the Spirit.

"But teacher, how can man come to this Spirit and cleansing with the water? Who has the power to change a man's heart and give him a new Spirit? In the ancient writings, the God of Israel said He would do these things, therefore, what form of man can take the place of God? Even the high priests are not given this!" The room fell silent and the followers turned to one another - what manner of question was this?

Yeshua gave no sign of misunderstanding the question. "No man can take the place of God; that which is born of flesh is flesh, and what is born of Spirit is

Spirit. Marvel not that I said unto you, you must be born again. This is no more a mystery than that of the wind. The wind blows where it will, and you hear the sound thereof, but cannot tell from where it comes or where it goes, so is everyone who is born of the Spirit."

"Aha, I can see all these things as the will of the God of our Father's, but how can these things be of man?" Nicodemus wasn't one to be put off; his teachings placed the God on High above the understanding of man, and these words he heard weren't of man.

Yeshua seemed taken aback by the continued questioning of the Pharisee, and said, "Are you a master of Israel and yet can't see these things?"

It was Nicodemus who was surprised at these words, but continued, "Master, I'm so accepted among men. What have I said in error? I know the promises of God unto Israel, and the cleansing of the body with water - haven't we all lived by this? I know God's word unto our father's about the instilling of a new Spirit, and this granted unto them in the days of old, but of this time, I know of no such promise." Nicodemus quickly defended his position.

"Listen to me, verily, I say unto you, I speak of that I know and testify of that I have seen; and you don't receive my witness." Yeshua wasn't smiling now.

"But teacher, aren't there other teachers who present similar ideas about these things? And don't they tell us they are the ones given of God? Should I be swayed by the speech and acts of each of these, or isn't it prudent to study their ways to avoid being deceived?" Nicodemus wasn't a fool; he wasn't one to be taken in by every itinerant teacher of the law. He moved to leave the house of Mary Magdalene. He hadn't received the answers he wanted, or so he thought. Instead, he had been called down for his love for the law. From this meeting, his need was to study and watch the progress of this Galilean.

Yeshua spoke again, "If I have told you earthly things and you don't believe, how shall you believe if I tell you of spiritual things? Hear me, believe this, no man has ascended up to heaven, but he that came down from heaven, even the Son of Man which was in heaven." Yeshua gestured unto himself as the one he spoke of.

Nicodemus and Joseph of Arimathaea drew in air sharply as this was near blasphemy. What manner of speech was this? Both stopped in their movement and stood transfixed on the spot. They seemed held there by a giant hand.

Yeshua continued, "Isn't it as written that Moses lifted up the serpent in the wilderness? Even so must the Son of Man be lifted up; that whosoever believes my teaching shall not perish but shall have everlasting life. For the God of Israel sent me not to condemn the world, but that the world through me might be saved. He who believes me is not condemned; but he who doesn't is condemned already. And this is the condemnation; that light has come into the world and because some men are evil in thought, word, and deeds, they love darkness rather than light. For everyone who holds to evil dislikes the light of truth and doesn't come to the light, lest he is reproved. But he who does honestly comes to the light so his deeds show that they are wrought in God."

Nicodemus was greatly undone by some of these words. He rent his robe to show his unhappiness and disbelief in these things. He stepped outside the house and took off his sandals and knocked off the dust gathered from the floor of the house of Mary Magdalene. Joseph of Arimathaea did likewise and followed his teacher, as was the custom. We then repeated the Shema, *"Hear, O Israel: the Lord is our God, the Lord is one."*

Nicodemus finally found his voice and called out, "Isn't it written that we are all son's of God? How then can you claim to be begotten of the Lord? This talk isn't of God, this is of man! Our God is one! Am I to believe that the God of the universe in his oneness has begotten a son? From whom? You speak as a gentile - they have gods who have intercourse with man and maid, and thereby begat sons of gods, isn't that so? Who's doctrine is this? What doctrine is this that Yahweh needs a son to forgive the sins of his people? Didn't David sing, 'Bless the Lord, O my soul, and forget not all his benefits; who forgave all the iniquities; who heals all thy diseases; who redeems thy life from destruction.'

Yeshua raised his hand, "Hold Nicodemus, why are you so hard of heart? Isn't it also written, 'Therefore the Lord himself shall give you a sign; behold, a virgin shall conceive, and bear a son, and shall call his name Emmanuel.' I am he!"

As Yeshua spoke, the group of followers became enchanted. Some were so filled with the Spirit of the sayings that they rolled on the bare ground and frothed at the mouth. Some shouted praises to the Lord, while others mumbled words that all couldn't understand. Some said they recognized the words of foreign tongues that these simple folk couldn't have known before that hour. Nicodemus stood his ground outside the house and became even more resolute in this position.

"May the Lord God of Israel forgive me of these things, for they are an abomination unto him. May your mouth be stopped. It's written, 'I am the Lord; that is my name: and my glory will I not give to another, neither praise to graven images.' And even as Isaiah cried out to the children of Israel, 'For I the Lord thy God, the Holy One of Israel, thy Savior...' Can it be that a man now says he is to take the place of Almighty God as the Savior of not only Israel but the world?"

Nicodemus continued, "No, and no again I say, for the Lord says, 'I, even I am the Lord, and besides me there is no Savior!' Have I not learned the Lord frustrates the tokens of liars, and makes diviners mad, who turns wise men backward, and makes their knowledge foolish?"

Ah Judas, all these things Joseph of Arimathaea told me of the night Nicodemus first met with Yeshua. What others may write I know not but these are his words.

Nicodemus rent his fine cloth under his outer garments, he was greatly distraught; and his disciple did likewise. "Look for me and mine no more, I find no truth in your sayings. The Lord God is the Savior of his people and the world if it is to be so, and the law is the fence against the gentile."

"Hear me, Nicodemus, study these things; I have seen in you the teacher without guile. We will meet again, and this I know, for it is given to me; you, oh, Nicodemus, will be by my side at the coming of the age!" Yeshua turned to those in the house and began instructing them again in the words of the Law and Prophets.

Nicodemus and his disciple stood outside the house of Mary Magdalene. Nicodemus was shaking from anger and frustration, and Joseph took off his own cloak and placed it over his masters shoulders. Nicodemus couldn't retire from the house but stood and listened to the discourse Yeshua presented unto his followers and the friends of Mary assembled there.

"Hear me, I say unto you no man has ascended up to heaven, but he who came down from heaven, even the Son of Man which was in heaven." And the listeners didn't understand him as none had learning to know these things.

Nicodemus couldn't stand these sayings and called out, "Then you are the Son of Man and you have been in heaven?"

"Yes, it is so." Yeshua answered as a simple truth.

Nicodemus was again upset and he ground his teeth and shook his fist at the house. He turned to me, his disciple, and cried in a loud voice such that those in the house could hear, "We must leave this place, Joseph, as God isn't here. This man sets himself up as the Son of God. This is blasphemy, pure and simple, even as all men are sons of God from creation, there is no one Son of God begotten of Him. The Lord needs no son to be lifted up to forgive the sins of his people; even as it is written, the Lord our God is the savior of his people." Nicodemus and Joseph left the house of Mary of Magdala for their own part of the city.

All these things Joseph of Arimathaea told me of the first meeting between his master, Nicodemus, and Yeshua. Now, dear Judas, can it be as he said, that Yeshua believes he is the Son of the living God? If he continues to say these things abroad, and allows others to make the same claims, and doesn't refute them, he is surely in trouble with those in authority. They won't leave a thing like this go unchallenged, and neither should it. Judas, I close this letter, hoping you'll return soon. *"Hear, O Israel: the Lord is our God, the Lord is one."*

There was a sketch of Joseph and Nicodemus as Ishmael saw them. I carefully stowed the letter in the packet. I would review these sketches many times before my meeting with some of these people. I was later to be thankful for Ishmael's hand as I knew many of them early on.

CHAPTER TWELVE

To Judea

"Judas, Judas, where are you?" It was the voice of Apuleius; he was running through the halls in a carefree manner. He had with him the transcripts of our travel papers, the ships' lists, and other necessary papers as he came into the room.

"Ah, there you are. We are set to sail this month. You'll never guess who is sailing in this same convoy? I'll tell you - Pontius Pilate and his entire entourage - that's who!"

"Judea's new governor?"

"Aye, the very one." He was excited about the prospects of leaving so soon and the good luck of the ships of the fleet accompany our vessel through the pirate-infested waters.

The days of preparation flew by. Packing and getting ready for the long stay for Apuleius, and the permanent stay for me was dealt with some sadness. Even so, many family parties were held for the going away of the only son of Lucius the elder.

The day we sailed was beautiful, but one dark element rested on us. Apuleius was to sail with his contingent, while Johnathan and I were to sail on a smaller craft. After some tears and farewells, we sailed with the tide. It was not long before I found I was standing on the deck of a sturdy craft plying the waters of the Aegean Sea.

The ship was considerably lighter than the war craft of the Roman army, broke away from the convoy, and sailed to Tarsus. It was here that I met the young Paul and his father once again. I had been in correspondence with Paul's father since the first year I returned to Jerusalem in the year 764. In accordance with the letters about my possible return, Bela Ard decided to take his son to the Holy City to study at the feet of Gamaliel. They were ready when the ship docked and we sailed as soon as the ship was refitted and resupplied.

We spent many hours during the voyage renewing old times and addressing the news we received from Jerusalem, Johnathan always near and offering his service when needed. Bela Ard was a mild-mannered man, but his son, Paul, was a firebrand. He had all the vigor of his youth behind his thoughts of what should be done with those who lived outside the law. His father more than once reprimanded him for his hasty conclusions about the different stories of those who believed in a Messiah. They had heard the stories in Tarsus. Some of the pilgrims from Jerusalem were full of these stories, and expressed the fanatical hope of throwing off the yoke of the Romans. It wasn't that Paul disagreed with these notions, but it was the way the different ones believed this could be done. To young Paul, the law was supreme, and all else was but a way to dilute it, and with dilution came loss of the House of Israel. I was happy to hear that he would study under Gamaliel, for there was a good teacher that knew how to instill the leveler in man; Paul would lose some thoughts of retaliation and retribution, and might gain some ideas of tolerance.

I showed them the sketches Ishmael made and recited the adventures he had while following the exploits of Yeshua. Paul's mind was closed on the subject, but was greatly interested in the sketches and studied them intently. It was as though he was burning them into his memory, to recognize these people whenever and wherever he might see them. He often remarked how well Ishmael's sketches were done and how lifelike the figures were. He said little other than this, yet I felt he thought it a gross transgression of the law.

Not many days passed when we landed in Caesarea. The speed of our smaller ship enabled it to catch the slower convoy of the armed ships before we entered port. We docked on the same day and nearly the same hour as the ships carrying the legion, Pontius Pilate, and his entourage. I searched for a glimpse of Apuleius and his officers, but it wasn't to be. As citizens, we were able to follow the troops but not to cause any obstruction of their travel. The disembarking troops were joined by a cohort of legionnaires from a garrison from Jericho who were to be relieved.

There was some delay as Pilate and his generals went to inspect his residence in Caesarea. Herod greeted him there but didn't join him in the trip to Jerusalem. After nearly two days of some revelry, the troops were again placed on the ships, and we also boarded our craft to sail to Joppa. The word was that Pilate decided the weather was too hot to make the extra miles on foot or on a litter. So it was that the entire legion and all left Caesarea for Joppa within the week. In all that time, I failed to contact Apuleius. Our vessel made better time than did the others and we landed at Joppa nearly a full day before the troops.

I had decided to wait and look for Apuleius once again when the troops disembarked at Joppa. I found quarters for us and we waited. The troops and Pilate's entourage arrived the following day. All were formed up in a receiving area and set to march after a brief rest to get the feel of the ground. The march from Joppa was one of nearly 40 miles Roman. The movement of a legion, nearly 6,000 men, would take more time than I could spare - I wanted to be home soon. Although unattached, we civilians from the ships were included in the march to Jerusalem. I had secured horses for Bela Ard, Paul, Johnathan, and myself and traveled along behind the troops. The march was one of Roman splendor; Pontius Pilate wasn't one to enter his new domain with less than the best. He was carried by litter bearers through the dusty streets of the villages and towns along the way.

Even in the heat of the day, the troops marched in quick step. Pilate was in a hurry to get to Jerusalem and make his presence known. In his hurry, he decided to bypass the palace in Joppa. So it was on to Jerusalem and let the people there know who is master.

The Roman eagle was uncovered and the guidons were unfurled. It was an awe-inspiring sight for those Romans living along the way, but a foreboding one to the Jews.

Pilate was a man who had marched with Germanicus through some bitter campaigns. He was a hardened soldier and one who knew the capacity for men to complain on the trail. He had instructed his generals to hold the men at quick step for some many miles and then let them walk at route step for another distance. Alternating this form of march gave the men needed rest without losing time. The dust of the roads soon coated the splendid uniforms of the men for it was exceedingly warm for this time of year. Rivulets of sweat caused the dust to stick to the men's bodies and armor.

It wasn't long before even the most hardy veteran was calling out to the Roman gods in less-than-honored addresses. All this and much more we could see as we were forced to follow them for some distance and the dust rolled back upon us. We, too, soon became covered with the silt of the roadway.

Because of the dust and discomfort of finding rooms along the way, I decided to get to Jerusalem before Pilate's entourage and cohorts entered the famous gate. I wanted to see Pilate's entry into the Holy City and I expressed this wish to my companions.

It was then I decided to pass the troops on their first rest stop from the grueling forced march. And so it was we passed the cohorts and Pilate while they were alongside the roadway on a wind break. With our horses held near a canter, we put the Roman army and Pilate behind us in short order.

The way was familiar to me as I had made this same trip three times before. I knew the best inns along the way and in these found the same good service and food in Lydda. We rested the horses there. We moved on to Emmaus and from there to Jerusalem. I drank in the familiar sights and sounds of this land of miracles and history of Israel. It was good to be near home. I described the scenes and activities along the countryside as we passed. This storytelling seemed to help the miles pass. It wasn't long before we were in sight of the gates of Jerusalem. My heart fairly sang with thanks to God for this moment.

HOME ONCE AGAIN

At that moment, I was torn between rushing full tilt into the city unto father's house and into the arms of my loved ones or delaying my arrival to see Pilate's entry! It wasn't often that such an occasion arose in my lifetime, and I might never again have a chance to see a Procurator enter Jerusalem. I knew the legion would be resting and at least two days on the roadway. I computed that we would have two and one-half days before the legion came over the hill into Jerusalem and seeing as they traveled on the Sabbath, they would arrive in the afternoon of the first day of the week. So I planned to go home and greet all, then see the arrival of Pilate on the first day of the week.

"Bela Ard, you and Paul must stay with us for a fortnight or so; to do otherwise would cause mother great grief. It's from there you can take your time in selecting a household for Paul. And of course, there's room in our house for Paul if he is of a mind to stay with us during his time before Gamaliel." I wanted Paul and his father to know of our gratitude for the time he had made Ishmael and I welcome when we were strangers in Tarsus some years before.

"Ah, it's a kind offer, Judas, and we would be less than honorable if we refused, and we would not cause your mother hurt in any way." Bela Ard spoke from a true heart. "Yet we wouldn't stay longer for I must be back to Tarsus by the end of this month. We have made arrangements with a distant relative for Paul and they will be expecting us."

"Aye, it is done. We will be well received this I can tell you." I set my horse in a canter and they followed, through the gate of the city and down familiar streets of merchants and craftsman we rode. I deliberately made a wide sweep of the area before heading for father's house. It was a heart-warming trip for me, while it was an eye-opening one for Bela Ard, Paul, and Johnathan. The sights and sounds of the old city brought memories surging back once more. Places and friends that were still as unchanged as when I left tumbled into view; it was I who had changed. Most of those I recognized as I rode by did not recognize me. Some called to me as Ishmael and thought it strange when I gave only a nod. I had been gone almost fourteen years, and had changed from the influence of Roman society.

When we reined up at the gate of father's house, Apius was first to greet us. He was a happy one. He nearly pulled me from the horse in his joy to see me again. It was easy for me to shed tears of joy at seeing him again. Without command on my part, he accepted control and had the horses of the others taken from them.

Atonis came running when he heard the shouts of happiness coming from us. He then alerted the rest of the household that the long-awaited errant son had returned to his proper place once again. With the household stirring, mother came with tears running down her cheeks. I was glad with all my heart to see her so well. She was still a woman of rare beauty and grace to me. I fell upon her shoulders and wept unashamed. After our tearful embrace, I introduced her to Bela Ard, Paul, and the young, free man, Johnathan.

I reminded mother that it was Bela Ard's household in Tarsus that took Ishmael and I in some years before. She was quick to remember and then offered her house unto them and wouldn't hear of any other arrangement. She saluted them in the manner of the day and bid them to follow the servants to the garden and to accept water for washing after the trip. I excused myself from mother and led them to the place for ablution. The servants brought clean clothes for me and the guests. Room arrangements were made by mother, and we were settled soon. It was then I ask about Ishmael for he hadn't greeted me.

"And where is that rascal, Ishmael? Here I arrive home and my twin isn't here to greet me." I pretended to be unhappy but I was curious at this turn of events.

"Your brother is on another one of his jaunts about the country seeking more about Yeshua. He's quite taken by him. I do hope you and he can talk about Yeshua for there are strange things happening here in Jerusalem." She looked worried about the situation.

"Ah mother, don't worry, Ishmael was always one quick to see the romance in any situation. He will tell me of these things when we see each other again. But for now, mother, I beg your indulgence for some political news I bring." She turned quickly. I could see she hadn't lost her interest in these things. "Apuleius and I were scheduled to sail together but alas, he had to sail with his contingent. This change was caused by orders from Caesar himself. Can you guess the cause?"

"Aha, do you speak of a change of politics? Have you news of the new Procurator?" She was sharp this lady of mine.

"You are too clever for me, mother. We were joined by a large convoy of warships and the flagship of this fleet was carrying the new Procurator of Jerusalem, a man called Pontius Pilate. Because of this, I was then left to sail on a lighter and faster service ship, and as I had made arrangements with Bela Ard to meet him in Tarsus, this I did. When we sailed from Tarsus, our ship, being faster, joined the warships before landing at Caesarea. After some troop interchange and a rest there by Pilate and the troops, we again boarded the ships and sailed to Joppa.

It was said Pilate saw no reason to march his men along the coast from Caesarea to Joppa when sea transportation was available. We landed at and traveled from Joppa here. I haven't seen Apuleius but he's with the cohort that will be stationed at Fort Antonia."

"But what has this to do with us?"

"It's my desire to see the entry of this Pontius Pilate into the city for I believe it will be the only one I shall ever see. With this in mind, I beg to leave you in a day or two to see him do so." I could see this wasn't pleasing to her as she didn't want to lose me so soon after fourteen years of absence.

I was still very lighthearted when Ishmael arrived home. Then my heart was raised to even higher ground as Ishmael greeted me at the gate. I fell on his shoulders and wept for joy. Here was blood of my blood and flesh of my flesh in the truest sense of the words.

"Stand back, Ishmael, and let me have a look at you! Ah, it's good, dear brother, and much has happened to us since we parted. Ishmael, you look different in some manner; have I changed so much?" I could see that some of his boyishness wasn't there and before me stood a man of the world.

Even without speaking, I knew he was changed in spirit and in grace. Had Yeshua instilled in Ishmael the ideas of the Messiah and the coming of a new and powerful Israel? I introduced him to my companions, Bela Ard, Paul, and Johnathan.

He moved back and looked at me for some time, "Aye, Judas, I have longed to see you with all my heart. My mind cried many times to see you. We will have much to talk about these next few days. Come, let's go into the garden and be more comfortable."

We moved into the garden; Bela Ard and Paul sat near mother, while Johnathan and Ishmael sat near me. Mother's face showed her happiness at having her sons home again.

"I have told Anath to come home for your homecoming celebration, Judas. After all, you have yet to meet her husband and family. Just think, three nephews and two nieces you haven't seen. Is that the way to start as an uncle? Oh Judas, may God keep you by my side these next few years, as I'm getting old and would have my family near." She motioned for us to come and join her on the bench under the trees.

The rest of the day passed pleasantly but I could tell Ishmael wanted to tell me of something that was even now more important to him than this homecoming party. He held his peace throughout the days of celebration, and I held my curiosity about his uneasiness. I met Anath's husband, one Lud, and it was said by my sister that he could trace his family back to the house of Shem, a son of Noah. Of all this I cared not for I judged a man not from his lineage. This much I learned from my time in Rome. I found as many men with evil intent with great historical accreditation as those of good dealings with none. It wasn't always a man's family that supported his honesty, but his love of God. Anath's family was beautiful and were brought up in the Lords' ways. I renewed old acquaintances and made some new ones. I introduced Bela Ard and Paul to my family and told of Paul's chance to sit at the feet of Gamaliel, the venerated teacher in Israel. The family was greatly impressed with the young man; he was a zealous young man with an excellent command of several languages. His manners were without cause to worry and he remained the apple of the young ladies' eyes among the guests.

Ishmael and I took Apius and Atonis with us as they had stood by us for many years and were eager to see this thing. Before we left, I introduced them to Johnathan, something I had failed to do earlier due to the excitement of our arrival. Both Apius and Atonis were interested in Johnathan's history but were restrained by the newness of their acquaintance. Both Bela Ard and Paul declined to go along; their attention was drawn to other things.

We arrived at the gate of the city and there joined some of the populace now forming to greet the new Procurator. He had sent some of his horseman ahead to bring news that he was on his way. Herod had informed Annas and Caiaphas and ordered them to meet Pilate with a goodly turn out.

By the time we reached the gate, we could hear the murmur of the crowd and see the column of dust rising from the roadway some distance away. It was amazing to us the sound the nailed boots of the troops made. It was a regular rhythm with a nerve-jarring noise of metal on the cobblestone. On they came; the people moved uneasily. Some of the merchants were already packing away their goods; they feared the force of the troops as they marched near their booths. Many had experienced the clean sweep of men in columns and knew that some refused to break rank for anyone. Some of these merchants and customers went inside their homes and closed their shutters and doors in a manner showing their displeasure. They were in no mood to accept another Procurator after Valerius Gratus had held them in ransom for so long.

We watched the troops top the rise. First came some German cavalry, then lancers and short swordsman, then came the litter bearers carrying Pilate. He was followed by the rest of the legion, each cohort separated by its commanding officers, nearly six thousand men and animals; a column stretched further than the eye could see from this lower spot.

As they came unto the gate, they sounded the march of triumphant on brass trumpets. It was a sight and sound that I will never forget. There was a great difference between the troops we saw en route and those entering Jerusalem. The difference was that all the guidons and war eagles of the Roman state were now covered.

My heart fluttered to see the great power agree to cover their colors and Roman eagles before entering the Holy City. It wasn't until later I heard that this was a trick of Pilate, and later, when he set them unfurled in the street of the city in the middle of the night, the people learned how devious he could be.

Through the streets they went until they came to the temple, for it was en route to Antonia. Pilate's entourage and the troops passed through the Court of the Gentiles. Although this was no abomination, it was gall to the people. Pilate then ordered his litter to be borne up the steps and into the inner temple - he would see what the Jews had inside this highly-touted seat of the Jewish God.

His progress was impeded by the high priest, Caiaphas, and his sons-in-law, the dressing priests, war priests, the Segan, the priest over the temple police, the police commander, senior priests, the administrator, the lay priests, and the Levites. Although unarmed, there was nearly twenty four hundred souls pressed before the litter and the entrance to the inner temple. Even Herod couldn't have brought forth a more impressive commission to meet the new Procurator. In their vestments, as set to the occasion, they looked the part of high dignitaries of the city. I was near enough to see that Pilate was duly impressed but whether or not to his liking, I couldn't be certain.

I could see Caiaphas was pale and eyes flashing as they stepped in front of the great doors of the inner temple. My heart fluttered to see their action but I felt great pride that these men moved to face the strength of the Romans.

In the background, I could hear a soft chanting of the Shema. I doubted if Pilate could understand its meaning but I knew the people near did. *"Hear, O Israel: the Lord is our God, the Lord is one and Him only shalt thou serve."*

Though some claimed these men corrupt and insensitive to the needs of the people, they had, at this moment at least, shown their commitment to the Lord of Israel. Yes, I was glad I had followed the Procurator and his entourage into the temple as I had seen this thing done before the Lord.

The late afternoon sun cast long shadows and made the vestments and armor of the troops so assembled dance before the eyes. Caiaphas raised his right arm in salute to Pilate, not as one showing lesser to greater, but as one who was equal.

"Hear me, oh Procurator," Caiaphas called from the steps of the inner court, "with all due respect to Rome, it is forbidden that any uncircumcised enter the inner temple. This has been recognized by Caesar himself."

And so it was for many years. Since Pompey, had this been recognized as the way of life of the Jews nor had any Caesar after, to this very hour, caused this to be denied as law. No Roman or gentile of their provinces had ever crossed the threshold of the temple.

Now, Pilate was keenly aware of this and visibly angered by this statement brought to his attention. He would have had his German riders force their way into the temple, but the call of the ram's horn caused the priests to close the great doors leading into the inner corridors. Pilate was furious at this obvious flaunting of his desires yet it seemed he didn't want to start in his new position under difficulties and wished not to disturb Rome as well with the news of a skirmish of any magnitude. From the number before him, it could very well be a serious confrontation. He also realized these Jews were not above sending a committee to Rome on just such matters. His face remained flushed, and no doubt his revenge would be planned soon.

Pilate commanded his troops to move through the Court of the Gentiles and out to the fort. We left the scene as the entourage traveled through the court and on toward the fort. We then hurried home while my heart sang the songs of David for I had seen the temple held sacred and the Lord move over the Romans this day.

APIUS SPEAKS

Some time later, all the family settled down and I approached Ishmael about his adventures since I received his last letters. He was more than willing to relate his travels and happenings. He began by explaining his whereabouts the day I arrived home from Rome - but I won't hurry his story. What he told me of those days was so.

Some time passed since Ishmael followed Yeshua and his little band, now known as disciples, as he was considered by them a teacher. Although he had little or no formal training at the feet of the doctors, he was so accepted among some of them and the people.

When Ishmael came to know of them again, Apius had last been with them. With Ishmael's permission, he followed Yeshua and was gone sometime before he returned to report what he had witnessed. He told some strange tales and had many questions about the practices of Yeshua and his followers. His was the eye of the Greek and not that of a Jew.

Apius said Yeshua was not being permitted to teach in the temple as is the custom these days for all who felt the Spirit of God. It was because some disagreement with the Sadducees - or so it was told. As a result, Yeshua gathered his disciples about him and traveled out of the Holy City to the North. His course wandered through many villages and towns. His time was his own, sometimes staying longer at one place than another. During this time, he taught no one other than his disciples. Travel was slow. He talked as they strolled through the countryside.

Wherever he traveled, some of the poor and infirm followed him crying out for him to relieve them from their discomforts. This he didn't do even along the way. The little group moved north-northeastward until they came near the waters of Aenon near Salim close to the border of Samaria. This was a quiet place some three days' walk from Jerusalem; here there was abundant food and water.

Although Apius didn't understand why Yeshua left the greater share of the needy and infirm in Jerusalem to travel to the little town of Salim, he found that they were away from most of the unbelievers, scoffers, and temple spies. He remained with them for their stay near the Jordan. During his stay, Apius traveled about the area when he couldn't find Yeshua. As he traveled thus, he came upon John ben Zechariah, who had traveled in the wilderness washing penitents and calling them to seek forgiveness from the God of Israel.

Because of his Greek background, Apius referred to John as *John the washer*, or *John the Baptist;* however, this wasn't a common practice among the followers of Yeshua or Yeshua himself, for to them he was still *John ben Zechariah.* And so it was that I became familiar with the term *John the Baptist.*

Apius was curious as to why this teacher also chose to come up from Jerusalem where the need was so great, but hadn't the heart to ask him. John was also using water from a spring-fed tributary of the Jordan to wash those who came to him for remission of their sins. Yeshua's disciples took on the practices of John in that they were also washing those who came to them as transgressors. Although Apius said he never saw their master do this thing, he washed not nor forgave them of their sins.

Apius said he didn't know the reason for the disciples of Yeshua washing the new followers of Yeshua as they hadn't been washed themselves, other than Andrew and John, who were known to have been followers of John before becoming disciples of Yeshua. But as far as the others, none were raised from the waters by John, yet they all washed others.

So John and the disciples of Yeshua washed penitents in nearly the same waters of Aenon. As many of these were washed unto the glory of God, they traveled back to their homes and carried the words of John and the disciples of Yeshua with them, each into his own city and town. Even as good news spreads of its own weight, so the news of the remission of sins was carried unto the countryside. Therefore, as Apius saw, some - as many as could be freed from other tasks - came to be blessed by these men of God.

Since not all understood what was said, they took with them many misconceptions of this act of washing. Some of those they met along the way listened to their stories of the changes they saw and heard happening by the power of this washing. The claims became grandiose and many of the new people expected much when they entered the water. Because of this, many came to the waters misinformed of its efficacy, expecting everything to happen to them from curing of bodily ills to being taken into heaven even as Elijah had. As often happens, the simple washing soon became a carnival atmosphere. On they came from Jerusalem and round about - the poor, sick, lame, blind, and even lepers. But what Apius didn't see was any of the Royal family, or any of the great and wealthy Sadducees. Oh, there were some Pharisees and scribes, but most stood aside to watch.

The lesser people Apius saw, some without food or water with them and no money to purchase such things. Many came as they were on the temple dole anyway and had no work to hold them, while others were from small villages where the work was of their own making. The merchant who had skills to sell and his employees weren't to be seen. Many became unruly at times, each believing his needs greater than the other. The crowds were so great that some were hurt and unable to reach the waters' edge. The cries of the infirm and blind were heard everywhere; "Hear and help us, men of God," became the cry repeated as most didn't know who was doing what, but they wanted some of whatever it was.

During these times, John did the washing of any that appealed to him for such and he deemed worthy. Those who were brought before him who couldn't confess their sins and accept his doctrine because of mental deficiencies, he wouldn't wash. Watching John, Apius found he demanded of those he washed these things among others, "He who has two coats, let him give to those who have none; he who has meat, let him do likewise; let him who drinks strong drink cease therefrom, even wine of the sacrament ye shall not drink; and let him who eats in excess cease therefrom, and let him mortify his body unto the Lord."

Some came to him thereafter and said, "All these things we have done since our beginnings." And John washed them. Some came to him thereafter and asked, "Master, what shall we do now?" John said, "Go and sin no more, put on clean raiment and with clean body stand before men as a new creature in the Lord unto the coming of the Messiah."

Afterward, some came again to John and asked how a man could sin no more, but Apius said he didn't hear John's remarks to them. Apius considered this an impossibility as he knew from some of the old teachings that sin was the breaking of the law, and no man kept the law.

Some that came before John were not so accommodated. Apius said John wouldn't wash a gentile for remission of sins unto the God of Israel. A number of certain devoted Greeks who were followers of the God of Israel, and kept the law as well as some Jews being washed, came to John and asked him thus, "Master, if we also believe in the Lord God of Israel and keep his commandments, why don't you baptize us?"

And John said, "Lest you are circumcised into the covenant of Abraham and counted as one of Israel's children, you cannot receive the benefits of the children of God!"

Nearly all the gentiles who heard this were undone and turned away from the teachings of John. It was whispered that some returned to their homes saying the God of Israel wasn't the all-powerful God of the world for He could not forgive their sins. They remembered no such limit was placed on the gods of Greece and Rome. All who applied were forgiven through the rituals of the day. This was indeed the mark of a supreme god; he that forgave the sins of all mankind regardless of the shape of his body, color of his skin, of his father's house, and mental capacity - he was the one true god.

Apius continued and told me while John washed only those he selected - those who met his standards - he was not able to wash as many as the disciples of Yeshua. Some who waited long for John to reach them became discouraged and went to the disciples of Yeshua. Some found these men didn't ask them the same commitments as did John. There were many who were unclean washed by the disciples. The already-baptized followers of John, even some of his disciples, were disturbed by this and went to John with this question, "Master, we believe in what you say. Yet he that we saw with you at the Jordan, the same you said was greater than you, baptizes, even as you, and not content with this, asserts himself unto setting you aside. Yea, the same permits his disciples to wash those who are unclean as seen from the law. Why then do you teach so?" And those who were of this mind pressed hard against John for an answer. Some shouted and called him a deceiver of men.

Apius said John seemed little disturbed by those who demanded to know who's teaching was in accordance with the law. He spoke loudly for the sake of the size of the crowd.

"What does it matter? Should I tremble or be angered at this? Hear me, a man can do nothing but that which is given from heaven!"

The crowd wasn't pleased by this remark and they continued to press John for a greater explanation. "How can this be? Have we not all a free will? If one cannot do but that which has been given from heaven, then aren't we pawns of God as the Greeks believe?" There was a great shaking of fists and noise making.

Some of the Pharisees called out to him passages from Proverbs. "Isn't it so that the simple believe every word; but the prudent man looks well where he is going? Here we have two teachers, which one is right and has the truth? How can we know who is given from heaven and who isn't? Who is in fault?"

John was quick to rise to their question. "It's neither who are in fault, but that you perceive not. Some of you bear me witness that I said I'm not the Messiah, but I'm sent before him who is. And so it is given to me, and so it will remain. I'm but the friend of the bridegroom. It's with joy I hear him happy in his recognition from heaven."

Some considered his words and one then said unto John, "But what is this to us? His disciples teach and baptize they who are unclean. How gain they remission of their sins if they are not first cleansed?" The leader of the group was a man of good standing known to John as Simon, the Pharisee.

John continued teaching but didn't satisfy them anymore. Apius said many talked of this thing of uncleanliness. He saw no great difficulty in this, but didn't know enough of the law to find fault in it. The crowd moved about, uncertain who to believe and who was speaking the truth. Soon the multitude split into two factions, those favoring John and those favoring Yeshua. Many were unlearned but recognized the representatives of the law in the Pharisees.

John said, "Don't let these men of the law confuse you. Hear me, and believe, the God of our Fathers loves his Son, and has given all things into his hands."

Apius said there were many that raised a great cry against John on hearing these words. They were prepared to press hard against him, and but for some of his followers, would have taken him with them to Jerusalem to appear before the great Sanhedrin.

These were the words that riled the crowd of lawyers from Jerusalem, "He of you who believe on the Son has eternal life, and he who doesn't shall not see life, but the wrath of God."

Yet those who found favor in the words of John held their ground and wouldn't let the lawyers and spies of the temple take John. So it was that John moved to another place.

Apius moved with the crowd for they now went up the stream until they came to where the disciples of Yeshua were teaching and washing. By that time, it was evening and the Sabbath day approached, so the disciples of Yeshua ceased the washing and moved into the house of one of the city of Salim. Here they prepared for the Sabbath.

Apius left the area and returned that same night. He and I spent much time going over these things he had seen and heard. And these I've told you this day.

And so it was I received the latest news of Yeshua from Apius through Ishmael. I was determined to become acquainted with Yeshua once again. But first, I must find Apuleius and have him join me in this pursuit, then I would see what these mysteries were all about.

BACK TO THE PRESENT

Suddenly, the speech synthesizer became garbled and the screen lost all intelligence. The computer switched to search mode. The system was offline while it tried to recapture the lost characters and sync words.

A sigh of exasperation came from John as he pressed the delay button, and proceeded to shut down the entire process. He turned to those at the consoles and with a gesture, indicated he was tired and welcomed the break. A quick glance at the elapse time meter indicated they were online for nearly four hours, and as was agreed before, four hours was enough. It was time for an evening meal.

John didn't wait for concurrence but proceeded to notify the university that he was taking the system offline for the rest of the day. They had been eight hours on the job; it was time for everything to rest until the next day.

"All those for dinner say aye." Agreement was quick. Each person moved to secure output material and was ready to leave in a short time.

They moved through the air interlock and into the hallway. John closed the door, inserted his keycard and notified security the laboratory was to be cleared for the rest of the evening, with access only at 0800 hours the next morning. John and Jean left in John's car. The meal was strictly a business-like dinner, a meat-and-potatoes affair, with apple pie as dessert. During coffee, the conversation was open for all.

"The more I see of this document, the more I'm beginning to believe the writer is being trapped into a situation of intrigue," said Ed.

"I will agree that it's been intriguing, and the storyteller has introduced some interesting characters. It's somewhat true to form, but have any of you noticed the lack of romance in this story?" It was Jean that raised the question.

"Well, I'm not surprised about that. It shows the male domination of those days rather clearly. But let's have a show of hands - can we agree that this isn't a story, but a genuine log or autobiography, if you will?" Chuck asked for this vote of confidence. There was little hesitation; the hands went up nearly in unison.

"Good," Chuck continued, "now, let me continue on the lack of romance - this writer wasn't interested in romance and has at this time in his journal concerned himself only with the happenings as he saw them or was told them. It's a good sign that almost none of the document indicates he knew what had transpired before his first-hand knowledge. Meaning that, unlike the Gospels, where there is a great deal of foreknowledge used to interpret current happenings, Judas writes differently. He has not added parenthetical phrases explaining what is really meant by the information in a certain line."

John asked, "What do you mean by that - no parenthetical explanations?"

"Well, for instance, in the Gospels, we have the line about the building and destroying of the temple, just as Judas reports it in his journal. The difference is that in the Gospel, the event is followed by the statement, "When he was risen from the dead, his disciples remembered that he had said this unto them…" while Judas reports the same happening but doesn't seem to know of Yeshua's subsequent rising."

Chuck took a long drink of coffee. "It means this: that when he wrote this statement, he didn't know of the subsequent happening and later, if he did know, which at the moment we can't deduce, he didn't go back and edit it as the others must have done."

"Okay, I see. This indicates Judas didn't know of Yeshua's rising from the dead at the time of his entry. Which means his writings may be older than the oldest acceptable New Testament now extant as those writings show that someone wrote or edited them at a later date." John was happy with this small bit of historical deduction. "I like that."

The waitress wearing a checkered apron brought fresh coffee for all. The restaurant wasn't too busy for this time of day. And with plenty of seats available for customers, the group wasn't interested in leaving the pleasant atmosphere. It was good to get away from the manuscript and let one's thoughts review the inputs of the day. So much early history had been viewed in a short time. Nearly twenty-five years of time in the life of Judas was translated by the system in three days.

"I was especially intrigued by the sketches that Ishmael made of these people, and was surprised to see them as part of this scroll. Judas must have thought enough of them to keep them for his lifetime. I was also amazed that the transponder could and did draw such fine graphics of these sketches. They were superb for the amount of detail; I'd say the machine is doing a fantastic job on this project." John was happy with the find and the work of the system on it.

"There's one thing sure. If we can believe the sketches drawn by Ishmael, these people weren't the beautiful persons now shown on every piece of religious literature in existence since the masters." Jean smiled, as she made the comment on the likeness of those depicted on the scroll. "Either Ishmael was not the artist Judas claims, or the people he saw were very homely, to put it kindly. I wonder what the reaction will be when these sketches are submitted to the religious community? After the many years of artwork done by the masters showing the primary personages in such good light, to see some of them as commonfolk now won't be as spiritually uplifting as before."

"It'll shock a few, I'm sure. But it's no great thing. Those who want to believe the masters will continue to do so, and those who might have some faith in this document will believe in these. After all, it's not looks that makes the difference anyway." Ed moved from one position to another; he was ready to leave. This wasn't so of the others; they were content and relaxed.

Chuck ignored the body language of Ed and moved on to another subject. "It's interesting to note of those who were of the twelve disciples, Judas, by his own story, seems to be the better qualified to write this sort of journal or exposé. I recall, some writing is attributed to Simon, later called Peter, John and Mark, who was thought to be known as John, also. But as in the case of Paul, John, the son of Mary of Cyrus, supposedly changed John to the Roman name of Mark when he went out into the field. While Luke, a contraction of Lucanus, who wrote one of the synoptics, wasn't one of the twelve. Of the twelve, it's claimed by some that they weren't learned men, and it's doubtful some of them could write well enough to be the originators of the Gospels. Of these, one named Levi, who is reported to be called Matthew, seems to be one of the more learned one of the twelve, other than Judas. He had a background of languages and mathematics sufficient enough to be chosen as the receiver of customs. He alone, of the twelve, other than Judas again, seems to meet the requirement of writing." Chuck took time to move his new cup of coffee around to the other hand.

Jean was puzzled and asked, "Just what are you driving at, Chuck?"

"Well, just this. We have no original text in any form, other than this Golden Scroll, and if we did, I was wondering just what the chances would be for the type of language used. By that I mean, what kind of structure would an original story have in text and grammar. If these men were simple fisherman, what would their dialogue be like? Just supposing Peter had written the first and second Peter. Can we really believe he would have written in the form accepted today? It seems to me that much of what we have in the New

Testament, in addition to being, at the earliest, two centuries old, must have been edited and copied many times by a variety of people before reaching us as it is."

"But what does this mean? Most Christian theologians agree to this," Ed stated, "and it's held that this isn't a thing of concern. The fact of the matter is that most believe that, learned or unlearned, the Gospel was transcribed as the writers were moved by the Spirit of the Lord."

"Hold on. I'm not arguing that point. All I'm saying is that of those who might be eligible to write something for posterity, without the guidance of the Spirit of God, Judas seems, by his own hand, the best qualified to do so.

Therefore, I feel that from the linguistics standpoint, his story, so far as I can discern from the system output, is well within structural validity." Chuck wasn't going to press his case any further.

"I agree with Chuck. The more we see of this scroll, the better it's presentation. But let's consider more of this after a good nights' rest." John was ready to leave.

"I'm sure we could stand the rest and relaxation," Ed was always one for time off.

"We'll see how things shape up tomorrow. I'll expect you all on time. Until then, Jean and I will be at my place for awhile, if that's ok, Jean?" John smiled in an easy way; he hoped he hadn't presumed too much.

"Of course. We'll see you tomorrow, fellows."

The group paid for their checks and left the restaurant. Jean and John drove to his apartment. They spent some time going over the days' inputs from the scroll.

There was a goodly bit of give and take about the meanings of the different parts of the scroll, but nothing serious developed about the material presented. The evening was spent with pleasant thoughts and hopes for continued success. Later, he took Jean home and returned to his rooms with the thoughts that it seemed a bit more lonely this time. After a quick shower, he was in bed and soon fast asleep.

And the evening and the morning were the fourth day.

The phone woke John. Had he slept through the alarm? He was temporarily confused by it all. The sunlight through the apartment window caused him to squint some as he reached for his glasses and the phone. There, he had them both - the world wasn't so bad after all.

"Good morning, John, and where are you? It's after 8 and I'm hungry." Through the mental haze, he recognized Jean's voice. He thought it was rather pleasant waking up to her call. "Are you there?"

"Well, yes, I guess I am. It seems I've overslept - boy, I didn't hear the alarm at all! Look, I'm sorry and I guarantee it wasn't planned this way. I'll be there in a jiffy. By the way, call Ed or Chuck and tell them I'm on my way." John was already moving about the room; the old cordless phone was helpful in this case.

Jean answered with a light laugh, wondering what John looked like in his moment of disarray. "Ok, no problem, and I'll call them both." Jean hung up and John was on his way to the shower. No further interruptions were forthcoming and things went without a hitch; in a matter of minutes, he was in his car and on his way to Jean's apartment. When he pulled up, she was waiting outside.

"Sorry about…" John started to say.

"Don't say that again. No harm will be done if you get me to the restaurant on time. Boy, I'm one hungry chick!" Jean stepped in and smiled at John. He seemed nonplused, much like a boy caught in the act of skipping school. The trip across town was done in good time. They entered the restaurant less than thirty minutes after her wake-up call.

John heard Ed's voice above the ambient noise. "Here, over here! We were just about to give up on you two and go ahead and order. Hey, friendship is one thing and starvation is another!"

"Well, I've all kinds of excuses on hand, but the truth is - I overslept. I'll bet each one of us has had that happen before."

John was about to continue when Chuck interrupted, "Here comes the waitress, we'll forgive you if you are ready to order."

The waitress was at the table before long. The morning breakfast was over quickly as all interests lay in the laboratory. Conversation was nil and one cup of coffee the order of the day.

They arrived at the laboratory door nearly at the same time; no time was wasted passing through security. Once inside, documents were prepared and consoles set up for the next phase of decoding. There was a question of finding the lost words, but everything had gone so well before that confidence was high on an early retrieval.

John punched in the codes of the day; the vertablinds closed automatically to darken the room.

"Everyone ready?" The trio nodded assent. John programmed in the translation phase. The system indicated a fault and the characters on the screen were unintelligible just as before. The first try wasn't successful. The blinds opened and the screen was placed in a standby mode.

The four sat with puzzled expressions as the system continued its search for the lost words. There wasn't anything to do but wait as all indications confirmed correct system operation.

The waiting was relieved by conversation. "Well, how about that? This is the first time we've been delayed by the system. It may be just a simple interface problem." John spoke with more hope than conviction. In truth, all of them had seen a short delay turn into a disaster.

"I hope you're right, but last time a simple interface problem lasted three days." Ed could always see the less optimistic side of anything. "I hope part of the scroll isn't obliterated or faded beyond recovery."

The search continued.

"We should consider that all the Golden Scroll may not be recoverable. However, for now, I'm pleased with the way the program is running. If the delay is great and caused by some scroll imperfections, we'll skip them and proceed with the next readable section."

All agreed it would be a wise move.

Chuck wasn't to be denied his chance to see as much as he could. "Of course, this means some of the writing recovered may be out of sequence." It was clear he was interested in speeding up the process without destroying the overall historical continuity.

They all continued to watch the screen for any change. John spoke slowly, "I think Jean should write a program enhancement to automatically jump search when the delay is more than ten minutes." He turned to her as he spoke.

"Be glad to, but I think it will take more time than we have at the moment. I'll start on it now during this down time. With luck, I'll have something soon." Jean was happy to have the assignment. She stepped over to another console and began to work.

While she was working on the program, the screen became alive again, and the voice synthesizer was activated. They watched and listened to the output. After a short time, the information stopped again, this time with an interrogation. They all sat trying to find an answer to the question.

"Well, what it is saying for the most part is that the information presented indicates two different writings of the same event, and those found at different times in the manuscript. The system can't make a decision as to which should take precedence, the event or the chronology of the event," John said, as they watched the split screen present two comparisons.

"We can either call for the event to be transcribed and forget the two different dates, or keep the dates and separate the different stories. But for now, we can't have both."

"I don't follow that, come again," Ed asked for clarification.

John punched the hold button. "As I see it, Judas has written two different descriptions of nearly the same event at different times. Evidently, the system has found the same event dressed in different clothes and told about different people. What the machine wants is a selection. Which story do we want? I say, for now, let's treat the event as one happening and accept what comes. Later, we can compare them." While John was acting project leader, he welcomed inputs. He pressed the clear control and inserted the answer to the question. The system went into action, the vertablinds closed, the lights dimmed, and the screen became sensible. The voice of the processor spoke.

CHAPTER THIRTEEN

Searching For Yeshua

Ishmael and I talked about our search for more information about Yeshua. We had decided to leave father's house and continue the search. To do this, we must first see to mother's care as we might be long in our quest.

"It's time we tell Anath that she provide care for mother. Not that mother is in want of servants or loving care, but I think she would like to have someone look in on her from time to time." Ishmael spoke the words of my heart as well. Yes, mother must be protected from loneliness while we are gone. Of course, with Atonis and the faithful handmaidens in the household, mother would want for nothing. It was because of these fine servants that I had no misgivings about leaving to solve what was already becoming a spiritual enigma.

"Good, let's send Apius to Anath with our resolve about this before we leave." I was of one mind on this. And so it was that Apius took to Anath our request for her to look after mother while we were gone. She accepted this chore of love and sent her blessings. It still wasn't easy for us to reveal our plans to mother, yet she accepted our decision. She was grieved at the news, but agreed it would be commendable work and gave her blessings.

With Apius at our side, we went to the fortress of Antonia to find Apuleius. We had dressed in the custom of the day to appear before the commandant. His adjutant welcomed us with an expression of contempt that would be credited to a slave or less. He was a haughty one, and was willing to show it freely.

"What is it you want, Jew?"

"If it pleases you, we inquire of one of your medical officers, an Apuleius Lucius by name." Although I had an immediate dislike for the man, I wouldn't let his manner grieve me. He would like nothing more than seeing us unhappy.

He turned without a word and looked over the roster of men stationed at the fort. His search was punctuated by a grunt of surprise.

"By my sword, he's here! Yet he isn't. He has been reassigned to the elite guard of the Procurator, and as such has been sent to the city of Capernaum. It seems his is to discover why there has been an outbreak of fever in the maniple station there." This information he blurted out - whether out of surprise or some other cause I don't know. But we were blessed by his laxity in security and found our leave before he decided to place us under house arrest for some trumped-up charge to cover his indiscretion.

We returned to our animals, mounted, and congratulated ourselves on God's blessing or good fortune, then returned home to get ready for the trip. We knew one thing. Regardless of where the adventure took us, we would go to Capernaum and see Apuleius.

Ishmael took his sketching materials, Apius prepared the animals, I assured mother we would send messages to her through Apuleius, and we moved up the road toward Samaria, which was necessary for us to travel through to get to Capernaum. This wasn't to our liking as the Samaritans were traditionally hostile to all from Judea.

After traveling some time, we arrived at El-Ascar, a small town near Jacob's well. We were cautious and weary, in need of water for ourselves and the animals. This well was a stopping place for many caravans passing from Jerusalem to Galilee and beyond.

Here at Jacob's well we rested near midday. As was the custom, we recited the noon prayers and proceeded to break bread. While eating near the well, those who weren't busy drawing water entered into conversation with the local people collecting the fee for use. The conversation turned to the happenings of the day, or in some cases, the events of the week. When such events occurred, try as they might, the local people couldn't get enough of the story. Each man tells the story over and over, relishing his part of the adventure and often coloring it to his taste. Each time the story is repeated, it becomes more and more personal to the teller. Many times, disagreements arise from the want of the teller to show his importance in the actual happening. As we ate and listened, so it happened among those at the well. An event of such magnitude had occurred and recently.

"But I tell you, *I* was the first to know," said the first of several men resting near the well. By their mannerisms, we knew they were local people.

"Aye, and you would have us believe you were brought here by an act of God no doubt," a second retorted, with a gesture of his hand and a raised eyebrow.

"I was the first called by Ramona to see this teacher at the well. I was first to believe her story. I saw him set right here where I'm now sitting." Some agreed and some didn't, but all agreed that Ramona was the aging matriarch of El-Ascar, the teacher Yeshua had asked for a drink of water.

The second speaker turned and looked at us, knowing from our dress we weren't Samaritans, and from our animals, probably Jews. They were quick to form an opinion that we were from Jerusalem - but it was for us to confirm or deny. Before entering Samaria, Apius had removed most of the markings to avoid additional hardships while traveling through Samaria. They knew we were from the south and drew upon this to conclude we were travelers from Jerusalem. Since we hadn't spoken to them, our speech and mannerisms didn't yet reinforce their suspicions.

One drew upon his suspicions to remark, "Ho there, do you know this teacher, Yeshua? They say he just came from Jerusalem and is on his way to Cana in Galilee. He spoke with a Galilean brogue."

I glanced at Ishmael and he at me; we didn't know if we should admit to knowing him or not. In many places it wasn't wise to acknowledge being friend or foe of some personage without first knowing the reason for the question. At times, it was asked to provide a means for reaction, and not altogether one that was expected.

"Aye, we have heard of him." I decided to be cautious about the matter. We could hardly deny knowledge of such a person for there was talk about him all along the trail. "But pray, tell us of what you speak."

He, as well as some others, was very willing to tell the tale over again. Each would interrupt the other to interject some missing bit or correction of time, but the second speaker continued nearly without pause. In his excitement to be the one to tell, he would sometimes fall into words which were not entirely familiar to us. This added to the difficulty of understanding the story but not sufficiently to destroy it any more than the interruptions of his co-speakers.

He told us of Yeshua's appearance at the well of Jacob, this very well, and asking for a drink - and this from the old matriarch - Ramona. All this news was secondhand as neither he nor the others were present when Yeshua first talked to the woman.

Ishmael was first to break the tale. "This teacher," here he avoided repeating the name, "was he alone? We have heard along the trail that he had disciples with him."

"Oh, he had some with him, though not when he addressed Ramona," a second speaker said, "we learned later that all were elsewhere - buying meat they said." Some laughed at this and moved their shoulders in a self-understanding way of these people.

"All these men left their teacher without drawing water for him to wash the dust of the road off or provide him with a drink?" Neither Ishmael nor I could understand such disrespect for Yeshua by his ardent followers. Even an apprentice follower wouldn't have left a prominent teacher in such a neglected condition. The search for food would have been secondary to relief of travel discomforts of their master.

"Aye, so it was, this I say, by the Mount of Gerizim." The speaker held his thought.

"But what of this Ramona?" asked Ishmael.

"Ah ha, that is another story," he said while shaking his head slowly. The others changed their attitude as well. It was as if none wanted to be first to speak of her. But as the rest of the story was dependent on her, the speaker plunged on.

"Ramona is nearly one hundred years old, and has lived through many adversities during her time, this I know. She is the matriarch who makes matches for the town of El-Ascar. She is a good woman and well respected hereabouts." He shook his head again and the others did the same in agreement. He would have continued but a newly-arrived caravan required his attention and we were left wondering. All of this was of great interest to us for we knew nothing as yet of the story that created such interest. What was this incident all about at the well of Jacob? That was the question!

STORY AT THE WELL

They continued to talk about the woman. Each had a tale to reveal about her. She was, in her younger days, a pretty wench and was known to tell a good story. Even now, at her age, she had a quick mind and was aware of the politics of the day. She held concern for others even after five husbands were lost - yes, lost to her - two by war, one struck down by armed robbers, one by the fever, and one to foreign slavery for his role as a Zealot. Five husbands and four sons she lost to the cause of freedom. Through all this she held fast to the faith of her fathers - Elohim would someday put things right. Even now, she cared for a grandson who lived with her after he was struck down by the Romans.

They all agreed - she was a good soul and a woman whose honesty wasn't questioned. Because of her kindly spirit, she was often at the well for water for others as well as herself. In warm weather, she would go to the well and take water to the men and women in the fields; it was then she met the stranger at the well.

Some said the face of God was turned from her for some evil before her time. According to the word among the men, she had a good heart but without blessing. Now, in her later years, she had taken to keep house for her grandson. So it was.

Here they all freely admitted that it was hearsay - the story they told - as none were present at the time of the incident. The tale finally settled around the woman's story about this stranger at the well. She was curious and asked if he traveled alone, to which he replied that his disciples had gone to Sychar to buy meat. She saw none with him and no skin or drawing instrument, so the teller said.

The woman, whom the man called Ramona, felt sorry for this stranger. His dress and body displayed the signs of the road. His feet were dirty from his walk, he was thirsty, and his hands and feet needed washing. When she told this to the women, none would believe it, for to travel in this country without a way to draw water from a well was idiocy. Even a dolt knew better than this! Thievery was common and a bucket was not above disappearing. So it was that many wells were left without implements to draw water; let the user beware. We found this to be true when we came to the well. Even with drawing implements, one must carry water bags because some wells ran dry this time of year.

Here, so her story went, he and she, the matriarch of Sychar, stood alone facing each other. She wasn't sure of his wants and was wary, for strangers were not to be befriended - especially if not Samaritans.

The stranger asked for a drink from the well. She was taken aback for a Jew seldom asked for such - they feared contamination - Samaritans were considered unclean.

"How did she know he was a Jew?" Ishmael asked.

The men talked among themselves for a moment and one said she surmised such from his dress and his Galilean tongue. He wasn't Samaritan, that she knew! The choosing of Jew was by guess as much as distinction and since he didn't deny it, she left it be.

She was about to give him a drink when he said to her that if she knew the gift of God, and who it is who asked her for a drink, she would ask him and he would give her a drink of living water. Upon hearing these words, she became confused, as it appeared to her he either wanted a drink or he didn't. His words led her to believe that there was another near because of his remark. But since there was just the two of them, she became even more confused and looked around for another who would give her a drink if asked. Yet as she described, there was no other.

She was nearly convinced he was a traveling mystic and would soon produce the living water from a rock as father Moses did for the ancients. She tried to understand his words, but failed and asked just where he was going to get the living water? From this time onward, she thought that he was twitting her for the beliefs of her fathers. Therefore, she decided to have fun with the stranger at the well as she did her own kind.

She asked him who it was who would give her a drink of living water; after all, if it was him, then why didn't he just say, ask me and I'll give it to you? She continued her prattle, even calling him teacher, and to her surprise, he showed no signs of her speaking an untruth about him. She asked if he thought he was greater than Jacob, whose hand was still on the well. Could he do such a thing? Could he bring forth water from a rock?

He returned her question with the statement that whosoever drank the water I offer shall never have to drink again - he will never thirst. Now she knew he would give her the living water. He spoke in a matter-of-fact manner, and she knew now to ask.

So she asked him to give her some of this water so she wouldn't thirst again or have to come to the well of Jacob - or any other. He ignored her request for this mystical water and gave her no reason for this. She stood looking at this man who said he would give or could give living waters and yet he honored not her simple request. She was about to leave him to the elements when he said to her to fetch her husband. She told him the truth; she had no husband, although she didn't know why he would want her to do such a thing.

She again turned to go to the fields and complete her mission of taking fresh water to the workers. He then said to her what she said was true. She had no husband, but had five during her lifetime and the man she now cared for wasn't her husband. She nearly dropped her water pitcher at these words. How came he by this information? She turned and said she knew him to be a mystic and had divined the pain of her losses. Who but a mystic or prophet could read the past and future? She addressed the differences between the beliefs of the Samaritans and Jews, and held her ground.

Here on the Mount of Gerizim is the place to worship, not in Jerusalem! So the fathers have said - the Jews have cut off their own. She reminded him it was the Judeans in turning away the help of the Samaritans at the rebuilding of the temple that brought the schism. She predicted that some day they would welcome her people to defend the temple.

He ignored her predictions. He said a stranger thing than all others, "Believe this: The time will come when the Elohim won't be worshiped here or in Jerusalem. You don't know what you worship where we do for in us is the salvation." From here, he accepted no interruption but spoke of strange things of worshiping anywhere and in Spirit and in truth.

None of these things could she understand or accept, but she wasn't unwise. She had heard the Jews speak of the coming of the anointed one who would set things right for them, yet also knew her people were excluded from these things. "Some day," she said, "the anointed one will come to the Samaritans as well, and he will tell us all things."

He told her of his presence there and who he claimed to be. His words just confused her, as he talked of water that would quench thirst for life. She continued to tell of his remarks about living water. She said although she didn't see him arrive at the well, felt he hadn't spoken to any of the local men. The stranger then told of her past losses of husbands and sons without her offering these.

Here, most laughed at this for they knew her as one willing to tell her story of loss to anyone and everyone - even those not wanting to hear. She then added to her banter the remark that she saw he was a prophet. The men laughed and swung their bodies from side to side in the humor of the situation for how would she know a prophet they didn't know? Who had seen a prophet these days?

I looked at Ishmael and he at me; yes, how would one know a prophet? Indeed, if one knew or was able to tell a prophet from someone else, how would one know if he was a true one, as was Elijah, or a false one?

This was the story as they told it with some disclaimers and embellishments; he and she talked for some time - he told of many things in her past life, but none of her future. Mystic, charlatan, or seer, she couldn't tell and while she listened, she wondered if her age was affecting her mind. She would take her story back to the counsel of Sychar where some of them would know if he was a seer or not. She set the pot of water before him and as she turned to leave, saw men approaching from the east. Fearing these to be unwanted visitors, she hurried to Sychar.

She turned to look once again at the well, and saw the men around the seer; they were obviously known to him. They were a rough-looking lot, so she hurried forth.

One of the men now came forward to add his part in this tale. He was somewhat older than the others and had their respect. He related how she came to the men of the town and told her story of the meeting at the well.

Her words were these, "Come and see a man who told me all things that I ever did, ho, I can't tell if he is a seer or a mystic! He claims he can make a living water that once drunk, no one will thirst again!"

Well, some were greatly interested while others marked it as the prattle of an old woman. Some went to see this seer at the well. When they arrived there, they found him with others he called disciples. He was instructing them at the time so all listened. His words made little sense to the good people of Sychar. He spoke only to his followers with words about sowing and reaping, laborers and labors, of fruit of eternal life, and many other things which caused great confusion in their minds, as well as the minds of his followers.

"How many were with him?" Ishmael asked.

This interruption caused a great deal of argument among the men present - some said four and others argued for more and less. The only thing one could safely say was that some that were at the well claimed to be followers and others just travelers refreshing themselves even as we were now. Ishmael and I considered what was said with some doubt as witnesses weren't agreeing and, according to the law, made all evidence inadmissible.

I spoke over the noise of the crowd, "And what then occurred?"

Silence reigned. The old man spoke. Some of the people of Sychar asked the man at the well to stay with them in the town. And so it was that Yeshua and some of his followers stayed in the town for two days. Now, the word was that many believed him to be a prophet, of this he wasn't sure. Some of the others raised and lowered their shoulders again to say they couldn't affirm or deny it. Ishmael and I held our silence on the matter.

The men of Sychar at the well considered this an important happening as the town wasn't one to be visited often by a man thought to be a prophet - at least by some.

"And who do you think he is?" asked Ishmael of the speaker.

The old man shook his head. Others were more vocal and sought to have their thoughts on this known. A prophet, some said, and others said a seer. One said the old woman and the followers tried to tell them he was the foretold Messiah of Israel, but all held that he wasn't the Samaritan prophet. Elohim would provide them a prophet from their own lineage - the true son of David - not a sojourner from Galilee! Most agreed to this.

And so it was told of this event at Jacob's well, and how some believed that he was a man of great truth. How some even believed him to be the Messiah of Israel. Although none knew what a Messiah looked like, some held he would ride on a white stallion and lead his troops into the gates of Jerusalem. These men didn't claim to be followers of his teachings and laughed at those who were so carried away by his stories of being the Messiah. They said some were even willing to say he was the Savior of the world; his close followers instigated this. They pointed out that nothing had changed in this city since his coming and some had forgotten their initial wonder while he was among them. Most held a true Messiah would have made greater changes in this city, country, and the world than had this itinerant teacher from Galilee. Nearly all of those enamored by his presence had returned to the teachings of their fathers.

Then, we were called by Apius to be on our way. So we left the people of Sychar at the well and their story of the seer they had met at the well of Jacob.

We often talked about this strange story and wondered just what the followers would say of this event and how much they would add to the tale.

ON TO SALIM

As we mounted our animals, Ishmael shouted to the men, "And where did he go after his stay in your fair village? Can you tell us this?"

"Aye, it was said by those with him that they were on their way to Galilee, but to what town we don't know," so answered the main teller of the story. "But how say you, what is meant to the Jews about the Messiah? Some here claim he is as he professed to be, and some say he is the Savior of the world. From what is the world to be saved?"

"We aren't his followers, and don't know what is meant by the Savior of the world." Ishmael tugged at my sleeve, a sign not to spend anymore time here. "We thank you and your city for the water, and may the Lord be with you and yours." We saluted these men and they nodded in return as we moved away. With the animals watered and rested, we were ready for the trip to Capernaum.

We moved along the road to the next city, but the evening of the third day was nearly upon us. Being in the country meant it would be better to be in some town to spend the night. There were many tales of small parties set upon by robbers and thieves for none of these roads were guarded by the troops. We came near Anneon near Salim which was but a short distance from the road we were on, yet it meant traveling across open country.

"Ishmael, isn't Salim the place where John and Yeshua performed washing on many?" I was interested in seeing this place.

"Aye, that it is." Ishmael looked at me with the expression that often indicated we were thinking of the same thing at the same time. It seemed that many times in our lives as twins, this sort of synchronism of thought occurred between us.

"You know, I would like to see this place and I'm sure Apius could find the way without difficulty. Apius, isn't it close enough to reach before evening prayers?"

"Aye, that it is, Master Judas." And with that he turned his horse for the open land and began to follow a small trail from the road to Scythopolis to the city of Salim. The horses walked a slower pace because of the trail, and headed in a due-easterly direction. Being close to the Jordan tributaries, the land grew a goodly amount of vegetation.

We soon came to the very spot were the water was abundant and Apius said here it was that John practiced the washing. The land still showed the markings of many people being on the bank of the stream that fed into the Jordan, like the remains of an encampment. We traveled on to the city of Salim.

We reached Salim before evening prayers and found an inn at the edge of the city. After arrangements were made and the animals taken care of by Apius, we took supper in the inn. The inn was inhabited by many travelers like us who didn't want to be on the road at night. Some were from passing caravans while others traveled in small companies. There were those from lands east of Jordan, those from Samaria itself, and those from Judea. Several different brogues were spoken by those at the rough-hewn tables of the inn. Many spoke openly of political troubles of the times. Those of the city of Salim still talked about the days of washing by the Jew from Jerusalem, and of his preaching and calling the people for repentance. As one who spoke with confidence about these things was near our table, Ishmael leaned across and spoke to him.

"Were you one of those washed by this man called John the washer, and is he still about?" I half expected the other to ignore the question, but he didn't.

He looked at us keenly before speaking. "Yes, I was one who repented of my sins against the Lord and was washed here in this very place. But as to John, he is no longer here." He leaned even closer and looked about carefully. "Haven't you heard of him?"

"No, we haven't and we have traveled far. What is the news?" Ishmael asked the question; we shared his interest. What could this man know of John?

"It was told me by a passerby that John had moved about the country after being here nearly a week. His call to the people was strong indeed." He again looked cautiously. "He included in his sermons the names of many of the house of Hanan and some of the Sanhedrin as well. It can be understood that this didn't lie well with those people, hah!" He turned and spat on the hard-pressed earth of the inn. "And the traveler told me the council brought charges against him and were about to arrest him. But his followers held them off and he was able to escape. This warning didn't stop John from calling for those in high places to repent of their sins and change their ways, for the Messiah soon comes." He ended his news with a sudden nod of his head.

The speaker then motioned for the innkeeper to bring him more wine. It was then we doubted his story, but couldn't leave even his story untold as we wanted news of John.

The speaker continued without any priming. "Well, it was in this wise," so said the traveler. "John had heard, and rightly so, that Herod had put aside his rightful wife - the daughter of Aretas, the king of Arabia Persia - and took Herodias, his own niece, daughter of Malthace, and his half-brother's wife, to wed. Ah, it's a double sin!"

To this we both agreed.

The speaker drank from the wine supplied by the innkeeper and then continued. "John called upon the house of Hanan to bring judgment against Herod, and called for Herod to repent and put Herodias away. His cries heard by many; it is indeed strange that you didn't hear of them as I can see you are from Jerusalem." He raised his eyebrows as he spoke his last sentence.

It was strange that we hadn't heard of these things, but this was a time when we were together for the first time and it was possible that we had not listened to the talk about us. Since I had just arrived from Rome, I hadn't talked with many from the byways.

We made plain to him that we had not heard of these things but were anxious to learn more. He continued, "Many of the people began to talk openly about the King and his sinful act. When Herodias came out, many jeered her as she passed through the city. Herodias became angry at this and called to task, or so it is said, and advised Herod to seize John on sedition and end his voice among the people. And so it was that as John was washing one day, the guard from the palace came and took him. So it is and so it shall be. It's said that even now, John lies in the dungeon of the palace fortress."

We were greatly grieved to hear this about John, as he was one of us from earlier days. To be in the prison at the palace was bad enough, but to be cut off from his calling to bring the people to repentance as a forerunner of the Messiah was a great hardship.

That evening as we lay in the inn, we talked of these things we had heard. Why had the Lord let this happen to his only mouthpiece at a time when he was needed among men? How could John be a forerunner in prison? Then, being very tired from the trip, and seeing nothing could be done, we called upon God to free John from the hands of Herodias as it was she who had instigated the arrest. Soon we were fast asleep.

TO NAZARETH

The sunlight woke Apius early and he, in turn, woke us. The animals were made ready and we said morning Shema. *"Hear, O Israel: the Lord is our God, the Lord is one."* We took our leave from the inn after a meager meal.

At Scythopolis, we crossed the valley and again came to the high road leading to Nazareth. It was there we thought we would see Yeshua teaching among the people. As we came into Galilee, we met more travelers who spoke of Yeshua and the things he had done among them. Many along the way were willing to tell of his concern for them and his talk about the coming of the kingdom of God here in earth. Although we listened to their stories, we didn't understand how he would accomplish this. After all, he had only a handful of followers. Why, even Judas of Galilee had more when the Romans hung him on a tree. It seemed that everywhere we stopped to water the animals and rest, there was talk of this man. Some claimed great deeds of healing done by him in the name of God, while others claimed otherwise, that he did these things of his own will. Some of those he passed by were not so kind and considered their needs greater than others he took time to help - from them came sounds of rancor.

As was the custom for travelers of the day, we proceeded to the village well to water our animals. As we approached, we recalled the time we had been to Nazareth as young boys. Our father brought the family here to celebrate the Feast of Purim with the household of Joseph and Mary. We stayed at the carpenter's house the full days of the celebration. Ah, that was many years ago; Ishmael and I were young, and Yeshua was very small. The days of Ester were celebrated with such merriment, and the reading of the roll of Ester signified cause to remember, "…cursed be Haman, blessed be Mordecai; cursed be Zeresh, blessed be Ester; cursed be all idolaters, blessed be all Israelites, and blessed be Harbonah who hanged Haman." It was a good time and yet I still remember the street and the house of Joseph. The city hadn't changed much from earlier days.

While at the well, we talked of going to see Mary and the family of Yeshua for they may have word of him. So it was said and so it was done.

Mary was a gracious hostess and, although not recognizing me at first, was quick to remember Ishmael from their meeting at the wedding feast at Cana. The fact that we were identical twins always helped many people remember either one of us when met. Although sometimes I wore a beard differently cut from that of Ishmael, in nearly all other respects, we were very similar in every way.

We stayed with Mary and her family for that evening and unto the next day. She told of Yeshua's call to do that which he said was his father's work. And this in the matter of spiritual things, for he was never one to practice carpentry. This was taken over by one of the others at an early age. She told us of Joseph's death and how the family had struggled to maintain its livelihood, and this through the efforts of all. As her sons grew, some were jealous of Yeshua as he was a dreamer and wanted to study the law without regard for family needs. He was forever with his head in the Law and Prophets, and seldom raised his hand to plane or saw to gain funds for the family. She was sure he had a calling greater than anything she might understand, and defended his natural leaning toward his studies over all else.

"And have you seen him of late?" I asked.

"Nay, not since Capernaum have we seen him. But we hear that even now he is with his disciples on his way to Cana." She spoke a little wistfully about this.

"Ah, then it is so what we hear along the way, that he is traveling here in Galilee. We search for him as others do. Should we find him, we will send you notice of his health and happiness." I found that I had nothing to say about what we really wanted with Yeshua and made small talk about things of the past.

Ishmael and I spent many hours talking to Mary about earlier history of her eldest son, his birth, and early life. We reviewed our family histories and my days in Rome. The time went quickly, but since we needed to find Apuleius, we moved on the road to Cana.

The distance is short from Nazareth to Cana. Ishmael remembered the way to the house of the wedding wherein Yeshua changed water into wine. There was no evidence of such when we passed as the wedding had taken place months before. Ishmael remarked that the couple had moved to Capernaum after the wedding, and the groom, Nathanael, was one of the disciples of Yeshua. We went to the well of the city to water the animals. Here we found the marketplace filled with the women doing their early morning shopping. Here and there small groups of men stood talking about the latest happening of import in the city.

We stood by while Apius watered the animals, and overheard one group of men speak of what they considered a miracle. It was distinctive as any in the country; some said that once heard, the speech of a Galilean was as telltale as a fingerprint and it seemed the more a Galilean tried to disguise this inherent speech pattern, the more predominate it became. I agreed and would add this: as they talked rapidly, they became less and less understandable to the untrained ear. As we stood nearby, their remarks were not clear to us for they were excited and took shortcuts in their expressions that were known only to them.

"Ishmael, do you comprehend all they are saying?" I asked my brother, for his ear was more in tune with their speech than mine. The time I spent in Rome had removed some of the capability of reading the dialects of the people here in the near east countries.

"No, but I gather they are excited about an act done by Yeshua here in Cana, and that not long ago. It would be to our advantage to ask one of them directly what it is that has the town so aroused." Ishmael was somewhat reluctant to call their attention to us for they were a rough-looking lot. But the need for information about Yeshua soon overcame this caution and he called out to the group hoping that one would provide a clearer word.

"Brothers, we would a word with you."

The talk among them stopped as if their mouths had been locked. Those not facing us turned slowly to see from whence came the question. These people were a suspicious lot, and weren't given to talking to strangers. They studied us with some care. Finally, they waited for a spokesman to make himself known.

"May God be with you. My name is Amos and we were discussing the words we received from Capernaum a fortnight ago." The others nodded in assent to his statement.

"Can we ask you to tell us of this thing that raises such feelings among you? As we came up from Jerusalem, we have heard of one Yeshua, a teacher. Have you seen him? We were told he passed this way." Ishmael had decided to keep our intimate knowledge of Yeshua a secret from these men so they wouldn't color their stories in any way to please us. I held that they wouldn't have done this at any rate for they were a fiercely independent lot, as all Galileans were known to be.

"Aha, I was here when one called Yeshua and his followers came into Cana. He came from Jerusalem and he and his group were known to be at Salim where he revealed unto some that he was a man of God. Some followed him from Salim begging for favor of all manner of things. He became disenchanted with their admiration over his ability to do strange and wondrous things."

The speaker turned to his comrades for their acquiescence, which, with different mannerisms, they indicated his truthfulness. "It is said by some that he changed the water into wine at a wedding feast of the household of Nathanael, one who was a true follower.

With our animals filled, Apius moved them to the shady side of the marketplace, and we moved with them. The speaker and his comrades were interested in our reaction to the story and therefore followed us to the shady part of the plaza.

"This is the event that causes your quickening of spirit?" Ishmael asked.

"No, this is caused by yet another happening which is mine to tell." Amos spoke as one who had been commissioned to expound this to the world. "I was present when a nobleman from the house of Herod came to the city looking for this teacher, one Joel. It was I who led him to this teacher for he first appealed unto me for direction. He was a man of goodly birth and nobility not often seen in Cana. He was from Capernaum and set over tax collectors there to provide unto Herod an accounting of the trade done along the coast of the Sea of Galilee. His jurisdiction and command was felt by many of the tradesman and fisherman of the area. Because of his level of influence, he had access to the finest physicians in the land. Yet it was this man that came to Cana to seek aid from this Yeshua, this I know from firsthand."

"He saluted Yeshua as a teacher for he had heard so addressed by some around him. His servants thrust aside some of the poor and ill to get to Yeshua. Yeshua took note of this with some unhappiness, but said nothing.

"Joel, what seekest thou?" thus said Yeshua as the nobleman approached. This was a great surprise to the nobleman that no one had delivered unto him the name of the King's servant. His servants were greatly astounded by this insight of this teacher, and began to whisper among themselves of his power.

"Master, how came you by my name?"

"It isn't of importance, Joel, come, what is it you seek?" Yeshua sat near the well, even near where you watered your animals.

Joel bowed to show his humble spirit, "I come with humble heart down from Capernaum to seek help for my son who is sick unto death. He has had a fever for some days and all the king's physicians cannot deliver him from this woe." This man was greatly troubled I can verify. We learned he was a cousin of Chuza, Herod's chief steward. "I heard from those that travel from Jerusalem, that you are a man of God and have His Spirit resting on you. I was told that you have the gift of healing in your heart. It is with a heavy heart that I ask you to come to my home and there lay hands on my son. I'm a rich man and could have my servants do this thing, but I'm greatly grieved at my son's illness, and wouldn't suffer anyone else to plead for his life. In truth, he is at the point of death."

I heard these things from the mouth of Joel as I stood nearby. The teacher continued to look at Joel who was now in prayerful posture, pleading for his son's life. The teacher spoke thus, "Except you see signs and wonders, you will not believe."

To this word Joel recoiled as if struck by a lash. His face became as white as snow, and his eyes filled with tears for he was of the impression that his request was refused. It was obvious that he didn't know where to turn and from his knees, he looked about him at the followers with Yeshua. As he looked at each one, he made a simple gesture of pleading, perhaps one of them would speak his case to their master; however, none moved to do so. He turned once again to Yeshua and spoke with a break of sorrow in his voice.

"There were those who spoke of your changing water into wine for a wedding feast at Cana. Some say this was an act of a common magi, and that you are thaumaturge, while others say it was indeed an act of the Most High through you."

He remained on his knees.

"I didn't come to ask for a trick to end my quandary. I need no proof that you are a man of God. Sir, if you have a son that you love dearly, as I do mine, you will not trifle with me. Even now, my son lies ill or dead. Come with me to Capernaum and lay hands on him that he might be saved." Joel pleaded with a sincere heart and many were swayed by his noble speech. And I, even Amos, the tanner, was moved by the needs of this noble-man and held no ill will against him for his wealth. His son was no different than my own. The crowd murmured in favor of Joel and petitioned Yeshua to have compassion on him.

Yeshua, seeing the sentiment of the crowd and the sincerity of the nobleman, had compassion on him. "Your belief in me is as great as any I've seen in all this land. Go your way, your son will live. My time isn't yet come to go to Capernaum. Return there for all is done as I've said."

Joel rose from the ground and believed Yeshua as of that moment. The crowd murmured greatly among themselves. Some said it was done as Yeshua said, but they didn't really know this as Capernaum was some distance away. Others said no man could do this thing; Joel and Yeshua were acting together and the boy wasn't sick at all. Some were determined to go to Capernaum with the nobleman and see this thing for themselves.

Joel wasn't disturbed by the crowds' murmurs and sang praises to God for permitting him to hear these words about his son's life being spared. Then Joel gave unto the one called John by the others a large sum of money in gracious thanks for his son's life. It was said that his sum became part of the treasury of the disciples and helped them feed and care for followers as they had no other income.

Here the storyteller stopped and the crowd grew larger about us. He was held suspect of reciting things from memory with more or less detail as the mood of the crowd dictated. Seeing the crowd was still with him, he continued. The nobleman then went directly to the synagogue in Cana where he gave thanksgiving offerings to God in accordance with the law. Joel remained one night to rest his animals, then left the city for his house in Capernaum. I'm unsure of this for I've not seen him since that day and hour.

He was about to speak on further when a second man moved to the front of the group; he was greatly agitated and was unable to speak well because of an impediment.

"Sirs, hear me, for I'm fortunate to know of the end of this act of God. I just came from Capernaum the day following and didn't know of this happening here in Cana. But as I rested along the way, I saw a nobleman and his entourage coming from Cana. He stopped where I was resting and rested his animals. He sang praises to God and threw some gold coins to me in his happiness. It was because of this I clearly remembered the happening."

Here the second speaker stopped to wipe his mouth with a dirty rag as he slobbered much when he spoke. He was anxious to tell his story. He was filled with the spirit of the story and was aware of his importance to the crowd of listeners. He continued his discourse with a great deal of hand motion, including slapping them together to release his tongue. This little ritual caused both Ishmael and I to smile cautiously; not all in the crowd considered his mannerisms humorous.

"It was while I was testing the coin," and here the man put a coin in his mouth and demonstrated his act of testing by biting down hard on the coin, "that I saw men approaching us and riding hard on well-lathered animals. They approached from Capernaum, and from a good distance were shouting, 'Master, Master, your son lives…' The nobleman's entourage gave a great shout for this seemed to be the cause of their praise before. Even then, I heard the nobleman tell what hour it was that the boy became well. The servants spoke above the noise of the group, that it was the seventh hour of the day before. It was then the nobleman left his animal to be by himself as he was overcome with joy. When he returned, he and his entourage left for Capernaum and I saw him no more. It is just now that I've heard the story of the nobleman's request for the healing of his son. It is as Yeshua had said, for the servants said his son was well and at the hour of Yeshua's word." He then broke away from the group near us and began to tell everyone he met of the story as he thought it to be.

We moved away from the well and returned to the road unto Capernaum. As we traveled, each of us had thoughts of the matter but kept them private.

Finally I said, "Let's see if we can learn the rest of the story, Ishmael."

"It's a good thing to do, and we must not forget to seek Apuleius; it may very well be that he has heard of this."

Ishmael was a good man of mind and reasoned that if the nobleman was of some importance to the city of Capernaum, it was possible that Apuleius may have met him. With this in mind, we set our horses in a canter.

It wasn't long before we came to Capernaum. It was a thriving city of some renown. In every town, there were places for finding out information. Some of these included the local marketplace, the synagogue, and the tax collector's office. Where there was a Roman station, troops were also well informed of the people in the city - it was to their advantage to know the moods of the people. All three are usually easy to find. Because of our unfamiliarity with Capernaum, we rode to the marketplace. It was there we learned the building which housed the maniple was near the port of Capernaum, and, according to the Adjutant of Fort Antonia, where we might find Apuleius.

It seemed like old times for an instant when Ishmael, Apius, and I rode down to the docks of the city. We saw the same sights we had seen some years before in Caesarea. The noise of the fisherman calling out their catches, the lesser people cleaning fish and repairing nets for what little they would receive. Many had strings through their ear lobes marking them as slaves. Through the maze of people both buying and selling, for this was the early catch and most of the well-to-do sent their servants to buy at this hour, we rode unto the Roman billets. The building at one time had been a fine home of one of the richer citizens of Capernaum. It was built in the model of Roman architecture with a goodly number of colonnades, porticoes, fountains, and baths. We were not permitted entry.

"Who goes there? State your business." We could see the guard near the entrance was alert. He was a likely-looking chap, straight and well-built, a model of the conqueror.

"We are three travelers from Jerusalem. We seek one Apuleius, a physician assigned here from Fort Antonia. We would have a word with him." We identified ourselves in the manner of the day. There wasn't much a Jew could say of his lineage that would make any difference to the troops of Rome. They were more concerned with your residence, for it was from certain parts of the country that most of the trouble for them came. The mere mention of some of these places cast great suspicions on the person attempting to gain any sort of boon from the Romans. With all its troubles, Jerusalem was not considered the nesting place of the Zionists. We were safe with the word Jerusalem.

"Dismount and stand to." The guard notified his corporal of the matter before him. The corporal of the guard went into the auxiliary room to find out what to do with us. We were not long waiting when he appeared again, and Apuleius with him.

A SABBATH CURE

He appeared in the uniform of the medic, and we could see that he was extremely tired. He walked hurriedly toward us, arms outstretched in a gesture of welcome. He motioned for us not to come forward to meet him. He stopped at the entrance of the outer gate and removed his medical clothing. He was wearing his informal Roman dress.

"Ah, Judas and Ishmael, how good it is to see you again, and what brings you so far from Jerusalem?" He came forward and gave us a brotherly grip. Yes, close up we could see he was a tired young man. He looked at Apius a long time but said nothing.

"We came for you, Apuleius, and hoped that you could ride with us for awhile in search of Yeshua. We first went to Antonia and there found you had been reassigned to this detachment here. Since we were interested in following the exploits of Yeshua and these moved this way, we came to seek you out. Our companion is Apius, the faithful servant unto us all these many years. You remember I spoke of him often when we were in Rome. This is he." Apius stood firm, and Apuleius came to him and offered his hand in friendship.

"It is well, Apius, you are in good company. Judas has spoken of you often even as he says and always with great honor. When we have time, you must tell me of your people for I see that you are Greek, is this not so?" Apuleius was attracted to this Greek who could have been a freeman many years ago but chose to stay as a servant in father's household.

"The honor is mine, Apuleius, and I have known of you and your kindness to master Judas while he was in Rome. It would be my pleasure to serve you, also."

"And how is it by you, Apuleius? What is the cause of your transfer from Antonia? We hear there is an outbreak of the fever among the troops, is that true? And Apuleius, can't we go inside out of this sun?" Ishmael was one to come to the point.

Apuleius hesitated for a moment. He looked about to see if anyone was close enough to overhear as he said, "Things have been better, Ishmael. I came here to find the contingent in great disrepair medically. But for this story we need to meet again as I must report to my station. Have you secured a place to stay here in Capernaum? If not, there is a small inn that is well known to us of the military for they give us a differential to stay there. It lies near the sea and if you move to the eastern part of the city, you will find it. You can't miss it as it's named King Solomon's Inn. There I will meet you near the sixth hour."

As he continued, he turned to look over his shoulder at the dog robber holding his medical garments. "Because of the fever, it's now well that you should enter this billet. So my dear friends, till we meet at the inn, I salute you." He raised his arm and left us there without waiting for our reply. We accepted his suggestion for we were bound by our need for housing and rest, and wanted to know more about his life here.

"God go with you, Apuleius." This was all the time we had to pass our regards while returning his salute. We mounted our horses to search for the inn he had mentioned.

It was Apius that found the place with apparent ease. We often marveled at his uncanny sense of direction even in the most remote or metropolitan places. Even as children, mother let us go different places as long as Apius was near. After taking care of the animals, we made arrangements to stay at the inn. This was arranged for a day-by-day schedule for we didn't know when Apuleius might be able to travel with us, if at all.

Time passed slowly for us as we waited for Apuleius. We had reserved rooms for four of us, hoping that Apuleius could stay until his duty call the next day. It was shortly after early evening prayers that Apuleius and an aide came to the inn. The aide returned his horse to the billet and would call for him in the morning before duty call, so it was arranged that Apuleius would stay with us through the night. We had the innkeeper set the table for us and began the evening meal. The conversation flowed better than rich wine, and much was said between us.

We insisted Apuleius tell his story of the conditions at the billet when we arrived. He was reluctant to do so, for it wasn't common for the Romans to hand out dirty laundry. Yet being among friends and filled with the indignity of it all, he continued his story.

"Even as I had said, things weren't well here. The commandant of this unit was a mercenary who was serving above his capability. He was a scoundrel at best and a traitor in the least. Suffice it to say he has been replaced at my request, and the new commandant, one Cornelius by name, is a Roman true. He was the lieutenant commander stationed here before the mercenary came from Rome. He was passed over because of his consideration for the Jews and their religious customs. To my mind, he was the better man from the beginning. Cornelius was well respected by the troops, the Jewish aristocracy, and the elders, also. I was told that he had given a large sum of money from his own earnings to them so they might build a synagogue here in Capernaum.

"But as to the first - he was of little good - and thorough lack of knowledge in the martial arts, led to the most miserable conditions in the lower ranks. It was because of his bungling that housekeeping slipped and the men fell ill to a fever. From what I could see, most of the illness came from the water. I found that most who drank a mixture of water and wine or water and vinegar were without the fever. Yet those who drank from the water barrels were ill. This, I believe, accounts for those stationed here being sick, while the civilian populous remained unharmed - it was the water barrels which weren't being maintained according to regulations. If the troops had followed procedures and kept their canteens well settled with vinegar, most of them wouldn't have become ill.

First one and then more couldn't report for duty. He had no recourse but to ask for recruits from Antonia, causing many eyebrows to raise. The search for an answer led to the formation of an inspector general to come here. It was with this group I arrived in Section A." Here Apuleius stopped to draw on a flagon of wine brought by the innkeeper.

"Ah, I see, then you are here as part of the medical team. And is this fever one that is only found among people who are strangers to Capernaum as well?" I was curious, for our search depended on good health.

"To this I can't say. It's a fever similar to that which you had, Ishmael, remember?" He turned to Ishmael with a smile of satisfaction. It was his hand that brought healing to Ishmael before we left Rome.

Ishmael nodded and shook his head, "Yes, it's one illness I'll not forget."

"Well, when I arrived, I found nearly all afflicted - the entire maniple! Some to greater and lesser degrees, but nearly all not feeling well. Some were so serious that I couldn't help them and they expired soon after." Apuleius hung his head for a moment. "None of the drugs would help. The others responded well and are now on the road to recovery. I've instituted a thorough house cleaning and some of the new techniques of sanitation we learned in Rome. A mixture of vinegar and water has become standard in the canteens. I'm pleased, as is the commandant, except for a Jewish lad who was ill when I came and failed to come about regardless of potions and normal remedies." He stopped again to look about at the crowd now at the inn. Many were Roman soldiers on holiday, some from the billet in Capernaum, and others from some of the outpost towns nearby. They all seemed in good health and having a good time relaxing from military strains.

"This young lad was the apple of the present commandant's eye, and the rest of the troops as well. His illness was of great concern to us for he was an excellent runner, and provided us with an honest and trustworthy intermediary between his people and our command, and had a personality that endeared him to all the men. Try as I might, none of the potions in my kit cured him, although some progress was being made. I finally went to the commandant and told him the boys life hung in the balance. It would be but another three days and he would either live or die. I had done all I could, the potions were capable of curing him but, even as in your case, Ishmael, time was the only thing left to me."

Apuleius lowered his head, and we could see that he was greatly grieved with his own prediction. "It was a simple case of waiting. Either I had caught the fever in time or I hadn't. The commandant was greatly upset by this news, and said that he had heard that a teacher known as Yeshua was nearby, as had some of us newly arrived from Jerusalem. Some of the local people claimed he could cure all manner of illnesses.

"Now, Cornelius was greatly interested in the history of the Jews, and had taken time to read and listen to some of their religious tenants. He wasn't one to hide his beliefs and held that prayers were helpful to man. He believed the gods played games in war. So he called to him some of the Jewish doctors. He told them of his concern for the lad and asked them if they would ask the teacher to come and lay hands on the lad and cure him.

"The commandant was liked among them, and although several didn't hold with the teaching of Yeshua, they were willing to go to him because of the liking for the man. They found Yeshua entering the city but yet some distance away, and appealed to him on behalf of the commandant. The teacher listened to his cause, and would have agreed to this but for some of those present that were not believers. They came back to the commandant with their report of a lack of success on his behalf. The commandant was greatly distressed as the request wasn't for him but for the lad. He called his aide and told him to get his animal ready as he would plead his case for the life of the lad once more."

Apuleius took time to rest from his tale. We sat enthralled as it was one similar to that heard in Cana.

"I remained with the boy; the commandant couldn't bear to stay and see the lad in such a condition. He gave me strict instructions not to leave the boy until he returned. When he left, I gave the lad the last of the potion and waited for his crisis to pass. I had been at his side nearly two days and nights. His condition continued to worsen throughout the time the commandant was gone. I feared that he would die and I would have naught but bad news for the commandant upon his return. I was near exhaustion and at times fell asleep during the watch. It was close to the seventh hour when I was awakened by the lad moving in his bed. It wasn't long before he roused sufficiently to sit on the edge of his cot, and even as you were better after the fever, Ishmael, so was he. The crisis had past and he was weak but on the road to recovery."

"It was soon after this Cornelius returned from his pleading for the teacher to cure the lad. When he saw the lad, he was filled with admiration for Yeshua and told me of their meeting. Now, Cornelius is a man of integrity and wouldn't surrender this for any cause. He asked me at what hour did the lad show signs of recovery, for he was greatly interested in this. I told him it was near the seventh hour. This I remember for I had turned the sand clock over after I had seen the lads' movement."

"Of this you are sure?"

"Yes, sir. I'm not one to leave a patient and his condition changed that hour."

When Cornelius said it had been done as the teacher said, I didn't understand what he meant, but was to learn as he continued his story, "I was received by this teacher and his disciples not far from here. I suppose it was because of my dress that I was let through the crowd. Centurions don't often come to these itinerant teachers, and therefore, the crowd was curious. Since I had sent some of the elders to speak with him on behalf of the lad, he had knowledge of my coming. I addressed him as teacher for this I had heard was his rank. From my point of view, he seemed no more or no less than a typical traveling teacher. Yahweh, their God, will send a Messiah to lead them once again into greatness. I told him again of my concern for the lad, and asked him to petition his God to save him. To this he was in agreement and would of that moment come to the billets to heal him. I didn't know if this fever was contagious or not, and not wanting to cause any illness to come upon the teacher, declined his offer to come and lay hands on the lad. It was a selfish act on my part. I knew if this Yeshua contracted the fever from coming here, there would be a great outcry by those who placed such faith in him. I told him it wasn't necessary for him to come to the billets and I believed that if it be the will of Yahweh, the lad could be cured from without."

"And this I truly believed, Judas - with gods, there can be no limit of power because of distance. And so it is that I believed that if he so desired and it was the will of their God, the lad would be cured then and there. He was greatly pleased with my words and told me to go, for it had been done as I had asked. It is because of this I wanted to know the time the lad improved. And as you have said, it was the same hour he told me it would be done. Judas, I'm no fool, and I've served in this land of the Jews nearly twenty years. It has been long enough to know them and their beliefs. I can't help believe that they have some mystique about them, and their God is more than the ones we see and hear stories about in Rome. Hear me, if I were a Jew, this man I would follow."

Apuleius ended his story with, "He looked in on the lad and gave me relief from the watch, and with it, time to rest myself. Cornelius returned to his quarters a happy man!"

We sat considering the similarity of it and the story we had heard in Cana, when I asked, "What are your thoughts on the matter of the lad's recovery, Apuleius?"

"It's hard to say, even as the fever Ishmael had a formal crisis that I looked for at the time, so the fever this lad had was a similar one. I know that the potion I gave him was enough to cure him, yet there is always the question of time. If I hadn't given the potion in time, then all was lost, but if I had, then all was well. One could say that the time Yeshua told Cornelius all would be well was coincidental with the reaction to the potion. Who knows? This I know, the commandant thinks the lad's recovery was directly caused by the will of Yeshua. Who am I to say otherwise? I still believe the potion had done its work and would have if Cornelius had waited with me in the billets. For my part, I'm glad it is over, and I can travel with you and see this Yeshua in person. As we see more of his work, we can be sure he is who the people claim." So ended the subject of the Jewish lad's healing.

We left the room where we ate, and moved up to a loft in the inn. This room had a large window that looked out over the Sea of Tiberias. As evening approached, the moon came up and set sail over the water. It was a pleasant scene. The conversation turned to the event we now called the healing of the noblemans' son. I, with some help from Ishmael, told of the things we had heard in Cana. Apuleius was greatly interested in the similarity of the two happenings. Some of his interest came from Yeshua curing two with the fever, or so it was said. We asked if Apuleius knew the nobleman named Joel, but he said not, for he, like us, was comparatively new in the area. He quickly added that he hadn't treated any civilians for the fever except the young lad. We again considered going in search of the nobleman and thereby confirming the tale but turned it aside as we were more interested in finding Yeshua and seeing him even as Ishmael had before.

Some time passed while Apuleius stayed with us at the inn. A few days later, duty called. When we next saw him, he told us that he had received orders to return to Jerusalem. We had yet to set out from Capernaum when we learned that Yeshua and his followers were on their way to Jerusalem to attend the feast of Purim. Apuleius joined our little group, as he traveled under his own recognizance.

We chose nearly the same route returning to Jerusalem that we used in our coming. I told Apuleius many of the tales we heard as we rode along. His interest was great enough to want to see the places wherein these occurred, so we found ourselves retracing steps through Cana, Nazareth, and even Salim, before we settled down to reaching our goal of Jerusalem.

In Cana, we still heard the stories of the water changed to wine, even as we had the first time here. But then we were more interested in the story of the healing and paid little attention to the hawking of miracle waters of the wedding.

Here and there were small shops selling water they said came from the very water pots used in the miracle. Each entrepreneur extolled the wine-like taste of the water he offered. Some claimed all sorts of healing powers in it, and these being directly proportional to the amount of water imbibed. Some had smaller vessels marked with special symbols which they pointed out were clean and contained only this water from the wedding feast. Ah, they were a crafty lot.

This turn of events outraged Ishmael, but he had been closer to the happening than many of those selling the water. I failed to see his sensitivity to this thriving business of selling water. After all, no one had to buy it or believe in its medicinal powers. Apuleius laughed at the many who were pressing close to spend their money for such water, and some of these, their last Gerah gained through begging.

"Ah, what's the difference between this and gambling - both depend on human frailties. One chances on good health, and the other on riches." Apuleius was right. There was no assurance of success in either case. The whole scene reminded me of those back in Rome when the priests of honored gods sold holy water.

Some of the merchants were unhappy with the results of their own hawking as the word traveled through the different communities - the sick, lame, blind, and poor of every kind came to lie around their booths crying out for some of the water. This infected crowd and their clamor for relief drove many of the well-to-do away, cutting into possible sales. Some had complained to the elders without success.

"See how foolish this thing of religion can become. Here people spend their last coin for a drink of water which probably comes from the town well or spring where it's free. I saw the same thing in Rome. My, how many of those so inclined became caught up in a belief in the efficacy of a potion offered by the priests of Juno and others. But I'm surprised at these people, for I thought they wouldn't fall for this form of skulduggery." He leaned far forward and gave one of the enterprising water merchants an Assarius for a ladle full of the miracle water.

Since he was thirsty, he drank with relish. "Ho, what is this, Judas, the taste of wine is there. I see these people aren't fools, they have added some wine to the water. At least, those drinking can't say they didn't get their money's worth. Maybe I should take some of this with me in my medical bag." He laughed again, threw what he didn't want onto the ground, and gave the ladle back to the merchant.

It seemed that the water had scarcely left the ladle when some of the ill able to move sprang on the wet spot on the ground to press their lips to it. I couldn't believe my eyes! Some of those were Jews forgetting that their help came from the Lord God of Israel and not from a few drops of water. Some came and took hold of our reins, begging for some of the water that we might not drink. The merchants drove them back for they wanted to sell more water to us.

Because of Apuleius' good report of the water, we all had some, which encouraged the merchants. After each one of us drank, the press of the crowd became greater, the clamor rose to high pitch, "Hear us, oh men of honor, we would want just what you don't drink. Grant us your leavings!" Such and more were the cries of those wretched people on the ground near the water booths. Apuleius suggested we leave the place, and soon!

As we left Cana, Ishmael was still mumbling to himself about this blasphemous commercial activity. He remained thoroughly convinced that the hand of God had moved to change the water into wine that day in Cana. While all this was going on between us, Apius remained silent - occupied by his own thoughts on the matter.

We saw the man who had told us the story of the healing of the nobleman's son, and by the crowd about him, was reliving the story. Many stood with eyes wide and mouths open greatly absorbed in his tale.

Some at the outer edge didn't respond as the others and jeered at the speaker. "You are a fool! Don't you know this carpenter's son from Nazareth? Have any of you seen the nobleman's son? Have any of you seen him healed? Ha, I see none of you have, so why believe this teller of tales? Isn't it written that a fool finds a snare in his tongue? Don't be deceived, the Lord God only is the healer of all, not this carpenters' son." Such were the words of some at the outer edge of the crowd. They weren't easy to put aside.

We left Cana and proceeded to Nazareth. There were many pilgrims along the way, some traveling to Jerusalem as we were. The crowds were large and varied in background and country. There was the usual pushing and shoving to get the best position on the trail. Some sat along the roadway crying to be carried to the Holy City. Occassionally, there was the clanging of a bell or din of spoon against plate to let everyone know that lepers were in the area; even the most obnoxious and belligerent stepped aside for these unfortunates. Their cries were pitiful, and their appearance quite frightening. People would scramble to escape their path.

"Ah, it's sad to see human beings in this state," said Apuleius. "I'd give much to be able to find a cure for that disease."

As we watched these poor people move along as best they could, I asked, "Isn't there a cure known, even in the Schula Medicorum of Rome?"

"Alas, there are many ills and bodily injuries that we have little knowledge of in the great school of Medicine. It's strange, Judas, but the school is just a starting place, not a finishing place. I have learned more about human illnesses since I left the school than I did studying all the books of the ancients and modern teachers. That's not to say the schools aren't necessary, but may the gods help those who practice medicine without the approval of Rome." Apuleius was a good man and had a great respect for human life. "Some day, there'll be one of these unfortunates cured by someone, this I know, and I hope that I'll be in the crowd when it happens." He looked off in a manner of seeing a dream come true.

"Well, I should, too," I said. The chances of seeing anyone cured of leprosy wasn't even in a dream stage, it was still in a miracle category. There hadn't been a healing of leprosy since Elisha had cured Naaman through the Spirit of Jehovah. Not in all the world was one cleansed of this disease among man since that time.

Ishmael sat quietly on his animal, sketchbook in hand; he drew lines rapidly. As I looked over his shoulder, the image of the lepers came to life. Apuleius pulled his horse alongside and looked at the sketch.

"Your talent could be of great value in my profession, Ishmael. Many young physicians could learn more quickly with your sketches before them when they study these diseases. You must draw every form of illness and disability we encounter along the way. I'll make a book of these things and will send them to the school of medicine. Great things come from your drawings." Ishmael's sketches impressed Apuleius and I was justly proud of him as well.

We arrived in Nazareth late that afternoon because of the want to see and hear the news along the way. We stopped many times to listen to some storyteller. Some told stories of our new Procurator, but these became silent when they saw the Legionnaire with us. Still others told stories about Yeshua. The stories ran the gamut of life's experiences filled with romance and the intervention of God to save the poor and helpless.

We rode by the home of Yeshua. His brothers were working on a house frame. As we rode by, one looked up from his work, shaded his eyes, and looked at us. We reined near the house. The brother of Yeshua continued to look from Ishmael to me. He showed some light of recognition in his eyes, but that faded soon as if he didn't want to recall the event that led to that remembrance. Ishmael called from without the house to those working in the shed next to the house.

"Ho there! Can we speak to Mistress Mary?" We had seen her not more than six weeks ago, and would speak with her again before we return to Jerusalem. A young lad ran into the house to announce us. It was Mary who came to see who the visitors might be.

"Oh, Ishmael, it's you!" She, too, shaded her eyes from the bright sun as she looked upward toward the rest of us. She was accustomed to people stopping and either inquiring about her eldest son, or telling her stories of his movement about the country. "Come in and sit awhile. Is that Judas with you?"

"Aye, it is, and we have with us Apuleius, the army physician that we spoke of when here before. He has an interest in Yeshua as he has heard of his healing people with the fever," Ishmael spoke as we dismounted and entered the house.

Mary saluted us and recognized the uniform of Apuleius. He gave her a gracious greeting even as he would have his own mother. He was one to recognize the goodness of women regardless of nationality.

"You are warm and in need of water. Son, see to the animals and water for their hands and feet. Come in to the center of the house as it's cooler there." She led the way through the little house as though it were a palace. Some of her daughters and their children were moving about the rooms taking care of chores. Those not having husbands glanced at the Legionnaire with some curiosity. They would like to know him better, and tried to move about the room as much as possible to gain added looks. Mary knew what they were about and permitted it for some time and then reminded them to hurry with their chores.

"We bring you news of Yeshua," Ishmael said.

"I thank the Lord for your kindness in telling an old woman of her son's ventures."

Ishmael then told of the healing of the nobleman's son, and of Apuleius telling of the healing of the servant to Cornelius, his commandant. She listened intently and would have had it all repeated but realized our need for continuing our travel and therefore didn't ask to hear them again. She admitted she hadn't seen Yeshua for some time as he hadn't stopped at Nazareth on his way to Cana or Capernaum. Her eyes misted some when she spoke of him. He was her firstborn and commanded a deep love in her.

We promised to return sometime and reveal any event in his life that may have come to our attention. We thanked her for the water and care of the animals. Having expressed our happiness in seeing her well, we told her that we would remember her to mother, and mounted our animals to leave. The young women came to the front of the house once again and stood by Mary as we rode away.

"Some of them are good looking, Judas," Apuleius stated in a matter-of-fact tone as we rode out of the city; he was in reference to the young women who were in the house. It was interesting to me for it was one of the few times I saw Apuleius show any recognition of the Jewish beauty. I smiled at him and let things be without comment. We turned our animals toward the main roadway and moved a canter to Jerusalem.

THE POOL OF BETHESDA

We continued to move along at a goodly pace, stopping here and there to listen to some traveling storyteller reveal the hidden mysteries of some ancient religious writings. Many called to the people to harken unto the Lord, "Repent, gain forgiveness, and be washed!" was the battlecry of most of them. It was as though the entire countryside was aflame with some prophetic cause. As we stopped to listen, some added to the phrase, "Unto the kingdom of God." Neither Ishmael nor I could answer Apuleius' question as to what the "kingdom of God" was. Nor could we understand how anyone but the priests could forgive sins and this only through the proper ritual.

"I can understand the kingdoms of the gods, Roman style, and I can imagine the seat where all the gods play their godly games, but what of your God, Judas? If he has no body and isn't contained or understood, then where and what is this kingdom of His?" His asking wasn't in fun, he was trying to visualize the thing offered to these poor people that listened to the passing storytellers and itinerant teachers. The poor and sick gathered around each one of these speakers, listening to their every word. Many showed signs of understanding them more than any of us, for they would smile and shake their heads to the remarks of freedom from pain and hunger.

"You know, Judas, it seems these people believe more that the kingdom of their God isn't a place or something, as much as freedom from something here that is nearly unbearable," so said Apuleius as we watched the crowd move, sometimes swaying back and forth with the speakers' words. Here and there, one would shout praises to the God of Abraham upon hearing a phrase now and again that meant something more than the others. I couldn't understand which phrase was the key to these feelings for all listeners seemed to nod and shout at different times. But I had to agree with Apuleius - some were lifted from their dreadful conditions for a moment to dream of times when they would have a better lot. Perhaps Apuleius was right that their kingdom of God wasn't a place as the gentiles knew it to be, but a condition - a condition of love.

As we came closer to Jerusalem, we met more patrols of troops leaving Jerusalem for the hills. The talk was that the Zealots had begun to cause trouble there.

We approached from the north road. At this end of the city, the roadway was often cluttered with various small animals needed for sacrifices. We passed several of the wash pools for sheep and goats. The temple officers and priests inspected the animals after they were washed. The good animals were then taken to the holding pens while those unacceptable were sold in the marketplace.

Near the north end of the city there was also a pool not used for animals but for humans. This pool, called the Pool of Bethesda by the local people, was said by some to have great healing powers at certain times. The pool existed for many years - though the claims of miraculous healings were recent - even I could remember when this was not the case. A number of porches surrounded an enclosure. The pool was spring fed and changed its level at times during the year. Temperature changes below the surface caused these infrequent but dramatic stirrings of the surface - by a rippling across the surface of the water. Such was the Pool of Bethesda.

There were many tales told of the healing efficacy of this pool. Many were totally unfounded and fabrications of the minds of the sick and dying who lay about the edge of the pool and among the porches. Those who kept positions near the pool were those called impotent folk, the blind, halt, withered, and retarded; all waiting for the moving of the water. Some said, when in motion, the Spirit of the Lord was upon the water, and cure was granted the first in the water of whatever his infirmity. So the tale went, but in all candor, neither I nor Ishmael had ever seen one cured.

"Surely, Judas, not all those poor souls believe in this story? Even if it were true, most of them can't get to the water anyway, let alone at the precise moment of surface movement." Apuleius was shocked at the many people lying near the pool without any attention. A strong stench hung over the area. The Pharisees and priests considered it an unclean place. None who kept the law came near without ablution later. Even Apuleius, who saw this sort of human degradation in his dealings with the military and war, pulled his cape over his face. "Who is responsible for this ill treatment of human beings?"

"Ah, Apuleius, it's one of the unfortunate truths that many believe in these tales. As to who is responsible for this, it must be said that King Herod is, for he supplies the funding to keep those who are living here in some form of meager food and water. The Romans haven't taken any interest in the plight of these people." It was a strong indictment against the Romans, but once said, I felt I had done no wrong. Apuleius said nothing in defense of the Roman attitude - I continued. "What would you have us do about this, dear friend?"

"This place should be closed and these people removed from here. Don't you know that much of this filth flows back into the ground, and from there into the very spring that feeds the city? By the gods, we may be drinking this in our water!" He was right, of course, and it was lucky that the upper city gained their water from different springs.

"Ah, it sounds so simple, but Apuleius, these people are here because they want to be, not because they don't have elsewhere to go! Remember, many believe these tales of miracle cures through the movement of the surface of the pool. They would resist as well as they could any attempt to remove them; they want a chance to be cured even if they die in the attempt. Don't you see, Apuleius, it isn't a simple matter of displaced persons - but a faith, no matter how ill-founded, in something greater than man can offer elsewhere." He was now nodding in a way that showed he understood more than before.

As we rode nearer, the waters of the pool started to rise and the surface became agitated. First, small ripples and then greater motion rode on the surface. Voices of those lying in the squalor near the pool rose to hysterical cries for help to get into the water.

We were horrified to see these wretches fight one another to be the first to reach the rippling water. One grabbed the legs of another to prevent him from moving ahead, while another that could see placed his crutch in front of a blind man. Some fell across others, and were bitten and scratched by those they fell across. It was everyone for himself; none wanted to give up his chance for good health to another. The thought of "love one another" wasn't the driving force at the edge of this Pool of Bethesda the day and hour the loving Spirit of God came on the waters.

At last, some entered the pool, but the ills remained. Great shouts of anger arose, some floundered about in the water, crying and pouring the water over themselves, but to no avail. Tears mixed with spring water that moment as many realized their chance was gone! The water became evil looking from the filth brought to it on the bodies of those seeking cures. Blood and pus rose to the top of the water. The shouts of anger continued, for now some in the water attacked others therein, claiming that had the others stayed out, a cure would have occurred. Some, locked in mortal combat within their limited capabilities and weakened by their efforts, fell near death at the edge of the pool. Nearly as soon as this had happened, it was over. Those with strength crawled out of the pool and lay back against the several porch steps, there to await another chance to receive the blessing of good health. None claimed the pool hadn't done its magic. Nearly all claimed the loss of healing because of the greed of another, for the saying was that when two or more entered the pool at the same time, its strength and blessing diminished.

So each claimed the other should have waited his turn. There were more curses said than prayers of thanksgiving on that movement of the pool.

"By the gods, I've never seen anything like that in all my days in the service of Rome. Even wounded military men haven't acted so - even in harsh times." Apuleius was emotionally drained, as were Apius and I. Only Ishmael seemed his calm self - his hand busy with the stylus.

We turned away and moved into the city. As we moved by the fifth porch, a voice called out from a straw pallet near the steps to the pool.

"Masters, was it truly a movement of the waters today? I heard such noise but I'm unable to reach even the second porch where I could see." I turned to look at the person having such a pitiful voice. "May God be with you, for it seems he isn't with me now these many years because of the sins of my fathers."

The voice belonged to a thin resemblance of a man lying on a pallet of straw. His body was naught but skin and bones. His hair and beard hadn't seen water, comb, or knife for nearly a lifetime. I peered down at him from my horse; I knew this man, but couldn't recall his name. Ishmael also must have known him, for I saw him rub his forehead; an early habit he executed when he tried to recall a particular event.

Apuleius was first off his animal. He had seen too much to remain disinterested anymore. His natural inclination to help people overcame his fear of any illness he might contact from such effort. He knelt near the man, and spent sometime examining him, his medical curiosity demanding such. As he felt each limb and moved them repeatedly, I suddenly remembered who the man was.

"Amal," I mused in disbelief, and then to Ishmael, "it's Amal, can you believe this?"

"Aye, you're right, Judas. I was sure I knew him also, but with his face mostly hair, I couldn't place him."

We both had known Amal since our travels in and about Jerusalem as young boys going to sit at the feet of Hillel. Apius recognized him before any of us, but had held his peace as always unless asked.

"You know this man?" Apuleius asked as he continued to examine him. I always felt reassured watching Apuleius for I felt he was a man of good practice; he was thorough.

"Aye, we have known him for many years. He is called Amal, and that by his own admission. He has been disabled for many years, I would say, nearly thirty or forty years, true Ishmael?"

"Aye, we have seen him elsewhere in the city. He hasn't always been here. Come, let's put alms in his box and be off for we have yet to prepare for the feast of Purim." Ishmael opened his purse and tossed the coins into the alms box while still on his animal.

"But Judas, this man can walk if he wants to. This I swear, for I find no fault in him that should keep him from rising from this mat. It's just a matter of convincing him to believe he can do it." This discovery excited Apuleius. "Climb down and help me get him to his feet. He will be weak but he can walk!"

I left my animal and walked to where Apuleius was now half supporting Amal with his arm under his shoulders. I helped Apuleius bring Amal to his feet, but he cried out in great fear.

"Hear me! I'm unable to do this thing, for my sins and those of my father rest heavy upon me." Tears of fear and discomfort rolled down his cheeks. The tears caused rivulets through the dirt on his face. He had no faith in what Apuleius was saying to him.

"Listen, you can walk if you will, but you must try. Can't you at least try? No sin is resting on you. Your illness comes from the mind, not the body. Hear me, I am a physician from the court of the Procurator, and I can see no hurt that would cause your incapacity. You can do this thing if you will." Apuleius tried to instill in Amal confidence in his own capability, but it was hopeless. Amal wouldn't try. We eased him back to his pallet and, after rinsing our hand with water from the clearer part of the pool, mounted our animals. Apuleius sat looking down at the pathetic figure on the mat; he was downcast.

"Ah, Judas, it's a sad day for me. First, I see such degradation of man, and then a man who won't try to overcome his infirmity though he can. I wish he was part of my command - I would command him to do this thing." Apuleius was both angry and frustrated for the moment. I couldn't help feel sorry for him and admire his patience through it all.

We left Amal and the pool, and moved through the city. Apuleius was still pondering the case of Amal, this I could tell from his apparent preoccupation. As we moved away, I had the strange feeling we would hear of Amal again.

The house stood as it always had, at the end of the street. It was good to see the gate again. Home at last, why was it that we all have such longings for our nesting place?

Apius was first to enter the gate. Atonis greeted him and then gave each of us a hug of warmth. The horses were taken care of and we approached the room of washing.

The servants now alerted by Atonis, brought water and clean clothes for all of us. It seemed strange to see Apuleius in something other than his Roman dress, but he made no objection and, in fact, enjoyed being considered one of the family. I knew he was somewhat ill at ease though as I could remember my first time wearing Roman dress at his father's house. Because of his military bearing, he wore the garments well.

After some rest and wine, we strode into the garden. Mother was yet in her afternoon nap, and I wouldn't have her disturbed. The garden was cooler than the rest of the house.

"What say you, Apuleius? It isn't the garden of Lucius the elder, but it's a resting place, don't you think?"

Even though it was smaller than the house and gardens of Lucius in Rome, I was still proud of father's house.

"Ah Judas, it's all you claimed it to be - a jewel in the desert of all Jerusalem. I can see now why you longed to return." Apuleius was sincere in his compliments and I was grateful for his comments. We now waited for the queen of the household - my mother.

CHAPTER FOURTEEN

The Story Of John

The household was preparing for the Feast of Purim for it was already the twelfth of Adar. I could remember the thirteenth wasn't to our liking as children - fasting wasn't a happy way to go. It was the fourteenth that meant happiness.

I described the Feast of Purim to Apuleius and told that part of our day would be spent in service at the temple. I reminded him that during this time he could do as he wished. Our house was his for as long as he wanted. He told us that he wasn't to report to the fortress for at least thirty days. He expressed the desire to see some of the service and this from the Court of the Gentiles. While we were talking, mother arrived.

She was prepared for company as her handmaiden told her of our return and the guest we brought to the house. We rose to greet her; she was as beautiful as ever. She greeted us with motherly hugs and kisses, and extended her hand to Apuleius. He saluted her in the custom of the Romans. She, having been in many of the homes of the Romans in Jerusalem, accepted his greeting with the graciousness of any Roman lady. He was impressed with her courtesy.

"My dear lady, I'm your servant. Your household is one of taste that only mirrors your elegance. I accept your hospitality with humbleness." I listened with some thought of this Roman speaking thus to a Jewish mother. Perhaps there was in Apuleius something that wasn't in some of the others.

"And what have you learned in your travels this past month?" mother asked.

First I, and then Ishmael told of the things we saw and did during the trip. We described our trip through Salim, Cana, Nazareth, and Capernaum. Ishmael capped the stories with our talking with Mary and her sending blessings to mother. The stories of the healing of the nobleman's son, and that of the Centurion's servant came to light, and all things some said of Yeshua and his followers.

We mentioned our distress upon hearing of John's arrest and imprisonment. Later, we learned that mother heard of this crime against John before we did. In fact, it was she who tried to warn John of his impending arrest but to no avail. John wouldn't cease his crying out against Herod and his wife.

We spent many hours that first day in conversation about the strange things that happened to us over the years.

Mother was greatly interested in Roman life, and the political arrangements that were made to bring Pontius Pilate to Jerusalem. Most of this news Apuleius was able to supply. He supplied much of the background of Pilate and what we might expect in the next few years from him.

The holiday of Purim passed in great joy for our family. For one thing, the blessings of the Lord were upon our household. All of the family, save father, was present; a thing not true for nearly sixteen years. Sister Anath brought her family home to greet us and meet Apuleius as well. Mother was indeed very happy with her family around her.

Yet thoughts of John being in prison remained a dark cloud in the normally clear sky of the season. Mother told us she heard from her clients that Herodias was pressuring Herod to silence John forever. It was also rumored Herod was afraid to take John's life because some of the people considered him a prophet. Herod, it seemed, still listened to Caiaphas on the mind of the people, and although he had little fear of God, he wanted to keep the people quiet. When they were quiet, the new Procurator, Pilate, remained in Caesaria or Tiberias and away from Herod's palace.

So given the choice, Herod didn't harm John - nor for the moment wanted to. He was satisfied the people would forget John and his radical ways if given enough time. He didn't fear the wrath of God resting on him because of his harming John, but did the possible recall to Rome because of an uprising. Herodias, on the other hand, had no such scruples and desired John dead at any cost. His call for the House of Hanan to deny her recognition of the marriage was a thorn in her side even though she held little respect for the people or their God. With John in prison, the people still jeered her whenever they came close enough to express their hatred. It was known to her that John was still making speeches from his cell to some camped outside his window. Once heard, these followers carried his words throughout Judea and within the city. It was the preaching by proxy that kept the fire of righteous indignation against Herodias burning. So it was that we were concerned for the life of John - now called "the washer."

AMAL HEALED

After the holidays, Ishmael, Apuleius, and I went to the marketplace to see the new goods made there. Apuleius was searching for things he might send home which would remind them of his service in Judea. His time wasn't yet upon him to report to the fort. As we walked through the marketplace, we approached the temple. There, in front of the gate of gold, was a large crowd. As we approached, we could hear the excited voices of many and the cross talk of these was such that we couldn't understand what it was about. We stood nearby to decipher the speech of many. We made our way through the crowd and found to our amazement, there standing in the midst, was Amal!

"By the gods!" exclaimed Apuleius.

"Praise the Lord!" cried Ishmael.

I stood unable to speak. There stood Amal, looking like a scarecrow being just skin and bones but such a difference! He was clean and it was obvious he had just come from presenting himself to the priests for cleansing of his spirit. He was clean of body, hair combed, beard trimmed, and his clothing, though ragged, was thoroughly washed. He stood without help, although not without some weaving. He moved slowly about as one showing off some new dance steps; he was proud of his ability to walk again. His words were full of praise to God for his return to wholeness. My first thought was echoed by Ishmael.

"Was it the pool of Bethesda?" he asked in awe.

Amal continued to praise God and chant thanksgiving verses. I couldn't hold my curiosity and shouted over the crowd.

"Hear me, Amal, start from the beginning and tell us of this thing that has befallen you. It seems your sins, or those of your fathers, are forgiven. Remember how we tried to have you walk just a fortnight ago? Don't you remember us?" I stood away from the crowd so that he could see me plainly.

He looked at me for some time, then at Apuleius, and then the others. His eyes fairly danced with a fire of the Spirit of God. He reminded me of John when I saw him after father's death. Amal's eyes, though shining like stars in the heavens, showed no recognition of any of us. He was as one in a trance.

"I knew he could walk if he would try, the question is who or what caused him to have the faith in himself to walk. As the gods know, I didn't have that ability to convince him of such." Apuleius studied the man before him with the eye of the physician robbed of his medical triumph by another. He wanted to hear the story of this man, also.

"Ah, hear me, and praise the God of Israel," cried Amal. "My healing was in this wise. I was at my place on the steps of the fifth porch on the Sabbath, when a teacher came to me. I knew him to be so only because some of his followers addressed him as such. He said he knew I had been there for sometime - how he knew this I don't know as I had never seen him before. He came near to me, bent down, and looked at me. I thought he would place something in the alms box, but he didn't do this. Instead, he asked me if I wanted to be made whole.

"I laughed and said what man wouldn't want to be. It was the second time I had someone tell me about my illness. The first was by a Centurion and his friends. They even tried to raise me, but all was for naught. I told the teacher I had no one to place me in the pool when the waters were disturbed; I couldn't make it to the water in time.

"I then told him how the sins of my father lay hard against me, and God had shut up his favor from me. He looked very sad and took my hand and said, "Rise up and take up your bed and walk." In his eyes I saw something that none other before him had. I couldn't refuse his command but held firmly onto his hand, and pulled myself up. I found I could stand without his hand in mine, yea, I could even walk, though not without pain for my bones hadn't seen this stress for many years."

Apuleius brought his hands together smartly, "I knew it, hear that Judas? He said he pulled himself up!" Apuleius continued to mutter about knowing of Amal's capability.

"Then he didn't ask you to believe in him or his sayings?" I interjected. "You didn't declare your belief that he could do this thing?"

He stopped as if to consider just what the teacher had done. "No, he neither asked nor did I give any such thoughts. I reached down and picked up my bed for he had thus instructed me to do. 'Go now and show yourself to the priest in accordance with the law.' Then he and his followers left as the press of the crowd was great after they saw what he did for me. Many cried for his help, but he didn't hear them and continued on his way. His followers held the crowd away from him as they went. He didn't give me his name but some told me his name was Yeshua, a teacher from Nazareth.

"I was about to show myself unto the priests when I heard some of those watching speak to me thus for they were lawyers, 'It's the Sabbath, and it's not lawful to carry your bed.' But I said unto them, 'Hear me, oh men of the law, the man that came to me and lifted me up said take up your bed and walk. His word to me is greater than all the law. Who of you can say this wasn't the will of the Lord?"

"And they then said unto me, 'Who was it that said these words to you?' I couldn't tell them as I didn't know. They were angry and threatened me, as they wanted his name. I left them and prepared myself for the priest, and then went to the temple as instructed.

"It was after receiving a blessing from the priest that I left the temple to tell others of my gift from God and once again met the teacher. I recognized him as the one called Yeshua. He said to me, 'Behold, thou art made whole, go and sin no more lest a worse thing come on you.' But this I knew I couldn't do - I couldn't sin no more. No man can do this thing; no man is free from transgression of the law. He spoke no further word on the subject. But I knew I was still weak and wobbly, yet I could walk and this well enough.

"After this, the Pharisees came to me by night and asked me who it was that made me well, and I said it was one called Yeshua, a man of God. And they left me saying they had just cause against him - not for that which he did on the Sabbath, for all know to do good on the Sabbath is not forbidden - but because he had told me to carry my bed. It's unlawful to carry ones' bed or even the Shofar on the Sabbath. This is all of my story."

"Hold," said Apuleius, "this is all he did - just lifted you up by the hand?"

"Aye, it was just as I said." With that, Amal left us to continue on his way telling all he met of his good fortune. He walked unsteadily, but he walked nonetheless.

My heart was filled with trembling, although I didn't reveal it to those with me. Ishmael was sketching the man as he did before while we were on the venture in Cana.

Later, when we examined the sketches, we were amazed at the likeness of Amal. In the sketch, Amal was shown as nearly a skeleton, having little flesh on his bones, and veins standing along his limbs and across his forehead. He was there on the papyrus even as we had seen him. As we continued on our way, we chatted about the strange happening we had just seen.

"I knew he could walk, I just knew it." Apuleius wanted us to know that it had been a possibility when he had first seen Amal. "The question is why did he believe this teacher and not me? What was it he saw in his eyes that wasn't in mine? It must have something to do with your religious background, you Jews are all alike. If I had offered him some kind of ancient saying with my suggestion he could walk, perhaps then he would have done so. So it is and so it will remain here in the east."

"Hold, this isn't anything against your skill, Apuleius. It is as you say, a thing in our background." Ishmael felt a kinship to Apuleius for both were sensitive to man's needs, and both found at times their skill short of what they would like. I felt sorry for them somewhat, but hadn't their interest - business was mine!

As time passed, Apuleius had to report to the fortress, Ishmael labored on improving his art, and I took on more accounts of those in the city. Our interest in the adventures of Yeshua waned some, as he had done little in the way of miracles and caused little to stir up the Pharisees of late.

We were well aware that the Pharisees had been seeking a just cause for his indictment. He was still claiming he was the Son of God and permitting his followers to do the same. It was this that caused the council to look for ways to limit his preaching. Yet their cause wasn't critical; many knew of men before Yeshua who had claimed to be the Messiah and were hung on a cross for their efforts. And history showed some who cried out they were the Son of God were stoned for their blasphemy.

His sayings were becoming better known and from some we heard stories of his sayings. We heard so many of these things we didn't know what to believe about the son of Joseph, the carpenter, from Nazareth. The people murmured against him in many circles. He was said to claim that he could do nothing except he had seen his father do it, yet all knew his father was a carpenter. Then he claimed his father was Yahweh, the God of his people. He spoke of his father raising up the dead; yet couldn't name one who was so raised. Yeshua said he was given the power to raise whom he would from the dead. His statements caused great confusion among the people.

Some claimed to hear him say, "Verily, verily, I say unto you, he that hears me and believes on him who sent me has everlasting life, and shall not come into condemnation but shall pass from death unto life." Some of those who listened to his words were very old and infirm even at this meeting. They were heard to cry out that they believed on him and him who sent him, and would have everlasting life as they didn't want to die. But even as they declared their belief in his words and in him who sent him, some expired. Those who saw this were disenchanted with Yeshua's words. They could readily see eternal life wasn't granted unto those who believed for they still died while crying their belief.

Many who heard his words and hadn't seen these aged people die continued to believe his sayings. Some left for their own countries with the belief they would never parish. They told many as they went of their belief and hope to receive everlasting life and never die. I didn't believe in this for no man knows the hour of his death and it's for man once to die - so it was written and so it's done.

Many still weren't happy with his reference to God as his father and cried out against this practice. When asked why he told the man to carry his bed on the Sabbath, he stated, "My father is working still, and I am working." This placed a great hardship on those listening to him as they remembered and believed as Moses said, "All to honor the Sabbath and keep it holy." Hadn't Moses recorded that a man who simply gathered sticks on the Sabbath to keep warm was stoned as directed by God himself?

Some who were gentiles accepted his words for they had known of such things from their religious histories. The stories of gods and goddesses mating with man and producing man-gods weren't new to them. The making of gods from living personages was happening every day. It had been happening since Caesar's time. But they didn't know how to address him. They wanted to bow down to him as they had for other gods before him, but felt the eyes of all his people on them and therefore refrained from showing homage. His own kind could find no release from the first great law, "Thou shalt have no other gods before me."

Some shouted, "If he be a god, why is he no different from one of us? He becomes tired, hungry, and thirsty. We see no light or pillar of fire near or about him!"

"Can Yahweh take the form of man and not consume him?" Some argued with his followers. "Hasn't Moses written for us, 'And the Lord said, thou cannot see my face; for there shall no man see me and live.' How then is this teacher living?"

And Yeshua counseled his followers not to answer. But this only gave full courage to the rabble and they cried even more, "Is he greater than Moses? Nay, he isn't the Son of the living God, but he is instead a blasphemer!"

Others raised their voices in other ways. "If he is what he claims to be, then let him show us, for this isn't an unreasonable request." They held that even a tradesman must show his wares.

The crowd milled about and shouted even more.

"Aye, for if a stranger claims to be the son of some man, do we not say, how do we know this? And doesn't he bring his father and mother forward as proof? Even those from far away places show the rings of the household. Where is this mans' proof? Where is his father or mother? Isn't his father dead and his mother Mary of Nazareth? And don't we know him to be the son of a carpenter? Show us your proof that you are the Son of God!" And they shouted for Yeshua to bring forth his proof of sonship.

"Show us a sign and we will bow down as do some of these gentiles to the man-gods." With that, some walked up and would touch him for they had no fear of him who claimed to be the Son of God. Their moves were stopped by the three followers who were ever between him and the people. Yeshua and his followers moved on to another spot, yet the crowd followed them shouting many of these things.

These and many more stories of his rejection by his own kind came to us from the streets of Jerusalem and through our servants.

A VISIT TO JOHN

We heard Yeshua had left Jerusalem and traveled northward to the Sea of Galilee which some called the Sea of Tiberias. But now things about us became more important than news of his travels. I had increased my wealth considerably through new and lucra-tive contracts with influential Romans and the elite of our own community. Ishmael had set about refining his sketches and bringing them into full illustrations. His time was spent laboring over these with the intent to make them into a small booklet - a scroll of pictures.

Apuleius was called away again to the near front in the hills. Whenever in Jerusalem, he would appear at our gate with regularity. However, recently, he mentioned these fre-quent visits were not being accepted very well by his superiors. They classed his intimacy as a mark of fraternization with the enemy as the trouble between the Roman troops and the Zealots grew from small skirmishes to serious conflicts along the borders. He was sad as he related some of the results of these short battles. He left us on the last visit with the announcement that he would be less frequent in his visits. Mother was greatly grieved to hear this as she had become accustomed to his presence.

During these visits, she tried to make Apuleius feel at home and was the first to listen to his comments about the political byplay among the new Procurator, Pilate, and the house of Hanan and Herod. She never lost interest in Roman politics. Besides her own clientele, Apuleius was an intimate source of intrigue. She bade him goodbye for what seemed to be the last time, and asked God to bless and keep him safe always.

Apuleius was taken to us as a family and had often said we erased some of his loneli-ness while here in Judea. We, Ishmael and I, watched him mount his animal and turn to salute us once more before leaving. It nearly brought us to weeping at his leaving, but we were consoled by the thoughts that we would see him again clandestinely, if no other way.

As time went on, mother became more apprehensive for John's life. It was whispered among her clientele that Herodias was unhappy at being put off by Herod. Herodias wasn't one to be refused, even by Herod. The rumors were flying that she was planning to catch Herod in a weak moment and force him to destroy John. Mother was troubled now that Herod's birthday celebration was near; she knew it was the custom of royalty to grant special gifts to those so applying during such occasions.

"My dear sons, I fear for John. Herodias isn't above asking for his life as a royal gift. We must try to gain Herod's ear and have John released before it happens. I'll try to get a message to Herod through his chief steward. You must go to Apuleius and seek his help in this matter. It's possible that Herod may desire to release John, and with the right pressure from the Romans, do so." She was preparing her finest beauty aids to tempt the wives of the court and thereby gain access to Herod's chief steward, Chuza. She knew what this might mean to her and her circle of friends who had provided much information unto her people about the policies of Rome. One wrong move would cost much.

Ishmael was already moving to leave for the fortress of Antonia. He shook his head in agreement, "We will find Apuleius and tell him of our concerns." I joined him and we rode to find Apuleius.

We once again found ourselves in front of the officer of the day in the main court of the fort. We were saddened to hear that Apuleius was in the field. The news he wasn't expected to return for some time brought us down some.

To return home with this news didn't seem right. The alternative left to us was to attempt to see John and change his present views or, at least, the views he had before going to the dungeon. We needed to cause him to cease his crying out against Herodias.

The gold coin with us to present to the chief guard would help. These men weren't above accepting bribes - or so we had heard. The chief guard and commandant of the prison were men who had heard much about John and were somewhat convinced his words were true. However, both were afraid of the King's royal guard that was made up of foreigners who held a great dislike of the Jews, and therefore refused the bribes. If the chief guard and commandant were found taking a bribe, it would cost them their lives. Yet to set aside time for someone to visit John in his cell wasn't a crime of negligence and they arranged such time for us. That isn't to say gold didn't change hands.

We stepped into the lower part of the prison wherein John was kept. The turnkey let us into his cell. John was resting on a straw mat; there was little else in the cell. As the door closed behind us, we moved to stand over his mat.

"John, John, son of Zechariah, can you recognize us?" I asked the question for there was precious little light coming from a very small window above him. "It's Judas and Ishmael of the house of Simon. We have come to see you and bring mother's blessings."

John tried to rise from his mat but didn't succeed. At last he spoke. "Ah, I've longed to see you but even now can't tell which is which." I could see John still remained himself and his spirit wasn't broken. "I fear my time is short. The Angel of the Lord has visited me and my work is near an end. May God be with you both and don't grieve at my condition as it's nought when compared with the reward I may soon receive."

As my eyes became accustomed to the light, I could see he was in a very weakened condition. Yet even in this low-level light, I saw his eyes burn with the fire of the Spirit. His was a cause which nothing on earth could abort. "Hear me, Judas. Some things still cause me pain. I'm but a man like yourselves and have my weaknesses. When I first received my call from the Lord to go into the wilderness, I feared neither man nor beast." He stopped; his head rolled back against the straw for a few moments as he rested. He was weak and tired from his confinement and ill treatment. My heart went out to him.

"I felt the hand of the Lord upon me and spoke out as the Spirit moved me. The greatest revelation came unto me when I washed Yeshua of Nazareth. It was then I thought I heard the voice of the Lord speak directly to me. The Lord said, 'This is my Son in whom I am well pleased.' My heart soared with the birds of the air, for these were the words that Israel was waiting for many generations. I became full of hope. Nothing could deter me from speaking out this truth and preparing many for the coming of the Messiah."

His head sank again and I feared for his life. He struggled to continue. Ishmael began to weep softly for he was a man of high feelings. I sank to my knees so that I might not miss a word of this testimony.

"I then heard of the crimes of Herod. How can we expect to gain the ear of the Lord when our leader under the Lord is corrupt? His crimes were an abomination to the Lord. I couldn't do less than point out to the people that his sins were upon them. I fear it was this that caused my loss of freedom." Although he didn't notice, I shook my head in affirmation of this judgment by him. "Oh Judas, have I done wrong in crying out against the sins of Herod and his wife? Have I cut down the flower to destroy the weed? I'm truly undone!" He, too, began to weep in despair.

Before he ended his lament, he turned and addressed Ishmael using my name. It was then I realized in the dim light John mistook Ishmael for me! I had changed a good deal since I came to Jerusalem; I had lost my pallor from my stay in Rome and had let my beard grow again. Many couldn't tell us apart. I remembered as children and young lads we often exchanged clothing and fooled all but our parents as to who we were. Later, I was to find this close similarity caused great hardships but to also have many rewards.

"Great despair is upon me, Judas. My soul cries out for proof of these things I've preached to others. The great deceiver has come to me in this darkness and filled my head with doubt. Many that gather outside my cell window are truly penitent and ask for remission of their sins and this I would gladly give them but I have no access to water! How can I wash away their sins without water? Oh Judas, my heart cries out for a word from Yeshua that I haven't been following a dream supplied by Satan. My soul is near lost!" And John grasped the garment of Ishmael and wept as before.

I tried to comfort him with what we had seen and heard. "Hear me, John. Don't despair; we have seen and heard of diverse things Yeshua has done for the sick and infirm. All these in the name of the Lord." I wasn't so convinced as others were that all I heard wasn't partly fanciful and partly real, and which was which wasn't clear to me. I couldn't help but feel a great need to give John some comfort in his hour of woe. "John, we have heard great things may yet be done for you. We have come to ask you to turn away from your preaching against Herodias, as it's from her your pain comes. If you can do this thing, we may be able to gain your release through a boon from Herod on his birthday. Even now, mother is appealing to the chief steward of Herod to hear her request for your release. John, will you refrain from speaking out against Herodias? What word can we give mother?"

Upon hearing my words his wailing increased; he was truly undone.

"Get thee hence, oh messenger of the great deceiver! Why have you come to torture me, Ishmael? Haven't I wrestled with this question of leaving my mouth stopped against Herodias enough?" He had addressed me as Ishmael again, but I made no effort to correct his error.

"Isn't it true that Israel now suffers from the sins of its king? The Lord comes down hard on his people because of the sins of its leader. It cannot be done, Ishmael! In my heart, when not troubled by the great deceiver, I know I'm but the voice of the Lord, and not the author of these words against Herod and his wife. God be with you; carry these words unto your mother; it is for this I was born and for this I will die!" He then motioned with his hand the meeting was over.

"Hear me, John! I'm truly grieved that this is your word. May the Lord be with you in your time of need." I touched his shoulder and raised Ishmael up to go.

We moved to the cell door, and the turnkey opened it for us. He was a big man, and looked to have the strength of several men. Yet his face was one of a babe, and the eyes of one not yet old enough to learn his letters.

"I have heard what this man says in his cell, and I'm a Jew of good family. I fear for his life for there is talk of Herodias wanting him dead. Is it true that a teacher Yeshua is the Messiah as this man says? Tell me, good men of Jerusalem." His eyes had a longing expressed in them that reflected the belief that someday a Messiah would lift the yoke of the Romans. "I believe that I'm a sinful man and would have my sins washed away, but we have no water here. Gentlemen, please tell me what to do for I'm a miserable man."

I had no answer to give to the man. Ishmael told him he might seek out Yeshua in the north country and through him find the answer to his troubles. The turnkey seemed happy with that answer and turned away singing a little song of praise. He was a simple man unable to understand much of what he heard; I felt some day we would meet again.

When we returned, we told mother what John had said. She was saddened by his words, and told us she was unable to get word to Herod. Our combined news wasn't pleasant; our fear for John increased manyfold. Mother's news was even worse; the rumors were strong that Herodias was courting ways to force Herod to acquiesce to her wishes. Should that come about, it would just be a matter of time that John's life would be taken.

We continued to observe the political winds in Herod's palace, hoping against hope that some good news about John might come forth. As Herod's birthday approached, mother again tried to talk with Chuza and through his mouth, the king. It was well known that Herod was concerned about the people and this kept him from listening to Herodias.

Our concern for John overshadowed our thoughts of the stories about Yeshua and his followers. Many things were told among the poor and infirm of his powers to do good. Since leaving Jerusalem, he had remained in the north, residing and traveling throughout

Galilee while visiting the towns of Nazareth, Capernaum, Naim, and Bethsaida. Nor had we heard of his returning to Jerusalem since the Passover.

Apius was one to listen to the stories of the travelers; he came to us with the stories of healings of many diverse illnesses by the word and hands of Yeshua. Also came the words of rejection from his own. The town of his early life, it was said, became greatly grieved at his teachings and threatened to cast him over a cliff near the town. They were not successful in this as Yeshua left Nazareth straightaway.

Things in and about Jerusalem became more important than the news of the whereabouts and travels of Yeshua. My accounting business had increased, leaving me little time for the call of adventure.

Mother became more involved with efforts to free John, while Ishmael was busy creating artistic trappings for Herod's birthday. Ishmael had been commissioned to do some of the mementos for the occasion; I thought his fees were excessive but I wasn't the purchaser. As the birthday approached, so did the court activity.

Many craftsmen wanted to supply something to the palace to show their talent, not that they cared anything for Herod, but that there was a need to be recognized. His likes and dislikes still had power in the marketplace. In addition, entrepreneurs of Jerusalem didn't want to be undone by foreign talent. The gold and silversmiths were busy creating trinkets for the occasion, and even the weavers were attempting to create a tapestry which would catch the eye of some courtesans wishing to impress Herod.

TIME TO TALK OF DEBTS

My business was conducted from the Upper City; this required riding to my accounting house. While riding there, I would daydream about stories of Yeshua. I would imagine what some of these events looked like; the placement of characters and their reaction to being well again. I could see the crowds of the sick and lame pressing against Yeshua to receive a cure with or without blessings. Ah, but these were just dreams as I had never seen any of these things, and the way business was, nothing indicated I ever would.

Once, while dreaming thus, my horse stopped in a strange alcove. As I looked around to find my bearings, I saw a single horseman bearing down on me. I was frightened as the figure was hooded. I rode to meet him, hoping to pass without incident. As I came alongside, a hand came from the cloak and caught the reins of my animal.

"Hold Judas, would you ride past an old friend?" As the figure spoke, the hood fell back and before me was - Shalazar. Shalazar, whom I hadn't seen for nearly three years. He showed no sign of aging and was as handsome as before. The cloak covered his strange dress; the material was not made from our weavers - this I knew.

His voice continued to rumble from the depths, "The time has come for us to talk about your debts!"

"Aye, I have often wondered what payment would be exacted and when." Ishmael and I had often talked about the strange rescues and what they might mean in the future. Even then I never spoke to Ishmael or mother about my striking a contract with Shalazar for Ishmael's release from prison. They were never aware that I knew the strange cause of his release. I had kept my side of the bargain and never told anyone.

"Is it so urgent as to require us talking here in the alleyways of Jerusalem? And isn't it time I know to whom I'm indebted?" I cautiously advanced the questions.

"One site is as good as another." He smiled but that quickly faded to show his seriousness, and he positioned his horse such that he faced me and our knees were touching. There was no one moving in the alleyway; we were alone - whether by his control, I couldn't tell. "Judas, time is running short, my name you know and it means nothing to you. This I say, I'm a prince in my own right, never fear. More power is mine than you can ever imagine. I owe allegiance only to the king and priest of this world, who, like Melchizedek, has no mother or father - no beginning or end, and no descendant; none other has claim on me! I do his bidding even as I expect you to do mine. Hear me: I know that before time began you were chosen for a special task. Hasn't it been revealed to you?"

His words tugged at my heart but not at my memory. I knew of no such revelation. Who was I to be greeted thus? Then the words between us from earlier times came to mind. The ones he had spoken before, that I carried hidden in my heart these many years, 'Oh Judas, I've known of you before time began, and have seen your progenitors come and go even unto this hour. Hear me, your part was written before Adam fell and the mark of the curse was upon Cain; it was known in heaven.' Could this be the beginning of a new meaning in my life?

"Your words have kindled an old memory within me, but I've no knowledge of any mission. Look to me, for I carry no ring or cloak of royalty! Who am I to be so chosen? It seems to me you have the wrong person!"

His face grew dark at this last remark. He wasn't pleased at the thought that he could be mistaken! "My time is short. You have much to do in your lifetime, Judas, and I'll help you. You have knowledge of the one claimed by some to be the Messiah - Yeshua of Nazareth. Isn't that so?" He bent down to look deep into my eyes. His gaze was so penetrating that I felt he was looking into my soul. I unconsciously moved back from him. "Why haven't you followed him?"

I felt ill at ease and searched for an answer to his questions. "Yes, I've known him as a lad, even unto this day. His work is his own; he isn't my teacher. Hillel was and still is the teacher I honor. But why do you ask?"

"Hillel is one of the past. This Yeshua is one of the future. Doesn't your heart call you to him?" He gave me no respite from his gaze.

"I must admit some curiosity about his movement and the sayings of the people about him, but I've no longing to become one of his followers." This was an honest answer; I had no urge to abandon all and walk with Yeshua.

"Then I say this to you! Your debts to me must be paid! You will leave your present way of life and follow Yeshua. Thus, I have requested and thus you will do." His voice dropped ever lower, giving the sound of one speaking from a deep well.

"How can I do this when I have much to do here in Jerusalem? My business is great and my mother needs me. All these things cannot be left for some frivolous move after some itinerant teacher. In this I mean no disrespect, but is there no other way for me to repay my debt? Yes, even to half of my property and fortune?" My mind reeled at his words. To leave my growing business and all I had worked for to follow Yeshua around the country as a poor man wasn't my thoughts of future success - not if I could change his mind about the repayment of my debts.

"Judas, Judas, do you think your wealth means ought to me? I'm a prince among the greatest in the world and the game I play has higher stakes than worldly wealth. Haven't I refused it before? All your total worth is of little use to me for I have greater wealth than you can imagine. It's your service I must have! Don't set your heart against me! Hear me, Judas, my time is nearly gone, you will suffer hardships known only to me and God until you become a follower of Yeshua. You have no other recourse, your debts will be paid and in the fashion I will. Expect to see me once more. Farewell."

He didn't wait for me to answer his questions; his words seemed an end to it. He wheeled his mount and left the alleyway. At the entrance, he stopped, turned, and gave me one last long, hard look and then disappeared from view.

I continued on to the countinghouse. Many were waiting for their bills and balance sheets. The day moved as a dream; it was as though I could see myself moving among the customers and conducting business as usual, yet not really wholly there. Shalazar! That name never left me the entire day. It, together with Melchizedek, kept reentering my thoughts at regular intervals. Who were they? And why me?

As the day wore on, I felt less and less interested in business. The words of Shalazar kept coming back to interrupt my thoughts of contracts and sales. At the close of the day, I was ready for rest. During the trip home, I wondered who I could tell of this meeting with Shalazar and the question of Melchizedek. Ah, if my old teacher Hillel was still living, he would know of this person and be able to advise me, but none other would I trust.

Ishmael? Was it time to tell Ishmael of the previous visit by Shalazar and my bargain with him for Ishmael's life? Or was it best to hold these things in my heart and continue as though nothing had happened?

I was preoccupied thus as I approached home. Apius met me as usual and saw to the horse. I went into the garden where Ishmael was working in clay. He had a contract with a local potter who owned one of the best clay fields in all Judea, or so it was said. Ishmael, who understood these things, held that this was so.

I strode up cautiously so that I might not disturb him. As I came close, I saw he was working on a bust of a man. At first glance, I thought it might be of one of his customers, or something for Herod's birthday. Many of his wealthy clientele were presupposed to having their own likeness made and given to others as gifts. I had always considered this a vain and unlawful practice, but it wasn't counted against me, so let it be done.

As I came closer, I recognized the emerging features of Yeshua, not from first knowledge, for I hadn't seen Yeshua since his childhood, but from the many sketches Ishmael had made and sent me. He was busy with this likeness; making lines here and there, taking out material to give true features, giving the beard the right amount of life with each turn of his knife; his hands moved over the clay with the ease of a surgeon. Ishmael was gifted beyond most in these things, and while I watched, I could feel the admiration for his talent well up inside me.

He stopped suddenly and stepped back to admire his handiwork. "What say you, Judas, does it meet with your approval?" His recognition of my presence surprised me for I thought I had approached him without being observed.

"Well, Ishmael, from the untrained eye, it's a most handsome likeness, but of course, I've never seen Yeshua since his youth. I've only your sketches to judge your work." I walked around the bust to view it from all angles. I knew he valued my opinion even though I wasn't an artist. I was his greatest admirer through all the years and was always one to encourage his abilities as he was to me in mine. We often laughed when we found that we were a mutual admiration society of two, I for his artistic talent, and he for my accounting and business sense. "Ishmael, would that I had such talent, but alas, it seems I've no real worth here. You will be long remembered by the family through your art, while I'll be soon forgotten, for who will remember this lowly accountant when all is done?"

"Thank you for your comments about the bust and Judas, you really don't know who will be remembered and for what, and that applies to all of us." He threw his arm across my shoulders. "Come, tell me, how was your day, and did the book balance?"

His question about my day brought back the meeting with Shalazar, his remarks about the person named Melchizedek, and the demands made against me. As happens between twins, Ishmael sensed something was different between us. I made light of the day, and covered them with the need for rest and washing before the evening meal.

"The day, as always, was filled with those wanting to buy without money and with some of our most religious leaders denying their legally-due bills. It would seem at times that the law means little to those of wealth. Those who have little are most apt to pay and pay on time. It's those with wealth and power who consider a debt a minor obligation;

it doesn't speak well of them." I turned from under his arm. He raised his shoulders and opened his hands in an attitude of helplessness about the truth of the statement.

I stood looking at the bust of Yeshua. This is the man I'm supposed to follow for the rest of my life to pay a previously-contracted debt. I saw that I was no better than those who would deny their debts to me. I was ready to deny the debt to Shalazar, and for this was heartily sorry. I quietly turned and went to my room, keeping these things to myself.

It wasn't long before the meeting with Shalazar slipped further back in my mind and the pressures of the business and household once again took precedence. The approaching of Herod's birthday became both the talk of the people and the cause of merchandizing as well. The people, although not great admirers of the king, recognized he was set over them, and since Yahweh had permitted this, they were to show him the grace of his office.

The old city was beginning to fill with many foreign dignitaries. Rooms at inns were fast becoming hard to find, and many families were gaining added coin from renting rooms to those from out of town.

Behind all this pageantry still lurked the worry about John. Mother still told of the court whispers about the guile of Herodias, and of her preparing a great surprise for Herod. It was after this she would ask a boon of Herod that he couldn't refuse. The word was that she still had great hatred for John and would see him dead.

Mother told us of being called to the palace and meeting Mary from Magdala, the well-known preparer of rare perfumes and ointments. She and Mary Magdala compared notes on the different wants of their clientele. Both mother and Mary were called to prepare beauty needs for the young daughter of Herodias, Salome. It was she who was to dance before the king on his birthday. She was a stepdaughter of Herod, being fathered by his brother Philip. The people were quick to make humor of the situation for after Herod married Herodias, Salome was both niece and stepdaughter to Herod. What was her greeting to him, father or uncle?

A WITHERED HAND?

The rumor throughout the court was that this young girl of less than fifteen was to perform a sensuous dance for the king. Mother saw the dancing costume and supplied beauty aids as commanded. Mary Magdalene provided some of the most exotic scents of her collection. Since this was to be a surprise for Herod, they were told the penalties were extreme for revealing this to anyone. Because of her religion, mother wasn't asked to swear to secrecy about the coming performance by Salome. From the costume and what was whispered around the court, mother had deduced that Salome's dance had much to do with Herodias and John.

Mother's fears for John multiplied each day. Because of this chance meeting with Mary Magalene, mother and she became sincere friends, and both shared concern for John. Mary, being more attracted to the sayings of John than mother, worked quietly among her clientele to gain John's release but to no avail - none wanted to cross Herodias.

It was some time later that my health began to deteriorate. At first, just little annoying aches and pains, and then these became more frequent and debilitating. Some weeks passed with great discomfort. At last, I found I couldn't use my right hand for normal skills. It became numb and remained that way throughout the greater part of the day. I showed this strange affliction to Ishmael, and even demonstrated how I could barely scribe a list of figures. I became more and more concerned; Ishmael even more so than I.

"Judas, dear brother, you must have your hand looked at by Apuleius. It may be something that requires a potion or salve. You can't hide this from mother much longer, and if she finds out, you know this will grieve her." He was right, it was getting more difficult to keep from dropping things lifted in my right hand, and mother was bound to notice soon. His advice was sound as the period for the repair of normal injury was fast exceeding limits.

"You're right, Ishmael. I'll send Apius to find Apuleius and ask him to visit us once again. Mother won't be alerted to anything in this wise." So it was I sent for Apuleius. More than a fortnight passed before Apuleius would visit us.

The day arrived and Apuleius rode up to the gate. Apius received him and took care of his animal. In the pouch he carried was his complete field medical kit; he was never without it. Apuleius was one prepared at all times. I can remember he had his medical supplies along when we traveled from Capernaum some months before.

He came straight to the garden and there greeted mother. She was delighted to see him, and it wasn't long before they were deeply involved in the politics of the day. He had been in the field and was now on a short holiday; he was happy to visit us once again.

Throughout the early evening and after the evening meal, we talked of the skirmishes between the Zealots and his troops. I noticed that Apuleius became interested in the talk about John and expressed the hope that something could be done to affect his release. He held that since John was in Jewish custody, and had broken no Roman law, there wasn't anything that the Romans could or should do. Interference in the observance of Jewish customs and of the operation of their sovereign, as long as it didn't abrogate Roman authority, was held outside Roman jurisdiction. That is as defined by Procurator Pilate. In fact, the accepted view at the fort was that whatever one Jew did to another was of little concern as long as Roman law wasn't broken in the process.

Mother grew weary and retired early; the events of the day and worry about John were telling on her more and more each day.

It was easy to see that Apuleius had noticed my care in handling things with my right hand, although he was careful not to make a point of it while mother was present.

"So Judas, what have we here? Why the care of the right hand?" He moved toward me and studied me as I had often seen him do others. "You haven't sent for me just to see me again, so out with it! What is your ailment?"

"I'm sure it's nothing that won't restore itself, but it's taken its time in doing so. My right hand has become weak and sometimes it becomes numb."

He moved over to my side and held my hand in his, studying it for some time. He recalled the time his chariot struck me many years ago, and how my side was injured then. I'd forgotten all of those things. Apuleius had me do different manipulations with my arm and hand while he felt the joints. He was of the opinion that it might be injury related, and this from the chariot incident. Aging might be taking its toll. After awhile, he gave me a potion to take every evening and made a sling to wear during daylight hours.

"I can't tell the cause of this trauma but we can treat it as a result of the old injury. Give your hand plenty of rest, use it little during the next three weeks, and I'll check you again when I return." He was very professional; I listened and thought he had forgotten I was his old friend. I was just another patient, another medical problem for the moment.

"Alas, mother will surely see this sling, and be upset at it. What shall I tell her? You know Apuleius, I'm nearly lost without the use of my right hand." I had never spoken truer words; if there ever was a right-handed person, I was!

"As to the recovery time, I can't tell, but you must not worry for I've seen many of these kinds of recurrent disabilities because of old wounds and injuries. It's common for some of the older troopers to be plagued with this sort of malady. A little rest and all should improve in three weeks. Don't be afraid to tell your mother of this simple weakness, and let her know all will be right soon; I dare she is stronger than you think. In the meantime, have your scribe do your writing for you, and you settle all with a mark, left handed or no!"

I thanked him for his good advice and prepared to follow his prescription to the letter. We then talked of other things as before. He remained with us for the next two days and then returned to his post. Mother wasn't nearly as alarmed as we thought and the words of Apuleius on the matter assured her all would be well.

For the next three weeks I followed the routine religiously, never going about during the day without the sling and taking the potion as prescribed. Yet as the weeks came closer to three, I saw no improvement. In fact, the hand was showing a lessening of strength and my concern grew from mildly curious to apprehensive.

Apuleius appeared as promised. He, too, showed more interest in the continued loss of strength, but the lack of any atrophy puzzled him. In the weeks that followed, he tried all of his skill poured over the many books he had, but nothing seemed to cause improvement.

Under mother's insistence, I showed myself to the priest and gave sacrifices in accordance with the law. In prayer, I called on the Lord of Hosts to heal my hand. I now feared some sin of old had caused this affliction and asked God to lift this sin from me. Yes, I, too, felt the tug of old beliefs about ills. If wholeness meant godliness, then illness must mean ungodliness - the story of ancient times.

After several visits, Apuleius said, "Dear Judas, I've tried everything I have learned about this ailment, and have sought in the text and advice of colleagues without success. I have to be honest, I have no solution - there is no cure. Nowhere can I find anything wrong with your hand. It shows no external sign of hurt. My opinion is that this condition is caused by something outside the body."

He looked so dejected that I felt no ill will toward him, and embraced him in brotherly fashion. He had tried his best in all these things. He took all his failures to cure with a deep sense of loss. It was I who must console him; even as it is in life, the one hurting must often be the physician for the one well.

"Apuleius, don't worry so. I know you have done your best and bare you no ill. But your words about the illness being caused by something outside the body gives me no rest. Does this mean you have thoughts of spirits and other instruments of ill will affecting the health of mankind? Have you come to the conclusion that not all illness has a physical source?" These things Apuleius and I had argued many times before; he was always quick to set aside any connection between the acts of the gods and physical well-being of men.

"No, Judas. I can't believe that your illness is the will of your God, nor the work of demons. But this I know: your illness isn't from your body, but may very well be from your mind. I feel there is something you haven't told me about this thing and how it came about. You know more about this than you care to admit."

He had come to this conclusion rightly, for I hadn't told him of the meeting with Shalazar some weeks ago, and of his saying, "You will suffer hardships known only to me until you become a follower of Yeshua." I stood looking down at my hand. I'd never told anyone of this meeting - not even Ishmael! Partly because of the press of the business and partly because I had felt no illness before this.

"Come, Judas, tell us. Haven't we been like three brothers? Can't you believe we have your well-being at heart?" Ishmael was very concerned and brought his kinship to bear on me.

"I agree I've not told you of these things, but I fear you wouldn't believe me. But because of this extending beyond the normal course of things, even as Apuleius has confirmed, I will tell you what I know." I told them of the meetings with Shalazar in Rome; the contract made there for Ishmael's release some years before; the meeting in the alleyway of the city about the future and his request for me to become a follower of Yeshua; his revelation about his princely position in the world; and his name, Shalazar.

A strange silence fell on them after they heard these things. Each was occupied by his own thoughts. Apuleius broke the silence.

"Who is this man, if he truly is a man? Shalazar is a foreign sound to me. I know of no prince in the Roman elite as such. I must admit he has strange and prophetic powers, as well as strength greater than any man I've met, be he citizen or man-at-arms. But such a strange request for payment of a debt!" He fell silent after this.

Ishmael had turned pale at the news of the contract made by me for his release from prison. He raised a shaking hand to his brow in a blow indicating unhappiness.

"I fear for you, Judas. This man isn't the good person we had first imagined so many years ago. There is little doubt of his power over man and nature, for this we have seen. What does it all mean? Why would he ask you to follow another, when it's certain he could do these things himself? Dear brother, could it be that you have bargained away your life for mine?" Ishmael was apt to be a bit more dramatic than others.

"It's not as bad as all that, Ishmael. What ill can come of it? We don't know that some of this isn't my imagination! But what to do about my hand is another thing."

"We have heard of the power of Yeshua to cure illness. Yet none of us has seen this." Apuleius spoke with his usual curiosity. "I have no right to hold you from seeing the man; I can't give you relief. If you believe he can help your hand, then see to it." Further discussion cleared nothing, so it was agreed that Ishmael and I would find Yeshua and ask him to cure this malady. It was time that we spoke of his abilities from first hand.

CHAPTER FIFTEEN

Yeshua's Healing

The following week I prepared for the trip to Capernaum as that was where Yeshua was reported to be. I told my scribes to take over the business while I was gone. Ishmael was ready even before me. We told mother only that we were going to see Yeshua in Capernaum; the reason remained a secret from her. Apuleius returned to the fort and was unable to join us. Apius prepared the animals and would ride with us. And so it was that we left Jerusalem the next day.

We traced our steps from Jerusalem through Samaria to Galilee, riding along the road-way through small villages and towns. The road led through the hills to Shechem and then a left fork to Nain in Galilee. Here we stopped to hear many stories about Yeshua. Each storyteller had his own version of these same or similar events, each claiming his was the true one! There were even those who claimed to be recipients of this healing and praised God every step of the way to their homes. Not all were so eager to reveal their stories, and some claimed that they had been ignored by Yeshua even as they cried for his help. They were often among those who scoffed at those who claimed help came to them through just the touching of his garments.

Much of this we saw and heard as we traveled across Galilee. We entered Nazareth before sunset, and after saying prayers and partaking of the evening meal, traveled to the home of Mary. We talked with her and she told us she didn't know where Yeshua was and hadn't seen him for sometime. We stayed in her home for the night as was the custom.

We left Nazareth with the rising of the sun for Cana. Cana hadn't changed except more shops were offering healing waters from the wedding bottles. Some shopkeepers were offering other things they claimed Yeshua had touched which had great powers of healing and comfort to those afflicted. Ishmael once again became incensed at this playing on the needs of the sick and poor. He nearly ran his horse over the booth of one rascal who was selling blessed water to a poor, ignorant pilgrim. One said that Yeshua and his followers had moved on to Tiberias, the town on the sea, so it was there we decided to go.

Along the way, we heard that Yeshua and his followers had just been this way. None could tell us where their next destination might be - either by design or forgetfulness, one couldn't tell - so we continued along the road to Tiberias, where we found the word around the well was that Yeshua had moved on to Magdala. It was said he had friends there and was to see them and teach in the Bet ha-knesset the next Sabbath.

We continued north to Magdala, the thought being that we would find a room at an inn and stay there until we found Yeshua. Since it was only a day's difference, we could be at the house of assembly and there see Yeshua as he read the Torah passage of the day. We could then approach him for help.

We found accommodations to our liking and Apius took care of the animals for we wouldn't need them in this small town; everything was within walking distance. At the inn, we heard stories about Yeshua and his followers. Some were of great deeds and the healing of many diseases, while others offered no such encouragement. The diverse tales gave me belief that all would be well, and also made me wonder if this wasn't an effort in futility.

After all, I had known Yeshua as a babe and as a lad. He showed no traits of being other than a boy with all boyish faults. He wasn't able to learn any of the games of the day any quicker than any other. He showed no intuitiveness when playing hide-and-seek. He had no insight to difficult or dangerous situations more than any other. Wasn't it true, I pondered, that his father was killed when he was old enough to know it? Some of the people claimed him to be clairvoyant. He could see into the future even as the prophet Isaiah. Others told of him great tales of raising the dead even as Elijah did.

It was true. I hadn't seen him for nearly sixteen years. It was possible that a great presence of God was in him now. I felt the truth of these sayings would be proved soon.

My hand steadily lost its strength but not its form. I learned to use my left hand well enough to permit some common acts, but was in great need of my right hand for things of accuracy. To relieve the feeling of uselessness of my right hand, I found that I often held it in my left hand. I was able to move my right arm without difficulty, but the hand itself was of little use; the hand was as a wooded one.

We prepared for the Sabbath day and the possibility of seeing Yeshua in the Bet ha-knesset. The synagogue was small; it was built within the walls of the village in accordance with the laws of travel. Nearly all in the village could reach the house of assembly in less than two thousand cubits. The word was that a goodly Roman Centurion had provided the money for its construction. The people were reluctant to reveal his name for fear of reaction from higher Roman authorities. They didn't want to see him removed as the authority over the city of Capernaum. The people devised a means of disguising his real identity when they spoke of him; they gave him a Hebrew name and family, thereby keeping some of the Roman spies from gaining his identity.

Once hearing the story of his kindnesses, I knew it was the officer of the fort in Capernaum, the commandant who had called upon Yeshua to heal his servant boy. Ishmael and I sealed this knowledge in our hearts, vowing never to reveal it to anyone.

We moved to the house of assembly in the early hours of the morning in accordance with the law. We stood near the entrance to the inner court waiting there for it was said Yeshua would read and interpret the Torah this day. There was a goodly crowd. Those of the house were present as well as those who had heard of his reading this day. Not all had come to hear his reading of the law; some were there to inquire of him his authority for doing so. There were doctors of the law present to hear his words as well. They stood some distance away in a small group quietly talking among themselves. As near as I could tell, they were men of rank in the law, and by their dress, from as far away as Jerusalem.

Many of the poor and ill pressed forward to see or touch the robes of Yeshua, and repeated many cries of despair. Some would have them silence their cries in accordance with the law for the Sabbath. But their pain and discomfort gave them no thought of such laws. Ordinarily, I would have been one of those quick to call for the quieting of their cries, but as I stood there holding my right hand in my left, things were different somehow; I could understand their plight better than ever before.

Soon the crowd started to murmur against Yeshua for he was late - this wasn't customary. The sun was up and the heat in the house of assembly increased steadily. Sweat ran down the faces of all waiting there for the word to be read. Many were calling for some other person to read the Torah, and satisfy the needs of the people.

Nearly as soon as these things happened, the crowd became quiet again and moved to make an opening for Yeshua and his followers to approach the altar. I recognized him from the many sketches Ishmael had made. The others with him, the one called Peter, his brother, Andrew, James and John, as well as Philip, and Nathanael, and others I didn't recognize as Ishmael's sketches didn't include them.

Yeshua was much smaller than I gathered from Ishmael's drawings. He wasn't much taller than his mother, Mary, and a good deal shorter than most of his followers. The one called Peter towered over him. Yeshua wasn't only small in stature, but also light in weight. In general, he was a small man. His face wasn't handsome, but he was not hard to look at either. He was a small image of his father Joseph. His hair was brown and held in the style of a Nazarene, untouched by blade. He was in all ways a Jew; his features showed no signs of interracial marriage as did many others of the day. He had no look of Babylonian, Persian, or Greek in him. As he came near, I could see the same fire in his eyes that John had some years ago. He was a man with a mission. He walked straight to the scroll and with the help of the others, read the lesson of the day.

"Remember the Sabbath Day and keep it holy. Six days you shall labor and do all your work, but the seventh day is a Sabbath of the Lord, your God. You shall not do any work - you, your son or daughter, your male servant, or your cattle, or the stranger, who is within your settlements. For in six days the Lord made heaven and earth and sea, and all that is in them, and He rested on the seventh day; therefore, the Lord blessed the Sabbath Day and sanctified it." He looked up to the heavens to gain strength to interpret the word.

"All these things you have known from your youth. Remember the Sabbath Day was made for man, not man for the Sabbath. Have we not kept these commands since Moses? Is it not a blessing for Israel to keep this day? This is the good thing for the people to do. All good things must be done everyday of one's life, but even more so on this day of God. Among you there are those who would tell you that it is better to do nothing on the Sabbath than to do good. They even call to mind the law of the ancients, "Yea, work ye must not do, but verily I say unto you that which is good you must do."

"Hear me, the Sabbath was not given to you to see others suffer while you observe the law, but to remind you that even as the Lord watches over you and keeps you on this day, so ought you move to save and protect the lives of others. God ignores neither rich nor poor, well nor sick, good nor evil on this day. Has he not caused the rain to fall and the sun to bring forth the new day? Can anyone of you argue against this? Can we but accept these blessings and emulate this love of our Father by being generous to our brothers?"

Some of the learned listening to his words shook their heads in agreement with his teachings of the Torah just read. There was none who challenged his words. Both Ishmael and I were proud to hear his discourse. He had given meaning to words that we had often heard before without consideration. While all considered his words, one stepped from the group and addressed Yeshua as one who desires to know more light in the law.

"Teacher, some have taught differently and they come well recommended. From your words, I see that you agree with the Pharisaic interpretation that it is legal to break the law given to Moses and perform healing on the Sabbath. But is it lawful to perform healing that could be done on another day? We agree that life-endangering sickness must be relieved, but we have heard that you have done otherwise. Tell us more of these things!"

The one who spoke was a goodly man, mild in his manner and showing respect to Yeshua in all things. He wore the dress of a Pharisee and proudly so. Later, Ishmael told he had a vague remembrance of the man, and as it turned out, he was right, for we discovered him to be a pupil of Nicodemus - a teacher of good report.

Yeshua acknowledged his question with a turn of his head in the direction of the speaker. "Is it so difficult? What man of you wouldn't rescue a distressed animal on the Sabbath? When you do this, do you consider it good or ill to leave the animal in the pit one more day? Do you not act as though it will die if left in the pit? How much more do you know of man's ills? How much more is man worth to God than the animal? If you act to save the animal and fear not the law, then why the hesitation about helping a man in distress? If a man's life is lost because of your negligence on the Sabbath, who then is guilty, God or man? Would you blaspheme God by saying it was God's fault for many to have illness on the Sabbath? My Father in heaven would come hard against those who think thus. Hear me, fear not the law and do good always, for it is the Lord's will, and doing less is to do evil."

ANOTHER SABBATH CURE

After saying thus, he came and stood before me and Ishmael. He didn't recognize us, or at least gave no indication of doing so. His act so surprised me that I couldn't speak. Because of the heat of the day, I wore no sling but simply held my right hand in my left.

"Stretch forth your hand," he softly commanded. I couldn't hold back. I answered by releasing my right hand and moving it forward, and as I did, so the numbness left it. He said no more and did nothing more. As suddenly as I had stretched out my hand, I found I could move it in complete freedom. I couldn't resist trying to grasp things with it and stretched forward even further to reach his robe.

He drew back from me, and I was unable to complete the act.

"Not now, friend. Be gone and praise God that this has come to pass. Your sin has been forgiven you." He then turned and gave the closing of the day. The Torah was returned to it's place of love. He and his followers left the house of assembly forthwith. None of those present could find fault with his teaching; all agreed that to do good on the Sabbath was within the law. Yet to move beyond the law to do these things without asking the priests was quite another thing. A group of Pharisees held that he was teaching well within their code, and none gave indications of any hurt against him. Yet it came to us some time later, that some Pharisees were grieved about his words and plotted to do him harm. I found this story hard to believe and found this tale was carried by some unfortunates who were willing to carry tales about anyone not of their own kind.

"Judas, have you ever seen such a thing? It's truly a miracle! God has favored us this day!" Ishmael was elated, he could barely refrain from following Yeshua. "Your hand, give it to me, let me feel the strength in your grip." Our right hands met in a firm grip; it felt good to use it again. "Judas, you must return to Jerusalem and show yourself to the priest, and to Apuleius. He'll want to know of this relief from your ailment." Ishmael was more excited than I; he moved about like a child. All along the way to the inn, he continued to jabber about the thing he saw and the strange way it happened.

Many others unknown to us stopped to ask about my hand. Some wanted to know if it truly was without strength before his words. Some refused to believe this was so even after Ishmael and I told them my hand was as one wooden before that same hour; each left with his own opinion about the truth of the healing. Some said it was a trick, and that we were secretly some of his followers who had taken on this illness to enable him to prove his power; some said they had seen others do the same for those claiming to be a Messiah.

"Don't you think it strange that he knew of your infirmity? And did you notice he plainly didn't recognize either of us? What power is given unto him to be able to cure that which is unknown to him?"

"Ishmael, don't become so excited. There are many reasons for all these things. What we have seen isn't as important as what he has taught us. Remember, I was just the tool by which he illustrated the point that we must care for all in distress and on all days." I felt had I not been there at that time, he would have found someone else who had an ailment and cured them as well. It wasn't who I was that meant anything, or what my infirmity was; anyone that stood before him at that moment would have received the blessing from God.

When we reached the inn, we addressed this subject and told Apius about the happening. He was happy for me and expressed the notion that Yeshua was indeed touched by the hand of the Jewish God. As soon as we had said our noon prayers and enjoyed the noon meal, I wanted to take up a stylus and try my hand at writing again, but this being the Sabbath, I couldn't do so. As it was the law, the use of a stylus was classed as work; I refrained from trying my newly-gained strength. The rest of the Sabbath passed in quiet reverence and closed with the prayer of thanksgiving.

In the morning, we gathered our things and left Magdala. Our minds and conversation centered on the happening in the house of assembly. We were anxious to get home and show both mother and Apuleius this thing. We didn't delay as we did on our trip to the north, but moved steadily along the road to Jerusalem. I was as a young boy riding with reins once again in my right. It was a pleasure to be able to do simple things with my right hand. With the close of the Sabbath, I took the stylus in hand and listed some figures. My hand moved well once again, and I gave thanks to the Lord for this even as Yeshua had said. What would mother say?

The ride from Magdala to Jerusalem was a full day, the distance being nearly 90 miles. We would again pass through Nazareth and, because of our promise to Mary to tell her about Yeshua, we planned to rest the horses there before continuing on home. We reached Nazareth in the early part of the day. Mary welcomed us and was anxious to hear any news we might have. She set before us refreshments and waited for us to tell our story.

Ishmael was quick to tell of the events as he was still in the spirit of it. I showed Mary my hand and stood by Ishmael's tale about it. Mary was exceedingly happy to hear of her eldest son, and praised God for this news. She was grieved to learn we couldn't tell her more of his doings. We had heard on the way that he was going again to Capernaum but couldn't be sure this was true. We stayed with Mary only long enough to rest ourselves and the animals. We left her household with promises to return when we could.

On the road, we passed through Shechem and stopped at Jacob's well. We waited our turn at the well as we were among many who came to water animals. At times, this was a busy place as I recalled from the time before.

Ishmael and I moved into the shade of a small tree while Apius waited with the animals. After he watered them, he brought us fresh water. The water from the well was sweet and cool, much better than what we carried as it was warm from the heat of the sun. We moved to a small hill on the outskirts of the well, where we could see all that went on at the well without being in the way. We ate our noon meal there. Jacob's well was an interesting place. Much history was told about it. Some of the stories bordered on the ridiculous, while others were more realistic.

A FATEFUL FUTURE

As we sat on the hill, we noticed an old man playing an old Chaldean game of bones wherein he claimed he could tell the future of one paying the price and he tossing the bones. As soon as Ishmael recognized this intent, he turned his head and eyes away even as it is written, but I, who had seen much in Rome, followed the scene. There were some from the trail drawn to the old faker; he would babble some, and then call out to those within earshot.

"Come, hear the future, spend a Gerah, Lepton, or a Kodrantes and see what the bones say." His head bobbed up and down as he repeated this little jingle in Hebrew, Aramaic, Egyptian, and some other languages not known to me. He covered nearly all nationalities in the area. As near as I could tell, he was a Babylonian and the game he was using to tell the future was from antiquity. A small crowd was near; some squatting and some standing. Many were foreigners, that is non-Jews. Among them I saw Apius. He had quietly left us and wandered down the hill. His Greek curiosity caused him to approach the old man calling out his wares. Even from this distance, I could see his eyes dancing with interest. Apius wasn't afraid of these soothsayers, and his religion found no fault in consulting them. He was his own man in these things and although I didn't like to see him waste his time and money so, I held my peace. While I watched, he and the old man haggled over price and product - if a vision of the future could be called a product.

"Here, old man, how much of the future can I gain for a half-shekel?"

"Aye, how can I tell something that is hidden from us until the bones are touched? Place your coins in the shone jar and I will toss the bones." The old faker fondled the bones, they were white and polished with use. Some were longer than others; it was said that each had its own meaning and the place and direction of landing gave the reader foreknowledge. Some said they were the wing and thigh bones of a Phoenix, but closer to the truth would be they were those of a chicken.

"Here you there, Greek! Wouldn't you like to play the game and see into your future? Many of your forefathers have done so. You have the wit to tell if my words are a hoax. Try me!" The old man looked at Apius; how he knew Apius was Greek surprised both of us. After all, Apius wore nothing that would indicate this was his nationality.

The others heard and crowded closer. They sensed Apius was one who would try the game and they wanted to see the results read from the bones. Apius looked at me for permission for he knew we were on our way home and time was short; if I had but motioned that we should leave forthwith he would have left the group and joined us.

Apius took a shekel from his pouch and held it between his thumb and forefinger of his left hand so the old man could see it. He turned his wrist so the Babylonian could see either side. He then let the coin fall into the palm of his right hand.

Closing his fingers over the coin, he said, "See old man, I'm no fool, I would have a game with you first. Prove your skill in predicting the unknown and I will pay your price and see the future."

Apius waited. The old man saw that much hung on his playing the game for now many were drawn to the circle. "Aye, and you would make a beggar of me, but I'll play your game; speak and we will play."

"I'll toss this coin into the air, and while it is so, you tell me what face will show when it's on the ground. If you call it correctly, I'll pay for a look into the future."

"Wait, as I must toss the bones for myself." The man was a sly one. I could see that he understood his audience. If he tossed the bones and guessed right, he was assured of more money than before. If he guessed wrong, he would claim he had merely read the bones wrong. In either case, the chance was worth the taking.

While the crowd grew, he chanted in his strange singsong incantations to some unknown spirit. As he continued this ritual, the crowd grew even more. At the end of his ritual, he shook the bones from a leather bag onto the ground. He was a showman and looked over the audience while he studied the lay of each bone. He suddenly looked up.

"Now, my fair Greek, toss your coin and I'll call what I've seen in the bones."

Apius tossed the coin into the air. It spun from his thumb and flashed as it turned over many times before striking the ground. There was none that could say it was anything but a true matter of chance, that is, declaring the face that would be revealed.

So the old man watched the coin reach its zenith and called out his choice. "Neither face shall reflect the sun this day!" He cried as the coin spun in the sunlight. Those who heard his words laughed for this was a silly answer - all knew it had to be one or the other.

All were quiet when the coin struck a loose stone on the ground and came to rest – on its' edge, leaning against a pebble! No side was reflecting the sun this day! Even Apius and I were taken aback. Did the bones really tell him this? Was this for good or ill? Had the old faker proved his connection with the world beyond?

The crowd murmured for many were given to accepting signs and words from oracles and soothsayers. Some started searching their purses for coins as they were now convinced of the Babylonian's power to read these things. I thought how little he had shown and how quickly these had become believers. I wasn't this sure of Apius; he wasn't one to easily accept such signs. Yet, since he had pledged his payment for a look into the future, he placed the shekel in the old man's pot. The old man smiled and replaced the bones in the bag and turned to Apius.

"Here, you hold the bones for it's from your hand the future is read."

Apius took the bag from the old man and held it gingerly. I became aware of some of my own watching and cast around for something to cover my interest in the show. Ishmael still stood with his back to the proceedings; I remained facing the crowd. I couldn't hear what passed between Apius and the old man when they talked low, but I stood on ground high enough to see it; later, Apius told us the missing parts of this story.

Almost as soon as Apius held the bag, the old man took it from him and shook out the bones. I could see the old man carefully pick up each bone, and tell Apius the future of his life in low tones. Sometimes he moved along in rapid motion, while at other times, he seemed to tell a long story and placed the bones of these carefully into the bag.

Once, I could see him hesitate as if afraid to pick up one of the bones and tell what was revealed to Apius. I saw Apius grow pale at some of his words. At one time, Apius fell to his knees as if struck a severe blow and remained on his knees until the end of the discourse. Finally, the last bone was placed in the bag and the session was over. The old man smiled triumphantly at his audience. Now, many were wide eyed because of what they had heard and were more than ready to spend their money for a look into the future. When Apius left to return to us, many in the crowd clamored to be next.

Apius turned away from us and walked some distance before stopping. He stood a long while looking out over the land with his back to us. Then, I could see him straighten his shoulders, turn and approach us. He had a troubled look about him; his usual look of confidence wasn't present. He walked passed us and gathered the animals and brought them to us. My curiosity was nearly out of control as I could see that some of the old man's sayings laid hard on Apius. I held my peace while we made ready, mounted, and were on our way.

Ishmael spoke, "I hope you two didn't bring God's wrath on us for your entertainment." Ishmael was still the one of sincere feelings for the law and keeping it to the letter - except for the making of images! Even when he practiced his art, he made special trips to the temple and added sacrifices for any possible misdoings. He had been and still was unhappy about our little escapade at Jacob's well.

"Ishmael, couldn't it be that God placed this old man before us to teach us something? Who can say what Apius has learned may not be for his and our good? If you feel otherwise, go to the temple tomorrow and pray that it's not held against you." I thought sometimes things weren't always what they seemed at the moment.

We rode for some time; Apius remained silent about the tales he had heard. My curiosity grew with each second; he remained a discrete distance to the rear.

"Apius, draw up to us, and tell us what the old Babylonian faker found in the bones."

Apius was reluctant to do as I asked. He looked away for sometime but finally came forward. He drew alongside; he was on my right and Ishmael on my left. We rode along in silence for a time, and my curiosity couldn't be contained any longer.

"Apius, what makes you so reticent? We don't believe in such sayings and they are good for conversation. We still have some space to go, and his tale of the future would at least lessen the boredom of this ride." He was still in a very pensive mood; this wasn't like him. Although not a chatterbox, he was usually willing to answer questions put to him.

"Master, I ask you not to demand I tell of his sayings. He was a mad old man, and babbled a good deal about ridiculous happenings he assigned to the future. He saw no more into the future than one holding a mirror. Consider it a thing that never happened." I could see that he wouldn't tell me without my insistence.

"Ishmael, wouldn't you like to hear what the old faker said about the future?" I turned to Ishmael for help; he was none.

"Judas, I agree with Apius, leave things as they are. Don't break the law; consulting with soothsayers, mediums, and witches is forbidden. For it's written, don't practice soothsaying in the law." No, Ishmael would be no help. Any information I got from Apius would be through my persuasion.

"Come Apius, don't hold back because of Ishmael, he can ride on ahead if he doesn't want to hear the story. I would have you tell me the old faker's words." Apius looked at me. He knew when I truly desired him to do a thing, and this was it. I wanted to know what was in the future. I would, like Saul, know of these things!

Ishmael, seeing Apius was about to tell the words of the old man, moved his horse ahead so as to not be a part of this sin, as he saw it. I moved closer to Apius for I would hear him well.

"Master Judas, I want you to know that I don't believe any of his sayings and set little in store by them and wouldn't tell you if I thought it were otherwise. From the time the bones struck the ground until he finished, it was all nonsense. But I am your servant in these things and will tell you his words. The old man's beginning was common enough; I've heard his song in many nations and in many languages. My life was to be long, my health would be good to the end, I would live comfortably and be held in your household.

"Then I asked the faker if the bones showed him anything else, and the old man said that I would live to see strange things come to pass, even to the death of one of my masters, and this just two years hence.

"When I heard this, I fell to my knees from shock. I asked him to read the bones again carefully and tell who it was that was in harms' way. He slowly removed the next bone, but there was no answer. All was at an end. My life was secure, but not for one of my masters. And so it was that he laughed and gathered up the bones, replaced them in the bag, and turned to another customer. This is the tale of the man. Pay it no mind."

I was shocked by this story, even more so at the knowledge of the old faker. What was the meaning of this tale? Ishmael, who had been looking back at us now and again, must have seen a change in me for he reined his horse. He waited for us to draw alongside.

"Judas, what is wrong? Your face shows nearly white under your tan. Now, haven't I told you not to listen to these stories? It's against the will of God. Oh, Judas, I fear for you!" He was sincere in his concern and could feel my discomfort.

I couldn't tell him of this news that one of us would die before long. He wouldn't listen to such prophecies anyway. "Ah, Ishmael, it's nothing but a silly story by an old Babylonian that knows nothing but lies. You know how these men are."

Ishmael didnt press me to tell what Apius had said, instead, turned his horse again toward Jerusalem. We all followed suit. I was now anxious to be home.

We weren't far from home when a rider came toward us with a loud shout. It was Atonis! It was unusual to see him so far from home. His horse was lathered and he was flushed from his ride.

"Masters, I come bearing bad news. Your mother is gravely ill. Apuleius is even now with her. Her body is racked with a strange fever. You must hurry home with me!" He barely took time to draw his breath, reined his horse about and started back along the road with Ishmael, Apius, and I in hot pursuit. Gone was the thought of the tale of the old faker, and the wonderment over my recovery. Only the sinking feeling that one I loved was in harms' way remained. Ishmael and I repeated prayers taught to us by our mother for God's blessing and aid for her. We rode hard with little thought of the horses. Atonis's horse began to falter and he reined him in to give him a blow, while the rest of us passed him on our way home. He would catch up when his mount was rested.

We rode through the north gate and on through the streets of Jerusalem with some abandon. People, animals, and fowl were scattered to the winds as we passed through the narrow streets of the city. Apius was first to pass through the gate. He quickly dismounted and took control of the animals. We ran through the courtyard and into the house. Our clothes were dusty and stained with sweat. As we passed through the hallway, Apuleius stepped out of an anteroom.

"Here, here, this will never do." He stepped before us blocking the way to mother's room. "Don't approach your mother thus. She is resting this moment and I wouldn't have you disturb her. Go wash away the road and prepare to meet her as she would wish."

"But Apuleius, we are fearful for her. Is she very ill?" Ishmael asked.

"Come, I'll tell you what I know while you refresh yourselves. While she sleeps, her body is repairing itself. I've given her a potion to give her rest from the fever." His voice bespoke of his authority, and we turned toward our rooms where we washed and changed clothes. The house was strangely quiet; the servants moved about with caution and brought wine and fruit for us.

"We have done as you asked, Apuleius. Now, tell us of this thing that is upon mother. You speak of a fever?"

"Judas, it's nearly the same as that I found in Capernaum. It's even similar in symptoms to that Ishmael had in Rome." Apuleius spoke in measured tones. It was as though he didn't want us to know of his deep concern. While he talked, he played with a small medical insignia that hung from a gold chain about his neck. I had always been fascinated by it; it was a gift from the School of Medicine in Rome. The form looked like a brass serpent on a pole, much like the one Moses raised in the wilderness in days of yore. It seemed a strange coincidence, this Roman symbol of medicine, and the healer of Israel.

"You are sure that she will recover?"

"As to this I can't say. It's different as she is older than any other I have treated for this malady. I can't deny you this, I'll do all I can, and if she is strong enough, all should go well. We must have faith in these things."

"Faith in what, dear Apuleius?" Ishmael asked. He had heard us argue about the existence of gods and their influence on the health of man.

"A good question, Ishmael. I presume that your faith will be in your God and his benevolence," he smiled, "while I will hold to the treatment."

"When can we see her?"

"Soon. The medicine will give her rest, and after that, there will be time enough. And now show me your hand."

In our excitement, we forgot the reason for our being gone. I gave him my right hand, and at the same time gripped his hand showing that strength had returned to it. He was very impressed. He knew that I had no strength in it when he treated it last.

"Come now. Tell me the story about the recovery." Before I could respond, Ishmael had plunged into the entire tale from beginning to end. Apuleius was returning my grip all the time the story was told.

"It's a wonderful happening! I must say, I respect this Yeshua. I know how useless your hand was just some time before. Someday, I'll go to see him do these things. I would like to learn his secrets and have the power to heal."

"Someday soon, you and I may see more than this," I remarked, as the thought struck me and to this day, I couldn't tell either of them why I said it. We separated and I retired to my room to say prayers of petition to the Lord, at the same time wondering why these things were happening in my household. First my hand, and now mother. Could there be something in the warning given to me by Shalazar? Was I only or was those near and dear to me to suffer because I resisted his will to follow Yeshua? If this be so, then what choice did I have but to join his little band?

All these and other things I turned over in my mind while looking out of my window. I could see the courtyard below. As I watched, somewhat disinterested in the happenings there, I saw Apuleius come from the house and join Apius there. I couldn't hear their conversation, but I could see what was said made a great impression on Apius. He glanced many times at the house, and after some time shook his head as if in disbelief. Finally, Apius took his leave from Apuleius, and Apuleius stood looking into the sky. He then came back into the house. I was curious about their conversation but was unable to ask about it for fear they would think I had been spying.

At evening time, Apuleius went to mother's chamber. When he emerged, he was frowning; he wasn't happy with what he found. Her condition wasn't improving.

"Judas and Ishmael, hear me. Your mother isn't responding as I would like. She is still under the fever. I'll prepare additional potions while you both go in to her as she wants to see you. Mind you, give her no reason to be discouraged. Do you understand?" He gave us a piercing look. "Remember, happiness cured more ills than tears."

We went in to mother. She looked so weak and worn. She lay just as father had some years ago. Our mother, who had seemed so indestructible, was now the small form in her bed. Her maidservant sat on a mat near her side. She had refused to leave mother's side. It was she who mother had saved from a slave auction some years before.

"Mother, we are here," Ishmael was first to speak.

She opened her eyes and slowly raised her hand from the bed.

"Ah, my sons, and where is my daughter?"

"She is on her way, this we know for we have sent for her. Mother, dear mother, are you quite comfortable?" I asked.

"Yes, Judas, and how is your hand? Did you see Yeshua?"

It was good to know she had interest in our trip. This meant she wasn't overcome by her own incapacity. I was much relieved. I smiled and held up my right hand and moved my fingers. I reached down and took her hand in mine and squeezed gently but firmly to let her know the strength had returned.

"It was a wonderful thing that happened to us when we stood before Yeshua in the house of assembly. Would you like to hear of it?" She was patient with Ishmael as he told the story of our trip and of the healing of my hand, of the excitement it caused in the Bet ha-knesset, and of the believers and nonbelievers who came away. Mother listened with the light of fever in her eyes, and when he was finished, she looked at me for some time.

"Surely it's a sign that you have been forgiven of some grave sin. May the Lord God of Israel accept this humble prayer of thanks for my son, Judas. But I am tired now, and would rest." She turned away and closed her eyes.

Ishmael and I quietly left her chambers. When we arrived in the hallway, we met our sister, Anath, who was in great distress. Her love for mother was as great as ours and the thought of mother being ill caused her extreme grief. She wanted to go to mother but we restrained her.

"Dear Anath, mother is now tired and asked to rest. Come, speak with us and wait awhile yet." I blocked her way into the chamber.

"Judas, I'm nearly undone. Mother is near to my heart. Is she faring well?"

"Yes, Apuleius, whom you know, is attending her. If anything can be done, he will do it. Come into the garden for we have something to tell you."

We went to the garden where Apuleius met us. We sat near the fish pond.

"First, I must tell you of our trip and visit with Yeshua."

When we were all comfortable, I told the story of our search and visit. The curing of my hand was told by Ishmael, which now had become his story. Anath was moved by the story and sang a song of thanks to God. We talked of many things, including our firsthand knowledge of Yeshua and his boyhood. Anath remembered things about him that we, as boys, didn't. The shadows lengthened as we sat in the garden.

One of the maidservants came for Apuleius. It seems that mother was again restless and not responding as one throwing off the fever. Apuleius left us without a word and went to mother's aid. We sat and waited.

Although Apuleius was frequently by her side and applied the latest potions of the day, mother failed to respond. As the days slipped by, it became apparent that medical knowledge and pharmacology wasn't sufficient to restore mother to reasonably good health. As was the practice of our people, prayers were sent to Almighty God on mother's behalf, prayers asking for her to be spared this illness, but her condition remained firm. Each time in the temple prayers were said, the thoughts of Shalazar's visit came back as a dream.

In my heart, the words of Shalazar would come forward during times of prayer, "Hear me, my time is nearly gone. You will suffer hardships known only to me and God until you become a follower of Yeshua." Was the loss of the use of my right arm and mother's illness his doing or just a coincidence? Would he harm others because of me?

During these times, the ancient history of Job came to mind. Wasn't Job beset with problems not of his own cause? And weren't others ravaged because of him? His sons, their wives, and all they possessed - wasn't it destroyed? The more I read the old books, the greater became my fears of the stranger and his power.

While these things were accomplished, I continued my usual business day. My trusty servants had given more than they had received during my illness, and the thought struck me that should I ever leave this business, I would turn it over to the faithful, but at that time, I had no such intentions.

Mother's condition deteriorated, and try as I might to prevent it, so did my faith in the healing of modern medicine. After one last visit with her, I began to prepare for a trip to Capernaum. I would again seek Yeshua!

I decided to make this trip alone. Ishmael, who normally wanted to travel with me, was less inclined to do so this time. His thoughts were occupied with mother and her illness; he would remain at her side. I agreed with Ishmael that his presence was needed here and not on the road, for who knew how long it would be before I located Yeshua?

Apius prepared a good animal for me and I gave orders to my trusted servants to watch the business while I was away. I reminded them I would have an accounting from them upon my return. I left within the hour to find Yeshua and ask him to make her well as he had my hand and Cornelius's servant.

As I crossed the city, I came across a group of young men holding street meetings. As I rode closer, I recognized the one speaking as Saul, the son of Bel Ard from Tarsus. He was giving a ringing speech. I wondered if Gamaliel would approve.

"Remove them, I say, remove them as it was told the ancients to remove those who would pollute the teachings of God. Don't protect those among you who would lead the young away from the law." His eyes shown brightly; his face was flushed with the excitement of the moment. I reined the horse for a moment to hear his words. He flung his arms wide as he spoke of people who would cause dissension among these people. "Who commissioned Yeshua to speak of the kingdom of God? Who was his teacher? I'll tell you who, no one! He is the son of a carpenter of Nazareth. Beware of his teaching; his followers would have you believe he is the Messiah!"

Some of the poor cried out against the young stranger in their midst. Strangely, I was moved to challenge Paul about his words against Yeshua, but this quickly faded when I caught sight of the Roman guard coming down the street. I moved my horse away for I wanted no delay in my mission to find Yeshua. I traveled through the city and out onto the road to Capernaum. Once on the road, I made good time. I moved the horse along at a good pace, and paused only for water and rest. The picture of mother resting so quietly in her bed kept returning to mind during the ride.

JOHN, THE SON OF ZEBEDEE

I arrived in Capernaum late in the afternoon. I secured a room in the same inn I had been in before. Tomorrow I would seek some news about Yeshua and his little band. With the favor of God, Yeshua might still be in the city.

I gave my horse to the innkeeper for care, and went to my room to prepare for prayers and the evening meal. After washing some of the dust from my body and resting for a few moments, I went to the rough eating area. There were many men there from the road, each had his own story to tell. Among them were the regulars of the city, most of them representing some merchant interested in the purchase of goods from foreign markets. Some of those stopping by were representatives of just such trades. This I could tell from my experience in the accounting trade and from the time I served my uncle in Rome.

As I ate, I listened to as many conversations as I could while being discreet. Impropriety could cost your life in this port city. I listened to the course of talk to hear something about Yeshua. It might be that some of the conversation would turn to him and his action in this city, and if so, I wanted to hear all.

Some time after the lamps were lit, three travelers came in the inn. They spoke to the innkeeper and then went to the center of the area. They were neither tradesmen nor salesmen by their dress. They had the look of seamen or fishermen. For some reason, their presence commanded quietness in the inn; the guests seemed to sense a need to hear what they would say. One of the three quickly recognized the attitude of the crowd and spoke out.

"Brothers, we bear news of one called Yeshua. We witness things he has done and said even to this hour." He spoke as those who lived in Galilee. Some present couldn't understand his speech, and even I had to listen closely to comprehend his thought.

"Of these things, we would have you know; people follow him wherever he goes in hopes he will cure them. People from Galilee, Decapolis, Jerusalem, Judea, and even from beyond the Jordan press against him to hear his words and feel his healing power. To many, his words are the awakening of the Spirit of Israel. He isn't afraid to speak of all things, things that the priests and lawyers still argue about. He speaks of the things a good man must do that are acceptable to God. He reminds us to respect the law, to love one another, to forgive one's brother before entering the temple with a gift, has taught us a new prayer, has brought many healings to pass, and even cast out demons."

These things and more the three men told as they stood before the patrons of the inn. Even when the hour became late I couldn't leave these storytellers. One told about a man whose withered right hand had been made well by the word of Yeshua. I drew in my breath as I recognized the storyteller was speaking of me.

"Hear me, oh teller of good news, where can we find this Yeshua?" I couldn't resist the urge to know where I could find him. I could feel the glances of many of those in the inn after I spoke.

"Ah, and who is it that asks of Yeshua?" The speaker looked at me through the dim lamp light. He left the others and came to me. "Haven't I seen you before among the others?" I could see he was studying me as one searching for the connection between his memory of a face and time.

"I'm Judas bar Simon from Jerusalem. My father's house was in Kerioth. I've never been one of the others." This was the truth, but I had received the blessing of Yeshua when my arm was restored some weeks before. "Even now, I search for Yeshua to ask for his blessing for my mother who lies near death in Jerusalem. And hear me, my time is short, as she has been ill of the fever for some days now and I fear for her life. Can you tell me where he is or where he will be within this week?"

"Aye, I'm heartily sorry to hear of your needs. If you can bring your cause before him, I'm sure he will see it is just and help you." He came even nearer; he continued to look at me as though he didn't know whether to believe me or not. "Your face is like one I've seen before in Cana, and yes, even in Capernaum, but your name isn't one I remember. Ah, time plays such tricks on the memory. My name is John bar Zebedee, and I'm one of Yeshua's followers. I will do better than tell where he is or will be. I'll take you to him! We will leave at daybreak. Now, I must return to the others and tell them the story of our teacher. Come, you must hear, also."

When he came closer, I recognized him as one of the close followers of Yeshua - even a disciple. The recognition came from the many sketches drawn by Ishmael. It was then I realized why he thought he knew me from some time before. It was that he saw Ishmael in me as many had before. I was about to tell him when he turned and made his way back to his fellow travelers. I remained in the background and listened to the wonderful stories they told. Some in the crowd accepted them with great interest while others showed no interest at all. Several called out to the innkeeper that these men were interrupting their good rest time, and wanted them removed. Others, tired from their long days on the road, were glad to hear any story to break the hours of the day. When they were finished, they left and I went directly to my room. I didn't meet the others. I knew only the one called John.

Sleep didn't come easily. Thoughts returned to the first nights in the inn with Ishmael, Apius, and Apuleius, and the strange story he told of the healing of Cornelius's servant. After evening prayers and request of blessings on mother, I finally fell asleep.

My sleep was troubled throughout the night. I was visited by Shalazar in a dream. The dream was so real I couldn't forget it when I awoke. Shalazar reminded me that my obligation unto him was threefold. As his image faded, I could see mother on the couch. I saw Ishmael, Anath, and Apuleius standing nearby in quiet sadness. I made attempts to call out to them but they didn't hear me. I was then awakened by the crowing of the cock; daylight was upon me.

John and his two companions were waiting for me in the courtyard of the inn. They traveled light. John suggested that I leave my horse stabled at the inn for Yeshua and the rest of his followers were closeby. I gave the innkeeper enough coins to care for my horse until I returned. Should it not be sufficient, I would pay him the difference when I returned.

With this done and some food secured for the trip, I left with John and his friends before sunup. John introduced his comrades to me as Kish, a Benjamite, or so it was said, and one Judah from the house of Judah. They were new converts to the teachings of Yeshua and freely talked of their change of heart. They both were considerably younger than John and I.

"Tell me, Judas, why is it that you look so familiar to me?" John finally expressed his puzzlement about me.

"Ah, the story is simple but a long one. It's simple in that I have a twin brother Ishmael. It's he who you've seen before. It's he you remember from Cana and even the house of Simon's mother-in-law. He was among you during the wedding feast in Cana and the family meeting in Capernaum. It's common for people to mistake us for one another. Don't feel badly over it." The last I added, not knowing if he would or not.

"Ah, that is the answer. I was sure I had met you before but something wasn't quite the same. Perhaps the cut of your beard or some mannerism is not the same. Where is your brother? How is it then, that you knew who I was, or so I thought from our first meeting?"

We walked close together because of the crowds moving toward the water.

"He is at our mother's side for she is very ill. The answer to the second question lies in his hand, John. The Lord has given him a glorious gift. He is a craftsman in art and had made detailed sketches of many he has met in his travels. Oh, yes, I've seen detailed sketches of Simon, James, and even Yeshua. Yes, I would know you anywhere."

"You know it is to the house of Simon's mother-in-law we go this morning. Yeshua is residing there until he decides to move elsewhere. Many of us were commissioned to go abroad and declare his teachings among the people. This was our commission at the inn last night. It's the reason we stopped there; to bring the news of the coming of the Kingdom of God. Have you heard this teaching?"

His question brought back memories of the subject in some of Ishmael's letters to me in Rome, including the story of the meeting of Nicodemus that night in the summer when Yeshua was in Jerusalem.

I recalled the strange words said by Yeshua, "Except a man be born again he cannot enter the Kingdom of God." I was about to ask him of these things when he motioned that we were near the house we sought, and because of this should be respectful in all manners. The house was just as Ishmael had drawn it in all respects. There were many poor souls lying on the ground near the wall that surrounded the entrance to the little cottage. They suffered from all sorts of human ailments; the blind, crippled, mentally infirmed, yes, even some lepers stood a few paces away from the others and used their pans and spoons to warn the others they were unclean. It was as Ishmael had told me when he was here months ago. These were all here seeking cures of ills through the power of Yeshua. They had no other recourse. Even as I had none. I was no better than they. I was a beggar; mother's illness had brought me to realize that all the wealth in the world couldn't make her well. When the love for another is great, wealth and pride cannot stand in the way of action.

We tread through and about those lying near the gate. Their cries for help were ever present on the ear. The gate was guarded against intruders. Simon held the gate.

"Ah John, I see you have returned from your mission. Come in, and your companions with you." John and the others passed through the gate. As I approached, a large muscular arm was thrown across the gate preventing me from entering. "What do we have here? And who might you be?"

My heart told me this was a man of purpose. He was one who decided what the world held for him and he meant to have it. At that moment, he didn't intend for me to interfere with his gaining what he thought was rightfully his. He faced me with fearless determination. He was, indeed, exactly as Ishmael had drawn him. My mind flashed quickly to the letters Ishmael wrote - so this was Simon, the fisherman's son!

"Now, Simon," said John, coming back toward us, "he is Judas bar Simon. Would I bring one of the temple spies with me? It's time you had some faith in the rest of us!"

"Ah, but John, sometimes I fear your good-heartedness. You see only good in all. I tell you I've seen some of the most innocent-looking men in the elite temple guard. Where did you come across this fellow?" Simon didn't remove his arm and continued to block the way into the little courtyard.

"We met during my telling the good news at an inn near the sea. He came from Jerusalem in search of Yeshua. Come, his mother is very ill and he would bring his cause to the master. Don't be so overbearing. Besides, I will stand for him." He placed his hand on the forearm of Simon and slowly lifted it from across the gate. Simon accepted his words rather reluctantly, or so it seemed to me. I stepped into the small yard by the house.

CHAPTER SIXTEEN

"I'll present you to Yeshua." John turned and we entered the house. It was much cooler inside. The room was very clean and the noon meal was being prepared.

Yeshua, whom I hadn't seen since the healing of my arm some weeks ago, reclined on a bench near the far wall of the cottage; there were people listening at his feet. Much later, I found it was a common practice for some to come and hear him address different topics of the law. A few came from distant lands, this I knew by their faces and dress as well as their mannerisms. Some were well-to-do and had servants with them.

I stood with John near the doorway. John waited while Yeshua told a story to the listeners. Some murmured about things happening throughout the countryside and of the evil which seemed to be in control everywhere.

"Declare unto us the story of the tares of the fields," said one near the door.

Yeshua shook his head in agreement. He told the story this way: "He that sows the good seed is here among you, and the field in which he works is the world. That isn't the world of things, but the world of hearts. The good seed can be likened unto the children of a great kingdom; when filled with goodness, they are the delight of the sower. In this world, there is one that sows seed of tares; the tares can be likened unto children of another kingdom. When filled with evil, they are a delight unto him, and from this seed comes evil. And the tares are the children of the worldly sower, and not that which is just. The worldly sower and his children with him are enemies of God. Even as there is a day of harvest in nature, so it will be in this story. And as a result of the harvest, the tares shall be gathered and thrown into the fire that they may not be confused with the wheat. So it will be in the kingdom of the good at heart. The children of the worldly sower will be excluded from seeing the face of the good sower, and so it will be in the end of this world. The good sower shall send forth his workers, and they shall gather out of his great kingdom all those who offend, and them which do wrong. They shall be cast into a furnace of fire; there shall be wailing and gnashing of teeth. Then shall the good children shine forth as sons in the kingdom of their Father. Who hath ears to hear, let him hear."

I leaned against John and motioned for his ear.

"What does this all mean? Who are the good seed and who are the tares? What does this have to do with the needs of the people under the heel of the Romans?" John took little note of my whisperings; his attention was on the face of Yeshua. All at the feet of Yeshua were happy with the story, and asked no more questions about its meaning. This wasn't true in my case, as I didn't understand it at all, but felt that some day I would.

Yeshua made a motion with his hand that the story was finished. The students and his followers left the cottage, leaving only John and I.

John went before me, knelt at the feet of Yeshua and said, "Greetings, Master," showing complete subservience to Yeshua. It was a different posture than normally taken by a student and teacher; instead, it was like one shown to a king or Caesar! He didn't bow and show the traditional respect, but remained on his knees. I thought this a strange attitude for him to take and expected Yeshua to reject this approach of reverence - but not so!

John finally rose after a word from Yeshua, and kissed his master on the cheek. Yeshua accepted this form of adulation with no show of embarrassment. Hillel wouldn't have accepted such a greeting! During this time, neither gave notice to my standing there.

"John, have you brought the good news to many this time?"

"Aye, master, I took young Kish and Judah with me. We spoke to many of the teaching you have given to us. Many would hear more and are coming to hear you."

Suddenly, John became aware of me again and added, "When we stopped at an inn to rest and teach, I met this man, Judas of Kerioth. His family is now of Jerusalem."

Yeshua slowly turned his head to look at me, he smiled, and from this I knew he recognized me.

"Judas, at last you have come. I've been expecting you. Your needs are even now known to me. Come, and give me greetings." He stood up and raised his arms indicating a brotherly embrace was wanted; I heard John take a quick breath, but I stepped forward. I greeted him as one might a long-lost relative. We embraced as was the custom. During the embrace, I had the feeling that John felt something was different between me and Yeshua than he and his master; and this not to his liking.

For some strange reason, my heart leaped as I came closer to Yeshua. I realized that here was a man of great spiritual power. It was different when we first met - the day my right arm was made whole. The entire scene was different.

Yeshua turned to John and said, "John, I would be alone with Judas." Even in the dim light of the house interior I could see John's face reflect a change, like one who had been rebuked. He looked at me a long time and then gave a deep bow to Yeshua and left us alone. From that time on, I felt uneasy among the others. It was as though I broke the perfect circle. I was a tare among the wheat!

"Yeshua, you know me and of my kin?" I could hardly believe that this was true, after all, he gave no such indication when Ishmael and I stood before him in the house of assembly some weeks ago. I didn't wait for his answer but plunged into the story of mother's condition.

"It's on behalf of my mother that I come, Yeshua. She helped watch over you when you visited the home of Zechariah - the many times you and your family came to Jerusalem to celebrate Pesach. Oh, it's of great urgency that I come. Mother is very ill, and now lies near death. I have come to ask your help."

"Ah Judas, I remember well the many trips we made to Jerusalem, and our yearly stays at Zechariah's. And your mother remains as dear to me as my own. Do you believe I can make your mother well? Think of what you ask, Judas, for it's with you that the success of many things depend."

"It's belief that has brought me in search of you. I have heard of the deeds done through your will, and yes, I've even experienced one personally. No, it isn't my belief that is of concern, but of your willingness to accept my pleas. I pray you, Yeshua, don't hold my unbelief against my mother and make her well on her goodness even as you have others." I stood looking down at him for I was taller by at least a half a cubit.

Even though he was very slim, he wasn't a weakling, nor was he the most handsome Jew I had seen. It was his eyes that held the key to his personality and character; they were the windows to the soul of every man, or so some ancient phrases said.

"So you have pleaded and so it is done; even this very hour your mother is well again." Here he hesitated while he studied me with care. "And now comes the mark of faith, Judas. Will you leave me again to see if your mother is really well, or will you follow me as your heart even now tells you to do?"

As I listened to his words, the desire to see mother well once more faded, yet the love I felt for her wasn't easily put aside. Then there was my business in Jerusalem that couldn't stand long without supervision. His voice came through my reverie; as Yeshua told of his calling, I could feel a magnetic quality that drew me closer to him and his cause - to bring the lost of Israel back to the kingdom of God here on earth - that's what I longed for! It had the ring of adventure and profit to it. Here was my forte, here I could contribute!

"Do you hear me, Judas?"

"Aye, it isn't that I don't believe that mother is even now well, but that I would like to tell her of her benefactor. Indeed, I would have Ishmael and the rest of my father's household know of this thing and how it came to pass. Shouldn't they have the same right to hear the good news as the strangers spoken to by John?"

"'Tis well said, Judas. Therefore, return to your home even on the morrow, but don't tarry there as much is to be done." We moved toward the doorway as we talked, much as old friends, no subservience here. I could see some of his followers lounging near the door. Their eyes followed their master's every move. Simon was pacing to and fro among the others; he stole glances at me often, and I felt a partial dislike for me. I walked too boldly with his master. Later I found he was a man of quick conviction and once decided on a like or dislike, he seldom changed it. Yeshua and I talked for a considerable time about earlier days and family history.

The followers couldn't understand my failure to show homage to Yeshua that most of them did. We stood as equals reminiscing; he telling me of all the recent travels and the feelings of the people upon hearing his teaching of the coming of the kingdom of God here on earth. While listening, I became more and more enamored with him and his desire for the kingdom to be restored. This teacher I had known as a lad was to be misunderstood by many I ventured. In him, I recognized all the elements of John the washer and more. He had an aura of the Spirit of God about him known only to the ancient prophets. As he spoke of the things he had done through the word of God, I thought of the stories of healings - even my own. Perhaps, in this man rested the salvation of Israel after all!

After awhile, I left Yeshua and his followers and returned to the inn. I gave the food I brought from the inn that morning to some of the beggars along the road. I secured my horse and was on my way home. I sang praises to God for his revelation and mother's recuperation. At last, a leader has been brought up by the Lord to bring His nation together and lift the heel of the Romans from their necks.

As I rode along, the idea of me joining Yeshua and his little band became more and more appealing. Me, the one who wasn't in favor of any such strong emotional trends. Me, the one who always weighed the gains and losses of such things. Ah, what was happening? What had this teacher done to me?

The time traveling home passed without incident and had the elements of a dream. I didn't eat a noon meal as I left before it was prepared at the household of Simon's mother-in-law. The feeling of hunger soon overcame the euphoric feeling of the moment.

I reined my animal near a small village well and, after watering him, I looked for an inn. Not far from the well was an inn. I found a goodly crowd, indicating either good food or the only inn for miles. I chose to believe the former. After some words with the innkeeper, I paid the price and received some date wine, smoked fish, and a flat cake of barley - not a king's banquet, but good food. My hunger made whatever was lacking in flavor and texture seem unimportant, and I ate all before me with relish.

My meal was interrupted by a noisy lot in the rear of the inn where a rather motley group was shouting at one another. Their apparent distress and the want to escape if necessary should they be discovered, caused me to listen to their noisy conversation. It seemed one of their number, a person named Joshua, who some in the group called Barabbas, was arrested on the order of the Procurator Pilate. From their excitement, I gathered that Barabbas, which I understood meant son of the father in Aramaic, was a prominent figure in the circle of the Sicarii.

This militant group had the backing of many of the Zealots, and no less amount of good will and money from some of the elite of our people. The great concern was not only for his life, but for the lives of many of those who belonged to the secret order supporting the guerrilla attacks on the Roman outposts there in Judea. Should he be tortured, as many in the group believed he would, and he revealed the names of his compatriots, then nearly all was lost. The Romans would, without a doubt, round up many of those attempting to force Rome to give more autonomy to our people, and under Pilate, crucifixions would undoubtedly be the result. All present at the inn were of one voice in this. Something must be done - but what?

At that moment, one of the men stationed at the door who had remained unnoticed by me until that very time, gave an imitation of a Roman military salute. This motion had a profound affect on those arguing at the far end of the room. They became more relaxed, more casual in demeanor, and the language which a moment before had involved the arrest of a leader, suddenly revolved around the days' markets of goats and sheep.

I looked about but saw no one I could identify as a Roman soldier or civilian elite. Nor did the group reestablish their conversation about the apparent tragedy in the loss of a valuable man called Barabbas. Instead, each man left the meeting place at different times and in different directions. The incident came and went as a dream, yet, I was to recall this meeting of men greatly concerned with a man named Joshua but called Barabbas.

I finished my meal, took care of the horse, and was on my way, this time with no intention of stopping until I was home in the courtyard. The rest of the trip went well and I arrived late that evening, arousing the entire household. Food and clean linens were brought immediately for the returning son. I was more interested in the story of mother's splendid recovery than of anything else. While I washed away the dirt and dust of the road, Ishmael excitedly told of the happenings while I was away. But it was the sight of mother that caused my heart to tremble. Had this young teacher done a miraculous thing, or had the potions Apuleius gave finally produced the cure?

She was truly made whole - not just well as recovering from a fever - but once again in full vigor. To see her was to doubt that she had ever been ill. Her entire being radiated new-found health. She was as alive and vivacious as ever and even more so. She walked with a light step, head high, and even though it was late, there was a great light in her eyes.

"Mother, you are well again, God has surely answered our prayers! We must be away to the temple and present our thanksgiving gift to Him."

"Did you see him?" Her first thoughts were of my encounter with Yeshua.

"Yes, even this day before noon I met and presented my plea. And how long have you been free from the illness?" I was interested in the time of her recovery.

"Ah, it left me like the shedding of one's old cloak, Judas. One moment, I was near death - or so they tell me - and the next, I was unable to stay in bed. The feeling of fire went through me and all strength that was gone for so long was mine again. I've found favor in the eyes of the Lord through Yeshua!" She left my embrace and danced around the room. "I must show myself to all my friends and tell them of this blessing granted by Yeshua."

Ishmael and Anath were rejoicing. Mother was given back to us at a time when we thought she was lost. It was then I became aware of an inner longing to see Yeshua again.

THE STRUGGLE

I left the happy group and went to my room to study these strange longings so newly born. It was there I began to argue, reason, and resist this longing to return to Capernaum yet that night. I brought before me all the advantages of staying in Jerusalem: the business and wealth from it, my friends and business associates, closeness to Apuleius, and my dear family. All these were mighty arguments against leaving and traveling to places Yeshua might lead. For well inside me, I couldn't deny the feeling of a modicum of truth that Yeshua was more than just an itinerant teacher with religious and philosophical precepts differing from those of the Sadducees and Pharisees. He was one with the power of God upon him and had shown this to me in two personal events.

While I struggled with this desire to stay in Jerusalem, the words of Shalazar crossed my mind, and the greeting of Yeshua. Shalazar demanding that I join the followers to pay debts and Yeshua expected me as well.

I thought of the many great things that might come about if Yeshua was indeed the Messiah and led our people into freedom and autonomy. It was easy to see that if this were true, then those closest to him would, of necessity, benefit from his rise to power. Power the ancient writers claimed beyond that of mortal man. Power of God himself to obliterate the forces against his people. In the hands of this Messiah, our people would again be a power for the rest of the world to reckon with in all forms of human endeavor.

And who would be those so blessed? Those who were declared his disciples - his followers! What did it matter about the accounting business in Jerusalem? What did it matter who were friends now? Even family might be a liability over the years; wasn't this the same as told by Yeshua to one of his followers when questioned about his dead father, "Follow me, and let the dead bury the dead?"

Wasn't it also as Ishmael had written, that when asked of his family, Yeshua said, "Who is my mother and my brethren? Hear me, whosoever shall do the will of God, the same is my brother, and my sister, and mother!"

My spirit was awakened to the desire to be gone and join Yeshua as soon as possible. There was no way I could balance the scales, for each part of my old life which I placed on the scale, the thoughts of my new life and its attractive long-term returns tipped the scale in favor of joining Yeshua. For God and Israel - I must go!

I didn't rest even though none of the family came to disturb me. They thought of my long trip and left me be. The rest of the evening I spent in study of some old writings, a thing that Hillel said would come to me even as it had other men. I made a diligent search for all the prophecies in the time I had left. During the search, all fell into place; I would go unto Capernaum and declare my fealty unto Yeshua.

And so it was, that after prayers and the evening meal and while the family still expressed thanks to the Lord and me for mother's recovery, I told them of my decision to join Yeshua. All were greatly surprised by my announcement, each for different reasons and to different degrees.

"Judas, what has brought this upon us? Have we just gotten you back from Rome to lose you again?" Ishmael was greatly grieved by this news.

"What are we to do while you follow Yeshua and what is to become of your business?" Anath was the practical one here.

But it was mother who surprised even me in this matter when she said, "Children, what has this to do with us? Can we make greater demands on Judas than the Lord? Haven't we seen the wonders and received blessings from Yeshua even this day? No, it's not for us to claim such rights. Judas, tell us of your coming to this decision."

With her encouragement and understanding manner, I reviewed many ancient writings pointing to the coming of the Messiah. I reminded them of the strange and mysterious happenings with respect to Yeshua that were well known to us; things known only to his own family and us. And for the first time, told of the many strange visits from Shalazar that both Ishmael and I saw during our early days. Mother and Anath were in great wonderment at these things.

"Dear ones, my heart tells me it's time for me to join Yeshua and all reasoning otherwise will avail nothing. I will divest myself of the business and prepare for my coming work alongside the other disciples. I can't do otherwise."

I didn't tell them of my thoughts about the meanings of the possible success of this venture. I withheld my deep feelings that someday I would be selected above all others to receive the highest award when Yeshua was recognized as the Messiah and was in power under the Lord. Oh, my heart sang with the thoughts of such a miracle, oh, that I should see that day - and soon!

"I shall go with you, Judas."

"No Ishmael, it's for you to stay here and honor our mother. There is time enough for you to join us later. Let it be as I've said." Ishmael was unhappy to hear me speak thus but held his peace. Anath spoke no word, but her eyes were soft as one looking at a dear one being taken from her.

"When will you leave?" Mother would have a family gathering to honor my decision. I recognized her intent and wished it not be so.

"Soon, as I would leave all, even this very night. Yet I have responsibilities to those who have served me well. To those I must give that which is due before I go." I had always thought I would give a share of my business to my faithful servants, and so it was to be, although earlier than I'd planned.

That evening, the family was both happy and sad. We all rejoiced in mother's recovery and they held a restrained peace about my leaving the house of my father.

And so it was that I disposed of my property in accordance with the law, giving to each of my faithful servants his rightful share and more. From them I received much blessing for they were Godly men of good report. That which I sold I converted into gold and gave to God a full tithe. I also gave enough to Apius and Atonis to care for them through their old age. The rest I left with Ishmael should I need it to relieve the needs of myself and others as I might direct. Ishmael was to remain home with mother and run the household for her until I should return. This I hoped would be after Yeshua had been declared the Messiah and seated on his throne. For so it was written by the ancients, "The Spirit of the Lord God is upon me; because the Lord hath anointed me to preach good tidings unto the meek; he hath sent me to bind up the brokenhearted, to proclaim liberty to the captives, and the opening of prison to them who are bound." It will happen, it must happen, and I shall be the one who causes it to happen!

That night I prayed for understanding and wisdom even as Solomon had so many ages ago.

ENHANCEMENT NEEDED

Suddenly, the speech processor output became garbled, and the screen lost all intelligibility; only gibberish remained. Then, the speech processor shut down completely. The system automatically switched to search mode, and went offline while it tried to recapture the lost characters and sync words. Each control panel indicated loss of contact with the memory bank of the International Science Museum. The system at Bradenton simply didn't hold lock. It was now a matter of waiting while the two systems searched through the maze of data and lock-on was achieved.

"From this console, it looks like the system has found a faulty or damaged portion in the Golden Scroll." John continued to try different system commands. These were often used to recapture lost threads of sense in routine documents, but this wasn't an ordinary document. The readouts continued to indicate a loss of date line or chronology in the scroll. The same information was reflected on the other consoles.

Without turning from his position, John said, "Jean, did you finish your enhancement program?"

"Yes." Jean held up the program disk.

"Good, the feedback I get indicates the system has intelligence and is ready to interpret, but cannot find the proper historical reference in the autobiography. So, what can we expect from your modification?"

"Well, as written and in place, the system should jump search over the time related events and present the story line irrespective of proper historical significance." She moved to the console and placed the enhancement program on the read/write unit. She booted up the system. "I'll dump it into the system; it's protected and none of the original program should be damaged."

The system came up and joined the ISM computer in Washington. Even with the modification in place, the system was struggling; there was more than one set of events that could be assigned to the same date. The query lamp came on, signifying a need of choice from the operator.

"As soon as the system recognizes a complete story line, give it the start command, John, and it should supply us a complete printout. It will then be up to us to decide by perusal of the text just where in history the story line belongs."

The laboratory light dimmed and the screen flashed with symbols but not intelligence. The search delay light came on as the system continued to look for a complete story line.

"Well, it looks like it will be another day before we see anymore of the hidden mysteries of the scroll."

And the evening and the morning were the fifth day.

The system continued to search between two events with the same story line; there was nothing to do but wait and review what was revealed during the past hours. Each of the four had hard copies and thumbed through the pages while waiting.

Ed commented as he looked over the copy on his console table, "More and more, I'm convinced this writer is being honest with those he's trying to address. In addition, I believe he wrote most of this at, or near, the time of occurrence. How he succeeded in doing so I'm not sure, as there was no simple way for anyone to carry the necessary writing and drawing instruments on these excursions about the countryside."

Chuck, who was one who often disputed with other linguists about the variances in the synoptic Gospels, suddenly remarked, "Well, one thing's sure, the language is consistent within itself. I'm happy to say that so far, we won't have to make any apologies about switching expressions or calling the same people different names. Judas, if it's truly his writing, and I'm nearly convinced it is, has given enough detail for us to say he is writing in his own time."

"How is that, Chuck?" Ed asked, looking up from his copy. Jean also showed some interest in this question and its answer.

"Well, you remember that Judas calls the person known to the Gospel writers as John the Baptist, John bar Zechariah. He has never deviated from this moniker, although he has noted that his servant and often companion, Apius, spoke of the name of Baptist being used by some. Even after acknowledging this use, he continues to hold to the name of John bar Zechariah. This is the sort of consistency I feel gives good report to this scroll. I never could rationalize the use of John the Baptist within an intimate group, as this was supposed to be, that the apostles and Yeshua would address John as - the Baptist!"

Jean asked in a rather light manner, "I guess you would find it hard to believe that someone in the group would shout, 'Hey, John the Baptist, what's new at the water's edge?' right?" Chuck laughed at this little jest, and the others relaxed some as well.

"I think that is the right idea. Lord knows, the complete formal nomen for some of the Caesars was eight to ten names long. I have no great insight, to what sort of nicknames, if any, was used by some in those days, but it is highly unlikely that the entire moniker was used each time. It's not been the case for other cultures for ages. And I might add that as situations become more desperate, the name becomes shorter and less descriptive. I'm sure Elizabeth didn't call her son John the Baptist, nor John bar Zechariah, in times of correction. Probably, when there was no danger of confusion, the name John was sufficient, but some other more intimate name could have been used even as we do today." The point was well taken, and like Chuck, the others agreed the wording held the key to acceptance.

"You know, John, the project leader," they all smiled at this jargon from Ed, "just to change the subject, what we should do is adjourn for an early lunch and let this system complete the search on its own. If not, I think I should check on the fabrication of the two models we ordered from the model shop. Hopefully, they have completed the initial phase of the job and placed them in the vault."

"Hey, let's do both! First, we'll take a break for lunch and then you can check on the model shop. When we are free, we should select a date and see what the system brings up." John carefully set in the command words for the system to continue handshaking with the unit at ISM. He then notified security of their intentions and left them aware of the continued unmanned search.

"Well, we can leave now for a bit of lunch."

"Sounds good to me," Ed said, and was out of his chair, placing the hard copies in security cabinets and slipping into his jacket.

They moved through the air lock and out into the corridor, John placed his ID in the sensor, and the lab door automatically closed to set the alarms. The trip down to the garage floor was quiet enough, and so was the ride to the restaurant. The meal wasn't anything special, and with good service, it was over soon. Yet there was always the lingering over coffee for a bit of off-the-record conversation.

"You know Ed, one thing obvious in this manuscript is the way the author, be it Judas or someone else, ties most of his events together. So far, there's none of the sudden changing of locales and events that are traditionally true in the accepted canonical writings of the Gospel. The subject matter is either directly known to Judas by his participation, or related to him by one directly involved or witnessing the events."

"How's that?" asked Jean.

"Yes, why is that so important? Many of the apologists seem to cover this dereliction easily enough, and excuse the pun, Lord knows, most of the established sects accept these aberrations without loss of faith." John showed his interest in this subject.

"That's so, John. I'm not arguing the point from the spiritual side, but from the secular. For instance, this writer let us know the temptation was witnessed by his brother Ishmael, as was the washing of Yeshua, and the wedding miracle at Cana. Even the story of the woman, known to him as Ramona, at Jacob's well, is told by those who lived there at the time. Notice, in the Gospels, none of this is true - in fact, just the opposite is true. Many of the events appear and no leads are given as to how the Gospel writers learn of all the details they are quick to present." Chuck signed to the waitress more coffee was needed.

"I still don't see the relevance, Chuck!" stated John.

"Well, from the secular, or venial history point of view, it's nearly inexcusable. For a moment - let's consider the story about Jacob's well and Ramona - the woman there. The Gospel writer - by the way, John is the only one who reports this event - states the disciples are gone away unto the city when all this takes place. Yet, he continues with his story as if he is present during the entire event - now one of the two can't stand - either he remained behind, which would make the statement ALL the disciples went shopping wrong, or he went and the story was told to him by Yeshua - a thing he neglects to report. In general, this is just poor historical writing."

He stopped here for a moment, glanced at his watch, then continued, "In addition, he reports what the woman said to her compatriots in the city away from Yeshua and themselves. How does he come by this knowledge? It seems hard to believe that anyone except the woman and those she addressed could possibly know these things. That's not to say John didn't come by these things later in the two days he was in the city, or what he wrote isn't true. It does raise the question of how he learned these things. Remember, he records little else. Although he considers this incident important to record, he doesn't think it's important to give us the number and names of those with him, the name of the city the disciple went to, and no name for the woman! What one might consider the first Christian convert is left anonymous - what an historical booboo!"

"Notice, this isn't the approach Judas takes - he furnishes the continuity of his journal through people on the scene. That's what I mean by his use of leaders, a quality not found in the Gospels." With that said, Chuck moved to go.

"Ok, I see. Well, there is some difference from that point of view!" This comment was voiced by Jean.

John, who was patient enough through this discourse, rose and placed his empty cup on the table; the others followed. They moved through the cashier line, left the restaurant, returned to the laboratory quickly enough, trooped off the elevator, and filed through the airlock sequentially. Wraps were stowed, and each went to his assigned console.

"Ed, before we make a second attempt, check on the prototypes," John directed Ed as he moved into the command chair.

"Check!"

Ed moved to the outer room and called the design engineers for information on the copies of the Golden Scroll. It wasn't long before he returned with the best possible news.

"Well, John, according to the project leader, they have made all the required measurements and purchased materials for the fabrication. It's just a matter of time. The costs are within budget so away we go." Ed was happy with the progress of the model shop people. He moved into his chair at the console and set up his board.

"Fine, glad to hear it, Ed. If everyone is ready, let's take a look at the output from the system." All gave the thumbs up sign often used by the men of Bradenton U.

John hit the interrupt key and keyed in the control word. The system responded with a query again. It had found the starting place lost earlier. It was just a matter of pressing the start button which John did. The synthesizer came to life, the screen filled with intelligence, the vertablinds closed, and the world of Judas once again moved to the present.

"Hear, O Israel: the Lord is our God, the Lord is one."

BARABBAS AND SHALAZAR

…The morning found me ready for the trip to Capernaum. Apius would travel with me. When we arrive at Capernaum, Apius would return home with the animals. I would travel as the others, whoever they might be. Ishmael told me of his attempt to bring Apuleius to see me off but because of military assignments elsewhere, Apuleius was not present. So it was, only the immediate family and servants were present when we left for Capernaum.

Mother gave me a new prayer shawl with her blessing for a good and full life with Yeshua. Ishmael and I embraced. The servants wept openly for they held me in high esteem, or so they said. Apius and I mounted and left the gate without looking back.

The trip to Capernaum went without incident. Before presenting myself to Yeshua, Apius and I went to the inn we visited before where I obtained a room. We remained there a full week as I made my final preparations to join the other followers. It was my hope that I might be chosen as one of a select group. It was in this inn I heard Yeshua was planning to form an intimate circle of men, not more than twenty, who would receive special and powerful teachings from him and no other. It was one of these I wanted to become. One of those who would receive the strange and mystical powers he alone had.

While we were at the inn, I saw a group of men talking of the need to gain release of one called Barabbas. I told Apius, who was still with me, of the strange happenings at an inn on the way home.

We listened intently to the arguments of these men. They were indeed desperate. They even talked of sacrificing one of their own to get Barabbas freed. Much of the success of their cause for freedom from the Romans depended on his release, or so they thought. To the Romans and some of the Sadducees, Barabbas was a desperate criminal - a known subversive. It was known that he and some of his followers had caused the deaths of both the hated Romans and some Sadducees who were considered turncoats. But to the Zealots, he was a hero and they were determined to gain his release. The question was - how?

To prevent spies, both Roman and those who had sold themselves to the Romans for political favors, from obtaining the secrets of the followers of Barabbas, they formed a secret order - a brotherhood! While in this brotherhood, they protected themselves from others by establishing a form of speech that held meanings other than the spoken word. Many times they spoke to one another in short tales or parables, the meanings known only to those enlightened through a ritual of initiation.

To those outside the circle, the common people and Romans, their parables were merely childish stories causing some reference to the silliness of grown men talking so simply to one another. Indeed, it was said that this same ritual provided them with certain signs and symbols that one member might know another in the dark as well as in the light. Ancient Hebrew passwords which were used during the building of Solomon's Temple found use here. These words were often difficult for those not trained in the ancient language from childhood to pronounce were used to ferret out the uninitiated. It was whispered that tests of sincerity of purpose and fidelity to the cause included torture.

Of all these I wasn't sure but Apius, one of goodly insight in those kinds of things because of his Greek heritage, assured me this wasn't an idle wives' tale. He held that to stumble into one of their meetings and not be able to convince them of your membership in the brotherhood, meant death. They were desperate men who worked for the overthrow of Rome in all Judea. It was they who placed in Herod the Great's mind the thought that a child of the house of David would take his throne. It was told that although he knew this was not possible, he feared this secret order of the Sicarii. And now it was known the same was true of Herod Antipas - he, too, feared them and would gladly have the Romans round them up and incarcerate them.

There were many merchants and tradesmen who willingly supported these freedom fighters. It became just as dangerous to say something against the Sicarii as it was to speak against the Romans. Some said that even Herod wasn't one to tread heavily on those suspected of being Sicarii members. He made no arrests of some desperate criminals because he feared being considered the brotherhood's enemy. It was whispered that he changed his elite guard to foreign mercenaries just to know that none were Sicarii.

I slept poorly that night. When the cock crowed, I was ready to approach what I considered my destiny. In the early morning hours, I gave Apius his final instructions, and bade him to take the animals and return home. He was reluctant to do so, but obeyed as was his custom. As he rode out of sight, I began to realize that I was alone in this world of Galilee. I, a Judean, a man who had lived among the hated Romans for over twelve years and moved among the greatest of these, was now in a desperate condition. I had but one robe, sandals, and a staff; a far cry from the silk and gold I wore in Rome. My heart was troubled; had I made the right decision?

I made my way through the streets of Capernaum to the little cottage of Simon's mother-in-law. There were many still about even at this early hour. The sick and lame lay near the wall by the gate and cried out for relief as before. Those desperately ill had succumbed and were quietly taken away by the servants of the people and their relatives. I was to find later that many did die at the very feet of Yeshua, and that he cured only those he decided were worthy. By what criteria he used I never knew; some I thought were in great need he ignored, while some I considered in lesser need he healed - sometimes not for their good, but for those about him. The condition of some of those present this morning and their wailing was enough to produce melancholy in the heart of one filled with good spirits. I passed around and over some of these poor unfortunates. It was early enough that some of the followers were rolled in their cloaks and still fast asleep in the courtyard. I stepped to the gate and rapped with my staff.

As before, the gate was manned by the ever-faithful Simon. His muscular arm again came across the gateway preventing me from entering. His keen eyes met mine. He recognized me from the time before but gave no outward sign. I felt in his gaze the deep dislike for those not from Galilee. He was determined to force me to ask for permission to enter; it was his way of lowering the status of one not considered in the inner circle of Galilean followers. I was just as determined not to give him any sign of weakness.

Finally, he spoke. "So we are blessed with the Judean again. The name is Judas bar Simon, isn't it? What is your cause this time? Would you have your fortune told?" He seemed to find great humor in this statement. His smile showed some uneven teeth which lacked care. He was a very rough fisherman and was unafraid of what one might think of him, and what anyone might think of his teacher because of his roughness.

Suddenly a voice behind me said, "Why is it you are so protective of your master? I've heard he has great power over things of this world, and by your own tongue, things not of this world. Why then, Simon, can't you see your strong arm isn't needed?" I turned to see who spoke. The person was in front of Simon. I could see from Simon's reaction the owner of this voice was known to him. The speaker's cloak was still over his head to ward off the early morning chill. He was a tall fellow, at least a head taller than me. Not easily impressed by others, Simon didn't drop his arm, but turned his eyes from me to the speaker.

"Why do you continue to bother us?" Simon called out. I knew then Simon at least had met this fellow before. I felt a flutter within me for the voice disturbed me, also. "If you're not with us, you're against us; therefore, leave us be, take your mischief elsewhere!"

"But Simon, you haven't answered my question. Haven't I stood among the crowds and heard of the feeding of them, and the healing of the sick, the quieting of the sea, and ho, even more, the raising of the dead? All these things and more I've heard from you and your brothers, and yet when I ask you to answer a simple question, your tongue sticks to the roof of your mouth or you seek another word."

The speaker came closer, and threw back his cloak. I recognized him - Shalazar - the person I had given my word to some months before and the one I met in the alleyway.

Ishmael's rescuer, and mine. The very person who demanded I join this group of followers. It was my tongue that clove to the roof of my mouth. I was as one cut from stone. It was the very same person, but why was he here and how did he come to know Simon? I couldn't help but wonder if Simon was also obligated to him in some manner!

"Speak loudly so all can hear, Simon! Do you believe all you have seen and heard, or is there some doubt that still holds you captive?"

The color drained from Simon's face for a few moments, and then the veins in his neck swelled; his face became flushed. His eyes filled with tears of rage. He shook with anger, but he made no move against the stranger. There was, I thought, some hidden reason for this act of restraint on his part.

Shalazar was enjoying this moment with Simon, and was about to press his advantage when Yeshua stepped from the house. Shalazar saw Yeshua, pulled the cloak over his head, and moved away from us, disappearing through the early morning mist. I made a mental note of this event and would later ask Simon of his knowledge of Shalazar. I felt that someday, both Simon and I would feel the power of Shalazar in our lives.

Simon dropped his arm to his side and turned to meet Yeshua. He remained at his post, ready to intercept any and all attempting to enter the small cottage gate.

"Master, we have one here who would speak with you, the Judean, Judas bar Simon. Shall I let him in?"

"Simon, must you always be so hard on those who aren't Galilean? Will you always hold such views? I pray that you won't fall into the trap of tradition - beware."

Yeshua turned and moved toward a small garden at the rear of the cottage. "Let him enter and come to me in the garden, I would have a word with him alone."

THE IMPORTANT QUESTION

Simon stepped aside, grudgingly, it seemed to me, but I let this pass and followed Yeshua into the small garden. I could feel the eyes of Simon and some of the others watching as I moved to the side of their teacher. He chose a small bench a goodly distance from them; it was obvious he wanted his words to me unheard by the others. It was the first time I saw Yeshua in this setting, a man at home in his environment; a person with no haughty or arrogant notions of self esteem showing. His features didn't show the nervous energy of John bar Zechariah. His eyes were quiet and, I thought, a bit moody in expression as he gazed at me. I tried not to be too obvious, and thereby reveal my extreme curiosity about him. Was he really strong enough to be the Messiah?

As we sat there for a few moments in silence, each studying the other, I recognized there were great differences between us. I finally moved into a position where my back was to those watching; I learned this from those in the Roman court when they wanted to avoid an unguarded facial expression from betraying the content of their conversation with another. I made a mark in the ground with my sandal as I waited for him to speak.

"It is good you have come, Judas. I've waited your return." He spoke softly, rolling his speech in the manner of Galileans. "And how was your mother when you left?"

"She was in good health when I left." I couldn't think of anything more astute than that to say. It seemed that with all my years in different courts of the land I could have returned with something better than she was well, but it wasn't so. I couldn't help wondering why he asked this question for he had spoken positively of her being well when I requested his help some days before. At that time, I had understood him to say, even then, at that moment she was well. I waited.

He looked at me as though he was reading my mind, but without continuing on with that subject, he turned and stood with his back to me.

"Judas, what have you heard of me?"

He didn't turn around after asking the question. I leaned on my staff for a moment watching him. He was, like John bar Zechariah, a small man in every way. I could see how it was that stories told of his great tiredness after some of his feats could be true. Also, how the big, rough fisherman, Simon, could carry his master with ease to places of safety when the crowd or weather pressed upon him.

"Ah Yeshua, much! I've heard of many wondrous things done by you. The healing of the sick, the casting out of devils, the quieting of the sea of Galilee, and the raising of one from the dead. I have been the beneficiary of two healings, one making my hand well, and the bringing of good health to my mother. Yes, I've heard many stories about you, Yeshua." I was about to add more to the stories when he turned to face me again. His face showed no great interest in what I had said.

"But Judas, have you heard who some say I am?"

I looked down at the ground. I knew what they said about him in the circle of his followers, and among some of the poor rabble in the lower city of Jerusalem. I knew of their insistence of his God-given appointment as the Messiah; even the cries of some that he was the Son of God! All these things I heard from some around the holy city.

Yet, with all this, I knew him as a lad, one not any different than others of his age, playing the same games and making the same mistakes. From what I knew of his family's visits to Jerusalem, there was nothing special about him. Today the Lord was with him, no one could deny unless, of course, it would cause hardships on their own kind. I looked up and tried to read his face for some inkling of what he wanted as an answer to his question. I hesitated to speak so freely at our first meeting.

It was the first time anyone challenged me to think on things I heard, and for my intentions for joining this little band. Although I didn't want to admit it, my real thoughts were still a mystery to me. Who or what was the real driving force that brought me here? Shalazar, Yeshua, or the Lord? I was about to supply an answer that I thought wouldn't close the door on my becoming a newly-initiated follower when he looked away for a moment. When he turned back he spoke before I could form my answer.

"It doesn't matter who some say I am, Judas, for all these things will be settled in time." He said this while he stood looking up at me.

"Truly, Judas, you will witness greater things than the making whole of your hand before our work is done. It doesn't matter why you've come. What truly is important is that you are here for so it's written. Many things hence are known to me; not all clearly as others, but this I know, Judas, you are of great value to me in this teaching of the coming of the kingdom of God.

"Your time of trial, even as mine, is yet to come. Your lot, even as mine, shall end with great tragedy, yet it will be to the glory of our God. We have but one purpose, Judas - before time began we were chosen, each of us to do the will of God! Each as it's required of him without fail! Aye, Judas, hear me, there's no turning aside!" His eyes were soft and dark; his speech showed great emotion; and I drew from this last utterance the conclusion that he knew more of this coming adventure than I did.

My thoughts were somewhat muddled by what he said. His words brought to mind the words of Shalazar; he spoke in like manner about my life. And what of the predictions of the old Chaldean sorcerer? They were a notice of evils yet to come. Yeshua's words brought no comfort. If God spoke to Yeshua in this regard, then why not to me?

"Yeshua, when will this trial be known to me and how, not knowing what it is, shall I prepare for it? Why hasn't God given me what you have? What am I, another Cain?"

Here I suddenly realized I was speaking to him as I had Hillel so many years ago. I had, without forethought, accepted him as an equal to Hillel, the master teacher and Rabbi of our people. What did it all mean?

His speech had set aside my earlier thoughts of being well off in the service of a successful Messiah. This wasn't the kind of language I wished to hear. I wasn't a man of sacrifice for others, but one of honest accounts and ledgers.

My heart trembled at the thought of what happened to Judas of Galilee, an earlier Messiah, and how many of his followers were crucified. I could see that this man wasn't one to rush to the sword; he moved away from the teaching of the Zealots. He was closer to the school of Hillel than of Shammai. I heard him repeat the two great commands given to Moses, first, "Love the Lord thy God with all thy heart," and second, "Love thy neighbor as thyself." Some said he added another burden to his followers with, "Love your enemies, bless them who curse you, do good to them that hate you, and pray for them which despitefully use you." This seemed hardly the words of one who would attack Rome or bring down the iron heel upon himself and his followers.

"Judas, dear friend, don't wonder and accept that which the Lord will give you. Don't fear the pain of this world for there is one moving about who can cause greater hurt to you than all the earthly enemies you can have. Someday you will have to chose between following the word of a stranger and that of God. In this matter, Judas, I'll have no power! Even the God of our fathers won't be able to force you to do other than your will."

He turned his face away. I stood as one struck by lightning, unable to move. Everything said confused me greatly. How much did Yeshua know of my past and future? Had Shalazar been the one Ishmael saw in the wilderness with Yeshua and was he the same Shalazar I struck the bargain with so many years ago? And what did that have to do with this? What did he mean, that Almighty God couldn't force me to do other than my will?

While we stood thus, he gazing off toward the rising sun, and me staring at him for want of composure, several voices were raised outside the gate.

"Hear us, we come from John bar Zechariah and would speak on his behalf with Yeshua!" The voice from outside the gate contained a tone of urgency. Yeshua turned from the east and moved in front of me toward the gate where the shouting continued. Simon let two men into the front courtyard.

They were travel worn and weary; they had no animals with them and wore the simple garb of the followers of John. They were of different ages; the younger of the two was more aggressive. He looked quizzically about the group which had grown in size as Simon had left his post and those who couldn't get past him were now pressing upon them to hear and see the event taking place. It was obvious from his hurried glances at one person then another that he didn't know who he was looking for except by name alone.

"Please, can anyone direct me to this teacher, Yeshua, that John spoke about so many times? It's to him I must deliver word from my teacher, John." His shoulders slumped a little with the nearness of the completion of his task. He was obviously a willing lad, but the strain of the hurried trip was now beginning to take its toll. He looked faint and turned to the elder companion for aid. Silence reigned for a moment as if everyone was waiting for the other to speak, then several began speaking at once; it was Simon's booming voice that was heard above the others.

"Here lad, he stands behind you." He moved aside such that the lad could see Yeshua standing beside me. He looked from me to Yeshua; neither I nor Yeshua gave an indication which of us was Yeshua. The lad chose Yeshua and strode to where he stood. Bowing in a manner taught the young to do before the elder, the lad spoke again.

"My lord, I'm called Dan and my companion is Judah. We have been washed by John and even now look for the coming of the kingdom of God. We have come from John's cell straight to this place and are bound to return in the same manner. It's from him we bring word." Yeshua motioned for him to rise and address him as a man might.

"My lord, Master John is in great uneasiness in both body and spirit. He even now lies in his prison cell unable to see the light of day or moon at night. His body is racked with pain and discomfort is in his heart. When I left him, his mind wasn't clear. He has heard much of your teaching yet still trembles for fear his own desires give substance to that which isn't real. He would have an answer to this for it troubles him even to his heart; art thou he that should come, or do I look for another is his cry!"

Seeing their plight, Yeshua moved close to them, embraced them, called to his followers and bade them to prepare food and drink for two faithful servants of John.

"You have done well, and I will give you the answer after you have rested and are ready to return. Stay in this house until I return for I must leave and go and pray yet a little while." He motioned for them to move into the house to receive food and rest therein. Simon's mother-in-law accepted them at her table without a word.

As many as seventy men forced their way into the little courtyard during this exchange between the young lad and Yeshua. All seemed ready for travel, every man carrying an extra cloak and staff. These I hadn't heard of before.

Three of those I saw in the sketches of Ishmael came from the crowd and stood near Yeshua. I moved to the outside of the group.

THE SERMON AND FEEDING

"Verily, the time has come." Yeshua spoke so all could hear, "Follow me." With the three - Simon, James, and John - moving the crowd aside, even as Ishmael had written so long ago in his letters, Yeshua and the rest passed through the gate and progressed up the road to a hill overlooking the city of Capernaum. I, too, followed near the leaders.

As this group passed through the streets of Capernaum, the curious and free were quick to follow, and I could see some shop owners closing to follow the crowd. These were people who needed no cause. They had one delivered by the years of Roman rule. To them, every gathering, either large or small, was a chance to vent their feelings against Herod and Rome. Politics and religion were rolled into one; this I saw in Rome as well.

The crowd grew, and when I topped the rise and looked back, there must have been as many as five hundred men following the leaders. Although later I heard from a passerby that the number was nearly five thousand, a difference of ten times what I beheld.

As they walked along, I could hear questions asked about the reason for this gathering and who the teacher was that was being so honored. I could hear Yeshua's name bandied about, and I could see that Simon, James, and John were flushed and this not from exercise alone.

From what I gathered, none knew the wherefor of the meeting on a small hill outside Capernaum. Except for those who were disciples, none really cared; if there was a chance to shout and thereby vent their feelings about what they believed to be injustice, and even blasphemy against the God of Israel, it was their desire, nay, their duty to do so.

The longer they walked, the more demonstrative they became about their dislikes of Herod and Tiberius. It was strange to see these men, quite unaware of what was the real purpose of this meeting, pushing and shoving to get to the top of the hill first. Some even broke off from the main body and ran on ahead, and then, picking a spot they thought would be the resting place and podium for the speaker, would encircle it only to find it wasn't the one Yeshua had in mind. As he walked on past them, they would beckon as hucksters would their wares, and when he didn't accept their offer, some gave vent to their frustration by adding his name to the list of Herod and Tiberius. It was obvious that not all this crowd was for anyone, but all were against someone.

The crowd was nearly all male; few women and no children were present. This was normally the case in this land and at this hour. Most women had their chores to do and the children their tasks and studies. It was a rare holiday when women and children were among such spontaneous gatherings.

At last, near the top of the hill and on the side facing Capernaum, Yeshua chose a large flat rock that stood high over the rest of the hillside. The summit was some distance higher. He stood facing the city; they stood facing him. He called the names of some of his followers and they approached. He then called to the assembly which had reached nearly a thousand souls, as near as I could judge.

"Hear me, sit here and wait for I must go further and pray alone." The crowd quieted and dutifully sat or reclined where they stood; none made any attempt to follow Yeshua to the summit. Deep inside each man was respect for a teacher, and this presently overrode their own personal desires for expression. The men he called by name arranged themselves in a manner that indicated to the crowd his words were to be taken seriously.

Of those called, I could recognize the following from Ishmael's sketches: Simon bar Jona, and his brother Andrew; James and John, his younger brother and the one I met in the inn; Philip and Nathanael, fellow townsmen of Simon and Andrew; Levi; Matthew, who looked like Levi; and James, Joses, and Judas, the only brothers of Yeshua who were among this gathering.

There were others in the group near the flat stone Yeshua selected as his podium. I didn't recognize them because they weren't included in Ishmael's sketches or I had simply not taken note of their appearance in them. I was sure many, if not all, were from Galilee. Their mannerisms, speech, and clothing set them apart from Judeans and Samaritans.

Yeshua didn't wait for the crowd to comply with his request, but continued on alone up the hill to the summit. It was there he knelt alone to pray even as he had said. The early morning sunlight played over him as he knelt there, the sunlight adding a soft gold coloring to his clothing and hair. The crowd sat quietly, some talking in low voices about the earlier saying and acts of Yeshua, and others in prayer.

Yeshua spent a good deal of time in this attitude and after awhile, the assembly became restless. There was a break in their respectfulness as they became more agitated by his lengthy stay. The thought of the ancients waiting for Moses came to mind, and how they became restless when he stayed on the mountain longer than they thought he should.

Some began to move about and ask each other why they came on this "fools' errand." It wasn't long before some of the more unruly shouted to his followers to call him down from his prayers and speak to them as it was approaching time for the noon meal. Since many just came for the show, and this wasn't to be forthcoming soon, they were ready for other diversions from the drudgery and boredom.

This noise and movement from the crowd continued for some time. It was Simon who finally broke the silence of the guarding group.

"What is this thing I see? Is this the respect men of Capernaum show the greatest teacher since Moses? Many of you have heard of his power over illness and spirits. Who of you can do these things? This I say to you, show your respect for this teacher, and learn what is to come. He will speak in his time." Simon sat down on a rock nearby. His speech calmed some of the crowd for awhile, but not all were satisfied with his prodding them about their lack of respect.

One shouted, "I haven't seen any of these things. Bring him down and show us and teach us before we faint from hunger!" The crowd found humor in it, but Simon didn't!

"I say to dismiss yourselves, those whose stomachs are greater than their heads and hearts. Your belly is your God. It was your forefathers who called for Moses to come down from the mountain before his time, and when he didn't, turned their hearts against the Lord. Go fill your bellies and turn away from this teacher as well."

Both Simon and the crowd were in an antagonistic mood. There was continued shouting and shaking of fists, some approached the group of followers as if to charge the summit and bring the teacher down by force. I stepped to the side of John and committed myself as one willing to defend Yeshua against the unruly mob. It was a strange and new act for me, done without my usual premeditation. Here we stood, following Simon's action, aligned in a row with staffs held horizontally across our bodies, ends of each staff touching in such a way as to prevent anyone from passing and proceeding up the hill.

It seemed pure folly. We were but forty against a cabal. Yet there was a calm determination of the few against the unorganized many, and the calm determination satisfied the crowd that their cause wasn't a valid one and they remained at bay. Their noise wasn't abated, however, and some of the wiser began to speak of the garrison sending troops up the hill if quiet didn't return. This was in no wise an idle thought for the Romans were in no mood these days for the gatherings of mobs.

As we stood thus, backs to the summit and facing the crowd, we suddenly realized a change in their mood. Without any signal among them, they started to seat themselves once again, and became less unruly. It was then we realized that Yeshua had finished his prayers and was coming down the hill.

As I stood with my back to the summit and facing the people, I suddenly realized how homogenous a gathering this was, and how this natural amphitheater on the slope facing Capernaum was far from the best for a meeting of this kind. The multitude consisted of nearly every kind of individual from the area. They, by custom, split themselves into small bands within the larger mass. The rich and poor separated because of their differences in status, that is, the rich were more interested in maintaining this segregation than the poor. The poor, who had nothing except the very ground they squatted on, were not about to move because of wants or desires of the rich.

The sick came slowly up the hill, some alone leaning on staffs for added support and others helped or led, as in the case of the blind, by those who had more heart than others. Many of the ill were those who were from around Simon's mother-in-law's cottage. Among all these were the professional poor, those who had existed for many years on the dole from the temple or begged along the by-roads and city streets of whatever city they came from. These passed through the assembly asking for alms or bread. They succeeded in securing relief as some present had enough forethought to bring along small amounts of foodstuffs. Those who took such precautions were few and far between, and as a general rule, the multitude was without food of any sort. Many had, however, under their cloaks, small bags of foodstuffs and some - even wine skins.

The lack of food and water wasn't a crucial one for most as Capernaum wasn't far away, but not all had access to food in Capernaum. I could see some weren't from Capernaum but from the outlying country and would go hungry if they stayed much longer.

Here and there I saw soldiers from the outpost in Capernaum. What was their reason for coming? I was sure they had seen many of these kinds of gatherings before as it was commonplace these days. People often followed a teacher or a storyteller. The fever of national rescue through the coming of a Messiah was hard upon the people, especially those simple folk who believed the words of early prophets. There were many who could read all sort of signs and symbols from the past into the present. From their point of view, present conditions and national servitude so long under the Romans made the Lord's quick intervention by bringing a deliverer only hours away.

The soldiers, often in close contact with the civilian populace, were well aware of the thin film of religious fervor that covered clandestine Zealot operations. The Romans were ill at ease for many saw eruptions develop from nationalism. They stood at the fringe of the crowd; they, too, were in small groups. Their attitude showed some haughtiness - my impression was that they didn't come out of pure curiosity but out of command.

Cornelius was in charge of Capernaum; he was a good man and didn't wish things to get out of hand. I wondered about these separate groups: the rich, poor, shopkeepers, Pharisees, Sadducees, Roman militia, and their differing interests in what Yeshua might say.

With such an assembly, I wondered how each would be able to hear, and even when hearing, how many would understand. None of our people were illiterate; as in accordance with the law, all males were taught to read the Torah. In fact, it was safe to say that our people as a nation was the most literate of the world. For those not Jews, even the Romans, I couldn't say how much they would understand - if anything.

"Teacher, give us words of comfort!" cried one of the poor at his feet. He spoke even before Yeshua was settled on the stone above them. In this place, nearly all could see him without great effort. The place was well chosen for another reason - the stone around this setting formed a natural outcrop that projected his voice as well as any amphitheater built by the Romans for their senate. Later, as I listened to Yeshua speak, I remarked to John that it seemed as though God had designed this place just for this purpose.

"Hear me, you men of Capernaum! Many of you have learned the Torah from childhood and have wondered about its sayings and of the Prophets as well. Hear then these words and be of comfort, for they are from the hidden meanings of the writings and them alone. How blessed are the poor of spirit for the reign of God is theirs. Blessed, too, are the sorrowing for they shall be consoled. Blessed are the lowly for they shall inherit the land. Blessed are they who hunger and thirst for holiness for they shall have their fill. Blessed are they who show mercy, for mercy shall be theirs. Blessed are the peacemakers, for they shall be called Sons of God. Blessed are those persecuted for holiness' sake, for the reign of God is theirs. Blessed are you who follow me when they insult you and persecute you and utter every kind of slander against you because of me. Be glad and rejoice, for your reward is great in heaven. Remember, they persecuted the prophets before you in like manner."

By the time he had stopped, the crowd was murmuring; some with happy expressions and others not so. I was at a loss. This was the first time I had heard Yeshua speak to a large group. I was amazed at the forcefulness of his voice. The crowd was strangely silent during this discourse. He taught through the day into late afternoon. It was the people that finally caused him to stop teaching. During the times he rested from his labors, he could hear some of the assembly murmur about their situation. Considering the number and their needs, he arose from the rock and addressed those I considered his disciples about the needs of the people.

"See, even now the day is goodly spent - the noon hour and these before us have had nothing to eat or drink. It's time to send them on their way, yet it wouldn't be wise nor compassionate for us to do so without relief from needs."

"Master, it would take much to feed such an assembly and we have naught in the treasury." The one called Philip called out for he was some distance from Yeshua. I was surprised to hear this as it was the custom of the day to provide for a teacher, and this usually by his followers. Why didn't they have anything in the treasury? Who was handling the funds of the little band? Maybe this is why God brought me to this group. If there was one thing I knew, it was how to balance books. I had more in my pouch than they had in their combined treasury. I could see, that should I be chosen as one of the intimate members of this band, I could contribute to its stability - I could be the treasurer!

While my thoughts wandered, the crowd had moved about joustling each other for a closer look and Yeshua. We still stood, like the men of Joshua, holding the crowd back.

"Have them arrange themselves first into groups of hundreds and then into tens. In this wise, it will be easier for every man to know he isn't forgotten in the count."

So the order was given, and all except the Romans and wealthy followed the word. The Romans remained on the outskirts of the crowd, while the wealthy and certain of the Pharisees and Sadducees moved toward the city and away from the masses. With the people arranged, passageways were made between the several groups, and the count was slightly over eight hundred men. Once accomplished, Yeshua said, "Search among the assembly and see if there isn't food and drink among them."

I joined the disciples in searching and asking those present if they had provisions with them. Many had nothing but some who had been on the road for days, carried the usual supplies of food and drink with them.

While doing this task, I heard the strong voice of Yeshua remind the crowd of the law: "If there be among you a poor man and one of your brethren within your gates in your land which the Lord your God giveth thee, you shall not harden your heart, nor shut up your hand from your poor brother." He added from Proverbs: "He who has pity on the poor lends unto the Lord; and that which he gives will he pay him again."

With these words ringing in their ears, many of the aggregation opened their hearts and hands to the one next to them. I saw many offer his neighbor food from a well-hidden pouch under his garments as I walked through the crowd. Still there wasn't enough for everyone, and many were without food or drink. We again gathered around Yeshua to tell of our findings when Andrew called out from the roadway that he had found a young lad from Capernaum carrying food.

"There is a lad here who has five barely loaves and two fish." Some hooting and whistling resulted from this announcement. "But what are they among so many?" He continued and turned to look heavenward as if expecting manna.

We were downcast about the needs of the people.

"Have the lad bring the fish and loaves," said Yeshua.

"But master, we have naught to pay for his goods and they are for his family." I couldn't resist what seemed to be an injustice here; to my mind, the loaves and fishes were his and his alone. We had no right to take them or even ask the lad to give the food away.

Simon was quick to ask, "Well, Judas, what would you have us do?"

"If the quantity is too small to feed the people, why take away from the mouths of those for which it's intended?" I countered. "Where is it written that the needs of one is to be considered greater than another? Where is it written that one must be forced to share?"

"Your position is well taken, Judas, but you avoid the question. Is that a common practice of the Judeans?"

"Aye, it's easy to call attention to another's birthplace when feeling the bite of truth, Simon. It comes to me that we must find out the lad's purpose for the fish and if he has freedom to dispose of them." I wasn't sure the lad had such freedom. It wasn't common for a lad as young as he was, to be walking down the road with five loaves and some fish without a purpose. To assume that his purpose was to supply food for this assembly would be a miracle nearly equal to the ravens feeding Elijah. "Let me speak with the lad."

I moved to where the lad stood mindful of the crowd and the teacher before him. He was a goodly lad and respectful in all ways.

"What is your name, lad, and from what house?"

"I'm Jeremiah, from the house of Benjamin." The lad was unafraid and spoke well of his family name.

"Ah, a good name is better than precious oils, so it is written. Jeremiah, I would have an answer to this. Are your fish and bread for sale?"

"The food is for my family's noon meal, and I'm already late, sir. This crowd distracted me from my chores and for this I'll pay. To sell this dinner would mean I must return to the city and secure more food; even later I would be." The lad was honest enough in his relating his mission and the lateness thereof.

"Hear me, Jeremiah. There are many here who are faint from hunger and your food would relieve them greatly. Would you sell your fish to relieve this need and make a profit for your family?" I was sure he would be happy to erase his lateness by contributing to his family's welfare. The added income would, by his looks, be useful.

"I would do so, if, after I purchase more food and deliver it to my family, I could be brought before the master and hear his discourse." His eyes were on Yeshua much of the time of our little chat.

"Aye, so it shall be done. When you have obeyed your parents, come back and I'll take you to the master. Remember, my name is Judas bar Simon and mark it well." I took more than enough to pay for the food from my pouch. Without regard of other things, I made mental note of the lightening of my pouch as was my habit in these days of high taxes. Some of the others willingly transferred the food from his carrying basket to one of many which was in the crowd and this took to Yeshua.

After selling his dinner, the young lad thanked me for the increase in wealth and tucked his empty basket under his arm and was away to Capernaum without delay.

I wondered what could be accomplished in the way of feeding this multitude with the small quantity now held by Yeshua. And even if these five loaves and two smoked fish could feed those not receiving food from others, who had some with them, I saw the need for water even greater than that of food. The day was hot and no clouds gave relief from the sun. The thoughts of dry bread and smoked fish without some form of drink were less than appealing. It was easy to see how quickly one would be filled on such a fare.

As it turned out, many who had no water refused food in deference to it, or as it were, took only the amount required to meet the minimum of the Pesach, "each shall have a portion as large as an olive."

Yeshua took the basket containing the food and held it high and called for God to hear his prayer of praise. "Blessed art thou, O God, King of the Universe, who brings forth bread from the earth." The people responded in like manner.

He then broke the bread and fish into pieces such that they were equally divided among twelve baskets. The baskets were very small ones used for table passing. These he gave to the disciples nearest him and instructed them to distribute unto all who hadn't sufficient to eat. With the men in small groups, and pathways between each of the groups of fifty, it was but a simple matter for the followers to give to those who waved their hands for a portion.

I could see that many didn't raise their hands, and this not for the want of food but for the need of water for the interpretation of the law - that no man shall eat without washing his hands. Even others didn't eat because of fasting.

At last, all ceased to wave hands and the feeding of the assembly was completed. In accordance with the law, the remaining food was gathered for it is the fool who wastes what he may desire later. After all who had need or desire had eaten, the prayer of the bounties of the Lord was said. Some who were close to the baskets said that gathered was greater than that provided. They called to many of their friends and told of what they saw - twelve baskets having food yet in them. By the time the story reached the roadway some distance from the collected food, it was said that the twelve baskets were running over. Yet, this I didn't see and even as I write, I cannot remember it being the case.

Because of Yeshua's teachings, many were filled with the Spirit of God. They left singing simple prayers of thanksgiving and repeated the story of the feeding of the multitude far and wide. Often times, I heard this feeding called the miracle on the slope near Capernaum, and the number grew to a "great multitude" - and this number ever growing.

Many traveled quickly to Capernaum. The word spread of this strange happening where the food in the baskets gained in quantity even though many had eaten of it. It was then that some of the Zealots living under the fever of Messianic folktales returned to the mount outside Capernaum. It was the young lad who sold us the fish and loaves who ran ahead and brought us the news of their intentions. He told me some were easily convinced that Yeshua was indeed the Messiah! They would bring him to their meeting house to set up a formal group to lead him into Jerusalem as it was written. They were even now looking for a pure white stallion to carry Yeshua through the gate of the Holy City as some old tales held. He would lead them, sword flashing in the sun, and conquer the Romans.

Upon hearing this, Yeshua hurried away from Capernaum with forty of his followers. I gave the lad a gold chain and shared with him some teachings of Yeshua and sent him back to his house. I wondered if and when I would meet young Jeremiah again as I watched him hurry on his way full of the Spirit of God; then I, too, followed Yeshua.

We traveled until the supper hour where we stopped at a small creek and there washed our hands, said our prayers for the bountiful gifts, and ate of the remaining food from the noon meal. The water from the creek was sweet after the afternoon's travel and lessons. The simple fare was near a banquet for those who hadn't eaten the noon meal because of lack of drink or ablution. It was good to be among some of these men.

Soon after evening prayers, Yeshua once again left the group to go pray alone to the God of our Fathers. He wouldn't have any follow him. As time passed into the early hours, some of the disciples became concerned about their master. Simon was of the opinion that a party should be formed and they should check on the welfare of Yeshua. His relentless cajoling of the others about Yeshua not returning reminded me of Shalazar's words once more. "Simon, can't you see your strong arm isn't needed?"

Most honored the wishes of Yeshua and didn't go where he was in solitude, but not Simon. He wanted to be near Yeshua always and this was apparent even to me, a relative newcomer to the fold. Simon seemed to gain in stature when near Yeshua, perhaps because of their difference in size or of the hidden power that was transferred between them. Not being long with these men, I couldn't tell which was true and what was imaginary.

When the fires had burned low, and Yeshua hadn't returned, there was no holding Simon any longer. James and John joined him and all set off into the dark to find him, while the rest of us remained by the fire although none slept soundly.

I awoke in the early light of the next day, somewhat confused. The lack of sound sleep and the inability to recognize the location made things seem as in a dream. The noise of the early camp brought me to the real world and that all before me wasn't a dream and the call to prayer settled the matter.

After prayers, Yeshua, Simon, James, and John appeared over the rise. They took their portion of the meager morning meal. Yeshua was greatly strengthened by his all-night vigil. He vigorously greeted each of the forty or so that came to him. I was curious of the night's happenings but decided I would learn most of these things in good time.

After he ate, he called to one and all. "The time has come for me to release you. Some of you are here as pupils and some to witness things not seen before. Hear me, for this is demanded of those who would be counted among my brethren. Those who, for whatever reason, wouldn't place their service unto me before this world isn't one of mine."

One of the forty, an elderly man, dressed better than most, asked, "Does this mean we deny those who are given by God as gifts of responsibility?"

Another, taking strength from the first, continued the vain and asked, "How can this be, for it is written, 'Honor thy mother and thy father that thy days may be prolonged on the earth and that it may go well with thee.'" He showed strength in his voice.

"Verily, I say unto you, there is no man that hath left house, or parents, or brethren, or wife, or children for the sake of the kingdom of God, who shall not receive manyfold more in this present time, and in the world to come - life everlasting," Yeshua answered.

Many of us couldn't believe nor understand these words. Many shouted their scripture verses unto him that refuted his statement. How can this be, some shouted? There was no small amount of animation among those before Yeshua. The words came to me as the setting aside of the law! I wasn't alone as many of those present murmured against these words. Some shook their fists at such sayings; it was easy to see they didn't fit the teachings of the law. Even Hillel had never asked his pupils to do such a thing! What teacher would ask his students to forsake his responsibilities as given by God? Forsake the children? Weren't children the greatest gift offered man? How then can he abandon them and gain favor in the sight of a just God?

Peter spoke, "This is so, we have left all, and have followed you!" He spoke for himself and some of the others. Simon had left his family, sons, daughters, wife, parents, and a good fishing enterprise. It was worded among the others that Simon's wife wasn't happy with his commitment. It was she and her mother who were left with the raising of his family. Simon's wife had threatened to go before the Sanhedrin for justice, or so it was said.

Even in my own case, I had done equally as well, if not better, for my life hadn't been as a Galilean fisherman, but as a Judean businessman. One who saw much of what the world had to offer - political prizes, wealth, sumptuous living, and great comforts - and had come to walk in the footsteps of Yeshua. Why? Was it fear of Shalazar and his power over me through the bargain to free Ishmael? Was it some political drive offered by this myth of the Messiah and a new government of Israel? Or was it as Yeshua had said - a mission yet to be revealed to me? One thing I knew it wasn't - it wasn't the call to everlasting life!

Yeshua moved to a position a bit higher than the rest of the ground so he could look down on all before him. The disciples, such as they were, stood quietly around him. The crowd had grown; there must have been nearly seventy or more men and boys there. They were from all walks of life - free men, runaway slaves, merchants, Zealots, some of the mystery men of the Sicarii, Pharisees, even some professional beggars. Strange, I thought - as near as I could tell, there were no Sadducees.

As I surveyed the crowd, I noticed the two messengers from John had recovered sufficiently to follow us and were now standing directly in front of Yeshua. Before he could speak again, the younger one, Dan, spoke.

"Forgive us, Master, but we have overstayed our time. John is gravely ill. We have sworn to bring your words to him, and this as soon as we were able. Give us, then, the words of comfort he needs; his heart is sorely pressed. Can't you give us a simple yea or nay - are you he that should come, or should we look for another?"

The lad was a sturdy fellow and not afraid to bring his cause before this man John had told him so much about. I couldn't help but remember the words Ishmael had written to me while I was in Rome about the discourse between John and Yeshua at his washing. According to Ishmael, John had declared Yeshua, his cousin, was the Messiah and more!

John and his family were close to Yeshua, both growing up as relatives - though distant ones. Even though Yeshua had never been to see John in prison, he knew that being in Herod's dungeon was trying to any man's heart. I could see from Yeshua's face that John's condition weighed heavily on his heart, yet there was a quiet firmness about his look that seemed to say - things were as they were meant to be.

This was an interpretation on my part which gave me pause to consider its meaning. Why wasn't Yeshua greatly concerned with the incarceration of the one person who both claimed to be the forerunner of the Messiah? Why hadn't Yeshua visited him or even spoken about him? So far as I knew, none of his close followers had been to see John for any reason. Why? Wasn't John deserving of at least this kindness? My mind whirled with these questions. As the others turned to Yeshua for comment, I couldn't remain silent.

"What the lad says is true, Yeshua," I found myself saying, although I couldn't honor the act with any real reason. "I saw John in the dungeon of Herod's palace. The lad speaks the truth for John's lot is a poor one, and Satan sat on the straw mat beside him, or so he said. He was sorely troubled both in body and soul when I spoke to him." Yeshua turned from the lad to me, as did the others.

"But, Master," interjected the lad, "he isn't in the palace dungeon!"

"Where, then?" This was a surprise to me.

"He is now in the prison at Fort Machaerus. It's from there we have come. Some say Herodias was offended by his continued preaching to followers from the dungeon and cajoled Herod into moving him away from the people in Jerusalem. He now suffers even more for he cannot reach anyone accept through bribing his guards. It cost us much to bring this word from him and will cost us again to take your words unto him."

Upon hearing this, many murmured against Herod. The faces of Simon, James, and John became flushed with anger; they wanted to do something to relieve John's discomfort. These three knew John before becoming followers of Yeshua and had great respect for the ministry and washing of John. These three were for quick and sometimes violent action!

"Master, what can be done for John? Can't you relieve him of this unjust trial?" Simon spoke, believing Yeshua could open the locks that held John and set him free. After all, he had seen him raise the dead, heal lepers, and do much outside the natural world.

"Yes, Lord, do this for John as he has yet to complete his mission," John spoke as he well knew of John's professed calling. Yet John hadn't even traveled more than one hundred miles - there seemed much to do. Nearly everywhere they went, few people were washed or knew of Yeshua as the Messiah. I had to agree with John - I saw little of John bar Zechariah's preaching in my travels to Capernaum and elsewhere.

Some of the others shook their heads in agreement. They wanted something done, but I was one who couldn't see this as a possibility. And even if it was possible, to what avail? Mere freedom without exoneration from Herod, and Herodias, would mean John could never minister or wash anyone again. No! Herod was the key; only through a complete change of his heart could John the washer be free to minister again, and this would indeed be a miracle! This wasn't to say I wouldn't relish witnessing such an act of the God of our fathers, but from what I could plainly see, this wasn't to be. To my mind, Herod wasn't a Jew, and never held his personal actions subject to the law of the God or Moses, our beloved teacher, and therefore was an abomination unto the Lord. The chance of softening his heart was even less than that of Pharaoh in the days of Moses.

There was another side to this that I couldn't set aright. Why hadn't Yeshua visited John? I was sure he knew of his imprisonment as it was the talk of many. Why wouldn't Yeshua want to visit his next of kin so woefully treated? Yes, there must be another side!

Yeshua turned from me to face Simon and the others. To me, his face showed an expression of disbelief; the look that is shown by one who discovers a flawed gem.

"Simon, of you I would have thought differently. You will be my greatest trial. It's to your heart Satan causes you to listen, not the will of God."

He turned to address the followers of John. "Hear me: that which must be cannot be disturbed for my personal desires. Go tell John that which he desires I cannot give, but be not deceived, blessed is he whosoever is not offended of me. Remind him again of the things he has already heard, and tell him I have knowledge that which he has started is sufficient unto the end."

"This then is the word we will take to John," Dan said, and he and his companion left the crowd for their journey to Fort Machaerus. Some who listened to this exchange started to fall away from Yeshua - they mumbled about the lack of attention they would receive if they were imprisoned. Some left that same hour to look for another claiming to be the Messiah as these were times of fierce nationalism; many of us wanted to be counted for our God and against the heathen gentile, but few wanted passivism over retaliation.

After the messengers left, Yeshua spent time extolling John and explaining his place in the Kingdom of God. But those who heard understood little of this, and neither did his disciples nor I.

It greatly confounded me that he didn't address these things about John while his followers were present. It was obvious to me that they weren't going to leave John for another, even Yeshua. So why hadn't they been privy to these good words about John? It was a thing I marked to consider later.

SELECTION AND PLEA

Yeshua turned away from the crowd and then turned back again to suddenly say, "Stand to - I would have a word with Judas alone." He motioned for them to stay and for me to follow to a place much above the rest. As I turned to follow, I could see expressions of jealousy and hate moving across the faces of the others.

"Judas, the time has come to chose some to be sent out among the people - some to carry the word and action of God through me. Many it cannot be, few it must be. And Judas, those few must be without serious flaw, even as a Passover lamb." He continued to climb up the hill as he spoke. Finally, he stopped and turned to face those below.

"Judas, look at them. Some are there to learn, some for personal gain, yea, even some with thoughts of war, each believing his turn of mind holds the real meaning and acts given to the Messiah." He turned toward me; I said nothing. As I stood facing the crowd below me, I noticed they were milling about even more. They were impatient and seeking answers from one another as this wasn't why they were here - to be held at bay. As they milled about, those men most familiar with Yeshua formed four groups of four - sixteen in all. All were plainly visible to me here on the knoll with Yeshua.

Yeshua continued, "The past night I wrestled with the selection of those few I must ordain. I looked inward with my Father to gain the foreknowledge to select, and select well. There are sixteen of those below us in four groups who will remain true, although some will barely make a mark in history, and because of this, be stripped of their rightful identity to finally be merged with others to form a new person with two names. You, Judas, are the seventeenth, and this I know - your identity will never be stripped from you and no other will carry your name or deeds! Your name will be linked to mine forever. There will be no mind that thinks of me that will not think of you." His eyes became like dark brown pools reflecting his sincerity and concern, but I couldn't tell whether from concern for me or himself. I still said nothing.

"Yes, Judas, there will be those who will use my name to curse others but not so of yours. To you, I reveal those I have chosen, mark them well as many will confuse them. Some will call them differently and Satan will cause some past honors to them not deserved." He turned again to view the milling crowd below us. Some of the early followers were clustered together and talking rather animatedly about something not clear to me at this distance. I couldn't help but think it was about me and why their master had chosen me to share things withheld from them. I still held my peace.

"Some you've had dealings with before, while others not so. These names carry with you always as you would carry your ciphers and sums. Simon, whose name I dislike, and Andrew, his brother, stand even now facing us in the most distant group. Bartholomew is to his right, while Thomas stands in front of Simon with his back to us. Bartholomew and Thomas you don't know, so mark them well. The group to the right is standing with John, whom you know, and to his right, James, my brother who believes in me. To his right and facing John is another Judas, and who also left the family to join me. And to his right, is Simon the Canaanite, a man of true birth. Notice, there is no peerage here, Judas. Each man has his chance to be what he will."

He turned and raised his arm to point to the left and third group.

"The group to your left is headed by James, the brother of John and son of Zebedee. Both of the Zebedee boys have voices like thunder; they command attention wherever they speak. To the left of James and facing us is Matthew. See how much he looks like the man standing to his left? That's Levi, and many times people confuse the two even when they know them well, so take care on this, Judas. The one remaining in the group and to the right of James is called Simon the Zealot - he has connections with the freedom fighters."

He dropped his arm and motioned to the group of four just below us, as he continued. "Philip you know, and he stands facing us in this group directly below us. To his left is one called Thaddaeus, and to his left, is Leddaeus; these two are destined to be confused and neither are extremely demonstrative. The one facing Philip is Nathanael, who is often mistaken for Bartholomew, although they are very different in looks and actions. There, Judas, you now know the people I will call to carry my teachings to all they can reach. You, Judas, have a more challenging roll in all this. It's not given to me to know all things, but in events I see dimly, you move about as a very special man among men." He ceased speaking just as quickly as he had started. My mind reeled from the sudden introductions and the mystical saying about me. Had it not been for Ishmael's sketches, all would have been strangers except John, who brought me to Yeshua.

What was this all about? Why was I permitted to know the selection even before those chosen? I could see this would only add to the ill will some might have toward me. I was about to speak when he motioned we should return to the crowd below.

"Come, we must return."

As we returned, they formed about Yeshua, all wanting to hear him speak again on the Kingdom of God on earth. It was this they wanted to know about. How the Messiah of old would someday rid them of their overseers and raise up the glorious kingdom of Israel and with it a government of righteousness. I, too, had visions of this being among the first acts of the Messiah.

"Hear me: these among you are now my apostles and leaders of faith. Those chosen will gain much but only through great sacrifice. The final choice is yours. Don't accept the call half-heartedly for nothing is gained from such a position. Consider and pray to the Father that you can be strengthened and never be given to evil. As I call you, step forward to my side or remain as you are, there is no compromise - follow me wholly or not at all."

Many, after hearing this, moved away. Only those interested in personal gain with no giving of themselves were quick to recognize this wasn't their Messiah. So the crowd was cut. Those remaining gathered close about Yeshua; some of his followers shoved others aside. I remained at his left hand and made marks on the wax tablet I had with me.

"Simon, you will be a stone to me since I don't like your name, and since there is another Simon who will follow, you shall henceforth be known as Peter. Andrew, the steady one, keep your brother in check and step now beside him." These two moved quickly to the right side of Yeshua and away from me. There was no hesitation in them, they were followers before and now wanted desperately to become apostles.

"James and John, may your voices ever roll like thunder when you speak about the Kingdom of God, yet never cause fear among the following." They, too, moved quickly to his right hand. I could see that because of their being picked early, some light of pride was in their faces. Who would be called last?

"Bartholomew and Nathanael, some will forever confuse the two of you, but among us, it will not be so. Here among us, Nathanael, your name will never be given to another."

These two moved to the right to join the others. It was then John looked about quizzically as one feeling something is wrong but not knowing what. He looked at Yeshua and me; Yeshua looked at him but said nothing. He hesitated, then broke ranks with those on the right and came over to my left. He touched my hand as he stepped next to me. It was then I realized how sensitive he was.

"Matthew and Levi, you will be the scribes for us, and many will be confounded by your works. There will be a day when only one of you will wear an appellation."

He called the rest: "James and Judas, Simon the Zealot, Simon the Canaanite, Philip, Thaddaeus, and Leddaeus; some are known to one another, others not so."

Each of these moved without hesitation to the side of Yeshua as his name was called. The rest of the crowd moved apart from us, and some showed great disappointment. Many were still filled with the excitement of the passing day.

"The one least known to you is the man to my left, he is Judas - Judas Ish Kerioth - the same name as my own brother. Him I have known for many years. His mother, Ruth, watched over me many years when I was a lad visiting Jerusalem during the Passover. He was as an older brother to me. He has shared much in the world; he has been to Rome, and he has much wisdom of the world in him. To him, I trust the purse of this young group; when he speaks of funding, his is the word for all in these matters."

The chosen few showed little emotion at this news, though all acknowledged my acceptance by Yeshua in one way or another. I hadn't expected to be greeted with brotherly embraces and the like, but the amount of reserve from the sixteen wasn't to my liking. This intimate group of men now had among it a Judean and stranger, one who wasn't one of them. The feeling of "wait and see" before total acceptance was apparent. Only John, the caring one, and the one that brought me to Yeshua, came forward after the announcement and gave me the kiss of friendship and brotherly love.

The rest of those present, nearly forty or so, milled about like sheep without a shepherd. Some shouted for Yeshua to attend to their plight; some, who were ill, cried for help. Before we left that afternoon, Yeshua had the disciples go among the crowd and form them into small groups. Those ill and in discomfort were brought before him and he healed many, and spoke words of encouragement to those seeking guidance in the search for a Messiah. To those seeking self gratification, he warned of the fruits of such mundane thoughts. What he said to all wasn't known to me as I wasn't near when each was brought forward to have him lay hands on them. Toward evening, all but the sixteen had gone.

"Master, what shall we do now that the day is near at end?" asked Simon. He was one always interested in Yeshua's welfare and the coolness of the evening caused him to ask about possible cover for the night.

"Aye, where can we all stay? Let's pool what is in our purses and find lodging," said one from the far edge of the group.

We moved along the path down from the knoll, Simon leading the way. Upon hearing this suggestion, some began to call out what moneys they had. There was some confusion because of the spontaneity of the act, and even though I had a quick mind for ciphering, I couldn't arrive at a true sum of that held by all.

As we came to the floor of the plain, Yeshua stopped. He turned to me and as the others gathered around, spoke these words: "It's good that you have considered this a common cause and offer your monies freely. Judas will accept your contributions and from them decide our worldly worth. He will hold the bag."

As he spoke, I moved to the head of the line and waited. After hearing his comment, each one filed past he and I. In so doing, they gave to me what little they had in their purses. When it was all done, I was surprised how little was their worldly worth. It took but a short time to count the coins.

"The total is not equal to that of a pair of doves," I said in disbelief.

"What would you have us be, Judean, rich merchants from Rome?" rolled the thunderous voice of James. I looked up to see he was not smiling. I could sense that these men were not going to let me forget that I wasn't a Galilean.

I held my peace, but nonetheless knew that some of these men weren't without goodly incomes from the fishing trade before they came to join Yeshua. At least five weren't poor in the same sense of those in their own cities. Simon, Andrew, James, and John still had vested interests in the fishing trade through their families while Levi was rich enough to be discussing his taxes with the tax collector when he was called by Yeshua. At least this much I remembered from Ishmael's letters to me in Rome.

I had the feeling that some were dissatisfied with the arrangement of me holding the bag of the group because they never knew just how much I contributed. This they all knew - I couldn't be absconding with any of the money for there wasn't enough to cause even the poorest thief to chance the deed. No, it was the lack of knowledge of my stake in their cause that really bothered some of them. Was I as committed as they? Could a Judean ever be trusted? Oh, I recognized their problem and foresaw someday it would cause them to declare against me.

"Come, let us return to Capernaum; those who wanted to declare me the King and Messiah are gone." Upon hearing this, I wondered how he knew this as none came to tell us so. Yeshua turned and moved down the trail toward Capernaum.

As we moved down the roadway, the sixteen fell into groups expressing hidden preferences, likes and dislikes, personalities, and background histories. I found that I was alone for most of the walk back to Capernaum. This didn't bother me as much as the sudden feeling of homesickness for Ishmael, and even my dear servant, Apius. It wasn't only a sudden longing but one of personal awareness of these both - the feeling that they were indeed very near. The impact was so great that I raised my eyes up and looked ahead, half expecting to see one or both waving at me in the distance. Ah, it was not so, but I marveled at this sudden excitement and decided to mark it even as I do now.

We came into the city in the afternoon. The populace moved about at their common tasks, and none seemed excited to see eighteen travelers go by. To their eyes, we were a common lot - there wasn't anything that set us apart from the others - or so it seemed to me.

We approached the center of the city in a short while and as Simon led the way, I could only surmise that he would again lead us to the cottage of Tirzah. I felt somewhat strange, for such a group as we had now to move on the house of a widow, and this without announcement or coin of any degree. It was Simon who made the decision; it was he who had the confidence of our acceptance into her home.

As it was, the individuals in the group changed position and I was near the front. It was here, near the old marketplace, that a young woman stepped from a small alcove to cause us to stop to avoid a collision with her. I could see, as the other's also, that she was a strange woman - a woman of the world. She wore no veil, and bore the mark of fire - she was a prostitute.

James and John forced her aside with their staffs as she was unclean and practiced a profession that was an abomination unto the Lord.

"Stand aside, can't you see our teacher comes?" asked James in a voice that rumbled as he spoke. But she trembled not, nor did she blush when she looked into his eyes.

"Oh, sirs, don't force me aside! I'm seeking one called Yeshua. I've met nearly every group coming in this way from the hills to find him. Give me this courtesy, tell me, is he among you?" She had a fine voice and was fair to look upon. It twisted my heart to know that one so young and comely should be in such straits, but the law was hard against such who practiced prostitution.

The group came to a halt and stood near but not touching the woman. Yeshua, who heard the young woman's words, moved near to her and looked with some compassion on her - this I could see from where I stood.

"I am he." His voice was much softer than either of the two Zebedee brothers.

"My lord, look upon me with favor and hear my plea."

"Say on," he answered. There was a murmur among the group; this wasn't the accepted practice for a teacher. Usually a prophet and holy man would move across the road to avoid closeness with the unclean. Here he stood speaking with this strange woman.

"My lord, some say you are a holy man and the Spirit of the Lord rests upon you, and though I haven't heard from your lips such things, other's say you speak forgiveness even of those not acceptable unto the law." She looked away as her voice broke.

"I'm the daughter of an indentured servant. My father had only daughters, and when he was forced into great debt, he sold himself into service - this even before I was born. When I was young, I was sold by the master - who wasn't of my father's house - unto prostitution. These many years I have found it intolerable and desire to be freed from this great sin." Here she could not contain her tears and turned away again to avoid showing of her shame and sorrow.

The group, to a man, smote their breasts in recognition of their pity for this woman. Some moved to a better position to hear - I also moved to gain a better view.

She said on, "I have appealed to the priests, but to no avail. They point to the transgression of the law and not the way to grant forgiveness. Even as it is written, 'Thou shalt not bring the hire of a whore into the house of the Lord,' and therefore they will not accept my penitence, nor will they accept an unblemished lamb if touched by me. Oh, Master, what am I to do for forgiveness, for I would be clean." She hid her face in her hands and fell to her knees in front of him; she was completely undone.

"Hear me, in the Lord is forgiveness for all sins; it's written, 'Saith the Lord; for I will forgive their iniquity, and I will remember their sin no more.' Truly I say forgiveness is yours because of your contrite heart. Give me your penitence, and I will see your sacrifice is brought to the temple within the law. Have faith in me; from this day your sins are forgiven you." He stepped forward, took her by the hand, and raised her from the ground.

Upon hearing his words, she stopped crying and from the fold of her garments, she gave him the amount set by the law. He in turn gave the sum to me.

"Now go in peace and sin no more." He turned away from her. She stood nearby for sometime with an astonished look on her face; she seemed not to know what to do. Suddenly, she ran from us to disappear into the alcove from whence she came.

"Yeshua, what shall I do with this money, for by law it is unclean, being the hire of a prostitute?" I asked still holding the coinage in my hand. I held no great fear of the sum for I had seen money from greater evil than this pass from one man to another. The question was, how was this forgiveness to be accomplished? This same thought moved about the rest and they murmured about the strange woman and what it all meant.

"Isn't the lamb and goat the expiation for sinful man? And how does the priest come to know who is sinful and who isn't? Isn't it man who knows he is sinful who brings the sacrifice? Even so, this woman is mindful of her sin and this a gift of God; so it must be. Hear me, when she knew of her sin and resolved not to be part of it anymore, she was already forgiven. It's now for us to satisfy the law. Tomorrow, one of you will take the penitence to Jerusalem and there present it to the Lord to cover the law, for so it's written." After he spoke, he moved on through the city and the seventeen followed.

I knew then I would be the one sent to the temple; this was to me the answer to the longing to see Ishmael and mother that came over me sometime before. My heart sang with the thought of seeing my family again even though I had been away only a few days.

Simon led us to his mother-in-law's cottage. She, although totally unprepared for such again, opened her home unto us. The evening meal was prepared and served. Evening prayers were said and all found resting places for the night. Yeshua, as the guest, went to the little room on the roof as he had before.

Simon greeted his family with a show of love. From where I was inside the small courtyard, I could hear all wasn't well in his household. Simon told his wife that he was a chosen one and would be following Yeshua from this day on. I could hear the words between them, as could the others.

"And my husband, who is to provide for your family while you are gone? Where does the writings of the prophets say you should abandon your family to follow a teacher? Isn't it the first law of man, that he should leave his parents and cleave to his wife? Is God so changeable that he now says you can leave your wife and children, his gift to you, without care, to follow an itinerant teacher?" Her questions tumbled from her lips like water over a falls. She was loud enough for all to hear.

"Woman, don't speak to your husband so! Yeshua isn't an itinerant teacher, he is the Messiah! Do you understand - the Messiah!" Simon spoke these words as if they were self-explanatory to the listener, but this was far from their effect.

"The Messiah, the Messiah, that's all I've heard all my life, and where has it gotten you? You have left a good fishing trade to go off roaming in the land with someone you say is the Messiah. It may surprise you to know that others are claiming the same thing about other teachers. You leave me and your family and I will bring just cause against you before the Sanhedrin!" She was not to be put off. I, like some of the others, covered my head with my robe and vainly attempted to sleep. They continued to argue about this cause for separation. The more I heard, the happier I was that I was not a married man.

I couldn't help but think of the young woman we met on our way into the city. She was good to look upon. Soon the action of the day fell heavy upon me and I fell asleep, even though Simon and his wife continued their domestic quarrel.

When morning came, some things were immediately apparent. One, that I was cold, stiff, and hungry; and two, I wondered who would go to Jerusalem; and three, who had struck the final blow in the quarrel.

After morning prayers and ablution, Tirzah brought some warm cakes with honey to each of us. I was very grateful for the food and gave thanks to both she and God.

No word was said about the quarrel heard in part during the night, yet neither Simon nor his wife gave any indication all was well. Soon after the morning meal, the group formed near the gate awaiting Yeshua.

As we waited there, a young man came to the gate and struck it soundly with his staff. Simon, who saw to these things, moved to answer.

"What do we have here?" asked Simon of the lad.

"I'm Nadab, the servant and runner for Simon the Pharisee of Capernaum. He has word that the teacher Yeshua is here. My master offers his house to your master and desires his presence at a small banquet, as he has heard of his deeds among the people. I'm commissioned to wait for an answer." The lad knew his place and didn't attempt to enter. "He has word that he is here."

Simon was suspicious by nature and didn't like the idea of Yeshua being invited anywhere without some of his disciples - a matter of protection, he said.

"I see your master has a good name, as it's as my own. Yeshua is here and I'll tell him your master's offer, but did your master say if he alone was to come, or can he bring guests as well?"

"He said no word for or against such. I have no authority to deliver such freedom, but this I know, my master is a generous man and has never refused guests of any man." The lad was loyal to his master and thought highly of him by his words.

"Good, so be it. Stand to, I'll take the offer to Yeshua." Simon left the gate and strode into the house. It wasn't long before he came back again to the gate. "Here is the word of our master, he accepts and will attend the banquet. We will be accompanied by four followers, do you need their names?"

"No, the number is sufficient; places will be arranged for all." At that, Nadab turned and left the gate. Then he turned again to Simon.

"Seeing as you don't know the city, I will return and lead you unto my master's house. Until then, God be with you."

"Aye, God *is* with us," returned Simon. I thought it curious and marked it well.

It was a good thing the lad offered to lead us to the house of Simon the Pharisee, as we found it wasn't an easy route through the city to his house.

Yeshua remained in study and prayers a good part of the morning. Toward noon, he sent one of Simon's sons to have me come to him in the garden at the rear of the house. It was there I saw him sitting on a small bench.

"Good morning, Judas. I trust you slept well."

"Aye, as well as one might on the ground at this time of year. I find my bones aren't as they once were, and I'm less adapted to this life than that in Jerusalem."

"Wonder not, Judas, as I've chosen you to go to Jerusalem and execute the sacrifice for the strange woman that approached us yesterday. I know of your longing to see your people, and this will be the answer to both conditions." He and I always spoke as dear friends more than disciple and teacher.

My heart jumped at the news.

"Very well. I cannot deny I long to see Ishmael, as it's hard for twins to be separated. I would bring Ishmael with me when I return. I would that he become one of us." I gave him my hand. "My needs are simple so I can be ready and on my way soon."

"Hold Judas, I would that you accompany me to the house of the Pharisee this afternoon. I've selected Simon, James, John and you to come along. So you won't leave for Jerusalem this day." He smiled to see my reaction to his news. I studied him some as it was the first time I'd seen him smile since arriving.

"Ah, it's good; it's my pleasure to join you." I remarked with some feeling.

"Till then, Judas," and he turned to his studies, and I left feeling more accepted than before. I was chosen among the many to move in the select group of James, John, and Simon. I wondered just what they thought of this Judean moving into their circle.

I left, and like the others, prepared for the banquet by washing body and clothes. I wouldn't disgrace Yeshua by appearing at the banquet unclean either in body or spirit.

The rest were told of the banquet and who were to attend and who weren't; those not were instructed to remain near. Some quietly spoke out against their not being included.

When the mid-day hour was near, the lad, Nadab, approached the gate. We joined him and he led the way through Capernaum to the Pharisee's house. This was a house similar to all others, but somewhat larger. This man was of goodly means. We entered the foyer and was brought into the main hall. To our surprise, some were already gathered and at places around three tables.

"Why weren't we greeted by the servant with water?" I whispered to John. I was of the old school and felt ill at ease stepping into a man's home without first removing sandals and washing my feet. But in this man's house, no one came to do this menial task. Since it was his house and his to rule, I would not breach the etiquette by asking for such washing.

"It's either the mark of forgetfulness or ignorance of good manners to treat our master thus," he whispered back. I could see color rising in the neck of Simon and knew that he also had noticed this irregularity in courtesy. I was afraid he would react in bad taste, but I saw Yeshua touch his hand and Simon relaxed.

The house servant showed us to our couches and we took our places; I was on a couch near the feet of Yeshua, while the others were separated from us at another table. The talk was mostly of local matters and I began to wonder why Yeshua was even asked.

ACT OF LOVE

After some time, the talk suddenly became guarded and most present turned to look toward the entrance to the main room. Coming into the room was the strange woman we met just the day before. Some mumbled but all seemed to accept her without accusing her of misdeeds. I was well aware then, that she was known to the master of the house in more ways than one. Yes, to me, many of these men weren't above reproach; she entered a Pharisee's house - a man of the law. Here was an anomaly.

She walked in grace; she was no common woman of the street. She removed her sandals before entering the house and yet she wore no veil. She wore clothes of good style and cost. She passed the master of the house, made a salute to him, and walked directly to Yeshua. The room was silent now. What was her purpose?

I could feel some leaned forward to be sure to mark the reaction of Yeshua. Here was one heralded as a teacher filled with the Spirit, and they wanted to see his reaction should this woman touch him. Not only did she touch him but she broke into weeping quietly as she did so. All those present knew her great happiness; those not with us didn't.

The chief of those not aware of her great joy on finding Yeshua was the master of the house. Although he did nothing to prevent her from continuing her will and ways, his face showed his disapproval. The rest of those in the room, upon seeing his face, also murmured against this scene being played in front of them.

The woman continued unconcerned. She was greatly overcome by the realization of the forgiveness of her sins the day before, and now wept and, while the guests of the banquet watched, let down her hair and wiped the tears from Yeshua's feet. I noted each tear left a white spot on his feet. This reminded me of the removing of sin from the soul of man. I was overcome with the act of the woman and marked it well. She continued until his feet were free of the filth of the roadway. She opened a small vial of fragrant oil, applied it to his feet, then kissed them. After awhile she rose, placed her hair in the style of the day with the pins removed before, bowed again to the company, and prepared to leave.

Then Yeshua stood and took her by the hand and said to her with all listening, "Your sins are forgiven you even as I have said." She then left with a look of one in love.

The master of the house continued to look with disfavor on the comings and goings of the woman.

"Master of the house, I would have a word with you," said Yeshua.

The master of the house, Simon, stepped over to Yeshua's couch.

"I can see by your face that you don't approve of this woman's acts to me and me to her. Is this not so?"

"Aye, for I have been told by some that you are a man of God and full of the Spirit. This scene causes me to wonder if this is so, or have I been deceived. It's known to us and also to you this is a strange woman, and from the scriptures, she is held to be unclean. Isn't it so that all Godly men and priests are to consider her so, even as it is written? So say on that I might learn, right or no." Many of the others now had moved from the reclining position on their couches to sitting the better to see and hear.

"I should remind you of your lack of courtesy. Neither I nor my companions were greeted with the kiss of friendship upon entering your house. Neither was I anointed with oil, as the guest of honor. No servant brought water for ablution. These things are not above the acts of good taste. But she, finding me, did all these things and more. Not because of custom, but because of love."

Yeshua stopped for a moment to see the reaction of these accusations, then continued. "I would tell you this, and hear your answer. There was a certain creditor who had two debtors, the one owed him five hundred pence, and the other fifty. And when he found they couldn't pay, he freely canceled the debts unto them. Now, Simon, tell me, which of them do you believe will love him the most?"

"Given no other parts to the story, I would think the one he forgave the most," Simon said.

"You have chosen rightly. You saw the woman did you not?" Yeshua waited. Simon the Pharisee, nodded. "You saw her wash my feet with tears and wipe them dry with her hair. I was greeted with no kiss when I came into your house. And, as an honored guest, my head wasn't anointed by your servants. Yet this woman, who wanted to show her gratitude, kissed my feet. Now this I say unto you, although her sins are many, and she isn't accepted in society because of the law, her sins are forgiven her for she had turned away from them and loved much."

Simon the Pharisee, dropped his head, for he knew he was in error, but his face showed that he couldn't accept the call with all those present. He turned and told his servants to dismiss the company, and so it was that we left the house of the Capernaum Pharisee. As the company left, I could hear some question others, "What manner of man is this who can forgive sins?" These things I kept and pondered them in my heart.

As we walked away from the house, we were again accosted by the strange woman.

"Hear me, master, I am without hope. I have no desire to return to my former abode and profession," she hesitated, looking at the four of us, "but I have nowhere to go that I am not known for my past. I appeal to you for help." She stood before us with eyes downcast. She had won the hearts of us for the tender act of love she had completed in the house of the Pharisee.

"Woman, what is your name?"

"Salome," she answered.

"It is well," said Yeshua, "your name will now be Miriam. I have a friend in Jerusalem who will take you in. Her name is Mary Magdalene. If you can be ready by the morrow, this man, Judas, will escort you to her. She has many friends who will give you a new start in life."

This bit of news came as a shock to me and those with me, as well as to her. I had no thought of taking anyone along to Jerusalem, let alone a woman! But it was said and she accepted with kisses on Yeshua's hands. She left on the run to gather her things and later came to follow us at a distance so that she wouldn't cast a shadow on Yeshua. Thus, we moved along the streets of Capernaum to the house of Tirza.

Late that evening, Levi, who was a man who understood figures and sums, as well as writing, came to me.

"Judas, I'm curious about this day, as I see a woman with you all. She is even now in the house with Tirza. Who is she and why is she here?" Now, Levi was a good man and not afraid to speak his mind. While others remained in the background and talked among themselves about this thing, he came forward to ask and end the suspicious talk. He was one who carried no tales or rumors.

I told him I was grateful that he asked about the day and proceeded to tell him in detail of the events. I didn't know then that some others would tell the story differently, and claim their story was the correct one and mine false. But this is another story.

After I told him things as I saw them to be, he was relieved, about what I never knew, and thanked me for my information. It was later that I learned he, too, maintained a journal of these happenings.

CHAPTER SEVENTEEN

A Commission And A Trap

The evening and starlit night passed without incident. The morning light brought the call to early morning Shema and I prepared for the journey to Jerusalem. While doing so, I reflected on the difference made in my plans by the presence of a strange woman now known to me and the others as Miriam. I had never traveled with a woman as a companion before, and wondered what must be done by me for her comfort and safety. To my surprise, before I completed my preparations, she came from the cottage, baggage in hand, such as it was. She was ready and willing to leave within the hour.

"Rest easy, I have some things to do before we leave," I told her and moved to the house to speak once again with Yeshua. He was finished with morning prayers and had moved into the garden.

"Yeshua, something isn't set aright. I still have the purse of the group but I'm going away. I would have you select someone else to carry it until my return." Although it sounded like a command, it wasn't meant to be so. He understood my remark and made no indication that it displeased him.

"This should be done, Judas. Give the bag and all that is in it, less that given to us by Miriam, to Levi. He is a shrewd businessman like yourself and will give us good advise. Yes, it shall be his honor." He returned to his studies and with a wave of the hand dismissed me. It was obvious he wanted no more to do with the trip and Miriam.

I searched for Levi soon afterward. I found him still at morning meal.

"Levi, I am away to Jerusalem, and have been instructed by Yeshua to give you the bag. It's yours to care for. Here it is with all the coins given to me less that of Miriam." I gave Levi the purse. He accepted it with some satisfaction. He was a man of good habits and a good command of the flow of funds. Although he wasn't a publican, he had set at the tax table for many friends and business associates to save them from the ruinous gouging of the tax assessors. It was his frequent trips to the tax table that caused some to believe him to be a collector of taxes. Although he tried desperately to erase this impression, it remained. It seemed to be a private joke among them, addressing him as "The Publican."

"I'll hold these spendthrifts to a fine line. There will be no frivolous spending while I hold the strings!" He was of good spirits, yet there was something about his words that rang true, and I was happy to be away.

The group gathered at the gate to see us off. Several not present at the first meeting and the banquet didn't understand what this was all about. I accepted the good wishes for a safe journey from those that knew, and ignored the slights and words of the others.

With Miriam at my side, I strode from the cottage gate through the streets of Capernaum. We passed the inn I had stayed at before. A strange longing came over me to see the inside of the inn once again. I turned into the inn and Miriam followed. As I stepped into the darkened room, it took a moment for my eyes to become accustomed to the dim light. My heart stopped, for I beheld the form and features of Apius! There he was, even as I imagined just the day before. Neither of us made any cry, but stepped together in a firm and brotherly embrace. I couldn't have been happier to see anyone other than Ishmael.

"Ah, Master Judas, it is good to see you again!" were the first words from Apius. His face was as wet as mine. I moved to arms length to have a better look at him. I could see for the first time he was aging, his beard and hair were nearly white now, and the wrinkles creased his face deeply - the realization of this nearly broke my heart. Why hadn't I noticed this before - after all, I had only been away a short while. He had been a young man when I was a lad of ten; the years had taken his youth even as they had mine.

"Oh, Apius, our faithful servant, how I longed to see you these days." I said as I guided him to a corner of the inn. "Rest here a moment for I must take care of my charge."

I brought Miriam into the same area and could see his expression change as he saw her. His brows knit together as he puzzled the woman and contemplated the meaning of her being with me. I said nothing for a moment, and then introduced her.

"Miriam, this is Apius, truly the finest soul among men. He has been with our family many years and was my greatest teacher of all manly things. Apius, this is Miriam - my charge to take to Jerusalem. She is to be delivered to Mary Magdalene forthwith."

Miriam said nothing but saluted Apius with respect and he returned the salute with honor. Here was a good beginning of the trip. But what brought Apius to Capernaum?

"Ah, dear Apius, there is some mystery about your being here, and it causes me some worry. I hope it's not some fault of mine." This I said in a lighthearted manner, at the same time fearing the worst.

"Don't worry. All is well at home. But Ishmael couldn't stand the loneliness and sent me to find you. He would hear of your adventures even if he couldn't be with you." He paused and showed the little twinkle in his eyes that used to mean his happiness. "But now that you are coming home, and this will be a surprise, he will be happy again."

There still was something strange in his manner and speech; I waited. The innkeeper came by and I ordered some wine for us.

"Did you come alone, you rascal?"

"Yea and nay," he said, still being evasive, "I came alone in person, but on the order of Ishmael, I brought an extra horse. His plans included a scheme for me to bring you back home - willingly or unwillingly." He chuckled a little at the thought of his little game - he was attempting to play. It reminded me of the many times he entertained Ishmael and me with riddles. He always had many interesting little word games for us as lads - they were his delight - these games of logic. It was these studies in thinking that made me see life and religion differently than others.

"Come, you schemer, tell all!" I begged. This I knew would be worth hearing.

"'Tis nothing - really! You know Ishmael, the dreamer he is. He gave me instructions - capture Judas and bring him home." He laughed at this. "His idea was to find you and get you drunk and bring you home across the back of the horse."

"I'm shocked that you would even entertain such an idea, Apius!" I remarked in feigned indignation - but I couldn't keep my mouth from turning up at the corners. Miriam, who stood nearby listening, look worried.

"This I didn't do, Judas, but you know how your brother and mother are when taken by an idea. They aren't easily put off. So I came, not to follow their instructions to the letter, but to learn of your life with these followers of Yeshua." He turned from me to look more closely at the girl beside me. He was a little more curious about her.

"Well, many plans of men are thwarted by the hand of God. You needn't use the song of wine to call me to Jerusalem." We talked of what to do. With the two horses, the trip home would be more comfortable and quicker. Yet, the woman, what to do about her?

"Apius, did you perchance bring gold with you?"

"Aye, and more than enough for our needs."

"Enough for us to gain the use of a donkey?" My mind had been considering the purchase of an ass for the girl; thus we would all be mounted.

"Aye, master," he was quick to see what must be done. He rose from the seat. "I'll secure one at the marketplace and we can be on our way."

"Good, we will stay here."

So it was that Apius went to the center of the city and returned soon with a sturdy animal. He had seen to its needs and had purchased soft riding blankets for the girl to use.

The day had moved through the morning and the mid-morning mealtime approached. Although our needs were small, some food was in order before starting for home. We stayed at the inn and prepared for the trip, indulging in a small noon meal. Apius saw to the animals and rations for the next leg of the trip.

Apius held that we should take a route from Capernaum through Magdal, Tiberas, Agrippina, to Scythopolis. This was a distance of nearly thirty miles over some of the best Roman roads. Here we should rest the animals as the time should be near sundown.

The time on the road was spent in conversation about home and the goings-on in Jerusalem. Apius told me that Herod, even as the followers of John said, moved John to Fort Machaerus. Not only that, but had sent out an edict that all his followers should be arrested and brought in for questioning. Herod was pressed by Herodias to consider all those associated with John's insurgents and attempting to gather the people against him. So many of John's followers were even now in prisons awaiting the people knew not what.

Miriam rode some distance behind us, and although she listened, showed no interest. She smiled when spoken to but offered no comments on her own. She was one subject to being seen but not heard. I noticed when our conversation shifted to the family and stories about the household, she drew closer the better to hear. When Apius told of mother's activities and her secret circle, Miriam listened intently, though spoke no word.

Our time should have been better, but the donkey wasn't one to be forced and the passenger he carried wasn't used to riding the animal as well. Apius solved some of the animals balkiness by fastening a line from the donkey to his horse. With this done, the donkey seemed more cooperative.

With the lowering of the afternoon sun, the city of Scythopolis came into view over the hill. The trip was pleasant enough for this time of year, and I was grateful that I wasn't walking these miles. Apius had already planned what should be done, and was a master of obtaining accommodations in any city. Scythopolis, although good sized, held no fear for him. With my consent, he rode ahead at a faster pace to arrange nights lodging for us; I trusted his selection without question.

While he was gone on ahead, Miriam and I had time to become better acquainted. She told me of her life as the daughter of a servant, and her family before their indebtedness caused their loss of freedom. Although it was unlawful for a Jew to hold another as a slave, it was lawful for one to accept the placement of indentured servants. Especially if this indenture saved possible slavery of a fellow Jew to a stranger - that is a gentile. So it was in this case, Miriam's father's loss was to a non-Jew, and his case was brought to the attention of another Jew who offered to pay his debts for his indenture to him. So it was that Miriam's father accepted the indenture. Because his family was part of his indebtedness, they, too, became part of the responsibility of the master of the house.

Her life there was pleasant enough until she was old enough to accept the responsibilities of womanhood. It was then she became a prostitute as the master had given her to another. All these things caused me to feel sorry for her and wish it wasn't so.

She, in turn, asked me of my life, and was surprised to learn I was a twin. She listened closely as I prattled on about my life. I was very comfortable with her and answered her questions in all honesty. The more we talked and rode near each other, the more I began to look at her differently than at first. She was not only good to look upon, but had pleasant ways about her. Her eyes, though dark, were clear and quickly registered sorrow and happiness as she talked or heard related tales from me. At times, her lips quivered as she talked of her loved ones not seen for some time. A small catch occurred in her voice when she spoke of her chances of becoming respectable again. She wanted all the things other women had - a home, husband, and family. Why was it, she asked me, that God had dealt with her thus? Was being born the daughter of an indentured servant a sin upon her even before she reached the age of accountability? Many of the questions she asked I couldn't answer from scripture or reason. She continued on with her comments. She told me her age was twenty five, and I suddenly found myself considering this difference between us - I was nearly forty-two. Why this seemed even vaguely important I couldn't guess - but there the thought was. I liked this girl, and believed she was indeed a victim of circumstances over which she had no control.

Before we reached the city, Apius came to us. He told us of his selecting an inn on the southern side of the city; hence, we could be on our way quickly in the morning. It wasn't the custom to travel at night in these parts. So it was, we traveled through the city of Scythopolis as the sun cast long shadows. It would soon be time for evening prayers, and I would be glad to be inside and have the animals taken care of for the night.

The inn was a popular one. Many of those resting there were Judeans. From their clothes and speech, I gathered they were merchants on regular routes to the cities near the sea of Galilee. As we ate the evening meal, I could catch bits of their conversations. Nearly all complained about the taxes and the unguarded roadways in these and other parts. There were too many robbers and rogues abroad these days. Most of these men were of good manners and company to one another. Though some talked in guarded tones and husky whispers, the majority were well into their wine and exhibited a relaxed mood.

There were some that had eyes for Miriam. One coarse straggler who came in late, upon sighting Miriam, considered her one of the house girls. His approach was aligned to his nature and he continued to make some noise about her presence. This continued until Apius approached him and said something to him quietly, his reaction was as one being issued an ultimatum with respect to his life. He soon finished his drink and left the inn. Apius never said anything when he returned and to this day, I don't know what passed between them - but I had my suspicions. It was Miriam who registered admiration of this act by Apius, and I secretly envied him for his act in her cause.

As the night came on, the thoughts of sleeping arrangements came upon me - this was the first night with a woman among us. I remarked about this and Miriam bravely answered she could sleep with the animals if her presence caused discomfort for us. She still felt the sting of her profession, partly because of the foregoing incident, and partly because of her own feelings of difference. Apius had already taken care of these arrangements and she was to have a corner next to us and he would sleep, as he used to with father, across the doorway to the room. He still held to the guarding of his master.

The night went quietly, though I was awakened at times by the street noises. It was a strange town with strange sounds reoccurring which brought me from a sound sleep to a half-awake condition. The sudden challenge of the night watch of someone in the street gave me such a start that my heart moved heavily in my breast. It was then I felt the hand of Miriam touching mine.

"What's this?" I asked quietly.

"Please, Judas, I'm frightened, and only desire your comforting arm to rest on," she said softly as she came near. I would feel her hair against my face as she rested her head against my arm which I had flung away from my body when I awoke. This was a new experience for me, and I didn't know what to make of it. I wondered what Apius might think if he found us thus. But the experience wasn't an unpleasant one, and I left my arm such that she could rest upon it. After awhile, it seemed the natural thing to do and soon I was overcome with sleep.

The night passed without any other happening and when I awoke, Miriam wasn't at my side. Nor was Apius present. I arose, said morning prayers, washed in water brought the night before by Apius, and moved about the room. I couldn't help but think of the incident and how pleasant it was to have Miriam's head on my arm.

"Master," came the voice of Apius from the doorway, "it's time for the morning meal and then to the road." He was a driver this Apius.

"Aye, and where is Miriam this morning?"

"She has eaten and is even now preparing for the trip."

"Have you also eaten?" I asked, wondering why I was permitted to rest so long.

"An old dog cannot learn new tricks. I've ever been an early riser, master, you know that. What food I need I've already taken." He turned to look out the window.

With all those answers heard, I sat cross-legged and ate a small portion of cheese, a flat barley cake, and took some wine. It was good to be on the way home.

The animals were ready when I finished. We moved out of the city quickly. Our plan was to make time and rest only as needed for the animals. Soon, we would enter Samaria. First, there was Salim, then the long mountain ride to Sychar. After Sychar, we would pass through some small towns until Jericho. Here we could see Fort Cyprus on a high hill; one of the many Herod had built to guard the borders of his land.

The conversation was good and the miles passed quickly. Noon was upon us while we were still on the road and between towns. We stopped to rest the animals, and secured a pleasant spot to spread a cover for the meal. The Lord had favored us with good weather. As we ate, the conversation turned to John bar Zechariah. My concern for him brought the subject to the front of our conversation. I asked Apius what he had heard or seen other than the news he had given us before.

Apius said mother had tried to secure his release once again through Joanna, the wife of Chuza, Herod's steward, but to no avail. Miriam asked about John and I told her about him - the stories about his birth, the strange way he began his preaching, his living in the desert with the Essenes, and finally, the strange way of washing all his followers. She was very quiet for the remaining part of the day.

It was late afternoon when we saw the towers of Fort Cyprus. We had come some fifty miles. Our destination, Jerusalem, lay only fifteen more miles away, but the animals and our bodies needed rest, so here we would stay this night.

AT JERICHO

The place selected by Apius was of minimal convenience. This was more of a khan than an inn. The comforts offered were few. The walls were made of stone; between the application of mud mixed with straw and palm leaves, holes left in the wall served as windows. For a price, there were separate rooms for those like ourselves who were traveling light. These rooms were positioned to the outside of the main walls, thus the noise of the roadway flowed through the openings into the sparse rooms. The rooms were little more than overnight resting places out of the weather; a stool and straw mats were all available. The dining room gave little comfort, and the entire entree consisted of dried fish, flat barley cakes, some goats' milk cheese, and a low-grade wine. I felt that Apius had done us some disservice in this selection, yet at the same time believed he had a reason for doing so, though what it was I couldn't fathom. It was my belief that he had less funds along than first said, and because of this, made less extravagant expenditures.

This building was on the road to the south of the city and would give us an early start without passing through the busy morning traffic of sheep and goats. Miriam and I found a small niche and there dined, and after prayers, prepared for sleep. Apius was uncomfortable about the animals and decided to remain with them; to lose the animals to some common night thief would end a pleasant trip. So Miriam and I lay huddled together on the single mat to keep warm and we were soon sound asleep.

Our sleep was interrupted by the barking of dogs held by the innkeeper to signal intruders. Following their noise came a rowdy group of armed men carrying torches. As they approached, I could see they were not Roman troops.

"What does this mean?" asked Miriam, now awake. I could feel her body tremble as it pressed against mine. I put my arm around her as a child knowing fear and cold.

"I don't know, but as near as I can tell in this dim light, two poor souls have been brought in from the roadway. I doubt if we would know them anyway, and therefore it's best we get our rest," I remarked as I still strained to see what they looked like. I knew the only heavily-armed troops permitted in this area, other than the Romans, were the royal guards of Herod. And because of what Apius told us the day before, I was curious to see who it was this company of guards had in custody.

Miriam slipped down and rested again on the straw mat near me. She sighed and pulled the blanket from the donkey close around her. I remained in a half-sitting position and watched the scene unfold through the opening in the wall used as a window. I could see only two in their control, one was young while the other was his senior by a goodly amount. I saw they were both bound, and from their staggering step, were near exhaustion.

Soon they were within shouting distance. The commander was a rogue of a fellow. These were ruffians in uniform, not men-at-arms. From their speech, I knew they were Idumean and not Roman or our people. These were part of the hired court guards of Herod, that was easy to see. They had no great love for my people or the Romans for that matter. Miriam started to breath deeply indicating sleep was upon her again.

"Ho there! You in the inn, come out and look to our needs," came the gravelly voice of the leader, and it was he that carried the trappings of command. The innkeeper suddenly overcame his sleepy condition and went forth to meet the ragamuffin patrol. They were close enough now to see the innkeeper salute the leader. The talk between them gave way to a noisy argument - the innkeeper held that he had little in his larder and didn't want to part with it without liberal compensation - hard coin - not promises. The officer, such as he was, claimed the King would make good any provisions and quarters they might use. The innkeeper wasn't so easily convinced and held his ground until the commander showed coin. It was an old trick of the military to demand services and provisions from the merchants on the word of the King and then never pay - many a commander kept the provisions and billet money for himself and the troops. The innkeeper was well aware of this action and held out for money on the spot. The entire company continued to approach the inn and with them the two prisoners.

I caught my breath as I recognized the two in the light of the burning brands. It was Dan and Judah, the followers of John bar Zechariah - the two who spoke to Yeshua just four days before. I could see they had both been badly treated by this group of ruffians.

My heart sank and I felt a little giddy. I was seized by anger and the helplessness of the situation. I wondered if Apius was awake and aware of this scene. There must be something I could do to save them. I stood up, trembling. Miriam awoke again.

"Judas, what is this to you?" she whispered. She didn't know of the mission of John's followers or their promise to John - a promise to bring the word of Yeshua to him.

"Alas, I must try to help them or at least find out if they delivered a vital message from Yeshua to John." I girded myself and prepared to step out to meet these men. I knew both Dan and Judah would recognize me. The question was, would they let on that they did, or would they play the game and give me the answers I wanted without alerting the commander of the company to my scheme?

"What are you going to do, Judas?"

"Don't worry, stay here and out of sight. Should Apius come, tell him I must talk with the prisoners. Tell him not to interfere regardless of the outcome." I continued to gather my robe about me for the night air was cold.

"Please, Judas, don't leave me; I'm frightened in this place." She was trembling again. I suddenly realized I was greatly drawn to her, but the quest was greater than the safety of the moment.

"Don't be afraid. Apius will be here soon, and I'm sure he will stay with you; tell him this I commission him to do. Should things get confused, he is to take you to mother's house. I cannot stay longer, I must find out what these men are up to." Saying thus, I strode out of the inn and toward the men standing over the two prisoners. I knew one thing might be in my favor - if all these men were Idumean, then it was doubtful they could understand Hebrew and I knew that either or both of their prisoners did.

When I stepped into the light of the torches, the leader turned to me.

"What is it you want, Jew? What have you to do with this? Return to your rest and cause us no hardships." He was suspicious of any other Jew. He hoped to move his prisoners quickly through the night to avoid other Jews from taking action against them. His voice was anything but pleasant. His face showed the high color of the Idumean people in the torch light. He and the rest of the company were well equipped for the taking of prisoners. I remained unshaken by his attempt to intimidate me. Yet, I couldn't believe that I, a person who had avoided any sort of personal encounter all my life heretofore, was now standing in front of a ruffian, if there ever was one, and this completely unafraid!

"Hear me, I'm a peaceful subject of Herod the King and have given you no cause to address me thus." My voice was solid and without any quaver. I couldn't believe the change that was upon me. I was almost a new person - it was like being born again!

"Have a care, I'm only interested in your prisoners. What is their charge? And how came you by them?" I was hoping I could bring him to feel his own importance enough to tell me these things. "It's a shame we don't know the exploits of our good troops these days. All we hear is the actions of the Romans."

His face changed and he became less belligerent. He looked at me for a long time, or so it seemed. Studying me, was I friend or foe? Was I one of the insurgents or no?

"Ho, the capture of these two was nothing. They were still on the road when we came upon them. But they gave us a merry chase before we caught them. Their charge is one of insurgence, they freely admitted they are followers of the one called John the washer, the one who spoke vile and villainous things about the King and his lady. It will be another feather in my cap for we have been looking for these two since they bribed a guard at Fort Machaerus. The guard is long since gone - head removed sometime ago. But these two, the cause of his downfall, were on our list, and now I have them." While he talked, his men nodded, agreeing with his every word. I knew these two were Dan and Judah without a doubt. I must find a way to talk to them.

"'Tis a fine piece of work, commander. Are they securely bound? I would like to speak with them but wouldn't want to be assaulted by them." I gave him the look of one curious but leery of getting too close.

"It's a bit irregular but I see no harm in your speaking with them. And I can assure you they are nearly immobile." He laughed again showing a set of uneven teeth.

The innkeeper came forward then with some food for the troops and this took precedence over concern about my request for the men and their commander.

"Go, speak to them if you wish, I don't care."

I made my way through the eating guards and finally came upon Dan and Judah. I motioned for them not to give any warning. I first addressed them in Aramaic for this would keep the commander from becoming suspicious.

"I hope you are aware of your awful deed. Joining with this John the washer wasn't wise." This I said loud enough that the guards heard it plainly. Then, in a lesser voice, I spoke to them in Hebrew.

"Were you able to reach John?" I watched to see if either recognized this statement. Ah, both looked up quickly - I knew they understood!

"No!" This wasn't the answer I wanted to hear, but was one I expected.

I changed my position so I could see the commander while I was speaking to Dan, "Don't lose hope, I'll try to reach him if you are held by these people. Is there any sign or symbol I must know to reach him?'" All this I asked in Hebrew.

Dan returned in like manner. "We don't know as our contact was put to the sword. Have a care, Judas, these are Godless men." I was about to continue when the commander came over - he was curious about our conversation.

"I've heard little between you and these wretches. Perhaps it's best if you stand away from them and speak louder, or even not speak with them at all." I could see my time with them was over. I must now move to reach John and give him the words of Yeshua.

"Aye, I've no further use of these unfortunates, I hope they will receive that which is coming to them."

"Never fear, these will be held in the dungeon of the palace - from them we hope to get the names of more followers of this man John." He went on, but my mind was already occupied with thoughts of their rescue or at least the delivery of their message to John. I thanked him for the opportunity to speak to them and left the area. I walked back to the inn and the room Miriam and I held for the night. Apius was with her as I said he would be. She came to me and embraced me as one does a lover. I was embarrassed as I had never known such an act by a woman before. Apius smiled at my momentary confusion.

I told Apius the complete story of these two followers and their attempt to get the message from Yeshua back to John. Apius listened intently. I told him I thought I would try to get the message to John at Fort Machaerus. His face showed great concern; he wouldn't hear of this. It was now in the wee hours of the night. The company with the prisoners moved on to a small clearing and there bedded down. I knew then that we would see them again in the morning. Apius returned to watch the animals, while we once more tried to get some sleep.

CHARGED AND ARRESTED

Sleep wasn't quick in coming for my mind turned over the happenings of the day. I tried to think of ways to free these men, but nothing seemed feasible. Why had God placed this hardship on John and his followers? Why was I always a party to these things? At last, I heard and felt nothing and sleep was my companion.

I was awakened by the rough hand of one of the soldiers. Miriam made a soft cry at seeing him standing over us.

"You there, the commander would have a word with you." In the early morning light, this man wasn't good to look upon. He held a sword in his hand and looked as if he would use it should he deem it necessary.

"Give me time to say Shema," I said.

"Save your prayer for later, you may need it more than now." He smiled at a personal joke. "Get along with you, and bring the wench along, he may want to talk to her also." He stood aside to let us pass into the morning light. I could see the commander sitting near the company of men and strode over to him. Miriam followed a short distance behind me. It was then I saw Apius moving away from the animals and approaching us.

I stood before the commander as I had the night before.

"Who are you and these with you?" He sounded even worse in the morning.

"My name is Judas bar Simon, and I'm from Jerusalem. This is my servant, Apius, a Roman citizen, and this woman is my charge." I decided not to mention her name unless forced to; it was immaterial anyway. "But commander, what is the reason for this interrogation, and what have we done to bring this about?"

"Ah, Judas, you are a clever one. You know there is one thing about being clever, you must always be sure that you are more so than others. What is your reason for being in this town?"

"I'm taking my charge to Jerusalem as I was commissioned by another. She is from Capernaum and is to be bound over in Jerusalem." This wasn't all fact, but I knew he wouldn't know the difference and it might protect the girl from questioning.

"I don't believe you, I believe you are a follower of this John, and, in fact, one of his leaders. What she is I don't know nor care, but you aren't what you say." He smiled, showing he knew something more than he let me know in that speech. I was surprised by this charge, and knew my manner reflected it.

I stood my ground not knowing what would come next. Apius had now come to stand by me and he now was wearing his broadsword. My heart skipped a beat or two as I was afraid for both he and Miriam.

"You were the only one who came from the inn to see these men and speak to them. You know what I think? I think you knew them and wanted information from them. Not only that, I think you were successful in doing so. Do you deny that you know these men?" He was a mean-looking man, and no doubt a cruel commander to his troops. What did he know, and how much?

"These men aren't known to me, but I cannot deny that in the dim light of the night torches I thought they were men I had seen on the road just days before near Capernaum. Because of this, I wanted to know what they had done. I spoke to them while you were watching. Where is the harm in that?" I felt I had to give some reason for wanting to talk to them regardless of how weak it might seem. I must take care for I wanted Apius and Miriam not involved in this, for if worse came to worse, they were my only contact with the outside world. Yes, they must not be taken with me, if it came to that.

"Hear me Jew. This I know, my man, lying in the dark near the prisoners, heard you speak in Hebrew to them. Now it was lucky for me and not so for you as he was once raised in the faith of your people. He has told me of your question and their answers. It's therefore my duty to place you under arrest with these other fellows." He stood up and motioned for his men to take me. Apius reached for his sword to prevent this act, but I motioned that he shouldn't do this thing. I was led away without a chance to tell either

Miriam or Apius another word. The guard formed up on me and moved me to a holding area near Dan and Judah.

Dan, Judah, and I were marched from near Jericho to Jerusalem at a relentless pace. We arrived in Jerusalem in one day, and I was placed in a cell in the palace.

For some reason, quite unknown to me, I was separated from Dan and Judah. My cell wasn't as bad as some of the others; this, too, seemed strange. Even so, my heart was low, here I was, moved from a man who had traveled with the elite of Rome to a prisoner in the palace of Herod. What had I done? Where was this commitment to Yeshua leading me?

I could see the light of morning through the window high above me. This was the second day of my arrest. I remembered that Apius and Miriam left me in haste and I felt that Apius, the servant of love, would take this news directly to mother and Ishmael. I felt that I would soon hear from them; it was this thought that kept me from complete despair.

The guard brought food, such as it was, twice a day. He was a humble man, and although not one of us, apparently held no animosity toward me. His was a dreary life, given to the care of both hardened criminals and political prisoners within the walls of the palace. I noticed he never spoke but simply nodded to my questions. Sometime later, I found that his tongue was cut out so that he couldn't reveal any secrets of this place. My heart went out to him, and a feeling of hate against those who would do such a thing to another human being crept in. Yet I had seen these things done before while in Rome, even some of the prisoners of war had suffered as much. These were bad times.

The cell wasn't one of great comforts but then again, it wasn't as poorly looked after as the one John was held in just a few months before. I consoled myself in this reasonableness of nature, but wished for freedom, home, and family.

The days went by slowly and I was forever expecting to see Ishmael or Apius approaching from the entranceway. Yet, it wasn't so. I started with the first day to make marks on the wall for everyday of my confinement. I judged the time for prayers and praise by the little light from the window high above me. There was no other light save for a brand on the wall that the jailor lighted when it suited him.

The routine came on slowly. I recognized I must move about to avoid complete loss of strength, so I paced the small cell. I would be ready when I was released, if ever.

At times, the loneliness was nearly beyond my strength. I prayed to the Lord to save me from this wasted life. Where were my friends and family? Why hadn't they come to gather me from this place? I received no answer to either prayers from the eternal questions about my loved ones.

It was now that I began to mentally list Miriam as one of my loved ones. Why this came to me as a proper relationship between us I cannot say, but there it was. And the longer and more I studied my strange confinement and its cause, the more mental pictures of Miriam came before me. The more I realized I was becoming greatly attached to an image so fleetingly known. Would she be waiting for me, for that matter, was she even concerned enough to inquire about me?

I counted the marks on the wall. It was three weeks since my arrest on the roadway near Jericho. What was happening in Capernaum and Jerusalem outside these walls? The guard was no help. When he was present, I could talk at him but not with him.

I was roused from a fretful sleep by a voice calling me. At first, I believed it a dream as many nights I dreamed of mother calling me to evening prayers. Slowly, I realized the voice wasn't part of a dream but of reality. I arose from the straw mat to look through the grated opening. There stood Apius and Ishmael even as I used to believe them to be!

"Judas, Judas, wake up and come to us!" Ishmael spoke softly. There was a break in his voice and I could see in the dim light tears streaming down his cheeks. I went to the opening as quickly as I could, and pressed my body against the door. Each took a hand and squeezed it warmly. The turnkey came and, between signs, accepted gold from Ishmael and opened the door. Ishmael and Apius entered the cell.

"Ishmael and Apius, how good to see you!" I embraced them again. The turnkey reset the lock and left us to ourselves. "Tell me, how is mother and Miriam?"

"What is this thing? You've placed Miriam in an honored circle of women!" He stood looking at the small cell. There was no place to sit other than the straw mat I slept on. The small amount of sunlight from the window broke the dark enough to permit recognition of the written word. "She is well and sends her love," he said with a smile.

"Who is *she?*"

He feigned a surprised look. "Mother, of course." I knew he was playing with me.

"Oh," I let my voice drop, "of course, I knew it all the time. Tell me, what has happened and what took you so long in coming to me? Am I a marked man now? Have I disgraced the name of Simon?" I would have continued but Ishmael held up his hand.

"I can't answer all these questions at once, Judas, so hear me out first and then I'll answer your questions as time is given to us." Apius rested against the wall of the cell; he looked very tired. I couldn't help wondering why, but did as Ishmael suggested and didn't ask any more questions.

"First, Apius and Miriam rode hard to bring us news of your plight. All was going well, but for the ass. He became a stumbling block to progress, so Apius commissioned a farmer in Bethany to hold and use the animal as he would for one year and then return it to us. My faith in human nature isn't as strong as that of Apius. He says the man will return the animal; I have my doubts and we shall see. Apius and Miriam made good time and came to us before evening prayers were said. Mother was greatly undone by the news of your arrest by the group of Herod's ruffians. It was Miriam who made her feel comfortable, rather than mother making Miriam feel at home. It was a case of who comforted the other more in this time of stress. Mother soon recovered and set things in motion to find where you were being held and by whom. Mother also took Miriam into her confidence and didn't send her to Mary Magdalene." Here, Ishmael stopped to gain his breath.

"I tell you, Judas, she is one fine girl, this Miriam. And, of course, she sends her love, this I know even if she spoke it not."

He moved the story along. "Mother talked to her circle of friends and they searched for you, but the palace and all in it were unaware of your arrest. Strange as it may seem, Judas, the men making the arrest weren't of this command, and even Joanna, the wife of Chuza, one of mother's most reliable sources of information in the palace, wasn't able to hear a word about your whereabouts. Nearly three weeks went by before word leaked out to members of mother's circle. It was only yesterday we found out where you were held. Many had whispered that you were with John in Fort Machaerus. It was Apius who rode posthaste to the fort and through subterfuge, managed to be assured that you weren't among those held there, and this was just a night away."

I reached out to touch the hand of Apius. He was a good man.

"Now Judas, it's one thing to know where you are and quite another to gain your release. Things aren't what they used to be. Herod, under the influence of Herodias, has written many death warrants on the followers of John, and Judas, most of these he doesn't know. They are just names on the execution papers put before him each month. Because of this, it's our great worry that unless we can remove your name from the rolls, he would sign such for you."

His voice dropped some as he said these words. He turned away for a moment. "Judas, all is being done that can be done. I have but one question. Why did you speak out in this thing? Why did you make this an issue?"

I couldn't see his face for he held his hands before it. He was greatly grieved. I felt great sorrow for him as I knew I would have felt if we were transposed in this act.

"Alas, dear brother, I cannot give you an acceptable reason for my actions that night in Jericho. I was taken by the knowledge that those commissioned to deliver the word of Yeshua to John weren't able to do so. I wasn't of their following and felt no great harm would come of my speaking with them. It was an act of God I was detected and brought to this end. I have tried to justify all things in this matter but to no avail. I feel no sorrow for my welfare. Have a care and don't become caught in this bit of intrigue." I couldn't shake the feeling I would be the cause of others being harmed. Why had I done this foolish thing?

"And what of Yeshua and the sixteen? What have you heard of them?"

"Ah, much is talked of among the people of Galilee and near towns, but here his works haven't been seen. The poor give him all power and call upon his name even when he isn't with them. The stories include many mystical happenings which some say are miracles. As for me, other than the day at Cana, I haven't seen these things."

"Hear me, Ishmael, if I'm not released from here soon, you must go and join the followers of Yeshua and bring me the stories firsthand. I must have a reliable witness of these things." I knew he would do this thing if asked.

"Aye, Judas, this I promise, if and only if you aren't released within the year."

"And I would have word about John. Is he still without the words of Yeshua?"

"This I don't know. I'm afraid to send Apius to Fort Machaerus again. It's a risky business with Herod's troops being well paid for the capture of John's followers." I agreed Apius wasn't to be sent to the fort again. I must depend on street talk for information. I thought of what John must be going through. For the first time, I really knew the pain of being deprived of freedom, friends, and family. It could break a man of lesser spirit.

During a moment of silence I could hear the turnkey coming down the hall.

"Hear me, Judas, this man is a good one and not given to betraying confidences. Never fear, we will find a way to get your freedom." Ishmael and Apius embraced me and stepped through the door. Suddenly, Apius reached down and handed me a bundle of clean clothes. The guard made no special note of this which surprised me, but later, I found he had gone through the clothes and found nothing suspicious. I was grateful for the change of raiment and when water was brought me, I washed and changed into better dress.

They left as quietly as they came; they knew where I was and how treated. It was now a matter of the Lord hearing my plea for freedom to rejoin Yeshua. I sank to the straw mat and said a prayer for them and guidance for any help that may be forthcoming. Then I turned to my side and fell fast asleep as one who worked a full day in the field.

When I was in the deepest part of sleep, I had a dream. I could see mother preparing exotic perfumes for use in Herod's court. She gave them to Joanna, the wife of Chuza; they talked of the coming of Herod's birthday. Mother spoke of the special beauty preparations she was making just for her most influential clientele. Then, she asked who reviewed the petitions of arrest made against John's followers, and who was responsible for their execution. It was known these were presented to the King once a month for his signature.

Joanna said these were reviewed by the chief steward of the King, that is, her husband. Mother then told Joanna of my arrest and how it was a mistake, that I wasn't a follower of John, but of Yeshua of Nazareth. The arresting officer acted indifferently to my statements of innocence, and had moved without authority in the matter. She told Joanna I was an honorary Roman citizen, being the adopted son of Lucius the Senator, and that it would behoove Chuza to remove the petition for my execution before it was carried out and the Procurator of Rome should hear of one of its citizens being treated thus.

I could then see Joanna become greatly disturbed at such news. She thanked mother for her graciousness in the word of advice, and assured mother that all would be done to remove the papers and initiate a writ of release as soon as possible. In addition, she was sure the officer of the little company that acted unwisely would receive reprimands worthy of his misconduct. Outside the palace, mother was joined by Miriam, whom she embraced, and the two women left the scene. My heart was rested and I fell into dreamless sleep.

When morning came, I fell on my knees and gave thanks for what I saw in the dream. Even as I believed in the dream about the release of Ishmael some years ago, I now believed this was the hand of God moving to gain my freedom. After Shema, I gave special thanks to our Father for his kindness to this unworthy wretch.

FREEDOM ONCE AGAIN

The days seemed to move slowly after the dream. It was but a few days when Apius and Ishmael came to visit once again - they were happier than before. They couldn't contain themselves. Ishmael burst forth with the news of my pending release. Ishmael told me of mother's success in managing the release and the papers were even now being drawn up. I held my peace for I couldn't reveal the story of my dream; it would have destroyed his joy and the joy of Apius, also. I knew someday I would be able to tell them.

We sat and talked of the happenings about Jerusalem. Soon, the turnkey came again, and this time, he held the release form in his hand. I had Ishmael give him a generous amount of gold for he had given me more of everything than he needed to, and this at his own risk. The door was unlocked and I moved out with my arms about two of the dearest men in my life. It was good to know that I was again free!

As we left the dungeon, we passed the cells of Dan and Judah which made my heart fall because of their distress. I stopped the guard long enough to introduce my companions.

"Alas, Dan, it's with a sad heart I leave you here, I will try to get your release if possible. Hold to your faith!" I gave them my hand and my blessings, as did Ishmael and Apius, in his own way.

"Don't concern yourself with us, it's John that is the true cause of your prayers for it's he who suffers the most." Dan was truly worried about John and had rightly expressed the thoughts of all of us. It was John's life that hung in the balance of a birthday party.

This meeting saddened us, yet we were happy enough to go to the temple to sing praises to the Lord for his goodness. It was to home and mother as quickly as possible. My, how good it seemed to me! Every noise, smell, and movement had a new meaning for me. It was as though being born again - a feeling that had come to me when standing fearlessly in front of the commander of the guards the night of the arrest. This was a phrase that would be told to me again under different circumstances later in life.

We were greeted first by the servants who were happy unto tears. Apius left us here, and Ishmael and I went into the house to be greeted by mother.

"Mother of mine, I humbly thank you for your service. Ishmael has told me of your ceaseless efforts to gain my release. No son has a more loving mother or is less deserving of her love." I knelt before her and kissed her hands. She ignored my untidy condition and embraced me and wept.

"It wasn't I, my son, but the gracious Lord that gave me the words to tell Joanna. It was these that caused her to give credence to my story. Let's not dwell on these things and I must not take all your time for another awaits your love. But before you meet, it would be well if the servants tend to your needs." She instructed them to prepare water for my bath, and new clothes to be laid out for me. The fatted calf was to be roasted and the family gathered to welcome the freed son. I rose and left with Ishmael for my room. I was much in need of a bath for prison had none.

All during my bath and care of hair and face, I kept wondering what I would do and say when I met Miriam. In a short time, I was a new man. When I entered the hallway to the garden, it was mother who met me again.

"I lost a son and now he has returned - praise the Lord - the Lord he is one Lord." She embraced me again, and I held her close for a short time, but strangely enough it was Miriam that commanded my attention!

I now beheld the figure of the girl I had brought from Capernaum standing in the noon sunlight at the entrance of the garden. She looked different than I remembered. Not the woman of the world I first saw in the street. No, mother had worked wonders on her, and before me stood one of the most beautiful women in the world, or so I thought. Mother was pleased at my recognition of her handiwork. She was also pleased with Miriam. This I could tell from the way she gently pushed me toward the garden.

I moved to Miriam; she gave me her hands. We walked to the bench near the small pool in the garden and sat down. She placed her forehead against my chest; she was so small, and her shoulders shook from the crying that overtook her.

"Here woman, this isn't the time for crying! I'm a free man again, and can take you to Mary Magdalene if you desire. As for me, I would have you stay!" I lifted her head and wiped away the tears. She smiled through brimming eyes.

"Oh, Judas, my heart was in deep despair when I saw you taken from me in Jericho. Your mother has accepted me as no other, and during this trial, has been my stay in all things. Oh, I'm but a poor, lost woman, and pray the Lord for forgiveness and love. Judas, I would be with you always." She moved toward me and I her. I kissed the tears still forming on her cheeks.

"Miriam, here is your new home. Like your new name, you will be born again a new person. You have overcome all the past and are now one of us. Come, let's go to mother and declare this thought."

We moved from the garden to a small study where mother stored many of the exotic oils and gums used in the making of beauty aids. Here, in the quiet corner of the house, she worked these materials into combinations that produced odors and skin softeners superior to any I smelled or felt in Rome. She was a mistress of her craft.

"Mother," I said quietly, "we have come to speak to you of a place for Miriam in our house." She looked up from her work and smiled, and moved her head to one side the better to hear us. It was this little gesture that made me realize that she, like Apius, was getting older. Where had the years gone?

"I would like Miriam to stay here with you."

"And Miriam, would you want to stay with an old woman?" Mother wasn't convinced that I had spoken the things in my heart, this I knew by the inflection in her voice. She knew me well, this mother of mine.

"Isn't my heart an open book? Have I tried to deceive anyone? In all my life I have desired but those things given to other women by the Lord. It's my desire to be with and to do whatever Judas may ask of me. For his people are my people and his God, my God." Miriam moved to mother's side and picked up her hand. "My family is now gone from me. I have none of my own because of an act beyond my control. This I hope to put aright, and only pray to prove this to the Lord and you."

Mother reached out and pulled Miriam close. Mother had but one daughter and had often wished for another. Here was a woman who needed mother more than any of her own, a woman once lost before God and man was now given to her as a daughter by the Lord. She couldn't turn her away - her past notwithstanding.

"It's written, 'Thou shalt not avenge, nor bear any grudge against the children of thy people but thou shalt love thy neighbor as thyself; I am the Lord.' So it is written and so it shall be done in this house. But now, Miriam, go to the room prepared for you as I would have a word with Judas alone." Miriam bent down and kissed mother as she would have her own, moved to my side and reached up on her toes to kiss me, and left the room. I wondered what Ishmael might say about all this.

"Come, Judas, sit by me for a moment." Mother moved over on the little bench she used while working at her craft. I sat down near her and waited.

"Judas, I grow old and see no sons giving me the name of their father. I have nearly lost hope for your father's namesake. Can it be true that this girl has won your heart?" she asked, reaching for my hand. She pressed it against her cheek.

"Ah, mother, I'm now forty-two years old and she is but a girl." I stammered. I could feel the color rising in my face.

"What's this? My own son doesn't understand my simple words?" she asked in mock disbelief. "What keeps the words of your heart from your lips?"

I slowly removed my hand from her grasp and stood up. I turned and walked about the room before coming back to her to say, "Dear mother, I'm confused by these feelings I have for Miriam. When I'm with her, I'm happy and when away, sad, but if this is heart or mind, I can't say! I know this, I have accepted the call of Yeshua to follow him and this for at least a year or so. During that time, I have nothing to offer any woman and don't know what this commitment means. Even that which I would - I cannot." I could see her face change from hope to near despair.

"My son, is Yeshua such a taskmaster that his followers are afraid to marry? Is his teaching above one of the first commandments of the Lord - be ye fruitful and multiply?" She was quite indignant about this possibility as to her, family was the first duty of man, and keeping alive the name of every man in Israel was a just cause.

Mother reminded me that Israel lived not by the spirit alone. It was man who carried the spirit - not the spirit who carried the man. I was astonished at her speaking thus, but she was a determined woman and through the years had often challenged interpretation of the writings even by Hillel, Gamaliel, and Shammai.

"Wasn't it Ishmael who told me that one Nathanael was married in Cana and isn't he among the followers of Yeshua? Aren't you the man he is?" She spoke again before I could gather my wits on her previous remarks. "My heart bleeds for your father - two sons and no namesake, ah, woe is me. What have I done to see these days?"

"Ah, mother, have you spoken thus to Ishmael?" I wanted to know what Ishmael said about such accusations of dereliction of family matters.

"Ishmael, Ishmael! Is he your guide to the law? His turn is coming - he will know of my sadness." She shook her finger at me. I couldn't help smiling within as I viewed this picture, a seventy-year-old mother shaking her finger at her forty-two-year-old son.

"So I take it that you want me to wed Miriam?" I couldn't help say this as I still wasn't sure Miriam had told mother all.

"Are you a priest? What have you to worry about? She is a kind soul and knows more of love than many these days. Give thanks to the Lord, as I do that she has been brought to this house. And wed her with my blessing." Mother then sat down again at her bench. I strode over to her and kissed her.

"Thank you, mother, and I'll attend to matters which should satisfy you. I've always tried to be an obedient son." She nodded and I left with much trepidation in my heart.

My head was in a whirl; what have I said? I strode quickly to my room. Ishmael was still there. In his hand was a sketch of Miriam. He had done it well.

"How goes it with mother?" he asked.

"With mother, some things are very obvious, and in addition - very direct. Ishmael, would you believe it, she asked me when I would wed, and has it in her mind that my bride should be Miriam!" I looked at him in mocked astonishment. He looked at me a long time and then turned away without speaking. I had expected more! What was this? Was Ishmael caring for Miriam and deeply so? I went to him and gently turned him around.

"What is this I see? Have you come to care for Miriam so much in just these weeks?" I studied his face closely. I knew Ishmael better than any other person in the world. His emotions were seldom hidden from me even though he often tried.

"What is there to say? From the day she came into this house, I've been her slave. I know she cares for me as well, but she will never leave your side."

"But why not?"

"Because she feels you are her first defender and wouldn't hurt you in any way. She is a good woman and I agree, Judas, I have no right to cause her love for you to lessen. Hear me, I've tried to avoid and crush my love for her, but find it tears me to do so." He was greatly disturbed but happier for his confession.

I was completely taken aback. I had forgotten the weeks she had been here and I in prison. I was even more confused at her failing to assert her wants. This was indeed a muddle. To think I was still wondering what to do, and here was the perfect solution! Although I cared a great deal for Miriam, and wished her to remain in our household, I was somewhat reluctant to wed her. I had even expressed this, although weakly.

Mother thought it was just a boyish embarrassment, but this wasn't the case. I truly didn't know in my heart that Miriam was the woman for me, or that I was ready for marriage. After all, I had just seen Simon and his wife play out a domestic scene before me just some five weeks before. Even then I had thanked the Lord that I wasn't married.

"Oh, Ishmael, go to Miriam now, and tell her of your love, and that I happily release her from any imagined ties." I stepped forward and embraced him. "Tell her I welcome her as a sister-in-law with all my heart and pray to God for her happiness."

"Ah, I'm blessed twice, one for a brother such as you, and once again, for the Lord finding me a love." He was away quickly.

Now I must tell mother of the change. I wondered if she would welcome that change as readily as I had. She would have her wish for grandsons, perhaps, God willing. And Ishmael would make a good father, this I knew.

Happy to be home, I stretched out on my bed, closed my eyes, and fell fast asleep.

Mother was more than pleased. Because of us not knowing the whereabouts of Miriam's family, mother made all arrangements and notified her circle of the coming event. The house was in a turmoil, the servants were happy for they had been waiting many years for this event. Ishmael and Miriam were greatly taken with each other and knew less of what was happening about them, or so it seemed to me.

Through it all, I thought I must go to Yeshua and soon. The stories of his healing the sick and his teaching came to me through the pilgrims that traveled to Jerusalem from Galilee and other places wherein he taught. I would remain here until after the wedding, and then go to find him and join the others.

The house took on the look of a festival. Mother was in her glory. The servants moved with great enthusiasm. All was happiness and light.

A CALL FOR A PHYSICIAN

It was during this time that Johnathan came to me with word that Apius wasn't well. This news gave me great pain for my love for Apius was like a son for his father. He had been with us since lads. I would see to him myself.

I went to his quarters and found him in no pain, but in poor spirits and a weakened condition. He had eaten little for sometime - so the other servants said. As he lay on his cot, I could see he wasn't the man he once was - even just a short time ago.

"Ah, Apius, dear comrade, what is this? Why haven't you come to me about your illness? Am I such a hard taskmaster?"

"'Tis naught to concern you, and with the house making ready for the wedding, I wouldn't disturb the household. I didn't know Johnathan went to you with this, and I'm sure it will pass." Apius was sincere in his thoughts, but my hand against his brow told me he wasn't as well as he thought, and his recovery might not be rapid at all.

"We will let Apuleius make the decisions about your condition. I'll have him come to look at you." I ordered two servants to look upon Apius and looked for Johnathan.

"Johnathan, go to the fort and seek out Apuleius. Tell him of our need." Johnathan was quick to make ready as he, too, liked Apius and was concerned for his life.

I could only hope that Apuleius was at the fort as I had heard nothing from him these weeks. I returned to the house and found mother moving about with happiness.

"Mother, I've some news that needs your attention," I took her by the arm and moved her away from the others. It's Apius. He's suffering from the fever and I fear for him. I've sent for Apuleius." She was startled to hear of her favorite servant's illness. "Tell me, mother, have you heard or seen Apuleius in these last few weeks?"

"Aye, it was he who provided me with the idea to plead for your life as a Roman citizen. I talked to him about your incarceration, and he would have come to you, but was sent out on patrol. He provided me with a writ that showed you were adopted by his father, Lucius, while you were in Rome. The writ was given without regard of the consequences, as we both know the penalty for claiming to be a citizen of Rome falsely. It was his father's seal that was placed on the writ, and I have much love for him because of this act." She then explained how all the plans were worked out that when completed, gave me freedom.

My heart fluttered as I listened. Apuleius was indeed a man among men.

"Was he to be long in the field?"

"I can't say. You know his words are few about his movements."

"Well, if he can be found, Johnathan will find him." I was still bothered by the news that he wasn't near.

I was determined to watch over Apius, and told Ishmael of my determination and had my bed moved where I could be near the old servant. He wouldn't want for anything during his illness; this I knew.

The day hadn't gone when Johnathan returned with the news that Apuleius was still out of Jerusalem, but expected soon. This he learned from some of the runners to the officers in the courtyard of the fort. I instructed Johnathan to go to the fort each morning and evening to seek out Apuleius and continue to do so until his return.

I kept my vigil alongside Apius; his condition deteriorated. He became disoriented. His mind would wander to times past. He called out warnings to Ishmael and me about boyhood dangers. My eyes filled with tears. I prayed for this good man. He was a Greek with the heart of a Jew.

Each day, Johnathan came back with his head down and told me that Apuleius hadn't returned. In desperation, we used all of the cures found among those known for fever. It wasn't enough. Apius wasn't better for it and he was getting weaker everyday.

The household was now much aware of Apius's condition and the wedding plans, though not put aside, were being done with some reserve. Ishmael came at least once a day to stand by for me, and on several occasions, Miriam came to the bedside of Apius as well. Mother, who was worried about Apius, was not one to be put aside as far as the wedding was concerned.

At last Johnathan brought word that Apuleius was on his way, and would be to us within a day. My heart was greatly relieved as I longed to see Apuleius and thank him for his part in my release.

His arrival was announced by the servants. He strode up the path to the servants quarters. He was still a handsome man, brown and trim, and walked with the step of a professional.

I greeted him outside the servants quarters.

"Ho, Apuleius! This house is yours. May you be well always." We embraced as long-lost brothers might.

"Judas, I've missed your companionship these many months. But let's look at the patient." Apuleius was a professional, and the sooner he could see the patient, the sooner it would mean a return to health. The examination was quickly done. He had grown more efficient in his days with the army. The need for quick decisions caused by the action of war had sharpened his medical skills. And the abundance and variety of traumas occurring because of combat gave him a wealth of experience.

"We must bring down his temperature. Have the servants apply wet cloths to his body. I'll leave a new potion for him. I've used it before and had good results in the cure of just such maladies." He took a small vial from his bag and gave it to Johnathan.

"Johnathan. It's good to see you again. The last time I saw you was after our arrival from Capernaum. You're looking well." Johnathan saluted Apuleius and spoke well of him. After Apuleius gave some of the potion to Apius, he gave the rest to one of the servants with instructions on the dosage and times. He turned from his patient and gathered the tools of his profession. We stepped outside.

"Judas, it's not good. Apius is well in his age, and I fear for him. I'll do all I can, but be apprised, it may not be enough." He pressed my arm. I remembered the day in Rome when he grasped my arm; he was still as strong as ever. I nodded that I understood and held my peace.

"What's this? The house looks in a festive mood. If I judge aright, I see the trappings for a wedding! Come now, Judas, have you been keeping something from me?" He smiled and continued to look about the house and gardens.

I was surprised. I had forgotten Apuleius didn't know about the recent decision of Ishmael to marry and wondered if he knew Miriam. Mother said nothing about a visit from him while I was in prison. I gathered from her conversation that a servant gave her the instructions and the writ as well from Apuleius.

I couldn't resist telling the news. "Hold on there, something is amiss." Now, it was *his* turn to be surprised, and he was.

"Ah, there must be something you aren't telling me. But first I must pay my respects to your mother." He turned and entered the house. He was completely at home here. Mother was in the garden and pleasantly surprised to see him.

She turned to greet him, "Dear boy, how good to see you. Once again, I must thank you for your guidance in securing Judas's release. I've asked the Lord to bless and keep you from harm. Have you seen Apius - what's his condition?" She was happy but reserved.

"I'm only too glad to be of service. And as to Apius, I think we can cure him, but time isn't on our side." He didn't lie to mother but held some of the truth from her by his careful wording, or so I thought.

Mother was satisfied with his answer and turned with a wave of her hand to all the changes made in the garden for the wedding. The canopy was in place and many candles carefully trimmed and in place. The time was near for this special event.

"Ah, I've seen Ishmael, but not so his bride-to-be," Apuleius said, looking around the garden - yet not expecting to see the bride - he knew the customs of our people well enough that this wasn't the time and place. "And how came Ishmael to be so lucky? I had always considered him too much in love with art to look at a woman. She must indeed be someone of rare beauty and refinement."

"Aye, that she is, and all the qualities to make him a good wife." Mother smiled as she was greatly pleased and was more than willing to show it. "I've a surprise for you Apuleius. She is in this house even now, and I want you to meet her. She's from Capernaum and Judas was bringing her to us when he was arrested." She turned and told her maidservant to secure the writ of adoption from the workroom.

"Your timely advice saved my son's life, Apuleius. Don't leave until I have introduced you to the one for whom all this is being done." Mother moved away and was soon joined by my sister, Anath. Together they continued to direct the gathering.

"What are your duties, Apuleius? Will you be free to come to this wedding?"

"Ho, I'm due some rest and wouldn't miss it for any cause. Come, let's go back to our patient and see his condition. Besides, I think we are in the way here." He turned and worked his way out of the garden, and I with him.

In the servants' quarters, they were still applying wet cloths to Apius. Apuleius held up his hand indicating they should stop. He knelt besides Apius and, studying his condition, shook his head. Apius looked better to me but it was more wishful thinking on my part.

"That's good!" Apuleius muttered as he studied Apius. "No more cooling, his temperature is lower now and the potion is working well. It's now just a matter of waiting and continuing this treatment. Make a weak beef broth and this he must take for it's necessary to build up his strength. Yes, I say, if all goes well, he should be up and around before the wedding. That is if it's not within the week."

I confided in him it wasn't to take place before a fortnight had passed. It looked like the entire world was in tune with this wedding as within a short time, Herod would celebrate his birthday. It was possible Ishmael's wedding would fall on Herod's birthday.

"Ah, never fear, Apuleius, mother will plan differently - she wouldn't allow this day to be so desecrated. Believe me, this wedding day will either be moved forward or backward to avoid such a possibility. Herod's birthday is an anathema to all good people." He nodded his agreement; we left Apius in the good hands of his fellow servants.

"Judas, who will take the place of Apius? You know he deserves continued rest after this fever. His days of hard riding and servitude are over." Apuleius was speaking as a doctor interested in the continued health of his patient. "What is his age anyway?"

"To tell the truth, I don't know. I only know the day of his birth as he told it to father many years ago. He was a young man of twenty when he was rescued by father from a slave caravan. He must be near sixty now. I will see his tasks are light." I hadn't thought about who would be my right-arm in times of stress. Apius had been for so long. "I can't say, but I know I must choose one among them."

"I would offer this, the man you brought from Rome with you is a good man and true. Johnathan, that one." Apuleius remembered his joining us when we left Rome.

"Aye, he is a good man, and has met all challenges well, but he is one of us, and there are times when it's better not so." I could remember many times and situations where Apius wasn't inhibited by religious laws and provided us service that one of our own couldn't. I wasn't sure this might be a factor to keep in mind when selecting a successor.

"If this is a point of argument, then by all means considerate it." Apuleius was now done with the matter. "Come, let's walk down the way, for I have a word for you." He turned to walk through the gate and away from the house.

We walked along in silence; I could see something was troubling him.

"Judas, this girl from Capernaum, Miriam, how did you come by her?"

In answer, I told him the story of Miriam and Yeshua in encapsulated form. He was surprised at the circumstances but was familiar enough with our customs to understand. I gave him no name other than Miriam and I thought no more of it. He continued to look puzzled but said no more and turned back to the house. As we arrived, mother greeted us with the writ in her hand. She gave it to Apuleius.

"You are coming to our wedding, aren't you?"

"Yes, dear lady, but the army being what it is, one cannot make promises." He bent down and kissed her as he would his own mother. Although it was the custom of our people to abhor and even avoid contact with the gentiles, it wasn't so in this house. Mother held that it was only through communication and reason that our people would ever avoid hardships under Roman rule. She, and those in her circle, had many friends and clients among the Romans in the city. She was a reasonable woman.

"Come to the garden, Apuleius, and meet the bride elect."

We moved into the garden, and there by the pool stood Miriam. She was more beautiful than the day before. As she became more accustomed to our household, she grew in stature, or so it seemed to me.

I heard Apuleius draw a quick breath and turned to look at him. He was pale and even though he attempted to recover, I could see he was shaken. I glanced at Miriam to see that she, too, was more than surprised to see this man before her. There was instant recognition between them. Ishmael stood beside her and held her hand. She spoke first and more calmly than I first thought.

"So this is Apuleius! My lord, Ishmael, has told me of your kindness to his brother and family." She smiled and saluted Apuleius as a member of the household.

"Well, Ishmael, you have found a rose among the weeds. I can see why you would be taken by her. I will be here to see you wed, but I must be off." He bowed and moved away without coming any closer. I followed him to the gate and to the servants' quarters. He had one final look at Apius. He strode to where his horse was waiting, placed his medical supplies on the animal, and mounted. He looked down at me for a moment.

"You didn't tell me the girl's name was Salome," he said, picking up the reins.

"No, for we had agreed to overlook her past and gave her a new name. How should I know that you knew her, and how so?" I stood stunned. He pressed the reins against the animal's neck and it responded, moving away from where I stood looking up at its rider.

"Come, Apuleius, get down and talk to me, don't leave with this a mystery." For Ishmael's sake, I wanted to know what was troubling Apuleius about Miriam.

"It's nothing that can't wait. There is no harm in it for Ishmael, of this I'm sure. Let it lay until I come again to see Apius." He then gave me a salute as of old and rode off.

I returned to the house, Ishmael came from the garden. He, too, had noticed the look and change of manner of Apuleius after meeting Miriam.

"What's this thing with Apuleius? Did he say what was troubling him?"

"No, he gave me no word."

"I feel he has been hurt by something before this meeting," said Ishmael, but the cloud slipped by and he joined Miriam a happy man.

CHAPTER EIGHTEEN

A Birthday, A Funeral, And A Wedding

The decree for the celebration of Herod's birthday to begin was read among all subjects. Friend and foe, visitor and subject, rich and poor - all were to be ready for a solid month of celebration. It was to be a gathering of many officials for nearly every province in the empire was notified. Games and other spectacles were to be provided in the hippodrome, and gala evening balls were in the offering. It was to these mother was commanded to attend. The ladies of the court were insistent that she come to all and bring with her many beauty aids. She was to sit with the elite and to see all. Yet, she was afraid there were things that were an abomination unto the Lord and these she must not see.

She set aside the wedding until the celebration and actual birthday of Herod was past. Ishmael and Miriam agreed that to wait was the better course, and so it was that the household awaited the birthday of Herod with some trepidation.

The fear for John bar Zechariah grew day by day. We had been unable to contact him or secure the release of his two followers, Judah and Dan. We had tried both money and pressure from those friends within the palace, but all for naught. John was still held in Fort Machaerus while his followers were in the palace dungeon. As near as we could find, no word from Yeshua had been passed to John. He was still without an answer to his questions of Yeshua. The guard force of the fort was manyfold and even our best efforts of subterfuge availed nothing. His fate remained in the hands of the Lord.

Time continued to move and Herod's birthday was within the week. A great many of the skilled artisans created objects for the house of Herod during this time. Ishmael sent a sculpture of one of the many fine animals owned by Herod. It was that of a horse. I thought it one of his finest works. Although we never saw it in the palace, Joanna, the wife of Chuza, said it was shown among the others. And she claimed that Herod held it high among the personal gifts he received.

The week went by and mother was pressed by the demands of the day as well as the night. She taught Miriam some of the simple operations of perfume and ointment making to give her more time to prepare the exotic formula. I could see she was becoming weary of these parties and banquets.

At last the birthday arrived. As the sun rose that morning, trumpets blared the news of Herod's day. He would have everyone know of this day. A great parade started early in the morning and lasted nearly the entire day. Of course, it wasn't as magnificent as those of Caesar, but then it would be dangerous for anyone to have a parade which was greater in size or splendor than Caesar's - many an official had lost his head for less.

Herod was a schemer and a good politician who had no fear of the God of Israel, but was well aware of our people and their respect for the high holy day. Yes, even the people's love of the Sabbath. He was careful not to force his celebration on the high priests, and invited both Annas and Caiaphas to witness his complete obedience to law of this day. He brought the sacrifice required to make atonement for his sins on this day, and it was whispered among the palace people that he gave to the temple a large weight of gold as well.

The parade was long and elaborate. It was opened by a command of temple guards followed by a course of priests. The priests were carrying lamps to light the way and give spiritual meaning to the celebration. The murmur of the crowd showed disfavor with this but they knew of the gift to the temple and thought no more about this show of false fealty. After the priests came the royal guard, most Idumean, who had little regard for the Lord. Then came mounted troops and well wishers of all countries. And finally, as though to keep the people in suspense, came the honored birthday celebrant and his wife. Both Herod and Herodias were carried through the streets of the city on a litter. Because their litter was so ornate, its great weight forced men to work in shifts to carry it and them. Teams of men would change without disturbing the flow of the parade; those not carrying would march behind the litter and rest shoulders, arms, and legs, and at the command of the leader, move like a centipede to exchange places with those carrying. It was an impressive sight.

As I watched from along the route, I remembered the noble parade held by Herod the Great when the Magi from the East came to visit Jerusalem so many years ago. This display reminded me of that parade and its ugly results afterward in Bethlehem.

Some remembered John bar Zechariah's words about Herod and turned their backs on him and Herodias as the litter past them. Even from where I stood, I could see Herodias grow pale through her makeup. She was an evil woman and bore the mark of Jezebel.

The parade continued until late into the day. When it was over, the people were free to do as they wished, though work wasn't required of anyone this day.

Back at home, I heard from mother that Herodias had a turn of heart, or so it was rumored. She had asked Herod to have John the washer moved from Fort Machaerus to the dungeon in the palace. This Herod was glad to do, for he had long felt that John's words against him were as rain off a duck's back and just as soon ignore his babbling. After all, John wasn't the only traveling self-styled Jewish prophet calling the people back to the old ways. There had been many before and would be many after; it was just a matter of ignoring his chatter about the God of Abraham, Isaac, and Jacob, sin, and its penalties. He had heard it all before. The people of Rome could care less about the God of Israel, and it was they who held the balance of his power.

He would have released John some time ago and ceased the arrest of his followers, except for the savage outburst of Herodias. It wasn't John, the people, or the Lord that Herod feared. It was Rome. To comply with Herodias's wishes, Herod sent a company of his fastest riders that same hour to Fort Machaerus to retrieve John. And so it was that John came to be in the palace on this, Herod's birthday. All these comments about Herod and his feelings about John were common knowledge throughout the palace, and mother had heard them all.

After the parade, the first of many banquets began. It brought many dignitaries from all provinces to the palace. Mother saw much entertainment - dancers, tumblers, musicians, magicians, and even storytellers.

As time wore on, the guests became bored with the entertainment as did Herod. The lamps were lighted in the great hall. A soft orange light cast a ruddy look to everyone. It was during this time of great drunkenness and revelry Herodias suggested that Salome, her daughter, be permitted to perform a dance for Herod. The king gave his permission with a wave of his hand.

A group of black slaves came to the fore and began a rhythmic beating of drums; they were joined by others on cymbals and harps. The rhythm became faster and faster until the mind reeled from the constant sound. Suddenly, it ceased and Salome burst from a curtained alcove near the throne. She stood for an instant in the soft light of the lamps. She wore a soft gown of thin material, fastened only at the neck, ankles, and wrists. Her body was only half hidden and half revealed through the thin material. Her young body was firm and supple, and slits in the material left her breasts uncovered as was the custom of the early Egyptian dancers. Her hair was in the coiffure of the Roman maids, and the largeness and softness of her eyes was enhanced by some of the ointments supplied by mother. In the orange light, she looked like a golden goddess and those seated near leaned forward to drink in this vision of beauty. Even the king stared open-mouthed at this young girl - his step-daughter and niece!

A WORD GIVEN

Salome wore small castanets on the fingers and thumb of each hand and brought them together in a sensuous rhythm while she danced. Small golden ankle bands bearing bells added to the musical accompaniment of her motion.

Her dance started with a slow motion of her hand and then her body moved slowly to and fro. The light of the oil lamps cast enlarged shadows of her moving body on the ceiling-high drapes near the throne. She moved with grace and beauty. The black drummers increased the beat in answer to her silent command. She continued to increase her motion in rhythm with the drums and brought her castanets together with a wondrous musical sound that excited all watching.

Salome danced in and about those reclining at the banquet tables; she came ever so close to each man but none dare touch her. Salome was feminine beauty personified, suggestive and sensuous. Finally, her gyrations became so fast that the eye could hardly follow. Then, in a twinkling, she darted through the curtains into the alcove near the throne and was gone. Herodias had left the throne, stood behind the curtains, and now welcomed her daughter with a motherly embrace; they were very near alike, this mother and daughter.

This sudden disappearing took all by surprise and silenced the crowd; it was uncommonly strange for an entertainer to leave the audience. They sensed she wasn't coming out again, and suddenly felt cheated of their chance to show their appreciation. There was no doubt Salome had won their hearts and they wanted to show their gratitude.

The reaction was swift; some stood up immediately and called out to the king for her to return. Others brought their drinking service together with a raucous noise. Some pulled off their jewelry and threw it on the floor in front of the curtained alcove; the slaves were quick to pick it up and pass it through the curtain to Herodias. Others shouted her name over and over - "Salome, Salome, queen of the dance!"

They wanted her to come out again and dance. Herod was proud his stepdaughter made such an impression on the dignitaries present and was interested in seeing another himself. He finally stood up and quieted the crowd. He motioned for his chief steward to fetch Salome. The steward left to take the message to her. He didn't bring her back but instead brought word from Herodias that Salome was tired and couldn't dance again. Herod couldn't hold to this and sent she should appear before him at once; his guests were waiting.

Herodias sent word that she would dance only if granted a boon. Herod was furious but kept it from his guests with wily smiles and jokes. He sent word to Herodias that he would grant Salome anything she might want up to half of his kingdom if she would only dance again.

His guests became sullen. The wine hadn't improved many of their personalities. The banquet hall was now hot and many of the guests called for water to freshen themselves again. The smoke from the lamps hung low in the hall because of the heavy air. The guests wanted more entertainment and it was to be more of the same. The noise began again. Herod's steward soon came out with the message from Herodias that Salome would dance again given assurance that he would keep his word.

Herod then arose from the throne and shouted over the noise: "Hear me! Salome would dance again, but she would that I grant her a boon; should I do so - has she danced well enough for such an act?" The answer was soon heard.

"Yes, grant to her, grant to her!" The voices of many rang throughout the hall. So it was that Herod, bending to the will of his guests, sent word to Herodias that he would indeed hold to his word even as the guests had heard.

Herodias was satisfied, and the music began to play. Salome appeared from the alcove. She had changed costume, and now wore a golden gown with a similar cut. Around her neck was a chain of gold and the bells around her ankles were silver. She danced as before and the guests were spellbound. Her young body glistened in the lamp light. The men were leaning forward each time she passed close. The exotic perfume mother had concocted for her provided a scent which drove the mind to things other than the dance. When Salome finished her dance, the hall became a bedlam again, more gold and silver trinkets were thrown at her feet. This time, she stayed longer, graciously bowed to her audience, and with a final wave of her hand, went behind the curtain over the alcove.

It was not long before Herodias sent a message to Herod which he received amid all the congratulations for his step-daughters' exhibition. He could hardly contain his pride, and accepted his guests good wishes with the air of one who could do no wrong.

The crowd became silent to hear what Salome's request might be. She came to Herod and knelt before him. The guests were duly impressed with her act of submission; a thing that any good daughter would do, they remarked to one another.

"Arise, Salome, and let's hear the gift you want from me." Herod was in a magnanimous mood at the moment and would have turned many a criminal free - if so requested! This had truly been a magnificent birthday celebration. While he waited for her reply, he thought for a moment of John the washer now in the dungeon below. On the morrow, he would release John, even if it was against Herodias's wishes. Yes, it would show the people that he had a good heart on his birthday.

"Dear father," said Salome; he smiled as this was the first time she had addressed him so. "I'm greatly distressed by those who have spoken harsh and cruel words about you and mother. If I could, I would rid your kingdom of those who trample on your name. I cannot take up the sword to do these things for you. I would be unkind if I thought of myself at this hour and ask for a common gift. My good king, I would stop one of those who cries out against you and raises the people unjustly against you. I ask now for the head of John the washer! I would have it in a charger and brought here as proof of your word!"

Herod reacted as though he had been struck in the face. His eyes bulged out and his face became flushed. He reeled back against his throne; he sat down as one who had lost all. He stared out at his guests in the hall with eyes that weren't focused on anyone.

The crowd, hearing this strange request, were also taken aback. Who would have thought that this young girl would ask for such a gory gift? Some now drew back and hid their faces. Some who were less delicate leaned forward in anticipation of Herod's action.

A man's life, although not a great price these days, as a gift of dance? The king was trapped by his own foolishness, and he knew it. His wasn't the will to refuse even such an evil request before his guests.

The scene unfolded as a nightmare wherein things moved unnaturally slow. As Herod searched for a way out of this dilemma, two white-robed figures approached from where they had been standing throughout the entertainment. One was quite old and the other not so - chief priests both - Annas and Caiaphas. It was they who opened the celebration and accepted Herod's gifts to the temple earlier in the week.

"Hear us, mighty Herod, this act you are requested to do is an abomination unto the Lord. The taking of a life is a serious thing, and to do so wantonly is to call down upon yourself and all who condone it the wrath of the God of our people. Be not so foolish as to do this thing." Caiaphas spoke with authority. He was a man who believed there was a line which must not be crossed and this, the taking of John's life without due process before the Sanhedrin, was unlawful. He wasn't above taking advantage of some gifts for the temple, but this wasn't so easily justified.

Herod, still reeling from the request, couldn't fully comprehend the warning by Caiaphas. He wasn't one to fear God, but the people and Rome, that was different.

"What is this? Haven't I heard your complaints about this man and his teaching's, and now you call the king to heel, while you send guards to seek out his followers? Begone, I'm not afraid of your God!" His words moved the foreign guests but many of the others moved back. His concern was political, not religious. Should the people become aroused and send a delegation to Rome over this matter - therein lay the crux of the act.

He remained seated while the assemblage moved about; some returning to their couches and the other entertainers, while others hovered near to hear the decree given or the request denied. Herod knew how much his name would be worth if he refused this girl her boon. The many foreigners and members of different governments were now wondering if he was a man of honor? Could he risk refusal?

Caiaphas and Annas left the hall to return to the temple, having done as they ought.

Salome still stood at the foot of Herod's throne. In the alcove, Herodias, partly hidden, listened to the conversations and waited for Herod's answer. Her hatred of John was well known among the people in the land. He had caused her to feel the prick of conscious and the ill will of the people. She would have him out of the way.

Herod finally stood up. He called for his chief steward, Chuza.

"It shall be as I promised. Go and fetch the prisoner's head. Bring it to us in a charger as Salome has asked." There, the dastardly decree was given. It was just a matter of time. Mother and many of her circle became ill upon hearing this order. They excused themselves from the court and left immediately. So ended the tale of the birthday celebration as mother had seen and heard it.

It wasn't until some time later that mother heard through Joanna, the wife of Chuza, what followed. She told the story as follows: Chuza gave the orders to the prison guards to behead John and bring his head to the banquet hall at once. So it was commanded and so it was done. According to Chuza, no one, other than the men of the execution, was with John at the time of his death. His last words were, so the executioner said, "Hear, O Israel: our God is one Lord. He who was to come has answered not. I'm sick unto my soul."

John's body was thrown outside the west wall of the palace in the place that held the bodies of criminals. His head was placed in a charger and brought from the dungeon to the throne room by the guards. They formed up in front of the throne and passed the charger to Salome who knelt in homage to Herod and carried the charger into the alcove to her mother. Some said they heard Herodias laugh at the sight of John's head. Herod became ill and cursed the day. He then dismissed the guests and went to his room. And

Herod's birthday ended. This is as told to mother by Joanna, the wife of the chief steward of the king.

From the story of Joanna, I knew the messengers of John, Judah and Dan hadn't reached him with the answer Yeshua had given. It was therefore reasonable to understand the statement attributed to him by the guards; he died with his faith in the oneness of the God of Israel undisturbed. To him, the Messiah hadn't come; his soul cried out for confirmation that never came. His belief in Yeshua that burned so brightly at the time of washing was changed to doubt by the lack of communication. It was indeed unfortunate that Yeshua didn't visit him in the prison. I was heartily sorry I didn't reach him before my arrest. Afterward it was impossible because of the increased guard at Fort Machaerus. I would never forget John, a boyhood chum. To me, he was the last great prophet; he gave his life for the cause he believed in, the announcement of the coming of one greater than he!

A GRUESOME SEARCH

It was that same night of the execution that a small band of men unknown to me appeared at the gate. Johnathan came to me with the news of this gathering.

"Master, they would have a word with you."

"What about? I and my family are in mourning for John and aren't to speak with anyone." I wouldn't shave or look into any reflecting surface.

"They have come to ask your help in retrieving the body of John. They say it is unlawful for it to remain in the hands of the Idumeans. They need a representative of his family to obtain the body and there is none. Since you were closest to him, perhaps you will identify his remains as there are more than one outside the prison."

I was shocked at this news but remembered the likelihood of others being executed by the sword because it was near the end of the month. I knew the bodies were thrown outside the prison in a heap, there to remain until the next of kin came to claim them.

It was an old method for capturing others in a family who were accused of insurrection. When they came to claim the body of their loved one, they were also cast into prison. It was an evil way to control those against the rulers. All knew it was unlawful for a man's family to leave his body exposed to the elements past sundown. The cruel guards stood by and waited like vultures picking the bones of the dead. It was just a matter of time that those obeying the law would come to claim the body, and then they would have them. So it was with John.

My heart trembled at the prospect of searching among the bodies and identifying that of John. Without his head, and having not seen him for sometime, I was afraid I wouldn't recognize the body. Yet, I understood these men and their desire to follow the law and give the body rest as was commanded.

I remembered as well, the probability of the bodies of Dan and Judah being among them. I called to Ishmael and had Johnathan bring Apius and Atonis with us. I and Ishmael made ourselves ready in accordance with the law and joined the party to retrieve the body of John. I had hoped that Dan and Judah had escaped this extreme penalty for being followers of John. Ishmael, Apius, and I talked of how we could be sure we obtained the right body. Each of us tried to recall some identifying mark, other than his face, that would give us a clue. This wasn't an easy task we were about to do.

Since most were afoot, we decided to walk to the palace. I was concerned about Apius for he had just recovered from the fever. His walk was sure and soon I forgot about his recent illness. We knew about where we would find the bodies. We passed through the city and approached the east wall of the palace. There was still some merriment going on as Herod had held over his birthday celebration to accommodate latecomers. We hurried past in order not to draw attention to our mission.

We passed through the Gennath gate and turned west along the wall past the palace towers to a dark and low place in the earth near the wall. Here it was that many bodies of those executed for crimes against the king were thrown. It was an evil place, and little care was given to some of the unnamed people that met this end. The bodies were left there until they were claimed by kin of the deceased, or the burial detail of slaves driven by guards of the prison came and interred them in a common grave in Gehenna south of the old city. It was forbidden to bury these people in the holy city.

So it was that we came upon the bodies of several who had suffered decapitation. It was a gruesome sight indeed. We were mindful of the law about touching corpses, and Ishmael and I knew we would have to wash in the blood of the red heifer and take sacrifices to the temple after this act, even though it was one of love.

By pooling our knowledge about John, we had remembered his birthmark and searched for the body showing this small design on the shoulder. Ishmael had recalled this mark because of his sketching of John after he had visited us shortly after father's death.

It wasn't long before we found the body of John. We carefully wrapped it in linen and placed it on a pallet to bear it through the city to the burial ground near his parents. The march through the gate and the city was accompanied by prayers and chants for the dead. Many joined in the march as was the custom although none knew who it was we carried. It was the thing to do for a fellow Jew.

We passed the palace fearing no man. God of our fathers was on our side. Who then could harm us? Those of his followers took his body and placed in the grave near his parents. Ishmael, Apius, Atonis, and I then returned home to tell mother of our deed. Even as we spoke, we couldn't help wondering why Yeshua wasn't present and decided that he didn't know of this cruel penalty paid by his cousin. Although I sent no word to Yeshua, word was sent by runner to Mary in Nazareth about John's death at the hand of Herod as I knew she would want to know. I received no answer from her or the family.

It took mother a long time to get over the death of John. Many prayers were sent to God to bless him, and curses against the name of Herod.

Mother's sorrow was somewhat lifted by the coming wedding of Ishmael. The household was in a joyous mood. The couple met all the traditional laws and prohibitions of the scriptures. Many people were invited. I was happy to see that Apius was better.

WEDDING DAY

Mother asked me about Mary, Yeshua's mother, and suggested I take a message to her and bring her to the wedding - if she was able. And so it was I left for Nazareth as soon as a horse was ready. I took Johnathan with me. The trip went smoothly and I spent the Sabbath with Mary and her family.

We talked of the wedding and her coming to visit mother during that week. She was surprised to hear it was Ishmael and wondered why I hadn't married. I recovered my surprise and simply said the Lord hadn't blessed me with such good fortune. She asked about Yeshua and I did the same of her. I told her of all the news about him, my selection as a follower, the sermon on the mount, the healing of my arm, the possible healing of mother, and much more. She listened with great interest. She told me of hearing of many wonders done by him, but she feared for him and his thoughts. Thoughts that she felt she had fostered throughout the years - stories of Messiahship and of him being selected above all others - that might now bring him to attempt something which would cost the lives of many. She prayed to God that all would be well with him. Finally, after Sabbath,

I again asked her if she would accompany me to the wedding. She declined and told me the reason.

"Ah, dear Judas, it's my youngest daughter; she suffers from a strong fever. I cannot leave her in this time of need. I wish I knew where Yeshua was. I hear he is still in Capernaum and will seek an audience with him as soon as I can get away." She told me of the illness that held Sarah captive and little they did relieved her condition. "I'll travel to Capernaum and find Yeshua and when he hears of his sister's illness, will surely come and give her comfort."

I feared for her and offered the search. "I'm sure of this and will ride to fetch him if you so desire - I'm your humble servant in this matter." I realized that Mary really wanted to see Yeshua for other reasons unspoken and accepted her refusal.

"Ah, thank you, but it's my desire to do this for Sarah, and I want to see Yeshua again and hear his lessons." I could remember mother's statement so long ago about seeing Ishmael and me.

It was with a sad heart I left her and traveled home. Mother was saddened as well but understood her concern for Sarah and their want to see Yeshua.

The wedding was one of style; mother and her circle saw to that. Many of mother's friends came to join in the celebration and for the most part, the death of John was nearly forgotten. The wedding celebration was a good week long. After that, I told mother I would leave and join Yeshua and would follow him until the commission was fulfilled.

CHAPTER NINETEEN

Among The Disciples

Once again, I left the house with Johnathan and moved along the high road to Capernaum. It was there I thought I would find Yeshua and the sixteen. I left Johnathan at the inn and instructed him to return with the animals and there await any word I might send. He left reluctantly. I went to the house of Simon's mother-in-law. I knew if anyone might know Yeshua's whereabouts, she would.

It was a pleasant surprise to find all there: Simon, Andrew, James and John, Matthew, Bartholomew, Thomas, Levi, Simon the Zealot, James and Judas, brothers of Yeshua, Simon the Canaanite, Thaddaeus, Philip, Lebbaeus, and Nathanael. All sixteen were there. Several came forward to greet me.

"Ho, Judas! It took you long enough to deliver one small girl." Simon was less than pleasant - but civil enough. Many of the others expressed happiness that I had returned and asked of my welfare and that of my family. John bar Zebedee, who always showed interest in the welfare of all, came to me.

"What is this thing we hear from the people of the road that you were arrested by men of Herod and thrown into prison? I was heartily grieved to hear of this; tell us of this uncommon adventure." He was a good man, this John, and ever forgiving of all things. Indeed, if he had any fault, it was his tendency to overlook even the most horrendous faults in any man, even Herod. It was this quality that endeared him to Yeshua, although some of the more belligerent of the group felt differently about this and often stated so privately.

Some of the others gathered around to hear the news and pass remarks about John. I told them all I knew of the arrest and imprisonment of John and myself; of the arrest of his followers, Judah and Dan, along the road near Jericho; how they failed to reach John with the message from Yeshua and were taken to the dungeon in the palace as I was; of my attempt to reach John and my subsequent arrest on the road near Jericho; and of my release through the subterfuge of my Roman friend, Apuleius.

They continued to asked questions and were greatly interested and smote their breasts at the news of John. They would have all the details of Herod's birthday celebration; the dance of Salome; her demand of a gift; the horror of her request; and the subsequent beheading of John. I completed the story by telling of the claiming of his body and how we managed to identify it; the search for his head, which we didn't find; and the final funeral march through the streets of Jerusalem and eventual burial beside his parents in their sepulcher. All these things I was first to tell them and that firsthand.

Some ran to tell Yeshua of these things. Yeshua sent for me and I stood before him as one man before another. At his request, I repeated the entire story from the time I left Capernaum to the return this day, even to that minute. He was greatly moved by the news of John and would be away to himself for awhile. He bade no one to follow him and was gone some days. This caused Simon great distress but he obeyed his command and remained with the rest. During this time, I was fortunate to hear of many of the deeds and visitations of the sixteen. In my absence, they had traveled much along the coast of Tiberias.

Many were interested in telling their adventures and the stories of their demand for a sign from Yeshua - how his family sought an audience with him, the many parables taught, the sea made calm, the healing of Gadarene man of demons, the raising of Jairus's daughter, the sight of blind men restored, the dumb healed, and the latest rejection of Yeshua as a Messiah by his own village.

All these I didn't experience but was told about as true happenings. I listened to many of these stories with some reservation. Some I openly questioned, and the story of the visit of Mary and his brethren seeking him out brought back the thought of Sarah's illness and the desire of Mary to once again look on her eldests' face.

WHO IS MOTHER AND WHO IS BROTHER?

"Who was here when Mary came?" I wanted to know those who witnessed this meeting. I wanted to know if Yeshua supplied the words to heal Sarah.

Levi, who was near, leaned across the open space and answered for the others.

"We all were present, isn't that so?" Of those I could see, they all nodded in agreement. It was strange to note that these men had once again formed into groups of four even as they did when Yeshua and I looked down from the hill before their ordination.

"Well, I have told you my story. Tell me what happened when Mary came to see Yeshua." I was wondering if I knew something they didn't; I already knew they knew something I didn't.

"Well, it was exceedingly strange." Levi continued to tell the story. "He was teaching a large group of people, mostly common folk, but there were some Pharisees present as well as those who came to heckle. I must say, and I think the others will agree, that he was somewhat disturbed by the press of the crowd. It was so great that there was hardly room to breathe, and the odors of their bodies came unto everyone's nostrils. The heat of the day had caused many to become weak and in need of water." He stopped here and looked about for a sign of agreement; seeing some, he continued.

"He was deep into the story of Jonah and the unclean spirits in the house which I understood not, nor many of the others. He was asked to explain this story by some of those seeking to heckle and was about to do so when word was passed from a far place to the edge of the crowd that his mother and brothers sought an audience with him. This was so because of the press of the crowd. His brothers wouldn't let Mary enter the crowd because of those with disease and running sores, and none who desired to see, hear, and touch Yeshua would leave his position to another. At times, there was much shoving and loud talking while he spoke. None of them moved aside to make way for Mary and she looked so small in the distance. The word of their presence was relayed along by one near to the master. He said boldly that Yeshua's mother and kin were standing to the edge of the crowd and would have a word with him. All of us heard him and many of the crowd as well. It seemed at first the master didn't hear him for he didn't turn from his teaching. The bold fellow spoke again in a louder voice. 'Hear me, teacher, your mother and some brethren stand without and desire to speak to you!' Some who heard turned to look in the direction the speaker motioned. Both Judas and James waved unto their mother and knew her in the distance. It was indeed Mary. Some later doubted it was her, but we all knew it was."

"What did Yeshua say to Mary and his kin?" I asked impatiently. I secretly wanted to know how Sarah fared. He stopped for a moment, drew from a goatskin bag at his side, and rinsed his mouth.

"Well, hear me, you're almost as impatient as those were around the master that day. Yeshua didn't even look up from those he was teaching. He gave no outward sign of recognition. He said a curious thing, 'Who is my mother and who my brethren?' Upon hearing this, the crowd murmured against what he said, as many knew he had brethren in Nazareth and yea, even sisters as well as his mother. Some like us attempted to answer his question, but to no avail. Even Judas and James, his brothers, showed some unhappiness at his remarks for they were indeed his brothers, and that's a fact."

Both James and Judas nodded and remarked they were amazed at Yeshua's question, but decided he asked the question not to be answered by them, but by himself.

"The master then stretched forth his hand so the crowd might know that we were favored as his kin above all others, and said, 'Behold my mother and my brethren! For whosoever doeth the will of my father, the same is my brother, sister, and mother!'"

"Well, what happened then? Didn't any of you go to the edge of the crowd to see what Mary wanted?" I was amazed at this incredulous story.

"There is nothing more to add, except he continued to teach and gave no further attention to his family. It was not long after that I and some of the others saw Mary weeping and resting heavily on the arm of her other son. They moved away before Yeshua completed his teaching." Levi ended his story thus, and waited for any others to dispute it, but none did.

"Again, didn't any of you leave to find out what Mary wanted, how about you - John?" I had always considered him to be the one of greatest compassion and would have given him the benefit of the doubt.

John hung his head. It was plain to see that none of them had left the side of Yeshua to even inquire of Mary's desire or needs. I felt that something was amiss and would bring this to Yeshua's attention when he returned.

"Then tell me, since you all received such a great teaching, what did he mean when he ignored his mother and brethren and said, 'Whosoever doeth the will of my Father which is in heaven, the same is my brother, sister, and mother?' Didn't Mary give her life to the Lord even before his birth? Hasn't she done the will of the God of Israel? Why wasn't she included in the wave of his hand?" I waited for answers to these questions but none came. Some fumbled with their girdles and robes, while other looked out across the courtyard of the small cottage. I couldn't conceive of Mary not being included in those doing the will of 'His Father in heaven.' I could still remember the announcement of Yeshua's birth for I was ten years old at the time. I doubted that any of these were even aware of this happening in the city of Nazareth so long ago. None of these had the privilege to know this family of Joseph as I had through the years. I knew things before Yeshua knew them, or so I thought.

On their failure to answer, I continued, "Let me tell you the reason for Mary making this trip." I was somewhat incensed at this great indifference to the mother of Yeshua by these men of God. Where was all the compassion Yeshua talked about earlier on the mount? What had he to teach at that instant that was so earth shaking that it couldn't wait long enough to honor his mother?

They came closer - except Simon. "Hear me, I visited Mary not more than two fortnights ago and she told me of the illness of her youngest daughter, Sarah. Aye, Judas and James, your own sister! I offered to come to Capernaum and find Yeshua for her but she wouldn't have it. She longed to see his face and feel the touch of his hand once more. Is there evil in that? In addition, she wanted to ask him for help to heal his sister. Mary told me of the many stories she heard of his healing powers, and she thought his sister was no less than some of the others he had healed. So it was that she came here seeking him. And now you tell me not one of you went forth to find out her needs. It would behoove Judas and James to find out how your sister is and ask your mother for forgiveness. Woe to those who care not for the cries of the needy!" After I said these words, many of them turned away from me and I knew then I wasn't to be held in the inner circle.

Levi remained and I spoke to him again.

DEMONICS

"Tell me of the trip to Gergesa?" I knew Levi had a journal and with it a good memory; none of his story was questioned by the others and I took this to mean it was true as they understood it.

"It was Gergesa, in the land of Decapolis."

"It was the town of Gadara!" came the voice of Mark from the edge of the little gathering. Levi turned and with a wave of his hand continued his tale.

"It was Gergesa, this I have it in my journal and so it is. We crossed over the Tiberias and came unto land. After walking a goodly distance, we came upon two possessed with unclean spirits…"

"There was only one!" Mark again interrupted.

"What's this? Were you both at the same place?" I looked around at the others. "Were you all there?" All those paying attention to what was being said nodded or in some other way indicated they were present. I looked at each one wondering why none of the others spoke, either to deny what was said or confirm it.

"Consider this, it cannot be both ways, either you all were at Gergesa or Gadara, and you all either saw one or two possessed. Let me take a count. Come near." I would have the truth of it before I heard the rest of the story. All of the sixteen came near. "Give me a show of count. Were you at Gadara or Gergesa? Those who were at Gadara confirm it."

And so it was, all except Levi gave indication that they went to Gadara. Ah, this opened a small rift among the group.

"And how many agree that only one man possessed came forth to meet you?"

Again the answer was the same. All except Levi indicated that only one man came from the tombs to challenge them. Levi ceased to object and also ceased to tell his story, but he remained resolute in this claim; I sometimes wondered why.

Since Mark had won the confidence of the group, he continued the story: "There was only one man, yet he was wild and had the strength of many; or so it was told by those who lived there, for we didn't really know. The people of the countryside made all sorts of claims about him. Some said that he was too strong to be bound, but I've never seen such a man, and doubt if the Roman's have either. After all, only Samson was such a man." He turned to the others and they all chuckled at this observation.

"Some said that he couldn't be tamed, but none could say for what reason it would be necessary. It was plain to see these people of Decapolis were tellers of falsehoods; they told so many stories about him that couldn't be true because of his age - he was too young to fulfill all their stories even if he was awake night and day." He smiled at this observation while the rest enjoyed his remark as well. The Decapoleans were known heathens and not worthy of great trust.

"It seemed strange to me, but few showed fear of him - they allowed that since he stayed where he was and didn't come into the city to bother anyone, they were not responsible for him, then what was there to fear? He could have the tombs - who wanted them anyway? Besides, he was a tourist attraction so to speak, and many from nearby towns came to see this poor possessed man. It was true that many local merchants gained some from his notoriety and weren't willing to see things change. They were comfortable, if not happy, with their civic attraction, and wouldn't have him disturbed. Yet, from his actions as we saw them, he was in a sorry state."

"Why did you go to Gadara? Isn't this a gentile state?" I was curious - this was the first time I knew of Yeshua going outside the province of Herod, since Decapolis was the province of Herod Philip II.

"We don't know. Perhaps it was to avoid the press of the crowds on this side of the lake." John spoke and the others agreed, to what I wasn't sure - the press of the crowd or some other reason.

"So you knew the man who approached Yeshua was possessed by the words of those who don't tell the truth?" I couldn't believe what I heard. Why listen to a liar?

"Was there any other signs of his being possessed - he wasn't simply a mad man?" I considered the many times I had seen those along the way that were said to be possessed but, oft times, according to Apuleius, were just mad, epileptic, or sometimes suffering the traumas of combat.

I remembered many trips I made with him in and about Rome to see some of these poor unfortunates. How people of different religious orders misunderstood the signs of madness and epilepsy. Apuleius often traveled some distance to study some poor wretch suffering from some common ailment who was hauled before the priests of Jupiter, and they declaring him to be possessed before all. He gave many nights and hours of time in attempts to cure, and often did, those so declared, by use of a potion or medical aid. He held that many a priest had made money by declaring an aging relative of some rich young beneficiary possessed and then offering to exorcise him.

After being with Apuleius on many of those investigations, I held the view that many very sick people were thought to be possessed.

"Oh, he was possessed; this was evident from his strange manners. He approached Yeshua without hesitation and fell on the ground in front of him. He said in a loud voice, 'What have I to do with thee, Yeshua, Son of the most high God? I adjure thee by God, that thou torment me not.' We were all taken aback that he should speak thus to our master." Mark turned to the others for support and I could see they agreed.

"How did he know this thing?" I asked.

"We don't know as we had never seen him before, as I have said, and none of the local people talk to him," John answered before Mark could find the words.

"Didn't Yeshua object to him calling out this way?"

Several answered in unison, "No!"

"What did he do on the ground, other than cry out?"

"He worshiped Yeshua." Mark said. He was beginning to tire of my questions.

"How did he do this?" I was curious how a heathen and gentile from a foreign country would worship the Son of the God of Israel! How did these disciples know he was worshiping Yeshua?

"He just remained in the posture of one in prayer, even as we do in temple." John was the one to answer quickly. It seemed strange to me that this heathen could know of such things. But not knowing the gods he followed, I couldn't deny their assumption.

"Why did he think Yeshua was tormenting him?" I wondered out loud. They all looked at me as if I was the one mad.

"Go on with the story. What happened after that?"

"Well," the master said, 'Come out of the man, unclean spirit!' and then he said unto him, 'What is thy name?'"

"And who answered?"

"The man! He said, 'My name is Legion, for we are many!'"

"Were all these Legions of unclean spirits in just one man?" I couldn't help but think that many in one man was a little more than necessary, after all one would seem enough. I noticed their faces and decided not to go too far with this.

"All in one man! And they besought Yeshua not to send them away out of the country." John spoke again. He was more interested in my reactions than some of the others. Some had wearied of the story and wandered off to other things.

"Out of the country?"

"Yes, out of the country!" John didn't change his story on that point.

"What does that mean?" I remarked quietly I didn't know that demons were more solicitous of one country than another. Apuleius would think this find a stroke of luck. None heard my remark and Mark continued with his recitation.

"Now there was a great herd of swine feeding nearby, and we heard the man say, 'Send us into the swine, that we may enter into them.'" It was Mark's turn to take a drink from his goatskin bottle.

"Why did these spirits ask for permission to leave the man? Who did they ask when they first entered the man of Gadara?" I couldn't imagine why these beings would ask for permission to leave the body of a man they had gained without permission.

"We don't know - you ask too many questions. I'm only the storyteller, not the understander of all!" Now, Mark was feeling my questions approached unbelief in his tale.

"I'm sorry Mark, consider my questions as wanderings of the mind, pray continue."

"Well, the master said, 'Go,' and there was a rushing of wind and suddenly the animals began to run about without purpose. The herders were unable to control them. Even the little piglets were running amuck. Then, the entire herd ran headlong into the nearby lake and, as we could plainly see, all drowned. Just as suddenly, the man who had been fierce sat down at our feet and became calm. Now, all this shocked the local people who were witness of these things and us as well."

"Those who were watching the swine were greatly provoked by this strange turn of events and shouted in their dialect about their loss; this seemed their right for they had a great interest in the herd which looked to be as many as two thousand animals. In addition, many looked ready for market in that country and worth much gold, although nearly worthless in our country." Mark stopped here and looked about for confirmation. All nodded in agreement with what he said - except Levi - but he held his peace.

"Those who had been herding the animals left, declaring their displeasure, and ran to the village for the owners. The owners, the village leaders, and priests of Jupiter came out to see this thing. They showed not only displeasure at this curing of the man, for he had been an attraction for some years, but also for the loss of the animals. The owners demanded recompense for their loss which they had every right to do according to the law. Some of us became frightened as we were in their jurisdiction and not well taught in the law of the land." I could see more than one agreed with his story about this fear of reprisal. They gave us fair warning that we should be gone from their country and not return as they were determined to have satisfaction. We had naught in the bag and couldn't give gold for their loss." This I could well imagine. They seldom had any gold in the bag, so poorly was their finances.

"We straightway went back the way we came and entered into our ship. It was then we discovered the newly-cured man was still with us; he begged to travel with us, if not as a follower, then as one of the crowd. Strangely, the master said that this could not be and that he should return to his friends and tell them the great things the Lord had done that day." Here he ended his tale with a long draught. He was satisfied with his story. I was about to ask Levi about his adventure when Mark spoke again.

"The man left us with great sadness in his heart or so he said; he was still afraid of the demons and would remain near his savior, our master, for protection. We could hear him cry out for a long time from the shore as we pulled away."

I was greatly puzzled by the story and thought of this lonely man left on the shore to his own devices after such a traumatic experience. I thought of Apuleius and how he stayed by the side of many of his patients - how he never wanted to hear them cry out for his help when he could give it.

"Whatever became of him, I wonder?" I thought of this man who now must face the strange world without a memory of things and friends to help him. A man who had been possessed for years - how could a heathen ever understand what it meant to know the great things the Lord had done for him?

"Oh, he departed and began to publish in Decapolis the great thing our master had done for him; and all men did marvel," Mark quickly added.

"And how do you know these things, that he published and all men marveled? Why would he tell people that Yeshua had done these things? Wasn't it commanded by Yeshua that he tell 'the great things the Lord has done' for him?" I had a difficult time reasoning that any one of these men ever went back to that part of Decapolis again this soon after the happening. Most had already indicated they were afraid of what might be done to them if they did! So how had they gathered this knowledge?

"Well, we have no real knowledge of this, but it must be so," John answered with confidence.

I held my peace about this last part of the story, but wondered how the man would tell his heathen kin about a strange God of Israel who had cured him? What confidence would the people have in a person some believed mad or possessed just days before telling this story? Indeed, I could understand the demons recognized and spoke to Yeshua, but after they were gone, would the man know of these things? So the story of the trip to Gadara came to an end.

"Judas, I would have a word with you." It was Levi who spoke in a low voice.

"Say on."

"I say there were two men, and I saw none worship the master as Mark says, and neither did they who were possessed ask to join us after they were cured, nor did I hear the master tell them to go about the country telling of this event." He was adamant about these things. "These things aren't in my journal and never will be. And another thing - the master didn't ask who they were either. Much of the rest was as Mark said."

He spoke softly and leaned close to me when he spoke of these things. He was a good man and had proved himself to be good with a story and accurate as well. "Levi, some things about this adventure amaze me but let's not dwell on this. If it's convenient, I would leave the purse with you, for I know your keen views of finance and I may be away soon." I had given it to him for safekeeping and he had it the days I wasn't among them.

"Aye, I can do this thing and have no fear, all will be guarded against the loss of one pence. This I know, we have little enough to manage, and since the master says that God will provide, the real need of the bag isn't here." He reached under his cloak and brought forth the bag. I inspected it and found nothing in it. I then took the gold I brought with me and placed it in the bag. I knew the amount for I was used to balancing the books; my right hand always knew what my left hand was doing in a purse. Uncle Benjamin often looked upon my dealings with admiration and considered my business ability a gift of God.

"Take what I have and be welcome to it. What is mine is also that of the group." He accepted the bag with the increase in riches and placed it again under his cloak.

Time rested heavily on the group as we waited for Yeshua to return. From where, we didn't know. I felt that he returned to Nazareth to see his family once more, but had no real reason to support this thought.

I told Johnathan to return to the inn every month and I would, if possible, leave my notes and requests for personal things with the master of the inn. I had hoped that I would be able to get back to Capernaum often enough to increase the money in the purse from my own account and to transmit news to Ishmael and hear that of home.

A SECOND COMMISSION

The days went by quickly enough and Yeshua soon returned. He called all to him soon after he was refreshed to tell us of his travels. It was as I suspected, he traveled to Nazareth to see his mother - but why alone I didn't know. I was happy to know this for I couldn't believe the story told about his uncaring act while teaching. His story filled the gap and restored my belief in his strength in maintaining family ties. He told of Mary's good health and her love for his brethren. He told of Sarah's illness and how she was now well and happy. He spoke little about some of his brothers and their lack of faith in him. He then changed his course of talk and spoke of our mission and limitations connected thereto.

"It's time you are sent into the world to learn the lessons from it without me at your side. You shall take my teachings to many and see their reactions to these even as I have. These things you must not do; don't go among the gentiles or Samaritans, yet stay within the cities and villages of our people. Listen to their causes, and teach them of the coming kingdom of God here on earth. Heal the sick, cleanse the lepers, raise the dead, and cast out devils. All these freely do, even as I did for you. Take nothing with you, save a staff only. Take no purse, no bread, no written word, and only one coat, but be shod." He told us of many things, warnings of persecutions from some, and rewards to those who received us.

After these instructions, we milled about for awhile. He gave us the command to go in pairs among the people - past experience and relations cause some to travel with those more compatible with them. All left in high spirits; all seemed to understand their commission and limitations except me. It wasn't clear to me, these words about the kingdom of heaven. In addition, I was left to myself. I wasn't invited to travel with any of them; the reason for this I couldn't tell. Although I was left with a feeling of rejection, I soon set that aside as other things troubled me more. I remained behind after all had left as I wanted to speak to Yeshua. After he sent the others on their way, he went in the little garden to pray. I followed him but remained some distance away.

He spoke as one to his father. "Father, forgive them for they don't know yet what they do. Give them the power in my name to do that which I've declared possible unto them. Bring each one back to me unharmed and unspoiled by their feelings of success. Hold the Great Deceiver from them; don't grant him the freedom to do them harm or destroy their faith in my word." He prayed in dead earnest. Sweat stood out on his forehead and the veins in his neck stood out. His eyes remained fixed on the heavens. He continued for some time in his request for help from his Father. After awhile, I could see his body relax in relief as though he had received an answer from the God on high. He was assured all was well. He turned to me. His eyes were sad but calm.

"Judas, you, more than any other, are dear to me. I'm glad you remained." He turned to the bench he often used and motioned for me to sit by him. Peter's wife brought out some cool water mixed with a fruit juice. It was pleasant and I welcomed it.

"Yeshua, I'm reluctant to go out, for I, of all the others, am not ready for such a commission. I've been away from your teaching more than the others, and feel this lack will cause me to do that which I shouldn't. I wouldn't want to lead anyone astray." I was finding it hard to explain my feelings at being the only one registering doubt and some quandary about his words. I couldn't understand how the others came to know the meaning of his discourse. There was a great gap between the apparent stories I heard and the things I believed true because of my early training under Hillel. I hoped to resolve these before I was sent out to teach. I could only envision my incompetence causing my listeners quandary, if not downright disbelief.

"Do you think each of them knows, without error, the meaning of all I've said unto them?"

"No, but therein lies the rub. Their lack of worldly knowledge is their stay, but it's not mine. I've seen more world and different religions than any of them, that isn't to say it is an advantage, but a disadvantage."

"But what have these to do with Israel and the God of our fathers?"

"Naught." I couldn't find any reason for the men of Israel to know of any other religion; all were unclean.

"What is it you fear?" He knew the reason of my hesitation - I was afraid! But of what? Of what Shalazar said long ago: "You will be given a great duty to perform for you have been selected from the beginning of time." *That* was what frightened me! He seemed to read my mind.

"Hear me, I, too, have fears - greater than you can ever imagine. Some of them I just expressed in prayer to my father. I can see the sins of Israel and the world weighing heavily on the scales of God and these out of balance. He demands justice and balance brought again. Good must eventually prevail. It is given to me to see, though dimly, that we, you and I, will be instrumental in restoring balance to this scale that's now askew." His voice had the ring of conviction and it impregnated me with a sense of will to perform and overcome my foolish fears. When was all this to take place, and where would the kingdom of heaven be on this earth? I was suddenly filled with the desire to see it happen now!

"Yeshua, your words have freed my mind from the fears of others I was once indebted to. What can I do now to bring about the balance wanted by the Lord?" I was more enthusiastic about this than my early desire to go to Rome, and that's what I would have done if asked!

"Go now to Jerusalem and stay there until I come. Do even as I have instructed the others. Have a care, Judas, the world is full of traps for those with much learning. Don't let the mind rule the heart when it's good in the balance. Remember, the greatest points of the law are these, 'First, love the Lord thy God with all thy heart, soul, and mind, and what is hateful to thyself don't do to others; this is then the law, all the rest is commentary.' Be gone unto Jerusalem for there it will be fulfilled in due time."

My heart jumped. Once again, I was to return to Jerusalem and there to remain until he came. It was then all would be revealed and come to pass! *Hear, O Israel: the Lord is our God, the Lord is one!*

IN JERUSALEM

I left the garden and moved through Capernaum to the inn. Here I stayed until Johnathan came at the end of the month. I made arrangements for service. In the time left me, I began transcribing my notes of the few days before. They included the stories of Yeshua's kin and the demon-possessed of Gadara. Or was it Gergesa? I spent time planning what I would do in Jerusalem while I waited for Yeshua's return. I gathered from his hesitance in saying when it would occur, that it would be at some later date not yet revealed to him. He, indeed, saw some events of the future as in a bronze mirror.

I hoped he would return to Jerusalem soon to announce his Messiahship and start the scales of justice balancing again. How this was to happen was a mystery to me as I'm sure it was to the others. Since I was a boy in Kerioth, it was told by some tannaim the Messiah was to come to Jerusalem riding on a white stallion. He would be a man, anointed by God as the elect redeemer for all mankind as well as Israel, he would have special powers granted to him, his name would be held in high esteem, and he would live apart from women. All these criteria Yeshua met. It was slow to come to me - these thoughts of the Messiah - about the relationship of Yeshua to all other prophets. Could it really be true?

I worked as quickly as I could on the transcription of these things - I wanted to lose nothing. I was proud of my accomplishments, and knew mother and Ishmael would read these words with great interest. I was determined to keep these notes for my lifetime and posterity; who knows, they may make a difference after the Messiah has established his government on earth. There was no boastfulness in this feeling for God and Israel, only the feeling of urgency - the time is right - he must act soon.

The days at the inn passed quickly. Soon, I heard the voice of Johnathan from the entrance of the inn inquiring about me. Ah, it was good to see him again. He was surprised to see me in the inn.

"Master Judas, this is a surprise! I thought you would be with Yeshua. When you left me just a month ago, you were committed to a year of travel and teaching or so you thought. What has come about?" He spoke as we moved to the room I held there.

"Ah, much has changed in this world since then," I said with much feeling. I could barely contain my thoughts and readily told him of the past days' adventures including the others' stories. He listened intently and willingly accepted all as truth as he heard it.

"Listen, Johnathan, I must be away to Jerusalem. I hope you brought the gold I wanted." I was in need of a horse and would either take Johnathan's animal or buy one.

"Aye, leave it to me, I'll find you one or you will ride mine." He was ready to search the city for a good animal, and left without delay.

It seemed a good while before he returned, but it wasn't long. With him was a sturdy mount. I paid my debt to the innkeeper and bade him goodwill for his services, gathered my belongings and we left Capernaum.

I wanted to set my course for Nazareth and once again see Mary but thought better of it, and instead, held close to the shore of the sea of Tiberias. We passed through Magdala, Tiberias, Philotena, and then followed one of the old trails to the south of the Jordan. As we passed Philotena, I thought of Gadara. I told the story of how the demonic was cured near there. Or was it Gergesa? I had the haunting feeling I should cross the river and find the healed heathen. I wondered if he remained free of the demons or had he fallen once again prey to their power?

Many things about this story bothered me: the sudden need of the demons to get permission to enter animals; and the obvious entry of demons into man without such, let alone Yeshua. Yet the urgency to return to Jerusalem overrode the yearning for confirmation of this story about demons and I left it as told to me and rode on south.

We made good time and was in sight of Jerusalem in two days. I was glad to see it sprawling on the hills below the Mount of Olives. We passed through the city without delay. The usual Roman checkpoints still were in effect. Finally, we arrived at the gate of home! We were met by some servants and the noise caused others to appear. Apius, the old wardog, came to see what the commotion was all about and helped me dismount. He greeted me as a son long lost. He added the new mount to the rest of the animals and saw to its needs. Johnathan received my thanks and I dismissed him for the day.

I entered the house and proceeded to repair the damages of the road. A bath and clean clothes gave me a brighter outlook on life. I went to the garden for refreshments. Mother

soon appeared and came to my side. She was curious about my sudden return from Capernaum, but was discrete and held her tongue until we had passed loving greetings.

"Judas, my heart sings again now that you have returned. I will set the house for
a family get together and we will then hear your stories." She had already signaled her
housemaid and arranged for the servants to notify the others.

"Ah, mother, my adventure was short lived. I have heard many stories and have grown
to understand much. I would be pleased to tell my tales to the others that they may know
of the coming of the Messiah." I would have said more but felt it not the time.

"Good. All will be present yet this week. I have some bad news for you, Judas. It has
been told to us by some at the fort that Apuleius isn't well." I was grieved to hear this and
turned to go to the fort.

"Stay, we have been told that he is suffering from the very fever he has so often cured
in others. From what is said, the potions that cured others don't have the same potency for
him. Oh, Judas, don't look so unhappy. I'm sure he will be alright. Come, give us some of
your days before you rush off unto him." She came close and took my hand. I was greatly
undone. Not many had been closer to me than Apuleius and to hear of his illness struck
fear in my heart. Was it Shalazar again? Apuleius had always been strong and careful about
his handling of those who were ill. I couldn't imagine him falling to this disease without
some just cause. I again thought of the warning of Shalazar. Had I done the wrong thing
by leaving the side of Yeshua? Was this a fault of mine charged to Apuleius?

"I bend to your will, mother, but as soon as I can, I will go to the fort and see this
thing for myself. If it is bad and he is not comfortable there in the barracks, I will ask to
have him released and brought here where we can nurse him back to health. Isn't that so?"
I looked at mother for assurance that it would be so.

"I wouldn't have it any other way. He shall come if it can be arranged. It wasn't long
ago that he placed his life in danger for you. If this is serious, you must write his family in
Rome." She was ready for this to take place. I would go to him tomorrow.

"Where is Ishmael?"

"Ah, so you noticed? He left to start a new life with Miriam in a home of his own. He
started a business in pottery and other art pieces. He will be here tomorrow and tell you of
his new home. I'm happy for him even though the house is a bit empty with both of you
gone. Would that I could hear the voices of the young again."

I sat down on the bench in the garden and watched the goldfish flash in the pool. I
always felt at home here. It was a feeling of being safe. Mother left to attend to the plans
of the day. She would have us all together again as happiness was family togetherness.

I was interested in the happenings after Herod's birthday, and decided to see if Apius
had any comments. I went to the servants' quarters and found him there.

"Apius, oh Apius, come and let me hear of the things going on in Jerusalem!" I called
to him from near the courtyard.

Apius came from his room and strode to me. We talked some time of the politics of
Palestine and the pressures on Herod to cooperate with the Romans. He reviewed the stories the street people told about the Sicarii and Zealots. The more I heard of these things
in and about Jerusalem, the more I felt the time was right for the coming of the Messiah.
There must be some way for me to speed up the time for balancing the scales of justice for
Israel and God as he desired. At last, the evening call to prayers came upon us; I left for
my room to call upon the Lord according to the law.

The evening meal was spent in the company of mother; it was a lonely time. We reminisced a good deal - she told me of letters received from Uncle Benjamin who asked about
the possibility of my returning to Rome. He still considered me a son and regretted my
leaving. I could still see his house and the stately garden I rested in while there.

Sleep came quickly that night. The morning brought thoughts of Apuleius and the desire to see him. The thoughts of him lying ill in a lonely barracks was depressing.

Soon the family came and the house was full of happy noises. Ishmael and Miriam greeted me with much emotion, and sister Anath and family wouldn't leave me alone. Her children were precocious and full of energy. Much of this was lost on an old bachelor uncle. It took all I could do to remember these young children were gifts from God.

The day passed with pleasant family games and at evening, the family rested and stories were told. I became the central figure in this scenario. I told them of all that happened to me from the first meeting with Yeshua in Capernaum unto the very day I returned. I told them of his words that I should return home and wait for his coming. I would do as I had done before and teach the lessons he had freely taught to me. It was the news of the coming of the kingdom of God on earth and the return to God with Israel's greatness that enthralled them all.

They were greatly interested in my stories but weren't convinced that Yeshua was the one Israel waited for these many years. Ishmael, who remembered Yeshua from earlier days, was least interested in this possibility. He was of the opinion that Yeshua wasn't forceful enough to lead Israel into a confrontation with the Romans. Try as I might, I couldn't convince them that it wasn't Yeshua of himself, but as an instrument of God that the balances of good and evil was to occur. All the family went to rest early and slept well except me - wasn't what I told them true? Had I even, as I told Yeshua, failed to give the message correctly - was I a failure as an apostle?

The families remained with us until the following day. After morning Shema, I told Ishmael I wanted to seek out Apuleius and see what I could do for him. If he was truly very ill, I wanted to bring him home and here care for him even as he would have for me were we in Rome. Ishmael agreed and we mounted and rode to the fort to see Apuleius.

The guard brought us to the officer of the day.

"What brings you here?" He was a big man and rough at that.

"We seek a friend, and officer, one Apuleius Lucius, of the medical brigade." I was patient for I wanted desperately to see Apuleius. I would have at this moment done anything outside of breaking the law to see him.

"Aye, and what is your business with him?" He started looking through the roster. I was grateful for this - we hadn't been escorted from the fort.

"Ah, here we are. He is in the infirmary and considered seriously ill!" I began to have a sinking feeling in my stomach.

"I am his adopted brother and have been told of his illness and would bring him word from his family in Rome." As I said this, I could see his face change from total disregard to interest. He looked from me to Ishmael and back again. We must have sounded like two Jews who had lost their minds to make such a statement. Finally, he motioned for the orderly to come forward.

"Go and see if Apuleius can verify this tale and if he wants to see these two." The orderly left with a forced step of a guard. "Stand aside until I hear from this man."

We moved to the door as he motioned and stood there in all meekness. Ishmael, as always, spent his time studying each man and appointments of the room for later sketches. He was a keen observer and it always showed in his work.

The orderly soon returned with a written message. He handed it to the officer and stepped back to his post.

"So, it's true, by Jupiter! This is a strange one. But it's his request and so it's done." He turned to the guard again. "Take these two to Apuleius. Mind, don't leave them out of your sight."

"Aye!"

The guard led us through a maze of hallways in the barracks. Many of the men there lounged against the walls or sat on bunks placed in files throughout the building. We entered the medical ward and soon were brought to the beside of Apuleius.

"Ah, Judas and Ishmael, it's good to see you! It seems fate has dealt me a cruel blow - I'm the patient and not the doctor." Apuleius lay on a cot covered with wet clothes to lower his fever. His condition caused me great distress. He had lost much weight and his eyes reflected the fever that now incapacitated him. His cheeks were hollow and were flushed with an unnaturally high color. I reached down to where he lay and took his hand in mine; Ishmael reacted in similar fashion. Ishmael, the emotional one, showed his concern of heart by wetting the cover with tears.

"Oh Apuleius, this is a fine state of affairs. Even now I was planning a banquet in honor of your birthday and here you have spoiled it." I was determined to hold to the brighter side of a bad situation. My real concern was the possibility of his removal from this stark dispensary to our home. "Hear me. Is it possible for you to sign yourself from this place and come home with me? Mother is greatly undone at the word of your illness, as we all are, and insists you come to us and be nursed back to health by her own hand."

"Yes, Apuleius, we owe much to you and would repay some little part of our debt…" Ishmael was too full to continue.

"Don't you fear the fever?" Apuleius was one to think of this possibility. I wasn't concerned and would be willing to give aid in any case.

"Apuleius, how many times did this concern you when facing this same illness? Come now, do you think this is an honest question? Don't try to hide behind such a mask. Can you sign out of this place and be brought to us or not?" Apuleius began to shiver from the chill of the fever. Now the cold presses were quickly removed and covers piled on him by the orderly in the infirmary. We waited as he became more stabilized.

"I can, yet I think I'm scheduled to return home within the season. It would be a traumatic voyage under these conditions." He spoke through chattering teeth. He was indeed a very sick man.

"Good, give this man your order and Ishmael will return home and bring men to carry your litter through the city." I saw no reason to delay any longer. It was obvious the treatments used were of little value, and mother, with the aid of her maids, would do just as well. Besides, his chances for recovery would be much better among those who cared as he would at the infirmary.

So it was, Apuleius was signed out on his own writ and brought across the city to father's house. Mother took command and he was soon in the most pleasant surroundings available anywhere. The rest of the family had departed and soon Ishmael and Miriam came and said they would go home.

As time passed, Apuleius's condition deteriorated. The use of the potions he brought with him did little to bring the fever under control. There were times when he wasn't rational. His mind wasn't his own, and he spoke of his younger days in Rome, sometimes shouting commands to men-at-arms and ordering others to their medical stations during battle. From these outbreaks, I learned how much he had experienced during his time of duty here in Judea. I couldn't help admiring him for his lack of hatred of our people but knew him to be a man of medicine and caring for any man irrespective of fortune or nationality.

Our prayers always contained his name. At last it was a critical time, something must be done or his life would run out. I called the household together and sent for Ishmael. When all were gathered, I told them of his condition and possible demise.

I left them and went to my room to attend to prayer one last time, pleading for the Lord to spare his life; not my will but his be done. It was while praying, I suddenly remembered the words of Yeshua, "I give to you the power to heal the sick, cleanse lepers, raise the dead, and cast out devils; all these things I freely give and see that you do likewise." My heart jumped within me! Surely this was a time to exercise this command. Yet hadn't the command included the admonition not to go among the gentiles? Oh, where was the justice in that? Weren't we taught from old, "One God - all children?" I couldn't abide by the command to avoid the need and cares of the gentiles when this gentile was Apuleius - love must rule over all!

A MIRACLE

I went to the room wherein Apuleius lay. It was evening and the oil lamps were lit and placed in the room. The sweet odor of perfume added to the mystical quality of the atmosphere. Apuleius lay on the bed as one near death. Even in the warm lamp light, he looked deathly pale. I softly called Ishmael close to me.

"Hear me, Ishmael. Some time before you said that you couldn't believe Yeshua was sent to be the Messiah, isn't that so?" I asked in a husky whisper. He nodded while still watching the slow breathing of Apuleius.

"You aren't the first to hold this view and won't be the last. But I tell you, he has the Spirit of God in him that no other has since Elijah, and has been given greater power than any other in the history of Israel." I stopped for a moment to listen to Apuleius breathe.

"But what has this to do with poor Apuleius? He is neither a follower nor a Jew." Ishmael was concerned about only one thing - the health of Apuleius.

"Hear me again. This power he has granted to each of his followers of which I am one. So I have said and so I will show you." I stepped forward and removed the coverlet from Apuleius. I knew that what I was to do wasn't for everyone's eyes, so I closed the heavy curtains between the rooms. Ishmael watched me move about the room but said nothing.

"Come to the bed, take the left hand of Apuleius in yours and place your right hand under his armpit. See even as I do, so you can lift him. I will do the same on his right side." Saying thus, I grasped the right hand of Apuleius and prepared to lift him in like manner.

"Hold, Judas, he is so weak and near death that we cannot support him thus and besides, to what end?"

"Hold your tongue and hear me out. Prepare yourself to see that which no others have seen in this city! Remember this, you must never tell another of what happens in this room this night - not even Miriam. Do you understand, and are you willing to do this?" Although I spoke harshly to him, I meant no harm.

"Aye," he said rather timidly - whether from fear or unbelief, I couldn't say.

"Remember Ishmael, some aren't ready to see these things or even to hear of them. Some would attach the wrong meaning to them, and through this meaning, give to some honors they don't deserve. This then takes from God that which is His." I looked sternly at him and wanted him to heed the warning for life. I was unhappy with his lack of faith. I knew I was given power to do this thing and this through God alone. Yet, I also knew it was hard for one brother to believe that special powers were granted to another.

Ishmael reluctantly obeyed my command and prepared himself to lift Apuleius.

As we both lifted, I prayed, "Hear me, O God, even as you heard Elijah so many years ago. O Lord God of Israel and Savior of all, grant to me the power to heal this gentle man. Now Ishmael, when I say the next words, lift Apuleius to a standing position!" Ishmael was wide eyed and opened mouthed at this ritual I was performing but he stood his ground, asked no more questions, and held Apuleius's hand in the grip of the Lion of Judah.

"In the name of Yeshua, I command you to be healed! Awake, Apuleius, and stand free from this fever!"

So it was said and so it was done! Apuleius awakened and stood alone with the fever gone and strength returned. Apuleius smiled and moved slowly about the room. He was steady but still weak. His bed clothes hung loosely about his thin frame. He was a sight to see - but a dear one.

"Ah, it's good, the fever has gone, and I feel much stronger. What happened? I remember little from the time I entered your house." I took his hand and guided him to bed. Ishmael followed him about not knowing what to expect. I stood back and watched the scene. I silently lifted my voice in praise to God.

I could see that Ishmael was bursting to tell Apuleius of his cure, but I motioned that this wasn't to be.

"You are well, Apuleius. It's now just a matter of getting your strength back." I turned, pulled the heavy curtains back, and gave orders to the servants to bring food. Suddenly, I noticed Ishmael was as pale as Apuleius had been just minutes before. "What's the matter, Ishmael? You look ill. Come, let's leave Apuleius rest and enjoy some food."

Mother came in and saw Apuleius and was amazed at his sudden recovery. She saw to the selection of his food.

"Apuleius, rest and get stronger. We will come again in the morning." I touched his hand and took the stunned Ishmael by the arm and whisked him away before he broke his promise and blurted out something that Apuleius or anyone else wasn't prepared to hear.

In my room, Ishmael moved like an automaton; he was still struck by the events of the moment. His color returned and so did his tongue.

"How did you do this thing?"

"Ishmael, what you have just seen is minor indeed to what you'll see when Yeshua assumes his rightful place as the Messiah. His name shall be used to do many wonders indeed!" I wanted him to understand that I didn't do the healing but the will of God through the name of the Messiah. I had no feeling of greatness from this act. I knew my place - I was but the instrument, not the musician.

"Is he truly healed or will he again succumb to the fever?" He was curious about this thing even as I was at one time.

"Listen. Apuleius will be as good as new as soon as he gains strength. The fever is forever gone from him. That isn't to say some other illness can't replace it and he succumb to that, but the fever is gone. In three days, he will be ready to travel back to his unit."

"But why three days?"

"This I don't know, but Yeshua has ever said this as if it has some hidden meaning that he is yet to know or we aren't ready to hear."

I wanted to say more but the evening was passing and I knew Ishmael wanted to be to his home. "Listen Ishmael, go home and ponder on what I've said about the coming of the Messiah. When this comes about, a select few will be honored, and one of these I intend to be!"

Ishmael left without more comment; I gave thanks to the God of Abraham, Isaac, and Jacob for granting me the power and insight to help Apuleius. I felt that it didn't matter whether one was Jew or gentile - *the Lord our God is one.* I went to my bed and fell into a dreamless sleep.

As days passed, Apuleius improved and then left us for his quarters in the fort. He never asked about his sudden recovery - whether he didn't think of it or didn't want to know remained a mystery to me. I was glad he never asked.

Mother asked many questions and often, but I was able to avoid the truth of the matter by expressing thoughts that the potions finally were sufficiently strong to cure him.

Apuleius came often to visit afterward, remarking he felt closer to us than before. We, too, were glad to have him call.

Ishmael's business prospered and I once again took to handling the finances of some of the Roman officers and officials stationed in Jerusalem. The days turned into months and I longed to hear that Yeshua was coming to Jerusalem but it was not so. I heard many stories of his accomplishments and some of the trials of his followers. I began to wonder if I had misunderstood him and should return to Capernaum, but none came to me and therefore I held to the word as I received it. I taught as much as I could in and about the city. At times, I was called to cure someone of a simple disease. Several times, I was called by the Sanhedrin to speak on behalf of Yeshua and the sixteen. The questions ranged from blasphemy to common disregard for customs. I was well known as the defender of the new movement - and became well known to Caiaphas and Annas.

I was careful never to express my thoughts on the coming of the Messiah unto them. They were good men in their way, but tradition and politics had nearly erased their respect for God's laws. The power of the Sanhedrin and the high priest had fallen on hard times.

Both offices were now politically controlled. Herod, an Idumean, was a puppet of Rome and had neither the will or morals to lead our people. Pontius Pilate, the Procurator, was always aspiring to be greater than he was capable and hated both our people and his post in Palestine. He had hoped for greater things when he came back from the German wars - but alas, he was stuck in this god-forsaken Jewish land. I continued to dream of the day of recompense - the day will come!

BACK TO THE PRESENT

...qwertyuiop...suddenly, the speech synthesizer output became garbled and the screen lost all intelligence. The system switched to search mode. Lock was lost and the system moved offline to search for the lost characters and sync words. It displayed a fault and shutdown.

Ed checked the hard copy and took material to the out baskets. The loss of information didn't bother the team as much as it did before. They had lived through this at least three times and always was able to locate a new starting place.

"Well, it's break time anyway. Let's call it quits and visit the restaurant." John placed the entire system on hold and notified security they were leaving. "Jean, your enhancement worked well." John wanted to thank Jean for her new system.

"Thanks. I know it's a good program and will pick up again when we return." She placed all her materials in the file and spun the tumblers.

"Well, much has happened in this segment." Chuck was the first to comment about the material that was seen and heard that morning.

The time taken for lunch was short. They were back at their consoles in less than an hour. John set the system in order, and punched in the code of the day. The automatic vertablinds closed and the room darkened.

"Here we go again - I hope." John crossed his fingers, but it didn't work - so much for luck. "It seems to be an old story," John said, as he watched the system struggle.

"In more ways than one!" Chuck added, and they all relaxed some from the comedy of the moment. It was an old story they were searching for at the moment - a very old story.

"Well, while we wait, we might as well look at what we have." John didn't want to waste time. They all began thumbing through the material.

"Suddenly, Ed called a page number for all to look at. "Look, one of the interesting things is the author's claim that there were more than twelve followers. He offers the names of as many as sixteen and seventeen counting himself. Traditionally, it's twelve."

Most checked through their copies for the page. "By the way, Ed, why is this held to be true? I know there are more than twelve names offered in the ancient copies. I know the rationale used to explain these differences, but isn't there room for doubt, and isn't there any other not talked about?" Jean asked, while scanning the pages before her.

"The early church held twelve to be an acceptable number first because the apostles themselves said there were twelve, though not in complete agreement as to who they were. Second, because of the prophesies from earlier Hebrew writings. They assumed a lesser number wouldn't be realistic because of the twelve tribes. The early church writers matched the number of teachers of the word to the number of tribes. Since then, it was to be transcribed, and held to be without error, and so it is today."

"I wonder how or even if Judas copes with this problem in later portions of his journal." John mused, as he looked at the text.

"I wondered the same thing," Chuck said, "I was thinking that he may find that although sixteen were ordained and dispersed, only twelve came back. Considering they are all average men with all the idiosyncracies of men, then it's entirely possible that only twelve hold fast to their cause." Chuck waited for some other comment - none came, so he continued. "Just imagine, if you were given the power to heal the sick, cast out devils, raise the dead, and cure the leper, what else would you need to become the most loved and powerful man in the world? From man's point of view, why would you ever return? I see no time limit given on these miraculous capabilities, or for that matter, that they should end! No! I find it hard to believe - from what is accepted as human nature - that some of these followers didn't turn away and remain out in the field functioning as their own emissaries."

They spent a quiet moment considering these statements by Chuck, each occupied with the immense possibility of human frailty overcoming the spiritual drive, the creation of several Frankenstein's - so to speak! There was more here than first meets the eye.

"This seems entirely possible, Chuck." Ed put a hand to his forehead and rubbed as if to remove some mental cobwebs. "Hmmm, let's see now...the passage I'm thinking of is written in Mark. To paraphrase, John points out to Yeshua that he saw one casting out devils in Yeshua's name, and the kicker here is, 'and he followeth not us.'" His hand came down and he looked up rather pleased with himself. The words had come back.

"The question is, how did anyone not associated with Yeshua gain the knowledge that such could be done in his name, let alone have the power to do this thing? From Mark, I understood it was a one-to-one exercise wherein Yeshua laid hands on each one and therewith gave his power to each disciple. Yet the way John writes, one would think he doesn't know this, 'one casting out devils in thy name.'" Ed again moved his hand to his head in the familiar motion of one brushing away some inhibitor.

"Now, in my mind at least, this implies the following: one, that it was possible to gain this power without ordination, and two, more than just twelve were given this special power, and one of those wasn't known to John! I'm of the opinion that this might be one of the early sixteen that didn't return but went on his own course. Notice, to believe otherwise is to agree that the ordination had nothing to do with the capability of someone to cast out devils, in other words, anyone could do it - both then and now!" He stood up and walked to the far end of the room. It was as though he was lecturing again in the classroom. The others watched and listened even as students would - none cared to interrupt.

"This opens questions to the repeating of the statement, 'Forgiven by the power vested in me as an ordained minister of the Gospel.' Just what does this mean and does it have any significance at all? I sincerely believe it's more show than substance. Of course, this is merely an educated guess, but I dare say, not anymore so than some of the others done with respect to these books." Ed stated the last with relish and walked back to his console; he didn't always agree with the traditionalists anyway. Well, this took some time and was the lecture of the day.

While the discussion was in progress, the system found and locked on a new story line and began to display information on the screen. The synthesizer became active as well.

They all forgot the discussion and moved to the consoles to gather information.

…It was in Abib near the time of Pesach and the festival of Unleavened Bread. The time passed with great events; as my journal states, the time I was in Jerusalem was nearly a year. I grew richer and so did Ishmael. Mother remained well and happy that her family was so near and the news of Miriam being with child reinforced her happiness. I wasn't as interested in the wealth I had made as with the waiting for Yeshua to come to Jerusalem and start the redemption of Israel.

Oh, I heard all the wondrous stories from the pilgrims and people on the roadway. They continued to tell of the miracles and teaching of Yeshua. Slowly, at first, then more stories came tumbling into the mainstream of Judea from Galilee. The Sadducees and some critical Pharisees became interested in this itinerant teacher from Galilee. He admittedly had no great learning yet was able to answer the most profound questions put to him by some of the more learned. Their attention bordered on dislike and, in the worst cases - hate.

Many who held strongly to the traditions of the past could only see these being broken down and leaving the people with nothing to protect them against the influx of gentile philosophies and religions. Many believed his teachings weren't well understood by the common and unschooled people, and who could tell where this would lead.

I could see no harm in any of the teachings I heard while in Jerusalem…

John shut down the system.

"What's happened?" he asked, as he stared at the screen. "This system has skipped at least a year in real time. The way this is being transcribed, the scroll is defective and nearly a year of the writings aren't available. Time has short changed us here." He wasn't happy about this sudden change in the operation of the system. He turned from the console and looked at the others.

"Look, the system has a mind of its own. From this chair, I believe, we need a rest from this work. I would like to take the day off and show Jean some of Bradenton - she just might like it well enough to stay here. So, what do you say? Let's play some hooky!" It was obvious he was tired and the same seemed true for the others. The scroll wasn't going anywhere - it hadn't done so for many years.

The others were mildly surprised at this change in John's "complete the project, all else be dammed" attitude but all accepted the call.

Chuck looked around the lab and swung his legs freely, "Don't see any chains on me, and I have some things I could do as well. I'm for the break until tomorrow."

So it was agreed; all were ready in a short time. The system shut down, material was stowed, and they were out the door and into the garage.

Ed waved before he got in the car, "Have a good one; see you early tomorrow!"

John and Jean were together in his car and on their way for an afternoon and evening of relaxation. They had a great time studying the campus, walking through each building, and John commented on each department. Afterward, they enjoyed an evening on the town. They finally called it a night in the wee hours of the morning, both happy and satisfied with the day of hooky!

And the evening and the morning were the sixth day.

CHAPTER TWENTY

Stories From Bethany

The next day they all arrived at nearly the same time. The laboratory was ready in good time. The consoles were placed online and the next phase of decoding the Golden Scroll began.

The system started and functioned well. John answered the query from the day before and the screen came alive with intelligent prose. "Ok, then, on with the show." John started the system again and the first words were: It was nearly 784 when the first knowledge of Yeshua coming to Jerusalem came to me. Yet I remembered that it was traditional for him to do so to honor Pesach and the days of the Feast of Unleavened Bread. The time of waiting was nearly over for me. I was soon to see the coming of the Messiah - coming in all his power and glory - glory for God and Israel! Soon, I would see the changes in the world as I often dreamed in the last months.

I was interrupted in my study by one of the servants. It was the announcement that a man stood at the gate and wished to see me. I left my meditation to attend to the matter. At the gate, I saw a man holding the reins to two animals. As I came to him, he saluted me and said he brought the animals to me as he was instructed. I had no knowledge of asking anyone to do this and was about to say he had the wrong household when Apius saw the animals and the man at the gate and came to us.

"Ho there! So you brought the animals." Apius shouted from some distance away; I could see he knew this fellow.

"Who is this fellow? What is this, Apius? I've no requirement for any more animals. Why have you purchased more?" I wasn't greatly disturbed by this act; it was just that I liked to know where my money was going.

"Master, don't you remember the ass we purchased in Capernaum over a year ago? The animal Miriam rode to Jericho?" I then recalled this purchase and the subsequent trip to Jericho, as well as my arrest.

"Oh, yes, but what has this to do with us now?"

"It was because of time I commissioned this man, Jeremiah, to take the animal and hold it for me until I called for it. For that, he was welcome to use it as he might. Well, he had use of it for a year, and the other day, I sent one of the others to seek it out. He came back with the message the man was grateful for the use of the animal and would return it as soon as it foaled."

So this was the story. This Jeremiah was bringing the animals back as he had said. I was very pleased and would have given the animals to him for his honesty but he refused them. It seemed he felt his use of the animals was more than enough to pay for the care of it and wouldn't impose any more on my generosity.

"Are you from Jerusalem?" I asked.

"No, my lord, I have a small garden farm near Bethany." He was a kindly fellow and looked in need of help. His skin showed the effects of the sun and his hands that of hard work. He had more than his share of wrinkles and when he spoke, I could see some of his front teeth were missing.

"Do we need these animals, Apius?" I inspected the animals; they were sturdy.

"No, master, we have all we need in the stables now." Apius was still the first servant of our household and knew these things well.

"Let's put it this way. You take the animals back to your small farm and use them as you need. Maintain their health as if they were your stock." I continued to consider a way to have him feel comfortable about taking the animals. "I have no immediate use for them and I would have to exercise them if I keep them, so you can do me a service by working them." His face suddenly lifted in countenance and he bowed to me with great style. "But hear me good, you must keep them well and available for me on a moments' notice. I wouldn't want you to sell or commit them to hire. Is that understood?"

"Aye, my lord, it will be so. But how will I know you want the animals on a moments' notice?" This was a logical question and deserved a reasonable answer.

"Consider this - any man who comes to you and says these words in this manner, 'The lord hath need of them,' to them or him you shall give both animals without concern or hesitation!" He repeated the sentence as though it was a part of scripture - he wouldn't forget. I doubted if I would ever send anyone for the animals and had decided he was worthy of their use for their lifetime. To my mind, this particular word grouping would seldom be used by anyone coming to take the animals, so it was that I dismissed Jeremiah and he took the animals and was about to leave with them when another thought struck me.

"Hold before you leave, Jeremiah. Come and join us for some refreshments and tell us of the news from Bethany. Leave the animals here. They will be safe." I turned and both Jeremiah and Apius followed. I moved to a shade tree within the gates but not in the courtyard for I saw no reason to raise the house. Apius had one of the servants bring some fruit and wine; this was in accordance with the custom of the day.

I wanted to hear the news from Bethany as it was on the route from Capernaum. It would be one of the stops made by those traveling to Jerusalem.

"Come now, Jeremiah, rest and tell us of the news in Bethany." He was a common man and not given to much gossip, but willing to tell what he knew as the truth about the happenings in the town. He was about to speak when I saw Apuleius ride up to the gate. Apuleius waved to us from the gate, dismounted, and came into the outer courtyard to us.

"Ho Apuleius! Come join us for news from Bethany. This is Jeremiah, a farmer who lives near there and is about to tell us some interesting stories." This I had no way of knowing as the truth, but winked at Apuleius and he accepted the signal as one of fun.

"Ha so! That is interesting for I've just come from Bethany, but I'll tell you my tale after this man has had his say." He turned to a nearby bench and removed some of his harness. Jeremiah stared at him. It was the first time he had ever seen a Roman accepted in the gates of his own kind without some warrant or force of arms. By the word of all the Pharisees, the Romans were considered unclean and an abomination unto the Lord. Some Pharisees even crossed the street to avoid bumping into Romans. Jeremiah had a hard time continuing, but after pouring water over his hands to meet the law, he took a few gulps of wine and moved ahead.

"Perhaps you haven't heard of these things. Both of these events concern the presence of an itinerant teacher called Yeshua. He was in our town for two months, Abib, and before that, Adar, teaching many of the coming of the kingdom of God. Yet the most peculiar thing is the miracle he performed there." Jeremiah was now in his element and the storytelling came easier. He stopped long enough to take some grapes and a sip of wine.

I wanted to tell him to hurry on, but held my tongue. I could see Apuleius smiling as he watched and listened to Jeremiah.

"It all happened in this wise: One called Lazarus, a brother to the woman known as Martha who lives in Bethany, became very ill and died sometime before Yeshua came to the town. I would say at least four or more days it was. I heard from the family members and professional mourners that this was so. Yeshua, as he was called by the others, came at the request of Martha and Mary, her sister. He had with him some eleven men - disciples they be. Some were not so handsome as others, and some ugly; that I say as the truth!" He stopped again, chuckled at his bit of humor about the followers, and helped himself to the wine and fruit. While he was so occupied, I turned to Apuleius.

"Apuleius, why were you in Bethany these days?" He set down his cup and took a grape, also.

"I had a sick soldier there. It turned out to be nothing but a poor choice of food on his part, and after purging, he was as good as new." He laughed at the incident, and turned back to listen to Jeremiah.

"Well, so the story was told to me, Lazarus was in the tomb for at least four days and the mourning was nearly done. Some of the mourners from Jerusalem and elsewhere were making ready to leave. They had been paid in full. It was then Yeshua came and mourned with the family. He asked to see where Lazarus lay. Now, here is the strange thing - before they went to the tomb, he had them take new clean clothes for Lazarus along; even Mary and Martha thought this exceedingly strange. It was some distance from the home of his kin to the tomb and many of the townspeople joined in the procession as is the custom. All those present warned Yeshua about removing the cover for the decomposition had already started. Yet, it was removed by some of the family at the request of Yeshua.

None wanted to do this as they didn't want to be declared unclean again. But so it was done. None there wanted to look upon the dead man again - it is not a good thing. As you know to be present or to touch a corpse is an unclean act, and purification must follow these acts. The teacher stood a goodly distance from the tomb and it was said by those present, he spoke in a loud voice 'Lazarus come forth!' in just that manner." Jeremiah raised his voice to mimic that of Yeshua in his command to the dead man. Some of those in the courtyard came to see what was about. I sent them away with a wave of my hand, and Jeremiah continued as though nothing unusual happened.

"Well, those I know personally who were there said that Lazarus rose from the place he was laid and came forth from the tomb! This I say even as I rest here! The scene was bedlam, the professional mourners departed in great haste, as well as some of the family. Some of the ladies and men also swooned and fell to the ground in fits. Many scrambled over one another to depart the place and great fear came upon them; some couldn't believe their eyes and thought it was a trick. You know, like those acts put on by the Chaldean mystics and traveling sorcerers."

Apuleius laughed heartily at his story; Jeremiah was greatly excited by his own telling of the tale. I noticed he spit a great deal while talking, this was primarily due to the lack of front teeth.

While he continued with his story, I noticed Apius remained leaning against the tree with his eyes closed as if the better to see the mental pictures he was hearing.

"Hear me, Jeremiah, how much of this do you believe and how much of this did you really see?" I wasn't one to believe some of the stories, and would much rather have them told by one seeing them firsthand.

"Ah, my lord, I saw much of this, for I came running as I heard the noise made by many of those frightened by this strange sight. Mind you, none had ever seen a man rise up from the grave before! I arrived just as he came stumbling out of the tomb. He was still wrapped in the customary burial cloth. He could barely walk because of the wrappings. I could see his face as the napkin fell away. His face was still covered with the ointment and looked pale as a ghost indeed. I reasoned some of that may have been due to the time spent in the tomb. Yeshua, noting his difficulty in walking, spoke to those still remaining to 'Loose him, and let him go.' Some of the family, who had not fainted, stepped cautiously forward and removed the bindings from him and placed on him the new clothes. I, not being one of the family, held my distance. It wasn't that I was afraid, but I was cautious. I will admit my heart pounded some." He paused to look at us and see the result of his story.

"Hold right there," Apuleius spoke. "I can add some to this story. While I was taking care of the disabled trooper, I, too, heard the raucous noise and went to investigate. It was the first time I had seen this Yeshua you've spoken so much about. He was there, even as Jeremiah says, and with him, near the tomb, was a strange sight indeed. Those who were family, I take it, were there, also, but the one standing apart from them looked more dead than alive." Apuleius stopped a moment, looked very serious, and drew on a cup of wine.

"Considering the great noise about all this, I would wonder if he was really alive at all. I made no thorough examination because what is done between Jews is often better left that way. From the distance between me and the near apparition standing alone like a scarecrow in new dress, he wasn't good to look upon. If this was an example of resurrection, then I wouldn't enjoy it for mine." He shook his head indicating a sad situation of life but not real life.

"But he was alive - you must admit that?" I asked.

"Oh yes, he was animated enough in a peculiar sense of the word. He walked as though all his joints were nearly locked, and moved his arms and hands as one would were he a puppet. His eyes were glazed over and moved little, while his tongue, which was dark, tended to protrude from his mouth. It seemed as though he had little control over his body. After I viewed this event for sometime and watched some of the women come to him and assist him in all ways, I left to return to my troops. Well, the noise had subsided anyway. There was no need of me staying there." He finished with a show of his open hands.

"Did you see this Lazarus later or did you return to the fort yet that day?"

"I had to stay to check some of the other troops in the maniple so I was there about a week. I saw him again when a small banquet was given in honor of the teacher. As near as I could see, he was still moving with the same difficulty, but he was seen by some of the troops to be eating and enjoying his notoriety. Word soon got around of this phenomena and people from Jerusalem and elsewhere sought him out. I would say that not many of your people came close to him. Most stood aside as they do for a leper. It seemed there was a religious law about touching a corpse or some such that kept them at a distance."

A PROBLEM

It was then Jeremiah solved some of the mystery. "After awhile, the people fell away and some went to Jerusalem to see Caiaphas."

"Why did they do such a thing?"

"Because of what is written about unclean things. It wasn't known what should be done - after all, this man was once a corpse! A corpse, mind! Many of the family wondered what should be done to make him clean again, and also what of those who were with him?"

He looked at me as if I hadn't reasoned well. Everyone should know the law! I didn't even know what should be done. When one touched a corpse or was even in the presence of a corpse, it was required by law to purify oneself by using water containing the ashes of a red heifer. How well I remembered, for this I had to do after I went to secure the body of John. I agreed all this was to be done when touching a corpse - but what was to be done when one had *been* a corpse? My mind reeled with the immensity of it all!

I shouldn't wonder that the Pharisees were turning over the pages of the Tradition and Law to find the answer. And, in fact, not finding anything, become somewhat undone by this new complication of religion. But I had drifted and he continued to tell the story.

"I heard some who went to the temple saw Caiaphas and he said that Lazarus wasn't really dead at all but just slept, while others said he should be dead for this would resolve the problem of uncleanliness. Others claimed the family had given him one of those potions from the far east that slows down all bodily functions, just so this trick would be done by the teacher, one like the Chaldeans kept with them in suspension acts. With this, I cannot agree, for Lazarus was dead to me on the day of the funeral." Jeremiah shook his head as he remembered the time and place.

"The family soon went into the house and I left and hadn't seen Lazarus until the other day." He moved to go but I wanted to hear more of the happenings.

"Stay, when did you see him again and was he well?"

"Aye, he was that, but as the Roman says, not as you or I. In fact, the family held a small banquet for the teacher who had brought Lazarus back to the land of the living. That was just a week ago." He settled down again and began his second tale.

"It was to be a banquet for the teacher and I was asked to bring some produce to them from my farm. I did so and was paid well. It seemed that it was an open house and all who wanted to see the teacher were welcome. It was said he would teach on the kingdom of God and the keeping of the law of love. So I chose to stay and hear him out. After the meal and while he was teaching, a woman came into the room, one Mary by name. She proceeded to anoint Yeshua with oil and wipe his feet with her hair. Well, the entire room was filled with the fragrance of the oil. I thought it was an ill-advised thing to do for the oil was very expensive and a little would go a long way, but I had naught to say about it."

"I noticed that some of the disciples chided the woman for the waste. I couldn't agree more, for the same sold at the marketplace would add to their coffers and part of this given to relieve the suffering of the poor. The teacher thought it wasn't becoming of them to object to her doing as she did, and called them to heel. He added this as well, 'The poor you always have with you, but me you have not always.' They were upset by this remark and murmured among themselves that they wouldn't have said it if it hadn't been for Judas."

He stopped suddenly, recalling my name as mentioned by Apius some time before. He looked at me a long time and then remarked, "Ah, there was one in the group of eleven named Judas but you aren't him. I thought for a moment I was telling this story for naught."

"No, I wasn't with them, if that's what bothered you," I answered.

"Well, some claimed him to be the keeper of the purse, but as to this I can't say. It seemed to me that none of the eleven wanted to take the blame for murmuring about the waste of the oil, and was willing to cast the shadow of guilt on one who wasn't there. I'm not such a learned man, but I couldn't help but wonder what was meant by the speech of the teacher. I really believe that many of the poor about him could have been saved both in life and limb if a bit more money was used. It was obvious to me that not all the poor could be saved by the little gained from the price of the oil - but was that just cause for not using it to lessen their suffering? I never heard a teacher accept such adoration, and not striving to stay it from happening!" He moved this time as his story was over. He was happy for our audience and evidently felt he had earned his repast. I gave him Godspeed and good will, and he left with the animals. Apius stood up and said nothing about the stories. He asked to be dismissed and left for the servants' quarters. I was deeply troubled by these stories. I knew now that Yeshua was but a short time from Jerusalem.

Apuleius and I talked at length about the condition of Lazarus but nothing came of it. He stepped into the house to give mother a good word and then mounted and left. After he left, I returned to my studies and thought considerably about the incident.

I had decided to scribe some of the stories I heard about Yeshua from the passing parade of human beings in Jerusalem. The stories were varied and at times hard to believe. Some bordered on the ridiculous while others, the sublime.

Some disturbed me greatly as I was mentioned in them, although I knew I wasn't even near the happenings described. It was as though someone among the sixteen still held me in contempt without just cause. After all, I had done nothing but obey Yeshua and resided in Jerusalem as he said to do.

One such story that caused me much concern was about the bag Jeremiah just told. I wanted to talk to Yeshua about these things when he came to the city.

A GRAND PLAN

I decided not to let Yeshua arrive as the Messiah without some acclamation. I called Apius and Johnathan to me. I told them to gather many people together and offer them a maneh each if they would prepare themselves and stay ready for the day of arrival. All that accepted the money were to gather palm branches and be ready to line the streets from the gate to the temple when Yeshua arrived. They would be signaled by the sounding of trumpets at the gate. Thus, we prepared the people to know of the arrival of the new King and Messiah. Both Apius and Johnathan did as I instructed. They took some of the others with them that they might cover much of the city. When they came to me again, they had contacted many people and I was happy to give them the money to seal the contract. I was sure Yeshua wouldn't be disappointed - a great crowd would meet him on the day of his entry into Jerusalem. I dispatched Atonis to the town of Bethany to wait and when Yeshua began his trek to the holy city, he was to ride on ahead and bring me the news. I would go out to meet Yeshua and order the trumpets blown to signal the arrival of the Savior of Israel.

So it was arranged and so it happened. Atonis came to me before Yeshua approached the city on a colt, and I hurriedly went to greet him before he was nigh to Jerusalem and before I called for the blowing of the trumpets. I wanted to talk to him before the crowds formed and sang to him.

He was a good distance when I rode up to he and the eleven. I gave greetings to all and noted how they were less than brotherly to me in their greetings. Most of this I felt was because of my absence from them for nearly a year. And, of course, they traveled over the arduous routes and difficult times with Yeshua. To them, I wasn't a comrade at arms, but a fair-weather companion who was never tried as they were. Yes, to them, I was a laggard.

I could see Yeshua was on a small colt accompanied by its' mother. As I came closer, I recognized the pair. Yes, it was the same, the very same I had lent Jeremiah some days before. As I came nearer, I asked the only question that would settle my mind.

"Yeshua, greetings in the name of the Lord, and the city is yours. But Yeshua, how came you by these animals?" I was consumed by curiosity.

"Greetings to you, Judas, and may the Lord be with you this day. As to the animals, do they look familiar to you?"

"Yes," I returned, looking down at him from my horse which was considerably larger than the little colt he was riding.

"Ah, well, I told Peter and Philip to go to Bethany and fetch me this pair as I had seen them sometime earlier. They are the property of someone you know, isn't that so?" He smiled. He was aware of my involvement - but how?

"Aye, I know him well, for I'm the owner of these two animals. But they were under the care of one Jeremiah, a local farmer near Bethany, and were to be held for me and let to no other." I was curious how and why Jeremiah let them go. We continued to ride along slowly so the eleven could remain with us. Some of them had now crowded around to hear our words.

"They came to me because I asked for them," continuing to say no more than he wanted.

"But, Yeshua, don't tease me. How did you get him to release the animals without telling me?"

"I told Peter to say unto the man thus, 'The Lord hath need of them,' and, according to Peter, when he said these words, the man said nothing and turned away. They then brought the animals to me - so it was said, and so it was done."

Ah! So that is the way of it. I said no more, but wondered how Yeshua knew the phrase I told Jeremiah. Then, I pondered an even more curious thing. How did *I* come by these words?

I turned to the few in number who were with Yeshua. Where were the others? Had they, like me, been assigned other places to wait until Yeshua would call them? Why - more than half weren't here! I counted eleven and with me, only twelve. I recognized immediately that only Peter, Andrew, Philip, James, Bartholomew, Thomas, Matthew, Simon the Zealot, Judas and James, the brothers of Yeshua, were present. While Levi, Simon the Canaanite, Thaddaeus, Lebbaeus, and Nathanael were missing. I wondered in my heart what had happened to these, the first fruits of Yeshua's labors? At some quiet time, I would ask Yeshua about those missing.

CHAPTER TWENTY-ONE

Greetings For A King

Soon we came within sight of the great gates of the city. I then told Atonis to ride on ahead and cause the trumpeters to sound the coming of Yeshua. This he did in a twinkling and the city was aroused. The people were brought together even as I had planned and came tumbling through the gates to greet the one they were told was the Messiah - Yeshua, the man from Galilee.

As prearranged, they brought olive branches and extra clothing to spread in his way. They sang the song of old as I had requested, 'Hosanna in the highest, blessed is he who comes in the name of the Lord.'

I could see by Yeshua's smile he was pleased with this greeting and because of this smile, I was more than amply paid for all my work. I had done something some of the others hadn't, and this pleased me as well.

The others, not aware of my participation in the stirring up of the crowd, thought it was all in spontaneity and gave much credit to his popularity. Although Yeshua's name and fame had spread throughout Galilee, and some areas to the north of Judea, the great city with all its cosmopolitan atmosphere wasn't so impregnated with his deeds. That isn't to say that many of the people didn't carry stories of his deeds in their hearts, for this was known to be true. In fact, many of the more learned Pharisees and Sadducees were well informed of his travels and teachings. What was also true was that many of those who were storytellers and carriers of his words in heart weren't with sufficient funds to leave their work and come to greet him. Even for one day, the costs would be prohibitive. So it was that I caused many of the lesser people to gather and greet Yeshua. This was little cost to me and great benefit to those who accepted the contract and came.

As the procession passed through the gates, some shouted, "Who is it that comes?" Some who were familiar with the writings of the sages asked, "Is it Mashiach ben Yosef or Mashiach ben David?" The answer that came ringing back was, "Hail, Yeshua, the Messiah from Galilee!" I could see many turn away - a Messiah from Galilee?

On they came, the paid jubilee and the curious singing and dancing. As the colt passed some of the learned, some shouted that the noise was enough to frighten angels away and bring on the Roman soldiers. A spokesman for some stepped forward and shouted above the crowd noise, "Teacher, bring some order among your followers. Don't cause the troops to come upon us!"

I heard Yeshua shout back, "If these should hold their peace, the stones would immediately cry out."

The spokesman for the others then shouted back, "Let them do it then - we would like to hear the stones speak!"

I watched Yeshua and hoped he would silence the crowd and show these learned men how the Messiah could cause the stones to speak - but he did nothing but smile and continued to ride on. In my heart, I was nearly destroyed - I had expected him to move now, but he gave no demonstration of his power! What had I done?

Those hearing the challenge of the learned men laughed as the procession with Yeshua on the colt moved on by - Messiah indeed! The procession passed down the streets of Jerusalem and to the temple itself. Here it stopped and those who had come at my contract were paid for work, but having the necessary pay for the day, many stayed to see the reason for this celebration.

Yeshua dismounted and went into the temple to pray and inspect it as he had done before. I remained there with the others. I sent Atonis to return the animals to Jeremiah in Bethany with my words of thanks for his following my instructions to the letter. After Yeshua finished his inspection, he came out and sat down on the steps of the porch. He was greatly disturbed with the money changers that were operating inside. The temple was the house of God, not the commercial center. He was very unhappy but bided his time.

While the others stood nearby, I came to Yeshua and spoke to him, "Soon it will be evening, Yeshua. Will you come to the house of my mother and bless us with your presence?" I wanted him to know in the great city there was one house he could call his own. I held my peace at the moment, but was burning with desire for him to come with the eleven and celebrate the Passover and Feast of the Unleavened Bread with my family.

"This night I will return to Bethany as I have yet to do that which I must there." I was humbled at this news and fought against this rejection. Surely, he had something more pressing than I could imagine but nonetheless, the refusal didn't go down easy.

"Ah, then, perhaps another day?" I hoped all my family could meet Yeshua - the boy they once knew - the man I now called the Messiah.

"It's possible, Judas, but even as I've told the others, time is getting short. Soon, I'll be called to do that which I must to bring the balance in the scales of justice. Remember, Judas, only you and I know these things." Some of the others murmured about these words and would have asked Yeshua to make them plain, but they remained silent. "You remain here. I'll come again tomorrow - look for me outside the gate again. The crowd will be gone tomorrow and the people will be gathering to make ready for the feast."

He stood up and motioned for the others to follow and they left me. I returned home to wait until tomorrow. Mother questioned me about his refusal to come to the house, but saw in my face the effects of the refusal and let it be.

"Judas, what will he do to celebrate the coming festival?" She would have him come as it had been a long time since he, as a lad with his family, had done so. In the early days, Joseph and Mary spent several festivals with Zechariah. But after Zechariah's death, Joseph's family celebrated the great days in a small upper room in the house of the "Pherohudria", or the sign of the carrier of the water-pot. The sign was very weather beaten but still hung over the door of the wayside inn as it had for years. Other times when alone, Yeshua celebrated the festival at the home of Mary Magdalene.

"I'll ask him and the others with him to come, but from his reactions today, I think he has already other plans in mind. So mother, don't look for these men to come here." I had my doubts of persuading him to do this thing.

"Well, should it be so, we have enough room for all, and servants to do the tasks. If not, I will open the house as we have often done, to those less fortunate than ourselves. Even as it is written, 'Let no man be without on this joyous day of redemption.'" She moved about the house without further comment.

I spoke again, "Since I'm one of his followers and, at present, he has only eleven with him, and that isn't enough to celebrate Pesach under the law, I will join him, wherever it might be." I could see she wasn't pleased to hear this. "It might be well if Ishmael takes over the preparation of the lamb, and brings the family together in my place."

She simply nodded and left me with the feeling of placing someone before her and the family. It wasn't the first time I would be separated from her on the day of Pesach, but I think the older she grew, the more it rested heavily on her heart. I would see that the next one I would spend here, God willing.

I went to my room to pray and consider the happenings of the day. I proceeded to scribe them into this journal. During this time, I received word from Apius that he would have a word with me. I met him in the courtyard and listened to his request.

"Master, I've come by some friends from Athens who have heard of Yeshua from some Jewish pilgrims in Athens. They are men of great talent and carry respected names among my people. They are students and travel the world studying science and religions of every nation."

"What is their names, and how long have they been among us?"

"Their names are Aristocles, Temaeus, and Xenocrates, all good men and true. They have been here nearly a year and have heard much of Yeshua. Aristocles tells me they have spoken to two followers of Yeshua, Philip and Andrew, but haven't heard from them again. Temaeus and Xenacrates must return home soon and would like to meet your teacher. I told them it might be possible, but some of your religious laws may be a stumbling block. Is there a possibility they may converse with Yeshua?" He was sincere in his request and aware of the feelings held by the teachers of our people and the gentiles.

"Ah, Apius, I have heard these names spoken in Rome. Perhaps it can be done, but I don't know when. Even this day, Yeshua told me that time was short and much is to be done and as you know, the feast is upon us. The city will be hard pressed to maintain order these days." I considered what might be done. "How long will these men be here?"

"They will be here a fortnight yet." He was confident of this.

"Well then, I will speak to Yeshua and tell you of the arrangements, if yes or no. Will your friends be available at any hour?"

"Yes."

"Good, then we shall see." Apius was satisfied and moved back to his quarters; I returned to my room pondering the strangeness of this request. Why were these Greeks interested in Yeshua and what had they heard?

In the morning, I would help Ishmael find a good animal for Pesach. I was hoping the market people and the temple officers wouldn't hold the prices too high this year. After supper with mother and evening prayers, I went to bed to dream of the days' happenings. It was but five days until the celebration and this caused me to dream and rest lightly.

The morning call to prayer gave me little time to wonder of the past. I was away early to join Ishmael and secure a lamb - one without blemish. We brought it home and made it ready for the trip to the temple. Ishmael would act as the head of the household and enter one of the courses to get the lamb sacrificed.

I strode out of the city early to await the arrival of Yeshua and the others. As I was early, I continued to walk away from the city along the road. I noticed a fig tree along the road and went up to it as I had no breakfast. It was on public land and therefore the fruit was for the use of any passerby. The law was that one could fill his belly but not his bag. So I looked for some fruit, but alas, there was none. I saw many leaves but no fruit, then I recalled it wasn't time for this tree to have mature figs. It was then I felt the fool and looked around to see if any of the local farmers were laughing at me for such an unwise act. Not noting any, I moved on down the road and soon met the others on their way to the city.

This time they were all afoot, and therefore later than the day before. I gave them the salute of the day and joined them.

"Yeshua, mother sends her blessings and requests that you and the others celebrate the coming festival within our house." I wanted to know early for the meal was dependent on the number of guests.

"Judas, give Ruth my blessings and thanks for her offer but it's not to be. I would celebrate the Pesach with only these I have chosen and still remain with me." His words settled the question and I wouldn't ask again. At the same time, I wondered again about the ones missing, and his words, "…only those I have chosen and still remain with me." I wanted to ask him of this thing but would do it only when we were alone.

A CURSE AND NOT A BLESSING

As we walked along, we saw the fig tree; the same one I had just passed. He walked over and looked at it even as I had just minutes before. He then said unto the tree as if it were a living thing, "Let no fruit grow on thee henceforth forever!" We all heard this plainly, and saw the fig tree wither away! We were aghast at these words against the tree. For what had the tree done to warrant this anathema? Hadn't I already seen it wasn't in season? And didn't I feel the fool for looking at it when any seasoned farmer wouldn't? Even so, if the tree had been barren in season, wasn't there some just cause?

"Yeshua, why do you curse the tree and deny to others the chance it might bear fruit for them?" I would have an answer to this mystery.

"There is more to this than meets the eye. I will tell you a story that illustrates it before the season is out." He said no more about the tree and his actions.

I, like the others, saw the tree now a withered and dried stub where once a beautiful tree stood. I couldn't let it rest as I had never seen him react thus to even an enemy.

"Yeshua, are you still hungry?" I asked, thinking this was the cause of his action.

"Yes."

"Then why didn't you cause the tree to bear fruit as quickly as you destroyed it, for I and some of the others are also hungry." After his story on the mount, love is better than bitterness; wouldn't it be better to bring fruit than to prevent fruitfulness forever?

He turned away and answered to those admiring the withered tree.

"I say to you; if you have faith and doubt not, you shall not only do this to a fig tree, but also if you say unto the mountain move, it shall be done. All things whatsoever you shall ask in prayer, believing, you shall receive."

John was quick to ask, "But master - *all* things?"

"Have I said other than the truth to you?" Yeshua asked of John.

"No."

"Then it's as I have said."

"But, master, there are things we have asked in prayer and believed yet haven't received," Thomas, the one with doubt, spoke. "Is there nothing else that must be done?"

"No."

"Then why haven't we received these things?"

Yeshua didn't answer, but continued on his way to the city.

I said nothing and pondered these things, wondering if it wasn't true of the others. If it was true that all prayers would be answered, then why had Israel suffered so long?

I knew of many true and Godly men who said prayers truly believing they would be answered and died still so, but none of their prayers were answered. Israel was still in the hands of the Romans! What did this mean, that all who pray and receive no answer aren't believing? Or not sufficiently? Or was there some other thing he hadn't told us; something that modified the word "all?" Some day I will ask these things.

Soon we came to the gate and passing through the streets, came again to the temple.

"Here is the teacher who can make stones cry!" Some of the people shouted and laughed. "Yes, make some stones cry!" they chanted as we passed by. Oh, I wished Yeshua would show his power over nature even as he had the fig tree and make the stones cry. But he continued to ignore their shouts and remained silent.

Yeshua and the twelve of us went therein and passed the many money changers and booths of dealer in animals for sacrifices. The more we passed, the more disturbed Yeshua became. With the many different kinds of people came different money, different languages, different customs, and different understandings of the law.

Many arguments were heard everywhere and the temple guards were hard pressed to keep order. This continual din from the traders in the Court of the Gentiles was grating on the ears. I knew the pilgrim's interest in securing his sacrificial lamb with the least amount of labor was seldom heard to complain about this impropriety. This wasn't true of Yeshua!

CLEANSING THE TEMPLE

"They ought not do these things in the temple!" He said as we walked the full distance. I thought he would stop and we would assemble around him and be instructed as before. But suddenly, he stopped and cried in a loud voice, "It's written, 'My house shall be called the house of prayer for all nations, but you make it a den of robbers!'"

We were taken aback at this sudden announcement. I remembered the letter Ishmael sent me in Rome, describing another time and happening similar to this one.

Suddenly, Yeshua girded himself for action. I turned to see that Peter, James, and John were doing likewise. I did nothing of the sort. After making this change, he stepped down the walkway and into the area of the booths. I stood some distance from the booths. He came to the first booth and with great force, lifted it and threw it over. The occupant was also spilled onto the ground, as well as his coins and other property. When he did this thing, he moved to another and repeated the process while shouting the scripture passage. Peter, James, and John did likewise. The area became bedlam. Some shouted for the officers of the temple to put an end to this unauthorized show of force against them.

I could see Yeshua in the middle of the fray. He was still shouting his battle cry about the den of robbers. It had now become a riot, and I knew that if it hadn't been in the temple, the soldiers would have enjoyed breaking heads to quell this riot.

The officers of the temple came running. The people got in each other's way. There was a mad scramble for money that continued to roll on the outer temple street from the booths. Several of the operators were accusing others of stealing their money from the ground. Much shouting and cursing came upon my ears; that this scene should happen within the temple appalled me.

As I studied the mass of humanity before me, I suddenly saw old Zichri - there he was, just as Ishmael had written before. He was still at his trade, but I noticed he had lifted his booth and was moving out of the temple. I could see his chin-whiskers moving up and down as he shouted for the guards. He was in a state of great agitation; he would have satisfaction this time.

When it was all over, the temple guards had restrained Yeshua and the other three. The rest of us hadn't joined in the skirmish and therefore weren't held with them. I strode to where Yeshua was being held. Now, perhaps I would see the power of Yeshua in his glory. He would surely show them they couldn't hold him. But alas, he now stood quietly held by the guards. Zichri was at the center of the argument. As I listened, I recalled the words Ishmael wrote so long ago. The man was almost repeating himself verbatim.

"He, *that one,* is a mad man!" He pointed a trembling hand at Yeshua. "He did this same thing last season. He came into the Court of the Gentiles and surveyed our booths, booths of honest merchants all, and all at work as is our custom at this time of year. All have paid our dues. We provide a good service to the temple as well as the pilgrims. He, this one called Yeshua, suddenly came upon us, for what reason I don't know. He upset the booths of many - he and his ruffians. Some say he is a gentle teacher, but I think he is mad and vicious and deserves forty lashes for this damage. Look at this carnage! Some of the animals are hurting, and ruined forever - no sacrificial animals here!"

Zichri pointed to some of the animals blemished in the fray. He was right, many now exhibited wounds and blemishes that would make them totally unacceptable for Pesach. As a man who once was in commerce, I felt that I understood their loss better than most. Both merchants and money changers had lost much in this cleansing of the temple.

"What is his cause and what is his right? Is he a member of the court, is he a member of the Sanhedrin? Is he even a minor priest? Is he any more a Son of God than I?" Zichri continued to badger the officers. "Give us satisfaction. Arrest him and bring him before the Sanhedrin - we have enough witnesses to this unjust deed."

The court officers took council among themselves. It wasn't a good thing to do this time of year - to arrest a teacher! This Yeshua was just welcomed only the day before into the city by a large crowd. The officers were unaware that much of the crowd was under my contract, and thought it would be unwise to bring Yeshua to trial before them.

"We hold what he did is improper and inexcusable, but are willing to withhold any action until after the celebration. In addition, the temple is now shutup unto him and his followers until that time." The chief officer gave his decision. The guards formed up around us and moved us outside the gateway.

Zichri shouted against this action as he wanted an arrest made. "How do we get satisfaction for our losses? What guarantee do we have that he won't go back to Galilee? Arrest him and hold him until after the feast and then try him. I will bring many witnesses against him," he shouted, but the guards paid no mind and closed the temple to us.

As we moved away from the temple, we were met by some of the poor and sick. Yeshua cured many and then tiring, moved to go, but remained long enough to tell many parables and lessons about duty and forgiveness, about the owner of a vineyard, about resurrection, about the great commandment, about David's son, warnings about the scribes and learned men, and many other stories I've left unrecorded in this journal. Those I've compiled in another book.

I saw his great tiredness and asked again, "Yeshua, will you grace the house of mother this day?"

"I will go to Bethany. Ah Judas, there is naught against you and yours, but it's my calling to do these things in accordance with a plan already set for me. I have no way to change these things, even a little bit. A change of even one moment isn't possible, and this you will learn in due time." I heard his words again, and turned cold to them. Why was this more reasonable and less time consuming than going to Bethany? I felt mother had been put upon once again. So he said and so it must be. I wondered how his friend in this city, Mary Magdalene, felt about this apparent refusal of her home as a resting place.

I saw her several times at the meetings and knew she held Yeshua in high esteem. Some held that she was in love with him, but others said it was not so. As for me, I didn't know if any of these were true or rumor. The question was, why was Mary and Martha more attractive to Yeshua than any others?

As we moved to go, I saw Apius and the Greeks coming up the street. I called to him and he brought his friends across the way to meet us. As they came toward us, I studied them and secretly tried to place the name with the face. Which was Aristocles, Temaeus, and Xenocrates? Not that it mattered but some day it might.

As they approached, I turned to Yeshua and spoke, "Yeshua, this is my most honored servant, Apius. He has with him three men from Athens who would meet you."

Yeshua said no word of rejection and instead, much to the surprise of some, including Philip and Andrew, stood quietly while the Greeks introduced themselves. Their spokesman, Aristocles, told of their search for truth and meaning of life. Yeshua was pleased and smiled as they talked on. I was grateful these men showed such respect for Yeshua. It pleased me that I saw this as I heard Yeshua forbid the rest to address the word unto the gentiles and Samaritans. After awhile, the men completed their respectful interrogation of his teachings and gave deep bows to Yeshua and parted with Apius for another part of the city. Yeshua then turned to leave the city.

I didn't go to Bethany but remained home and helped prepare for the feast.

Mother was greatly disturbed by the news that Yeshua wouldn't join us for the festival and, as I recall, said she would surely speak to him about it. I was tired and after much preparation, rested until the evening meal. After that, I was quick to bed. I began the mental preparation for the next meeting with Yeshua.

In the morning, I searched for Yeshua and the others throughout the city, but was unable to find them. I heard from some of the street people that Yeshua went into hiding to prepare for the festival. I thought it strange that he said nothing to me about this day of exile, yet I could see he was extremely tired the day before, and could accept his need for rest away from the crowds. Many people now followed him about after the fracas at the temple expecting to see some more of the same or some great deed done before their eyes.

In addition, the learned men and others were watchful so that he didn't enter the temple again, and sent spies on the movements of the followers. I felt their glances for this was my city and I was known to Caiaphas and Annas as well as some of the Sanhedrin. I was also known as the defender of the followers and his teachings.

Yes, I would say I knew more about Caiaphas and the Sanhedrin than even Yeshua. In the last few days, some Pharisees came to me in the night, and sought to bring Yeshua to trial on several charges, one of which was the incident in the temple which was repeated a second time. Some of the other charges weren't so well founded and bordered on the ridiculous, namely, the call to blasphemy. There were some very good men who were Pharisees; not all were held as deniers of the truth over tradition. Some were solid in their belief of the law and were well grounded in it. I know, for I studied under one - Hillel.

The day went slowly without the others to talk to and Yeshua to listen to. The preparation for the feast went on without pause. The city was flooded with outsiders and the population grew to about two hundred thousand. The city pulsed because of this increased populous - each night, great numbers left to rest in tents outside the city and then returned again the next morning to perform what thing each needed to do in the way to prepare for the feast.

The water supply was taxed to the extreme as many prepared for the great day by cleaning the house and home to meet the law. Many carried great pots of water from the central source to do the necessary ablution. It was easy to see many men and women moving through the city with water pots on their heads.

While I roamed the city in search of Yeshua, I came across Peter and John. The press of the crowd was great, and everywhere there were men and women plying their trades and carrying all sorts of products. Many people passed us carrying pots on their heads, the contents of which only they knew, as well as their destinations. Peter and John were watching each one intently, oblivious of me. They were busy calling to one another.

"Hold Peter, I think it's him!" shouted John. He waved his hand in the direction of a young man carrying a pot on his head.

"I say no, it's this one here, see how quickly he strides, he knows where he's going," Peter answered. By then, another approached and they both became undecided again. I could hear them discussing what to do about this problem.

"Ah, Peter, these instructions aren't plain enough. There are hundreds of men carrying water pots, or at least some kind of pots on their heads." John was more confused than Peter, or so it seemed from where I stood. What instructions had they been given? And why weren't they with the others. In fact, just where *were* the others?

"Ha so, Peter and John, how's by you this day?" I came upon them before they could move away. I didn't know that they would. They turned sharply to view me, and for a moment gave up their search.

"We are fine. Well, that's not entirely true." John was downcast. Peter pulled his arm as an indication that he would rather not have all known to me. "We have been sent by Yeshua to find a place for us to celebrate the feast and aren't succeeding in finding it." John was always an honest man, but Peter was one to try to bluster his way through any crises.

"What's the difficulty? I'm familiar with the city; maybe I can help." I wanted to save them from the embarrassment of returning to Yeshua without finding a room.

"Well, that is so, Judas. You've been here most of your life. I remember you telling us that. Peter, let's see if he can help us." He turned to Peter for authorization, it seemed. "After all, the day is running short and there are thousands of people on the streets."

"Alright, but it's you who has given up in the search, not me." Peter wasn't about to have the loss of completion charged to him. He wanted Yeshua to know that he would have continued until the night was upon them before he would cease his search.

"Listen Judas, this is our problem. When we left Yeshua this morning, he said to us, 'Go to the city and find us a room to use for the feast.'"

"And how shall we know the place?" John asked of Yeshua.

"You shall meet a man bearing a pitcher of water and follow him. Wherever he goes, there you shall go also and speak to the man, and he will let the room to you. There you will make ready for us." John repeated the words as near as he could recall. Peter added some corrections to John's story but nothing of any real import. The problem was obvious, there were just too many men carrying pitchers of water.

"Tell me again, are you sure that it was a man carrying a pitcher of water, or a *place* of a man carrying a pitcher of water?" I was hoping that something had been lost in their story. "Hear me, there is a place in the lower part of the old city that has a sign over the door which displays a man carrying a water pitcher. It has been there for many years. The man who runs the inn is an old Greek and has let rooms to pilgrims for many years during the time of Pesach. He prefers to lease to Greek pilgrims but those who appeal to him first are usually accepted. I remember Yeshua and his family sometimes used that inn and the upper room for the celebration." I was about to say more when John interrupted.

"That's it! That's what he said! I remember now, it wasn't to follow the man with the pitcher but to follow the street to the man with the pitcher. Remember, Peter?"

"I can't remember such, but if there is such a place, let's high to it." He was preparing to go.

"Hold, Peter, there you go again not waiting for additional instructions," John said, with some feeling in his voice. "Judas, lead on."

"Aye, the lower city isn't the easiest to search as it has many odd streets. Let me take you and you will save much time." I wanted to talk to them about the next evening as it would be the day of the feast and I wasn't told yet what time or where to meet them. I knew I was to be included as I was one of the twelve, and the law and tradition held that no fewer than twelve should gather together for the eating of the supper. And if there be less, then open the door to some less fortunate to share and make up the number.

So it was that I led them to the spot and they were in time to let the room.

"Our master said thus, 'Where is the guest chamber, where I shall eat the Pesach with my followers?' and we say the same to you, good man of the lodge." Peter towered over the innkeeper.

"Aha! It's been a long time since I've heard those words. It must be Yeshua and his family, isn't that so? The room is ready as I have always had is so." He was a good-hearted man and willing to trade words as any good innkeeper would. I was amazed that he would remember Yeshua after all the years, but some do have such a facility. He spoke again, "What is the need - for the day or festival?" It was obvious he didn't know how many followers there would be for the day or week.

"The number is twelve and the time is for the celebration of the supper only," John told the man.

"Then I'll expect you to be out of the room before the beginning of the festival of the Unleavened Bread as I'll let it to some others." John and Peter agreed this would only be fair.

I was surprised to find they didn't have the money to let the room, so I paid the innkeeper from my own purse. It was again a service not noted by the others for they were already thinking of seating and other arrangements.

After all was arranged, Peter and John thanked me for the service and payment and reminded me about the time. They then told me that Yeshua was still in Bethany but had moved from Martha's to the home of Simon the Leper. I remembered that Simon had a small house outside the town for no leper was permitted to live in any of the communities. Here Yeshua was safe from the crowds as few people wanted to approach the house of Simon, even though many knew of his being made whole by Yeshua and that he had been seen by the priests and declared well. They still were less than enthusiastic about personal contact with him or his house. And so it was that Yeshua was at peace and feared neither the curious nor enemies at Simon's house.

Peter and John left soon after arrangements were made. I went home and joined Ishmael, who, with Miriam, was to spend the feast day with mother. Today was the fifth day of our calendar; tomorrow at the sounding of the shofar, the day of Pesach would begin.

Everything was ready in our household. It had been thoroughly cleaned and searched for any leavening and found wanting. The house was ready for the angel of the Lord to pass by.

NIGHT VISITOR

I went to bed wondering what the next day would bring at the inn. As I closed my eyes, I could see the arrangement as laid out by John. What would Yeshua say to us, that was the burning question? I soon relaxed and sleep came to me.

While sleeping, I suddenly became aware of someone in my room. Was this so or was I dreaming? The room was filled with light brighter than the sun. In the center of the light, I could see a figure of a man clad in a white robe. I held my hand before my eyes to shield them from the light, much as Moses had so many ages before. I must be dreaming for no such light could exist from any lamp, yet it was still in dark hours. The light lessened, either by plan or imagination, and I could see the face of the man. He was like no other I had seen before. I was quite disturbed and trembled some. Even with my years of experiences in a number of lands, this wasn't common to them.

"Judas, fear not, for I have come to reveal to you that which has been held from you until now." The voice was kindly and deep - as if from a man of goodly age; this being wasn't a lad.

"Aye, who are you and what do want of me?" I spoke rather boldly seeing as I didn't know in whose presence I was. Yet, it was my own room and the feeling of security was still there.

"I'm Raphael, the Prince of Healing, who bears aloft to the Throne of Mercy the contrite prayers of men. It has been given to me to reveal your mission in this life. Before the next night is over, Judas, you must do that which no other man in this world, born of woman, before you, now, or after, can do!" He turned so I could see his features better. I had never seen such a one. He was without blemish and had no beard. His face was light, not dark as one of us; his eyes were light blue, a thing I had seldom seen in any man; he was tall and well built.

My heart trembled in my breast; now, I was much afraid. This wasn't an ordinary dream. This was an answer to the lifelong question from God on High to the many prayers I said about the words of Shalazar. What was this great deed that I had been born to do? Yes, as he said, "...even before time began."

"Hear me, Judas, my time is short. Come near and look at what I have in my hand. What do you see?"

"I see a jewel of great beauty, and it has many facets. But what is its' name? I haven't seen any like it, no, not even in Rome."

"It has but one name and one existence; the name is Thummim. It was once in the breastplate of the High Priest, then because of evil, was lost to man forever. Now, look deep into the different facets and tell me what you see." Raphael spoke encouragingly.

"I see the twelve, me included, reclining at the table for celebration of Pesach. We are all reminiscing - times of good things. Some are doing a great deal of cross talking. All are in good spirits. I hear them telling each other of miracles not seen by me that are predominate in their minds - Peter's mother-in-law cured; the curing of the leper; the raising of the son of the widow of Naim; the calming of the sea; Yeshua walking on the sea; and several others that bring great happiness. Then some talk of those happenings which were not so pleasant. Some boast of the fealty and bravado."

I turned away to look upon the angel again.

"Ah, so it is, but look again."

"I now see the time of celebration is over and the mood is solemn; the joviality is gone. Yeshua speaks of death. All are quiet. He speaks of one betraying him. He is taking a sop. He speaks, 'He that dippeth his hand with me in this dish, the same shall betray me.' Suddenly, the jewel grows dark - I can't see anything more. Will I be shown the man?"

And so it was, the facet turned dark and the scene was lost!

CHAPTER TWENTY-TWO

Jewel Of The Future

"Soon you will see, but not in this facet." Raphael rotated the jewel until new facets were showing. He placed his finger on another. "Look, Judas, learn and speak."

I feared to look. Why, I couldn't tell. Yet, I couldn't refrain, and look I did.

"I see a group of men gathering to make an arrest. They are mostly gentiles, Samaritans, and Idumeans. All our people are at the tables of Pesach. The arresting party is awaiting a messenger to supply them with directions and identification. I see a man coming in the night. He approaches and they greet him. I cannot see his face, he is turning my way. The facet turned cloudy, I didn't see who it was. Raphael, won't I know who this man is?" The mystery was growing; who was this man so clearly involved and what was the plot?

Raphael ignored my question and turned the jewel again. I looked this time without instruction; I wanted to know this man and the result of his treachery.

"I see a man dressed in a purple robe. He has a crown of thorns on his head and a wooden scepter in his hands. He is turned from me. There are many officers of the temple around him and they are abusing him. This ought not to be! The Sanhedrin must be notified at once, how can I reach them?" I was greatly incensed at the scene and tried to stop them, but they paid me no mind. I turned to Raphael for help.

"Don't waste your breath, Judas, they cannot hear or see you. These are things yet to be if nothing is done to change their course; you have been given a glimpse of the future. Look again! Can you see who the man is they are abusing?"

I was afraid to look, what if it was me? Yet, the magic of the moment overcame my fear - I looked deep into the jewel.

I cried out in great agony, "It's Yeshua! This is madness - show me no more!"

"Look, what must be will be!"

"What has he ever done to call such evil from the hearts of man? Has the God of our fathers left us all? Is this the way the anointed one is to be used? I cannot look more!" I flung myself on the bed and hid my eyes from it all. Perhaps Raphael would disappear and the dream, which was now a nightmare, would also fade away and I would be free of it all. What man wants to see the future at this cost? If naught can be done to change it, then only pain is the result of knowing. Yet I must look again. Perhaps I will learn the identity of the man who caused Yeshua to fall into this trouble.

Raphael remained steadfast. "We aren't yet done with this jewel, Judas! Peer again into the facet and tell me what you see!"

"I see three crosses! It's a crucifixion! Dear God, I cannot look more!" I pulled away, frightened beyond my reason. Who were the three? Was one of them me? Had I been too close to Yeshua and found guilty of some trumped-up charge, and therefore hung on a tree? My mind reeled and legs turned to water, and even in this dream, I swooned. How long I was unconscious I couldn't say before I heard the voice of Raphael speak again.

"Hear me, Judas, you must look again. Your personal fright is unfounded. Look, this I command you!"

I found I couldn't resist and look I did. I saw three crosses again. Each poor wretch was in great agony. As I studied the features of each, I recognized only one. It was the features of Yeshua! Torn and twisted by the pain, yet I recognized him.

"Has God left his heaven? This shouldn't and cannot be the future! The Messiah is to bring salvation to Israel, not die as a common thief on a cross. What is the meaning of this?" I looked toward Raphael and he was weeping, and then I saw many angels of lesser degree with him also weeping.

"Ah, Judas, the men of this world don't understand this Messiah isn't of this world. He isn't Messiah ben Joseph, the warrior king who will overcome all Israel's enemies or Messiah ben David, who would rule at the end of days in peace for evermore. He has come to establish no worldly kingdom but a righteous and spiritual one here on earth. A kingdom of God on earth. Yet to bring this about he must die so that man might live." Raphael wept more. "Now, look again in the jewel and learn your part in this plan to bring men back to God, and to balance the scales of justice."

"Must I?"

"Yes, there is no alternative."

So I looked into the jewel. I now saw the sop given to me! I was the one chosen to identify my teacher in the dark - the man coming to greet the men waiting to make the arrest! Why was I born to do this thing and not Ishmael, my twin?

Raphael ceased to weep. He was now readying to leave, this I could see.

"Judas, you have been selected even as Yeshua! There can be no other, even as there can be no other spiritual Messiah other than Yeshua. You and Yeshua were spiritually and physically entwined before time began even as you and Ishmael were before birth. Your lives and those of your progenitors have been carefully watched and sometimes protected. Remember, even as Yeshua was protected from Herod as a babe in arms, so you have been saved from an assassination in the old marketplace and later, a drowning while at sea. These weren't happenstances or whims of God, they were to keep chance from upsetting the plan. Hear me, my time is nearly gone. Pray that the God of Abraham, Isaac, and Jacob will grant you understanding of this and give you strength to do that which has been foretold in the stars and cannot wait, not even an hour longer. You will yet be tried. You have a free will! Not even God will force you to do this thing! The souls of all mankind could be lost and your soul with them! Don't be caught in a trap of false love. I leave you to your own mind and heart." With that said, he was gone and the light failed; the room was dark and I fell fast asleep again.

The early sunlight woke me. I trembled with fear and dread. Ishmael came to my room to see about my well being.

BROTHER AGAINST BROTHER

"Judas, did you sleep well? I and Miriam thought we heard you cry out in the night." As always, Ishmael vaguely experienced traumas that affected me.

"Ishmael, the questions have finally been answered! You remember the meeting with Shalazar many years ago, in the alcove, when we were set upon by robber-assassins?"

"Ah, yes, that day in the marketplace before we went to Rome," he answered while still watching me dress.

"Remember how this person we know now as Shalazar said, "Oh, Judas, you are a man among men; it's not well for you to know of events before their appointed time and place?" I looked closely at him to see if he truly understood and recalled the meetings and conversation. I had told he and Apius about it many years ago. His eyes told me he knew of the time and story.

"Well, I had a dream this night. And Ishmael, it was a terrible dream. My heart and soul are shaken to their utmost." My hands still shook although the dream must have taken place some hours before I awoke.

"Judas, you must tell me of this dream that disturbs you so!" Ishmael came over and placed his arm around my shoulders as he often did when I was mentally torn by some misdeed or the result of a boyish prank. He understood me better than any other.

"Hear me, Ishmael. It's not a pleasant thing I have seen this night. I was visited by the angel, Raphael, and he has told me what Shalazar never told me." I told Ishmael all from the greeting to the ending. As he heard, he stiffened and withdrew his comforting arm. His face drained of color and eyes flashed fire. I was amazed at his reaction. Never had I seen Ishmael show such fire and concern in all our dealings. I almost became afraid of my own brother - my other soul.

"Judas, forget this dream, it's the work of Satan. You must erase it from your mind and heart. Hear me, Yeshua is more than just a person, he is the Messiah!" It was my turn to be surprised! What is this thing, what was Ishmael's interest in Yeshua? It wasn't he who had traveled part of the world with Yeshua - but me!

"Why are you so concerned about this? I never knew you to be a follower of Yeshua. When did you find time to seek him out?" I was some confused by his agitation.

"I have found in my heart a strong need for him and his teachings since Miriam came to this house. It was she who told me of her forgiveness by him and the change in her life because of belief in his words. It was she who took me to him and because of her, we were washed as one by James, the brother of Yeshua." He began pacing up and down in the room as he told his story of his belief in the words of the old friend and son of Joseph and Mary. I still couldn't remember any of this happening. It must have occurred when I was busy with business details after Yeshua sent me to Jerusalem, and months after Ishmael's marriage to Miriam.

"Ishmael, why didn't you tell me of this admiration of Yeshua? We have never kept secrets from one another."

"Ah, you were the busy one and occupied by other happenings away from home." He looked down at me for I was still sitting on the bed. "Give me your word that you won't do this thing. You won't have anything to do with the seeking out of Caiaphas and giving information to the temple guards." He held out his hands to plead his case.

"Hold on, I can't give you such a promise. I'm not so sure the words aren't indeed from God. Yeshua has said many times he is to die for the sins of many. I heard him say, 'As Moses lifted up the serpent, even so must the Son of Man be lifted up.'" I began to defend my position in earnest and began to walk about the room. "Now listen, Ishmael, even as I told you, Raphael showed me three crosses and on one was the figure of Yeshua. Isn't that being lifted up, even as the serpent was lifted up in the days of Moses?" My voice had grown louder as I asked the question.

He accepted the challenge and returned at nearly the same volume. I suddenly realized we were shouting at each other; a thing we hadn't done since childhood. What was this secret element that was forcing us apart after all these years?

"This is madness, Judas, what makes you believe you're so special? Leave it be, I pray you!" He was extremely unhappy.

Our shouting brought mother to the room and Miriam quickly followed. They stood outside the room and looked at us - mother, as if she was seeing two strangers in her house.

Never in her life has she looked upon her two sons in such a violent mood. I couldn't accept his point of view and was willing at this time to defend my position even if it meant violence. Ishmael, on the other hand, felt strongly called to defend Yeshua and also, if necessary, to prevent me from the meeting with the others at the supper.

Mother tried to separate us and bring reconciliation but to no avail. I wouldn't tell her of my dream and left it to Ishmael if she was to learn of the command I felt God had given me.

Ishmael told all I had spoken about earlier to both mother and Miriam. Mother collapsed and fell weakly into the chair in the room. Miriam ran to Ishmael for support, either for herself or to aid Ishmael.

We stood apart for some time. Finally, I spoke.

"I'm not above leaving this be, even as Ishmael asks, but I must now go to the Garden of Gethsemane to the place Yeshua has often gone, and there, alone, near the great rock, I will call upon God to guide me. If it's his will, then how can I or any of you stand against it?" I waited for comment then slowly turned and left the room. None followed. The last I saw them, mother had her head bowed and hand held against her breast, and Ishmael and Miriam in each other's arm. I then recalled the words of Yeshua, 'Think not that I am come to send peace, but a sword.' This is the reality of the words!

I left the house and went to the Garden of Gethsemane at the foot of the Mount of Olives. There were few people here as most were taking care of last minute preparations for the coming feast. I was familiar with this place as we had met here with Yeshua. He liked the quietness and shade of the garden. I felt the need for prayer and the comfort it could give. How many of my forefathers had resorted to prayer to settle things that bothered them? I spent a great deal of time placing my cause before God. Time moved by while I was deep in prayer. As I looked up from my prayer shawl, I saw another figure near the stone at the entrance to the cave of love, as Yeshua often called it. It was there we met to hear him teach. I sat up to see more plainly. The light of the morning sun revealed the features of Shalazar!

NEW MEETING

"What is this, how did you come here? Have you been listening to my prayers?"

He smiled, and spoke quietly, "Not long, and your prayers aren't mine to act upon. Fear not, Judas, none of the rest of the eleven are near." He was just as handsome as ever. "I see you had a visitor last night."

I was shocked at hearing his words. How did he know of this dream and the contents thereof? Was he everywhere? His remarks brought me back to the words of Raphael. I must hurry to lay plans and do what I was bid by God.

"Ah, don't be in a hurry, Judas. You remember your debt to me, and that threefold, don't you? I see by your actions you do. I see your visitor was Raphael. I know him well. He speaks only truth, but Judas, not *all* the truth." He laughed as if he heard a good joke. I was afraid that he would call attention to us. "Don't worry, Judas, none care about either of us here in the morning mist. I know they don't even hear us so our speech is safe."

"What do you want, your thirty pieces of silver?" I couldn't help but think of the silver and debt together.

"Before I answer, let me show you some of the things Raphael forgot or didn't want to show you." He opened his left hand and in it was a black stone. It was a jetstone and was also faceted. "Look into these facets! What do you see?"

I looked as I wanted to learn all I could of these coming events.

"I see my reflection everywhere, on all facets." This was the truth - each facet was so black that it reflected what was before it.

"Aye, and look again. This time, don't look at it but into it."

"Before I look again, tell me, Shalazar, does this curious stone have a name?"

"Aye, but this is of little use to you."

"But tell me its' name so I can see better." I was trying to buy time for I didn't care to look at the stone. It was an evil-looking jewel.

"Its' name was given many thousand years ago by God. It's called Urim. It was lost by man and all the sight of the future with it." He was impatient for me to look. "Now, time is short, look!" He raised his hand and pointed at it.

I did so and began to see different events as was in the stone held by Raphael. "I see a man in a garden in prayer - it's Yeshua." I pulled away from the stone. I didn't want to intrude on his prayers. Shalazar was angry now; a thing I hadn't seen before.

"Don't delay, look again and tell me what you see."

"I see him in prayer as I have said. He is crying out to the Lord, 'O my Father, if it be possible, let this cup pass from me; nevertheless, not as I will but as you will.'" I was ashamed to hear his prayer; it wasn't mine to hear. What evil is done here by this Shalazar?

"Ha! See, is that a prayer of a Messiah? The anointed one? He is human just as you, and has failures just as you have! He isn't certain of the future anymore than you. Listen as he prays, '…if it be possible…' He doesn't know what the future brings, and neither do you. Now, hear me Judas, would you want this man to waste his life? You saw his suffering to come on the cross - perhaps! If that is foretold as truth, and Raphael hold it so; if you could, wouldn't you rather see it not happen?" Shalazar stood feet spread apart and hands on hips. He was in dead earnest.

"Hear me, Shalazar, if there is a way to avoid this I would but it is so written and will so be done." I couldn't see any way a mere human, like me, could stay this event.

"Notice, Judas, even Yeshua knows he has the power in himself to deny this plan. He will pray to avoid this responsibility even as you have seen as part of the future. There is still time! But let's look at another facet in time."

He turned the stone as Raphael did. I looked at a new facet. I could see some men coming into the garden and being led by a man of my build and looks. It was me. I identified Yeshua so no mistake was made in the arrest. I couldn't look longer but fell back against the rock. Dear God, why have you forsaken me?

"Come, Judas, see how this is a monstrous plan? Do you really believe that God would depend on men to carry out his most ingenious plan to save mankind? Think on it! All eternity and the saving of all mankind from the past until the end of time resting on the free will of two men? The forces of heaven and hell now awaiting the decisions of one man - you, Judas! This is all a story! It cannot be true. It's a great waste; we must cooperate to end this farce!" He could see I wasn't convinced but wavering.

"Listen to me - let me show you one more facet, and then we will speak of my plan to save Yeshua."

He brought the stone up again. I looked and spoke this time what I saw.

"I see a man being hanged on a tree by a mob. They think he is part of those who betrayed their leader. He begged for his life but to no avail. Oh, my heart stopped; my blood ran cold. Shalazar, who is this poor soul who lost his life?" I tried to see who it was but was unable to do so.

"Here, I'll help you." He shifted the stone again.

"Ah! Eeeee! It's Ishmael! My God, not my own brother! Not my twin soul. What has he done to receive such a fate?" I fell again a broken man. My mind wasn't able to accept all these events revealed to me. I stared at Shalazar. "Oh, are these things that happen because of what I must do, or are these events just shadows of what might be?"

"Rest easy, Judas. These are things that might be! Now, hear me well. We, you and I, can change these future events. If you will pay your debt to me in silver from the

Sanhedrin and follow my directions, not only will Yeshua not die, but neither will your brother suffer at the hands of others." He began turning the stone again. I was now greatly interested. "I'll show you the same scene Raphael did of the future, after you follow my instructions. Notice how the scene will change for the better. Look and believe I can do that which I say." He held the stone out toward me again.

I looked deep into the stone again. I saw the three crosses again. The men were writhing on them. I wasn't much disturbed this time. I strained until I could see the features of the man on the center cross. It wasn't Yeshua! It was another I didn't know.

"Who is the vicar?"

"It's a man called Barabbas, a chief insurrectionist and a member of the Sicarii. He is a murderer as well and deserves to die, and is so sentenced, but hear me, Judas, if things aren't changed, he will go free, and Yeshua will be hanged in his place!"

My heart turned to stone. How could this man be freed and Yeshua nailed to the cross in his stead? Who had such evil plans? Where was the justice of God on High? I turned and looked at Shalazar; he looked hopefully at me for the decision to fall his way.

"Come now, Judas. Would you have the blood of Yeshua and Ishmael on your hands? How could you live with that? God would ask no man to do such a thing." He came over and sat on the rock near me. "Listen to me, all isn't lost. Will you at least listen to what is another course?"

"Aye, but my mind is now used up!"

"You can follow these simple instructions. Hear me well, you must first go to the Sanhedrin or Caiaphas and gain his confidence by accepting the thirty pieces of silver. Remember, Judas, they are mine! They will save you." He held up a clenched fist.

"Then you must go to the supper, for to do otherwise would only raise suspicion. See Judas, even in this matter, Yeshua doesn't know all - he will believe you to be what you can't be. You must accept the sop, and leave at once, even as Raphael's faceted stone showed. Hear me, this thing must be done - you cannot go near the men about to make the arrest nor give them any assistance. They are Herod's men, temple guards, and a maniple. The Roman soldiers have a writ issued by Pilate, but they need witnesses to identify Yeshua. Without one of his own band to guide them, the writ is worthless. It's Roman law, the writ can only be served on the one scribed on it. They aren't sure and wouldn't want to make an error. Don't go near the band of men or the garden. Instead, come to the main gate and as soon as you get the thirty pieces of silver and the sop, I'll meet you there and from then on, all will be well." He smiled and took my hand.

I suddenly became exhausted and fell against the rock. When I looked up again, Shalazar was gone. Soon Ishmael and Apius came looking for me.

"It's time to come to the house and you must get ready for your supper with Yeshua and the others," Ishmael reminded me. He acted as though nothing had taken place earlier in the morning. I left it well enough alone, but was determined to tell him of this conversation with Shalazar.

I must make ready and get to the inn soon. Since it was known to me, I wasn't concerned. I would be there on time.

"Aye, Ishmael, I'll get ready. Are you alright? There's nothing on your mind that causes you depression?" I was cautious, but the words and scenes of the stones kept reoccurring. Oh, Ishmael, take care! "Oh, yes, I must be away to the temple to give a sacrifice before the supper. Go on home and I'll soon follow."

Ishmael agreed and left the garden with Apius. I went first to the temple and then called at the house of Caiaphas. I asked if he was interested in the whereabouts of Yeshua? I reminded him that I was aware of his interest in Yeshua and of hearing through the street people about his desire to forgive Yeshua for the harm done to the temple. The interruption of the exchange and purchase of animals was still to be resolved and Yeshua hadn't been in the temple since the action of the guard against him. Caiaphas was more than pleased and was very willing to pay for the information. But why he wanted this information when he had spies watching Yeshua and us, I couldn't tell.

AN ARRANGEMENT

"Why do you need someone supply information you already have, Caiaphas? You and I know that your spies have been aware of our movements for some time. And what is the need this night?" I knew from the visit of Raphael that this was given to him as the time for this event, as he said, "...which was foretold in the stars and cannot wait - no, not even an hour longer." But how did Caiaphas come by this night as one written in heaven?

"Come, Judas, we have known each other for some years. You know as well as I do these servants are far from trustworthy. You would be surprised at the amount of misinformation I've received from my trusted men. I cannot act on rumors - I must act only on facts. You will provide these facts for I'm willing to pay for them. Now, as to the reason for this night being so important. Hear me, I have it on good authority that Herod has wanted Yeshua, like John, out of the way."

"Hold, Caiaphas, on who's good authority?" I was interested in who might have such privy to the King and who would dare to bring such word without fear of reprisal.

"It's a long-standing confidant of Herod's, one who has his ear on many things. He comes and goes at his will; even Herod doesn't question his advice. His name escapes me at the moment, but it's of little concern in our case, believe me, he speaks well of you." He smiled and was about to continue.

"Such a person knows me?" I was bewildered; I knew of no such person. Suddenly, I saw the picture of Shalazar in my mind. He then was the connection of all these events and the guiding force. "Was he a handsome and strange one?" I had to know!

"Aye, he told me of your willingness to help us, and so you have offered. Now back to Herod. He and Herodias still feel the ill will of the people and truly feel that the people follow Yeshua even as they did John, and more so.

"Herod knows if the people rise up and go to Rome again, he might be deposed, even as his predecessor was. It's he who petitioned Pilate that Yeshua is raising the people to acts against Caesar as many believe him to be the Messiah. Herod, at the insistence of Herodias, asked Pilate to authorize a writ for Yeshua's arrest and prosecution. Now, Herod also has spies, and they told him of the annual visit of the Galilean to the temple on Pesach. So the writ is dated and so it is to be served. You and I know that Yeshua has no intentions of bringing force against Rome, but that doesn't resolve the question.

"Hear me, there are those that hold this office in low esteem, and me with it. I tell you, unless you walk in these shoes, God's hand isn't on you. I would that none of us suffer crucifixion under the hand of Rome, Yeshua included. The only way this can be done is to cause Yeshua to plead not guilty to the questions asked by Pilate, for there he will go. There is no alternative. Only God himself can erase this event from the calendar of man. Ask Yeshua to hear us. I and the council will meet this night, for so I have ordered them. They will be ready after Pesach and assemble in my house. Here we will listen to Yeshua's words and attempt to dissuade him from saying anything incriminating before Pilate. You must help us! Now what is it you want for the information? And when can you deliver him? It must be before the morning!" He was a sly fox, this one. "You know the treasury is nearly empty these days. The hateful Idumean takes everything he can; says he is building the temple for the glory of God, but to my mind, it's for his edification." He looked about to see that no others heard his last statement. He knew very well his position as high priest was dependent on Herod and the Procurator as well.

"What you say is true, but it will still take thirty pieces of silver, and that struck from the temple treasury - that and no other. Don't take me for a fool. I know the difference between coins." Caiaphas knew very well of my stay in Rome and had often wondered what power I had assembled there. I also knew now that Shalazar had a hand in this and would accept no other coin.

"Don't be touchy, Judas. This is a business deal with me, and if you want only coinage from the treasury, so it will be. This word you bring will have to be taken to the Roman check station. We are to make the arrest; it's a religious matter, not a civil one. Remember, there are those who would put Yeshua to death for treason, yet, you and I know this is an unreasonable charge. I have heard that some have been paid to testify against him before Pilate. Not Jews, mind, but foreigners, Idumeans and the like, ones not held by our laws. They will masquerade as Jews and cry out for his life. Although we, that is Annas, I, and the great council, don't agree with his teachings, we are less want to see a Jew brought before the Procurator on false charges and crucified. We must gain access to Yeshua before he is taken before Pilate. It's only through you we have a chance to do this. Give us this chance, Judas. We fight for Israel, and every soul in our care. *Hear, O Israel: the Lord is our God, the Lord is one.*" He moved about the house and finally came to me with a lambskin bag filled with the coins. I opened it and counted the coins.

"Why Judas, you shame me! Would you believe I would give less than contracted for? I would give you much more if you had so demanded. It is so contracted before God and it will so be done. Isn't that so?" The fox wasn't one to forget the law. He knew full well that a contract made before God was a binding one.

"It shall be done. It's not a shortage I was looking for but an overage. The money isn't for me, it's for another who contracted for thirty coins, no more and no less. He drives a hard bargain. The wrong amount would be cause for denying the contract paid."

Caiaphas shook his head. While listening to Caiaphas, I began to have the feeling that Shalazar was speaking; he also wanted to prevent harm coming to Yeshua. I wondered what Shalazar would say when I told him of this arrangement? He had promised that all would be well if I followed his instructions. It had better be so.

I left the home of Caiaphas with the bag of coins. I had met the first demand of Shalazar - now for the feast. I must be at the inn and ready for the supper before the sounding of the shofar.

The trip home was like a dream. The crowd was still pressing to get things done; people were beginning to settle in for the celebration. Here and there I was jostled by someone in near flight to take home some bitters or salt.

I reached the house in good time. I went to my room and began to prepare for the supper. Clean body and clean clothes. I secured the bag of coins under my cloak and girded myself for the trip across town.

"Mother and Ishmael, this will be a night to remember!" I told them of Shalazar and all that transpired. I told them I would follow Ishmael's admonition and not do the thing as shown to me in the dream by Raphael. They were happy once again. I left the house; they were dressed for the celebration. My heart was pulled to join them in this most desired family ritual. This was the night of remembrances; the night many in exile dreamed of over and over again. "Yeshua has told us of many things and this night is to reveal a new turn of events. As near as I know, we are only going to spend Pesach at the inn. Where Yeshua and the rest of us will spend the Feast of Unleavened Bread is yet to be told us. Don't wait up for me. I will stay with the others wherever it might be."

A NIGHT TO REMEMBER

"Oh, Judas, I have a feeling this is a night not only to remember, but one to dread. You recall, when you were younger I spoke of great trials in your life, and even now I feel they will be soon. My son, I pray for you. God go with you and save you from all harm." Mother was very sad. My heart turned over as she spoke these words. She couldn't have known about my dreams, but was surely close to my thoughts about them. I, too, partially dreaded this night.

"Cease this prattle, mother, all is as it should be." I tried to cover my concern. "Mother, I was wondering, have you heard anything from Apuleius these days?"

"No, the circle has said nothing about any action at the fort other than the reinforcement and new checkpoints have been placed in and about the city. This is common each year at this time. Apuleius must still be in the city. Why do you ask?"

"I would talk to him, that's all." I wished I could tell him of my dreams, and ask him about the possibility of Yeshua being charged with treason or insurrection. I knew well that prosecution and sentencing for both of these was crucifixion. I began to feel sick. I must leave the house and now! I kissed mother and Ishmael, threw on a cloak to fend off the night air, and left without further words.

I hurried. The sun will soon be taken as low enough in the evening sky and the sighting of the first stars would signal the beginning of the celebration. I ran part way; I wished I had ridden an animal, but it was too late to return now. The crowds were gone. The streets belonged to foreigners. Our people were already in their homes and the doors shut tight against intruders; this was an intimate family ritual. Doors would remain shut until opened in expectation of Elijah.

I was last to climb the stairs at the inn of the water carrier. All the others were in place. The u-shaped tables were covered and ready for the service to begin. Yeshua sat as the father-instructor of this feast supper. The oft-repeated story of the Passover was retold.

Before the sounding of the shofar, the group relaxed and reminisced even as I had seen and heard in my dream. Spirits were high. This was to be a night to remember!

The sounding of the Shofar brought the group to attention and the service began. It progressed in accordance with custom and the law. Yeshua answered the question put forth by John, the youngest. Soon the ritual was over with the final washing done.

Then, Yeshua did a curious thing. He called for additional food and drink to be brought as the ritual feast was over and the meat was finished in accordance with the law. They were told by the master of the inn to keep a sharp eye on the band in the upper room, and when the ritual was over, to clear the room. It was let for use by other guests. So it was that Yeshua sent John to have the servants bring some bread and wine.

After receiving these things, he took bread and broke it into small pieces and took one of them and blessed it as was the custom. He then said, "This is my last Pesach." He paused, and I heard all inhale because of the shock of his words. My heart fluttered like a bird in my chest as I remembered my dream was still with me. Did this mean I had no choice in the matter and Shalazar was lying to gain some other end?

He passed twelve pieces among us, saying, "Take eat, this is like unto my body."

All sat like made of stone! None ate! I couldn't believe what I heard; the others likewise. All were holding the piece of bread in hand; some partially to their lips, and others still with hands resting on the table. None of us seemed able to speak at the revulsion the command brought to us. My mind reeled with the proposition!

Wasn't it written that the human body was not to be considered as clean for consumption? How then could we accept this allegory - this eating of his body? This wasn't Jewish - this was Persian! It was they who practiced the eating of bread and drinking of wine to represent body and blood in rituals of the eternal fire. Rituals that were an abomination unto the Lord God of Israel. Oh yes, I remember seeing these in Rome.

The band began to murmur among themselves. I couldn't contain my thoughts on the matter.

"Yeshua, isn't it written that man shall not eat of human flesh?"

"Aye, so it is written." He could see the reaction of the others to his command. They were afraid to speak, where I wasn't.

"Yeshua, since none of our people has ever eaten the flesh of another, why then do you say we should eat this bread as a symbol of your body? You command this thing as if we had done a similar thing before and shouldn't be surprised at these words. Is this a new covenant?" I wasn't at all happy with the idea I should consume this bread as his body after asking God to bless it for its' natural use.

He made no excuse or explanation for his strange request of us. "Judas, I see that all are taken aback by this command. Verily, what I do you don't know now, but you shall know hereafter. Therefore, if you would be one of mine - do this thing."

After hearing these words, all of us ate the bread - though I had some reservations in my heart. We all wanted to enjoy the oneness with him in the great adventure of a new Israel and God's kingdom on earth. Their visions of the Messiah were still grand; mine were now less so.

He then took a cup of wine and blessed it, and passed it to each of us, saying, "Drink you all of it, for this is like unto my blood shed for the remissions of the sins of many and a new covenant."

The reaction was nearly the same. Those about to drink - hesitated. To drink blood of any animal was strictly forbidden and that of a human not even considered. The shochet and priests had for years performed the slaughtering ritual so the blood was drained from any clean animal before consumption or sacrifice. Now Yeshua again referenced an act that was revulsion unto us. I didn't care for this thing, but followed the rest and drank the wine.

After this, Yeshua returned to the bread and broke a piece of it away from the loaf. All watched him not knowing what to expect after the two other changes to the celebration of Pesach.

"Verily, I say this, one of you will bring the soldiers and others against me tonight." You could have heard a cricket chirp in the room it was so quiet after he spoke those words.

My heart jumped within me and color left my face as I felt weak and nearly sick. Parts of Raphael's words came flooding back to me. How much did Yeshua know of this thing? Had Raphael visited him as well? Why was he so positive about this? Hadn't I just seen him in the garden praying to his father to remove this cup if possible?

I could barely keep my chin and body from shaking. Yet none looked at me! So they didn't know; of this I was sure now! They were all looking unto themselves! Not only did they not know who it was, but were questioning their own acts. I gave no sign.

"I say again, one of this little band will inform on me tonight." They all seemed unsure of themselves as each began again to question him on the matter; all but me!

"Is it me?" Each man asked in turn. I couldn't help wondering if each of them had been visited by Raphael and Shalazar as well. Why would these men of God wonder if they would be the one who brings the troops on their beloved teacher?

Were they so unsure of themselves? Or was it they had no idea what the word betray meant? I surely didn't!

How could one betray anyone that wasn't in a clandestine operation? I couldn't reason that this little band had been so occupied; everyone from Caiaphas to the common people knew of their travel and teachings. Even the old fox, Herod, knew of Yeshua and where to find him. All knew of his affinity for the temple and the Mount of Olives. Where was the need for any of this?

"It's he who accepts this sop." With that, he dipped the bread into a small cup of wine, and held it up without making a motion toward any one of the little band. Glances darted from all in the room - all looking for the one who it would be - none knew if it wasn't them. None dare move!

I reached for the sop. When I touched his hand to accept the sop, the thrill of mutual companionship on a deed that might be done passed between us.

"Is it me?" I asked, not to cover a covert act, but because I was still not sure if the deed would be done! Could I bring about the pain and suffering to this man as I had been shown by Raphael?

"It has been so written. Judas, you and I are one in this. Don't fail, for there is no other before heaven to do this thing." He spoke low yet I heard the words clearly above the others murmuring. My heart wasn't in it, yet I knew he understood my place in the history of this thing. I looked at the others, and plainly saw they didn't know the meaning behind his words. I knew then Yeshua hadn't told them of the plan of God to bring about the balance to the scales of justice - right and love must prevail. The sin of man must be erased for justice to once again have meaning. I also knew they would never know what my mission was all about. They would, until they died, believe I was traitor and their enemy.

"Go," he said in a quiet voice, "that you would do, do quickly!" My heart stopped again. These were the very words mother had said to me some years before when I left her to go to Rome. So they once again haunted me! I gathered my cloak about me and left the upper room. I would retire to the city gate and there meet with Shalazar.

The streets were clear and only stragglers and foreigners were about. I passed through the checkpoint quickly. The night was light and a bright silver moon now slowly rose over Jerusalem and gave light to the crooked streets of the lower city. The bright moon was a good sign on the night of Pesach, or so it was said of old. The old tale was the angel of the Lord was able to see the blood on the lintels the first night because of a full moon, and therefore, all looked to see it again on succeeding celebrations of the Passover.

For some reason, I became confused and lost my way. It seemed like the finger of God had changed things. I was concerned as this wasn't common to me. I had always been better at directions than Ishmael and we often laughed at this difference. I used to believe he became so interested in the artistic things he saw that he lost his way. I must solve this confusion; I want to meet Shalazar in good time to set aside this crime - if I could. I must save Yeshua and Ishmael if I can! But why must I make such a decision? If I had been born second of us two, would Ishmael now be doing this and not me? Had the midwife tied the string on the wrong arm? My head was full of these thoughts as I attempted to find my way along the back streets of the lower city.

As I turned the next corner, I beheld a light in the end of the alleyway. I turned that way seeking the reason and maybe here I would recognize some landmark to guide me to the gate. There at the end of the alcove stood Raphael!

"So, Judas, you are far off your path. Aren't you to meet with the men-at-arms at the fourth checkpoint?"

Aye - he was right about that, I was off the path. I was about to ask him why he sought me out again when he continued.

"Haven't you made a contract with Caiaphas to carry to them the identification of Yeshua? Wasn't this contract made before God?" He was right again. I had deep reservations about this meeting with Shalazar but I kept seeing the images of Yeshua and Ishmael in their trial and pain. My God, why was this brought to bear upon me?

He turned that I might see his face again. It showed signs of his weeping. "Oh, Judas, don't you know what you must do?"

My heart shrank from his last question. I reeled and fell against the well of the alleyway. My legs turned to quicksilver and I cried out against this sentence. What had been my crime? Was I born without a heart of my own? Was love of brother less than love of duty to God? I also wept!

"Hear me, I'm but a man, and my heart isn't given to these harsh things. I was shown by one called Shalazar that I could change these things and save the lives of Yeshua and my brother, Ishmael. I cannot do this thing." I began to weep harder.

"Judas, listen to me. Shalazar has caused you much pain, and this is to his liking. He isn't interested in saving Yeshua, but in gaining your soul and the death of all mankind as well. But go, and do as it comes to you. Only you have control over your destiny because God gave you and all mankind a free will." Suddenly, there were other angels of lesser degree with him weeping. The alley was again dark and I found I was near the gate.

My mind reeled with the immensity of what I had been told. God gave each man the right to make the decision for good or evil, and it was again his will that man should choose.

I approached the gate with some trepidation. There in the shadows stood Shalazar. He had two horses with him. He came forward and grasped my hand, and as he did so, a heavy cloud came across the face of the moon. It was so dark I could barely discern his features.

"Ah, Judas, I thought for a moment you had been waylaid. It's good to see you have done so well. The others didn't challenge you did they?"

"No, and none followed me." I then took the bag of silver coins from beneath my cloak and held it out to him.

"Here are the coins even as I said. I have kept my part of the bargain. Tell me, what I must do to save Yeshua and Ishmael?" I was anxious to get the deed done. He took the bag of coins and cast them on the ground near his feet. He laughed with great pleasure.

"Ah, it's good. I've nearly brought this servant to my will. O God and master of all, how does your servant look to you this night? I think he isn't the match of Job!" He was very animated - he cavorted about like a man winning a great victory.

I then thought I heard a voice from heaven say, "Ah, Shalazar, the night's not over yet, and my servant, Judas, is still free to choose." He also must have heard for he stopped his wild dance and returned to me.

"Aha, the deed is nearly done. You have but to mount this horse and travel to Egypt; all else is arranged!" He handed me the reins of one of the horses.

"To Egypt?" His proposal boggled my mind. Leave Jerusalem and my family?

"Oh, Judas, it's a simple thing. I've friends there in a seaside town of Pelusium. There you will receive all the good things of this life - power, riches, friends, and good health for as long as you live. Your brother will be freed from his straits, live well here, and give your mother many grandsons. Yeshua will go free and live his life out as a teacher among the people. The evil Barabbas will receive the punishment he deserves. Those that want Yeshua destroyed will receive their ounce of blood and be satisfied. Here I will help you aboard." He moved to get me mounted for the flight to Egypt.

THE DECISION

"Hold! You said nothing about the need for going to Egypt!" I wasn't interested in leaving my homeland and friends without just cause.

"Haven't you contracted with the Sanhedrin to deliver Yeshua? Do you think you can stay in Jerusalem or even Judea a free man and not be taken to task for fraud? It might well be that you be on the cross because of that decision." He was fidgeting with the reins. "Hear me, Judas, time is running out. You can't play for both sides. I've little patience. Either you are with me or against me."

"And what would you have me do with this silver?" I pointed to the bag on the ground. Once I had given it to him I was no longer bound to him. I could return it to Caiaphas and the contract with him would no longer be valid. Even before God, a debt paid was a contract fulfilled or purchased.

"I don't care about the silver! I've more silver and gold than any man or animal can carry. Don't mock me, Judas, I've more power than any man on earth." He was now getting angry. "Don't forget the things I've shown you. Your brother's life now depends on your moving quickly to join me. Be not deceived, I will work my will on those you love."

"It's as you say, the contract was made in the sight of God, whereas I have no contract with you as you accepted the silver. Why do you still try me? It's now given to my heart to follow the call for which I was brought into this world. Even as you have said. I believe God has set me free to do that which will shackle evil evermore. I cannot leave this country and holy city. So I must be off to meet the man of Rome!" I dropped the reins and moved to go back through the gate and into the city. "Hear me, Shalazar, if you have so much power, why don't you destroy me and then go on with your plan through another?"

At that moment, the cloud left the face of the moon and I could see my way and his features very well. His face twisted with hate. His hands shook.

"This isn't given to me, Judas. But others are under my hand and they will pay for your choice."

I turned to look again at Shalazar. His face was now greatly distorted and ugly to look upon. There seemed to be much hate in his eyes.

"You have just sealed the fate of both Yeshua and Ishmael; upon you is their blood, and all men will hate you from this night onward. Your act will be recorded as the most dastardly deed known to man, and your name will be written ever to be damned by man. Your mother will die of a broken heart. And even as I've said, Barabbas, the killer, will go free, and Ishmael will die!" He shook his fist at me, and turned to shake it in the face of heaven. "Here, take this bag back to those who gave it to you, I've no need of it!"

He threw the bag at my feet. I then picked it up with the determination to return it to Caiaphas as proof to God that I didn't need to be paid for that which I was chosen to do. I, of my own free will, do this to complete the plan of God. Where it will lead I don't know but believe I'm the instrument of God even as Yeshua, and this from the beginning of time.

Because of his output of evil words, I was greatly frightened and hurried to meet the maniple at the fourth checkpoint as I'd been instructed by Caiaphas. As I traveled through the city meeting place, I thought I heard singing in the air. My heart began to sing as well. I knew then, even if all the world spoke evil of me, I was doing the will of God, even though Shalazar had declared otherwise. *Hear, O Israel: the Lord is our God, the Lord is one.*

I hurried through the streets to the meeting place told me by Caiaphas. The bag of silver weighed heavy against me. I would have thrown the purchase price in the face of Caiaphas earlier, but now it seemed his act was no more than a steering of the hand of God. Besides, I had only secured the money to pay the long-standing debt to Shalazar, and how because of his deceitfulness I was free of it. Yes, that's what I will do - return the money - and good riddance.

I debated within whether I had time to do this thing before I met with the maniple, but finally chose the latter. I would seek out the maniple and the temple guards first and then return the money.

AT THE CHECKPOINT

I followed the usual course through the city to the checkpoint. Every year at this time, it was set up to control the flow of people. It was instituted by the first Procurator to harass the people during this festival, and was a show of force to let the people know Roman presence even during the Passover. These checkpoints were a thorn in the sides of all of us and were hated for their intrusion.

I came to the place I saw in my dream, and approached from the darkened roadway. The bright moonlight spun off the armor of the men waiting for me. The night was quiet except for the sounds of metal and leather working against each other as the men moved about. The commander stood out from the others. The highest rank in the maniple was a lieutenant, this I knew from my stay in Rome. There were several officers from the temple, one I recognized, Malchus, steward to Caiaphas. I saw him often in the temple court and was one of those listening to the complaints on the day Yeshua overturned some booths and tables. I didn't like the man and refused to give him a greeting in the Lord. Yet as I approached, I could see a higher-ranked officer with them.

"Ho there! Who approaches this checkpoint?" one on post shouted. He was a point guard and stationed some distance from the rest of the band.

"I'm here to meet with the commander of this company," I answered. "I've information for him about the writ he has in his possession."

"Follow me." He turned and we crossed the open space; the moonlight fell upon us.

"Sir, this fellow says he has information about the writ." The post guard was short in his words; I didn't want them to know me other than to identify Yeshua, then be gone.

"So what took you so long? We've been waiting for sometime." He was a young man. Now that I was close to the band, and considered the mixture of men present, I wondered just who was in charge of this arresting party.

I understood, as every other Jew, that civil charges, especially those of major crimes, were under the jurisdiction of Rome, while the religious ones were generally left to the forces of Herod and the temple guards. But here, all three were present: Roman troops, Herod's finest, and the officers from the temple as well.

As I saw it, the charge or charges were being brought by the officers of the temple. In fact, Caiaphas told me, as the faithful guardian of the temple, he was bringing charges against Yeshua. The minor one being the disrupting of business and destroying property within the gates of the temple. The major one being the ridiculous charge of blasphemy - one that could hardly be taken seriously. In either case, the action was to be taken on religious laws, so why the need for the Romans? Something was amiss here!

The officer of higher rank then stepped forward and into the moonlight. Then I recognized him!

"Apuleius!" I whispered as loud as I could, "what are you doing here?" He stiffened and stared toward me. He came forward and grasped my arm.

"Lieutenant Ancus Marcius, stand to, I would have a word with this man in privy." The officer saluted and stood aside as we strode some distance away from the contingent.

"Judas, what's this ugly deed you do?" He talked in hushed tones.

"Oh, Apuleius, how I've longed to talk to you about this thing. It isn't what it seems. We don't have time to spend on this, but believe and trust me as a dear friend ought. What is done here tonight is for the good of all." My voice broke; I couldn't keep the pain of this deed from my voice. "My heart is breaking for what I do isn't for all men to know."

"Judas, are you mad? Do you know what is about to happen? The writ held by Lieutenant Ancus is one for conspiracy to commit treason against Caesar!" His grip on my arm was like a steel band. He spoke between his teeth as his jaws were clenched.

"I know what that means. But there can be no treason here. The charges are of a religious nature - I have spoken to Caiaphas and no civil cause is here. I know of things not known to you. Things that are from the beginning of time in the history of our people." Oh, God, if I just had time to explain, he could understand and not turn against me, too!

"Do you know why I'm here?"

"No!"

"I'm here to take care of three who are to be scourged!" He was greatly disturbed. Both he and I knew what that meant. "By Jupiter, I hate this. I'm a medical man who's taken the oath to cure and heal for the good of all mankind. And here I'm called upon to patch up those scourged and keep them alive to undergo crucifixion. Is there no end to this madness?" He let go of my arm and turned away. The troops were still waiting in the shadows, no firebrands were lit, but I could see them resting against the walls of the building. Each of these dripped with oil and were ready for the march. The march to a place I only could show them.

"Who are the three?" I remembered the three crosses shown to me by both Shalazar and Raphael.

"I know only one who was transferred from the fort at Caesarea to Antonia this week, a Barabbas. He is a hard one, a member of the Sicarii and responsible for the death of many a good Roman. I'm sure he is getting no more or less than he deserves. The other two are common thieves who stole taxes - stealing from Caesar is a capital crime."

"Ah, Apuleius, time is running out. That which I must do cannot wait. Hear me and trust me to tell you what I know about this after it's done." I turned to go. He took my arm again.

"Listen," he whispered again, "the man's name on that writ is Yeshua! Do you know that? So you believe this is a religious matter? Hah! Judas, you're being played for a fool. In fact, you *are* a fool to believe Caiaphas and that old cynic Annas aren't playing politics with the life of your teacher. And you're a bigger fool if you believe that Pilate doesn't know what the word Messiah means in this empire! And what of Herod? Why are his men here? Do you think Herod gives a sesterce about religion? He has long wanted to place Yeshua in a position of pain and then ask him to bring forth a miracle. Believe me, this man will try to take Yeshua away from us, mark my words!"

"You don't really believe there is a chance that Yeshua would be convicted of treason! He is and always has been a mild-mannered teacher who offers no threat to Caesar. Come, admit to me, you don't think he will be convicted?" We turned back to the others.

"As to that, I can't say. But if it were me, I wouldn't want to be in that position on this night. I heard from the guards at Antonia that Pilate was in a foul mood all week. He didn't want to come down here in the first place, hence anything that brings him discomfort will bring summary action. Pray to your God Yeshua isn't one of those discomforts!"

COME, LIGHT THE FIREBRANDS!

We arrived at the band and I went to the Lieutenant as Apuleius went to his group of medics. I noticed some nondescripts had joined the band; whether a bloodthirsty mob or those genuinely interested in what was to take place, I couldn't tell. I knew there were often men and young boys who followed the Roman troops when serving a writ or making an arrest. These were zealous people that like to harass the Romans at any action taken against our people. They would do nearly anything to stand in the way of the arresting of our own.

"Come, light your firebrands and follow me to the inn of the water carrier. It's the last place he used for the celebration of the feast and he should still be there." It was to my mind the best place to take them, would be few to witness the taking, and less harm done.

As we strode through the city, a small crowd of curiosity seekers joined behind the troops. In the dark and with the brands waving in the night, it looked like a large contingent, but in reality only one maniple was with me: one hundred and thirty men, three medics, the officers of the temple, and their men-at-arms. The Romans were equipped with the standard implements of war, while the officers of the temple and their men carried small bludgeons - the Procurator having restricted their use of swords during the festival. Pilate wasn't about to give our people any weapons to encourage riots. The others who followed had no official capacity in this action. As we went through the streets, more and more free from the celebration and interested in the passing of the troops joined us.

When we arrived at the inn, a large group of men were in the area. I went into the inn and up to the room. It was empty! Yeshua and the eleven had left. But gone where?

"What's this, you were to give us direction and identification, and now you have led us on a goose chase!" Ancus was disturbed.

"Come, I know his usual haunt. We must leave the city and go to the Mount of Olives."

I turned them about and led them through the city streets again and out the Gate of Water past the temple west wall to Gethsemane. I was familiar with this garden. I had just spent the afternoon here in prayer.

"Hold, take care with the firebrands. Don't harm the trees." The Lieutenant warned his men; his words were lost on the others, they weren't under his command and could care less about his concerns.

The bright moonlight was a distinct advantage for this endeavor. I could see the little band and Yeshua a short distance from the hill.

"Hold, I see them a short distance away. Consider this, I want no mistake here." The young Lieutenant was cautious. "What can we see in this moonlight that would provide positive identification of the man?"

"Hear me, look to me. The man I greet as teacher is your man. Take him and no other." I felt the shame of it all. I was about to commit the deed that would result in the arrest and charge of Yeshua. Who was to make the arrest was not yet told me. After I told the Lieutenant, he called over one of the officers of the temple.

"Now hear this, the writ is for the arrest of one Yeshua and this is for a criminal offense. My warrant is for probable cause of treason." He was about to continue when the highest-ranking officer of Herod's men spoke.

"Look Lieutenant, we also have a criminal charge against this man. It's well known that both the king and Pilate have sworn to let the King have jurisdiction over our people. It would be wise if we took him. See this mob surrounding us? They are just looking for a reason to cause trouble. I know these people and these times. Their feeling of oneness is extremely high this night of all nights. It might prove very costly for you to arrest him."

This man was no fool. He wanted to take Yeshua without Roman interference. Not that he wanted to do the Romans a favor, but he wanted a free hand to do with the prisoner as he would. "I'm not one to tell the Roman authorities what to do, but in this case, a rash act ending in violence could be heard clear to Rome."

I could see the young officer bristle, and then as he relaxed, he continued to explain the situation. He was young and new at the game in Palestine, but no fool. From where we stood on the hill, some twenty-five thousand tents stood reflecting assorted silver shapes from the valley floor. Even Lieutenant Ancus knew a heavy skirmish with the rabble on the hill would raise enough noise to alert those in tents below. And it was a simple thing to understand this could bring more than fifteen thousand irate pilgrims and indigenous populace to the scene. Discretion was the better part of valor in this case. He wouldn't want to be the cause of the fort commander sending out a legion; Jupiter forbid!

"Lieutenant?" I heard the voice of Apuleius.

"Yes, sir."

"I think that the man is right. I've been in this same situation many times and it's best to allow these people to take their own troublemakers." Apuleius spoke from much experience this I knew. The Lieutenant folded the writ and put it in his bag.

"This then should be done. You will make the arrest and I will provide support. When the arrest has been made, you will take charge of the prisoner with the understanding that should he escape, you will be charged with his crime. Lastly, should he be found not guilty by your Sanhedrin, he will still stand charged by us and must be given over to us."

I could see the officer of Herod's troops smile and look at the others, he knew what was said to him. He slowly nodded his head and accepted the word of the Lieutenant.

IDENTIFICATION AND ARREST

Herod's troops moved to the fore; their leader spoke, "Let's move on the group!"

I led them up a small knoll. As I came close, the eleven recognized me. They made a clucking sound with their tongues indicating their hate and disdain for me. I felt the full force of their enmity; these good men who were just taught to love their enemy! I stepped before Yeshua and greeted him with the honorary kiss between teacher and pupil.

"Yeshua, the time has come, this we both know." I spoke low so the others couldn't hear. "I must obey the will of God even as you!"

"Aye, but Judas, must this be done with a kiss?" He knew it must be done, yet he was unhappy at the signal used. He turned toward the soldiers and officers of the temple.

"Who do you want?" Yeshua asked. Even though he had been identified, he still asked this question.

"Yeshua, one known to be a Galilean and teacher of sedition," the officer of the temple returned. Yeshua was taken aback and the others as well. The others moved closer about him and shouted angrily at this remark. A seditionist he wasn't, but teacher, yes.

"I am Yeshua, the teacher of these men, but a seditionist I am not! These are of no concern of yours, leave them be." He motioned to the eleven who stood by him.

After I stepped aside, Herod's officers and some of the temple guards came forward to place Yeshua under arrest. Peter, who had a sword, suddenly brought it down hard against the helmet of Malchus. The blade slid from the top of the helmet and severed the right ear of Malchus, who fell to his knees from the force of the blow. The act was quick and unexpected. All stood still for a moment, and those near ceased to speak.

Yeshua spoke to the silent gathering. "Put away your swords; leave it be." Peter, who was frightened by his own act, dropped the sword as he had no scabbard. Neither he nor any of the others ever carried anything other than a staff; it was obviously a borrowed weapon. His act was anything but that of one who knew tactics, and these I knew from the training Apuleius gave me when we lived in Rome.

Yeshua turned to Peter and rebuked him, saying thus, "Is your arm mightier than mine? Don't you know I can call more than twelve legions of angels?" Peter bowed his head and moved behind him. He then spoke quietly but those near easily heard his remarks. Many took a step or two away from him.

Ah, my heart soared! Here at last was the answer! Now I would see the Messiah in all his heavenly glory even as he had said! This maniple and small number of Herod's men would be no match for twelve legions of angels. Praise the Almighty God of Israel!

It seemed an eternity was passing - time stood still - the Father and heavenly hosts awaited his prayer. The earth and stars were without movement. I waited his command that would change the world and all that was in it. I could see each face of the eleven; they were as enthralled as I was at his words. Surely now, with his life and those of his followers at stake, he would move to bring aid to this little band and the start of righteous justice.

Still nothing moved! Why was he taking so long? Why had he spoken thus and brought no relief?

Then as a flickering of the eye, all moved again. He spoke in soft Galilean tones, this time as to himself, with his voice breaking from the pain of it all, "But how then shall the scriptures be fulfilled, as thus it must be?" He gave no call to his Father - instead, he stood there as a lamb before the knife of the priest!

I suddenly realized this wasn't the Messiah of old. Not the Messiah ben Joseph or Messiah ben David tradition had taught us. No Jew could accept this Messiah - no, not even his disciples - they started to scatter as hens before the fox.

My heart plummeted to the depths of despair - so this then was the meaning of it all - not glory on earth for the Messiah and his followers but pain and despair! Suddenly, the reality of it all was with me again.

Malchus was still bleeding and on his knees, stunned by the blow. I was wondering through the haze of lost hopes for the rise of Israel, what the young Roman officer might do? He did nothing - his lack of experience generated hesitation. Yeshua stooped low and picked up the ear and placed on the now-bleeding head of Malchus. The ear became attached and was whole again. Malchus rose to his feet and showed no effect from the blow except for the blood that had run down his face and neck. He acted as if he hadn't received a blow at all. He gave no thanks for the restoration, and I doubted in his stunned condition he even knew anything serious had happened. I knew one who had partly seen the act and was interested - Apuleius, who stepped forward to give aid to the man looked closely at the ear and then saw nothing needed to be done and stepped back to my side.

The maniple under the command of Lieutenant Ancus moved aside. The eleven quickly dispersed and were soon lost in the crowd. None stayed with Yeshua - no, not one! He was the only one taken in custody. None of the arresting officers or men made any attempt to seize any of his followers, nor did any attempt to follow them and ferret out their hiding places. This I thought strange at the time. Usually, under such serious charges as treason and sedition, the Romans were dogmatic about arrests. Not only was the leader arrested, but any and all of his supporters were also hunted down and brought to court. I knew of the arrest and prosecution of Judas of Galilee, as did all the people, and in that case, many of his followers were arrested, charged, and found guilty; even his sons paid the price. Why then had Lieutenant Ancus said that the writ was one charging treason against Yeshua but ignored his followers? This was indeed strange - though not unappreciated by me!

When one of the Roman soldiers picked up the fallen sword and gave it to his officer, there was no sudden command to run down the culprit, no search party was formed, and no reaction at all except to turn aside and permit Herod's men take over. The presence of the Roman troops was a farce; someone had been duped as to the seriousness of this police action. The command would hear of this calling out of a maniple for a simple arrest of a teacher of twelve fisherman! The officer simply remarked that the sword wasn't the best blade in the world, and it wouldn't have lasted long in action.

Some of the men were greatly relieved at the ease of the arrest. Evidently, some of the officers of the temple who had heard of the miracles were expecting at least some sort of mystic repulsion or retaliation - but none occurred - much to my loss of faith in Yeshua as the Messiah. Later, I heard them joking about some of them falling down out of pure fright when he spoke, each claiming the other fellow did, and all claiming the rookies were done in by his voice. They were a boisterous lot now that all was over.

I moved along with the crowd. The maniple retired after arriving in the city and returned to Antonia, but Apuleius stayed with me. I would leave as soon as I was through and return the silver to Caiaphas. It would be a pleasure to throw it into his hall and tell him I couldn't be bought neither by silver, nor the threat of life. As I walked along, I could feel the sting of tears in my eyes for Yeshua and Ishmael. I thought of the many trials of Job. Was this true again? Was I the one selected to be tried even as he had been so many centuries ago? If this was true, then I had resisted the hand of Satan! Glory to God on high!

As we walked along with the prisoner, the temple officers and Herod's men, I thought of the writ still held by Lieutenant Ancus.

"Apuleius, what will Lieutenant Ancus say to his superior about the failure to bring Yeshua to the fort?" It seemed a waste of manpower to send a maniple and an officer to assist in a simple arrest. In addition, when a writ of the magnitude of treason was written, and signed by the Procurator, it could seldom be put off by a field lieutenant.

"From my understanding, the writ was established in agreement between Herod and Pilate, that it was to be served if and only if the Idumeans didn't succeed. There was some fear on the part of Herod the people would cause a disturbance."

The crowd walked faster now and soon passed through the streets. The night was fast passing. It would soon be in the midnight watch before the Feast of Unleavened Bread.

"I heard from the men at the fort that Pilate wanted to avoid any of this; not because he held any fear or friendship with any of the others, but that he wanted to attend a banquet given by Vitellius, the governor of Syria. However, since the banquet would have lasted through your Feast, always known as a troubled time in Jerusalem, he thought it better in the eyes of Rome if he were here."

"Fear or friendship of others - which others?"

"Herod, Annas, and Caiaphas. Some have the idea that Pilate is concerned about what Herod and yes, even Annas and Caiaphas think or do, but believe me, Pilate is a man concerned about only one thing, and that is Rome."

"Well, that may be all well and good, but if he fears nothing but Rome, then why did he make an appearance?"

"He came here because the previous Procurators set up a weak system and he has yet to break it, but he will. After all, he has only been here six years."

The crowd had moved into the area of the Hasmonean Palace and were turning toward the house of Caiaphas. The walk was a long one. The column stopped and an argument started about where Yeshua should be taken. Herod's guards held that they had the prisoner left in their care by the Romans, and the officers of the temple held that he should first go to the house of Caiaphas. As a result, there were raucous voices heard and a scuffle between the two agents with Yeshua in between.

I and Apuleius watched from a small rise in the street. It was plain that each faction wanted control of the prisoner and were pummeling each other and him to get control. Soon Apuleius, who feared for the life of Yeshua, stepped into the fray. Even though he was a medical officer, he was still bound to military law to quell any riot or potential riot in his view, just as it was the duty of those so commanded to cease and desist on command of any such officer. Failure to do so and harm came to the Roman officer who could bring harsh reaction from the men stationed at Fort Antonia.

I was sure they wouldn't heed his calls and he would be left for dead soon. Yet, it wasn't so; some of the cooler heads recognized the Roman officer among them and stepped aside. He was then able to move to the relief of Yeshua. Herod's guards gave way to the will of the temple officers and retired some distance from them, but it was obvious they hadn't given up their intentions of having the prisoner for themselves sometime.

The temple officers reformed and proceeded down the street. Apuleius held them long enough to look at Yeshua and found no great harm done. As they moved on, he rejoined me.

"You know, it's a strange thing, but twice tonight I thought I would need to patch someone up, yet it hasn't materialized. The damage to the ear of the temple officer, what was his name?" Apuleius turned to me believing I knew the man.

"Malchus."

"Yes, that's it, Malchus. I thought sure, with all the blood that first showed, that there was severe damage, but when I looked, I could only see a scratch." He pulled at his nose while he mused about this action in the garden.

"Then you didn't see the ear of Malchus on the ground?" I couldn't believe he didn't see this.

"No, from where I stood, I only saw a good deal of blood and knew there had been damage done by the force of the blow. You know the one called Peter is a big one." He never admitted that he had seen the ear severed from Malchus.

"Well, I can tell you, the ear was completely severed from the head of Malchus and fell to the ground. It was Yeshua who restored it and made it whole." I spoke with proud assurance that I was right.

"Ha, as to that I can't say, but the injury as I saw it was small. And here, just a moment ago, I thought I saw one of the men hit in the eye with a bludgeon, yet when I came upon him, all was well. This is surely a strange night." We walked along in silence.

"I'll be glad when this night is over," he said. I couldn't help agree.

Looking back, I could see a lonely figure of the big man Peter walking in the moonlight. He, of all the others, other than myself, was still following his master. He wasn't the bravest man, but far from a coward. I couldn't help feeling great admiration for him; there was none who liked me less, but given his convictions, I couldn't hold it against him. I knew, as I watched him plod along behind us, he would be one who would seek me out with a vengeance when this was over. I would have to be on my guard against reactions from the eleven, but more than any other, Peter!

ISHMAEL AND TWO

It was very early in the morning. I looked around at the different people who were still interested in this arrest and noticed three others in the moonlight. I faintly recognized them, that is to say, I felt I knew them from some time past. As they came closer, I strained to see who they were. I took a short breath; one of them was Ishmael! The other two were evidently known to him as well.

"Apuleius, look! There's Ishmael! I wonder what brings him out this night of all nights. Let's see why he is in this crowd." I began to move to the edge of the band, but Apuleius caught my arm and restrained me.

"Listen, Judas," he whispered, "I've a feeling you shouldn't do this thing."

"Why not?"

"Because it's you who caused this arrest. What do you know of the feelings of Ishmael about Yeshua?" What he said made me quickly realize that many people touched by the hands of Yeshua would be devastated by his arrest and possible death. I would be marked as the man who brought this about. None would know or understand my God-given mission. All, even as Shalazar had said - truthfully - all would now hate me, and my name would symbolize infamy and treachery of the highest degree! Now, even with God's forgiveness, man would never forgive or forget - woe is me! How will I live out my life?

"I must see what has brought Ishmael to this event." I pulled away and was soon at his side; I knew of our argument the morning before, but had given no thought that Ishmael would leave mother and Miriam to come to this place. How did he hear of this thing?

"Ishmael, what brings you to this place?" He turned to face me; the moonlight plainly showed the pain of his emotions. He held me off.

"You didn't know? Even after our talk this morning?" I knew he was serious.

"But how did you hear of the arrest?" I wondered if Yeshua told him of his possible betrayal into the hands of the gentiles. If true, then I could better understand Ishmael's violent reaction to my announcement that morning.

"I heard from Nicodemus and Joseph of Arimathea that this arrest was to be attempted. Now, I find he is arrested and you had a hand in it." He turned away. This was the first time he and I had been so cut off from one another. My heart began to break; now I knew what the words of Shalazar meant.

"Ishmael, it's not what you think. There is more to this than you see, and after it's all over, you will understand." I knew I didn't have time to explain all to him, but perhaps he would accept these words and hold them in his heart. "Listen, return home to Miriam this night. All that happens here is not for you and your friends. Remember me to mother."

It was then I recognized the other two as the learned Pharisee, Nicodemus, and his student, Joseph of Arimathea. I recognized them from the sketches Ishmael had sent me while I was in Rome. Even in the moonlight and the years between, they hadn't changed much. It was evident they had become followers of Yeshua. Knowing Ishmael, I knew no other words would change him at the moment and I turned away to where Apuleius stood some distance away. He hadn't come with me for reasons of his own.

"My heart can't stand much more of this, Apuleius. Ishmael has found life without Yeshua nearly lost. From his own lips he rejected me." I leaned against him. Oh, Shalazar, you have an evil heart.

"Judas, I care for Ishmael nearly as much as you. I don't know him as well, but I feel he will forgive all and not hold this against you even as I won't when I know the truth." My heart sang at his words. Oh, Apuleius, God has given you the first knowledge about this fulfillment of his plan. My action wasn't in accordance with the wish of the Great Deceiver, but in the will of God. Someday, the world will know the truth.

Time now seemed to move as a fast stream. The house of Caiaphas appeared around the corner. It was a place of quality, this I knew from my frequent visits there to argue the cause of Yeshua earlier in the ministry. Nothing but the best for Caiaphas; his complaint about the treasury wasn't reflected in the appointments of his home.

The house of Annas was close by. The crowd had now dwindled down to less than before the arrest and consisted of Herod's men, mostly Idumeans, many poor that were here to support their teacher, and one or two Pharisees. Almost no Sadducees and the like were seen; after all, they weren't interested in being seen at this arrest of a Galilean. They all knew nothing good could come out of Galilee - so what was new in this arrest?

The crowd sans the maniple was far from large. It was true that most pilgrims were outside the city in their tents either fast asleep or already preparing for the Feast of Unleavened Bread. The few I saw here were the homeless and officers of the temple. Even so, these carrying burning brands and torches gave some semblance of a large and unruly mob to the eye at night. When the large street gate that gave access to the courtyard of Caiaphas's house was opened, the crowd with the prisoner at its head all tried to enter at the same time. There was a great deal of shouting and shoving - all wanted to enter first and be near the action, whatever it might be.

Yeshua remained silent and gave no resistance along the way. At times, I did see him stumble from tiredness, for this he was roughly pulled forward and upbraided. Herod's guards kept their distance but were close by when the crowd came to the gates of the house of Caiaphas. I could see the house was dark except for the night lamps. I knew the old fox was in his darkened bedroom, or had went to bed leaving instructions to be awakened at the first sign of someone at the gate.

The first to reach the gate pounded on it with exuberance. To them, the arrest had been a rousing success and that's what they intended to do to Caiaphas - rouse him. The boisterous crowd soon raised the servants of the household and lamps began to move about the house. Servants came on the run to open the gates. They didn't want them destroyed and that seemed to be the intent of the crowd.

With the gates flung open, those in the back pushed those in front into the courtyard. They squirted through like pigs through a sty when chased by an animal of prey. They reformed inside and Yeshua was pushed to the fore. I left Apuleius as he preferred to remain outside and off the property of Caiaphas. I entered the gate and worked my way to the front. The servants entered the house to give the message to Caiaphas that the deed had been done, and smoothly at that. The many firebrands and torches lighted the courtyard and produced grotesque shadows that moved about and danced on the walls of the house.

I noticed Peter had moved under the steps of the house where a burner of coals was going to fend off the early morning chill. I could see some of the temple guards and others gathering there. I was surprised to see Ishmael, Nicodemus, and Joseph of Arimathea near the front, attempting to give aid and comfort to Yeshua, a dangerous thing to do in this hall; I would give them credit for that.

It was hard for me to reason that Ishmael would be so caught up with the teachings and personality of Yeshua. To my knowledge, Ishmael had never shown any interest in this sort of thing. He was an artist and craftsman, not often given to politics and even to religious thought. Oh, that's not to say he wasn't a good Pharisee, for he was. So why the interest in Yeshua as the Messiah? I did remember the day I came to find Ishmael doing the bust of Yeshua; he never explained why he had chosen to do it. Even now as I watched, he stood next to Yeshua during this trial - closer than any of his followers, me included. This was my brother - my twin?

CHAPTER TWENTY-THREE

Suddenly they came - the members of the Sanhedrin. Some borne on litters and others walking, all with servants bearing oil lamps to lead the way. It was still the midnight watch. It amazed me, this call to the Sanhedrin at this hour and in the holy season. Caiaphas said it would be so and so it was. The servants of the members pushed and shoved their way through the crowd. I began to count those I recognized from my years in Jerusalem. I knew Peter down below didn't know them even when he saw them; the same was true of Yeshua. I continued to count. Nearly all the members were present. The Sadducees took the highest count, then the Pharisees. I recognized Gamaliel, Joseph of Arimathea, Nicodemus, and many more. At last, the assembly hall of Caiaphas was filled to overflowing; more than those called were present. Many were servants of these men, especially of the older men - the elders.

It was soon obvious the hall must be cleared of those not with authority or business on this night. The hall was not yet quiet, and the noise and questions flew between the council members and spectators as well. I stepped into the room and stood near the front of the hall which was filled with benches arranged in two semicircles. There were several seats before the benches, and in front of them, two larger chairs facing the benches. These chairs, nearly throne size, were now occupied by Gamaliel and Caiaphas. It was Gamaliel who was the president of the council, but when the high priest came to call on the council, he took the seat to his left. Because this meeting was held in the house of Caiaphas, and because it wasn't an official court session, Gamaliel took the lesser role in the proceedings. Gamaliel was the grandson of Hillel, my teacher, whom I knew well.

The elders were in the furthest row behind and facing the Chairs of Judgement. The senior and junior members sat in the rest of the benches in accordance with their seniority. Two scribes stood near the Judgement Seats, one to the left and one to the right. Each had the instruments of his profession. The prisoner and his guards stood further to the left.

Caiaphas was patient. Some of the council members were not young and time must be given for them to be seated; at last all seventy were seated. As I quickly counted again, I could see that more than seventy were present. Counting Gamaliel and Caiaphas, there were seventy two, this made the council greater than required.

Finally, Caiaphas stood up, raised his arms, and spoke. "I salute you, good men of Israel. Normally, this isn't the time for such meetings but we have no choice - a teacher's life hangs in the balance. Because this is an extremely delicate matter, I ask you to send your servants from the hall." He sat down to wait the emptying of the hall. Shouts rose from those who claimed to have business with the assembly or those claiming support for the accursed but they were cleared from the room.

I saw Ishmael remain at the side of Nicodemus and was satisfied he had reasons sufficient to keep him there. I knew that he would tell the others after the meeting what happened. Caiaphas's servant came to me; I sent word that I would remain if so desired by Caiaphas. The message brought back was to remain as there might be questions asked of me. So I stood in the front of the hall near the Judgement Seat during the meeting.

The room was soon cleared and only the council and those holding Yeshua were present. There were no others; not one apostle was present other than myself. Even Peter wasn't in the hall; he was in the lower level near the burner under the steps.

"Each of you are now in the register. The prisoner is one Yeshua, a teacher from Galilee." The council murmured in finding who it was before them. Some had heard of Yeshua but had never seen him; there was a craning of necks to see this notorious Galilean. "A man whose teaching has become known to many of you. He was arrested by command of Herod and this office. He now stands before you."

Yeshua was indeed standing at the right of the semicircle of the council and the left of Caiaphas. He was a very tired man.

His outer garments were in complete disarray. His general appearance was disheveled and worn to say the least. His hands hung limply at his sides. He looked more like a beggar than a Messiah or king. The council studied this somewhat pathetic figure. Some not realizing the seriousness snickered at this sight of a Galilean teacher - this brought a stern reprimand from Gamaliel.

I knew many had heard of his deeds, teachings, and the cleansing of the temple. I also knew that some were sympathetic with his action in the Court of the Gentiles. For many years, there was an outcry from both the Sadducees and Pharisees against the booths set up inside the temple walls. He was just the one who took charge and did what others didn't have the nerve or calling of God to do! So this was the man some said was the Savior of Israel! A soft murmur went through the council. The gist of this was a question, "*This* is the Messiah?"

There was a disturbance at the door to the hall and in came Annas - the high priest emeritus. The council rose to a man in respect to old Annas. Caiaphas was taken aback some by his appearance but welcomed him with graciousness. He was yet a figure held in high esteem. A special chair was brought into the hall for Annas. When he was seated, the council did likewise.

Yeshua was brought forward to the dock. Caiaphas walked to where he stood and questioned him as to his teachings and followers. I knew that most of the council were aware of all these things, but it was in accordance with precedents, and although not a court matter, it permitted each member to review the facts. Yeshua remained silent on these questions. His reticence brought some to their feet.

"How can we help one who won't help himself?" one of the elders spoke. Yet, I could understand Yeshua's reluctance to tell all about his followers for they also became targets of arrest should the information leak from this room. Caiaphas continued to ask many questions about his teachings and how these differed from those of the law.

Finally, Annas stepped forward. Caiaphas, seeing him approach, moved aside in deference to his standing and age. Annas asked some of the same questions in a different manner.

Yeshua finally broke his silence to say, "I taught in the House of Assembly in many villages, even in the temple where our people came often as you know. I've nothing to hide and therefore have said nothing in secret. But why not ask those who heard me? They know what I've said."

He had scarcely said these words when a guard standing nearby struck him, saying, "Is this a way to answer one such as Annas?"

At this, Yeshua turned quickly to face the man and boldly answered the blow saying, "Why did you strike me? If I have broken the rule in answering, then tell it to me, but don't strike me!"

The reaction was swift. The council, led by Nicodemus and Joseph of Arimathea, stood as one man and demanded the guard be withdrawn.

"The accused has said nothing improper, and this man has done an unjust thing!" the voice of Gamaliel rang out. Annas had to agree, and since he saw that naught was gained by his questions, he returned to his chair. Indeed, the guard had done an unjust act, for it's written that no prisoner in the dock shall be treated poorly. Caiaphas relieved the guard and he was taken from the hall by his superior to await the judgement of the court at a later date. He would stand before the Sanhedrin in the court in the entrance to the Mount.

After this, Caiaphas caused the servants of the court to circulate among the people in the courtyard to bring forward any who wanted to witness on behalf of Yeshua. Many witnesses were brought forward but their testimony was found not agreeing. They were a confused lot, many bringing with them tales of his comings and goings that were pure hearsay. Most admitted on further examination that they had not seen or heard these things themselves, but were quick to add those that spread them were godly men and true, and therefore worthy of belief. The council was amused by some of these remarks. In general, the council sat patiently while each of these witnesses were brought forth, challenged, and then dismissed as unreliable.

Some of the less educated took great pride in telling of Yeshua saying, "I am able to destroy the temple of God and to build it up in three days." Some argued and said these were his words, "I will destroy this temple that is made with hands, and in three days, I will build another, not made with hands."

Finally, the council became involved. The argument of this being possible, and if he were serious, brought the entire story to an abrupt end. As the council quieted down from this repartee, Caiaphas dismissed the witnesses as unreliable. It wasn't that they were false in the sense of bearing false witness, it was just that they had natural differences of opinion as anyone would given the circumstances. The guards were sent out again, and each time I thought Peter would come forth as he was just below the staircase in the courtyard. Yet, he wasn't among those speaking for Yeshua.

Time was running out and Caiaphas became tired and desperate; he wanted to find a solution to this tricky and thorny problem. He wanted to be able to have Yeshua plead innocent and promise not to claim he was the Messiah before Pilate! It was essential that this be done, it was only in this way the Sanhedrin could hope to bring about an escape for him. Caiaphas spoke to them for some time. All agreed they would stand by the decision rendered here. Caiaphas finally approached Yeshua again.

"Hear me well. This I ask of you and the answer will tell us all of your chance to avoid the penalty at the hand of Pilate!" He stopped here for a moment. "But before I ask it, I would address the council without the prisoner present." With that said, he had Yeshua taken from the hall. I noticed as the passed though the doorway, I could see some of Herod's Idumeans had come into the house and moved to escort Yeshua to the other room.

I was torn between staying and listening to Caiaphas and going to talk to Yeshua. But considering what was about to happen, I felt it wise to stay in the hall of the assembly.

After Yeshua was through the door, Caiaphas stood in front of the assembly and began to speak his mind.

CAIAPHAS SPEAKS

"This I know, that some have been encouraged, yes, even paid to bring false witness against this man when he is brought before Procurator Pilate. It's their word against his and ours." He slowly turned and walked to the side of his assembly. He was a showman this man - he knew his act must be good.

"The charge is a simple one. Insurrection! He will be charged with attempts to convince large groups of people that he is the Messiah! Now good men of the Sanhedrin, is this so wrong? Haven't we seen these would-be Messiahs before? Have these pseudo-Messiahs ever changed Israel? No! If we then aren't to demand his freedom be taken for his teachings, then what of this meeting? Why have we brought him here?" He moved to the other side of the room and raised his arms to hush the murmur of the assembly.

"Good men of Israel, the problem lies in the memories of the Romans. To them, the title of Messiah brings strange pictures of revolution - and challenge to their control! We know Pilate is no fool and he knows the story of a Messiah leading our people to victory over the enemies of God!" He brought his hands together with a loud bang; some of the older men who were nodding just a bit sat boldly upright at this noise.

"I say again, Pilate is no fool. He knows what the word Messiah means to the masses. He has heard all the romantic tales of our ancient and modern heros, and Pilate won't abide by such talk. He fears Rome too much to let it be. He will, without compunction, find any and all persons guilty of treason, this teacher Yeshua included, and bring the ultimate penalty to bear. Pilate will not and can not give exception to one who claims to be King here and now, or of some world populated by gods! All are the same to him; Caesar is both emperor and god!" Here the assembly roared their disapproval with the last part of the speech. There was only one God - the God of Israel!

He held up his hands again. "It could mean greater harm to all of us this time as Pilate is a cruel man and vindictive as well. He, with Herod, desires to see this just body diminished in authority over the people. They both would have us sit only on cases of religious transgressions. With their will expressed, all rights to try criminal cases would be stripped from us - blasphemy included. So, with Yeshua could go much of our power to restrain the people. So it is that we must know what his answer will be before Pilate. If he is asked - 'Are you the Messiah?' he must say he is not! Hear me, he must say he isn't!"

The speech was a long one for Caiaphas. The council agreed to his evaluation of the situation and I did as well. In fact, from what I saw in the garden, I could safely say Yeshua wasn't the Messiah our people had been waiting for these centuries. There wasn't one who would say that he was, not even his own followers - they had left him! Deep inside I knew Yeshua would never deny what he believed was his appointment with destiny by God.

Caiaphas, after speaking and listening to the remarks of the council, including Gamaliel and Nicodemus, called for the prisoner be brought before him. When Yeshua was before the dock, Caiaphas came to him. He stood such that all could see them both.

"This now I ask you, have a care, for on your answer rests your case before Pilate. Tell us, as the God of our fathers is your witness, do you believe yourself to be the Messiah?" Gamaliel and Annas stood up, and some of the others leaned forward to better hear his answer. All waited.

"I am, even as you say." The council moved and groaned.

Gamaliel now raised his voice, "Perhaps the question wasn't worded properly. I'll put it to you this way to remove the doubt of belief - are you the Messiah?"

"I am!" This statement was like a dagger in the heart of all, even me. Many of the older men fell against their benches; they were indeed the words they least wanted to hear.

Caiaphas spoke once again with a tremulous voice, "Is this the answer to this question when put to you by Pilate?"

"It is so!"

Tears ran down the face of Caiaphas, he was completely undone. He slowly raised his vestments and rent his clothes.

"This is to show my great grief for this man. He has surely doomed himself by these words. He isn't guilty of blasphemy, as none can be found guilty of his own mouth, and he spoke not, nor have we found two witnesses or more who can agree that he spoke the name of the Lord, or spoke evil of Him." His voice broke with the great distress of the moment. The entire council agreed, Yeshua would surely be put to death if asked this question by Pilate and he answered the same. If he wouldn't deny his Messiahship - then he was lost!

Caiaphas fought to control his grief. He turned again to the council, many of whom were as distressed, not necessarily for Yeshua but for the reflection on the council and the possible repercussions on it. "This then, good men of Israel, I say to you, we have heard enough, we have no need of more witnesses. What he has said seals his doom when spoken before Pilate. The time is too short to do other than we have. It's now time to rest and be ready for any action that might call us out again. Go home and pray for this man and Israel; we are one and the same, hear me, as he goes - so goes Israel. I can see naught but trouble from this thing - the nation will rue this day!" He turned away from the council and hid his face in his vestments. Gamaliel and others were greatly distressed as well. I then realized I hadn't been asked to testify for or against Yeshua. My heart was torn again as I saw them lead him from another room and knew that Ishmael, Nicodemus, and Joseph were still thunderstruck at the outcome of this meeting.

Ishmael averted his eyes and wouldn't approach me. I left to join those in the court-yard and watched as the council members, some seventy in all, slowly left the house of Caiaphas. Many were greatly downcast and murmured about the coming events yet later in this morning. Some talked of going to the Hall of Judgement, but the elders were declining because of age and wanted to celebrate the coming festival.

It was near time for the sun to appear and life in Jerusalem to take on the look of the festival. Look what God has wrought.

It was then I thought of the silver I still had in my bag. I returned to the hall and found Caiaphas.

He was still in great discomfort, but willingly admitted me to his chambers.

"Ah, Judas, there are few who now or in the future will understand my words this day. I have had a dream. I have seen both Jew and gentile struggle against one another about this night. There is more to come! I'm afraid there will be more souls lost than saved before this is history." He sadly shook his head as he spoke. I wasn't ready for this speech - I had decided he was not a man of strong decisions. He moved with the wind and like the wil-low made sounds that were more theatrical than honest.

"Ah, Caiaphas, it's good that you see me. I have sinned by accepting the silver for the deed done this night. I knew some things about this that you didn't and took the silver under false pretenses. I now give it back to the temple and ask for forgiveness." I held the bag toward Caiaphas, but he couldn't bring himself to touch it.

"Hear me, Judas, I've also known some things of this matter. I wasn't entirely truthful with you. I've seen in many dreams in these years the part I must play. I fought against these acts - God knows. I would this night hope to save your teacher from this ordeal - but it isn't to be so!" He couldn't continue; he was greatly troubled, not knowing if he had done right.

I spilled the coins on the floor - I knew they couldn't be returned to the treasury. "Lis-ten, you have been saved from a terrible mistake this night. You have tried, even as I have, to do that which is contrary to the mind of God." I knew I couldn't tell Caiaphas what was in my heart and what the angel Raphael had said about Yeshua. No man on this earth could know other than me and Yeshua. No man on this earth could know other than me what was *really* happening between man and God at this very moment. I knew each time Yeshua passed the test of man, the angels sang!

"What do I want with the money, Judas? I've lost the battle to save a fellowman, a Jew of good standing. Keep the money and welcome to it. Your deed was well done. You brought him before us and it's we who have failed this day."

I could see he still didn't understand his good fortune or the hand of God in guiding his acts this day. Would there ever be a day that such was known to all men?

I couldn't wait any longer. He was distressed beyond the point of reasonableness. I saluted him and left the hall again. I wandered around in a daze for some time. As I passed through the crowd, I heard some strange stories of what went on in the council hall. Many of these stories now circulated so soon after the investigation were entirely false; I was much troubled. There were monstrous stories of cruelty done to Yeshua that were completely foreign to the course of the night. My head swam with the effects of these stories - most told by people not even near the hall during the time of the inquisition - let alone in it. Things like the striking of Yeshua by the guard had now grown to wholesale attacks wherein Yeshua was blindfolded and asked to identify who struck him. This and many other acts didn't occur. I knew it, as I was there.

Why were these people so happy in their telling of these tales? Who encouraged them? I listened and heard each story and none asked to verify any of it but just repeated it with apparent relish. The more coarse the better. After listening to several of these stories and wanting to tell all in the courtyard that they were wrong and untrue, I noticed in the dim light the figure of Shalazar. He was enjoying the stories and repeating some to other's himself. He hadn't given up on others even if I had withstood his hand through the gift of God.

A DENIAL

I continued to walk about the courtyard listening to the stories of the laggards. There were many who weren't commonfolk and some who were but weren't preparing for the coming feast. I was one, and as near as I could tell, so was Ishmael, but not as certainty for I hadn't seen him since Yeshua was led into the other room. From what I could gather from the guards still stationed about, Yeshua was to be kept on the premises until the morning, then taken to the Judgement Hall of Pilate.

It was very chilly and I wandered to the charcoal burner where others stood and warmed themselves. The group was large and all jostled one another trying to eke out a bit of heat by standing close to the wrought iron heater. Those near were housemaids, guards, runners, and scribes attached to the Sanhedrin. I stood silent in the circle that pressed against each other around the heater, wondering what to do after this was over, and what I should do until morning. I couldn't go home, unless it was to gather some belongings and leave again. I then heard someone talking about an incident that just took place.

"I say he was!" It was the voice of the housemaid. She was addressing someone her equal, for to speak in that tone to a better would have brought a blow upon her.

"How do you know this?" another questioned.

"Because of his speech. He was definitely a Galilean, you know how they change words." She then mimicked a Galilean; some snickered at her efforts.

"Well, just because one is a Galilean doesn't mean he is a party to or follower of the accused - this Yeshua." A man now spoke from the opposite side of the circle.

"Tis so!" said another.

I began to listen closer. I thought of Peter being in company with some of these when I went into the hall. In fact, he stood at this very burner under the steps.

"Let the maid speak again. What did you say to him?" One from behind moved up to where he could see as well as hear.

"I said to him, you also were with this Yeshua of Galilee, isn't that so?" She was more than willing to tell her part of the story. "But he denied before us all and said, 'I don't know what you're saying.'" She laughed a hard laugh. "Now, you know he understood what I asked, after all, he wasn't dumb. He couldn't stand to see me looking at him, so he left the fire and went out onto the porch, and I watched him but didn't hear him anymore."

"Yes, he stood looking up into the house and I said to one of the maids, 'This fellow was also with Yeshua, the accused,' but he heard me and swore an oath of Jupiter to show he wasn't one of his followers." A second bystander added his part to the story.

I couldn't contain my curiosity any longer, and spoke out. "Was this a big man?" I knew that many don't often remember a person's clothing but often do size.

"Aye, that he was, and looked powerful as well," came the answer from one close to the burner. "I would say he was not only a Galilean but was a fisherman as well."

"What would give you that idea?" I had never thought a person's trade could be so readily observed in light such as this. I had my doubts about all of this; I had just seen Shalazar encouraging these people to tell outrageous stories about the goings on in the hall.

"That's simple," the man answered, "I'm a fisherman myself and I know the strong shoulders it takes to pull in nets, and if anyone had them, he did." He held up a powerful arm to support his observation. Many at the burner hooted and whistled at this show.

"Well, anyway, he was accused once again by another," said someone else.

"Aye, that was by me. I said to him, 'Surely you also are one of them; your speech betrays you.' At this, he became very angry. I don't know the reason, but I had moments of fear he would attack me, but he didn't. He just spoke evil words unbecoming anyone who followed this kindly teacher, so I'm content he didn't." He turned away from the fire and left us with the final word.

"It was a strange thing indeed," remarked another, "he changed in his demeanor when he heard the sounding of the trumpet at the fort." The man continued near me in hushed tones. "He muttered something about a cock crowing, as to what he meant I don't know, but have often noted how that trumpet from Antonia sounds like the crowing of a cock. You know, there are stranger things in this world." With that, he moved on. I wondered what it all meant as well.

Why would Peter deny his association with Yeshua? Unless he feared he would be brought in the hall and forced to testify at the investigation. He was an impetuous one. He had a reputation of saying the wrong thing at the right time. He wasn't afraid as a man of strength isn't in times of combat, even as the happening in the garden this night indicated. It was the fear of saying the wrong thing and thereby placing his master in danger - that was his nemesis! So where was Peter now? I looked for him among those yet in the courtyard but didn't find him. If he was still present, he was staying out of sight.

It was about this time I recalled Apuleius was outside the gate, or so I thought. Time had left me and I doubted he remained there all this time. The weather didn't warrant it and his interest in this session wasn't a driving force. He was, after all, here at the request of his command, and that to see to the care of the prisoner when in the hands of his troops.

I didn't find him at the high spot in the street where I left him before the trial. As I peered into the semi-darkness in search of him, a boy came to me. He was a goodly lad, although I didn't know why he was out at this hour; nonetheless, he gave me a good salute and asked in all respect, if I was one named Judas? I said I was, and he gave me a message and said he was paid well to give it to me. The note was from a Roman officer who was called away by a runner. All this he said in truth. I gave him my blessings and noted how much he looked like the lad who had carried the baskets of loaves and fishes nearly two years ago on the mount near Capernaum. He left the scene as quickly as he could and I had no chance to ask his name or why he was out at this hour.

I walked to where a wall brand was still throwing a ruddy glow and opened the note scribbled on the military papyrus often carried by Apuleius. It was written with a small nib he carried with some of his field kit.

"Judas, I've been called to the fort. Some changes have been brought about. Till we meet again, Apuleius." That was all the note said; I knew this was in accordance with his custom. His military operations were never privy to me. What had been the call to the fort? I had a feeling I would soon find out.

Great tiredness came upon me. I must seek a place to rest and home wasn't the place. I must be near as I knew from the talk in the hall, all would be called together again. I wanted to be present and follow this to the end. I couldn't believe that the Lord wouldn't protect the Messiah of Israel from all harm. Hadn't he done so soon after his birth? Hadn't Israel suffered enough at the hands of oppressors through the years?

If he is the Messiah - then surely the Lord won't desert him! This thought kept repeating itself in my mind - I must believe it!

I finally joined some of the others at the outer gate and there lay down, pulled my cloak about me and fell into a troubled sleep of one tired in mind and body but unable to divorce all of the days' happenings. *Hear, O Israel: the Lord is our God, the Lord is one.*

I wasn't as young as I once was and the chill of the night caused me to change positions often to keep my joints from aching. Each time I looked about the courtyard of Caiaphas, all was quiet. When the sunlight tinged the sky, I knew three things immediately: I was very stiff, hungry, and dirty. I wanted my old room and all it stood for: warmth, ablution, and food. The need for these things caused me to wonder about Yeshua and Ishmael. Yeshua, as near as I could tell, was held in the house of Caiaphas through the night. I believed Ishmael went with Nicodemus and Joseph to the house of Nicodemus.

I went to one of the wells and washed the nights' dust and grime away. I returned to the courtyard and entered through the open gate. My hunger made all the smells of morning food more intense.

A ROMAN SCRIBE

Through the years, I established many friends within the city and now was the time to call on one who lived near. Seeing nothing afoot at the house of Caiaphas, I moved through the streets of the city until I came to the house of a man, Quintus Gaius Tiberius, a distant relative of the royal family, although he seldom boasted of that. At times, I do believe he wasn't proud of his heritage. He was in the shipping trade and I met him while in Rome working as bookkeeper for Uncle Benjamin. He was a good man even though a gentile. Several of his family's ships plied the seas from Caesarea to Rome carrying olive oil and wool to cities along the route. He was near counterpart of Uncle Benjamin in Rome, except he being Roman while uncle was a Jew. In the time before joining Yeshua and while in business here, I had many dealings with him and managed his books for trade done from Jerusalem. His was a lucrative contract for me and I honored it well. I had visited his home often in those days, although he seldom found time to do the same to ours.

He moved his family to Jerusalem some years ago, and by this time, knew our ways and ancient history very well. He was, like Apuleius, appreciative of our God and teachings. That was not to say he was swayed by these, but had respect. I would call on Quintus Gaius Tiberius this day.

I was early, but shema was said, so I felt Quintus and his house would be awake - he knew when and what this day meant to us. I called at the gate and asked the servant to announce me to his master. I was ushered to the door of the pleasant house of Quintus. I refused to bring the days' filth into his house and declined to enter as was the custom. Water was sent and I bathed feet and hands to leave the street uncleanliness behind. I asked and received from one of the servants a trimming of my hair and beard. As I looked into the bronze mirror, I noticed how much I looked like Ishmael. I began to wonder who could tell the difference between us at a distance. I entered the house to be greeted by Quintus.

"Ah, Judas, it is Judas, isn't it? You know, for a moment I thought otherwise, and you were Ishmael. By Jupiter, good health to you, Judas! This house is yours as always." Quintus came forward and gave me his hand and grip in brotherly love and friendship.

"And may your house find the face of the Lord toward it." He hadn't changed much in the last year or so. His family soon moved elsewhere and he and I went to a large room to relax and talk. Food was quickly brought and this I enjoyed with some relish. As we sat sipping wine afterward, we talked of things going on during the first day of the feast. We exchanged stories and comments about our respective families and then his thoughts turned to the news his servants brought to him in the early morning. The news of an arrest and inquisition at the house of Caiaphas. He was very curious about the event and asked me if I had any knowledge of it.

I told him of the happenings of the night before, and explained my part of it and the reason for my being close to his home on the first day of the Feast of Unleavened Bread. He was surprised to hear all this and wondered what the world was coming to.

"It's hard enough to do business with your people these days without more trouble here. I hope that all this will blow over soon. I've got to make another trip to Rome and would like to be spared explaining more trouble here to my customers." He waved his hands in an exasperated manner. "By the way, I suppose the teacher of yours will be brought to trial before the governor, right?" I wondered why his interest in this thing, and was soon to find out.

"Yes, so it was given by our august body, and from the writ in possession of Lieutenant Ancus. I must hurry to join those going to the Judgement Hall. But why do you ask?" I made ready to go as I waited for his answer.

"Oh, it's simple enough. My son is an apparitores for the Governor and is always asked to record all statements of the Governor, witnesses, and prosecutors during such a trial. He is often called to this work in the secretarium, and has in the past received commendations from the Governor for his steady hand and precise copy work." He was proud of his son's accomplishments in this work. I knew, though, he wanted his son to follow him in the sea trade.

"Aha, and which son is this?" I knew he had more than one, but was sure he spoke of his eldest, Titus.

"It's Titus. I've given up all hope of him joining me in the trade, but my other sons are ready and willing, so all is not lost." I suddenly had an idea and asked if it was possible to talk to Titus.

"Ah, yes, he hasn't left for the Praetorium yet." He sent a servant for the young man. Soon, Titus appeared in his garb of office. He saluted his father and me.

"Titus, this is Judas, an old friend as you remember from your youth." Titus gave me his hand. "He would speak to you."

I returned the greeting and spoke of how well he looked and how much like his father when younger. Smiles passed between them at this.

"This I would like to ask of you. My interest in this case is great. This man to be tried is my teacher, and my heart is deeply distressed at this trial. I would have firsthand knowledge of all that is said in confidence." Here I stopped and watched his reaction. I knew his position required secrecy but of what in a Roman court I didn't know.

"Hold sir, this is one of the proprietaries of the court and I wouldn't dare to compromise it. I can, however provide all that's normally transmitted to the forum. Will this be of help?" His answer was as it should be.

"Yes, I know this trial will be conducted in private and even though I am among those outside the Praetorium, I will hear and see little. I would have more. Yet I wouldn't have you compromise your trust for I know the penalties are severe." I could ask no more.

"Then this I can do," he said with a nod of confidence, "is there something else I might do for an old friend of my father?"

"Well, yes, I would impose on you once more. I have a friend, Captain Apuleius, by name, who is now assigned as the surgeon to the prisoners in the dock. He will be there. If it's possible, please speak with him and tell him to meet me here after his assignment is over. This I beg of you." I began to show my distress and turned away.

"Don't be so undone. Titus will do as you asked, yes?" Quintus spoke to his son.

"Yes, so he asked and so it shall be done." He bowed to us and left.

"And now, Judas, tell me more of this trial and your connection with it." Quintus came to me and took my arm to move me to a chair.

As briefly as I could, I told him of my involvement sans my betrayal of Yeshua. I then asked if I could return here to receive the words of Titus and Apuleius.

"Of course, dear friend, and I'll prepare food and wine for you and Apuleius as well. Tell me, will you stay with us this night after the trial? You know this house is yours and your friends are mine as well." He followed me to his foyer.

"I think all this will be over without much repercussion in the world of shipping, Quintus, but I have imposed on your hospitality too long. As to this night I can't say. It may be possible, yet I don't know if Apuleius will have to report to the fort afterward. For now, I must go back to the house of Caiaphas and see what is to be done in this thing." I turned and thanked him and his house for the morning kindness. I then reminded him that it was his obligation to return this favor to me by visiting my mother's household. I left his house the better for the visit, feeling cleaner and better prepared for the rest of the morning.

When I arrived at the house of Caiaphas, much was stirring. A new bed of coals had been added to the burner and many of the same people were about it. Yet Peter I still didn't see.

Some of the members of the Sanhedrin who came early entered the house; I followed and entered the hall. After awhile, I could see that many were not present. Many of the elders had not returned from the night before. Caiaphas entered the hall and set things in motion by having the scribes enter the names of those present. The count showed there was enough for a quorum as slightly more than twenty three were now seated in the hall. As Caiaphas sat waiting for the hall to quiet down, I noticed his haggard look. The evening and early hours of the morning had taken its toll - he was a very tired man.

Caiaphas finally brought the members to order, and had Yeshua brought into the hall. Yeshua was so forlorn looking that my heart nearly broke. Some of the members whispered to one another about his poor condition, and they spoke of the law and treatment that was to be given all prisoners, and more especially, those whose life may be in jeopardy.

"Men of the council, the time has come. We have no alternative but to send this man unto the Judgement Hall and appear before Pilate. The full council, as was present, agreed that if naught was changed, and he persisted in his claim to be a Messiah, he would surely be found guilty of the charge of treason. Is this still the belief of this most just body? If so, stand and be counted."

And so it was as I watched, each member present rose, faced the prisoner and told him in their words his transgression of the Roman law as they understood it, and warned him of the penalty it would bring upon him. It was done as the law required - for so it was written - at least two must warn the lawbreaker of the law he breaks and of the penalty he will bring upon himself following his course. During this procedure, I couldn't help but notice Ishmael, Nicodemus, Joseph of Aramathea, and Gamaliel weren't present, neither in seats nor in the hall. After this, Caiaphas dismissed the assembly and prepared the prisoner for his trip across town to the Praetorium.

It was then the captain of Herod's watchdogs spoke to Caiaphas from the entrance to the hall. He was a large Idumean and reminded me of the officer that arrested me on the road to Jericho a year before. His manner was coarse.

"Here, high priest! It's Herod's command that we take the prisoner to him, why is it you prepare him for Pilate?"

His mannerisms angered the tired Caiaphas. "He goes to Pilate, and if Herod wants to see him, he can go to the Praetorium to do it!" I had known Caiaphas was not altogether sympathetic with the wishes of Herod and knew he took his high calling to be above this Idumean set over the people by Rome. Herod's officer scowled but held his peace; he knew better than to stand between Caiaphas and Herod.

So it was that the temple guards and some of the members of the Sanhedrin moved slowly out of the house toward the Praetorium. Neither Caiaphas nor any other priests went with them, but returned to the temple to start their courses on this, the fifteenth of Abib and the beginning of the Feast of Unleavened Bread. This was the busiest time of the year for the temple and no priest was excused from service. Even those impure could have no affect on the outcome of the ritual. All were to work this day. The thoughts of them gathering at the Praetorium to see this trial was ridiculous.

IN THE PRAETORIUM

I followed the lowly procession from the courtyard of the home of Caiaphas through the streets. The city was beginning to come alive. The many pilgrims from the tent cities outside the walls were beginning to bring their sacrifices to the temple. It was near time for the blowing of the trumpets, signifying the sacrifice of the two young bullocks. There were other offerings as well and this day was one of relief from work. The people were free to enjoy this holiday.

As we walked through the city, the officials and stewards of the temple, Herod's men, Yeshua, and some curiosity seekers paused to look, but few were deterred from their celebration. It wasn't uncommon to see a prisoner walked to the Judgement Hall. There were the usual catcalls and snide remarks about and to the prisoner, none apparently interested in the innocence or guilt of the one in custody. Most of those who stopped to watch looked happy that it wasn't them and looked to heaven in prayers of thanks.

I wondered just where the Apostles and followers of Yeshua were as they weren't here in this body. Not more than four days before, a great crowd, partly paid by me to assemble and give homage, came to greet Yeshua at the gate of this very city. Now, where were they? I knew, and fully expected the people I had bought not to appear, but what of the others? The others so many talked about, who so often followed him about the country and city when he was teaching and healing? Where were the poor and sick - the ones that always cried out, "Help us, O son of David!" How about Mary Magdalene, Martha, and their newly-risen brother, Lazarus? And those who shouted, "Hosanna, thou son of David who comes in the name of the Lord!" I saw no multitude joining this sad procession along the way. Even the sick and lame had fallen away - this was a lonely Messiah!

Soon the palace came into view. It was here Pilate was residing during this festival week, and here he would hold the trial. The courtyard of the palace faced the street and the gates were guarded night and day. As we approached, I saw a large crowd outside the gates. This was strange, as they hadn't come with us. They must have come another way and for another reason. Who were these men?

As we approached, the guards caused the procession to wait. The news of the approach of the company was delivered to Pilate's steward. Word came back to have only the prisoner, his guards, and the temple officers enter and bring the prisoner to the Praetorium. The crowd, which was large but by no means a multitude, pressed against the gate and walls in front of the palace.

I continued to survey the crowd for someone I might know and converse with about the trial, but none of these men looked familiar. Many weren't from Jerusalem. From their dress, some were from distant provinces and foreign countries; some Jews, this was true, but even those weren't from this area.

As I listened, I recognized the brogue of many. I had to listen closely to understand them. They were a suspicious lot, and were apt to silence when I roamed too close. These men were certainly a cloak-and-dagger group of the same brotherhood as the Sicarii.

The time spent in this crowd was long as the trial was entirely in a closed session in the Praetorium. This case was to be tried in the Secretarium and only the officers of the court and a few witnesses were permitted in the courtroom. Even the witnesses were held outside the Secretarium. Only when Pilate wanted information did any approach the Judgement Seat. The curtain shut off the courtroom from the nearby rooms and the forum. I could see no apostles anywhere in this crowd or going in or out of the hall.

After a time I knew who these men were! Though dressed in different costumes, that is, wearing clothes of priests and members of the Sanhedrin, they were members of the secret society - the Sicarii!

This I reasoned by their language and subject of conversation I overheard. Some weren't so careful in their speech. Some were Zealots and together presented a large crowd.

As time went on and no word came from the Praetorium, these men became restless and began to cry out slogans they had prepared before this trial. It was obvious they weren't interested in this trial, but in the possible prosecution of their leader - Barabbas!

Barabbas, the man Shalazar mentioned and whom I knew as an insurrectionist and murderer. Barabbas, the man I heard talked about in the inn at Capernaum over two years ago by the men Apius said knew each other in the dark as well as in the light! Men who had a secret language and signs to distinguish between member and nonmember of their order. Men who wouldn't hesitate to kill an intruder to or a turncoat to their order.

These men now stood outside the Praetorium and chanted the slogan, "Release to us Barabbas, release to us Barabbas! Crucify all, but release Barabbas! Crucify all but Barabbas!"

They continued this absurd cry without ceasing. They knew their leader was guilty of insurrection and sedition, but weren't afraid of any man for their cause was just in their eyes. At length, the governor's personal guard stepped from the Praetorium and came to the gate. The centurion came forward and spoke to the crowd.

"Know this, your plea is without merit. The governor has no intention of complying to the howling of jackals. The trials are now over and the results announced forthwith." He stopped for a moment as the crowd became even more unruly. He raised his hand again for quiet. "Hear me, your actions give us no alternative but to call for men from the fort. They will round you up and place you in hold until you can be sentenced and sent into slavery. See to it yourselves! On you rests the outcome!" He then turned and dispatched a runner to the fort, then turned to salute the Praetorium. The vellum was opened and Pilate was in the Judgement Seat. Three prisoners were on his right. He spoke from the seat.

"These are now found guilty and shall receive the prescribed punishment. One, they each shall be scourged, and two, they shall be taken to a place called Calvary and there crucified in accordance with the law. All have been found guilty of sedition. There is no appeal. There is no precedent for the release of one prisoner as the vicar of another, on this day, or any other! But I feel magnanimous this day, and therefore will release one prisoner to you." Here Pilate paused. The crowd roared approval! He smiled at their willingness to accept his word. What fools these simple Jews were!

When the crowd quieted down, he spoke again, "This I say unto you, it's not because of your bellowing I do this but because of my good will; see that you remember it! I give you Barabbas!" The rabble near me were joyous and slapped one another on the back. Some shouted, "Hail Pilate, hail Pilate!"

He then continued, "On the others these sentences are summary. Now disperse or fall!" He meant every word. He wasn't a man to be easily intimidated and this crowd felt their hope for their leader was sustained. So Shalazar was right in that Barabbas would go free; how could this be justice? Even as they moved away, the troops from the fort were coming at a forced march step and already in sight. Pilate watched for awhile, drew the vellum, and knew these men he saw below him in the street would live to fight again.

My heart nearly failed me at the announcement from the Judgement Seat. It was true, this Messiah wasn't going to bring his angels down from heaven to rescue him and reset the scales of justice in balance. What did it all mean - this teaching, promises of God's blessings, forgiveness of sins, his coming again, and a comforter to us?

I staggered from the forum and wandered aimlessly down the street, guided only by the realization that soon the life of Yeshua would be over. The eleven men he had given so much to were now somewhere in great disillusionment, considering, like me, where had it all gone wrong?

I knew I couldn't see the crucifixion of my teacher. I remembered the appointment with Titus and Apuleius at the house of Quintus. It was there I must go to find out what happened, even though I knew in my heart, Yeshua hadn't recanted when asked if he was the Messiah. He had, just as Caiaphas had intimated earlier in the morning, refused to deny his Messiahship and this was interpreted as an act placing himself above Caesar. Even though he might have held that his kingdom was not of this world, it was all the same to Pilate. Caesar thought himself to be a god and any kingdom out of this world was his, also.

I had enough hold on reality to know I must first go to mother and explain as best I could what had happened and why. I must move my residence from the house and accept quarters elsewhere. I was afraid of the eleven and more especially of Peter.

I moved along the streets now filled with happy people. The festival was under full swing. The old city was full of people from all walks of life. It brought tears to my eyes when I realized that nearly all of these were completely unaware of the tragedy that was even now unfolding at a place called Calvary.

I continued to walk as fast as I could and soon reached home. I went directly to the servants' quarters. Apius was at his usual station near the gate. He greeted me with a kind heart. I went to his room and there broke down. He sent all others from the quarters and sat with me in silence at I continued to weep. At last, I became calm enough to tell Apius the entire story from the beginning - from the visits of Raphael and Shalazar through the sentence just heard from Pilate. He sat and listened with great patience and interest. He was and always had been a man of understanding.

I told him of what I thought I must do. I told him I had little time, as I must meet Apuleius and Titus at the house of Quintus. I must take some of my belongings from the house to other quarters. I couldn't remain here with my twin set against me; Apius agreed. After awhile, I decided to once again see mother and try to explain why this must be done.

Apius told me Ishmael hadn't returned from the day before; he didn't know where he was or when he would return. A runner came for Miriam earlier in the morning and she also wasn't in this house - whether at her own home, he didn't know.

A MOTHERS' LOVE

I left the servants' quarters and went into the house to search for mother. I found her weeping in the room she used for formulating exotic scents. I knelt at her side.

"Oh mother, don't weep, please don't. I have done that which I was born to do. I have, to the best of my heart, done only that which God desired me to do. Believe me, there are men who don't understand and would, if they find me, take my life. Give me your blessing even as you did when I was a child on your lap. I must now leave and take up new quarters. I will send a messenger to you when I have selected such a place. Pray, give me your word you won't tell this to Ishmael. Give me now for the last time your blessing and forgiveness." I began to weep, also. My efforts to explain things to her were not complete.

She held me close and said, "Oh Judas, how much you look like your brother. At first, when you came in, I thought it was Ishmael coming home to tell me all was well. But now I know this unjust act done by the Romans. Dear son, I remember the day many years ago when I prophesied you would some day be facing a great decision. It has come to pass. I have a mother's heart and cannot nor care to understand it all. You now have my blessings and a prayer to God to go with you until we meet again." We kissed and I left her without looking back. I must be away before Ishmael comes. I wouldn't have him do anything he would be sorry for against me.

I gathered what possessions I thought I might need both in the city and if I was forced to leave the city. I left the house and found Apius waiting for me with a mount ready. I lashed all the things to it and gave him a long embrace, mounted, and rode through the gate for perhaps the last time.

A SLIGHT OF HAND

I must hear the words of Apuleius and Titus. I rode to the house of Quintus where I entered the gate and was shown to a place I could remove the dust of the day. I then went to the masters' room. Quintus was away for the moment and I was shown a place to wait. He soon came into the room.

"Ah Judas, you have come at the ideal moment for Titus has just arrived and is now in the garden. He has brought much news for you. So let us go and hear his story." He turned and led me through the hallway to his garden where I had been before.

Titus was seated on a bench near a little pool. He motioned for me to sit nearby, handed me a goblet of wine, and said, "This has been a trying day. The courtroom has never had a scene like this while I have been the secretary." He sipped his wine. Quintus moved to a small stool with a back rest.

"The trial began simply enough. Two others were charged with sedition - one, Barabbas, and the other, Gastas. Roman witnesses were brought and sworn in. Their testimony was without flaw and both Barabbas and Gastas were found guilty without pause. They were then taken to be scourged in accordance with the law." He took another sip. "By the way, Judas, I not only met Apuleius, but was able to converse with him and he is to come here as soon as the crucifixion is over. He has to attend as he will make the decision to break their legs, if necessary." When he said this, I swooned away and wasn't aware of anything around me for sometime. Then, I heard the voice of Quintus calling to me. I slowly awakened to see the two of them bending over me.

"Dear Judas, you have had a trying day and day before. I don't know if I should continue while you are so tired." I sat up slowly and took some wine. I was weak but not such that I couldn't hear his story.

"Carry on, I'm sorry for my weakness, but I have great feelings for Yeshua."

"So be it, but this you must know. Apuleius will be here as soon as he is relieved." He forced me to take some more wine.

"The next case was the one of your master. Pilate had me read the name of the prisoner and his place of birth. It was given on the writ as Yeshua, a Galilean. At first, Pilate was of a mind to send him to Herod, but thought the old fox knew of this, hadn't acted before and doubted if he would do anything anyway, so held his peace. No word nor prisoner was sent to Herod. According to Pilate, time was short. He was expected at a banquet held by Vitellius and wouldn't let a simple thing like the trial of any Jew hold him."

"After reading the charges before the prisoner, he asked him if he was aware of what they meant. If your teacher understood his possible penalty? I have inscribed that your teacher said naught. Pilate then called witnesses even as he had for the others. Their names are not privy to us. They were men of some substance. Some claimed to be, and were proven so, servants of the high priest. They brought charges to light of Yeshua, saying he claimed he was a Messiah of your people. Pilate certainly knows what this means. The political point of view that your Messiah will come to conquer all and thereby subject all, even Rome and more especially, Caesar, to the will of your God, isn't accepted as an idle threat. Your teacher didn't deny his claim to being a Messiah, but did finally answer that his kingdom wasn't of this world. Pilate didn't know or make much sense of this and asked him again if he were a king. Your teacher answered he was and to that end was he born.

"Well, this was enough for Pilate! He was about to pronounce sentence when a hue and cry outside the gates came to his ears." Titus stopped here and rose to walk around. He was greatly interested in his own telling of the story.

"He sent one of his men to circulate among the people outside and bring word of what the noise was about. The man came back and said that the large mob outside were of the impression that there was a 'privilegium paschal' set by previous governors. It was this they demanded and they wanted Barabbas released to them even at the cost of any other.

"At first, Pilate sat there with his mouth open, completely dumbfounded by these words. Then he began to laugh until he cried, tears ran down his cheeks and he slapped his leg. He then shouted so all could hear, 'Who do they think they are? And who do they think I am, some weak-kneed Jewish vassal king like Herod? I know who they are, these men of the Sicarii and Zealots! I know them even though they dress in the robes of priests!' He began to laugh again as if he knew something they didn't. 'If they were truly priests, they would be at the temple on this day; do these Jews really think I don't know their religious laws and festivals? I'll give them a privilege to think about!' There was more commotion outside the gate. He waited a few moments and then continued, 'Let's just see how wise they are!' He was in a villainous mood; he wasn't above playing deadly pranks - this man. He stood up, moved from the Judgement Seat, and walked about like one on a stage. For a moment, he was oblivious of the prisoners and trial proceedings. Although he gave me no sign, I continued to record his words. He finally sent for his elite guard. The captain of his guard came to him; they stood so close to me I overheard their conversation, although this I tell you in strict confidence." Titus stopped here to see that the servants were not near and then leaned forward to give this detail of the happening.

"He gave these instructions to his Captain, 'Go now and find me a man in the ranks that looks like Barabbas, mind you, one who is so near that he can pass at close range. Bring him to me, here in this room. Don't take too long for this is important, go!' The captain left immediately on a fast mount. Pilate passed the time by strutting up and down with his arms folded. He muttered to himself about the audacity of these Jews. Then he would burst out in loud peals of laughter - a joke of jokes was to be played. It was not long before the Captain returned and had with him a man from the ranks who looked so like Barabbas that even I was astounded. Pilate had this fellow taken to the prisoner holding area and dressed in the clothes of Barabbas. He was then returned; the transformation was now complete. Pilate instructed the Captain to make arrangements for this imposter to be given to the rabble after the crucifixion as Barabbas. Do you see this picture? Not the real Barabbas, but a Roman imposter!" He stopped again and looked about the room.

"Pilate knew this crowd; they were not to be trifled with. This man's life was to be protected, so the exchange would be made in the forum where the troops would protect the impostor after discovery. He well knew they would attempt to kill the look-alike if given the chance, so this was to be the bargain: Barabbas was to be released to the people only after the crucifixion - this he repeated. He told his men to go that moment and gain their confidence. So in a short while some were yet calling for the release of Barabbas, and the deal was struck. Barabbas was to be given to them in the forum after the execution of the others. The word was soon spread around and the rabble quieted; they thought they had forced the governor to do their bidding. This was the word you heard, Judas."

"But this Pilate is no fool, and an experienced fighter. He knows tactics and is a wily one. After this, he sent your teacher out to be scourged with the others in preparation for the supreme penalty. Pilate then had the prisoners brought forth and he went to the Judgement Seat. He commanded the curtains be opened and he read the sentence as you must have heard in the forum." Titus ended his story and sat down again to enjoy his drink.

"I must thank you for your kindness, Titus. Some of this I knew as I was in the street below. But from what you say, Barabbas will also be crucified this day?" I was bothered by the words of Shalazar, for he had threatened me with the possibility that Barabbas would go free, while Yeshua would not!

"Aye, that is indeed how the orders have been given to the troops. There will be three hung this day, and according to my court orders, they are Barabbas, Gastas, and Yeshua. The idea of Pilate offering that rabble a choice is ludicrous, and if you know Pilate as I do in these matters, not only ludicrous, but preposterous at best. Anyone who thinks he would stoop so low in command as to accept the Jew's direction on a decision that he must report to Rome is daft." Now he was laughing.

"Hold, Titus, just what do you mean?" I didn't understand his words. There were those in the crowd who thought he would listen to them about the release of Barabbas.

"Well, first, the rabble at the gate dressed themselves as priests and officers of the temple - why? Surely not to deceive the Jews - they know better - who then?"

"The gentiles!"

"Correct. It was those who didn't know every priest was needed at this time who would believe that the rabble were priests acting with the power of the temple - they hoped Pilate would believe it. Not only that, but the rabble at the gate, which you were among at the time, knew or should have known, that even Pilate has enemies here in Judea. Not necessarily Jews! Do you agree?" He stopped here to look for an answer.

"Yes, I know there are Romans in this city who would like to see him removed." That was true. Some of the more wealthy tradesmen from Rome wanted him removed - they felt his strong-arm tactics weren't conducive to increased commerce.

"Now, look what the release of Barabbas would mean!" He stopped again to sit down and lean toward his father and me. He brought his hands together fiercely. "To anyone of political influence, and friend of Caesar, it would mean Pilate wasn't operating as a governor at all, but as a traitor!"

"Aha!" exclaimed Quintus.

Titus continued with his political intrigue, "After all, anyone who would turn a known guilty insurrectionist free in this part of the empire, and one who especially threatens the life of Caesar, as Barabbas surely did, is asking for his enemies to call attention of this to Caesar! How long do you think Pilate would last? Anyone who believes a story like this is either an ignoramus, a fool, or a liar; take your pick." He started laughing again. Even Quintus laughed. So I thought Shalazar wasn't achieving as much as he thought when he showed me the vignette in the stone.

"It's good. I was told by Apuleius that Barabbas was a hard one and deserved his sentence if anyone did. But still Barabbas has a long walk to the place of execution and he will surely claim he is the real Barabbas, will he not?" I remained skeptical of this plan; there were many armed men at the gate. My heart was low indeed.

"Aye, that's true, but Judas, have you ever looked upon a man after he was scourged?" This question by Titus brought me back to his conversation.

"No!"

"Why, I'll tell you, Judas, I have, and it's not a pleasant sight. But the important thing is this, after such an ordeal, it's seldom a man's own wife or mother can recognize him. Not only that but they still have to face crucifixion, and many claim they are innocent or some other person wrongly being led to execution. Believe me, Judas, none will listen to his cries along the way and it's felt his clan will believe he will come to them unharmed at the forum after all this is done."

"I can't deny your words. I know I would believe it were I one of his followers and would remain at the forum to welcome his release." I could believe Pilate would be the one laughing all the way to Caesarea, not the Sicarii and Zealots.

"Come, Judas, it's time we took our noon meal. You are welcome to join us, or if you want, to take rest until later in the day." Quintus was a good man, remembered the ritual of our people, and knew many of us ate but twice a day. I asked to be taken to a room where I might rest until Apuleius came. I then decided to remain there the rest of the night and asked Quintus about this. I told him I had things on my horse still standing at the gate or so I thought. This was not true, as Quintus had sent his man to take of my animal long since. Not only this, but also my things had been placed in a room for me. He not only welcomed me, but since my fainting spell, would have it no other way than I stay there the night. I hope someday to repay him for this kindness.

I was shown a guest room and there fell across the bed wishing I had not been born Judas of Kerioth. I placed my prayer shawl over my head and brought my petition for forgiveness of whatever I had misunderstood as the Lord's commands. I asked that nothing I did or said that day would be held against any man, and the same for me. I lay upon the bed to rest until there was some news of Apuleius; I fell fast asleep.

I awoke to feel the hot winds blowing in the opening in the room and the sky very dark, yet it was only near the third hour. This I knew from the call of the servants below. Quintus had his servants call the time every hour by the sundial. The wind blew steadily and the clouds hung low in the sky over Calvary, and I thought of those being placed on crosses. Although it didn't rain, there was some lightning and thunder; some peals I thought were loud enough to wake the dead.

Because of all this, I had difficulty becoming oriented and couldn't grasp just where I was. Slowly, the awful truth of the past hours came upon me. My heart went from the depths of despair to race with high expectations that Apuleius might even now be below me waiting to tell his story. Perhaps, just perhaps, he would tell of how Yeshua acted as the true Messiah and brought this cruel event to an end - angels had freed him and set the balances of justice aright. Yes, perhaps the world was now experiencing a new era - the God of our father's had moved to restore Israel to its' greatness! I prepared for a meeting with my host and possibly Apuleius.

I went to join Quintus in the garden and, although it was windy there, it was still comfortable. I found Quintus and greeted him. He recognized my want to know about Apuleius and told me my friend hadn't returned. Food and drink was brought for me. The servants had lighted some of the oil lamps in the house to light the rooms without windows.

Quintus remarked on the strange weather. The heavy cloud cover at this time of year was uncommon. I agreed but knew of stranger things in this land of ancient history.

"Here, Judas, please have something to strengthen you." He was determined to make my stay pleasant even through this trial.

We began to reminisce about the days' happenings and he told me more of what Titus had told him in private. He said his son remembered Pilate remarking he must be on his way, but would remain one more day to close the books on this trial. He asked Titus to prepare a full copy of the proceedings including the trick played on the rabble; especially, he noted, so Caesar would not listen to any stories contrary to the facts as he commanded. These he signed, sealed, and prepared for transmission to Rome. Pilate wasn't one to let things stand. He was an old military who knew the value of timely reports and the importance of first news. Above all, he wanted to avoid the possibility of any enemy providing the first account of this trial to Caesar or the Senate. As soon at it was copied, the courier was on his way to Rome.

After that, Pilate and his lady prepared for their trip to Syria and to the banquet now in progress, or so he said to his commander near Titus. They would remain at the palace until his guard would be gathered, and after that, it would be a forced march to the palace of Vitellius. Titus was then dismissed and left the palace for home.

The talking continued until late in the afternoon. About the ninth hour, the sky suddenly lightened and the storm which hadn't produced any rain was over. The wind decreased and less sand was in motion in the garden. The air was left somewhat cooler from the overcast conditions.

THE RETURNING SOLDIER

I became restless. Where was Apuleius? I strode to the foyer and looked toward the gate. Quintus followed me. As we watched, a lone figure of a Roman officer came into view. My heart quickened. It was Apuleius, and he was studying the house of Quintus critically. I left Quintus and ran to the gate. I stepped outside and motioned to Apuleius. He waved back, dismounted and strode to me through the gate.

We clasped hands in silence. He looked somewhat older to me. Could this day have taken such a toll? For a moment, we stood at the gate and I told him of my friend Quintus, who now sent his servant to take the animal and prepare it for the night. We moved to the house and into the foyer.

Quintus greeted Apuleius as an old friend to show me respect. Quintus was a man of his word and any friend of mine was indeed welcome in his home.

"Greetings, my house is yours." Quintus brought his servants forward with a clap of his hand. "Please, sir, follow my servants - take off your harness and boots. Use the water and accept more comfortable dress that he will bring." Apuleius accepted the offer and followed the servant. He appeared sometime later completely in new Roman dress without his military gear.

"Come with us to the garden to rest and refresh yourself." The food and drink was already laid out for us in the garden. Apuleius was a tired man. He had welcomed the release from the uniform he wore. The day was hot and his work tiring. He accepted and drank a small goblet filled with wine in one long draught.

"Sir, Judas has kindly agreed to stay the night and honor my house. I would be pleased if you would do the same. It's not often I have the opportunity to have the honor of one from the garrison in my house," Quintus offered as soon as Apuleius was comfortable. "I sincerely hope that you now have a few days to yourself after this terrible ordeal."

"Aye, and thank you for the offer. I have a fortnight to my own and would be only too glad to accept your offer but wouldn't want to impose…" Apuleius was about to continue when Quintus held up his hand.

"Nonsense, it's my pleasure, and it may be that we have mutual acquaintances in Rome that would be brought to mind." Quintus was interested in the history and family of this young medic, Apuleius Lucius. I had just told him enough about Apuleius to wet his appetite about his family.

Titus soon joined us. He no longer wore his clothes of office, but had on a handsome toga with the beading of a Roman citizen. He and Apuleius greeted each other again as friends. They were comrades-at-arms so to speak, both having endured a trial and prosecution of the ugliest sort.

Although I was greatly interested in the happenings of the day as seen through the eyes of Apuleius, I wasn't so impatient as to force the issue. The tale from Apuleius would be told at his convenience and not before.

Most of the early evening was spent in small talk about Rome and the families of Apuleius and Quintus. They reviewed in detail their deeds and city life. All this I thought was good for them; as the talk continued, I could see Apuleius relax.

The time came when we were notified that the meal was soon to be offered and as guests, we were honored. I knew the shofar would soon signal the call to prayer and the start of the first high holy day of the new feast. I asked to be excused and returned to the room I had used before where I prayed and enjoyed the solace of the early evening. After prayers and ablution, I went to meet with the family of Quintus and Apuleius for the meal.

Quintus introduced all to us and this in rank. Most of his family was known to me but all were introduced for the benefit of Apuleius. The meal was near a banquet and time was taken to enjoy all. The food and eating style was Roman. Once the meal was over and thanks given to the lord and lady of the house, we adjourned to the garden. Apuleius asked Titus of his experiences in the courtroom, and after learning what had happened there, asked me of the events outside the gate of the Hall of Judgement.

Once learning all, he sat and watched the evening sky for awhile and drank wine. Lamps were brought into the garden and the golden glow gave all a ruddy look. The soft air caused the flame of the lamps to move, giving animated shadows under their light.

"These are the things I've seen and heard this day," Apuleius began his story. I was determined to hold all his words in my heart and someday transcribe them even as this day.

"To begin, I was called away from the street in front of the house of Caiaphas while Judas was still in the hall. I left a note with a lad to let him know of the new orders. When I returned to the fort, I was ordered to take those I wanted and report to the palace and there remain until I was commanded otherwise. I came upon a bad scene; there were two prisoners in the compound at the palace. One I knew, Barabbas, and the other I didn't but found his name to be Gastas. Both were bound and in good condition, this I know for I was assigned their care.

"After looking to their condition, I was free to move about that portion of the palace held by the troops. I knew the guards and talked with the officer in charge. I walked with him as he made the rounds in the early hours. At the gate, he was especially attentive to the crowd that was assembling. They were a scurvy lot, yet he wasn't so sure of their looks. He had some doubts that they were what they pretended to be. Beneath their robes, they looked to be a well-fed transient group, and their robes said they were priests - this he said plainly they weren't. Yet, he was greatly disturbed by their presence. He told his men not to relax as some would be challenged.

"I returned to my post and there assigned others in shifts to prevent the prisoners from committing suicide. This act would deprive the state of its right of prosecution and penalty and wasn't to be tolerated." He shook his head at the wonder of it all. The others and myself also were at a loss in this regard.

"I then took my rest in preparation for the day soon to be upon me. The morning started with the feeding and check of the prisoners. The one called Barabbas was in good spirits, while the other wasn't. Gastas was a small man accused of killing a Roman merchant during a robbery. He wasn't the bravest man and whimpered a good deal. He was a Jew and asked to be permitted a time to pray. This I granted for I felt he was in need of his God. Barabbas was also a Jew. He was a rascal of the highest order. I listened to his prayers and they were for the overthrow of Caesar, the Roman government, and all else whom he considered an abomination unto the God of Israel. It was an odd thing, though. He gave me the impression that he truly believed he wouldn't be hung on the tree. How he came to such a conclusion I couldn't see for if there ever was a man guilty of his crimes, he was. While talking to his guard, I found he had one visitor during the night." He stopped and looked at me for a long time.

"According to the guard, the man was of good stature, well built, well dressed, with smooth voice and manners. His permission was granted by writ from the office of the governor. The man spoke to Barabbas in quiet tones and the guard was unable to hear what passed between them, but it was after he left, that Barabbas suddenly gave the impression of one unafraid of his charge. One might say he believed his chances for freedom were guaranteed by someone of power greater than Pilate." Apuleius took a long drink of wine. The rest of us were greatly interested in this adventure and leaned forward on his words. Apuleius was a good storyteller and I hoped to capture his every word for my journal.

"You didn't see this person then?" I asked, thinking of Shalazar.

"No, but I thought of the man that saved us from the sea, as his description was nearly as romantic as that. Be that as it may, the trial started even as Titus had said. Each of the prisoners were brought before Pilate in order. The trials of Barabbas and Gastas went smoothly enough. They were soon brought to the troops below and there prepared for scourging. Each man was stripped down, tied to a rack that stretched his skin tight, and then scourging began. At first, they resisted the pain, but later, even the strong one, Barabbas, pleaded for relief. I'm not one to see these things for I am sworn to give aid to all men and this treatment of human beings is sickening to me. I left the scourging until I was called upon to tend their wounds. I gave each one a deadening solution and this I knew was a chance I took for it wasn't legal to do so!"

CHAPTER TWENTY-FOUR

The Trial And Death

I looked at the others and saw the horror registered in their faces. My throat was parched and I drank some wine. I wanted to run away from this tale but couldn't.

"The last man to be brought before Pilate was Yeshua. While I was not privy to the court proceedings, I heard much of the action in the holding room. Judas, your teacher was a brave man indeed. Once during the trial, he was brought to the holding area and flogged. After this, he was returned but for what reason this took place, I don't know. Now, this wasn't a scourging but a flogging. After the trial was over, he was brought to the scourging rack. He held his peace well throughout the scourging. At times, I thought he was using some mystical power even as some of the far easterners do during their cult initiations. In the end, all were helped to the Judgement Seat and shown to the people in the forum. As Titus has already said, Pilate gave the sentences for all three."

"After sentencing, they were prepared for the walk to the hill. Before I knew what was about, some of the soldiers guarding Yeshua began to mock him and dress him as a king. They even called him names and spoke to him as the King of the Jews. This is indeed what the writ for the cross claimed. Evidently, one had spent much time for he brought forth a crown of thorns he made the night before and placed it on the head of Yeshua. The pain of this crown pressing into his head must have been nearly unbearable but he didn't speak or cry out. Some located a scarlet robe and placed it about his shoulders. After awhile, since he gave no outcry or fought back, the troops became disenchanted with the play and took off the robe. They ceased the play and spoke of him with admiration. They knew a man when they saw him. I filed a complaint with the commander about this treatment of a man already sentenced to death; reprimands and punishing for the guard's acts against their prisoner will be forthcoming."

The talk momentarily ceased and the servants came into the garden and filled the lamps again. The light which had weakened while Apuleius was speaking again flooded the garden. We were all awaiting the next words.

"As you might know, men who have received such treatment seldom have strength enough to walk, much less carry a cross. It is a rule that a man so sentenced must carry his own tree. As a medical officer, I ruled that it wasn't possible, and if permitted to follow this course, the crucifixion might not take place for all were near death from the scourging. So it was that substitutes were found in the streets of Jerusalem. There were three chosen from those held on minor charges in the holding area to carry the trees of the malefactors. The guard that chose these men said the one carrying the tree for Yeshua was called Kish, and was slightly addled. He was the son of a woman from Samaria called Ramona. It seems she had met Yeshua in her country when visiting a place called Jacob's well near the town of

Sychar. And since, she and her son had followed Yeshua for years. She hoped that someday Yeshua would heal Kish - but till now, not so." Apuleius reached for more wine.

"Strange," I muttered aloud, "I once talked with some men of Sychar about this very woman a long time ago. I was told her son was addled by a blow from the lance of a Roman foot soldier. So she was following in the crowd?" I looked at Apuleius.

"Well, not exactly. According to the guard, Kish was arrested for stealing bread from some vender. Not a criminal offense of any great magnitude. But he was one in the compound. His mother, who was very old, told him to volunteer for the act to relieve Yeshua - and so he did." Apuleius set his cup down.

"I'll tell you an interesting thing about this later. We now walked through the city, Kish carrying the tree for Yeshua, and finally came to a place called Golgotha. The men at the fort said it had been the sight of many such deaths. The one called Barabbas kept screaming that he was Barabbas and wasn't to be executed on the word of Pilate. I thought he was more addled than the young lad carrying Yeshua's tree. None of the people or troops gave him much attention; by Jupiter, I didn't as I knew he was guilty and guilty men often claim innocence as well as the law having the wrong person. The guards forced him in line and kept it moving. He was persistent about this being all wrong and called on those along the route to bring the governor to his aid. Even called some names of men not known to me that would help if they were just notified. Most laughed at his request for someone to bring the governor. When these men were about to be stretched on the tree, I gave them a mixture to deaden the pain of the nails. Judas, your teacher just tasted the drink and then refused to drink any more. The others welcomed it and were more comfortable.

"The trees were finally raised with great effort; the stony ground gave little support. The position was such that they formed a triangle and when viewed from any angle, the cross bearing Yeshua was predominate. There weren't many followers of any of the men crucified there. Even those of Barabbas weren't to be seen. Barabbas was abusive to the others in every way, he fought and struggled to avoid his punishment. Because of this, the troops were less than gentle with him; and because some knew his history of hate and killing their comrades, they were glad to do this thing to him. Barabbas seemed to think he would be saved. He kept screaming about the governor guaranteeing his freedom. Finally, he railed out against Yeshua and called out for him, 'If you're a Messiah, save yourself and us!' The other malefactor rebuked Barabbas, shouted for forgiveness and said, 'Lord, remember me when all is over.' Then, Yeshua shouted back to him with nearly all his strength gone, 'Hear me, this day you shall be with me in the garden.'"

"So Barabbas was truly hung on the cross?" I asked. Shalazar wasn't right about two things and maybe not about the third - Ishmael's death - was my happy thought.

"Some women finally appeared and stood at the foot of the cross of Yeshua. I don't know who they were - relatives I imagine. After awhile, a single man approached and stood by them. The noise of the wind and darkness was still upon the hill. I could hear the men moaning and screaming at times for God to take them and then against their enemies. I wanted to end their suffering as soon as permitted. Your teacher spoke several times during his torture on the tree, and so did the others. Mostly things of little relevance for he was soon out of his mind with the pain, as were the others. Some called for their mothers and others cursed the day they were born. Barabbas cursed the Romans and all who had done this to him. Yeshua spoke some words not heard distinctly by me and I doubt any of the others. He was getting weaker all the time. Sometimes he spoke in Hebrew and not Aramaic, this I knew." Apuleius stopped his story and hung his head in the shame of it all. He was a doctor, not a hangman and this night had drained him.

He continued after a rest. "This lasted for nearly three hours. After the sounding of the trumpet at the fort for the ninth hour, the sky lightened and the wind laid. They were all tiring fast. Their attempts to relieve the strangulation forced upon them by their position on the trees became less and less. The time had come to break their legs. Their pain would then shorten even if they didn't know it. As I turned to order this done, I heard Yeshua call to the woman standing at the foot of the cross, 'Woman, behold your son.' And to the man, 'Behold, your mother.' Soon after, he said he was thirsty, and then he said, what sounded to me like, 'It is finished' and I could see by his natural functions he died at that moment." Tears ran down the face of Apuleius unabashed. He couldn't for the moment continue. I and the others looked sadly about the room; all of us were emotionally involved.

"I then gave the orders to break the legs of the others." This he said while his face was resting on his hands. "The others died shortly thereafter. Since I was busy, things were said by all those in torment, but I heard only these things. As soon as my assignment was over, I gave word to the Centurion who headed the detail that all were dead. The three observers, whom I later found to be Ishmael, Joseph of Arimathea, and Nicodemus, left to seek an audience with Pilate, or so they said as they walked by. It was their desire to remove the body of Yeshua because of some religious law or other. Now, whether this was done, I don't know as I left the hill shortly thereafter and came directly here."

"Apuleius, what of Kish, the one who carried the tree for Yeshua? I thought you said there was something you would tell of this."

"Ah, yes. When I left, I met the one called Kish by the guard. I don't know how addled he was before this, but I can tell you that he was normal now as you or I. I talked with him for some time and he struck me as a person of good reasoning. I must say that the woman's faith in Yeshua may have been justified after all."

I noticed Apuleius was sweating profusely, and I began to worry about him and all others who had been cured through Yeshua. Would the fever again attack Apuleius? Could it be possible that with Yeshua also died the effects of this word unto his followers? This had been a trial unto him. He rested against the back of the bench then began again.

"Hear me, Judas, I almost forgot. Ishmael and two others I didn't know were at the crucifixion. He came to me and challenged me on the matter. I told him I was given orders and must follow command - I was a soldier. He asked where you were. I told I was to meet you after this at the home of one Quintus. He asked where this would be. I told him what I could of the directions as given to me by Titus. He gave no reason for his wanting to know, but returned to his friends." He opened his hands to indicate his innocence of the matter. As I looked around, I noticed again that it had tired us all this night and its stories.

The silence was unbearable. All were occupied by their own thoughts on the happenings of this day. As a Jew, I wondered what the trick against the Zealots and Sicarii would bring upon us. And the Romans were interested in the effect on the trade.

Suddenly there was a commotion at the gate. The servants went to set it aright. Soon one came to Quintus; he listened for a short time and then turned to me.

"It seems Ishmael is outside and wishes to speak with you." I stood up and went to the foyer. There stood Ishmael! He had changed. I could see this ordeal was too much for his sensitive soul. Quintus, who came to the foyer, was also distressed to see Ishmael in such a state. He ordered his servants to bring wine. Ishmael refused food or drink.

"Oh, Ishmael, my heart goes out to you. I would that you understood what is done this night." I knew this remark wouldn't be heeded as he wasn't in his true mind. Quintus asked him to go to the room I had used and there to lie down until he was more composed. He would have none of it.

"Judas, I've little time and the same is true for you. We met with one of Pilate's lieutenants and received permission to remove Yeshua's body. We have buried it in the tomb of

Joseph; it's now within the law. There are those who would take your life and are even now searching this city for you. They have taken me twice to be you and would have hanged me if it were not for my companions. There is no safe place for you in this city, you must go and soon." Having said this, he nearly fell at my feet. I caught him and held him up. "I'll now say goodbye. Although I don't understand your part in this, I'll forever pray for your forgiveness. I must be away as they now watch mother's house as well. Miriam is there alone and needs me. They feel you will return there and then they will take you. Don't go there. I don't feel they have followed me and so you will be safe here for the night, but after that, the street people are watching for you - beware!"

He turned and pulled from my arms and dashed out into the night; to where, I don't know. My heart trembled. Was this the last time I would see my twin - my other heart?

I began to weep. I asked to be forgiven and left for the room prepared for me. After some moments, I realized I couldn't stay the night in the house of my friend Quintus. I wouldn't jeopardize his reputation and the lives of his family by using his home as a place to hide from those seeking my life. I gathered my things and made my way to the foyer. I placed these near the doorway. I went into the garden and found Apuleius and Quintus speaking about the scene just played in the foyer. Both turned to greet me.

"Hear me, Quintus, dear friend, I cannot stay in your house this night. Should any have followed Ishmael it would be best if I were elsewhere." He started to protest, but I held up my hand. "You have been and always will be in my heart for the kindness of this day, and the offer this night. I must find another place where no one except me will be threatened by any misguided people who intend me harm. I leave my animal with you, please see that it is taken to my home at your convenience." Apuleius strode up to me.

"Judas, it's fortunate I'm here. We, that is the men of the corp, have an apartment open to us and friends. You will be safe there, that I can guarantee. It's but a stones' throw from here and under the cover of darkness, we will not be noticed." I was eager to be away. Quintus knew his pleading to do otherwise would be to no avail, so left it well enough alone. He provided a servant to travel with us. Apuleius redressed in his military gear. I said my farewells to Quintus and his family, and Apuleius did likewise.

We then checked that the way was clear and left the house of Quintus forthwith. We hadn't traveled far when we were accosted by a band of marauding ruffians. Apuleius had put his uniform on before he left the house and was prepared for any trouble. They were a bad lot. They were about to set upon us when a squad of soldiers came around the bend. Seeing how many was in the squad, the mob of evildoers left the scene. I was glad that Apuleius was along for I was subject to arrest so said the officer of the squad.

"Ho, Lieutenant, what is this? Why all the troops about tonight?" Apuleius asked the officer in charge.

"Some of the troublemakers have just found out that Barabbas wasn't released after all, and was executed this afternoon. Pilate's subterfuge isn't being taken lightly by the followers of Barabbas. They are making life miserable for us tonight. A curfew is in place, and that's why we nearly placed you under arrest. These people have formed small bands and are roaming the city attacking the lightly-protected checkpoints and outposts; they have caused some loss of life and much damage to different installations. But we will have it under control soon." He saluted and called his men together. "Have a care! Get to where you need to be quickly and stay there this night."

They left us on a loop to sweep the streets of all Jews who ignored the curfew. We traveled quickly to the apartment Apuleius spoke about.

Once inside, the gate was barred, we entered the house, and the servant was sent home. Several officers were already there and resting from the days' tour of duty. Some recognized Apuleius. Words were exchanged about his day at the execution. He motioned for a non-commissioned officer to give us some assistance. The man did so sullenly. He knew I was a Jew, and from his view, not to be given the time of day, let alone courtesy. I ignored this and went with Apuleius to a small room. Here, I knew I would be safe until I could leave the city. And this is what I would do as soon as I could manage transportation.

I stayed in the room that night and slept fitfully. Apuleius was up early and went out to see what damage was done during the night. I heard him ask and receive an animal to ride. When he was gone, I said shema and other prayers of thanks. I found a small amount of food and was happy with that. He was gone most of the day. I never left the room. I sat watching for him to return through an opening that let air and sunlight into the room.

ISHMAEL IS LOST

I could see from the opening as he approached he looked very downcast. I knew when I saw his countenance, that all wasn't well. Under his arm was a bundle of clothing. He came to the room and laid the clothing on the bed. He came to me without comment and embraced me.

"What's this, Apuleius? I can see by your face all isn't well! Have the marauders caused damage to father's house? Or have some caused harm to my family?" I was nearly in shock.

"I have brought you clothes to use as a disguise during these next few days." He turned away from me and went to the opening that I had stood by nearly all morning.

"Judas, I must tell you some bad news. Please bear with me. I am not sure how to do this." He was struggling to word the news properly - this I could tell. Why doesn't he just tell me? Am I a child that has never had a disappointment?

"It's Ishmael. Judas, sometime last night, your dear brother and my friend was hanged on a tree outside the wall of the city." He turned quickly and put out his arm to steady me. I was near swooning. What did he say? What did I hear? My blood ran cold.

"Ah, what is this, Apuleius? What kind of game is this?" I couldn't believe his words - they made no sense!

"It's as I say, Ishmael's body is even now resting at your home. Are you steady enough to hear what is thought to have happened?" He led me to the bed and I sat down for my legs had turned to water. "First, perhaps you had better put on these clothes and prepare yourself for the trip home. I'll tell you as you dress."

I began the change. "It's this way. I left here on a good mount to survey the work of the vandals. I traveled a goodly distance throughout the city. As I passed one of the gates to the valley of Kidron, I saw a small crowd so I investigated. There in the corner of the wall on a sturdy tree was the body of a man. Not knowing if he was still alive or why he was hung, I dispersed the crowd and went to his side. Believe me, Judas, I had no idea who I would find. It was Ishmael! I was about to cut him down when I heard a voice from the crowd say, 'Touch him not, this is my honor.' I turned to see who it was that spoke and I recognized Apius. And so he and I cut down your brother's body and moved it from the view of the onlookers. Apius covered him with his cloak and prepared to take him home."

"He was astride but dismounted and placed Ishmael's body across the back of the horse. He then paused and told me this story. According to those in the area, some men brought Ishmael to this spot where few lived with the intent of ending his life. Those nearby said the marauders accused Ishmael of being in league with Pilate. They called to him that he was seen at the gate of the forum just that morning and was not one of them. They claimed he knew of the deception brought on them by Pilate and were now ready to end his life as they had some others for the same reason."

I could hear him continuing with the story, but my mind left him and flashed back to the morning before when I stood in front of the gate in the forum. I recalled walking among these men as they watched me closely. They were studying my every move and I not the wiser. So it was poor Ishmael who gave his life for me. Suddenly, I heard Apuleius again.

"Ishmael pleaded for his life, so nearby people said, but to no avail. They proceeded to hang him without just cause. The authorities are now looking for some of the renegades. Oh, Judas, this is a terrible thing." He was nearly as shocked and undone as I was.

He continued, "While Apius and I were deciding what to do, some others came running. None I knew. I asked them what was their business there, and they said they thought this man was one of their compatriots. Seeing a Roman there, they didn't want to identify themselves with him more than this. I said, 'Not so fast, give me your names.' They said they were James and John bar Zebedee. Apius knew them immediately but said nothing. They then said, 'We would look upon him and see if we know him.' Apius let them look at Ishmael's body. They were satisfied that Ishmael was really you! Mind you, they thought they were looking at the face of their fellow apostle - Judas of Kerioth. They then said, 'Aye, it has happened as our teacher had said - woe to that man by whom the Son of Man is betrayed. It would be better if he had not been born. It is Judas and this without doubt.' Apius and I said nothing. Each moved closer to look again at Ishmael. They then spat on the ground and left without offering to help or a kind word about him or a word of solace to his family. From what I could see, they were glad this happened and were not about to dirty themselves in the matter. Apius later said they were followers of Yeshua and he recognized them from sketches. I don't know, but this I say to you, if they are honest men and true in their feelings, then I am glad I don't follow them. May their God help them." He was unhappy with their disinterest in another's misfortune, neither asking about family or friends of the deceased. I knew then I would not forget their coarse act. I recognized at that moment I would be more a Jew and less a follower than ever before.

I was ready when he had finished and we moved toward the door. So Shalazar had collected an interest payment on his loan even after I paid. Well, we will see!

A RESURRECTION

We left the apartment and headed for father's house, a place of great mourning this day. The trip was made in silence as both of us thought of the night and the terrible things brought about by the arrest and conviction of Yeshua.

The crowd was less than the day before. The Roman checkpoints were increased and most of our people were off the streets. The troops patrolled the city and were ordered to take no remarks from the local or pilgrim populace.

With Apuleius at my side, I was able to get through the checkpoints without the usual harassment. We finally came to the house I had lived in much of my life while in Jerusalem. It was now the scene of the preparation for Ishmael's funeral. I went first to the servants' quarters to see the preparations and then to the house.

Mother and Miriam were in deep despair. All the mirrors and reflecting surfaces were draped and the house was given to the spirit of death. I went to mother and Miriam. Both turned away and marked me as the murderer of my brother. It was as if Cain had come from the hunt and found Adam and Eve turned against him. My heart was broken. They must be made to listen and understand this mission of my life. God had selected me and no other for this task in the garden. All the rest followed as naturally as the sun follows the moon. The death of Ishmael was the doing of Shalazar if anyone's doing at all. I could conjure up the picture of Shalazar smiling at this bit of success - but his loss was greater - I, like Job before me, had won the prize God had offered. I, his faithful servant, had obeyed his command - no other betrayer would ever be needed!

I left them and went unto the room wherein Ishmael's body lay. It was even now prepared for interment. It was time to show them that God still stood by me - his trusted and obedient servant! I was alone in the room. I stood over Ishmael's body and called upon God to deliver him from the hands of Shalazar! I called upon God to hear my prayer and give me the power to do that which I asked; then, I took the hand of Ishmael and said, "Hear me, Ishmael bar Simon, arise and come alive, this I command in the name of God."

And so I had said, and so it was done, and Ishmael arose and was whole again. I took the coverings off his body and gave him a new cloak to wear. He spoke to me in a strong voice and asked for some wine. His throat, although still sore, was soon completely healed. The bruise of the rope remained and could easily be seen.

While we were still alone, he told me of his attackers and how they thought he was really me. How he begged them to reconsider and how they laughed; they were caught up in the frustration of the moment! Their leader had been taken from them and the rest of the world was to blame. He remembered his final words and then darkness. He came to realize what I had done and considered it a miracle - to which I agreed - but not of myself. I reminded him not of my own will but that which God had granted. I sought some more wine and he drank with ease.

He and I talked of many things and understood some of the mysteries of my selection and blessings from God; also, the strange way these events unfolded, and the possible distortion that others would make of them. I told him I must leave as there couldn't be two Ishmael ben Simon's in this city. The eleven would surely seek out one of us when they learned of their error in identification. I was a marked man and therefore must leave my home forever.

He was about to object when I held up my hand, "Hear me, Ishmael, God isn't through with me yet. I have more to give to this new order than others may know."

I called mother and Miriam to come see what God had wrought. They came and swooned at the sight of Ishmael once again with them. I called for Apius and Apuleius to come see. They were amazed and gave thanks to God as well as they could, both being gentiles. I gave Ishmael more wine and gave thanks to God for granting me this plea.

When Apuleius had awakened both mother and Miriam, they began to realize what had happened. They wanted me to tell them of this thing I had caused to come about. I told them all that none should hear of this thing, and the servants should be warned against telling anything about it. They realize that those who heard it wouldn't believe and say that Ishmael was taken down before he had expired. Ishmael and Miriam wanted to touch me as if I, of myself, had done this thing, but I put them off.

What to do to cleanse ourselves and not bring the wonderment of all upon the house came upon us. I was torn between preparing for the necessary cleansing by the blood of the red heifer as was declared by the law, or just to deny all. Since I was leaving, I left it up to Ishmael and mother to do as they interpreted the law about the dead. What to do if one was once a corpse still wasn't known to me. Even Apuleius was quiet and didn't challenge this happening as he had those of Yeshua.

The house was given to life and happiness again. I knew none of the followers of Yeshua would ever believe I had done this thing. And if they heard it, they would deny it as that done by Beelzebub. I also knew they would never enter this house where I once lived to give their condolences to mother on my apparent death. As I saw it, they were a very vindictive lot, and the love of friend or enemy wasn't in them. So it was best I leave.

I would accept no thanks from the family for none was expected. Instead, I immediately prepared for the trip to Rome. I wanted Johnathan to join me in this venture and he was more than willing. These last three years in Jerusalem hadn't been as expected and he was ready to go back to Rome. He and I worked feverishly to complete our readiness.

Apuleius left within the hour after declaring Ishmael as good as new in every respect known to his medicine. He had time coming to him for a trip home and this is what he decided to request on his return to Antonia. I was to meet him as soon as I was ready and we three would ride to Caesarea. There, as before, to catch a ship to the great city of Rome!

Mother was a new woman, and moved again with all grace and energy. She gave me her blessings and prepared a small amount of provisions to take along. The money I had left in Ishmael's care was in part brought to me. I shared this with a grateful Johnathan in case we should be parted somewhere along the way. I signed my share of the estate from mother over to Ishmael with my blessings.

In the last few moments, I told the family of my thoughts on what had happened and what was still to occur. I believed Yeshua would rise again from the dead and then go to his father even as he had taught us in the last days. I told them not to be taken in by those who claimed to be the true leaders and speakers of his teachings, but to listen to their own hearts. Those who were true would live on and those who spread false teachings would fail. Watch and wait for Yeshua's return after his ascent. I gave them all my blessings and joined Johnathan. We left the house and this for the last time; this was on the sixteenth day of the month of Abib, the year of Tiberius Caesar, 780 ann uris codite.

TO ROME

Johnathan and I rode to Antonia as we had arranged with Apuleius. There we found him astride and ready for the voyage home. His papers and orders were processed in haste by a friendly fort commander. And so it was, we left Jerusalem that same hour.

We followed the same route we used before. We booked passage on a vessel of the Quintus line. It was loaded with jars of olive oil and bales of wool for Rome. I spoke to the captain of the vessel about Quintus - the owner of this ship line. I told him about speaking with Quintus just the day before; after this, he was very accommodating. I then made a note to write Quintus from Rome and thank him for his kindness the night of the trial. The ship made the usual stops for provisions and water. We arrived in Rome some fifteen days later little worse for the wear. The ship lay out of port for the night; we docked in the early morning mist. The shoreline was beautiful to us gone so long.

Apuleius would have nothing else than we go with him to his father's house. It had been nearly three years since he had been home. I declined the offer, knowing his family would be overwhelmed at his unannounced coming. He would have none of it, and we followed him to a place of slaves and there secured the use of one to carry our things. Apuleius would send him back after we were home.

We moved through the old city and enjoyed every moment. The sights and smells of Rome were different than any other in the world. The crowds were as fluid as ever in Rome - a sea of human beings.

We progressed well even though we hadn't recovered our land legs as yet.

At last, we came to the gate of the house of Lucius the elder. As we stood outside, Apuleius had tears in his eyes. It was strange, but that was the first time I realized this was a moment of deep feelings for him just as it had been for me years ago in front of my own father's house. His pounding on the gate brought action. The older servants recognized him and came with a shout that raised the entire household. The family welcomed him in every way possible. Embraces, tears, and laughter were the modus operandi of this moment. Johnathan and I stayed in the background of this most intimate family reunion. Sometime later, when some semblance of order had been established in the household, Apuleius, ashamed for his not bringing his two travelers into the meeting sooner, introduced us and we also received the warm welcome of his house.

I met again Lucius the elder and his wife; the entire family wasn't present as many were now married and had residences of their own. I then said I would like to see my Uncle Benjamin and visit his family. Lucius wouldn't hear of our leaving so soon. He begged me to stay and Johnathan with me. Apuleius introduced Johnathan as a free man and all accepted him in the household. His servant status was now forgotten, at least in the home of Apuleius. I agreed to stay two days and then I was to see my only uncle.

The activity in the home of Lucius was high. Runners were sent to the other family members and friends of Apuleius, telling them he had returned from the wars. A family gathering of such as I had never seen was planned in a short time. I was especially intrigued by the efficiency of the second oldest sister, Paulina, in making these arrangements. I remembered her from the days I spent in this house before I left for Jerusalem. She wasn't wed when I left and I could see she wasn't now. I would talk to her someday, this I knew.

The next two days went by with friends and relatives from far away places keeping the house in happiness. Johnathan and I were shown the love and care from members of the family. By the end of those days, we were ready for leave to visit the house of Benjamin.

Lucius the elder wouldn't accept any denial of his request for me and Johnathan to stay in his house. Apuleius was also of the mind that I would live with him in this house. I said I would consider this offer and was honored above my station for it.

Johnathan and I left the house of Apuleius and taking nothing with us, rode in a chariot to the gate of Benjamin the Jewish sea merchant of Rome. Some of the servants at the gate ran to tell the master of our presence. We were admitted in grand style. Uncle Benjamin was happy beyond words and wept to see me again - here was a son lost now found. He immediately brought the cloth of the house to me and placed his ring on my finger. He said that now no more would I leave his house but would be his son forever.

I refused all these things until I could talk to him alone. I left Johnathan waiting for I knew I wouldn't be long. Either Uncle Benjamin would understand and accept my story or he wouldn't. So Johnathan waited in the great hall.

Uncle Benjamin and I spent some time in the garden alone that morning. I told him of my adventures in Jerusalem as a disciple of Yeshua, of his death, and the threats on my life which caused me to flee Jerusalem. I told of mother's prayers that he would give me honor and accept me as I was and not believe any strange stories of my life.

Uncle Benjamin listened with a kind heart and then, on the presentation of the letter from mother, gave to me his hand and the ring again.

"From this day forth, you have nothing to fear from me or my family. Today, and from this day onward, you shall be known as Judas bar Simon the son of the Jewish sea merchant of Rome. Not from me or mine shall anyone hear of your days in Jerusalem."

I thanked my uncle for his kind heart and accepted him as my father. We returned to the others in high spirits. From then on, the house and all in it was ours. Johnathan was accepted as a free man by my uncle and sat in the family circle. I was happy this courtesy was shown to him. Johnathan had been more than a servant to me for the three years and I would take nothing less than his rise to an accepted status.

The parties and family gatherings began all over again but this time in the house of Benjamin. After three days of celebration, we grew tired and asked to be relieved of all this.

The house came back to normal and work was the order of the day. Uncle Benjamin wanted to know if I was of a mind to join him again in the sea trade and I told him I was, but was also interested in a business of my own. He was somewhat unhappy about this news but then showed his true colors and offered to be my first backer. He was now up in years and had a great desire to see Jerusalem again. I joined uncle as a partner and was within a short time back into the swing of the sea trade.

I accepted the offer of Lucius the elder and became a member of his household. Johnathan, whom I found had a good head for books, became my assistant and lived elsewhere in the good old city.

The Lord blessed me in all ways. I had good health and was increasing in wealth everyday. Uncle Benjamin and I spent many hours going over the books of his prosperous business. I told him of my friend Quintus and of his kindness to me on the night of Yeshua's death. I was able to join the Quintus fleet of ships to our log.

Later, Uncle Benjamin and my dear aunt secured passage to Judea. They left some time later to visit mother in Jerusalem. I sent many letters with them telling all of my success and the love I still had for all there at home.

In that same year, Apuleius left the service and became a practicing physician in the good old city. To my surprise, he married and started a family even though late in life. Later, he took over running the household of Lucius the elder. The elder left the Senate and retired a gentlemen on his estate and a member of the two hundred. Many still sought his advice on all things political.

Uncle Benjamin and my aunt spent a year in Jerusalem and was pleased to celebrate a Passover there. Mother and Uncle Benjamin sent letters of their good time and blessings.

He told me stories Yeshua told throughout the land. Many had grown into great tales and miracles I had never heard or saw while there. His first story was of Joseph of Arimathea and Nicodemus securing permission to take down the body and prepare it for burial, on the day before the Sabbath so the law might not be broken. How Yeshua was laid in the tomb of Joseph, and not in the family tomb in Nazareth. Why this was done and Mary not insistent he should be buried in the tomb of his father, he couldn't say.

He related about the resurrection of Yeshua as told by some of his followers. How some of the women saw him first and then the eleven.

"Did he show himself to the high priest?" I asked.

"None said so!"

"Did he show himself to Pilate or any of the public officials?"

"No," Uncle Benjamin was quick to answer.

"Was he seen by Herod?" I asked again.

"No!" was the answer again. I wondered why he didn't do these things. It would have been a show of the power of God for him to do this. As the Messiah of Israel, all would have soon known about his resurrection had he shown himself to the powers of the world - even Caesar! The power of the Great Deceiver would have been diminished and many would bless the God of Israel if this had been done; but it was not so.

Uncle Benjamin told the sayings of many. One such story was told about a man called Matthew, the man I knew as Levi, for Matthew wasn't one of the eleven, and this is what he spoke: "It was the Sabbath and some of the lesser officers of the temple went to Pilate and asked for a guard to be placed on the tomb as they knew of his saying in three days he would rise again from the dead. Pilate cared less about their superstition and was in a hurry to leave the city so he authorized their use of a small detachment. Some of the officers of the temple heard that the body was in the tomb of Joseph of Arimathea. They searched out the tomb and set a guard upon it and sealed it. Now, during the night there was a great earthquake and the seal was broken and the stone rolled away. The men were frightened about all this and ran to tell the temple officials Yeshua had risen. The officials would have none of it and gave each man money to say his followers came and stole the body away while the guards were sleeping. The guards were fearful of Pilate but were told by the officials of the temple not to worry as they would make it right with Pilate."

I couldn't believe this story. I wondered what Apuleius would say about Roman guards accepting bribes - to say nothing of admitting sleeping on guard duty! I was skeptical indeed about the story, and I remembered how Levi maintained there were two possessed with devils and the place was Gergasa while the ten disagreed with both number and place. Levi could get some of his stories twisted this I knew. I could see this happening in this case.

I knew Pilate was already making ready for his trip to Syria when I was still there. I was amused that anyone knowing Pilate believed he would accommodate any Jew, temple officials or no, with a detachment of Roman soldiers, and this to guard against a ghost! Pilate was no friend of Annas and Caiaphas, but to grant Jews power over his Roman troops at any time was obviously the figment of someone's imagination - probably Levi's. For some temple officials to be able to bribe the guards and say they could "persuade Pilate" and thereby guarantee the guards safety from military justice was too much! I smiled when I heard this story. Yet I knew that many would believe it - and so it was.

"How came those not disciples to know of his prediction of resurrection when none of the disciples did?" I asked Uncle Benjamin.

"I don't know. Why do you ask?"

"Because I know, if I knew of such a thing happening and was free to do so, I would have stayed up all three days and nights to see it. Yet none of the disciples did this; it is nearly a breach of his love. They didn't even assemble near the tomb on the third day. Now uncle, if you were a disciple of someone and had seen him raise the dead and cure the blind and lepers, wouldn't you be interested enough in his word to go where he is laid and wait for him to come forth?" He was taken aback at my sayings on the matter. He said nothing in answer. Why would such a story be told? What was the need? As I saw it, neither believer nor nonbeliever had reason to carry this story about.

"Was this story told by any other?" I asked.

"None."

"Let it be and continue." I was more interested in the rest of the stories.

Uncle Benjamin then told of the several appearances of Yeshua before his followers and finally his ascension into the air, which many claimed was his return to the Father. Oh, there were many other stories he brought back with him. And when the nights were long and I was visiting him in his old age, he would relate more of these. Some I found had a ring of truth, while others sounded a bit more like the ancient writings of our people.

I was greatly interested in the miracles and asked if there had been any more raising from the dead by the followers of Yeshua since he died. Was anyone telling of such? Uncle said that he never heard of such in the years he was there. So I concluded that I was the last to do this thing when the Lord granted me the power to raise Ishmael - my twin!

CHAPTER TWENTY-FIVE

Moments Of The Past

Later, one of those I had befriended in the teachings of Yeshua told a story of Judas that was now told in Jerusalem by those who addressed themselves as Apostles. It was the story of my betrayal of Yeshua and told in truth as the most evil of deeds, of how these good men found me hanging of my own hand, and how my intestines had gushed out from the force of evil that had been in me!

All these things I knew were untrue, as it wasn't *me* that died that night of hanging - but Ishmael! Besides, how would these men know that a man hanging had died of his own hand? Many times, I was moved to tell those repeating the story the truth of the matter; but to what avail? None of those who repeated this story to me in Rome knew me as Judas of Kerioth and the possible betrayer as I went by the name of Marcus Lucius.

My heart went cold at these tales told to pilgrims by the eleven who remained in Jerusalem and elsewhere in the empire. I could feel the hand of Shalazar in mine and hear his words ringing clear, "Your act this night will be recorded as the most dastardly deed known to man, and your name will be written ever to be damned."

As time passed, I left the sea trade a wealthy and influential man of Rome. Even as a Jew, I was asked to sit in meetings about state functions. All these honors meant little compared with helping both slave and free man in Yeshua's studies and his true teachings. I heard many stories of his glories. Some I knew were false and others I knew as neither true nor false, but only that I wasn't present when they happened or were told by Yeshua.

I heard from the later pilgrims that Yeshua was raised from the dead even as he said he would be, and this within three days of his death. I realized I could have been there had I not hurried to Rome in fear of my life. And this not of the Romans, but of the eleven!

Others told that he ascended to his Father in heaven, but promised to those he loved he would return; because of confusion and lack of faith, his beloved disciples returned to the fishing trade rather than follow his teachings; that he appeared to those near to him again to commission them to teach of the Kingdom of God; that he appeared to the young Paul, who I had taken to Jerusalem to study at the feet of Gamaliel, and commissioned him to teach the gentiles; that the Spirit or word was given to the Apostles some fifty days after his death and they spoke in tongues thereafter; these and many more things I heard even unto my old age.

I was told some of these men were preparing journals of their own to perpetuate the word as they lived it for generations to come, and that my name was never left without the accusing finger of the Great Deceiver - even as he had said. It is because of these stories and misunderstandings and yes, even falsehoods, that were placed in the hearts of man by the Great Deceiver so long ago that I am now finishing this journal.

Man must have the truth when he is able to understand it and not before. So this scroll must be hidden away until the hand of God brings it forth. Then and only then will man hear and understand, see and perceive, and in his heart say this is the truth.

Time moved on and Uncle Benjamin died an old man of good reputation among all who knew him. He was an honest man in all respects and did no man harm in any dealings. I loved Uncle Benjamin as one would a father. I suffered no small amount at his death.

The rest of this journal is as follows for my time is short. Apius stayed with mother even unto her death, then died some years after her. Ishmael and Miriam gave mother many grandsons before her death. Ishmael and Miriam still live in Jerusalem, though I hear by letter they aren't well. They grow old even as I.

For many years, I wondered if anyone in Jerusalem heard of the raising of Ishmael, but while in Rome, no pilgrim ever spoke of it. So it was that Ishmael and his family never revealed this last miracle of his raising to anyone in accordance with my word. And I never tried to do that thing again, though tested times to do so.

Later in life, before Lucius the elder died, I was honored by being adopted by him as his second son, received the name Marcus Annaeus Lucius in an honorable ceremony, and became a Roman citizen. So as I grew older and wealthier, I went by the name of Marcus Lucius; I wanted to return to the land of my birth, but there was a new element of control. The young man called Paul had changed the course of the teaching of Yeshua. His teachings I couldn't abide and therefore never returned to Jerusalem.

I helped many a young Jewish person, both free man and slave, following the teaching of Yeshua, and even helped start small assembly houses in the homes of these people. I used both money and influence to reinforce these humble beginnings of the teachings of Yeshua. All this without notice to myself or earthly reward from those receiving help as I used my Roman name.

God gave me a good life in Rome. Another journal detailing my life and times in Rome and that of those near and dear to me from the year 784 to 813 I leave with Apuleius. I hope it will become part of the family history of Lucius, and remain in their library to someday be joined with this journal of my life as the servant of God, to form a complete book of God. Only God knows. And now in the year of 813 ann uris codite, at the age of seventy-six, I hear the call of God.

This journal, bearing the truth of these things, is to be enclosed in a Golden Scroll. The scroll is of itself a work of art dedicated to God and under his protection. I have but one desire - that this journal be someday brought to the eyes of the people of the world, and that my name once again be held among men as it has been and is now forever before God. "Behold, this is Judas, my beloved servant, in whom I am well pleased!"

I have commissioned the grandson of Apuleius to take this scroll and my body to the land of my birth and there inter them together, and this as God may direct. To this end I sign and seal this journal, Marcus Annaeus Lucius, one and the same Judas, son of Simon, also known as Judas of Kerioth. *Hear, O Israel: the Lord is our God, the Lord is one.*

LETTER FROM APULEIUS

I, Apuleius Lucius, physician to all who apply to me needing such, have this day witnessed the death of Marcus Annaeus Lucius, my adopted brother and Jewish teacher of some thought. His Jewish name was Judas, and he was the son of Simon of Kerioth. He has lived his life in the strict belief that the God of his people gave him a special task to do and even though at great personal danger and mental stress, did accomplish that task. He died in the belief his God honored him before time began and will do so ever afterward.

It is to honor his wishes that I set my hand and seal to close this journal from his own hand, adding only this of Barabbas from my own hand.

Because of the story circulated by those known as Apostles and others of a secret order that Barabbas is alive, I add this story as told to me by Judas yet not found in his journal as given to me. Why he chose to ignore it or to exclude it is his to know.

From the annals of the Military Library in Rome, I have secured a copy of a letter from Captain Marcus Lucius, the Secretary of the forces at Fort Antonia. This I have inserted in this journal to support the word of Judas. As he wrote in his journal, Barabbas was and is dead - this is the truth of the matter.

Lucius Annaeus Seneca
Keeper of the Library
Rome - 794 a.u.c.

Greetings, Honorable Seneca,

May the gods find favor in your life and endeavors. As your humble servant, I send you this letter concerning an enigma of a member of the Sicarii and insurgent known to us only as Barabbas. According to the teller, it has a direct bearing on your history of the civil unrest, lawful proceedings against, and eventual execution of the accused, one Yeshua ben David, in Jerusalem on or about 784.

These are the events immediately preceding and subsequently following as told to me by Marcus Sejanus, a Lieutenant of the Elite guard of Herod. Lieutenant Marcus Sejanus was one of Herod's guards detailed to assist the Romans during the trial and execution of Yeshua ben David on the hill called Golgotha. At the time of the telling, he was nearly seventy years old though still of good health and keen mind. Although his story differs from traditional versions, I see no reason to deny it as a possibility. So I have heard and so I have put my hand to.

Captain Marcus Lucius
Secretary - Fort Antonia
Year - 793 a.u.c.

It was my good fortune as a Lieutenant of Herod's Elite guard to be assigned a company of men who joined with a Roman maniple to apprehend one Yeshua ben David. After apprehension, we guarded the prisoner and marched him to and from the Governor's office and Herod's palatial estate. I was present, although in the background, at the prosecution of the prisoner - Yeshua. I witnessed his scourging and final presentation before the crowd. I witnessed the selection of an openly and widely known insurgent and murderer, one known to me only as Barabbas, for release by the crowd in the forum.

Both of the accused were charged by the hand of one Judas of Kerioth as insurgents. It was his complaint brought against them, sealed by the secret fraternity from a small town called Bethlehem, and signed by the Procurator Pilate. I later learned this secret order was seeking retribution for the tragedy of Bethlehem. It was this charge which brought both the accused condemnation and death.

The following events were either witnessed by me or brought to my attention through reports of Herod's spies. All these things occurred in the eighteenth year of the reign of Tiberius and of the time of 784 a.u.c. I swear by Jupiter and Mars that these events occurred even as I give them utterance.

After the scourging, the party and prisoners marched to Golgotha from the forum. Among these were members of a secret society, the order of the Death Star, who were members of the

Sicarii, and some Zealots. After the crucifixion, they returned to the forum; many of these men were assembled in the square before the sentence and crucifixion. My orders obeyed, I was free to observe the happenings, which I did and saw things this wise.

The crowd awaited the release of this mighty leader - Barabbas! They heard the proclamation of Pilate read - Barabbas would be freed! Pilate gave his word to release their leader, but only after the crucifixion of Yeshua ben David - the one they had rejected. They saw the crucifixion and were satisfied; they felt they had won a minor victory.

That afternoon, the Roman troops from the fort were sent to the forum and formed around the square. A full thousand men flanked all sides of the forum. A horse troop was also standing by should they be needed. Thus they stood - men and their animals - waiting. It seemed they were always waiting - waiting for food, pay, exercise, and the commands of their officers. The heat and flies made the waiting even more irritating - but soldiers they were and wait they did.

In the square moved members of the order of the Death Star of Bethlehem and among them the Sicarii, all dressed as priests of the temple - which even the Romans knew they weren't. And I, as a member of Herod's Elite Guard, had seen these men dressed as priests before to disguise their real intentions - this was an old trick. The experienced troops knew they weren't priests.

The crowd moved around like a pot of barley brought to a boil. Their motion was random; they too were waiting. Waiting to hail their leader's release and hope for another strike against these same Romans - with the hated symbol of sheaf and axe everywhere - who now stood so quietly watching them.

The afternoon was hot. The men of the first corps were restless but not so free to move as the rabble. A dark cloud hung over Golgotha; it was an evil omen to some. This day it was the place of execution.

The mob moved about cautiously while glancing frequently at the place of the skull. There, except for some queer turns of fate, Barabbas would be at this moment. Most queer was the arrest and conviction of an itinerant teacher, Yeshua ben David of Galilee. Convicted, by Pilate, for sedition and this on the day Barabbas was to be sentenced and hung for the same charge! The charge brought by Judas of Kerioth, a master of the order of the Death Star. Also queer, the apparent change of heart of the Procurator! Some said he fears the people! Even the heart of Pilate, like that of Pharaoh, could be moved!

But to release a prisoner - any prisoner - regardless of his crime, against the State? How? Just say the word - the one the rabble selected goes free! No writ from Caesar, no pardon from the Senate? Ridiculous! Now hear this, Pilate releases a convicted seditionist - Barabbas! What a twist of justice - the law has gone mad or a miracle has indeed occurred. So the proclamation was read and so it was to be done!

The third strange twist of fate was that the rabble, now milling about in the forum - believed this proclamation, believed Pilate, this egomaniac, would release their leader - a revolutionary - unto them. This mob, who cared nothing for Roman authority and honor, and showed even less respect for it, now stood in the heat of the day awaiting an act to be done for them! An act from a Governor who's very life was to them a lie!

Their acts of sedition were based on the concept that this man and his government were evil in every way, including being dishonest. While on the hill, Pilate said another was being put to death, with two others who cried out for mercy. One they had freely rejected. The trumpets sounded! The formal guards came forward from behind the velum. With them was Barabbas! The rabble murmured some - he seemed different to them. After scourging and torture, though, any man would look less himself.

"Barabbas, Barabbas!" they shouted. "Give us Barabbas!"

The horse soldiers moved forward and forced the crowd back from the podium. The prisoner stood silent - not acknowledging the acclamation - almost indifferent to their salute. The irons were struck from him before them. With each blow of the hammer, the mob roared its approval. This was worth waiting for. The chief of their cause - freed! "Barabbas, Barabbas! Hail Pilate!" There was a mixture of joyous calls.

The last chain fell away and the tired figure of one who looked like Barabbas stood alone. The robes of prison fell away. The calls of joy stopped in the throats of those near to the podium; then those further back stopped their shouts as well. The man before them had changed - was this the man they knew so many months ago? Had his trial and days in prison changed him so much?

Only personal contact - and that close - would dispel the sudden doubt in the minds of all. They were stunned and their mouths were shut up! I was amazed at their quietness.

The Captain stepped forward and read. "This day, 781 ann uris codite, this prisoner, one Barabbas, is released unto you. This in accordance with the will and pleasure of your Governor and Procurator Pontius Pilate." He turned toward the man. "Step forward. Now, you see him free and clear even as the Governor said." The man stepped forward to leave the podium and the guards stopped him.

The Captain received another writ from the secretary. "Hear ye, this second order from the Governor. In accordance with the law of the Empire, this man, Barabbas, is now arrested for charges of murder. Take him away." The guards surrounded him and moved him behind the velum!

The rabble was stunned and stood like statues for a moment. Then it roared its disapproval and entered an insane rage. Pilate had tricked them! This man wasn't Barabbas - he wouldn't stand so reticent before their call of honor! And if so - why the arrest? Woe is he who is the fool of another!

The mob erupted into a raging destructive force - they charged the podium only to be forced away by the calvary. They swore oaths against Pilate and Rome. They took to the streets of the city. This is a day Jerusalem would remember!

Cooler heads of the secret society were already asking - where was Barabbas? And should the others be told of his whereabouts if found?

Where was Barabbas? Suddenly, they began to see! The man crying out that he was Barabbas while carrying his tree to Golgotha - was indeed their beloved Barabbas! The one some of them ignored as he cried out to them for help. The very one they thought was an impostor, was their man!

The committee formed to visit Golgotha and see what had come to pass. They climbed the hill and came to the crosses, lifted their eyes to the third cross, and although his face now greatly distorted and swollen in death, it was indeed Barabbas!

They were overcome with remorse. But what to do? Could they let the rest of the followers know of this gruesome trick played by Pilate? No, said the masters, and no again. Barabbas must not die an ignominious death on the cross! He must live on as a symbol of their cause. What Pilate had started as a joke would now haunt him - every man of the order would now carry the story of how Barabbas escaped hanging for his crimes through the whim of Pilate. Yes, even Rome and Caesar would hear of this release of Barabbas! Pilate would live to regret this as a comedy of errors on his part. He would rue the day he tricked them!

They left the body of Barabbas on the tree; to take it down would throw suspicion on the order - no, the body must remain there even if it was against the Law of Moses and the Lord God. There must be no recognition of this man on the tree; the order and followers must never know the truth - nay, not even the world! Barabbas must forever be a man praised but never seen after release. The order would see to this.

This closed circle now created a new Barabbas! They would tell all how he was ferreted away after his release and placed on a ship for Rome - a ship that never arrived there! Yes, he would live on and die as a hero at sea! They gave their signs of secrecy and dispersed to carry the tale throughout the Empire. And the first to be told of his release as fact - the eleven who now *called themselves disciples of this Yeshua ben David. They must be assured that none of those hung on the tree with Yeshua was Barabbas! Search them out was the word - find these followers and convince them of Barabbas's release by Pilate.*

They must be the ones to carry the word! The order knew they would tell this story as gospel! Later I heard these things even as they had planned. I, Lieutenant Marcus Sejanus, heard this same story of the release of Barabbas from one Matthew of Galilee. A story he told as true - but is known to me to be false.

Who was the man released and re-arrested? The soldier, Gallus Trajan Aelius, who played the part of Barabbas so successfully. A man who had an amazing resemblance to Barabbas, even as I can attest to! He was the man arrested again before the rabble. I heard later he was sent home to Rome with honors and no small amount of gold as a gift from Pilate. There he was mustered out of the army and lived out his life as an attache over shipping. He became a government consul and often met Marcus Annaeus Lucius, or Judas, the wealthy Jewish sea merchant about matters of international trade.

Some say they knew each other well and often spoke of the strange part each played in the story of the conviction and death of one Yeshua ben David.

The writ, which was read before the crowd the day Callus played the part of Barabbas, was given to Lucius Judas as a memento. It remained in his possession until his death in 813 ann uris codite.

Thus, I reveal the story of Barabbas, his life of crime, and his death on the cross at Golgotha, as well as the story of his apparent escape.

Signed Marcus Sejanus
Captain of Herod's Elite Guards
Retired 793 a.u.c.

This is the story as told to me, Apuleius Lucius, late in life by my adopted brother and dear companion, Judas Marcus Lucius.

In accordance with his wishes in this year of 820 a.u.c., I have commissioned my grandson to take his body and this Golden Scroll to Jerusalem where they, both scroll and body, will be interred in an unmarked grave to rest until God shall cause it to be found and this document revealed. All his other writings shall remain with me and my family so long as it is the will of God. Perhaps these, too, will be added, even as he prayed, to the others to make the secret writings of Judas, the son of Simon. So it is written and so it is done.

Apuleius Lucius
Physician of the first house Aesculapius
Signed, Apuleius Lucius
"magna est veritas et praevalebit"

And the evening and the morning were the seventh day.
The system ceased is operation and the screen held the last bits of information.

TO THE PRESS

The four remained in their chairs staring at the screen. Only the soft hum of the equipment was heard. Some long breaths were expelled. Time seemed to stand still in this complex laboratory as if it, nor those in it, wanted to return to the present. Finally, John moved to shut down the entire operation. He said nothing and moved slowly and quietly as he could, as if in respect to some distant love. The others also came to life and moved quietly as well. None wanted to be the first to speak, yet all knew someone would. As the system shut down, the characters faded from the screen, the lights came up, and the vert-ablinds moved to accommodate the need for light. It was the increase in light that finally broke the spell of ancient history. The here-and-now came back to them.

"Lord, what a great experience!" Chuck exploded with a good deal of feeling.

"I second the motion," Jean spoke her mind, "I'm just about wrung-out!"

"I can see my first wish - to find the other journals of the author!" John spoke as he still looked at the blank screen. "I wonder…"

Even though nothing more was said, the rest also had the urge to go to Rome and search for the lost journals so briefly mentioned at the end of the Golden Scroll. Could they be found after all these years? What would they reveal?

John continued to put things in order. The project and its control were of major importance. The material must be protected and properly stored, then it's time to talk.

"I believe I've never had a richer religious experience, either from visiting the ancient Christian ruins or in the reading of manuscripts, regardless of their age." These were the words of Ed Stuart, one of the most traveled and well-read men in modern day religious history.

They said little more but continued to complete their separate tasks. Finally, the work was done and all was in ship-shape condition.

"Well, I guess you'll have to return the award for the find of the year, John!" Ed said as he moved this final copy into the safe.

"How is that?"

"Well, near the end of the journal, Judas prays that with God's will, 'this scroll must be hidden away until the hand of God brings it forth' and that is precisely what happened."

The others stopped and listened. Ed was dead serious, not so much about returning the award, but of the way the scroll was discovered.

"You know, that is an interesting thing, John. I remember the days on the site. We had worked that area several times without discovering anything. In fact, the consensus was that we should move on. Then, a sudden rain came up and we couldn't move the equip-ment or lines. It was the rain that opened the hole and led to the discovery of the crypt." Jean was the only one other than John who had been at the site.

"I can't deny that some coincidences have occurred, but let's not get carried away with the romance of the moment." John wasn't about to give in to this religious thought of God's moving in mysterious ways in his life.

"There was another thing," Jean added to the probability that all wasn't just coin-cidence. "That rain occurred only once in that entire month. And as I recall, we both remarked at the time what a small cloud it was; the rain barely covered a thousand square meters on the ground." She shook her head at the wonder of it all.

"I think you are all barking up the wrong tree." John turned away from them and started to work on his reports. The time and use of the equipment as well as the computer time at headquarters must be accounted for to the University Board.

"There's still another thing that interests me," Chuck now entered the discussion. "That site wasn't very large was it?"

"No, not more than a kilometer square, and out of that we were working about a hundred square meters."

"And it had been used as practice for years. This I know by the school records. In all this time, no one came up with a clue that the Golden Scroll was hidden in a crypt just below. My, my, and you say your discovery was purely a coincidence?" Now, Chuck was in the swing of things.

"Well, I'm not about to give the award back no matter what kind of circumstantial evidence you all bring against me!" John tried to make light of their comments.

"Look, John, we don't care about the award, Lord knows the school needs the publicity of this discovery, but the timing and place of this find is a bit too unusual to be relegated to chance. I, for one, found not only the journal revealing and interesting, but also historic, and vote that we don't throw away its' religious significance as coincidence. There is more mystery here than at Lourdes."

"Hear, I think we should consider ourselves and this school the one selected for its' revelation and deliver this document and its' story to the world," Jean said, indicating her conviction about the journal and what was in it.

"Fine, so you have said and so it will be done," John agreed. With that, the lights of the laboratory went down and the four left through the air-lock and headed for their favorite restaurant. Tonight would be a good meal for a job well done! Tomorrow, the press, and later, the search for other journals written by Judas Marcus Annaeus Lucius, the beloved betrayer.

www.ingramcontent.com/pod-product-compliance
Lightning Source LLC
Chambersburg PA
CBHW080830280626
47161CB00018B/3106